THE
JEEVES OMNIBUS

Volume 3

Books by P. G. Wodehouse

Fiction

Aunts Aren't Gentlemen
The Adventures of Sally
Bachelors Anonymous
Barmy in Wonderland
Big Money
Bill the Conqueror
Blandings Castle and
  Elsewhere
Carry On, Jeeves
The Clicking of Cuthbert
Cocktail Time
The Code of the Woosters
The Coming of Bill
Company for Henry
A Damsel in Distress
Do Butlers Burgle Banks
Doctor Sally
Eggs, Beans and Crumpets
A Few Quick Ones
French Leave
Frozen Assets
Full Moon
Galahad at Blandings
A Gentleman of Leisure
The Girl in Blue
The Girl on the Boat
The Gold Bat
The Head of Kay's
The Heart of a Goof
Heavy Weather
Hot Water
Ice in the Bedroom
If I Were You
Indiscretions of Archie
The Inimitable Jeeves
Jeeves and the Feudal Spirit
Jeeves in the Offing
Jill the Reckless
Joy in the Morning
Laughing Gas
Leave it to Psmith
The Little Nugget
Lord Emsworth and Others
Louder and Funnier
Love Among the Chickens
The Luck of Bodkins
The Man Upstairs
The Man with Two Left Feet
The Mating Season
Meet Mr Mulliner
Mike and Psmith
Mike at Wrykyn
Money for Nothing
Money in the Bank
Mr Mulliner Speaking
Much Obliged, Jeeves
Mulliner Nights
Not George Washington
Nothing Serious
The Old Reliable
Pearls, Girls and Monty Bodkin
A Pelican at Blandings

Piccadilly Jim
Pigs Have Wings
Plum Pie
The Pothunters
A Prefect's Uncle
The Prince and Betty
Psmith, Journalist
Psmith in the City
Quick Service
Right Ho, Jeeves
Ring for Jeeves
Sam the Sudden
Service with a Smile
The Small Bachelor
Something Fishy
Something Fresh
Spring Fever
Stiff Upper Lip, Jeeves
Summer Lightning
Summer Moonshine
Sunset at Blandings
The Swoop
Tales of St Austin's
Thank You, Jeeves
Ukridge
Uncle Dynamite
Uncle Fred in the Springtime
Uneasy Money
Very Good, Jeeves
The White Feather
William Tell Told Again
Young Men in Spats

Omnibuses

The World of Blandings
The World of Jeeves
The World of Mr Mulliner
The World of Psmith
The World of Ukridge
The World of Uncle Fred
Wodehouse Nuggets
  (edited by Richard Usborne)
The World of Wodehouse Clergy
The Hollywood Omnibus
Weekend Wodehouse

Paperback Omnibuses

The Golf Omnibus
The Aunts Omnibus
The Drones Omnibus
The Jeeves Omnibus 1
The Jeeves Omnibus 2

Poems

The Parrot and Other Poems

Autobiographical

Wodehouse on Wodehouse
  (comprising Bring on the Girls,
  Over Seventy, Performing Flea)

Letters

Yours, Plum

THE
JEEVES OMNIBUS

Volume 3

P. G. Wodehouse

Hutchinson

London Sydney Auckland Johannesburg

First published in this collection 1991
© in this collection The Trustees of the Wodehouse Estate 1991
Ring for Jeeves © P. G. Wodehouse 1925
The Mating Season © P. G. Wodehouse 1934
Very Good, Jeeves © P. G. Wodehouse 1947

Random Century Group Ltd
20 Vauxhall Bridge Road, London SW1V 2SA

Random Century Australia (Pty) Ltd
20 Alfred Street, Milsons Point, Sydney, NSW 2061, Australia

Random Century New Zealand Ltd
PO Box 40-086, Glenfield, Auckland 10, New Zealand

Random Century South Africa (Pty) Ltd
PO Box 337, Bergvlei, 2012, South Africa

Reprinted 1991

BRITISH LIBRARY CATALOGUING-IN-PUBLICATION DATA

Wodehouse, P. G.
    The Jeeves Omnibus 3. – (P. G. Wodehouse trade paperback series)
    I. Title II. Series

    823[F]

ISBN 0-09-174833-X

Set in Ehrhardt by Falcon Typographic Art Ltd
Printed and bound in Great Britain by Mackays of Chatham PLC,
Chatham, Kent

Contents

RING FOR JEEVES

1

The waiter, who had slipped out to make a quick telephone call, came back into the coffee room of the Goose and Gherkin wearing the starry-eyed look of a man who has just learned that he has backed a long-priced winner. He yearned to share his happiness with someone, and the only possible confidant was the woman at the table near the door, who was having a small gin and tonic and whiling away the time by reading a book of spiritualistic interest. He decided to tell her the good news.

'I don't know if you would care to know, madam,' he said, in a voice that throbbed with emotion, 'but Whistler's Mother won the Oaks.'

The woman looked up, regarding him with large, dark, soulful eyes as if he had been something recently assembled from ectoplasm.

'The what?'

'The Oaks, madam.'

'And what are the Oaks?'

It seemed incredible to the waiter that there should be anyone in England who could ask such a question, but he had already gathered that the lady was an American lady, and American ladies, he knew, are often ignorant of the fundamental facts of life. He had once met one who had wanted to know what a football pool was.

'It's an annual horse race, madam, reserved for fillies. By which I mean that it comes off once a year and the male sex isn't allowed to compete. It's run at Epsom Downs the day before the Derby, of which you have no doubt heard.'

'Yes, I have heard of the Derby. It is your big race over here, is it not?'

'Yes, madam. What is sometimes termed a classic. The Oaks is run the day before it, though in previous years the day after. By which I mean,' said the waiter, hoping he was not being too abstruse, 'it used to be run the day following the Derby, but now they've changed it.'

'And Whistler's Mother won this race you call the Oaks?'

'Yes, madam. By a couple of lengths. I was on five bob.'

'I see. Well, that's fine, isn't it? Will you bring me another gin and tonic?'

'Certainly, madam. Whistler's Mother!' said the waiter, in a sort of ecstasy. 'What a beauty!'

He went out. The woman resumed her reading. Quiet descended on the coffee room.

In its general essentials the coffee room at the Goose and Gherkin differed very little from the coffee rooms of all the other inns that nestle by the wayside in England and keep the island race from dying of thirst. It had the usual dim religious light, the customary pictures of *The Stag at Bay* and *The Huguenot's Farewell* over the mantelpiece, the same cruets and bottles of sauce, and the traditional ozone-like smell of mixed pickles, gravy soup, boiled potatoes, waiters and old cheese.

What distinguished it on this June afternoon and gave it a certain something that the others had not got was the presence in it of the woman the waiter had been addressing. As a general rule, in the coffee rooms of English wayside inns, all the eye is able to feast on is an occasional farmer eating fried eggs or a couple of commercial travellers telling each other improper stories, but the Goose and Gherkin had drawn this strikingly handsome hand across the sea, and she raised the tone of the place unbelievably.

The thing about her that immediately arrested the attention and drew the startled whistle to the lips was the aura of wealth which she exuded. It showed itself in her rings, her hat, her stockings, her shoes, her platinum fur cape and the Jacques Fath sports costume that clung lovingly to her undulating figure. Here, you would have said to yourself, beholding her, was a woman who had got the stuff in sackfuls and probably suffered agonies from coupon-clipper's thumb, a woman at the mention of whose name the blood-sucking leeches of the Internal Revenue Department were accustomed to raise their filthy hats with a reverent intake of the breath.

Nor would you have been in error. She was just as rich as she looked. Twice married and each time to a multi-millionaire, she was as nicely fixed financially as any woman could have wished.

Hers had been one of those Horatio Alger careers which are so encouraging to girls who hope to get on in the world, showing as they do that you never know what prizes Fate may be storing up for you around the corner. Born Rosalinda Banks, of the Chilicothe, Ohio, Bankses, with no assets beyond a lovely face, a superb figure and a mild talent for *vers libre*, she had come to Greenwich Village to seek her fortune and had found it first crack out of the box. At a studio party in Macdougall Alley she had met and fascinated Clifton Bessemer, the Pulp Paper Magnate, and in almost no time at all had become his wife.

Widowed owing to Clifton Bessemer trying to drive his car one night through a truck instead of round it, and two years later meeting in Paris and marrying the millionaire sportsman and big game hunter, A.B. Spottsworth, she was almost immediately widowed again.

It was a confusion of ideas between him and one of the lions he was hunting in Kenya that had caused A.B. Spottsworth to make the obituary column. He thought the lion was dead, and the lion thought it wasn't. The result being that when he placed his foot on the animal's neck preparatory to being photographed by Captain Biggar, the White Hunter accompanying the expedition, a rather unpleasant brawl had ensued, and owing to Captain Biggar having to drop the camera and spend several vital moments looking about for his rifle, his bullet, though unerring, had come too late to be of practical assistance. There was nothing to be done but pick up the pieces and transfer the millionaire sportsman's vast fortune to his widow, adding it to the sixteen million or so which she had inherited from Clifton Bessemer.

Such, then, was Mrs Spottsworth, a woman with a soul and about forty-two million dollars in the old oak chest. And, to clear up such minor points as may require elucidation, she was on her way to Rowcester Abbey, where she was to be the guest of the ninth Earl of Rowcester, and had stopped off at the Goose and Gherkin because she wanted to stretch her legs and air her Pekinese dog Pomona. She was reading a book of spiritualistic interest because she had recently become an enthusiastic devotee of psychical research. She was wearing a Jacques Fath sports costume because she liked Jacques Fath sports costumes. And she was drinking gin and tonic because it was one of those warm evenings when a gin and tonic just hits the spot.

The waiter returned with the elixir, and went on where he had left off.

'Thirty-three to one the price was, madam.'

Mrs Spottsworth raised her lustrous eyes.

'I beg your pardon?'

'That's what she started at.'

'To whom do you refer?'

'This filly I was speaking of that's won the Oaks.'

'Back to her, are we?' said Mrs Spottsworth with a sigh. She had been reading about some interesting manifestations from the spirit world, and this earthy stuff jarred upon her.

The waiter sensed the lack of enthusiasm. It hurt him a little. On this day of days he would have preferred to have to do only with those in whose veins sporting blood ran.

'You're not fond of racing, madam?'

Mrs Spottsworth considered.

'Not particularly. My first husband used to be crazy about it, but it always seemed to me so unspiritual. All that stuff about booting them home and goats and beetles and fast tracks and mudders and something he referred to as a boat race. Not at all the sort of thing to develop a person's higher self. I'd bet a grand now and then, just for the fun of it, but that's as far as I would go. It never touched the deeps in me.'

'A grand, madam?'

'A thousand dollars.'

'Coo!' said the waiter, awed. 'That's what I'd call putting your shirt on. Though for me it'd be not only my shirt but my stockings and pantie-girdle as well. Lucky for the bookies you weren't at Epsom today, backing Whistler's Mother.'

He moved off, and Mrs Spottsworth resumed her book.

For perhaps ten minutes after that nothing of major importance happened in the coffee room of the Goose and Gherkin except that the waiter killed a fly with his napkin and Mrs Spottsworth finished her gin and tonic. Then the door was flung open by a powerful hand, and a tough, square, chunky, weather-beaten-looking man in the middle forties strode in. He had keen blue eyes, a very red face, a round head inclined to baldness and one of those small, bristly moustaches which abound in such profusion in the outposts of Empire. Indeed, these sprout in so widespread a way on the upper lips of those who bear the white man's burden that it is a tenable theory that the latter hold some sort of patent rights. One recalls the nostalgic words of the poet Kipling, when he sang 'Put me somewhere east of Suez, where the best is like the worst, where there ain't no ten commandments and a man can raise a small bristly moustache.'

It was probably this moustache that gave the newcomer the exotic look he had. It made him seem out of place in the coffee room of an English inn. You felt, eyeing him, that his natural setting was Black Mike's bar in Pago-Pago, where he would be the life and soul of the party, though of course most of the time he would be out on safari, getting rough with such fauna as happened to come his way. Here, you would have said, was a man who many a time had looked his rhinoceros in the eye and made it wilt.

And again, just as when you were making that penetrating analysis of Mrs Spottsworth, you would have been perfectly right. This bristly moustached he-man of the wilds was none other than the Captain Biggar whom we mentioned a moment ago in connection with the regrettable fracas which had culminated in A.B. Spottsworth going to reside with the morning stars, and any of the crowd out along Bubbling Well Road or in the Long Bar at Shanghai could have told you that Bwana Biggar had made more rhinoceri wilt than you could shake a stick at.

At the moment, he was thinking less of our dumb chums than of something cool in a tankard. The evening, as we have said, was warm, and he had driven many miles – from Epsom Downs, where he had started immediately after the conclusion of the race known as The Oaks, to this quiet inn in Southmoltonshire.

'Beer!' he thundered, and at the sound of his voice Mrs Spottsworth dropped her book with a startled cry, her eyes leaping from the parent sockets.

And in the circumstances it was quite understandable that her eyes should have leaped, for her first impression had been that this was one of those interesting manifestations from the spirit world, of which she had been reading. Enough to make any woman's eyes leap.

The whole point about a hunter like Captain Biggar, if you face it squarely, is that he hunts. And, this being so, you expect him to stay put in and around his chosen hunting grounds. Meet him in Kenya or Malaya or Borneo or India, and you feel no surprise. 'Hullo there, Captain Biggar,' you say. 'How's the spooring?' And he replies that the spooring is tophole. Everything perfectly in order.

But when you see him in the coffee room of an English country inn, thousands of miles from his natural habitat, you may be excused for harbouring a momentary suspicion that this is not the man in the flesh but rather his wraith or phantasm looking in, as wraiths and phantasms will, to pass the time of day.

'Eek!' Mrs Spottsworth exclaimed, visibly shaken. Since interesting herself in psychical research, she had often wished to see a ghost, but one likes to pick one's time and place for that sort of thing. One does not want spectres muscling in when one is enjoying a refreshing gin and tonic.

To the captain, owing to the dimness of the light in the Goose and Gherkin's coffee room, Mrs Spottsworth, until she spoke, had been simply a vague female figure having one for the road. On catching sight of her, he had automatically twirled his moustache, his invariable practice when he observed anything female in the offing, but he had in no sense drunk her in. Bending his gaze upon her now, he quivered all over like a nervous young hippopotamus finding itself face to face with its first White Hunter.

'Well, fry me in butter!' he ejaculated. He stood staring at her. 'Mrs Spottsworth! Well, simmer me in prune juice! Last person in the world I'd have dreamed of seeing. I thought you were in America.'

Mrs Spottsworth had recovered her poise.

'I flew over for a visit a week ago,' she said.

'Oh, I see. That explains it. What made it seem odd, finding you here, was that I remember you told me you lived in California or one of those places.'

'Yes, I have a home in Pasadena. In Carmel, too, and one in New York and another in Florida and another up in Maine.'

'Making five in all?'

'Six. I was forgetting the one in Oregon.'

'Six?' The captain seemed thoughtful. 'Oh, well,' he said, 'it's nice to have a roof over your head, of course.'

'Yes. But one gets tired of places after a while. One yearns for something new. I'm thinking of buying this house I'm on my way to now, Rowcester Abbey. I met Lord Rowcester's sister in New York on her way back from Jamaica, and she said her brother might be willing to sell. But what are you doing in England, Captain? I couldn't believe my eyes at first.'

'Oh, I thought I'd take a look at the old country, dear lady. Long time since I had a holiday, and you know the old proverb – all work and no play makes Jack a *peh-bah pom bahoo*. Amazing the way things have changed since I was here last. No idle rich, if you know what I mean. Everybody working. Everybody got a job of some kind.'

'Yes, it's extraordinary, isn't it? Lord Rowcester's sister, Lady Carmoyle, tells me her husband, Sir Roderick Carmoyle, is a floorwalker at Harrige's. And he's a tenth baronet or something.'

'Amazing, what? Tubby Frobisher and the Subahdar won't believe me when I tell them.'

'Who?'

'Couple of pals of mine out in Kuala Lumpur. They'll be astounded. But I like it,' said the captain stoutly. 'It's the right spirit. The straight bat.'

'I beg your pardon?'

'A cricket term, dear lady. At cricket you've got to play with a straight bat, or . . . or, let's face it, you don't play with a straight bat, if you see what I mean.'

'I suppose so. But do sit down, won't you?'

'Thanks, if I may, but only for a minute. I'm chasing a foe of the human species.'

In Captain Biggar's manner, as he sat down, a shrewd observer would have noted a trace of embarrassment, and might have attributed this to the fact that the last time he and Mrs Spottsworth had seen each other he had been sorting out what was left of her husband with a view to shipping it to Nairobi. But it was not the memory of that awkward moment that was causing his diffidence. Its roots lay deeper than that.

He loved this woman. He had loved her from the very moment she had come into his life. How well he remembered that moment. The camp among the acacia trees. The boulder-strewn cliff. The boulder-filled stream. Old Simba the lion roaring in the distance, old Tembo the elephant doing this and that in the *bimbo* or tall grass, and A.B. Spottsworth driving up in the car with a vision in jodhpurs at his side. 'My wife,' A.B. Spottsworth had said, indicating the combination of Cleopatra and Helen of Troy by whom he was accompanied, and as he replied 'Ah, the memsahib' and greeted her with a civil '*Krai yu ti ny ma pay*', it was as if a powerful electric shock had passed through Captain Biggar. This, he felt, was It.

Naturally, being a white man, he had not told his love, but it had burned steadily within him ever since, a strong, silent passion of such a calibre that sometimes, as he sat listening to the hyaenas and gazing at the snows of Kilimanjaro, it had brought him within an ace of writing poetry.

And here she was again, looking lovelier than ever. It seemed to Captain Biggar that somebody in the vicinity was beating a bass drum. But it was only the thumping of his heart.

His last words had left Mrs Spottsworth fogged.

'Chasing a foe of the human species?' she queried.

'A blighter of a bookie. A cad of the lowest order with a soul as black as his fingernails. I've been after him for hours. And I'd have caught him,' said the captain, moodily sipping beer, 'if something hadn't gone wrong with my bally car. They're fixing it now at that garage down the road.'

'But why were you chasing this bookmaker?' asked Mrs Spottsworth. It seemed to her a frivolous way for a strong man to be passing his time.

Captain Biggar's face darkened. Her question had touched an exposed nerve.

'The low hound did the dirty on me. Seemed straight enough, too. Chap with a walrus moustache and a patch over his left eye.

Honest Patch Perkins, he called himself. "Back your fancy and fear nothing, my noble sportsman," he said. "If you don't speculate, you can't accumulate," he said. "Walk up, walk up. Roll, bowl or pitch. Ladies half-way and no bad nuts returned," he said. So I put my double on with him.'

'Your double?'

'A double, dear lady, is when you back a horse in one race and if it wins, put the proceeds on another horse in another race.'

'Oh, what we call a parlay in America.'

'Well, you can readily see that if both bounders pull it off, you pouch a princely sum. I've got in with a pretty knowledgeable crowd since I came to London, and they recommended as a good double for today Lucy Glitters and Whistler's Mother.'

The name struck a chord.

'The waiter was telling me that Whistler's Mother won.'

'So did Lucy Glitters in the previous race. I had a fiver on her at a hundred to six and all to come on Whistler's Mother for the Oaks. She ambled past the winning post at –'

'Thirty-three to one, the waiter was saying. My goodness! You certainly cleaned up, didn't you!'

Captain Biggar finished his beer. If it is possible to drink beer like an overwrought soul, he did so.

'I certainly ought to have cleaned up,' he said, with a heavy frown. 'There was the colossal sum of three thousand pounds two shillings and sixpence owing to me, plus my original fiver which I had handed to the fellow's clerk, a chap in a check suit and another walrus moustache. And what happened? This inky-hearted bookie welshed on me. He legged it in his car with me after him. I've been pursuing him, winding and twisting through the country roads, for what seems an eternity. And just as I was on the point of grappling with him, my car broke down. But I'll have the scoundrel! I'll catch the louse! And when I do, I propose to scoop out his insides with my bare hands and twist his head off and make him swallow it. After which –'

Captain Biggar broke off. It had suddenly come to him that he was monopolizing the conversation. After all, of what interest could these daydreams of his be to this woman?

'But let's not talk about me any more,' he said. 'Dull subject. How have you been all these years, dear lady? Pretty fit, I hope? You look right in the pink. And how's your husband? Oh, sorry!'

'Not at all. You mean, have I married again? No, I have not married again, though Clifton and Alexis keep advising me to. They are sweet about it. So broad-minded and considerate.'

'Clifton? Alexis?'

'Mr Bessemer and Mr Spottsworth, my two previous husbands. I get them on the ouija board from time to time. I suppose,' said Mrs Spottsworth, laughing a little self-consciously, 'you think it's odd of me to believe in things like the ouija board?'

'Odd?'

'So many of my friends in America call all that sort of thing poppycock.'

Captain Biggar snorted militantly.

'I'd like to be there to talk to them! I'd astonish their weak intellects. No, dear lady, I've seen too many strange things in my time, living as I have done in the shadow-lands of mystery, to think anything odd. I have seen barefooted pilgrims treading the path of Ahura-Mazda over burning coals. I've seen ropes tossed in the air and small boys shinning up them in swarms. I've met fakirs who slept on beds of spikes.'

'Really?'

'I assure you. And think of it, insomnia practically unknown. So you don't catch me laughing at people because they believe in ouija boards.'

Mrs Spottsworth gazed at him tenderly. She was thinking how sympathetic and understanding he was.

'I am intensely interested in psychical research. I am proud to be one of the little band of devoted seekers who are striving to pierce the veil. I am hoping to be vouchsafed some enthralling spiritual manifestation at this Rowcester Abbey where I'm going. It is one of the oldest houses in England, they tell me.'

'Then you ought to flush a spectre or two,' agreed Captain Biggar. 'They collect in gangs in these old English country houses. How about another gin and tonic?'

'No, I must be getting along. Pomona's in the car, and she hates being left alone.'

'You couldn't stay and have one more quick one?'

'I fear not. I must be on my way. I can't tell you how delightful it has been, meeting you again, Captain.'

'Just made my day, meeting you, dear lady,' said Captain Biggar, speaking hoarsely, for he was deeply moved. They were out in the open now, and he was able to get a clearer view of her as she stood beside her car bathed in the sunset glow. How lovely she was, he felt, how wonderful, how . . . Come, come, Biggar, he said to himself gruffly, this won't do, old chap. Play the game, Biggar, play the game, old boy!

'Won't you come and see me when I get back to London, Captain? I shall be at the Savoy.'

'Charmed, dear lady, charmed,' said Captain Biggar. But he did not mean it.

For what would be the use? What would it profit him to renew their acquaintance? Just twisting the knife in the wound, that's what he would be doing. Better, far better, to bite the bullet and wash the whole thing out here and now. A humble hunter with scarcely a bob to his name couldn't go mixing with wealthy widows. It was the kind of thing he had so often heard Tubby Frobisher and the Subahdar denouncing in the old Anglo-Malay Club at Kuala Lumpur. 'Chap's nothing but a bally fortune-hunter, old boy,' they would say, discussing over the gin *pahits* some acquaintance who had made a rich marriage. 'Simply a blighted gigolo, old boy, nothing more. Can't do that sort of thing, old chap, what? Not cricket, old boy.'

And they were right. It couldn't be done. Damn it all, a feller had his code. '*Meh nee pan kong bahn rotfai*' about summed it up.

Stiffening his upper lip, Captain Biggar went down the road to see how his car was getting on.

2

Rowcester Abbey – pronounced Roaster – was about ten miles from the Goose and Gherkin. It stood – such portions of it as had not fallen down – just beyond Southmolton in the midst of smiling country. Though if you had asked William Egerton Bamfylde Ossingham Belfry, ninth Earl of Rowcester, its proprietor, what the English countryside had to smile about these days, he would have been unable to tell you. Its architecture was thirteenth-century, fifteenth-century and Tudor, its dilapidation twentieth-century post-World War Two.

To reach the abbey you turned off the main road and approached by a mile-long drive thickly encrusted with picturesque weeds and made your way up stone steps, chipped in spots, to a massive front door which badly needed a lick of paint. And this was what Bill Rowcester's sister Monica and her husband, Sir Roderick ('Rory') Carmoyle, had done at just about the hour when Mrs Spottsworth and Captain Biggar were starting to pick up the threads at their recent reunion.

Monica, usually addressed as Moke, was small and vivacious, her husband large and stolid. There was something about his aspect and deportment that suggested a more than ordinarily placid buffalo chewing a cud and taking in its surroundings very slowly and methodically, refusing to be hurried. It was thus that, as they stood on the front steps, he took in Rowcester Abbey.

'Moke,' he said at length, having completed his scrutiny, 'I'll tell you something which you may or may not see fit to release to the press. This bally place looks mouldier every time I see it.'

Monica was quick to defend her childhood home.

'It might be a lot worse.'

Rory considered this, chewing his cud for a while in silence.

'How?' he asked.

'I know it needs doing up, but where's the money to come from? Poor old Bill can't afford to run a castle on a cottage income.'

'Why doesn't he get a job like the rest of us?'

'You needn't stick on side just because you're in trade, you old counterjumper.'

'Everybody's doing it, I mean to say. Nowadays the House of Lords is practically empty except on evenings and bank holidays.'

'We Rowcesters aren't easy to place. The Rowcester men have all been lilies of the field. Why, Uncle George didn't even put on his own boots.'

'Whose boots did he put on?' asked Rory, interested.

'Ah, that's what we'd all like to know. Of course, Bill's big mistake was letting that American woman get away from him.'

'What American woman would that be?'

'It was just after you and I got married. A Mrs Bessemer. A widow. He met her in Cannes one summer. Fabulously rich and, according to Bill, unimaginably beautiful. It seemed promising for a time, but it didn't come to anything. I suppose someone cut him out. Of course, he was plain Mr Belfry then, not my lord Rowcester, which may have made a difference.'

Rory shook his head.

'It wouldn't be that. I was plain Mr Carmoyle when I met you and look at the way I snaffled you in the teeth of the pick of the County.'

'But then think what you were like in those days. A flick of the finger, a broken heart. And you're not so bad now, either,' added Monica fondly. 'Something of the old magic remains.'

'True,' said Rory placidly. 'In a dim light I still cast a spell. But the trouble with Bill was, I imagine, that he lacked *drive* . . . the sort of drive you see so much of at Harrige's. The will to win, I suppose you might call it. Napoleon had it. I have it, Bill hasn't. Oh, well, there it is,' said Rory philosophically. He resumed his study of Rowcester Abbey. 'You know what this house wants?' he proceeded. 'An atom bomb, dropped carefully on the roof of the main banqueting hall.'

'It would help, wouldn't it?'

'It would be the making of the old place. Put it right in no time. Still, atom bombs cost money, so I suppose that's out of the question. What you ought to do is use your influence with Bill to persuade him to buy a lot of paraffin and some shavings and save the morning papers and lay in plenty of matches and wait till some moonless night and give the joint the works. He'd feel a different man, once the old ruin was nicely ablaze.'

Monica looked mysterious.

'I can do better than that.'

Rory shook his head.

'No. Arson. It's the only way. You can't beat good old arson. Those fellows down in the east end go in for it a lot. They touch a match to the shop, and it's like a week at the seaside to them.'

'What would you say if I told you I was hoping to sell the house?'

Rory stared, amazed. He had a high opinion of his wife's resource-fulness, but he felt that she was attempting the impossible.

'Sell it? I don't believe you could give it away. I happen to know Bill offered it for a song to one of these charitable societies as a Home for Reclaimed Juvenile Delinquents, and they simply sneered at him. Probably thought it would give the Delinquents rheumatism. Very damp house, this.'

'It is a bit moist.'

'Water comes through the walls in heaping handfuls. I suppose because it's so close to the river. I remember saying to Bill once, "Bill," I said, "I'll tell you something about your home surroundings. In the summer the river is at the bottom of your garden, and in the winter your garden is at the bottom of the river." Amused the old boy quite a bit. He thought it clever.'

Monica regarded her husband with that cold, wifely eye which married men learn to dread.

'Very clever,' she said frostily. 'Extremely droll. And I suppose the first thing you'll do is make a crack like that to Mrs Spottsworth.'

'Eh?' It stole slowly into Rory's mind that a name had been mentioned that was strange to him. 'Who's Mrs Spottsworth?'

'The woman I'm hoping to sell the house to. American. Very rich. I met her when I was passing through New York on my way home. She owns dozens of houses in America, but she's got a craving to have something old and picturesque in England.'

'Romantic, eh?'

'Dripping with romance. Well, when she told me that – we were sitting next to each other at a women's lunch – I immediately thought of Bill and the abbey, of course, and started giving her a sales talk. She seemed interested. After all, the abbey is chock full of historical associations.'

'And mice.'

'She was flying to England next day, so I told her when I would be arriving and we arranged that she was to come here and have a look at the place. She should be turning up at any moment.'

'Does Bill know she's coming?'

'No. I ought to have sent him a cable, but I forgot. Still, what does it matter? He'll be only too delighted. The important thing is to keep you from putting her off with your mordant witticisms. "I often say in my amusing way, Mrs Spottsworth, that whereas in the summer months the river is at the bottom of the garden, in the winter months – ha, ha – the garden – this is going to slay you – is at the bottom of the river, ho, ho, ho." That would just clinch the sale.'

'Now would I be likely to drop a brick of that sort, old egg?'

'Extremely likely, old crumpet. The trouble with you is that, though a king among men, you have no tact.'

Rory smiled. The charge tickled him.

'No tact? The boys at Harrige's would laugh if they heard that.'

'Do remember that it's vital to put this deal through.'

'I'll bear it in mind. I'm all for giving poor old Bill a leg-up. It's a damn shame,' said Rory, who often thought rather deeply on these subjects. 'Bill starts at the bottom of the ladder as a mere heir to an earldom, and by pluck and perseverance works his way up till he becomes the Earl himself. And no sooner has he settled the coronet on his head and said to himself "Now to whoop it up!" than they pull a social revolution out of their hats like a rabbit and snitch practically every penny he's got. Ah, well!' said Rory with a sigh. 'I say,' he went on, changing the subject, 'have you noticed, Moke, old girl, that throughout this little chat of ours – which I for one have thoroughly enjoyed – I have been pressing the bell at frequent intervals and not a damn thing has happened? What is this joint, the palace of the sleeping beauty? Or do you think the entire strength of the company has been wiped out by some plague or pestilence?'

'Good heavens!' said Monica, 'bells at Rowcester Abbey don't ring. I don't suppose they've worked since Edward the Seventh's days. If Uncle George wished to summon the domestic staff, he just shoved his head back and howled like a prairie wolf.'

'That would have been, I take it, when he wanted somebody else's boots to put on?'

'You just open the door and walk in. Which is what I am about to do now. You bring the bags in from the car.'

'Depositing them where?'

'In the hall for the moment,' said Monica. 'You can take them upstairs later.'

She went in, and made her way to that familiar haunt, the living room off the hall where in her childhood days most of the life of Rowcester Abbey had centred. Like other English houses of its size, the abbey had a number of vast state apartments which were never used, a library which was used occasionally, and this living room, the popular meeting place. It was here that in earlier days she had sat and read the *Girl's Own Paper* and, until the veto had been placed on her activities by her Uncle George, whose sense of smell was acute, had kept white rabbits. A big, comfortable, shabby room with french windows opening into the garden, at the bottom of which – in the summer months – the river ran.

As she stood looking about her, sniffing the old familiar smell of tobacco and leather and experiencing, as always, a nostalgic thrill and a vague wish that it were possible to put the clock back, there came through the french window a girl in overalls, who, having stared for a moment in astonishment, uttered a delighted squeal.

'Moke . . . *darling!*'

Monica turned.

'Jill, my angel!'

They flung themselves into each other's arms.

3

Jill Wyvern was young, very pretty, slightly freckled and obviously extremely practical and competent. She wore her overalls as if they had been a uniform. Like Monica, she was small, and an admirer of hers, from Bloomsbury, had once compared her, in an unpublished poem, to a Tanagra statuette. It was not a very apt comparison, for Tanagra statuettes, whatever their merits, are on the static side and Jill was intensely alert and alive. She moved with a springy step and in her time had been a flashy outside-right on the hockey field.

'My precious Moke,' she said. 'Is it really you? I thought you were in Jamaica.'

'I got back this morning. I picked up Rory in London, and we motored down here. Rory's outside, looking after the bags.'

'How brown you are!'

'That's Montego Bay. I worked on this sunburn for three months.'

'It suits you. But Bill didn't say anything about expecting you. Aren't you appearing rather suddenly?'

'Yes, I cut my travels short rather suddenly. My allowance met those New York prices and gave up the ghost with a low moan. Ah, here's the merchant prince.'

Rory came in, mopping his forehead.

'What have you got in those bags of yours, old girl? Lead?' He saw Jill, and stopped, gazing at her with wrinkled brow. 'Oh, hullo,' he said uncertainly.

'You remember Jill Wyvern, Rory.'

'Of course, yes. Jill Wyvern, to be sure. As you so sensibly observe, Jill Wyvern. You been telling her about your sunburn?'

'She noticed it for herself.'

'It does catch the eye. She says she's that colour all over,' said Rory confidentially to Jill. 'Might raise a question or two from an old-fashioned husband, what? Still, I suppose it all makes for variety. So you're Jill Wyvern, are you? How you've grown!'

'Since when?'

'Since . . . since you started growing.'

'You haven't a notion who I am, have you?'

'I wouldn't say *that* . . .'

'I'll help you out. I was at your wedding.'

'You don't look old enough.'

'I was fifteen. They gave me the job of keeping the dogs from jumping on the guests. It was pouring, you may remember, and they all had muddy paws.'

'Good God! Now I have you placed. So *you* were that little squirt. I noticed you bobbing about and thought what a frightful young excrescence you looked.'

'My husband is noted for the polish of his manners,' said Monica. 'He is often called the modern Chesterfield.'

'What I was about to add,' said Rory with dignity, 'was that she's come on a lot since those days, showing that we should never despair. But didn't we meet again some time?'

'Yes, a year or two later when you stayed here one summer. I was just coming out then, and I expect I looked more of an excrescence than ever.'

Monica sighed.

'Coming out! The dear old getting-ready-for-market stage! How it takes one back. Off with the glasses and the teeth-braces.'

'On with things that push you in or push you out, whichever you needed.'

This was Rory's contribution, and Monica looked at him austerely.

'What do you know about it?'

'Oh, I get around in our Ladies' Foundation department,' said Rory.

Jill laughed.

'What I remember best are those agonized family conferences about my hockey-player's hands. I used to walk about for hours holding them in the air.'

'And how did you make out? Has it paid off yet?'

'Paid off?'

Monica lowered her voice confidentially.

'A man, dear. Did you catch anything worth while?'

'I think he's worth while. As a matter of fact, you don't know it, but you're moving in rather exalted circles. She whom you see before you is none other than the future Countess of Rowcester.'

Monica screamed excitedly.

'You don't mean you and Bill are engaged?'

'That's right.'

'Since when?'

'Some weeks ago.'

'I'm delighted. I wouldn't have thought Bill had so much sense.'

'No,' agreed Rory in his tactful way. 'One raises the eyebrows in astonishment. Bill, as I remember it, was always more of a lad for the buxom, voluptuous type. Many a passionate romance have I seen him through with females who looked like a cross between pantomime Fairy Queens and all-in wrestlers. There was a girl in the Hippodrome chorus –'

He broke off these reminiscences, so fraught with interest to a fiancée, in order to say 'Ouch!' Monica had kicked him shrewdly on the ankle.

'Tell me, darling,' said Monica. 'How did it happen? Suddenly?'

'Quite suddenly. He was helping me give a cow a bolus –'

Rory blinked. 'A –?'

'Bolus. Medicine. You give it to cows. And before I knew what was happening, he had grabbed my hand and was saying, "I say, arising from this, will you marry me?"'

'How frightfully eloquent. When Rory proposed to me, all he said was "Eh, what?"'

'And it took me three weeks to work up to that,' said Rory. His forehead had become wrinkled again. It was plain that he was puzzling over something. 'This bolus of which you were speaking. I don't quite follow. You were giving it to a cow, you say?'

'A sick cow.'

'Oh, a sick cow? Well, here's the point that's perplexing me. Here's the thing that seems to me to need straightening out. *Why* were you giving boluses to sick cows?'

'It's my job. I'm the local vet.'

'What! You don't by any chance mean a veterinary surgeon?'

'That's right. Fully licensed. We're all workers nowadays.'

Rory nodded sagely.

'Profoundly true,' he said. 'I'm a son of toil myself.'

'Rory's at Harrige's,' said Monica.

'Really?'

'Floorwalker in the Hosepipe, Lawn Mower and Bird Bath department,' said Rory. 'But that is merely temporary. There's a strong rumour going the rounds that hints at promotion to the Glass, Fancy Goods and Chinaware. And from there to the Ladies' Underclothing is but a step.'

'My hero!' Monica kissed him lovingly. 'I'll bet they'll all be green with jealousy.'

Rory was shocked at the suggestion.

'Good God, no! They'll rush to shake me by the hand and slap me on the back. Our *esprit de corps* is wonderful. It's one for all and all for one in Harrige's.'

Monica turned back to Jill.

'And doesn't your father mind you running about the country giving boluses to cows? Jill's father,' she explained to Rory, 'is Chief Constable of the county.'

'And very nice, too,' said Rory.

'I should have thought he would have objected.'

'Oh, no. We're all working at something. Except my brother Eustace. He won a Littlewood's pool last winter and he's gone frightfully upper class. Very high hat with the rest of the family. Moves on a different plane.'

'Damn snob,' said Rory warmly. 'I hate class distinctions.'

He was about to speak further, for the subject was one on which he held strong opinions, but at this moment the telephone bell rang, and he looked round, startled.

'For heaven's sake! Don't tell me the old boy has paid his telephone bill!' he cried, astounded.

Monica took up the receiver.

'Hullo? . . . Yes, this is Rowcester Abbey . . . No, Lord Rowcester is not in at the moment. This is his sister, Lady Carmoyle. The number of his car? It's news to me that he's *got* a car.' She turned to Jill. 'You don't know the number of Bill's car, do you?'

'No. Why are they asking?'

'Why are you asking?' said Monica into the telephone. She waited a moment, then hung up. 'He's rung off.'

'Who was it?'

'He didn't say. Just a voice from the void.'

'You don't think Bill's had an accident?'

'Good heavens, no,' said Rory. 'He's much too good a driver. Probably he had to stop somewhere to buy some juice, and they need his number for their books. But it's always disturbing when people don't give their names on the telephone. There was a fellow in ours – second in command in the Jams, Sauces and Potted Meats – who was rung up one night by a Mystery Voice that wouldn't give its name, and to cut a long story short –'

Monica did so.

'Save it up for after dinner, my king of raconteurs,' she said. 'If there is any dinner,' she added doubtfully.

'Oh, there'll be dinner all right,' said Jill, 'and you'll probably find it'll melt in the mouth. Bill's got a very good cook.'

Monica stared.

'A cook? These days? I don't believe it. You'll be telling me next he's got a housemaid.'

'He has. Name of Ellen.'

'Pull yourself together, child. You're talking wildly. Nobody has a housemaid.'

'Bill has. And a gardener. And a butler. A wonderful butler called Jeeves. And he's thinking of getting a boy to clean the knives and boots.'

'Good heavens! It sounds like the home life of the Aga Khan.' Monica frowned thoughtfully. 'Jeeves?' she said. 'Why does that name seem to ring a bell?'

Rory supplied illumination.

'Bertie Wooster. He has a man named Jeeves. This is probably a brother or an aunt or something.'

'No,' said Jill. 'It's the same man. Bill has him on lend-lease.'

'But how on earth does Bertie get on without him?'

'I believe Mr Wooster's away somewhere. Anyhow, Jeeves appeared one day and said he was willing to take office, so Bill grabbed him, of course. He's an absolute treasure. Bill says he's an "old soul", whatever that means.'

Monica was still bewildered.

'But how about the financial end? Does he pay this entourage, or just give them a pleasant smile now and then?'

'Of course he pays them. Lavishly. He flings them purses of gold every Saturday morning.'

'Where does the money come from?'

'He earns it.'

'Don't be silly. Bill hasn't earned a penny since he was paid twopence a time for taking his castor oil. How could he possibly earn it?'

'He's doing some sort of work for the Agricultural Board.'

'You don't make a fortune out of that.'

'Bill seems to. I suppose he's so frightfully good at his job that they pay him more than the others. I don't know what he does, actually. He just goes off in his car. Some kind of inspection, I suppose it is. Checking up on all those questionnaires. He's not very good at figures, so he always takes Jeeves with him.'

'Well, that's wonderful,' said Monica. 'I was afraid he might have started backing horses again. It used to worry me so much in the old days, the way he would dash from race-course to race-course in a grey topper that he carried sandwiches in.'

'Oh, no, it couldn't be anything like that. He promised me faithfully he would never bet on a horse again.'

'Very sensible,' said Rory. 'I don't mind a flutter from time to time, of course. At Harrige's we always run a Sweep on big events, five-bob chances. The brass hats frown on anything larger.'

Jill moved to the french window.

'Well, I mustn't stand here talking,' she said. 'I've got work to do. I came to attend to Bill's Irish terrier. It's sick of a fever.'

'Give it a bolus.'

'I'm giving it some new American ointment. It's got mange. See you later.'

Jill went off on her errand of mercy, and Rory turned to Monica. His customary stolidity had vanished. He was keen and alert, like Sherlock Holmes on the trail.

'Moke!'

'Hullo?'

'What do you make of it, old girl?'

'Make of what?'

'This sudden affluence of Bill's. There's something fishy going on here. If it had just been a matter of a simple butler, one could have understood it. A broker's man in disguise, one would have said. But how about the housemaid and the cook and the car and, by Jove, the fact that he's paid his telephone bill.'

'I see what you mean. It's odd.'

'It's more than odd. Consider the facts. The last time I was at Rowcester Abbey, Bill was in the normal state of destitution of the upper-class Englishman of today, stealing the cat's milk and nosing about in the gutters for cigar ends. I come here now, and what do I find? Butlers in every nook and cranny, housemaids as far as the eye can reach, cooks jostling each other in the kitchen, Irish terriers everywhere, and a lot of sensational talk going on about boys to clean the knives and boots. It's . . . what's the word?'

'I don't know.'

'Yes, you do. Begins with "in".'

'Influential? Inspirational? Infra red?'

'Inexplicable. That's what it is. The whole thing is utterly inexplicable. One dismisses all that stuff about jobs with the Agricultural Board as pure eyewash. You don't cut a stupendous dash like this on a salary from the Agricultural Board.' Rory paused, and ruminated for a moment. 'I wonder if the old boy's been launching out as a gentleman burglar.'

'Don't be an idiot.'

'Well, fellows do, you know. Raffles, if you remember. He was one, and made a dashed good thing out of it. Or could it be that he's blackmailing somebody?'

'Oh, Rory.'

'Very profitable, I believe. You look around for some wealthy bimbo and nose out his guilty secrets, then you send him a letter saying that you know all and tell him to leave ten thousand quid in small notes under the second milestone on the London road. When you've spent that, you tap him for another ten. It all mounts up over a period of time, and would explain these butlers, housemaids and what not very neatly.'

'If you would talk less drivel and take more bags upstairs, the world would be a better place.'

Rory thought it over and got her meaning.

'You want me to take the bags upstairs?'

'I do.'

'Right ho. The Harrige motto is Service.'

The telephone rang again. Rory went to it.

'Hullo?' He started violently. 'The *who*? Good God! All right. He's out now, but I'll tell him when I see him.' He hung up. There was a grave look on his face. 'Moke,' he said, 'perhaps you'll believe me another time and not scoff and mock when I advance my theories. That was the police.'

'The police?'

'They want to talk to Bill.'

'What about?'

'They didn't say. Well, dash it, they wouldn't, would they? Official Secrets Acts and all that sort of thing. But they're closing in on him, old girl, closing in on him.'

'Probably all they want is to get him to present the prizes at the police sports or something.'

'I doubt it,' said Rory. 'Still, hold that thought if it makes you happier. Take the bags upstairs, you were saying? I'll do it instanter. Come along and encourage me with word and gesture.'

4

For some moments after they had gone the peace of the summer evening was broken only by the dull, bumping sound of a husband carrying suitcases upstairs. This died away, and once more a drowsy stillness stole over Rowcester Abbey. Then, faintly at first but growing louder, there came from the distance the chugging of a car. It stopped, and there entered through the french window a young man. He tottered in, breathing heavily like a hart that pants for cooling streams when heated in the chase, and having produced his cigarette case lit a cigarette in an overwrought way, as if he had much on his mind.

Or what one may loosely call his mind. William, ninth Earl of Rowcester, though intensely amiable and beloved by all who knew him, was far from being a mental giant. From his earliest years his intimates had been aware that, while his heart was unquestionably in the right place, there was a marked shortage of the little grey cells, and it was generally agreed that whoever won the next Nobel prize, it would not be Bill Rowcester. At the Drones Club, of which he had been a member since leaving school, it was estimated that in the matter of intellect he ranked somewhere in between Freddie Widgeon and Pongo Twistleton, which is pretty low down on the list. There were some, indeed, who held his IQ to be inferior to that of Barmy Fotheringay-Phipps.

Against this must be set the fact that, like all his family, he was extremely good-looking, though those who considered him so might have revised their views, had they seen him now. For in addition to wearing a very loud check coat with bulging, voluminous pockets and a crimson tie with blue horseshoes on it which smote the beholder like a blow, he had a large black patch over his left eye and on his upper lip a ginger moustache of the outsize or soupstrainer type. In the clean-shaven world in which we live today it is not often that one sees a moustache of this almost tropical luxuriance, and it is not often, it may be added, that one wants to.

A black patch and a ginger moustache are grave defects, but that the ninth earl was not wholly dead to a sense of shame was shown by the convulsive start, like the leap of an adagio dancer, which he gave a moment later when, wandering about the room, he suddenly caught sight of himself in an old-world mirror that hung on the wall.

'Good Lord!' he exclaimed, recoiling.

With nervous fingers he removed the patch, thrust it into his pocket, tore the fungoid growth from his lip and struggled out of the check coat. This done, he went to the window, leaned out and called in a low, conspiratorial voice.

'Jeeves!'

There was no answer.

'Hi, Jeeves, where are you?'

Again silence.

Bill gave a whistle, then another. He was still whistling, his body half-way through the french window, when the door behind him opened, revealing a stately form.

The man who entered – or perhaps one should say shimmered into – the room was tall and dark and impressive. He might have been one of the better-class ambassadors or the youngish High Priest of some refined and dignified religion. His eyes gleamed with the light of intelligence, and his finely chiselled face expressed a feudal desire to be of service. His whole air was that of a gentleman's gentleman who, having developed his brain over a course of years by means of a steady fish diet, is eager to place that brain at the disposal of the young master. He was carrying over one arm a coat of sedate colour and a tie of conservative pattern.

'You whistled, m'lord?' he said.

Bill spun round.

'How the dickens did you get over there, Jeeves?'

'I ran the car into the garage, m'lord, and then made my way to the servants' quarters. Your coat, m'lord.'

'Oh, thanks. I see you've changed.'

'I deemed it advisable, m'lord. The gentleman was not far behind us as we rounded into the straight and may at any moment be calling. Were he to encounter on the threshold a butler in a check suit and a false moustache, it is possible that his suspicions might be aroused. I am glad to see that your lordship has removed that somewhat distinctive tie. Excellent for creating atmosphere on the race-course, it is scarcely vogue in private life.'

Bill eyed the repellent object with a shudder.

'I've always hated that beastly thing, Jeeves. All those foul horse-shoes. Shove it away somewhere. And the coat.'

'Very good, m'lord. This coffer should prove adequate as a

temporary receptacle.' Jeeves took the coat and tie, and crossed the room to where a fine old oak dower chest stood, an heirloom long in the Rowcester family. 'Yes,' he said, ''Tis not so deep as a well nor so wide as a church door, but 'tis enough, 'twill serve.'

He folded the distressing objects carefully, placed them inside and closed the lid. And even this simple act he performed with a quiet dignity which would have impressed any spectator less agitated than Bill Rowcester. It was like seeing the plenipotentiary of a great nation lay a wreath on the tomb of a deceased monarch.

But Bill, as we say, was agitated. He was brooding over an earlier remark that had fallen from this great man's lips.

'What do you mean, the gentleman may at any moment be calling?' he asked. The thought of receiving a visit from that red-faced man with the loud voice who had bellowed abuse at him all the way from Epsom Downs to Southmoltonshire was not an unmixedly agreeable one.

'It is possible that he observed and memorized the number of our car, m'lord. He was in a position to study our licence plate for some considerable time, your lordship will recollect.'

Bill sank limply into a chair and brushed a bead of perspiration from his forehead. This contingency, as Jeeves would have called it, had not occurred to him. Placed before him now, it made him feel filleted.

'Oh, golly, I never thought of that. Then he would get the owner's name and come racing along here, wouldn't he?'

'So one would be disposed to imagine, m'lord.'

'Hell's bells, Jeeves!'

'Yes, m'lord.'

Bill applied the handkerchief to his forehead again.

'What do I do if he does?'

'I would advise your lordship to assume a nonchalant air and disclaim all knowledge of the matter.'

'With a light laugh, you mean?'

'Precisely, m'lord.'

Bill tried a light laugh. 'How did that sound, Jeeves?'

'Barely adequate, m'lord.'

'More like a death rattle?'

'Yes, m'lord.'

'I shall need a few rehearsals.'

'Several, m'lord. It will be essential to carry conviction.'

Bill kicked petulantly at a footstool.

'How do you expect me to carry conviction, feeling the way I do?'

'I can readily appreciate that your lordship is disturbed.'

'I'm all of a twitter. Have you ever seen a jelly hit by a cyclone?'

'No, m'lord, I have never been present on such an occasion.'

'It quivers. So do I.'

'After such an ordeal your lordship would be unstrung.'

'Ordeal is the right word, Jeeves. Apart from the frightful peril one is in, it was so dashed ignominious having to leg it like that.'

'I should hardly describe our recent activities as legging it, m'lord. "Strategic retreat" is more the *mot juste*. This is a recognized military manoeuvre, practised by all the greatest tacticians when the occasion seemed to call for such a move. I have no doubt that General Eisenhower has had recourse to it from time to time.'

'But I don't suppose he had a fermenting punter after him, shouting "Welsher!" at the top of his voice.'

'Possibly not, m'lord.'

Bill brooded. 'It was that word "Welsher" that hurt, Jeeves.'

'I can readily imagine it, m'lord. Objected to as irrelevant, incompetent and immaterial, as I believe the legal expression is. As your lordship several times asseverated during our precarious homeward journey, you have every intention of paying the gentleman.'

'Of course I have. No argument about that. Naturally I intend to brass up to the last penny. It's a case of . . . what, Jeeves?'

'*Noblesse oblige*, m'lord.'

'Exactly. The honour of the Rowcesters is at stake. But I must have time, dash it, to raise three thousand pounds two and six.'

'Three thousand and five pounds two and six, m'lord. Your lordship is forgetting the gentleman's original five-pound note.'

'So I am. You trousered it and came away with it in your pocket.'

'Precisely, m'lord. Thus bringing the sum total of your obligations to this Captain Biggar –'

'Was that his name?'

'Yes, m'lord. Captain C.G. Brabazon-Biggar, United Rovers Club, Northumberland Avenue, London WC2. In my capacity as your lordship's clerk I wrote the name and address on the ticket which he now has in his possession. The note which he handed to me and which I duly accepted as your lordship's official representative raises your commitments to three thousand and five pounds two shillings and sixpence.'

'Oh, gosh!'

'Yes, m'lord. It is not an insignificant sum. Many a poor man would be glad of three thousand and five pounds two shillings and sixpence.'

Bill winced. 'I would be grateful, Jeeves, if you could see your way not to keep on intoning those words.'

'Very good, m'lord.'

'They are splashed on my soul in glorious Technicolor.'

'Quite so, m'lord.'

'Who was it who said that when he or she was dead, the word something would be found carved on his or her heart?'

'Queen Mary, m'lord, the predecessor of the great Queen Elizabeth. The word was "Calais", and the observation was intended to convey her chagrin at the loss of that town.'

'Well, when I die, which will be very shortly if I go on feeling as I do now, just cut me open, Jeeves –'

'Certainly, m'lord.'

'– and I'll bet you a couple of bob you'll find carved on my heart the words "Three thousand and five pounds two and six".'

Bill rose and paced the room with fevered steps.

'How does one scrape together a sum like that, Jeeves?'

'It will call for thrift, m'lord.'

'You bet it will. It'll take years.'

'And Captain Biggar struck me as an impatient gentleman.'

'You needn't rub it in, Jeeves.'

'Very good, m'lord.'

'Let's keep our minds on the present.'

'Yes, m'lord. Remember that man's life lies all within this present, as 'twere but a hair's breadth of time. As for the rest, the past is gone, the future yet unseen.'

'Eh?'

'Marcus Aurelius, m'lord.'

'Oh? Well, as I was saying, let us glue our minds on what is going to happen if this Biggar suddenly blows in here. Do you think he'll recognize me?'

'I am inclined to fancy not, m'lord. The moustache and the patch formed a very effective disguise. After all, in the past few months we have encountered several gentlemen of your lordship's acquaintance –'

'And not one of them spotted me.'

'No, m'lord. Nevertheless, facing the facts, I fear we must regard this afternoon's episode as a set-back. It is clearly impossible for us to function at the Derby tomorrow.'

'I was looking forward to cleaning up on the Derby.'

'I, too, m'lord. But after what has occurred, one's entire turf activities must, I fear, be regarded as suspended indefinitely.'

'You don't think we could risk one more pop?'

'No, m'lord.'

'I see what you mean, of course. Show up at Epsom tomorrow, and the first person we'd run into would be this Captain Biggar –'

'Straddling, like Apollyon, right across the way. Precisely, m'lord.'

Bill passed a hand through his disordered hair.

'If only I had frozen on to the money we made at Newmarket!'

'Yes, m'lord. Of all sad words of tongue or pen the saddest are these – It might have been. Whittier.'

'You warned me not to let our capital fall too low.'

'I felt that we were not equipped to incur any heavy risk. That was why I urged your lordship so vehemently to lay Captain Biggar's second wager off. I had misgivings. True, the probability of the double bearing fruit at such odds was not great, but when I saw Whistler's Mother pass us on her way to the starting post, I was conscious of a tremor of uneasiness. Those long legs, that powerful rump . . .'

'Don't, Jeeves!'

'Very good, m'lord.'

'I'm trying not to think of Whistler's Mother.'

'I quite understand, m'lord.'

'Who the dickens *was* Whistler, anyway?'

'A figure, landscape and portrait painter of considerable distinction, m'lord, born in Lowell, Massachusetts, in 1834. His *Portrait of my Mother*, painted in 1872, is particularly esteemed by the *cognoscenti* and was purchased by the French Government for the Luxembourg Gallery, Paris, in 1892. His works are individual in character and notable for subtle colour harmony.'

Bill breathed a little stertorously.

'It's subtle, is it?'

'Yes, m'lord.'

'I see. Thanks for telling me. I was worrying myself sick about his colour harmony.' Bill became calmer. 'Jeeves, if the worst comes to the worst and Biggar does catch me bending, can I gain a bit of time by pleading the Gaming Act?'

'I fear not, m'lord. You took the gentleman's money. A cash transaction.'

'It would mean choky, you feel?'

'I fancy so, m'lord.'

'Would you be jugged, too, as my clerk?'

'In all probability, m'lord. I am not quite certain on the point. I should have to consult my solicitor.'

'But I would be for it?'

'Yes, m'lord. The sentences, however, are not, I believe, severe.'

'But think of the papers. The ninth Earl of Rowcester, whose ancestors held the field at Agincourt, skipped from the field at Epsom with a slavering punter after him. It'll be jam for the newspaper boys.'

'Unquestionably the circumstance of your lordship having gone into business as a Silver Ring bookmaker would be accorded wide publicity.'

Bill, who had been pacing the floor again, stopped in mid-stride and regarded the speaker with an accusing eye.

'And who was it suggested that I should go into business as a Silver Ring bookie? You, Jeeves. I don't want to be harsh, but you must own that the idea came from you. You were the –'

'*Fons et origo mali*, m'lord? That, I admit, is true. But if your lordship will recall, we were in something of a quandary. We had agreed that your lordship's impending marriage made it essential to augment your lordship's slender income, and we went through the Classified Trades section of the telephone directory in quest of a possible profession which your lordship might adopt. It was merely because nothing of a suitable nature had presented itself by the time we reached the T's that I suggested Turf Accountant *faute de mieux*.'

'*Faute de* what?'

'*Mieux*, m'lord. A French expression. We should say "for want of anything better".'

'What asses these Frenchmen are! Why can't they talk English?'

'They are possibly more to be pitied than censured, m'lord. Early upbringing no doubt has a good deal to do with it. As I was saying, it seemed to me a happy solution of your lordship's difficulties. In the United States of America, I believe, bookmakers are considered persons of a somewhat low order and are, indeed, suppressed by the police, but in England it is very different. Here they are looked up to and courted. There is a school of thought which regards them as the new aristocracy. They make a great deal of money, and have the added gratification of not paying income tax.'

Bill sighed wistfully.

'*We* made a lot of money up to Newmarket.'

'Yes, m'lord.'

'And where is it now?'

'Where, indeed, m'lord?'

'I shouldn't have spent so much doing up the place.'

'No, m'lord.'

'And it was a mistake to pay my tailor's bill.'

'Yes, m'lord. One feels that your lordship did somewhat overdo it there. As the old Roman observed, *ne quid nimis*.'

'Yes, that was rash. Still, no good beefing about it now, I suppose.'

'No, m'lord. The moving finger writes, and having writ –'

'Hoy!'

'– moves on, nor all your piety and wit can lure it back to cancel half a line nor all your tears wash out one word of it. You were saying, m'lord?'

'I was only going to ask you to cheese it.'

'Certainly, m'lord.'

'Not in the mood.'

'Quite so, m'lord. It was only the appositeness of the quotation – from the works of the Persian poet Omar Khayyám – that led me to speak. I wonder if I might ask a question, m'lord?'

'Yes, Jeeves?'

'Is Miss Wyvern aware of your lordship's professional connection with the turf?'

Bill quivered like an aspen at the mere suggestion.

'I should say not. She would throw fifty-seven fits if she knew. I've rather given her the idea that I'm employed by the Agricultural Board.'

'A most respectable body of men.'

'I didn't actually say so in so many words. I just strewed the place with Agricultural Board report forms and took care she saw them. Did you know that they issue a hundred and seventy-nine different blanks other than the seventeen questionnaires?'

'No, m'lord. I was not aware. It shows zeal.'

'Great zeal. They're on their toes, those boys.'

'Yes, m'lord.'

'But we're wandering from the point, which is that Miss Wyvern must never learn the awful truth. It would be fatal. At the outset of our betrothal she put her foot down firmly on the subject of my tendency to have an occasional flutter, and I promised her faithfully that I would never punt again. Well, you might argue that being a Silver Ring bookie is not the same thing as punting, but I doubt if you would ever sell that idea to Miss Wyvern.'

'The distinction is certainly a nice one, m'lord.'

'Let her discover the facts, and all would be lost.'

'Those wedding bells would not ring out.'

'They certainly wouldn't. She would return me to store before I could say "What ho". So if she comes asking questions, reveal nothing. Not even if she sticks lighted matches between your toes.'

'The contingency is a remote one, m'lord.'

'Possibly. I'm merely saying, whatever happens, Jeeves, secrecy and silence.'

'You may rely on me, m'lord. In the inspired words of Pliny the Younger –'

Bill held up a hand. 'Right ho, Jeeves.'

'Very good, m'lord.'

'I'm not interested in Pliny the Younger.'

'No, m'lord.'

'As far as I'm concerned, you may take Pliny the Younger and put him where the monkey put the nuts.'

'Certainly, m'lord.'

'And now leave me, Jeeves. I have a lot of heavy brooding to do. Go and get me a stiffish whisky and soda.'

'Very good, m'lord. I will attend to the matter immediately.'

Jeeves melted from the room with a look of respectful pity, and Bill sat down and put his head between his hands. A hollow groan escaped him, and he liked the sound of it and gave another.

He was starting on a third, bringing it up from the soles of his feet, when a voice spoke at his side.

'Good heavens, Bill. What on earth's the matter?'

Jill Wyvern was standing there.

5

In the interval which had elapsed since her departure from the living room, Jill had rubbed American ointment on Mike the Irish terrier, taken a look at a goldfish belonging to the cook, which had caused anxiety in the kitchen by refusing its ants' eggs, and made a routine tour of the pigs and cows, giving one of the latter a bolus. She had returned to the house agreeably conscious of duty done and looking forward to a chat with her loved one, who, she presumed, would by now be back from his Agricultural Board rounds and in a mood for pleasant dalliance. For even when the Agricultural Board know they have got hold of an exceptionally good man and wish (naturally) to get every possible ounce of work out of him, they are humane enough to let the poor peon call it a day round about the hour of the evening cocktail.

To find him groaning with his head in his hands was something of a shock.

'What on earth's the matter?' she repeated.

Bill had sprung from his chair with a convulsive leap. That loved voice, speaking unexpectedly out of the void when he supposed himself to be alone with his grief, had affected him like a buzz-saw applied to the seat of his trousers. If it had been Captain C.G. Brabazon-Biggar, of the United Rovers Club, Northumberland Avenue, he could not have been much more perturbed. He gaped at her, quivering in every limb. Jeeves, had he been present, would have been reminded of Macbeth seeing the ghost of Banquo.

'Matter?' he said, inserting three Ms at the beginning of the word.

Jill was looking at him with grave, speculative eyes. She had that direct, honest gaze which many nice girls have, and as a rule Bill liked it. But at the moment he could have done with something that did not pierce quite so like a red-hot gimlet to his inmost soul. A sense of guilt makes a man allergic to direct, honest gazes.

'Matter?' he said, getting the word shorter and crisper this time.

'What do you mean, what's the matter? Nothing's the matter. Why do you ask?'

'You were groaning like a foghorn.'

'Oh, that. Touch of neuralgia.'

'You've got a headache?'

'Yes, it's been coming on for some time. I've had rather an exhausting afternoon.'

'Why, aren't the crops rotating properly? Or are the pigs going in for smaller families?'

'My chief problem today,' said Bill dully, 'concerned horses.'

A quick look of suspicion came into Jill's gaze. Like all nice girls, she had, where the man she loved was concerned, something of the Private Eye about her.

'Have you been betting again?'

Bill stared.

'*Me?*'

'You gave me your solemn promise you wouldn't. Oh, Bill, you are an idiot. You're more trouble to look after than a troupe of performing seals. Can't you see it's just throwing money away? Can't you get it into your fat head that the punters haven't a hope against the bookmakers? I know people are always talking about bringing off fantastic doubles and winning thousands of pounds with a single fiver, but that sort of thing never really happens. What did you say?'

Bill had not spoken. The sound that had proceeded from his twisted lips had been merely a soft moan like that of an emotional red Indian at the stake.

'It happens sometimes,' he said hollowly. 'I've heard of cases.'

'Well, it couldn't happen to you. Horses just aren't lucky for you.'

Bill writhed. The illusion that he was being roasted over a slow fire had become extraordinarily vivid.

'Yes,' he said, 'I see that now.'

Jill's gaze became more direct and penetrating than ever.

'Come clean, Bill. Did you back a loser in the Oaks?'

This was so diametrically opposite to what had actually occurred that Bill perked up a little.

'Of course I didn't.'

'You swear?'

'I may begin to at any moment.'

'You didn't back anything in the Oaks?'

'Certainly not.'

'Then what's the matter?'

'I told you. I've got a headache.'

'Poor old thing. Can I get you anything?'

'No, thanks. Jeeves is bringing me a whisky and soda.'

'Would a kiss help, while you're waiting?'

'It would save a human life.'

Jill kissed him, but absently. She appeared to be thinking.

'Jeeves was with you today, wasn't he?' she said.

'Yes. Yes, Jeeves was along.'

'You always take him with you on these expeditions of yours.'

'Yes.'

'Where do you go?'

'We make the rounds.'

'Doing what?'

'Oh, this and that.'

'I see. How's the headache?'

'A little better, thanks.'

'Good.'

There was silence for a moment.

'I used to have headaches a few years ago,' said Jill.

'Bad?'

'Quite bad. I suffered agonies.'

'They do touch you up, don't they?'

'They do. But,' proceeded Jill, her voice rising and a hard note creeping into her voice, 'my headaches, painful as they were, never made me look like an escaped convict lurking in a bush listening to the baying of the bloodhounds and wondering every minute when the hand of doom was going to fall on the seat of his pants. And that's how you are looking now. There's guilt written on your every feature. If you were to tell me at this moment that you had done a murder and were worrying because you had suddenly remembered you hadn't hidden the body properly, I would say "I thought as much". Bill, for the last time, what's the matter?'

'Nothing's the matter.'

'Don't tell me.'

'I am telling you.'

'There's nothing on your mind?'

'Not a thing.'

'You're as gay and carefree as a lark singing in the summer sky?'

'If anything, rather more so.'

There was another silence. Jill was biting her lip, and Bill wished she wouldn't. There is, of course, nothing actually low and degrading in a girl biting her lip, but it is a spectacle that a *fiancé* with a good deal on his mind can never really enjoy.

'Bill, tell me,' said Jill. 'How do you feel about marriage?'

Bill brightened. This, he felt, was more the stuff.

'I think it's an extraordinarily good egg. Always provided, of course, that the male half of the sketch is getting someone like you.'

'Never mind the pretty speeches. Shall I tell you how I feel about it?'

'Do.'

'I feel that unless there is absolute trust between a man and a girl, they're crazy even to think of getting married, because if they're going to hide things from each other and not tell each other their troubles, their marriage is bound to go on the rocks sooner or later. A husband and wife ought to tell each other everything. I wouldn't ever dream of keeping anything from you, and if it interests you to know it, I'm as sick as mud to think that you're keeping this trouble of yours, whatever it is, from me.'

'I'm not in any trouble.'

'You are. What's happened, I don't know, but a short-sighted mole that's lost its spectacles could see that you're a soul in torment. When I came in here, you were groaning your head off.'

Bill's self-control, so sorely tried today, cracked.

'Damn it all,' he bellowed, 'why shouldn't I groan? I believe Rowcester Abbey is open for being groaned in at about this hour, is it not? I wish to heaven you would leave me alone,' he went on, gathering momentum. 'Who do you think you are? One of these G-men fellows questioning some rat of the Underworld? I suppose you'll be asking next where I was on the night of February the twenty-first. Don't be such an infernal Nosy Parker.'

Jill was a girl of spirit, and with girls of spirit this sort of thing soon reaches saturation point.

'I don't know if you know it,' she said coldly, 'but when you spit on your hands and get down to it, you can be the world's premier louse.'

'That's a nice thing to say.'

'Well, it's the truth,' said Jill. 'You're simply a pig in human shape. And if you want to know what I think,' she went on, gathering momentum in her turn, 'I believe what's happened is that you've gone and got mixed up with some awful female.'

'You're crazy. Where the dickens could I have met any awful females?'

'I should imagine you have had endless opportunities. You're always going off in your car, sometimes for a week at a stretch. For all I know, you may have been spending your time festooned with hussies.'

'I wouldn't so much as look at a hussy if you brought her to me on a plate with watercress round her.'

'I don't believe you.'

'And it was you, if memory serves me aright,' said Bill, 'who some two and a half seconds ago were shooting off your head about the necessity for absolute trust between us. Women!' said Bill bitterly. 'Women! My God, what a sex!'

On this difficult situation Jeeves entered, bearing a glass on a salver.

'Your whisky and soda, m'lord,' he said, much as a President of the United States might have said to a deserving citizen 'Take this Congressional medal'.

Bill accepted the restorative gratefully.

'Thank you, Jeeves. Not a moment before it was needed.'

'And Sir Roderick and Lady Carmoyle are in the yew alley, asking to see you, m'lord.'

'Good heavens! Rory and the Moke? Where did they spring from? I thought she was in Jamaica.'

'Her ladyship returned this morning, I understand, and Sir Roderick obtained compassionate leave from Harrige's in order to accompany her here. They desired me to inform your lordship that they would be glad of a word with you at your convenience before the arrival of Mrs Spottsworth.'

'Before the what of who? Who on earth's Mrs Spottsworth?'

'An American lady whose acquaintance her ladyship made in New York, m'lord. She is expected here this evening. I gathered from what her ladyship and Sir Roderick were saying that there is some prospect of Mrs Spottsworth buying the house.'

Bill gaped.

'Buying the house?'

'Yes, m'lord.'

'*This* house?'

'Yes, m'lord.'

'Rowcester Abbey, you mean?'

'Yes, m'lord.'

'You're pulling my leg, Jeeves.'

'I would not take such a liberty, m'lord.'

'You seriously mean that this refugee from whatever American loony-bin it was where she was under observation until she sneaked out with false whiskers on is actually contemplating paying hard cash for Rowcester Abbey?'

'That was the interpretation which I placed on the remarks of her ladyship and Sir Roderick, m'lord.'

Bill drew a deep breath.

'Well, I'll be blowed. It just shows you that it takes all sorts to make a world. Is she coming to stay?'

'So I understood, m'lord.'

'Then you might remove the two buckets you put to catch the water under the upper hall skylight. They create a bad impression.'

'Yes, m'lord. I will also place some more drawing pins in the wallpaper. Where would your lordship be thinking of depositing Mrs Spottsworth?'

'She'd better have the Queen Elizabeth room. It's the best we've got.'

'Yes, m'lord. I will insert a wire screen in the flue to discourage intrusion by the bats that nest there.'

'We can't give her a bathroom, I'm afraid.'

'I fear not, m'lord.'

'Still, if she can make do with a shower, she can stand under the upper hall skylight.'

Jeeves pursed his lips.

'If I might offer the suggestion, m'lord, it is not judicious to speak in that strain. Your lordship might forget yourself and let fall some such observation in the hearing of Mrs Spottsworth.'

Jill, standing at the french window and looking out with burning eyes, had turned and was listening, electrified. The generous wrath which had caused her to allude to her betrothed as a pig in human shape had vanished completely. It could not compete with this stupendous news. As far as Jill was concerned, the war was over.

She thoroughly concurred with Jeeves's rebuke.

'Yes, you poor fish,' she said. 'You mustn't even think like that. Oh, Bill, isn't it wonderful! If this comes off, you'll have money enough to buy a farm. I'm sure we'd do well running a farm, me as a vet and you with all your expert farming knowledge.'

'My what?'

Jeeves coughed.

'I think Miss Wyvern is alluding to the fact that you have had such wide experience working for the Agricultural Board, m'lord.'

'Oh, ah, yes. I see what you mean. Of course, yes, the Agricultural Board. Thank you, Jeeves.'

'Not at all, m'lord.'

Jill developed her theme.

'If you could sting this Mrs Spottsworth for something really big, we could start a prize herd. That pays like anything. I wonder how much you could get for the place.'

'Not much, I'm afraid. It's seen better days.'

'What are you going to ask?'

'Three thousand and five pounds two shillings and sixpence.'

'What!'

Bill blinked.

'Sorry. I was thinking of something else.'

'But what put an odd sum like that into your head?'

'I don't know.'

'You must know.'

'I don't.'

'But you must have had some *reason*.'

'The sum in question arose in the course of his lordship's work in connection with his Agricultural Board duties this afternoon, miss,' said Jeeves smoothly. 'Your lordship may recall that I observed at the time that it was a peculiar figure.'

'So you did, Jeeves, so you did.'

'That was why your lordship said "Three thousand and five pounds two shillings and sixpence".'

'Yes, that was why I said "Three thousand and five pounds two shillings and sixpence".'

'These momentary mental aberrations are not uncommon, I believe. If I might suggest it, m'lord, I think it would be advisable to proceed to the yew alley without further delay. Time is of the essence.'

'Of course, yes. They're waiting for me, aren't they? Are you coming, Jill?'

'I can't, darling. I have patients to attend to. I've got to go all the way over to Stover to see the Mainwarings' Peke, though I don't suppose there's the slightest thing wrong with it. That dog is the worst hypochondriac.'

'Well, you're coming to dinner all right?'

'Of course. I'm counting the minutes. My mouth's watering already.'

Jill went out through the french window. Bill mopped his forehead. It had been a near thing.

'You saved me there, Jeeves,' he said. 'But for your quick thinking all would have been discovered.'

'I am happy to have been of service, m'lord.'

'Another instant, and womanly intuition would have been doing its stuff, with results calculated to stagger humanity. You eat a lot of fish, don't you, Jeeves?'

'A good deal, m'lord.'

'So Bertie Wooster has often told me. You sail into the sole and sardines like nobody's business, he says, and he attributes your giant intellect to the effects of the phosphorus. A hundred times, he says, it has enabled you to snatch him from the soup at the eleventh hour. He raves about your great gifts.'

'Mr Wooster has always been gratifyingly appreciative of my humble efforts on his behalf, m'lord.'

'What beats me and has always beaten me is why he ever let you go. When you came to me that day and said you were at liberty, you could have bowled me over. The only explanation I could think of was that he was off his rocker . . . or more off his rocker than he usually is. Or did you have a row with him and hand in your portfolio?'

Jeeves seemed distressed at the suggestion.

'Oh, no, m'lord. My relations with Mr Wooster continue uniformly cordial, but circumstances have compelled a temporary separation. Mr Wooster is attending a school which does not permit its student body to employ gentlemen's personal gentlemen.'

'A school?'

'An institution designed to teach the aristocracy to fend for itself, m'lord. Mr Wooster, though his finances are still quite sound, feels that it is prudent to build for the future, in case the social revolution should set in with even greater severity. Mr Wooster . . . I can hardly mention this without some display of emotion . . . is actually learning to darn his own socks. The course he is taking includes boot-cleaning, sock-darning, bed-making and primary-grade cooking.'

'Golly! Well, that's certainly a novel experience for Bertie.'

'Yes, m'lord. Mr Wooster doth suffer a sea change into something rich and strange. I quote the Bard of Stratford. Would your lordship care for another quick whisky and soda before joining Lady Carmoyle?'

'No, we mustn't waste a moment. As you were saying not long ago, time is of the . . . what, Jeeves?'

'Essence, m'lord.'

'Essence? You're sure?'

'Yes, m'lord.'

'Well, if you say so, though I always thought an essence was a sort of scent. Right ho, then, let's go.'

'Very good, m'lord.'

It was with her mind in something of a whirl that Mrs Spottsworth had driven away from the door of the Goose and Gherkin. The encounter with Captain C.G. Biggar had stirred her quite a good deal.

Mrs Spottsworth was a woman who attached considerable importance to what others of less sensitivity would have dismissed carelessly as chance happenings or coincidences. She did not believe in chance. In her lexicon there was no such word as coincidence. These things, she held, were *meant*. This unforeseen return into her life of the White Hunter could be explained, she felt, only on the supposition that some pretty adroit staff work had been going on in the spirit world.

It had happened at such a particularly significant moment. Only two days previously A.B. Spottsworth, chatting with her on the ouija board, had remarked, after mentioning that he was very happy and eating lots of fruit, that it was high time she thought of getting married again. No sense, A.B. Spottsworth had said, in her living a lonely life with all that money in the bank. A woman needs a mate, he had asserted, adding that Cliff Bessemer, with whom he had exchanged a couple of words that morning in the vale of light, felt the same. 'And they don't come more level-headed than old Cliff Bessemer,' said A.B. Spottsworth.

And when his widow had asked 'But, Alexis, wouldn't you and Clifton *mind* me marrying again?' A.B. Spottsworth had replied in his bluff way, spelling the words out carefully, 'Of course we wouldn't, you dumb-bell. Go to it, kid.'

And right on top of that dramatic conversation who should pop up out of a trap but the man who had loved her with a strong silent passion from the first moment they had met. It was uncanny. One would have said that passing the veil made the late Messrs Bessemer and Spottsworth clairvoyant.

Inasmuch as Captain Biggar, as we have seen, had not spoken his love but had let concealment like a worm i' the bud feed on his tomato-coloured cheek, it may seem strange that Mrs Spottsworth should have known anything about the way he felt. But a woman can always tell. When she sees a man choke up and look like an embarrassed beetroot every time he catches her eye over the eland steaks and lime juice, she soon forms an adequate diagnosis of his case.

The recurrence of these phenomena during those moments of farewell outside the Goose and Gherkin showed plainly, moreover, that the passage of time had done nothing to cool off the gallant captain. She had not failed to observe the pop-eyed stare in his keen blue eyes, the deepening of the hue of his vermilion face and the way his number eleven feet had shuffled from start to finish of the interview. If he did not still consider her the tree on which the fruit of his life hung, Rosalinda Spottsworth was vastly mistaken. She was a little surprised that nothing had emerged in the way of an impassioned declaration. But how could she know that a feller had his code?

Driving through the pleasant Southmoltonshire country, she found her thoughts dwelling lingeringly on Captain C.G. Biggar.

At their very first meeting in Kenya she had found something about him that attracted her, and two days later this mild liking had become a rather fervent admiration. A woman cannot help but respect a man capable of upping with his big-bored .505 Gibbs and blowing the stuffing out of a charging buffalo. And from respect to love is as short a step as that from Harrige's Glass Fancy Goods and Chinaware department to the Ladies' Underclothing. He seemed to her like someone out of Ernest Hemingway, and she had always had a weakness for those rough, tough devil-may-care Hemingway characters. Spiritual herself, she was attracted by roughness and toughness in the male. Clifton Bessemer had had those qualities. So had A.B. Spottsworth. What had first impressed her in Clifton Bessemer had been the way he had swatted a charging fly with a rolled-up evening paper at the studio party where they had met, and in the case of A.B. Spottsworth the spark had been lit when she heard him one afternoon in conversation with a Paris taxi driver who had expressed dissatisfaction with the amount of his fare.

As she passed through the great gates of Rowcester Abbey and made her way up the long drive, it was beginning to seem to her that she might do considerably worse than cultivate Captain Biggar. A woman needs a protector, and what better protector can she find than a man who thinks nothing of going into tall grass after a wounded lion? True, wounded lions do not enter largely into the ordinary married life, but it is nice for a wife to know that if one does happen to come along, she can leave it with every confidence to her husband to handle.

It would not, she felt, be a difficult matter to arrange the necessary preliminaries. A few kind words and a melting look or two ought to be quite sufficient to bring that strong, passionate nature to the boil. These men of the wilds respond readily to melting looks.

She was just trying one out in the mirror of her car when, as she rounded a bend in the drive, Rowcester Abbey suddenly burst upon her view, and for the moment Captain Biggar was forgotten. She could think of nothing but that she had found the house of her dreams. Its mellow walls aglow in the rays of the setting sun, its windows glittering like jewels, it seemed to her like some palace of Fairyland. The little place in Pasadena, the little place in Carmel, and the little places in New York, Florida, Maine and Oregon were well enough in their way, but this outdid them all. Houses like Rowcester Abbey always look their best from outside and at a certain distance.

She stopped the car and sat there, gazing raptly.

Rory and Monica, tired of waiting in the yew alley, had returned to the house and met Bill coming out. All three had gone back into the living room, where they were now discussing the prospects of a quick sale to this female Santa Claus from across the Atlantic. Bill, though feeling a little better after his whisky and soda, was still in a feverish state. His goggling eyes and twitching limbs would have interested a Harley Street physician, had one been present to observe them.

'Is there a hope?' he quavered, speaking rather like an invalid on a sickbed addressing his doctor.

'I think so,' said Monica.

'I don't,' said Rory.

Monica quelled him with a glance.

'The impression I got at that women's lunch in New York,' she said, 'was that she was nibbling. I gave her quite a blast of propaganda and definitely softened her up. All that remains now is to administer the final shove. When she arrives, I'll leave you alone together, so that you can exercise that well-known charm of yours. Give her the old personality.'

'I will,' said Bill fervently. 'I'll be like a turtle dove cooing to a female turtle dove. I'll play on her as on a stringed instrument.'

'Well, mind you do, because if the sale comes off, I'm expecting a commission.'

'You shall have it, Moke, old thing. You shall be repaid a thousandfold. In due season there will present themselves at your front door elephants laden with gold and camels bearing precious stones and rare spices.'

'How about apes, ivory and peacocks?'

'They'll be there.'

Rory, the practical, hard-headed businessman, frowned on this visionary stuff.

'Well, will they?' he said. 'The point seems to me extremely moot. Even on the assumption that this woman is weak in the head I can't see her paying a fortune for a place like Rowcester Abbey. To start with, all the farms are gone.'

'That's true,' said Bill, damped. 'And the park belongs to the local golf club. There's only the house and garden.'

'The garden, yes. And we know all about the garden, don't we? I was saying to Moke only a short while ago that whereas in the summer months the river is at the bottom of the garden –'

'Oh, be quiet,' said Monica. 'I don't see why you shouldn't get fifteen thousand pounds, Bill. Maybe even as much as twenty.'

Bill revived like a watered flower.

'Do you really think so?'

'Of course she doesn't,' said Rory. 'She's just trying to cheer you up, and very sisterly of her, too. I honour her for it. Under that forbidding exterior there lurks a tender heart. But twenty thousand quid for a house from which even Reclaimed Juvenile Delinquents recoil in horror? Absurd. The thing's a relic of the past. A hundred and forty-seven rooms!'

'That's a lot of house,' argued Monica.

'It's a lot of junk,' said Rory firmly. 'It would cost a bally fortune to do it up.'

Monica was obliged to concede this.

'I suppose so,' she said. 'Still, Mrs Spottsworth's the sort of woman who would be quite prepared to spend a million or so on that. You've been making a few improvements, I notice,' she said to Bill.

'A drop in the bucket.'

'You've even done something about the smell on the first-floor landing.'

'Wish I had the money it cost.'

'You're hard up?'

'Stony.'

'Then where the dickens,' said Rory, pouncing like a prosecuting counsel, 'do all these butlers and housemaids come from? That girl Jill Stick-in-the-mud –'

'Her name is not Stick-in-the-mud.'

Rory raised a restraining hand.

'Her name may or may not be Stick-in-the-mud,' he said, letting the point go, for after all it was a minor one, 'but the fact remains that she was holding us spellbound just now with a description of your domestic amenities which suggested the mad luxury that led to the fall of Babylon. Platoons of butlers, beauty choruses of housemaids, cooks in reckless profusion and stories flying about of boys to clean the knives and boots . . . I said to Moke after she'd left that I wondered if you had set up as a gentleman bur . . . That reminds me, old girl. Did you tell Bill about the police?'

Bill leaped a foot, and came down shaking in every limb.

'The police? What about the police?'

'Some blighter rang up from the local gendarmerie. The rozzers want to question you.'

'What do you mean, question me?'

'Grill you,' explained Rory. 'Give you the third degree. And there was another call before that. A mystery man who didn't give his name. He and Moke kidded back and forth for a while.'

'Yes, I talked to him,' said Monica. 'He had a voice that sounded as if he ate spinach with sand in it. He was inquiring about the licence number of your car.'

'What!'

'You haven't run into somebody's cow, have you? I understand that's a very serious offence nowadays.'

Bill was still quivering briskly.

'You mean someone was wanting to know the licence number of my car?'

'That's what I said. Why, what's the matter, Bill? You're looking as worried as a prune.'

'White and shaken,' agreed Rory. 'Like a side-car.' He laid a kindly hand on his brother-in-law's shoulder. 'Bill, tell me. Be frank. Why are you wanted by the police?'

'I'm not wanted by the police.'

'Well, it seems to be their dearest wish to get their hands on you. One theory that crossed my mind,' said Rory, 'was – I mentioned it to you, Moke, if you remember – that you had found some opulent bird with a guilty secret and were going in for a spot of blackmail. This may or may not be the case, but if it is, now is the time to tell us, Bill, old man. You're among friends. Moke's broad-minded, and I'm broad-minded. I know the police look a bit squiggle-eyed at blackmail, but I can't see any objection to it myself. Quick profits and practically no overheads. If I had a son, I'm not at all sure I wouldn't have him trained for that profession. So if the flatties are after you and you would like a helping hand to get you out of the country before they start watching the ports, say the word, and we'll . . .'

'Mrs Spottsworth,' announced Jeeves from the doorway, and a moment later Bill had done another of those leaps in the air which had become so frequent with him of late.

He stood staring pallidly at the vision that entered.

Mrs Spottsworth had come sailing into the room with the confident air of a woman who knows that her hat is right, her dress is right, her shoes are right and her stockings are right and that she has a matter of forty-two million dollars tucked away in sound securities, and Bill, with a derelict country house for sale, should have found her an encouraging spectacle. For unquestionably she looked just the sort of person who would buy derelict English country houses by the gross without giving the things a second thought.

But his mind was not on business transactions. It had flitted back a few years and was in the French Riviera, where he and this woman had met and – he could not disguise it from himself – become extremely matey.

It had all been perfectly innocent, of course – just a few moonlight drives, one or two mixed bathings and hob-nobbings at Eden Roc and the ordinary exchanges of civilities customary on the French Riviera – but it seemed to him that there was a grave danger of her introducing into their relations now that touch of Auld Lang Syne which is the last thing a young man wants when he has a fiancée around – and a fiancée, moreover, who has already given evidence of entertaining distressing suspicions.

Mrs Spottsworth had come upon him as a complete and painful surprise. At Cannes he had got the impression that her name was Bessemer, but of course in places like Cannes you don't bother much about surnames. He had, he recalled, always addressed her as Rosie, and she – he shuddered – had addressed him as Billiken. A clear, but unpleasant, picture rose before his eyes of Jill's face when she heard her addressing him as Billiken at dinner tonight. Most unfortunately, through some oversight, he had omitted to mention to Jill his Riviera acquaintance Mrs Bessemer, and he could see that she might conceivably take a little explaining away.

'How nice to see you again, Rosalinda,' said Monica. 'So glad you found your way here all right. It's rather tricky after you leave the main road. My husband, Sir Roderick Carmoyle. And this is –'

'Billiken!' cried Mrs Spottsworth, with all the enthusiasm of a generous nature. It was plain that if the ecstasy occasioned by this unexpected encounter was a little one-sided, on her side at least it existed in full measure.

'Eh?' said Monica.

'Mr Belfry and I are old friends. We knew each other in Cannes a few years ago, when I was Mrs Bessemer.'

'Bessemer!'

'It was not long after my husband had passed the veil owing to having a head-on collision with a truck full of beer bottles on the Jericho Turnpike. His name was Clifton Bessemer.'

Monica shot a pleased and congratulatory look at Bill. She knew all about Mrs Bessemer of Cannes. She was aware that her brother had given this Mrs Bessemer the rush of a lifetime, and what better foundation could a young man with a house to sell have on which to build?

'Well, that's fine,' she said. 'You'll have all sorts of things to talk about, won't you? But he isn't Mr Belfry now, he's Lord Rowcester.'

'Changed his name,' explained Rory. 'The police are after him, and an *alias* was essential.'

'Oh, don't be an ass, Rory. He came into the title,' said Monica. 'You know how it is in England. You start out as something, and then someone dies and you do a switch. Our uncle, Lord Rowcester, pegged out not long ago, and Bill was his heir, so he shed the Belfry and took on the Rowcester.'

'I see. Well, to me he will always be Billiken. How are you, Billiken?'

Bill found speech, though not much of it and what there was rather rasping.

'I'm fine, thanks – er – Rosie.'

'Rosie?' said Rory, startled and, like the child of nature he was, making no attempt to conceal his surprise 'Did I hear you say Rosie?'

Bill gave him a cold look.

'Mrs Spottsworth's name, as you have already learned from a usually well-informed source – viz Moke – is Rosalinda. All her friends – even casual acquaintances like myself – called her Rosie.'

'Oh, ah,' said Rory. 'Quite, quite. Very natural, of course.'

'Casual acquaintances?' said Mrs Spottsworth, pained.

Bill plucked at his tie.

'Well, I mean blokes who just knew you from meeting you at Cannes and so forth.'

'Cannes!' cried Mrs Spottsworth ecstatically. 'Dear, sunny, gay, delightful Cannes! What times we had there, Billiken! Do you remember –'

'Yes, yes,' said Bill. 'Very jolly, the whole thing. Won't you have a drink or a sandwich or a cigar or something?'

Fervently he blessed the Mainwarings' Peke for being so confirmed a hypochondriac that it had taken Jill away to the other side of the county. By the time she returned, Mrs Spottsworth, he trusted, would have simmered down and become less expansive on the subject of the dear old days. He addressed himself to the task of curbing her exuberance.

'Nice to welcome you to Rowcester Abbey,' he said formally.

'Yes, I hope you'll like it,' said Monica.

'It's the most wonderful place I ever saw!'

'Would you say that? Mouldering old ruin, I'd call it,' said Rory judicially, and was fortunate enough not to catch his wife's eye, 'Been decaying for centuries. I'll bet if you shook those curtains, a couple of bats would fly out.'

'The patina of Time!' said Mrs Spottsworth. 'I adore it.' She closed her eyes. '"The dead, twelve deep, clutch at you as you go by,"' she murmured.

'What a beastly idea,' said Rory. 'Even a couple of clutching corpses would be a bit over the odds, in my opinion.'

Mrs Spottsworth opened her eyes. She smiled.

'I'm going to tell you something very strange,' she said. 'It struck me so strongly when I came in at the front door I had to sit down for a moment. Your butler thought I was ill.'

'You aren't, I hope?'

'No, not at all. It was simply that I was . . . overcome. I realized that I had been here before.'

Monica looked politely puzzled. It was left to Rory to supply the explanation.

'Oh, as a sightseer?' he said. 'One of the crowd that used to come on Fridays during the summer months to be shown over the place at a bob a head. I remember them well in the days when you and I were walking out, Moke. The Gogglers, we used to call them. They came in charabancs and dropped nut chocolate on the carpets. Not that dropping nut chocolate on them would make these carpets any worse. That's all been discontinued now, hasn't it, Bill? Nothing left to goggle at, I suppose. The late Lord Rowcester,' he explained to the visitor, 'stuck the Americans with all his best stuff, and now there's not a thing in the place worth looking at. I was saying to my wife only a short while ago that by far the best policy in dealing with Rowcester Abbey would be to burn it down.'

A faint moan escaped Monica. She raised her eyes heavenwards, as if pleading for a thunderbolt to strike this man. If this was her Roderick's idea of selling goods to a customer, it seemed a miracle that he had ever managed to get rid of a single hose-pipe, lawnmower or bird-bath.

Mrs Spottsworth shook her head with an indulgent smile.

'No, no, I didn't mean that I had been here in my present corporeal envelope. I meant in a previous incarnation. I'm a Rotationist, you know.'

Rory nodded intelligently.

'Ah, yes. Elks, Shriners and all that. I've seen pictures of them, in funny hats.'

'No, no, you are thinking of Rotarians. I am a Rotationist, which is quite different. We believe that we are reborn as one of our ancestors every ninth generation.'

'Ninth?' said Monica, and began to count on her fingers.

'The mystic ninth house. Of course you've read the *Zend Avesta of Zoroaster*, Sir Roderick?'

'I'm afraid not. Is it good?'

'Essential, I would say.'

'I'll put it on my library list,' said Rory. 'By Agatha Christie, isn't it?'

Monica had completed her calculations.

'Ninth ... That seems to make me Lady Barbara, the leading hussy of Charles II's reign.'

Mrs Spottsworth was impressed.

'I suppose I ought to be calling you Lady Barbara and asking you about your latest love affair.'

'I only wish I could remember it. From what I've heard of her, it would make quite a story.'

'Did she get herself sunburned all over?' asked Rory. 'Or was she more of an indoor girl?'

Mrs Spottsworth had closed her eyes again.

'I feel influences,' she said. 'I even hear faint whisperings. How strange it is, coming into a house that you last visited three hundred years ago. Think of all the lives that have been lived within these ancient walls. And they are here, all around us, creating an intriguing aura for this delicious old house.'

Monica caught Bill's eye.

'It's in the bag, Bill,' she whispered.

'Eh?' said Rory in a loud, hearty voice. 'What's in the bag?'

'Oh, shut up.'

'But what *is* in the . . . Ouch!' He rubbed a well-kicked ankle. 'Oh, ah, yes, of course. Yes, I see what you mean.'

Mrs Spottsworth passed a hand across her brow. She appeared to be in a sort of mediumistic trance.

'I seem to remember a chapel. There is a chapel here?'

'Ruined,' said Monica.

'You don't need to tell her that, old girl,' said Rory.

'I knew it. And there's a Long Gallery.'

'That's right,' said Monica. 'A duel was fought in it in the eighteenth century. You can still see the bullet holes in the walls.'

'And dark stains on the floor, no doubt. This place must be full of ghosts.'

This, felt Monica, was an idea to be discouraged at the outset.

'Oh, no, don't worry,' she said heartily. 'Nothing like that in Rowcester Abbey,' and was surprised to observe that her guest was gazing at her with large, woebegone eyes like a child informed that the evening meal will not be topped off with ice cream.

'But I want ghosts,' said Mrs Spottsworth. 'I must have ghosts. Don't tell me there aren't *any*?'

Rory was his usual helpful self.

'There's what we call the haunted lavatory on the ground floor,' he said. 'Every now and then, when there's nobody near it, the toilet will suddenly flush, and when a death is expected in the family, it justs keeps going and going. But we don't know if it's a spectre or just a defect in the plumbing.'

'Probably a poltergeist,' said Mrs Spottsworth, seeming a little disappointed. 'But are there no visual manifestations?'

'I don't think so.'

'Don't be silly, Rory,' said Monica. 'Lady Agatha.'

Mrs Spottsworth was intrigued.

'Who was Lady Agatha?'

'The wife of Sir Caradoc the Crusader. She has been seen several times in the ruined chapel.'

'Fascinating, fascinating,' said Mrs Spottsworth. 'And now let me take you to the Long Gallery. Don't tell me where it is. Let me see if I can't find it for myself.'

She closed her eyes, pressed her fingertips to her temples, paused for a moment, opened her eyes and started off. As she reached the door, Jeeves appeared.

'Pardon me, m'lord.'

'Yes, Jeeves?'

'With reference to Mrs Spottsworth's dog, m'lord, I would appreciate instructions as to meal hours and diet.'

'Pomona is very catholic in her tastes,' said Mrs Spottsworth. 'She usually dines at five, but she is not at all fussy.'

'Thank you, madam.'

'And now I must concentrate. This is a test.' Mrs Spottsworth applied her fingertips to her temple once more. 'Follow, please, Monica. You, too, Billiken. I am going to take you straight to the Long Gallery.'

The procession passed through the door, and Rory, having scrutinized it in his slow, thorough way, turned to Jeeves with a shrug of the shoulders.

'Potty, what?'

'The lady does appear to diverge somewhat from the generally accepted norm, Sir Roderick.'

'She's as crazy as a bed bug. I'll tell you something, Jeeves. That sort of thing wouldn't be tolerated at Harrige's.'

'No, sir?'

'Not for a moment. If this Mrs Dogsbody, or whatever her name is, came into – say the Cakes, Biscuits and General Confectionery and started acting that way, the store detectives would have her by the seat of the trousers and be giving her the old heave-ho before the first gibber had proceeded from her lips.'

'Indeed, Sir Roderick?'

'I'm telling you, Jeeves. I had an experience of that sort myself shortly after I joined. I was at my post one morning – I was in the Jugs, Bottles and Picnic Supplies at the time – and a woman came in. Well dressed, refined aspect, nothing noticeable about her at all except that she was wearing a fireman's helmet – I started giving her courteous service. "Good morning, madam," I said. "What can I do for you, madam? Something in picnic supplies, madam? A jug? A bottle?" She looked at me keenly. "Are you interested in bottles, gargoyle?" she asked, addressing me for some reason as gargoyle. "Why, yes, madam," I replied. "Then what do you think of this one," she said. And with that she whipped out a whacking great decanter and brought it whizzing down on the exact spot where my frontal bone would have been, had I not started back like a nymph surprised while bathing. It shattered itself on the counter.

It was enough. I beckoned to the store detectives and they scooped her up.'

'Most unpleasant, Sir Roderick.'

'Yes, shook me, I confess. Nearly made me send in my papers. It turned out that she had recently been left a fortune by a wealthy uncle in Australia, and it had unseated her reason. This Mrs Dogsbody's trouble is, I imagine, the same. Inherited millions from a platoon of deceased husbands, my wife informs me, and took advantage of the fact to go right off her onion. Always a mistake, Jeeves, unearned money. There's nothing like having to scratch for a living. I'm twice the man I was since I joined the ranks of the world's workers.'

'You see eye to eye with the Bard, Sir Roderick. 'Tis deeds must win the prize.'

'Exactly. Quite so. And speaking of winning prizes, what about tomorrow?'

'Tomorrow, Sir Roderick?'

'The Derby. Know anything?'

'I fear not, Sir Roderick. It would seem to be an exceptionally open contest. Monsieur Boussac's Voleur is, I understand, the favourite. Fifteen to two at last night's call-over and the price likely to shorten to sixes or even fives for the SP. But the animal in question is somewhat small and lightly boned for so gruelling an ordeal. Though we have, to be sure, seen such a handicap overcome. The name of Manna, the 1925 winner, springs to the mind, and Hyperion, another smallish horse, broke the course record previously held by Flying Fox, accomplishing the distance in two minutes, thirty-four seconds.'

Rory regarded him with awe.

'By Jove! You know your stuff, don't you?'

'One likes to keep *au courant* in these matters, sir. It is, one might say, an essential part of one's education.'

'Well, I'll certainly have another chat with you tomorrow before I put my bet on.'

'I shall be most happy if I can be of service, Sir Roderick,' said Jeeves courteously, and oozed softly from the room, leaving Rory with the feeling, so universal among those who encountered this great man, that he had established connection with some wise, kindly spirit in whose hands he might place his affairs without a tremor.

A few moments later, Monica came in, looking a little jaded.

'Hullo, old girl,' said Rory. 'Back from your travels? Did she find the ruddy gallery?'

Monica nodded listlessly.

'Yes, after taking us all over the house. She said she lost the influence for a while. Still, I suppose it wasn't bad after three hundred years.'

'I was saying to Jeeves a moment ago that the woman's as crazy as a bed bug. Though, arising from that, how is it that bed bugs have got their reputation for being mentally unbalanced? Now that she's over in this country, I expect she'll soon be receiving all sorts of flattering offers from Colney Hatch and similar establishments. What became of Bill?'

'He didn't stay the course. He disappeared. Went to dress, I suppose.'

'What sort of state was he in?'

'Glassy-eyed and starting at sudden noises.'

'Ah, still jittery. He's certainly got the jumps all right, our William. But I've had another theory about old Bill,' said Rory. 'I don't think his nervousness is due to his being one jump ahead of the police. I now attribute it to his having got this job with the Agricultural Board and, like all these novices, pitching in too strenuously at first. We fellows who aren't used to work have got to learn to husband our strength, to keep something in reserve, if you know what I mean. That's what I'm always preaching to the chaps under me. Most of them listen, but there's one lad – in the Midgets Outfitting – you've never seen such *drive*. That boy's going to burn himself out before he's fifty. Hullo, whom have we here?'

He stared, at a loss, at a tall, good-looking girl who had just entered. A momentary impression that this was the ghost of Lady Agatha, who, wearying of the ruined chapel, had come to join the party, he dismissed. But he could not place her. Monica saw more clearly into the matter. Observing the cap and apron, she deduced that this must be that almost legendary figure, the housemaid.

'Ellen?' she queried.

'Yes, m'lady. I was looking for his lordship.'

'I think he's in his room. Anything I can do?'

'It's this gentleman that's just come, asking to see his lordship, m'lady. I saw him driving up in his car and, Mr Jeeves being busy in the dining room, I answered the door and showed him into the morning room.'

'Who is he?'

'A Captain Biggar, m'lady.'

Rory chuckled amusedly.

'Biggar? Reminds me of that game we used to play when we were kids, Moke – the Bigger Family.'

'I remember.'

'You do? Then which is bigger, Mr Bigger or Mrs Bigger?'

'Rory, really.'

'Mr Bigger, because he's father Bigger. Which is bigger, Mr Bigger or his old maid aunt?'

'You're not a child now, you know.'

'Can you tell me, Ellen?'

'No, sir.'

'Perhaps Mrs Dogsbody can,' said Rory, as that lady came bustling in.

There was a look of modest triumph on Mrs Spottsworth's handsome face.

'Did you tell Sir Roderick?' she said.

'I told him,' said Monica.

'I found the Long Gallery, Sir Roderick.'

'Three rousing cheers,' said Rory. 'Continue along these lines, and you'll soon be finding bass drums in telephone booths. But pigeonholing that for the moment, do you know which is bigger, Mr Bigger or his old maid aunt?'

Mrs Spottsworth looked perplexed.

'I beg your pardon?'

Rory repeated his question, and her perplexity deepened.

'But I don't understand.'

'Rory's just having one of his spells,' said Monica.

'The old maid aunt,' said Rory, 'because, whatever happens, she's always Bigger.'

'Pay no attention to him,' said Monica. 'He's quite harmless on these occasions. It's just that a Captain Biggar has called. That set him off. He'll be all right in a minute.'

Mrs Spottsworth's fine eyes had widened.

'Captain Biggar?'

'There's another one,' said Rory, knitting his brow, 'only it eludes me for the moment. I'll get it soon. Something about Mr Bigger and his son.'

'Captain Biggar?' repeated Mrs Spottsworth. She turned to Ellen. 'Is he a gentleman with a rather red face?'

'He's a gentleman with a very red face,' said Ellen. She was a girl who liked to get these things right.

Mrs Spottsworth put a hand to her heart.

'How extraordinary!'

'You know him?' said Monica.

'He is an old, old friend of mine. I knew him when . . . Oh, Monica, could you . . . would you . . . could you possibly invite him to stay?'

Monica started like a warhorse at the sound of the bugle.

'Why, of course, Rosalinda. Any friend of yours. What a splendid idea.'

'Oh, thank you.' Mrs Spottsworth turned to Ellen. 'Where is Captain Biggar?'

'In the morning room, madam.'

'Will you take me there at once. I must see him.'

'If you will step this way, madam.'

Mrs Spottsworth hurried out, followed sedately by Ellen. Rory shook his head dubiously.

'Is this wise, Moke, old girl? Probably some frightful outsider in a bowler hat and a made-up tie.'

Monica's eyes were sparkling.

'I don't care what he's like. He's a friend of Mrs Spottsworth's, that's all that matters. Oh, Bill!' she cried, as Bill came in.

Bill was tail-coated, white-tied and white-waistcoated, and his hair gleamed with strange unguents. Rory stared at him in amazement.

'Good God, Bill! You look like Great Lovers Through The Ages. If you think I'm going to dress up like that, you're much mistaken. You get the old Carmoyle black tie and soft shirt, and like it. I get the idea, of course. You've dolled yourself up to impress Mrs Spottsworth and bring back memories of the old days at Cannes. But I'd be careful not to overdo it, old boy. You've got to consider Jill. If she finds out about you and the Spottsworth –'

Bill started.

'What the devil do you mean?'

'Nothing, nothing. I was only making a random remark.'

'Don't listen to him, Bill,' said Monica. 'He's just drooling. Jill's sensible.'

'And after all,' said Rory, looking on the bright side, 'it all happened before you met Jill.'

'All what happened?'

'Nothing, old boy, nothing.'

'My relations with Mrs Spottsworth were pure to the last drop.'

'Of course, of course.'

'Do you sell muzzles at Harrige's, Rory?' asked Monica.

'Muzzles? Oh, rather. In the Cats, Dogs and Domestic Pets.'

'I'm going to buy one for you, to keep you quiet. Just treat him as if he wasn't there, Bill, and listen while I tell you the news. The most wonderful thing has happened. An old friend of Mrs Spottsworth's has turned up, and I've invited him to stay.'

'And old friend?'

'Another old lover, one presumes.'

'Do stop it, Rory. Can't you understand what a marvellous thing this is, Bill! We've put her under an obligation. Think what a melting mood she'll be in after this!'

Her enthusiasm infected Bill. He saw just what she meant.

'You're absolutely right. This is terrific.'

'Yes, isn't it a stroke of luck? She'll be clay in your hands now.'

'Clay is the word. Moke, you're superb. As fine a bit of quick thinking as I ever struck. Who is the fellow?'

'His name's Biggar. Captain Biggar.'

Bill groped for support at a chair. A greenish tinge had spread over his face.

'What!' he cried. 'Captain B-b-b –?'

'Ha!' said Rory. 'Which is bigger, Mr Bigger or Master Bigger? Master Bigger, because he's a little Bigger. I knew I'd get it,' he said complacently.

8

It was a favourite dictum of the late A.B. Spottsworth, who, though fond of his wife in an absent-minded sort of way, could never have been described as a ladies' man or mistaken for one of those Troubadours of the Middle Ages, that the secret of a happy and successful life was to get rid of the women at the earliest possible opportunity. Give the gentler sex the bum's rush, he used to say, removing his coat and reaching for the poker chips, and you could start to go places. He had often observed that for sheer beauty and uplift few sights could compare with that of the female members of a dinner party filing out of the room at the conclusion of the meal, leaving the men to their soothing masculine conversation.

To Bill Rowcester at nine o'clock on the night of this disturbing day such an attitude of mind would have seemed incomprehensible. The last thing in the world that he desired was Captain Biggar's soothing masculine conversation. As he stood holding the dining room door open while Mrs Spottsworth, Monica and Jill passed through on their way to the living room, he was weighed down by a sense of bereavement and depression, mingled with uneasy speculations as to what was going to happen now. His emotions, in fact, were similar in kind and intensity to those which a garrison beleaguered by savages would have experienced, had the United States Marines, having arrived, turned right round and walked off in the opposite direction.

True, all had gone perfectly well so far. Even he, conscience-stricken though he was, had found nothing to which he could take exception in the captain's small talk up till now. Throughout dinner, starting with the soup and carrying on to the sardines on toast, the White Hunter had confined himself to such neutral topics as cannibal chiefs he had met and what to do when cornered by headhunters armed with poisoned blowpipes. He had told two rather long and extraordinarily dull stories about a couple of friends of his called Tubby Frobisher and the Subahdar. And he had recommended to Jill, in case she should ever find herself in need of one, an excellent ointment for use when bitten by alligators. To fraudulent bookmakers, chases across country and automobile licences he had made no reference whatsoever.

But now that the women had left and two strong men – or three, if you counted Rory – stood face to face, who could say how long this happy state of things would last? Bill could but trust that Rory would not bring the conversation round to the dangerous subject by asking the captain if he went in for racing at all.

'Do you go in for racing at all, captain?' said Rory as the door closed.

A sound rather like the last gasp of a dying zebra shot from Captain Biggar's lips. Bill, who had risen some six inches into the air, diagnosed it correctly as a hollow, mirthless laugh. He had had some idea of uttering something along those lines himself.

'Racing?' Captain Biggar choked. 'Do I go in for racing at all? Well, mince me up and smother me in onions!'

Bill would gladly have done so. Such a culinary feat would, it seemed to him, have solved all his perplexities. He regretted that the idea had not occurred to one of the cannibal chiefs of whom his guest had been speaking.

'It's the Derby Dinner tonight,' said Rory. 'I'll be popping along shortly to watch it on the television set in the library. All the top owners are coming on the screen to say what they think of their chances tomorrow. Not that the blighters know a damn thing about it, of course. Were you at the Oaks this afternoon by any chance?'

Captain Biggar expanded like one of those peculiar fish in Florida which swell when you tickle them.

'Was I at the Oaks? *Chang suark!* Yes, sir, I was. And if ever a man –'

'Rather pretty, this Southmoltonshire country, don't you think, Captain?' said Bill. 'Picturesque, as it is sometimes called. The next village to us – Lower Snodsbury – you may have noticed it as you came through – has a –'

'If ever a man got the ruddy sleeve across the bally wind-pipe,' proceeded the captain, who had now become so bright red that it was fortunate that by a lucky chance there were no bulls present in the dining room, 'it was me at Epsom this afternoon. I passed through the furnace like Shadrach, Meshach and Nebuchadnezzar or whoever it was. I had my soul tied up in knots and put through the wringer.'

Rory tut-tutted sympathetically.

'Had a bad day, did you?'

'Let me tell you what happened.'

'– Norman church,' continued Bill, faint but persevering, 'which I believe is greatly –'

'I must begin by saying that since I came back to the old country, I have got in with a pretty shrewd lot of chaps, fellows who know one end of a horse from the other, as the expression is, and they've been putting me on to some good things. And today –'

'– admired by blokes who are fond of Norman churches,' said Bill. 'I don't know much about them myself, but according to the nibs there's a nave or something on that order –'

Captain Biggar exploded again.

'Don't talk to me about knaves! *Yogi tulsiram jaginath!* I met the king of them this afternoon, blister his insides. Well, as I was saying, these chaps of mine put me on to good things from time to time, and today they advised a double. Lucy Glitters in the two-thirty and Whistler's Mother for the Oaks.'

'Extraordinary, Whistler's Mother winning like that,' said Rory. 'The consensus of opinion at Harrige's was that she hadn't a hope.'

'And what happened? Lucy Glitters rolled in at a hundred to six, and Whistler's Mother, as you may have heard, at thirty-three to one.'

Rory was stunned. 'You mean your double came off?'

'Yes, sir.'

'At those odds?'

'At those odds.'

'How much did you have on?'

'Five pounds on Lucy Glitters and all to come on Whistler's Mother's nose.'

Rory's eyes bulged.

'Good God! Are you listening to this, Bill? You must have won a fortune.'

'Three thousand pounds.'

'Well, I'll be . . . Did you hear that, Jeeves?'

Jeeves had entered, bearing coffee. His deportment was, as ever, serene. Like Bill, he found Captain Biggar's presence in the home disturbing, but where Bill quaked and quivered, Jeeves continued to resemble a well-bred statue.

'Sir?'

'Captain Biggar won three thousand quid on the Oaks.'

'Indeed, sir? A consummation devoutly to be wished.'

'Yes,' said the captain sombrely. 'Three thousand pounds I won, and the bookie did a bolt.'

Rory stared. 'No!'

'I assure you.'

'Skipped by the light of the moon?'

'Exactly.'

Rory was overcome.

'I never heard anything so monstrous. Did you ever hear anything so monstrous, Jeeves? Wasn't that the frozen limit, Bill?'

Bill seemed to come out of a trance.

'Sorry, Rory, I'm afraid I was thinking of something else. What were you saying?'

'Poor old Biggar brought off a double at Epsom this afternoon, and the swine of a bookie legged it, owing him three thousand pounds.'

Bill was naturally aghast. Any good-hearted young man would have been, hearing such a story.

'Good heavens, Captain,' he cried, 'what a terrible thing to have happened. Legged it, did he, this bookie?'

'Popped off like a jack rabbit, with me after him.'

'I don't wonder you're upset. Scoundrels like that ought not to be at large. It makes one's blood boil to think of this . . . this . . . what would Shakespeare have called him, Jeeves?'

'This arrant, rascally, beggarly, lousy knave, m'lord.'

'Ah, yes. Shakespeare put these things well.'

'A whoreson, beetle-headed, flap-eared knave, a knave, a rascal, an eater of broken meats; a beggarly, filthy, worsted-stocking –'

'Yes, yes, Jeeves, quite so. One gets the idea.' Bill's manner was a little agitated. 'Don't run away, Jeeves. Just give the fire a good stir.'

'It is June, m'lord.'

'So it is, so it is. I'm all of a doo-dah, hearing this appalling story. Won't you sit down, Captain? Oh, you are sitting down. The cigars, Jeeves. A cigar for Captain Biggar.'

The captain held up a hand.

'Thank you, no. I never smoke when I'm after big game.'

'Big game? Oh, I see what you mean. This bookie fellow. You're a White Hunter, and now you're hunting white bookies,' said Bill with a difficult laugh. 'Rather good, that, Rory?'

'Dashed good, old boy. I'm convulsed. And now may I get down? I want to go and watch the Derby Dinner.'

'An excellent idea,' said Bill heartily. 'Let's all go and watch the Derby Dinner. Come along, Captain.'

Captain Biggar made no move to follow Rory from the room. He remained in his seat, looking redder than ever.

'Later, perhaps,' he said curtly. 'At the moment, I would like to have a word with you, Lord Rowcester.'

'Certainly, certainly, certainly, certainly, certainly,' said Bill, though not blithely. 'Stick around, Jeeves. Lots of work to do in here. Polish an ashtray or something. Give Captain Biggar a cigar.'

'The gentleman has already declined your lordship's offer of a cigar.'

'So he has, so he has. Well, well!' said Bill. 'Well, well, well, well, well!' He lit one himself with a hand that trembled like a tuning fork. 'Tell us more about this bookie of yours, Captain.'

Captain Biggar brooded darkly for a moment. He came out of the silence to express a wistful hope that some day it might be granted to him to see the colour of the fellow's insides.

'I only wish,' he said, 'that I could meet the rat in Kuala Lumpur.'

'Kuala Lumpur?'

Jeeves was his customary helpful self.

'A locality in the Straits Settlements, m'lord, a British Crown Colony in the East Indies including Malacca, Penang and the province of Wellesley, first made a separate dependency of the British Crown in 1853 and placed under the Governor General of India. In 1887 the Cocos or Keeling Islands were attached to the colony, and in 1889 Christmas Island. Mr Somerset Maugham has written searchingly of life in those parts.'

'Of course, yes. It all comes back to me. Rather a strange lot of birds out there, I gather.'

Captain Biggar conceded this.

'A very strange lot of birds. But we generally manage to put salt on their tails. Do you know what happens to a welsher in Kuala Lumpur, Lord Rowcester?'

'No, I – er – don't believe I've ever heard. Don't go, Jeeves. Here's an ashtray you've missed. What does happen to a welsher in Kuala Lumpur?'

'We let the blighter have three days to pay up. Then we call on him and give him a revolver.'

'That's rather nice of you. Sort of heaping coals of . . . You don't mean a *loaded* revolver?'

'Loaded in all six chambers. We look the louse in the eye, leave the revolver on the table and go off. Without a word. He understands.'

Bill gulped. The strain of the conversation was beginning to tell on him.

'You mean he's expected to . . . Isn't that a bit drastic?'

Captain Biggar's eyes were cold and hard, like picnic eggs.

'It's the code, sir. Code! That's a big word with the men who live on the frontiers of Empire. Morale can crumble very easily out there. Drink, women and unpaid gambling debts, those are the steps down,' he said. 'Drink, women and unpaid gambling debts,' he repeated, illustrating with jerks of the hand.

'That one's the bottom, is it? You hear that, Jeeves?'

'Yes, m'lord.'

'Rather interesting.'

'Yes, m'lord.'

'Broadens the mind a bit.'

'Yes, m'lord.'

'One lives and learns, Jeeves.'

'One does indeed, m'lord.'

Captain Biggar took a Brazil nut, and cracked it with his teeth.

'We've got to set an example, we bearers of the white man's burden. Can't let the Dyaks beat us on code.'

'Do they try?'

'A Dyak who defaults on a debt has his head cut off.'

'By the other Dyaks?'

'Yes, sir, by the other Dyaks.'

'Well, well.'

'The head is then given to his principal creditor.'

This surprised Bill. Possibly it surprised Jeeves, too, but Jeeves' was a face that did not readily register such emotions as astonishment. Those who knew him well claimed on certain occasions of great stress to have seen a very small muscle at the corner of his mouth give one quick, slight twitch, but as a rule his features preserved a uniform imperturbability, like those of a cigar-store Indian.

'Good heavens!' said Bill. 'You couldn't run a business that way over here. I mean to say, who would decide who was the principal creditor? Imagine the arguments there would be. Eh, Jeeves?'

'Unquestionably, m'lord. The butcher, the baker . . .'

'Not to mention hosts who had entertained the Dyak for weekends, from whose houses he had slipped away on Monday morning, forgetting the Saturday night bridge game.'

'In the event of his surviving, it would make such a Dyak considerably more careful in his bidding, m'lord.'

'True, Jeeves, true. It would, wouldn't it? He would think twice about trying any of that psychic stuff?'

'Precisely, m'lord. And would undoubtedly hesitate before taking his partner out of a business double.'

Captain Biggar cracked another nut. In the silence it sounded like one of those explosions which slay six.

'And now,' he said, 'with your permission, I would like to cut the *ghazi havildar* and get down to brass tacks, Lord Rowcester.' He paused a moment, marshalling his thoughts. 'About this bookie.'

Bill blinked.

'Ah, yes, this bookie. I know the bookie you mean.'

'For the moment he has got away, I am sorry to say. But I had the sense to memorize the number of his car.'

'You did? Shrewd, Jeeves.'

'Very shrewd, m'lord.'

'I then made inquiries of the police. And do you know what they told me? They said that that car number, Lord Rowcester, was yours.'

Bill was amazed. 'Mine?'

'Yours.'

'But how could it be mine?'

'That is the mystery which we have to solve. This Honest Patch Perkins, as he called himself, must have borrowed your car . . . with or without your permission.'

'Incredulous!'

'Incredible, m'lord.'

'Thank you, Jeeves. Incredible! How would I know any Honest Patch Perkins?'

'You don't?'

'Never heard of him in my life. Never laid eyes on him. What does he look like?'

'He is tall . . . about your height . . . and wears a ginger moustache and a black patch over his left eye.'

'No, dash it, that's not possible . . . Oh, I see what you mean. A black patch over his left eye and a ginger moustache on the upper lip. I thought for a moment . . .'

'And a check coat and a crimson tie with blue horseshoes on it.'

'Good heavens! He must look the most ghastly outsider. Eh, Jeeves?'

'Certainly far from *soigné*, m'lord.'

'Very far from *soigné*. Oh, by the way, Jeeves, that reminds me. Bertie Wooster told me that you once made some such remark to him, and it gave him the idea for a ballad to be entitled 'Way Down upon the *Soigné* River'. Did anything ever come of it, do you know?'

'I fancy not, m'lord.'

'Bertie wouldn't have been equal to whacking it out, I suppose. But one can see a song hit there, handled by the right person.'

'No doubt, m'lord.'

'Cole Porter could probably do it.'

'Quite conceivably, m'lord.'

'Or Oscar Hammerstein.'

'It should be well within the scope of Mr Hammerstein's talents, m'lord.'

It was with a certain impatience that Captain Biggar called the meeting to order.

'To hell with song hits and Cole Porters!' he said, with an abruptness on which Emily Post would have frowned. 'I'm not talking about Cole Porter, I'm talking about this bally bookie who was using your car today.'

Bill shook his head.

'My dear old pursuer of pumas and what-have-you, you say you're talking about bally bookies, but what you omit to add is that you're talking through the back of your neck. Neat that, Jeeves.'

'Yes, m'lord. Crisply put.'

'Obviously what happened was that friend Biggar got the wrong number.'

'Yes, m'lord.'

The red of Captain Biggar's face deepened to purple. His proud spirit was wounded.

'Are you telling me I don't know the number of a car that I followed all the way from Epsom Downs to Southmoltonshire? That car was used today by this Honest Patch Perkins and his clerk, and I'm asking you if you lent it to him.'

'My dear good bird, would I lend my car to a chap in a check suit and a crimson tie, not to mention a black patch and a ginger moustache? The thing's not . . . what, Jeeves?'

'Feasible, m'lord.' Jeeves coughed. 'Possibly the gentleman's eyesight needs medical attention.'

Captain Biggar swelled portentously.

'My eyesight? *My* eyesight? Do you know who you're talking to? I am Bwana Biggar.'

'I regret that the name is strange to me, sir. But I still maintain that you have made the pardonable mistake of failing to read the licence number correctly.'

Before speaking again, Captain Biggar was obliged to swallow once or twice, to restore his composure. He also took another nut.

'Look,' he said, almost mildly. 'Perhaps you're not up on these things. You haven't been told who's who and what's what. I am Biggar the White Hunter, the most famous White Hunter in all Africa and Indonesia. I can stand without a tremor in the path of an onrushing rhino . . . and why? Because my eyesight is so superb that I know . . . I *know* I can get him in that one vulnerable spot before he has come within sixty paces. That's the sort of eyesight mine is.'

Jeeves maintained his iron front.

'I fear I cannot recede from my position, sir. I grant that you may have trained your vision for such a contingency as you have described, but, poorly informed as I am on the subject of the larger fauna of the East, I do not believe that rhinoceri are equipped with licence numbers.'

It seemed to Bill that the time had come to pour oil on the troubled waters and dish out a word of comfort.

'This bookie of yours, Captain. I think I can strike a note of hope. We concede that he legged it with what appears to have been the swift abandon of a bat out of hell, but I believe that when the fields are white with daisies he'll pay you. I get the impression that he's simply trying to gain time.'

'I'll give him time,' said the captain morosely. 'I'll see that he gets plenty. And when he has paid his debt to Society, I shall attend to him personally. A thousand pities we're not out East. They understand these things there. If they know you for a straight shooter and the other chap's a wrong 'un . . . well, there aren't many questions asked.'

Bill started like a frightened fawn.

'Questions about what?'

'"Good riddance" sums up their attitude. The fewer there are of such vermin, the better for Anglo-Saxon prestige.'

'I suppose that's one way of looking at it.'

'I don't mind telling you that there are a couple of notches on my gun that aren't for buffaloes . . . or lions . . . or elands . . . *or* rhinos.'

'Really? What are they for?'

'Cheaters.'

'Ah, yes. Those are those leopard things that go as fast as race-horses.'

Jeeves had a correction to make.

'Somewhat faster, m'lord. A half-mile in forty-five seconds.'

'Great Scott! Pretty nippy, what? That's travelling, Jeeves.'

'Yes, m'lord.'

'That's a cheetah, that was, as one might say.'

Captain Biggar snorted impatiently.

'Chea-*ters* was what I said. I'm not talking about cheetah, the animal . . . though I have shot some of those, too.'

'Too?'

'Too.'

'I see,' said Bill, gulping a little. 'Too.'

Jeeves coughed.

'Might I offer a suggestion, m'lord?'

'Certainly, Jeeves. Offer several.'

'An idea has just crossed my mind, m'lord. It has occurred to me that it is quite possible that this race-course character against whom Captain Biggar nurses a justifiable grievance may have substituted for his own licence plate a false one –'

'By Jove, Jeeves, you've hit it!'

'– and that by some strange coincidence he selected for this false plate the number of your lordship's car.'

'Exactly. That's the solution. Odd we didn't think of that before. It explains the whole thing, doesn't it, Captain?'

Captain Biggar was silent. His thoughtful frown told that he was weighing the idea.

'Of course it does,' said Bill buoyantly. 'Jeeves, your bulging brain, with its solid foundation of fish, has solved what but for you would have remained one of those historic mysteries you read about. If I had a hat on, I would raise it to you.'

'I am happy to have given satisfaction, m'lord.'

'You always do, Jeeves, you always do. It's what makes you so generally esteemed.'

Captain Biggar nodded.

'Yes, I suppose that might have happened. There seems to be no other explanation.'

'Jolly, getting these things cleared up,' said Bill. 'More port, Captain?'

'No, thank you.'

'Then suppose we join the ladies? They're probably wondering what the dickens has happened to us and saying "He cometh not", like . . . who, Jeeves?'

'Mariana of the Moated Grange, m'lord. Her tears fell with the dews at even; her tears fell ere the dews were dried. She could not look on the sweet heaven either at morn or eventide.'

'Oh, well, I don't suppose our absence has hit them quite as hard as that. Still, it might be as well . . . Coming, Captain?'

'I should first like to make a telephone call.'

'You can do it from the living room.'

'A private telephone call.'

'Oh, right-ho. Jeeves, conduct Captain Biggar to your pantry and unleash him on the instrument.'

'Very good, m'lord.'

Left alone, Bill lingered for some moments, the urge to join the ladies in the living room yielding to a desire to lower just one more glass of port by way of celebration. Honest Patch Perkins had, he felt, rounded a nasty corner.

The only thought that came to mar his contentment had to do with Jill. He was not quite sure of his standing with that lodestar of his life. At dinner, Mrs Spottsworth, seated on his right, had been chummy beyond his gloomiest apprehensions, and he fancied he had detected in Jill's eye one of those cold, pensive looks which are the last sort of look a young man in love likes to see in the eye of his betrothed.

Fortunately, Mrs Spottsworth's chumminess had waned as the meal proceeded and Captain Biggar started monopolizing the conversation. She had stopped talking about the old Cannes days and had sat lingering in rapt silence as the White Hunter told of antres vast and deserts idle and of the cannibals that each other eat, the Anthropophagi, and men whose heads do grow beneath their shoulders.

This to hear had Mrs Spottsworth seriously inclined, completely switching off the Cannes motif, so it might be that all was well.

Jeeves returned, and he greeted him effusively as one who had fought the good fight.

'That was a brain wave of yours, Jeeves.'

'Thank you, m'lord.'

'It eased the situation considerably. His suspicions are lulled, don't you think?'

'One would be disposed to fancy so, m'lord.'

'You know, Jeeves, even in these disturbed postwar days, with the social revolution turning handsprings on every side and Civilization, as you might say, in the melting pot, it's still quite an advantage to be in big print in *Debrett's Peerage*.'

'Unquestionably so, m'lord. It gives a gentleman a certain standing.'

'Exactly. People take it for granted that you're respectable. Take an earl, for instance. He buzzes about, and people say "Ah, an Earl" and let it go at that. The last thing that occurs to them is that he may in his spare moments be putting on patches and false moustaches and standing on a wooden box in a check coat and a tie with blue horseshoes, shouting "Five to one the field, bar one!"'

'Precisely, m'lord.'

'A satisfactory state of things.'

'Highly satisfactory, m'lord.'

'There have been moments today, Jeeves, I don't mind confessing, when it seemed to me that the only thing to do was to turn up the toes and say "This is the end", but now it would take very little to start me singing like the Cherubim and Seraphim. It was the Cherubim and Seraphim who sang, wasn't it?'

'Yes, m'lord. Hosanna, principally.'

'I feel a new man. The odd sensation of having swallowed a quart of butterflies, which I got when there was a burst of red fire and a roll of drums from the orchestra and that White Hunter shot up through a trap at my elbow, has passed away completely.'

'I am delighted to hear it, m'lord.'

'I knew you would be, Jeeves, I knew you would be. Sympathy and understanding are your middle names. And now,' said Bill, 'to join the ladies in the living room and put the poor souls out of their suspense.'

9

Arriving in the living room, he found that the number of ladies available for being joined there had been reduced to one – reading from left to right, Jill. She was sitting on the settee twiddling an empty coffee cup and staring before her with what are sometimes described as unseeing eyes. Her air was that of a girl who is brooding on something, a girl to whom recent happenings have given much food for thought.

'Hullo there, darling,' cried Bill with the animation of a ship-wrecked mariner sighting a sail. After that testing session in the dining room, almost anything that was not Captain Biggar would have looked good to him, and she looked particularly good.

Jill glanced up.

'Oh, hullo,' she said.

It seemed to Bill that her manner was reserved, but he proceeded with undiminished exuberance.

'Where's everybody?'

'Rory and Moke are in the library, looking in at the Derby Dinner.'

'And Mrs Spottsworth?'

'Rosie,' said Jill in a toneless voice, 'has gone to the ruined chapel. I believe she is hoping to get a word with the ghost of Lady Agatha.'

Bill started. He also gulped a little.

'Rosie?'

'I think that is what you call her, is it not?'

'Why – er – yes.'

'And she calls you Billiken. Is she a very old friend?'

'No, no. I knew her slightly at Cannes one summer.'

'From what I heard her saying at dinner about moonlight drives and bathing from the Eden Roc, I got the impression that you had been rather intimate.'

'Good heavens, no. She was just an acquaintance, and a pretty mere one, at that.'

'I see.'

There was a silence.

'I wonder if you remember,' said Jill, at length breaking it, 'what I was saying this evening before dinner about people not hiding things from each other, if they are going to get married?'

'Er – yes . . . Yes . . . I remember that.'

'We agreed that it was the only way.'

'Yes . . . Yes, that's right. So we did.'

'I told you about Percy, didn't I? And Charles and Squiffy and Tom and Blotto,' said Jill, mentioning other figures of Romance from the dead past. 'I never dreamed of concealing the fact that I had been engaged before I met you. So why did you hide this Spottsworth from me?'

It seemed to Bill that, for a pretty good sort of chap who meant no harm to anybody and strove always to do the square thing by one and all, he was being handled rather roughly by Fate this summer day. The fellow – Shakespeare, he rather thought, though he would have to check with Jeeves – who had spoken of the slings and arrows of outrageous fortune had known what he was talking about. Slings and arrows described it to a nicety.

'I didn't hide this Spottsworth from you!' he cried passionately. 'She just didn't happen to come up. Lord love a duck, when you're sitting with the girl you love, holding her little hand and whispering words of endearment in her ear, you can't suddenly switch the conversation to an entirely different topic and say "Oh, by the way, there was a woman I met in Cannes some years ago, on the subject of whom I would now like to say a few words. Let me tell you all about the time we drove to St Tropez."'

'In the moonlight.'

'Was it my fault that there was a moon? I wasn't consulted. And as for bathing from the Eden Roc, you talk as if we had had the ruddy Eden Roc to ourselves with not another human being in sight. It was not so, but far otherwise. Every time we took a dip, the water was alive with exiled Grand Dukes and stiff with dowagers of the most rigid respectability.'

'I still think it odd you never mentioned her.'

'I don't.'

'I do. And I think it still odder that when Jeeves told you this afternoon that a Mrs Spottsworth was coming here, you just said "Oh, ah?" or something and let it go as if you had never heard the name before. Wouldn't the natural thing have been to say "Mrs Spottsworth? Well, well, bless my soul, I wonder if that can possibly be the woman with whom I was on terms of mere acquaintanceship at Cannes a year or two ago. Did I ever tell you about her, Jill? I used to drive with her a good deal in the moonlight, though of course in quite a distant way."'

It was Bill's moment.

'No,' he thundered, 'it would not have been the natural thing to say "Mrs Spottsworth? Well, well," and so on and so forth, and I'll tell you why. When I knew her . . . slightly, as I say, as one does know people in places like Cannes . . . her name was Bessemer.'

'Oh?'

'Precisely. B with an E with an S with an S with an E with an M with an E with an R. Bessemer. I have still to learn how all this Spottsworth stuff arose.'

Jeeves came in. Duty called him at about this hour to collect the coffee cups, and duty never called to this great man in vain.

His arrival broke what might be called the spell. Jill, who had more to say on the subject under discussion, withheld it. She got up and made for the french window.

'Well, I must be getting along,' she said, still speaking rather tonelessly.

Bill stared.

'You aren't leaving already?'

'Only to go home and get some things. Moke has asked me to stay the night.'

'Then Heaven bless Moke! Full marks for the intelligent female.'

'You like the idea of my staying the night?'

'It's terrific.'

'You're sure I shan't be in the way?'

'What on earth are you talking about? Shall I come with you?'

'Of course not. You're supposed to be a host.'

She went out, and Bill, gazing after her fondly, suddenly stiffened. Like a delayed-action bomb, those words 'You're sure I shan't be in the way?' had just hit him. Had they been mere idle words? Or had they contained a sinister significance?

'Women are odd, Jeeves,' he said.

'Yes, m'lord.'

'Not to say peculiar. You can't tell what they mean when they say things, can you?'

'Very seldom, m'lord.'

Bill brooded for a moment.

'Were you observing Miss Wyvern as she buzzed off?'

'Not closely, m'lord.'

'Was her manner strange, do you think?'

'I could not say, m'lord. I was concentrating on coffee cups.'

Bill brooded again. This uncertainty was preying on his nerves. 'You're sure I shan't be in the way?' Had there been a nasty tinkle in her voice as she uttered the words? Everything turned on that. If no tinkle, fine. But if tinkle, things did not look so good. The question, plus tinkle, could only mean that his reasoned explanation of the Spottsworth-Cannes sequence had failed to get across and that she still harboured suspicions, unworthy of her though such suspicions might be.

The irritability which good men feel on these occasions swept over him. What was the use of being as pure as the driven snow, or possibly purer, if girls were going to come tinkling at you?

'The whole trouble with women, Jeeves,' he said, and the philosopher Schopenhauer would have slapped him on the back and told him he knew just how he felt, 'is that practically all of them are dotty. Look at Mrs Spottsworth. Wacky to the eyebrows. Roosting in a ruined chapel in the hope of seeing Lady Agatha.'

'Indeed, m'lord? Mrs Spottsworth is interested in spectres?'

'She eats them alive. Is that balanced behaviour?'

'Psychical research frequently has an appeal for the other sex, m'lord. My Aunt Emily –'

Bill eyed him dangerously.

'Remember what I said about Pliny the Younger, Jeeves?'

'Yes, m'lord.'

'That goes for your Aunt Emily as well.'

'Very good, m'lord.'

'I'm not interested in your Aunt Emily.'

'Precisely, m'lord. During her long lifetime very few people were.'

'She is no longer with us?'

'No, m'lord.'

'Oh, well, that's something,' said Bill.

Jeeves floated out, and Bill flung himself into a chair. He was thinking once more of that cryptic speech, and now his mood had become wholly pessimistic. It was no longer any question of a tinkle or a non-tinkle. He was virtually certain that the words 'You're sure I shan't be in the way?' had been spoken through clenched teeth and accompanied by a look of infinite meaning. They had been the words of a girl who had intended to make a nasty crack.

He was passing his hands through his hair with a febrile gesture when Monica entered from the library. She had found the celebrants at the Derby Dinner a little on the long-winded side. Rory was still drinking in every word, but she needed an intermission.

She regarded her hair-twisting brother with astonishment.

'Good heavens, Bill! Why the agony? What's up?'

Bill glared unfraternally.

'Nothing's up, confound it! Nothing, nothing, nothing, nothing, nothing!'

Monica raised her eyebrows.

'Well, there's no need to be stuffy about it. I was only being the sympathetic sister.'

With a strong effort Bill recovered the chivalry of the Rowcesters. 'I'm sorry, Moke old thing. I've got a headache.'

'My poor lamb!'

'It'll pass off in a minute.'

'What you need is fresh air.'

'Perhaps I do.'

'And pleasant society. Ma Spottsworth's in the ruined chapel. Pop along and have a chat with her.'

'What!'

Monica became soothing.

'Now don't be difficult, Bill. You know as well as I do how important it is to jolly her along. A flash of speed on your part now may mean selling the house. The whole idea was that on top of my sales talk you were to draw her aside and switch on the charm. Have you forgotten what you said about cooing to her like a turtle dove? Dash off this minute and coo as you have never cooed before.'

For a long moment it seemed as though Bill, his frail strength taxed beyond its limit of endurance, was about to suffer something in the nature of spontaneous combustion. His eyes goggled, his face flushed, and burning words trembled on his lips. Then suddenly, as if Reason had intervened with a mild 'Tut, tut', he ceased to glare and his cheeks slowly resumed their normal hue. He had seen that Monica's suggestion was good and sensible.

In the rush and swirl of recent events, the vitally urgent matter of pushing through the sale of his ancestral home had been thrust into the background of Bill's mind. It now loomed up for that it was, the only existing life preserver bobbing about in the sea of troubles in which he was immersed. Clutch it, and he was saved. When you sold houses, he reminded himself, you got deposits, paid cash down. Such a deposit would be sufficient to dispose of the Biggar menace, and if the only means of securing it was to go to Rosalinda Spottsworth and coo, then go and coo he must.

Simultaneously there came to him the healing thought that if Jill had gone home to provide herself with things for the night, it would be at least half an hour before she got back, and in half an hour a determined man can do a lot of cooing.

'Moke,' he said, 'you're right. My place is at her side.'

He hurried out, and a moment later Rory appeared at the library door.

'I say, Moke,' said Rory, 'can you speak Spanish?'

'I don't know. I've never tried. Why?'

'There's a Spaniard or an Argentine or some such bird in there telling us about his horse in his native tongue. Probably a rank outsider, still one would have been glad to hear his views. Where's Bill? Don't tell me he's still in there with the White Man's Burden?'

'No, he came in here just now, and went out to talk to Mrs Spottsworth.'

'I want to confer with you about old Bill,' said Rory. 'Are we alone and unobserved?'

'Unless there's someone hiding in that dower chest. What about Bill?'

'There's something up, old girl, and it has to do with this chap Biggar. Did you notice Bill at dinner?'

'Not particularly. What was he doing? Eating peas with his knife?'

'No, but every time he caught Biggar's eye, he quivered like an Ouled Nail stomach dancer. For some reason Biggar affects him like an egg-whisk. Why? That's what I want to know. Who is this mystery man? Why had he come here? What is there between him and Bill that makes Bill leap and quake and shiver whenever he looks at him? I don't like it, old thing. When you married me, you never said anything about fits in the family, and I consider I have been shabbily treated. I mean to say, it's a bit thick, going to all the trouble and expense of wooing and winning the girl you love, only to discover shortly after the honeymoon that you've become brother-in-law to a fellow with St Vitus's Dance.'

Monica reflected.

'Come to think of it,' she said, 'I do remember, when I told him a Captain Biggar had clocked in, he seemed a bit upset. Yes, I distinctly recall a greenish pallor and a drooping lower jaw. And I came in here just now and found him tearing his hair. I agree with you. It's sinister.'

'And I'll tell you something else,' said Rory. 'When I left the dining room to go and look at the Derby Dinner, Bill was all for coming too. "How about it?" he said to Biggar, and Biggar, looking very puff-faced, said "Later, perhaps. At the moment, I would like a word with you, Lord Rowcester." In a cold, steely voice, like a magistrate about to fine you a fiver for pinching a policeman's helmet on Boat Race night. And Bill gulped like a stricken bull pup and said "Oh, certainly, certainly" or words to that effect. It sticks out a mile that this Biggar has got something on old Bill.'

'But what could he possibly have on him?'

'Just the question I asked myself, my old partner of joys and sorrows, and I think I have the solution. Do you remember those stories one used to read as a kid? The *Strand Magazine* used to be full of them.'

'Which stories?'

'Those idol's eye stories. The ones where a gang of blighters pop over to India to pinch the great jewel that's the eye of the idol. They get the jewel all right, but they chisel one of the blighters out of his share of the loot, which naturally makes him as sore as a gum-boil, and years later he tracks the other blighters down one by one in their respectable English homes and wipes them out to the last blighter, by way of getting a bit of his own back. You mark my words, old Bill is being chivvied by this chap Biggar because he did him out of his share of the proceeds of the green eye of the little yellow god in the temple of Vishnu, and I shall be much surprised if we don't come down to breakfast tomorrow morning and find him weltering in his blood among the kippers and sausages with a dagger of Oriental design in the small of his back.'

'Ass!'

'Are you addressing me?'

'I am, and with knobs on. Bill's never been farther east than Frinton.'

'He's been to Cannes.'

'Is Cannes east? I never know. But he's certainly never been within smelling distance of Indian idols' eyes.'

'I didn't think of that,' said Rory. 'Yes, that, I admit, does weaken my argument to a certain extent.' He brooded tensely. 'Ha! I have it now. I see it all. The rift between Bill and Biggar is due to the baby.'

'What on earth are you talking about? What baby?'

'Bill's, working in close collaboration with Biggar's daughter, the apple of Biggar's eye, a poor, foolish little thing who loved not wisely but too well. And if you are going to say that girls are all wise nowadays, I reply "Not one brought up in the missionary school at Squalor Lumpit." In those missionary schools they explain the facts of life by telling the kids about the bees and the flowers till the poor little brutes don't know which is which.'

'For heaven's sake, Rory.'

'Mark how it works out with the inevitability of Greek tragedy or whatever it was that was so bally inevitable. Girl comes to England, no mother to guide her, meets a handsome young Englishman, and what happens? The first false step. The remorse . . . too late. The little bundle. The awkward interview with Father. Father all steamed up. Curses a bit in some native dialect and packs his elephant gun and comes along to see old Bill. "*Caramba!*" as that Spaniard is probably saying at this moment on the television screen. Still, there's nothing to worry about. I don't suppose he can make him marry her. All Bill will have to do is look after the little thing's education. Send it to school and so on. If a boy, Eton. If a girl, Roedean.'

'Cheltenham.'

'Oh, yes. I'd forgotten you were an Old Cheltonian. The question now arises, should young Jill be told? It hardly seems fair to allow her to rush unwarned into marriage with a rip-snorting roué like William, Earl of Rowcester.'

'Don't call Bill a rip-snorting roué!'

'It is how we should describe him at Harrige's.'

'As a matter of fact, you're probably all wrong about Bill and Biggar. I know the poor boy's jumpy, but most likely it hasn't anything to do with Captain Biggar at all. It's because he's all on edge, wondering if Mrs Spottsworth is going to buy the house. In which connection, Rory, you old fat-head, can't you do something to help the thing along instead of bunging a series of spanners into the works?'

'I don't get your drift.'

'I will continue snowing. Ever since Mrs Spottsworth arrived, you've been doing nothing but point out Rowcester Abbey's defects. Be constructive.'

'In what way, my queen?'

'Well, draw her attention to some of the good things there are in the place.'

Rory nodded dutifully, but dubiously.

'I'll do my best,' he said. 'But I shall have very little raw material to work with. And now, old girl, I imagine that Spaniard will have blown over by this time, so let us rejoin the Derby diners. For some reason or other – why, one cannot tell – I've got a liking for a beast called Oratory.'

10

Mrs Spottsworth had left the ruined chapel. After a vigil of some twenty-five minutes she had wearied of waiting for Lady Agatha to manifest herself. Like many very rich women, she tended to be impatient and to demand quick service. When in the mood for spectres, she wanted them hot off the griddle. Returning to the garden, she had found a rustic seat and was sitting there smoking a cigarette and enjoying the beauty of the night.

It was one of those lovely nights which occur from time to time in an English June, mitigating the rigours of the island summer and causing manufacturers of raincoats and umbrellas to wonder uneasily if they have been mistaken in supposing England to be an earthly Paradise for men of their profession.

A silver moon was riding in the sky, and a gentle breeze blew from the west, bringing with it the heart-stirring scent of stock and tobacco plant. Shy creatures of the night rustled in the bushes at her side and, to top the whole thing off, somewhere in the woods beyond the river a nightingale had begun to sing with the full-throated zest of a bird conscious of having had a rave notice from the poet Keats and only a couple of nights ago a star spot on the programme of the BBC.

It was a night made for romance, and Mrs Spottsworth recognized it as such. Although in her *vers libre* days in Greenwich Village she had gone in almost exclusively for starkness and squalor, even then she had been at heart a sentimentalist. Left to herself, she would have turned out stuff full of moons, Junes, loves, doves, blisses and kisses. It was simply that the editors of the poetry magazines seemed to prefer rat-ridden tenements, the smell of cooking cabbage, and despair, and a girl had to eat.

Fixed now as solidly financially as any woman in America and freed from the necessity of truckling to the tastes of editors, she was able to take the wraps off her romantic self, and as she sat on the rustic seat, looking at the moon and listening to the nightingale, a stylist like the late Gustave Flaubert, tireless in his quest of the *mot juste*, would have had no hesitation in describing her mood as mushy.

To this mushiness Captain Biggar's conversation at dinner had contributed largely. We have given some indication of its trend, showing it ranging freely from cannibal chiefs to dart-blowing headhunters, from headhunters to alligators, and its effect on Mrs Spottsworth had been very similar to that of Othello's reminiscences on Desdemona. In short, long before the last strawberry had been eaten, the final nut consumed, she was convinced that this was the mate for her and resolved to spare no effort in pushing the thing along. In the matter of marrying again, both A.B. Spottsworth and Clifton Bessemer had given her the green light, and there was consequently no obstacle in her path.

There appeared, however, to be one in the path leading to the rustic seat, for at this moment there floated to her through the silent night the sound of a strong man tripping over a flowerpot. It was followed by some pungent remarks in Swahili, and Captain Biggar limped up, rubbing his shin.

Mrs Spottsworth was all womanly sympathy.

'Oh, dear. Have you hurt yourself, Captain?'

'A mere scratch, dear lady,' he assured her.

He spoke bluffly, and only somebody like Sherlock Holmes or Monsieur Poirot could have divined that at the sound of her voice his soul had turned a double somersault, leaving him quivering with an almost Bill Rowcester-like intensity.

His telephone conversation concluded, the White Hunter had prudently decided to avoid the living room and head straight for the great open spaces, where he could be alone. To join the ladies, he had reasoned, would be to subject himself to the searing torture of having to sit and gaze at the woman he worshipped, a process which would simply rub in the fact of how unattainable she was. He recognized himself as being in the unfortunate position of the moth in Shelley's well-known poem that allowed itself to become attracted by a star, and it seemed to him that the smartest move a level-headed moth could make would be to minimize the anguish by shunning the adored object's society. It was, he felt, what Shelley would have advised.

And here he was, alone with her in the night, a night complete with moonlight, nightingales, gentle breezes and the scent of stock and tobacco plant.

It was a taut, tense Captain Biggar, a Captain Biggar telling himself he must be strong, who accepted his companion's invitation to join her on the rustic seat. The voices of Tubby Frobisher and the Subahdar seemed to ring in his ears. 'Chin up, old boy,' said

Tubby in his right ear. 'Remember the code,' said the Subahdar in his left.

He braced himself for the coming tête-à-tête.

Mrs Spottsworth, a capital conversationalist, began it by saying what a beautiful night it was, to which the Captain replied 'Top hole'. 'The moon,' said Mrs Spottsworth, indicating it and adding that she always thought a night when there was a full moon was so much nicer than a night when there was not a full moon. 'Oh, rather,' said the captain. Then, after Mrs Spottsworth had speculated as to whether the breeze was murmuring lullabies to the sleeping flowers and the captain had regretted his inability to inform her on this point, he being a stranger in these parts, there was a silence.

It was broken by Mrs Spottsworth, who gave a little cry of concern. 'Oh, dear!'

'What's the matter?'

'I've dropped my pendant. The clasp is so loose.'

Captain Biggar appreciated her emotion.

'Bad show,' he agreed. 'It must be on the ground somewhere. I'll have a look-see.'

'I wish you would. It's not valuable – I don't suppose it cost more than ten thousand dollars – but it has a sentimental interest. One of my husbands gave it to me, I never can remember which. Oh, have you found it? Thank you ever so much. Will you put it on for me?'

As Captain Biggar did so, his fingers, spine and stomach muscles trembled. It is almost impossible to clasp a pendant round its owner's neck without touching that neck in spots, and he touched his companion's in several. And every time he touched it, something seemed to go through him like a knife. It was as though the moon, the nightingale, the breeze, the stock and the tobacco plant were calling to him to cover this neck with burning kisses.

Only Tubby Frobisher and the Subahdar, forming a solid bloc in opposition, restrained him.

'Straight bat, old boy!' said Tubby Frobisher.

'Remember you're a white man,' said the Subahdar.

He clenched his fists and was himself again.

'It must be jolly,' he said, recovering his bluffness, 'to be rich enough to think ten thousand dollars isn't anything to write home about.'

Mrs Spottsworth felt like an actor receiving a cue.

'Do you think that rich women are happy, Captain Biggar?'

The captain said that all those he had met – and in his capacity of White Hunter he had met quite a number – had seemed pretty bobbish.

'They wore the mask.'

'Eh?'

'They smiled to hide the ache in their hearts,' explained Mrs Spottsworth.

The captain said he remembered one of them, a large blonde of the name of Fish, dancing the can-can one night in her step-ins, and Mrs Spottsworth said that no doubt she was just trying to show a brave front to the world.

'Rich women are so lonely, Captain Biggar.'

'Are *you* lonely?'

'Very, very lonely.'

'Oh, ah,' said the captain.

It was not what he would have wished to say. He would have preferred to pour out his soul in a torrent of impassioned words. But what could a fellow do, with Tubby Frobisher and the Subahdar watching his every move?

A woman who has told a man in the moonlight, with nightingales singing their heads off in the background, that she is very, very lonely and has received in response the words 'Oh, ah' is scarcely to be blamed for feeling a momentary pang of discouragement. Mrs Spottsworth had once owned a large hound dog of lethargic temperament who could be induced to go out for his nightly airing only by a succession of sharp kicks. She was beginning to feel now as she had felt when her foot thudded against this languorous animal's posterior. The same depressing sense of trying in vain to move an immovable mass. She loved the White Hunter. She admired him. But when you set out to kindle the spark of passion in him, you certainly had a job on your hands. In a moment of bitterness she told herself that she had known oysters on the half-shell with more of the divine fire in them.

However, she persevered.

'How strange our meeting again like this,' she said softly.

'Very odd.'

'We were a whole world apart, and we met in an English inn.'

'Quite a coincidence.'

'Not a coincidence. It was destined. Shall I tell you what brought you to that inn?'

'I wanted a spot of beer.'

'Fate,' said Mrs Spottsworth. 'Destiny. I beg your pardon?'

'I was only saying that, come right down to it, there's no beer like English beer.'

'The same Fate, the same Destiny,' continued Mrs Spottsworth, who at another moment would have hotly contested this statement, for she thought English beer undrinkable, 'that brought us together in Kenya. Do you remember the day we met in Kenya?'

Captain Biggar writhed. It was like asking Joan of Arc if she happened to recall the time she saw that heavenly vision of hers. 'How about it, boys?' he inquired silently, looking pleadingly from right to left. 'Couldn't you stretch a point?' But Tubby Frobisher and the Subahdar shook their heads.

'The code, old man,' said Tubby Frobisher.

'Play the game, old boy,' said the Subahdar.

'Do you?' asked Mrs Spottsworth.

'Oh, rather,' said Captain Biggar.

'I had the strangest feeling, when I saw you that day, that we had met before in some previous existence.'

'A bit unlikely, what?'

Mrs Spottsworth closed her eyes.

'I seemed to see us in some dim, prehistoric age. We were clad in skins. You hit me over the head with your club and dragged me by my hair to your cave.'

'Oh, no, dash it, I wouldn't do a thing like that.'

Mrs Spottsworth opened her eyes, and enlarging them to their fullest extent allowed them to play on his like searchlights.

'You did it because you loved me,' she said in a low, vibrant whisper. 'And I –'

She broke off. Something tall and willowy had loomed up against the skyline, and a voice with perhaps just a quaver of nervousness in it was saying 'Hullo-ullo-ullo-ullo-ullo'.

'I've been looking for you everywhere, Rosie,' said Bill. 'When I found you weren't at the ruined chapel . . . Oh, hullo, Captain.'

'Hullo,' said Captain Biggar dully, and tottered off. Lost in the shadows a few paces down the path, he halted and brushed away the beads of perspiration which had formed on his forehead.

He was breathing heavily, like a buffalo in the mating season. It had been a near thing, a very near thing. Had this interruption been postponed even for another minute, he knew that he must have sinned against the code and taken the irrevocable step which would have made his name a mockery and a byword in the Anglo-Malay Club at Kuala Lumpur. A pauper with a bank balance of a few meagre pounds, he would have been proposing marriage to a woman with millions.

More and more, as the moments went by, he had found himself being swept off his feet, his ears becoming deafer and deafer to the muttered warnings of Tubby Frobisher and the Subahdar. Her eyes he might have resisted. Her voice, too, and the skin he had loved to touch. But when it came to eyes, voice, skin, moonlight, gentle breezes from the west and nightingales, the mixture was too rich.

Yes, he felt as he stood there heaving like a stage sea, he had been saved, and it might have been supposed that his prevailing emotion would have been a prayerful gratitude to Fate or Destiny for its prompt action. But, oddly enough, it was not. The first spasm of relief had died quickly away, to be succeeded by a rising sensation of nausea. And what caused this nausea was the fact that, being still within earshot of the rustic seat, he could hear all that Bill was saying. And Bill, having seated himself beside Mrs Spottsworth, had begun to coo.

Too little has been said in this chronicle of the ninth Earl of Rowcester's abilities in this direction. When we heard him promising his sister Monica to contact Mrs Spottsworth and coo to her like a turtle dove, we probably formed in our minds the picture of one of those run-of-the-mill turtle doves whose cooing, though adequate, does not really amount to anything much. We would have done better to envisage something in the nature of a turtle dove of stellar quality, what might be called the Turtle Dove Supreme. A limited young man in many respects, Bill Rowcester could, when in mid-season form, touch heights in the way of cooing which left his audience, if at all impressionable, gasping for air.

These heights he was touching now, for the thought that this woman had it in her power to take England's leading white elephant off his hands, thus stabilizing his financial position and enabling him to liquidate Honest Patch Perkins' honourable obligations, lent him an eloquence which he had not achieved since May Week dances at Cambridge. The golden words came trickling from his lips like syrup.

Captain Biggar was not fond of syrup, and he did not like the thought of the woman he loved being subjected to all this goo. For a moment he toyed with the idea of striding up and breaking Bill's spine in three places, but once more found his aspirations blocked by the code. He had eaten Bill's meat and drunk Bill's drink . . . both excellent, especially the roast duck . . . and that made the feller immune to assault. For when a feller has accepted a feller's hospitality, a feller can't go about breaking the feller's spine, no matter what the feller may have done. The code is rigid on that point.

He is at liberty, however, to docket the feller in his mind as a low-down, fortune-hunting son of a what not, and this was how Captain Biggar was docketing Bill as he lumbered back to the house. And it was – substantially – how he described him to Jill when, passing through the french window, he found her crossing the living room on her way to deposit her things in her sleeping apartment.

'Good gracious!' said Jill, intrigued by his aspect. 'You seem very upset, Captain Biggar. What's the matter? Have you been bitten by an alligator?'

Before proceeding the captain had to put her straight on this.

'No alligators in England,' he said. 'Except, of course, in zoos. No, I have been shocked to the very depths of my soul.'

'By a wombat?'

Again the captain was obliged to correct her misapprehensions. An oddly ignorant girl, this, he was thinking.

'No wombats in England, either. What shocked me to the very depths of my soul was listening to a low-down, fortune-hunting English peer doing his stuff,' he barked bitterly. 'Lord Rowcester, he calls himself. Lord Gigolo's what I call him.'

Jill started so sharply that she dropped her suitcase.

'Allow me,' said the captain, diving for it.

'I don't understand,' said Jill. 'Do you mean that Lord Rowcester –?'

One of the rules of the code is that a white man must shield women, and especially young, innocent girls, from the seamy side of life, but Captain Biggar was far too stirred to think of that now. He resembled Othello not only in his taste for antres vast and deserts idle but in his tendency, being wrought, to become perplexed in the extreme.

'He was making love to Mrs Spottsworth in the moonlight,' he said curtly.

'What!'

'Heard him with my own ears. He was cooing to her like a turtle dove. After her money, of course. All the same, these effete aristocrats of the old country. Make a noise like a rich widow anywhere in England, and out come all the dukes and earls and viscounts, howling like wolves. Rats, we'd call them in Kuala Lumpur. You should hear Tubby Frobisher talk about them at the club. I remember him saying one day to Doc and Squiffy – the Subahdar wasn't there, if I recollect rightly – gone up country, or something – "Doc," he said . . .'

It was probably going to be a most extraordinarily good story, but Captain Biggar did not continue it any further for he saw that his audience was walking out on him. Jill had turned abruptly, and was passing through the door. Her head, he noted, was bowed, and very properly, too, after a revelation like that. Any nice girl would have been knocked endways by such a stunning exposé of the moral weaknesses of the British aristocracy.

He sat down and picked up the evening paper, throwing it from him with a stifled cry as the words 'Whistler's Mother' leaped at him from the printed page. He did not want to be reminded of Whistler's Mother. He was brooding darkly on Honest Patch Perkins and wondering wistfully if Destiny (or Fate) would ever bring their paths together again, when Jeeves came floating in. Simultaneously, Rory entered from the library.

'Oh, Jeeves,' said Rory, 'will you bring me a flagon of strong drink? I am athirst.'

With a respectful movement of his head Jeeves indicated the tray he was carrying, laden with the right stuff, and Rory accompanied him to the table, licking his lips.

'Something for you, Captain?' he said.

'Whisky, if you please,' said Captain Biggar. After that ordeal in the moonlit garden, he needed a restorative.

'Whisky? Right. And for you, Mrs Spottsworth?' said Rory, as that lady came through the french window accompanied by Bill.

'Nothing, thank you, Sir Roderick. On a night like this, moonlight is enough for me. Moonlight and your lovely garden, Billiken.'

'I'll tell you something about that garden,' said Rory. 'In the summer months –' He broke off as Monica appeared in the library door. The sight of her not only checked his observations on the garden, but reminded him of her injunction to boost the bally place to this Spottsworth woman. Looking about him for something in the bally place capable of being boosted, his eye fell on the dower chest in the corner and he recalled complementary things he had heard said in the past about it.

It seemed to him that it would make a good *point d'appui*. 'Yes,' he proceeded, 'the garden's terrific, and furthermore it must never be overlooked that Rowcester Abbey, though a bit shop-soiled and falling apart at the seams, contains many an objet d'art calculated to make the connoisseur sit up and say "What ho!" Cast an eye on that dower chest, Mrs Spottsworth.'

'I was admiring it when I first arrived. It's beautiful.'

'Yes, it is nice, isn't it?' said Monica, giving her husband a look of wifely approval. One didn't often find Rory showing such signs of almost human intelligence. 'Duveen used to plead to be allowed to buy it, but of course it's an heirloom and can't be sold.'

'Goes with the house,' said Rory.

'It's full of the most wonderful old costumes.'

'Which go with the house,' said Rory, probably quite incorrectly, but showing zeal.

'Would you like to look at them?' said Monica, reaching for the lid.

Bill uttered an agonized cry.

'They're not in there!'

'Of course they are. They always have been. And I'm sure Rosalinda would enjoy seeing them.'

'I would indeed.'

'There's quite a romantic story attached to this dower chest, Rosalinda. The Lord Rowcester of that time – centuries ago – wouldn't let his daughter marry the man she loved, a famous explorer and discoverer.'

'The old boy was against Discoveries,' explained Rory. 'He was afraid they might discover America. Ha, ha, ha, ha, ha. Oh, I beg your pardon.'

'The lover sent his chest to the girl, filled with rare embroideries he had brought back from his travels in the East, and her father wouldn't let her have it. He told the lover to come and take it away. And the lover did, and of course inside it was the young man's bride. Knowing what was going to happen, she had hidden there.'

'And the funny part of the story is that the old blister followed the chap all the way down the drive, shouting "Get that damn thing out of here!"'

Mrs Spottsworth was enchanted.

'What a delicious story. Do open it, Monica.'

'I will. It isn't locked.'

Bill sank bonelessly into a chair.

'Jeeves!'

'M'lord?'

'Brandy!'

'Very good, m'lord.'

'Well, for heaven's sake!' said Monica.

She was staring wide-eyed at a check coat of loud pattern and a tie so crimson, so intensely blue horseshoed, that Rory shook his head censoriously.

'Good Lord, Bill, don't tell me you go around in a coat like that? It must make you look like an absconding bookie. And the tie! The cravat! Ye gods! You'd better drop in at Harrige's and see the chap in our haberdashery department. We've got a sale on.'

Captain Biggar strode forward. There was a tense, hard expression on his rugged face.

'Let me look at that.' He took the coat, felt in the pocket and produced a black patch. 'Ha!' he said, and there was a wealth of meaning in his voice.

Rory was listening at the library door.

'Hullo,' he said. 'Someone talking French. Must be Boussac. Don't want to miss Boussac. Come along, Moke. This girl,' said Rory, putting a loving arm round her shoulder, 'talks French with both hands. You coming, Mrs Spottsworth? It's the Derby Dinner on television.'

'I will join you later, perhaps,' said Mrs Spottsworth. 'I left Pomona out in the garden, and she may be getting lonely.'

'You, Captain?'

Captain Biggar shook his head. His face was more rugged than ever.

'I have a word or two to say to Lord Rowcester first. If you can spare me a moment, Lord Rowcester?'

'Oh, rather,' said Bill faintly.

Jeeves returned with the brandy, and he sprang for it like Whistler's Mother leaping at the winning post.

11

But brandy, when administered in one of those small after-dinner glasses, can never do anything really constructive for a man whose affairs have so shaped themselves as to give him the momentary illusion of having been hit in the small of the back by the Twentieth Century Limited. A tun or a hogshead of the stuff might have enabled Bill to face the coming interview with a jaunty smile. The mere sip which was all that had been vouchsafed to him left him as pallid and boneless as if it had been sarsaparilla. Gazing through a mist at Captain Biggar, he closely resembled the sort of man for whom the police spread drag-nets, preparatory to questioning them in connection with the recent smash-and-grab robbery at Marks and Schoenstein's Bon Ton Jewellery Store on Eighth Avenue. His face had shaded away to about the colour of the underside of a dead fish, and Jeeves, eyeing him with respectful commiseration, wished that it were possible to bring the roses back to his cheeks by telling him one or two good things which had come into his mind from the *Collected Works of Marcus Aurelius*.

Captain Biggar, even when seen through a mist, presented a spectacle which might well have intimidated the stoutest. His eyes seemed to Bill to be shooting out long, curling flames, and why they called a man with a face as red as that a White Hunter was more than he was able to understand. Strong emotion, as always, had intensified the vermilion of the captain's complexion, giving him something of the appearance of a survivor from an explosion in a tomato cannery.

Nor was his voice, when he spoke, of a timbre calculated to lull any apprehensions which his aspect might have inspired. It was the voice of a man who needed only a little sympathy and encouragement to make him whip out a revolver and start blazing away with it.

'So!' he said.

There are no good answers to the word 'So!' particularly when uttered in the kind of voice just described, and Bill did not attempt to find one.

'So you are Honest Patch Perkins!'

Jeeves intervened, doing his best as usual.

'Well, yes and no, sir.'

'What do you mean, yes and no? Isn't this the louse's patch?' demanded the captain, brandishing Exhibit A. 'Isn't that the hell-hound's ginger moustache?' he said, giving Exhibit B a twiddle. 'And do you think I didn't recognize that coat and tie?'

'What I was endeavouring to convey by the expression "Yes and no", sir, was that his lordship has retired from business.'

'You bet he has. Pity he didn't do it sooner.'

'Yes, sir. Oh, Iago, the pity of it, Iago.'

'Eh?'

'I was quoting the Swan of Avon, sir.'

'Well, stop quoting the bally Swan of Avon.'

'Certainly, sir, if you wish it.'

Bill had recovered his faculties to a certain extent. To say that even now he was feeling boomps-a-daisy would be an exaggeration, but hc was capable of speech.

'Captain Biggar,' he said, 'I owe you an explanation.'

'You owe me three thousand and five pounds two and six,' said the captain, coldly corrective.

This silenced Bill again, and the captain took advantage of the fact to call him eleven derogatory names.

Jeeves assumed the burden of the defence, for Bill was still reeling under the impact of the eleventh name.

'It is impossible to gainsay the fact that in the circumstances your emotion is intelligible, sir, for one readily admits that his lordship's recent activities are of a nature to lend themselves to adverse criticism. But can one fairly blame his lordship for what has occurred?'

This seemed to the captain an easy one to answer.

'Yes,' he said.

'You will observe that I employed the adverb "fairly", sir. His lordship arrived on Epsom Downs this afternoon with the best intentions and a capital adequate for any reasonable emergency. He could hardly have been expected to foresee that two such meagrely favoured animals as Lucy Glitters and Whistler's Mother would have emerged triumphant from their respective trials of speed. His lordship is not clairvoyant.'

'He could have laid the bets off.'

'There I am with you sir. *Rem acu tetigisti.*'

'Eh?'

'A Latin expression, which might be rendered in English by the

American colloquialism "You said a mouthful". I urged his lordship
to do so.'

'You?'

'I was officiating as his lordship's clerk.'

The captain stared.

'You weren't the chap in the pink moustache?'

'Precisely, sir, though I would be inclined to describe it as russet
rather than pink.'

The captain brightened.

'So you were his clerk, were you? Then when he goes to prison,
you'll go with him.'

'Let us hope there will be no such sad ending as that, sir.'

'What do you mean, "sad" ending?' said Captain Biggar.

There was an uncomfortable pause. The captain broke it.

'Well, let's get down to it,' he said. 'No sense in wasting time.
Properly speaking, I ought to charge this sheep-faced, shambling
refugee from hell –'

'The name is Lord Rowcester, sir.'

'No, it's not, it's Patch Perkins. Properly speaking, Perkins, you
slinking reptile, I ought to charge you for petrol consumed on the
journey here from Epsom, repairs to my car, which wouldn't have
broken down if I hadn't had to push it so hard in the effort to catch
you . . . and,' he added, struck with an afterthought, 'the two beers
I had at the Goose and Gherkin while waiting for those repairs to be
done. But I'm no hog. I'll settle for three thousand and five pounds
two and six. Write me a cheque.'

Bill passed a fevered hand through his hair.

'How can I write you a cheque?'

Captain Biggar clicked his tongue, impatient of his shilly-shallying.

'You have a pen, have you not? And there is ink on the premises, I
imagine? You are a strong, able-bodied young fellow in full possession
of the use of your right hand, aren't you? No paralysis? No rheumatism
in the joints? If,' he went on, making a concession, 'what is bothering
you is that you have run out of blotting paper, never mind. I'll
blow on it.'

Jeeves came to the rescue, helping out the young master, who was
still massaging the top of his head.

'What his lordship is striving to express in words, sir, is that while,
as you rightly say, he is physically competent to write a cheque for
three thousand and five pounds two shillings and six pence, such a
cheque, when presented at your bank, would not be honoured.'

'Exactly,' said Bill, well pleased with his lucid way of putting the thing. 'It would bounce like a bounding Dervish and come shooting back like a homing pigeon.'

'Two very happy images, m'lord.'

'I haven't a bean.'

'Insufficient funds is the technical expression, m'lord. His lordship, if I may employ the argot, sir, is broke to the wide.'

Captain Biggar stared.

'You mean you own a place like this, a bally palace if ever I saw one, and can't write a cheque for three thousand pounds?'

Jeeves undertook the burden of explanation.

'A house such as Rowcester Abbey, in these days is not an asset, sir, it is a liability. I fear that your long residence in the East has rendered you not quite abreast of the changed conditions prevailing in your native land. Socialistic legislation has sadly depleted the resources of England's hereditary aristocracy. We are living now in what is known as the Welfare State, which means – broadly – that everybody is completely destitute.'

It would have seemed incredible to any of the native boys, hippopotami, rhinoceri, pumas, zebras, alligators and buffaloes with whom he had come in contact in the course of his long career in the wilds that Captain Biggar's strong jaw was capable of falling like an unsupported stick of asparagus, but it had fallen now in precisely that manner. There was something almost piteous in the way his blue eyes, round and dismayed, searched the faces of the two men before him.

'You mean he can't brass up?'

'You have put it in a nutshell, sir. Who steals his lordship's purse steals trash.'

Captain Biggar, his iron self-control gone, became a human semaphore. He might have been a White Hunter doing his daily dozen.

'But I must have the money, and I must have it before noon tomorrow.' His voice rose in what in a lesser man would have been a wail. 'Listen. I'll have to let you in on something that's vitally secret, and if you breathe a word to a soul I'll rip you both asunder with my bare hands, shred you up into small pieces and jump on the remains with hobnailed boots. Is that understood?'

Bill considered.

'Yes, that seems pretty clear. Eh, Jeeves?'

'Most straightforward, m'lord.'

'Carry on, Captain.'

Captain Biggar lowered his voice to a rasping whisper.

'You remember that telephone call I made after dinner? It was to those pals of mine, the chaps who gave me my winning double this afternoon. Well, when I say winning double,' said Captain Biggar, raising his voice a little, 'that's what it would have been but for the degraded chiselling of a dastardly, lop-eared —'

'Quite, quite,' said Bill hurriedly. 'You telephoned to your friends, you were saying?'

'I was anxious to know if it was all settled.'

'If all what was settled?'

Captain Biggar lowered his voice again, this time so far that his words sounded like gas escaping from a pipe.

'There's something cooking. As Shakespeare says, we have an enterprise of great importance.'

Jeeves winced. '"Enter*prises* of great pith and moment" is the exact quotation, sir.'

'These chaps have a big SP job on for the Derby tomorrow. It's the biggest cert in the history of the race. The Irish horse, Ballymore.'

Jeeves raised his eyebrows.

'Not generally fancied, sir.'

'Well, Lucy Glitters and Whistler's Mother weren't generally fancied, were they? That's what makes this job so stupendous. Ballymore's a long-priced outsider. Nobody knows anything about him. He's been kept darker than a black cat on a moonless night. But let me tell you that he has had two secret trial gallops over the Epsom course and broke the record both times.'

Despite his agitation, Bill whistled.

'You're sure of that?'

'Beyond all possibility of doubt. I've watched the animal run with my own eyes, and it's like a streak of lightning. All you see is a sort of brown blur. We're putting our money on at the last moment, carefully distributed among a dozen different bookies so as not to upset the price. And now,' cried Captain Biggar, his voice rising once more, 'you're telling me that I shan't have any money to put on.'

His agony touched Bill. He did not think, from what little he had seen of him, that Captain Biggar was a man with whom he could ever form one of those beautiful friendships you read about, the kind that existed between Damon and Pythias, David and Jonathan, or Swan and Edgar, but he could understand and sympathize with his grief.

'Too bad, I agree,' he said, giving the fermenting hunter a kindly, brotherly look and almost, but not quite, patting him on the shoulder. 'The whole situation is most regrettable, and you wouldn't be far out in saying that the spectacle of your anguish gashes me like a knife.

But I'm afraid the best I can manage is a series of monthly payments, starting say about six weeks from now.'

'That won't do me any good.'

'Nor me,' said Bill frankly. 'It'll knock the stuffing out of my budget and mean cutting down the necessities of life to the barest minimum. I doubt if I shall be able to afford another square meal till about 1954. Farewell, a long farewell . . . to what, Jeeves?'

'To all your greatness, m'lord. This is the state of man: today he puts forth the tender leaves of hopes; tomorrow blossoms, and bears his blushing honours thick upon him. The third day comes a frost, a killing frost, and when he thinks, good easy man, full surely his greatness is a-ripening, nips his roots.'

'Thank you, Jeeves.'

'Not at all, m'lord.'

Bill looked at him and sighed.

'You'll have to go, you know, to start with. I can't possibly pay your salary.'

'I should be delighted to serve your lordship without emolument.'

'That's dashed good of you, Jeeves, and I appreciate it. About as nifty a display of the feudal spirit as I ever struck. But how,' asked Bill keenly, 'could I keep you in fish?'

Captain Biggar interrupted these courteous exchanges. For some moments he had been chafing, if chafing is the right word to describe a White Hunter who is within an ace of frothing at the mouth. He said something so forceful about Jeeves' fish that speech was wiped from Bill's lips and he stood goggling with the dumb consternation of a man who has been unexpectedly struck by a thunderbolt.

'I've got to have that money!'

'His lordship has already informed you that, owing to the circumstance of his being fiscally crippled, that is impossible.'

'Why can't he borrow it?'

Bill recovered the use of his vocal cords.

'Who from?' he demanded peevishly. 'You talk as if borrowing money was as simple as falling off a log.'

'The point his lordship is endeavouring to establish,' explained Jeeves, 'is the almost universal tendency of gentlemen to prove uncooperative when an attempt is made to float a loan at their expense.'

'Especially if what you're trying to get into their ribs for is a whacking great sum like three thousand and five pounds two and six.'

'Precisely, m'lord. Confronted by such figures, they become like the deaf adder that hearkens not to the voice of the charmer, charming never so wisely.'

'So putting the bite on my social circle is off,' said Bill. 'It can't be done. I'm sorry.'

Captain Biggar seemed to blow flame through his nostrils.

'You'll be sorrier,' he said, 'and I'll tell you when. When you and this precious clerk of yours are standing in the dock at the Old Bailey, with the judge looking at you over his bifocals and me in the well of the court making faces at you. Then's the time when you'll be sorry . . . then and shortly afterwards, when the judge pronounces sentence, accompanied by some strong remarks from the bench, and they lead you off to Wormwood Scrubs to start doing your two years hard or whatever it is.'

Bill gaped.

'Oh, dash it!' he protested. 'You wouldn't proceed to that . . . what, Jeeves?'

'Awful extreme, m'lord.'

'You surely wouldn't proceed to that awful extreme?'

'Wouldn't I!'

'One doesn't want unpleasantness.'

'What one wants and what one is going to get are two different things,' said Captain Biggar, and went out, grinding his teeth, to cool off in the garden.

He left behind him one of those silences often called pregnant. Bill was the first to speak.

'We're in the soup, Jeeves.'

'Certainly a somewhat sharp crisis in our affairs would appear to have been precipitated, m'lord.'

'He wants his pound of flesh.'

'Yes, m'lord.'

'And we haven't any flesh.'

'No, m'lord. It is a most disagreeable state of affairs.'

'He's a tough egg, that Biggar. He looks like a gorilla with stomach ache.'

'There is, perhaps, a resemblance to such an animal, afflicted as your lordship suggests.'

'Did you notice him at dinner?'

'To which aspect of his demeanour during the meal does your lordship allude?'

'I was thinking of the sinister way he tucked into the roast duck. He flung himself on it like a tiger on its prey. He gave me the impression of a man without ruth or pity.'

'Unquestionably a gentleman lacking in the softer emotions, m'lord.'

'There's a word that just describes him. Begins with a V. Not vapid. Not vermicelli. Vindictive. The chap's vindictive. I can understand him being sore about not getting his money, but what good will it do him to ruin me?'

'No doubt he will derive a certain moody satisfaction from it, m'lord.'

Bill brooded.

'I suppose there really is nobody one could borrow a bit of cash from?'

'Nobody who springs immediately to the mind, m'lord.'

'How about that financier fellow, who lives out Ditchingham way – Sir Somebody Something?'

'Sir Oscar Wopple, m'lord? He shot himself last Friday.'

'Oh, then we won't bother him.'

Jeeves coughed.

'If I might make a suggestion, m'lord?'

'Yes, Jeeves?'

A faint ray of hope had stolen into Bill's sombre eyes. His voice, while still scarcely to be described as animated, no longer resembled that of a corpse speaking from the tomb.

'It occurred to me as a passing thought, m'lord, that were we to possess ourselves of Captain Biggar's ticket, our position would be noticeably stabilized.'

Bill shook his head.

'I don't get you, Jeeves. Ticket? What ticket? You speak as if this were a railway station.'

'I refer to the ticket which, in my capacity of your lordship's clerk, I handed to the gentleman as a record of his wager on Lucy Glitters and Whistler's Mother, m'lord.'

'Oh, you mean his *ticket*?' said Bill, enlightened.

'Precisely, m'lord. As he left the race-course so abruptly, it must still be upon his person, and it is the only evidence that exists that the wager was ever made. Once we had deprived him of it, your lordship would be in a position to make payment at your lordship's leisure.'

'I see. Yes, that would be nice. So we get the ticket from him, do we?'

'Yes, m'lord.'

'May I say one word, Jeeves?'

'Certainly, m'lord.'

'How?'

'By what I might describe as direct action, m'lord.'

Bill stared. This opened up a new line of thought.

'Set on him, you mean? *Scrag* him? Choke it out of him?'

'Your lordship has interpreted my meaning exactly.'

Bill continued to stare.

'But, Jeeves, have you *seen* him? That bulging chest, those rippling muscles?'

'I agree that Captain Biggar is well-nourished, m'lord, but we would have the advantage of surprise. The gentleman went out into the garden. When he returns, one may assume that it will be by way of the french window by which he made his egress. If I draw the curtains, it will be necessary for him to enter through them. We will see him fumbling, and in that moment a sharp tug will cause the curtains to descend upon him, enmeshing him, as it were.'

Bill was impressed, as who would not have been.

'By Jove, Jeeves! Now you're talking. You think it would work?'

'Unquestionably, m'lord. The method is that of the Roman retiarius, with whose technique your lordship is no doubt familiar.'

'That was the bird who fought with net and trident?'

'Precisely, m'lord. So if your lordship approves –'

'You bet I approve.'

'Very good, m'lord. Then I will draw the curtains now, and we will take up our stations on either side of them.'

It was with deep satisfaction that Bill surveyed the completed preparations. After a rocky start, the sun was coming through the cloud wrack.

'It's in the bag, Jeeves!'

'A very apt image, m'lord.'

'If he yells, we will stifle his cries with the . . . what do you call this stuff?'

'Velours, m'lord.'

'We will stifle his cries with the velours. And while he's grovelling on the ground, I shall get a chance to give him a good kick in the tailpiece.'

'There *is* that added attraction, m'lord. For blessings ever wait on virtuous deeds, as the playwright Congreve informs us.'

Bill breathed heavily.

'Were you in the First World War, Jeeves?'

'I dabbled in it to a certain extent, m'lord.'

'I missed that one because I wasn't born, but I was in the Commandos in this last one. This is rather like waiting for zero hour, isn't it?'

'...ensation is not dissimilar, m'lord.'

'He should be coming soon.'

'Yes, m'lord.'

'On your toes, Jeeves!'

'Yes, m'lord.'

'All set?'

'Yes, m'lord.'

'Hi!' said Captain Biggar in their immediate rear. 'I want to have another word with you two.'

A lifetime of braving the snares and perils of the wilds develops in those White Hunters over the years a sort of sixth sense, warning them of lurking danger. Where the ordinary man, happening upon a tiger trap in the jungle would fall in base over apex, your White Hunter, saved by his sixth sense, walks round it.

With fiendish cunning, Captain Biggar, instead of entering, as expected, through the french window, had circled the house and come in by the front door.

12

Although the actual time which had elapsed between Captain Biggar's departure and return had been only about five minutes, scarcely long enough for him to take half a dozen turns up and down the lawn, pausing in the course of one of them to kick petulantly at a passing frog, it had been ample for his purposes. If you had said to him as he was going through the french window 'Have you any ideas, Captain?' he would have been forced to reply 'No more than a rabbit'. But now his eye was bright and his manner jaunty. He had seen the way.

On occasions of intense spiritual turmoil the brain works quickly. Thwarted passion stimulates the little grey cells, and that painful scene on the rustic seat, when love had collided so disastrously with the code that governs the actions of the men who live on the frontiers of Empire, had stirred up those of Captain Biggar till, if you had X-rayed his skull, you would have seen them leaping and dancing like rice in a saucepan. Not thirty seconds after the frog, rubbing its head, had gone off to warn the other frogs to watch out for atom bombs, he was rewarded with what he recognized immediately as an inspiration.

Here was his position in a nutshell. He loved. Right. He would go further, he loved like the dickens. And unless he had placed a totally wrong construction on her words, her manner and the light in her eyes, the object of his passion loved him. A woman, he meant to say, does not go out of her way to bring the conversation round to the dear old days when a feller used to whack her over the top-knot with clubs and drag her into caves, unless she intends to convey a certain impression. True, a couple of minutes later she had been laughing and giggling with the frightful Rowcester excrescence, but that, it seemed to him now that he had had time to simmer down, had been merely a guest's conventional civility to a host. He dismissed the Rowcester gum-boil as negligible. He was convinced that, if one went by the form book, he had but to lay his heart at her feet, and she would pick it up.

So far, so good. But here the thing began to get more complicated.

She was rich and he was poor. That was the hitch. That was the snag. That was what was putting the good old sand in the bally machinery.

The thought that seared his soul and lent additional vigour to the kick he had directed at the frog was that, but for the deplorable financial methods of that black-hearted bookmaker, Honest Patch Rowcester, it would all have been so simple. Three thousand pounds deposited on the nose of Ballymore at the current odds of fifty to one would have meant a return of a hundred and fifty thousand, just like finding it: and surely even Tubby Frobisher and the Subahdar, rigid though their views were, could scarcely accuse a chap of not playing with the straight bat if he married a woman, however wealthy, while himself in possession of a hundred and fifty thousand of the best and brightest.

He groaned in spirit. A sorrow's crown of sorrow is remembering happier things, and he proceeded to torture himself with the recollection of how her neck had felt beneath his fingers as he fastened her pen—

Captain Biggar uttered a short, sharp exclamation. It was in Swahili, a language which always came most readily to his lips in moments of emotion, but its meaning was as clear as if it had been the 'Eureka!' of Archimedes.

Her pendant! Yes, now he saw daylight. Now he could start handling the situation as it should be handled.

Two minutes later, he was at the front door. Two minutes and twenty-five seconds later, he was in the living room, eyeing the backs of Honest Patch Rowcester and his clerk as they stood – for some silly reason known only to themselves – crouching beside the curtains which they had pulled across the french window.

'Hi!' he cried. 'I want to have another word with you two.'

The effect of the observation on his audience was immediate and impressive. It is always disconcerting, when you are expecting a man from the north-east, to have him suddenly bark at you from the south-west, especially if he does so in a manner that recalls feeding time in a dog hospital, and Bill went into his quaking and leaping routine with the smoothness that comes from steady practice. Even Jeeves, though his features did not lose their customary impassivity, appeared – if one could judge by the fact that his left eyebrow flickered for a moment as if about to rise – to have been stirred to quite a considerable extent.

'And don't stand there looking like a dying duck,' said the captain, addressing Bill, who, one is compelled to admit, was giving a rather close impersonation of such a bird *in articulo mortis*. 'Since I saw you two beauties last,' he continued, helping himself to another whisky and soda, 'I have been thinking over the situation, and I have now got it all taped out. It suddenly came to me, quick as a flash. I said to myself "The pendant!"'

Bill blinked feebly. His heart, which had crashed against the back of his front teeth, was slowly returning to its base, but it seemed to him that the shock which he had just sustained must have left his hearing impaired. It had sounded exactly as if the captain had said 'The pendant!' which, of course, made no sense whatever.

'The pendant?' he echoed, groping.

'Mrs Spottsworth is wearing a diamond pendant, m'lord,' said Jeeves. 'It is to this, no doubt, that the gentleman alludes.'

It was specious, but Bill found himself still far from convinced.

'You think so?'

'Yes, m'lord.'

'He alludes to that, in your opinion?'

'Yes, m'lord.'

'But why does he allude to it, Jeeves?'

'That, one is disposed to imagine, m'lord, one will ascertain when the gentleman has resumed his remarks.'

'Gone on speaking, you mean?'

'Precisely, m'lord.'

'Well, if you say so,' said Bill doubtfully. 'But it seems a . . . what's the expression you're always using?'

'Remote contingency, m'lord?'

'That's right. It seems a very remote contingency.'

Captain Biggar had been fuming silently. He now spoke with not a little asperity.

'If you have quite finished babbling, Patch Rowcester –'

'Was I babbling?'

'Certainly you were babbling. You were babbling like a . . . like a . . . well, like whatever the dashed things are that babble.'

'Brooks,' said Jeeves helpfully, 'are sometimes described as doing so, sir. In his widely read poem of that name, the late Lord Tennyson puts the words "Oh, brook, oh, babbling brook" into the mouth of the character Edmund, and later describes the rivulet, speaking in its own person, as observing "I chatter over stony ways in little sharps and trebles, I bubble into eddying bays, I babble on the pebbles".'

Captain Biggar frowned.

'*Ai deng hahp kamoo* for the late Lord Tennyson,' he said impatiently. 'What I'm interested in is this pendant.'

Bill looked at him with a touch of hope.

'Are you going to explain about that pendant? Throw light upon it, as it were?'

'I am. It's worth close on three thousand quid, and,' said Captain Biggar, throwing out the observation almost casually, 'you're going to pinch it, Patch Rowcester.'

Bill gaped.

'Pinch it?'

'This very night.'

It is always difficult for a man who is feeling as if he has just been struck over the occiput by a blunt instrument to draw himself to his full height and stare at someone censoriously, but Bill contrived to do so.

'What!' he cried, shocked to the core. 'Are you, a bulwark of the Empire, a man who goes about setting an example to Dyaks, seriously suggesting that I rob one of my guests?'

'Well, I'm one of your guests, and you robbed me.'

'Only temporarily.'

'And you'll be robbing Mrs Spottsworth only temporarily. I shouldn't have used the word "pinch". All I want you to do is borrow that pendant till tomorrow afternoon, when it will be returned.'

Bill clutched his hair.

'Jeeves!'

'M'lord?'

'Rally round, Jeeves. My brain's tottering. Can you make any sense of what this rhinoceros-biffer is saying?'

'Yes, m'lord.'

'You can? Then you're a better man than I am, Gunga Din.'

'Captain Biggar's thought processes seem to me reasonably clear, m'lord. The gentleman is urgently in need of money with which to back the horse Ballymore in tomorrow's Derby, and his proposal, as I take it, is that the pendant shall be abstracted and pawned and the proceeds employed for that purpose. Have I outlined your suggestion correctly, sir?'

'You have.'

'At the conclusion of the race, one presumes, the object in question would be redeemed, brought back to the house, discovered, possibly by myself, in some spot where the lady might be supposed to have dropped it, and duly returned to her. Do I err in advancing this theory, sir?'

'You do not.'

'Then, could one be certain beyond the peradventure of a doubt that Ballymore will win –'

'He'll win all right. I told you he had twice broken the course record.'

'That is official, sir?'

'Straight from the feed-box.'

'Then I must confess, m'lord, I see little or no objection to the scheme.'

Bill shook his head, unconvinced.

'I still call it stealing.'

Captain Biggar clicked his tongue.

'It isn't anything of the sort, and I'll tell you why. In a way, you might say that that pendant was really mine.'

'Really . . . what was that last word?'

'Mine. Let me,' said Captain Biggar, 'tell you a little story.'

He sat musing for a while. Coming out of his reverie and discovering with a start that his glass was empty, he refilled it. His attitude was that of a man, who, even if nothing came of the business transaction which he had proposed, intended to save something from the wreck by drinking as much as possible of his host's whisky. When the refreshing draught had finished its journey down the hatch, he wiped his lips on the back of his hand, and began.

'Do either of you chaps know the Long Bar at Shanghai? No? Well, it's the Café de la Paix of the East. They always say that if you sit outside the Café de la Paix in Paris long enough, you're sure sooner or later to meet all your pals, and it's the same with the Long Bar. A few years ago, chancing to be in Shanghai, I had dropped in there, never dreaming that Tubby Frobisher and the Subahdar were within a thousand miles of the place, and I'm dashed if the first thing I saw wasn't the two old bounders sitting on a couple of stools as large as life. "Hullo, there, Bwana, old boy," they said when I rolled up, and I said "Hullo, there, Tubby! Hullo there, Subahdar, old chap," and Tubby said "What'll you have, old boy?" and I said, "What are you boys having?" and they said stingahs, so I said that would do me all right, so Tubby ordered a round of stingahs, and we started talking about *chowluangs* and *nai bahn rot fais* and where we had all met last and whatever became of the *poogni* at Lampang and all that sort of thing. And when the stingahs were finished, I said "The next are on me. What for you, Tubby, old boy?" and he said he'd stick to stingahs. "And for you, Subahdar, old boy?" I said, and the Subahdar said he'd stick to stingahs, too, so I wig-wagged the barman and ordered stingahs all round, and, to cut a long story short, the stingahs came, a stingah for Tubby, a stingah for the Subahdar, and a stingah for me. "Luck, old boys!" said Tubby. "Luck, old boys!" said the Subahdar. "Cheerio, old boys!" I said, and we drank the stingahs.'

Jeeves coughed. It was a respectful cough, but firm.

'Excuse me, sir.'

'Eh?'

'I am reluctant to interrupt the flow of your narrative, but is this leading somewhere?'

Captain Biggar flushed. A man who is telling a crisp, well-knit story does not like to be asked if it is leading somewhere.

'Leading somewhere? What do you mean, is it leading somewhere? Of course it's leading somewhere. I'm coming to the nub of the thing now. Scarcely had we finished this second round of stingahs, when in through the door, sneaking along like a chap that expects at any moment to be slung out on his fanny, came this fellow in the tattered shirt and dungarees.'

The introduction of a new and unexpected character took Bill by surprise.

'Which fellow in the tattered shirt and dungarees?'

'This fellow I'm telling you about.'

'Who was he?'

'You may well ask. Didn't know him from Adam, and I could see Tubby Frobisher didn't know him from Adam. Nor did the Subahdar. But he came sidling up to us and the first thing he said, addressing me, was "Hullo, Bimbo, old boy", and I stared and said "Who on earth are you, old boy?" because I hadn't been called Bimbo since I left school. Everybody called me that there, God knows why, but out East it's been "Bwana" for as long as I can remember. And he said "Don't you know me, old boy? I'm Sycamore, old boy." And I stared again, and I said "What's that, old boy? Sycamore? Sycamore? Not Beau Sycamore that was in the Army Class at Uppingham with me, old boy?" and he said "That's right, old boy. Only it's Hobo Sycamore now."'

The memory of that distressing encounter unmanned Captain Biggar for a moment. He was obliged to refill his glass with Bill's whisky before he could proceed.

'You could have knocked me down with a feather,' he said, resuming. 'This chap Sycamore had been the smartest, most dapper chap that ever adorned an Army Class, even at Uppingham.'

Bill was following the narrative closely now.

'They're dapper in the Army Class at Uppingham, are they?'

'Very dapper, and this chap Sycamore, as I say, the most dapper of the lot. His dapperness was a byword. And here he was in a tattered shirt and dungarees, not even wearing a school tie.' Captain Biggar sighed. 'I saw at once what must have happened. It was the old, old story. Morale can crumble very easily out East. Drink, women and unpaid gambling debts . . .'

'Yes, yes,' said Bill. 'He'd gone under, had he?'

'Right under. It was pitiful. The chap was nothing but a bally beachcomber.'

'I remember a story of Maugham's about a fellow like that.'

'I'll bet your friend Maugham, whoever he may be, never met such a derelict as Sycamore. He had touched bottom, and the problem was what was to be done about it. Tubby Frobisher and the Subahdar, of course, not having been introduced, were looking the other way and taking no part in the conversation, so it was up to me. Well, there isn't much you can do for these chaps who have let the East crumble their morale except give them something to buy a couple of drinks with, and I was just starting to feel in my pocket for a *baht* or a *tical*, when from under that tattered shirt of his this chap Sycamore produced something that brought a gasp to my lips. Even Tubby Frobisher and the Subahdar, though they hadn't been introduced, had to stop trying to pretend there wasn't anybody there and sit up and take notice. "*Sabaiga!*" said Tubby. "*Pom bahoo!*" said the Subahdar. And I don't wonder they were surprised. It was this pendant which you have seen tonight on the neck . . .' Captain Biggar faltered for a moment. He was remembering how that neck had felt beneath his fingers. '. . . on the neck,' he proceeded, calling all his manhood to his aid, 'of Mrs Spottsworth.'

'Golly!' said Bill, and even Jeeves, from the fact that the muscle at the side of his mouth twitched briefly, seemed to be feeling that after a slow start the story had begun to move. One saw now that all that stingah stuff had been merely the artful establishing of atmosphere, the setting of the stage for the big scene.

'"I suppose you wouldn't care to buy this, Bimbo, old boy?" this chap Sycamore said, waggling the thing to make it glitter. And I said "Fry me in olive oil, Beau, old boy, where did you get that?"'

'That's just what I was going to ask,' said Bill, all agog. 'Where did he?'

'God knows. I ought not to have inquired. It was dashed bad form. That's one thing you learn very early out East of Suez. Never ask questions. No doubt there was some dark history behind the thing . . . robbery . . . possibly murder. I didn't ask. All I said was "How much?" and he named a price far beyond the resources of my purse, and it looked as though the thing was going to be a washout. But fortunately Tubby Frobisher and the Subahdar – I'd introduced them by this time – offered to chip in, and between us we met his figure and he went off, back into the murk and shadows from which he had emerged. Sad thing, very sad. I remember seeing this chap Sycamore make a hundred and forty-six in a house cricket match at school before being caught low down in the gully off a googly that dipped and swung away late. On a sticky wicket, too,' said Captain Biggar, and was silent for a while, his thoughts in the past.

He came back into the present.

'So there you are,' he said, with the air of one who has told a well-rounded tale.

'But how did you get it?' said Bill.

'Eh?'

'The pendant. You said it was yours, and the way I see it is that it passed into the possession of a syndicate.'

'Oh, ah, yes, I didn't tell you that, did I? We shook dice for it and I won. Tubby was never lucky with the bones. Nor was the Subahdar.'

'And how did Mrs Spottsworth get it?'

'I gave it her.'

'You *gave* it her?'

'Why not? The dashed thing was no use to me, and I had received many kindnesses from Mrs Spottsworth and her husband. Poor chap was killed by a lion and what was left of him shipped off to Nairobi, and when Mrs Spottsworth was leaving the camp on the following day I thought it would be a civil thing to give her something as a memento and all that, so I lugged out the pendant and asked her if she'd care to have it. She said she would, so I slipped it to her, and she went off with it. That's what I meant when I said you might say that the bally thing was really mine,' said Captain Biggar, and helped himself to another whisky.

Bill was impressed.

'This puts a different complexion on things, Jeeves.'

'Distinctly, m'lord.'

'After all, as Pop Biggar says, the pendant practically belongs to him, and he merely wants to borrow it for an hour or two.'

'Precisely, m'lord.'

Bill turned to the captain. His mind was made up.

'It's a deal,' he said.

'You'll do it?'

'I'll have a shot.'

'Stout fellow!'

'Let's hope it comes off.'

'It'll come off all right. The clasp is loose.'

'I meant I hoped nothing would go wrong.'

Captain Biggar scouted the idea. He was all buoyancy and optimism.

'Go wrong? What can possibly go wrong? You'll be able to think of a hundred ways of getting the dashed thing, two brainy fellers like you. Well,' said the captain, finishing his whisky, 'I'll be going out and doing my exercises.'

'At this time of night?'

'Breathing exercises,' explained Captain Biggar. 'Yoga. And with it, of course, communion with the Jivatma or soul. Toodle-oo, chaps.'

He pushed the curtains aside, and passed through the french window.

13

A long and thoughtful silence followed his departure. The room seemed very still, as rooms always did when Captain Biggar went out of them. Bill was sitting with his chin supported by his hand, like Rodin's *Penseur*. Then he looked at Jeeves and, having looked, shook his head.

'No, Jeeves,' he said.

'M'lord?'

'I can see that feudal gleam in your eye, Jeeves. You are straining at the leash, all eagerness to lend the young master a helping hand. Am I right?'

'I was certainly feeling, m'lord, that in view of our relationship of thane and vassal it was my duty to afford your lordship all the assistance that lay within my power.'

Bill shook his head again.

'No, Jeeves, that's out. Nothing will induce me to allow you to go getting yourself mixed up in an enterprise which, should things not pan out as planned, may quite possibly culminate in a five year stretch at one of our popular prisons. I shall handle this binge alone, and I want no back-chat about it.'

'But, m'lord –'

'No back-chat, I said, Jeeves.'

'Very good, m'lord.'

'All I require from you is advice and counsel. Let us review the position of affairs. We have here a diamond pendant which at the moment of going to press is on the person of Mrs Spottsworth. The task confronting me – I said me, Jeeves – is somehow to detach this pendant from this person and nip away with it unobserved. Any suggestions?'

'The problem is undoubtedly one that presents certain points of interest, m'lord.'

'Yes, I'd got as far as that myself.'

'One rules out anything in the nature of violence, I presume, placing reliance wholly on stealth and finesse.'

'One certainly does. Dismiss any idea that I propose to swat Mrs Spottsworth on the napper with a blackjack.'

'Then I would be inclined to say, m'lord, that the best results would probably be obtained from what I might term the spider sequence.'

'I don't get you, Jeeves.'

'If I might explain, m'lord. Your lordship will be joining the lady in the garden?'

'Probably on a rustic seat.'

'Then, as I see it, m'lord, conditions will be admirably adapted to the plan I advocate. If shortly after entering into conversation with Mrs Spottsworth, your lordship were to affect to observe a spider on her hair, the spider sequence would follow as doth the night the day. It would be natural for your lordship to offer to brush the insect off. This would enable your lordship to operate with your lordship's fingers in the neighbourhood of the lady's neck. And if the clasp, as Captain Biggar assures us, is loose, it will be a simple matter to unfasten the pendant and cause it to fall to the ground. Do I make myself clear, m'lord?'

'All straight so far. But wouldn't she pick it up?'

'No, m'lord, because in actual fact it would be in your lordship's pocket. Your lordship would institute a search in the surrounding grass, but without avail, and eventually the search would be abandoned until the following day. The object would finally be discovered late tomorrow evening.'

'After Biggar gets back?'

'Precisely, m'lord.'

'Nestling under a bush?'

'Or on the turf some little distance away. It had rolled.'

'Do pendants roll?'

'This pendant would have done so, m'lord.'

Bill chewed his lower lip thoughtfully.

'So that's the spider sequence?'

'That is the spider sequence, m'lord.'

'Not a bad scheme at all.'

'It has the merit of simplicity, m'lord. And if your lordship is experiencing any uneasiness at the thought of opening cold, as the theatrical expression is, I would suggest our having what in stage parlance is called a quick run through.'

'A rehearsal, you mean?'

'Precisely, m'lord. It would enable your lordship to perfect yourself in lines and business. In the Broadway section of New York, where

the theatre industry of the United States of America is centred, I am
told that this is known as ironing out the bugs.'

'Ironing out the spiders.'

'Ha, ha, m'lord. But, if I may venture to say so it is unwise to waste
the precious moments in verbal pleasantries.'

'Time is of the essence?'

'Precisely, m'lord. Would your lordship like to walk the scene?'

'Yes, I think I would, if you say it's going to steady the nervous
system. I feel as if a troupe of performing fleas were practising
buck-and-wing steps up and down my spine.'

'I have heard Mr Wooster complain of a similar malaise in moments
of stress and trial, m'lord. It will pass.'

'When?'

'As soon as your lordship has got the feel of the part. A rustic seat,
your lordship said?'

'That's where she was last time.'

'Scene, A rustic seat,' murmured Jeeves. 'Time, A night in summer.
Discovered at rise, Mrs Spottsworth. Enter Lord Rowcester. I will
portray Mrs Spottsworth, m'lord. We open with a few lines of dialogue
to establish atmosphere, then bridge into the spider sequence. Your
lordship speaks.'

Bill marshalled his thoughts.

'Er – Tell me, Rosie –'

'Rosie, m'lord?'

'Yes, Rosie, blast it. Any objection?'

'None whatever, m'lord.'

'I used to know her at Cannes.'

'Indeed, m'lord? I was not aware. You were saying, m'lord?'

'Tell me, Rosie, are you afraid of spiders?'

'Why does your lordship ask?'

'There's rather an outsize specimen crawling on the back of your
hair.' Bill sprang about six inches in the direction of the ceiling. 'What
on earth did you do that for?' he demanded irritably.

Jeeves preserved his calm.

'My reason for screaming, m'lord, was merely to add verisimilitude.
I supposed that that was how a delicately nurtured lady would be
inclined to react on receipt of such a piece of information.'

'Well, I wish you hadn't. The top of my head nearly came off.'

'I am sorry, m'lord. But it was how I saw the scene. I felt it,
felt it *here*,' said Jeeves, tapping the left side of his waistcoat. 'If
your lordship would be good enough to throw me the line once
more.'

'There's rather an outsize specimen crawling on the back of your hair.'

'I would be grateful if your lordship would be so kind as to knock it off.'

'I can't see it now. Ah, there it goes. On your neck.'

'And that,' said Jeeves, rising from the settee on which in his role of Mrs Spottsworth he had seated himself, 'is cue for business, m'lord. Your lordship will admit that it is really quite simple.'

'I suppose it is.'

'I am sure that after this try-out the performing fleas to which your lordship alluded a moment ago will have substantially modified their activities.'

'They've slowed up a bit, yes. But I'm still nervous.'

'Inevitable on the eve of an opening performance, m'lord. I think your lordship should be starting as soon as possible. If 'twere done, then 'twere well 'twere done quickly. Our arrangements have been made with a view to a garden set, and it would be disconcerting were Mrs Spottsworth to return to the house, compelling your lordship to adapt your technique to an interior.'

Bill nodded.

'I see what you mean. Right ho, Jeeves. Goodbye.'

'Goodbye, m'lord.'

'If anything goes wrong –'

'Nothing will go wrong, m'lord.'

'But if it does ... You'll write to me in Dartmoor occasionally, Jeeves? Just a chatty letter from time to time, giving me the latest news from the outer world?'

'Certainly, m'lord.'

'It'll cheer me up as I crack my daily rock. They tell me conditions are much better in these modern prisons than they used to be in the old days.'

'So I understand, m'lord.'

'I might find Dartmoor a regular home from home. Solid comfort, I mean to say.'

'Quite conceivably, m'lord.'

'Still, we'll hope it won't come to that.'

'Yes, m'lord.'

'Yes ... Well, goodbye once again, Jeeves.'

'Goodbye, m'lord.'

Bill squared his shoulders and strode out, a gallant figure. He had summoned the pride of the Rowcesters to his aid, and it buoyed him up. With just this quiet courage had a Rowcester of the seventeenth century mounted the scaffold at Tower Hill, nodding affably to the headsman and waving to friends and relations in the audience. When the test comes, blood will tell.

He had been gone a few moments, when Jill came in.

It seemed to Jeeves that in the course of the past few hours the young master's betrothed had lost a good deal of the animation which rendered her as a rule so attractive, and he was right. Her recent interview with Captain Biggar had left Jill pensive and inclined to lower the corners of the mouth and stare mournfully. She was staring mournfully now.

'Have you seen Lord Rowcester, Jeeves?'

'His lordship has just stepped into the garden, miss.'

'Where are the others?'

'Sir Roderick and her ladyship are still in the library, miss.'

'And Mrs Spottsworth?'

'She stepped into the garden shortly before his lordship.'

Jill stiffened.

'Oh?' she said, and went into the library to join Monica and Rory. The corners of her mouth were drooping more than ever, and her stare had increased in mournfulness some twenty per cent. She looked like a girl who is thinking the worst, and that was precisely the sort of girl she was.

Two minutes later, Captain Biggar came bustling in with a song on his lips. Yoga and communion with the Jivatma or soul seemed to have done him good. His eyes were bright and his manner alert. It is when the time for action has come that you always catch these White Hunters at their best.

'Pale hands I loved beside the Shalimar, where are you now, where are you now?' sang Captain Biggar. 'I . . . how does the dashed thing go . . . I sink beneath your spell. La, la, la . . . La, la, la, la. Where are you now? Where *are* you now? For they're hanging Danny Deever in the morning,' he carolled, changing the subject.

He saw Jeeves, and suspended the painful performance.

'Hullo,' he said. '*Quai hai*, my man. How are things?'

'Things are in a reasonably satisfactory state, sir.'

'Where's Patch Rowcester?'

'His lordship is in the garden, sir.'

'With Mrs Spottsworth?'

'Yes, sir. Putting his fate to the test, to win or lose it all.'

'You thought of something, then?'

'Yes, sir. The spider sequence.'

'The how much?'

Captain Biggar listened attentively as Jeeves outlined the spider sequence, and when he had finished paid him a stately compliment.

'You'd do well out East, my boy.'

'It is extremely kind of you to say so, sir.'

'That is to say if that scheme was your own.'

'It was, sir.'

'Then you'd be just the sort of fellow we want in Kuala Lumpur. We need chaps like you, chaps who can use their brains. Can't leave brains all to the Dyaks. Makes the blighters get above themselves.'

'The Dyaks are exceptionally intelligent, sir?'

'Are they! Let me tell you of something that happened to Tubby Frobisher and me one day when we —' He broke off, and the world was deprived of another excellent story. Bill was coming through the french window.

A striking change had taken place in the ninth Earl in the few minutes since he had gone out through that window, a young man of spirit setting forth on a high adventure. His shoulders, as we have indicated, had then been square. Now they sagged like those of one who bears a heavy weight. His eyes were dull, his brow furrowed. The pride of the Rowcesters appeared to have packed up and withdrawn its support. No longer was there in his bearing any suggestion of that seventeenth-century ancestor who had infused so much of the party spirit into his decapitation on Tower Hill. The ancestor he most closely resembled now was the one who was caught cheating at cards by Charles James Fox at Wattier's in 1782.

'Well?' cried Captain Biggar.

Bill gave him a long, silent mournful look, and turned to Jeeves.

'Jeeves!'

'M'lord?'

'That spider sequence.'

'Yes, m'lord?'

'I tried it.'

'Yes, m'lord?'

'And things looked good for a moment. I detached the pendant.'

'Yes, m'lord?'

'Captain Biggar was right. The clasp was loose. It came off.'

Captain Biggar uttered a pleased exclamation in Swahili.

'Gimme,' he said.

'I haven't got it. It slipped out of my hand.'

'And fell?'

'And fell.'

'You mean it's lying in the grass?'

'No,' said Bill, with a sombre shake of the head. 'It isn't lying in any ruddy grass. It went down the front of Mrs Spottsworth's dress, and is now somewhere in the recesses of her costume.'

14

It is not often that one sees three good men struck all of a heap simultaneously, but anybody who had chanced to stroll into the living room of Rowcester Abbey at this moment would have been able to observe that spectacle. To say that Bill's bulletin had had a shattering effect on his companions would be, if anything, to understate it. Captain Biggar was expressing his concern by pacing the room with whirling arms, while the fact that two of the hairs of his right eyebrow distinctly quivered showed how deeply Jeeves had been moved. Bill himself, crushed at last by the blows of Fate, appeared formally to have given up the struggle. He had slumped into a chair, and was sitting there looking boneless and despairing. All he needed was a long white beard, and the resemblance to King Lear on one of his bad mornings would have been complete.

Jeeves was the first to speak.

'Most disturbing, m'lord.'

'Yes,' said Bill dully. 'Quite a nuisance, isn't it? You don't happen to have any little-known Asiatic poison on you, do you, Jeeves?'

'No, m'lord.'

'A pity,' said Bill. 'I could have used it.'

His young employer's distress pained Jeeves, and as it had always been his view that there was no anodyne for the human spirit, when bruised, like a spot of Marcus Aurelius, he searched in his mind for some suitable quotation from the Emperor's works. And he was just hesitating between 'Whatever may befall thee, it was preordained for thee from everlasting' and 'Nothing happens to any man which he is not fitted by nature to bear', both excellent, when Captain Biggar, who had been pouring out a rapid fire of ejaculations in some native dialect, suddenly reverted to English.

'*Doi wieng lek!*' he cried. 'I've got it! Fricassee me with stewed mushrooms on the side, I see what you must do.'

Bill looked up. His eyes were glazed, his manner listless.

'Do?' he said. 'Me?'

'Yes, you.'

'I'm sorry,' said Bill. 'I'm in no condition to do anything except possibly expire, regretted by all.'

Captain Biggar snorted, and having snorted uttered a tchah, a pah and a bah.

'*Mun py nawn lap lao!*' he said impatiently. 'You can dance, can't you?'

'Dance?'

'Preferably the Charleston. That's all I'm asking of you, a few simple steps of the Charleston.'

Bill stirred slightly, like a corpse moving in its winding sheet. It was an acute spasm of generous indignation that caused him to do so. He was filled with what, in his opinion, was a justifiable resentment. Here he was, in the soup and going down for the third time, and this man came inviting him to dance before him as David danced before Saul. Assuming this to be merely the thin end of the wedge, one received the impression that in next to no time the White Hunter, if encouraged, would be calling for comic songs and conjuring tricks and imitations of footlight favourites who are familiar to you all. What, he asked himself bitterly, did the fellow think this was? The revival of Vaudeville? A village concert in aid of the church organ restoration fund?

Groping for words with which to express these thoughts, he found that the captain was beginning to tell another of his stories. Like Marcus Aurelius, Kuala Lumpur's favourite son always seemed to have up his sleeve something apposite to the matter in hand, whatever that matter might be. But where the Roman Emperor, a sort of primitive Bob Hope or Groucho Marx, had contented himself with throwing off wisecracks, Captain Biggar preferred the narrative form.

'Yes, the Charleston,' said Captain Biggar, 'and I'll tell you why. I am thinking of the episode of Tubby Frobisher and the wife of the Greek consul. The recollection of it suddenly flashed upon me like a gleam of light from above.'

He paused. A sense of something omitted, something left undone, was nagging at him. Then he saw why this was so. The whisky. He moved to the table and filled his glass.

'Whether it was Smyrna or Joppa or Stamboul where Tubby was stationed at the time of which I speak,' he said, draining half the contents of his glass and coming back with the rest, 'I'm afraid I can't tell you. As one grows older, one tends to forget these details. It may even have been Baghdad or half a dozen other places. I admit frankly that I have forgotten. But the point is that he was at some place somewhere and one night he attended a reception or a *soirée* or whatever they call these binges at one of the embassies. You know the sort of thing I mean. Fair women and brave men, all dolled up and dancing their ruddy heads off. And in due season it came to pass that Tubby found himself doing the Charleston with the wife of the Greek consul as his partner. I don't know if either of you have ever seen Tubby Frobisher dance the Charleston?'

'Neither his lordship nor myself have had the privilege of meeting Mr Frobisher, sir,' Jeeves reminded him courteously.

Captain Biggar stiffened.

'Major Frobisher, damn it.'

'I beg your pardon, sir. Major Frobisher. Owing to our never having met him, the major's technique when performing the Charleston is a sealed book to us.'

'Oh?' Captain Biggar refilled his glass. 'Well, his technique, as you call it, is vigorous. He does not spare himself. He is what in the old days would have been described as a three-collar man. By the time Tubby Frobisher has finished dancing the Charleston, his partner knows she has been in a fight, all right. And it was so on this occasion. He hooked on to the wife of the Greek consul and he jumped her up and he jumped her down, he whirled her about and he spun her round, he swung her here and he swung her there, and all of a sudden what do you think happened?'

'The lady had heart failure, sir?'

'No, the lady didn't have heart failure, but what occurred was enough to give it to all present at that gay affair. For, believe me or believe me not, there was a tinkling sound, and from inside her dress there began to descend to the floor silver forks, silver spoons and, Tubby assures me, a complete toilet set in tortoiseshell. It turned out that the female was a confirmed kleptomaniac and had been using the space between her dress and whatever she was wearing under her dress – I'm not a married man myself, so can't go into particulars – as a safe deposit.'

'Embarrassing for Major Frobisher, sir.'

Captain Biggar stared.

'For Tubby? Why? He hadn't been pinching the things, he was merely the instrument for their recovery. But don't tell me you've missed the whole point of my story, which is that I am convinced that if Patch Rowcester here were to dance the Charleston with Mrs Spottsworth with one tithe of Tubby Frobisher's determination and will to win, we'd soon rout that pendant out of its retreat. Tubby would have had it in the open before the band had played a dozen bars.

And talking of that, we shall need music. Ah, I see a gramophone over there in the corner. Excellent. Well? Do you grasp the scheme?'

'Perfectly, sir. His lordship dances with Mrs Spottsworth, and in due course the pendant droppeth as the gentle rain from heaven upon the place beneath.'

'Exactly. What do you think of the idea?'

Jeeves referred the question to a higher court.

'What does your lordship think of it?' he asked deferentially.

'Eh?' said Bill. 'What?'

Captain Biggar barked sharply.

'You mean you haven't been listening? Well, of all the –'

Jeeves intervened.

'In the circumstances, sir, his lordship may, I think, be excused for being distrait,' he said reprovingly. 'You can see from his lordship's lacklustre eye that the native hue of his resolution is sicklied o'er with the pale cast of thought. Captain Biggar's suggestion is, m'lord, that your lordship shall invite Mrs Spottsworth to join you in performing the dance known as the Charleston. This, if your lordship infuses sufficient vigour into the steps, will result in the pendant becoming dislodged and falling to the ground, whence it can readily be recovered and placed in your lordship's pocket.'

It was perhaps a quarter of a minute before the gist of these remarks penetrated to Bill's numbed mind, but when it did, the effect was electric. His eyes brightened, his spine stiffened. It was plain that hope had dawned, and was working away once more at the old stand. As he rose from his chair, jauntily and with the air of a man who is ready for anything, he might have been that debonair ancestor of his who in the days of the Restoration had by his dash and gallantry won from the ladies of King Charles II's Court the affectionate sobriquet of Tabasco Rowcester.

'Lead me to her!' he said, and his voice rang out clear and resonant. 'Lead me to her, that is all I ask, and leave the rest to me.'

But it was not necessary, as it turned out, to lead him to Mrs Spottsworth, for at this moment she came in through the french window with her Pekinese dog Pomona in her arms.

Pomona, on seeing the assembled company, gave vent to a series of piercing shrieks. It sounded as if she were being torn asunder by red-hot pincers, but actually this was her method of expressing joy. In moments of ecstasy she always screamed partly like a lost soul and partly like a scalded cat.

Jill came running out of the library, and Mrs Spottsworth calmed her fears.

'It's nothing, dear,' she said. 'She's just excited. But I wish you would put her in my room, if you are going upstairs. Would it be troubling you too much?'

'Not at all,' said Jill aloofly.

She went out, carrying Pomona, and Bill advanced on Mrs Spottsworth.

'Shall we dance?' he said.

Mrs Spottsworth was surprised. On the rustic seat just now, especially in the moments following the disappearance of her pendant, she had found her host's mood markedly on the Byronic side. She could not readily adjust herself to this new spirit of gaiety.

'You want to *dance*?'

'Yes, with *you*,' said Bill, infusing into his manner a wealth of Restoration gallantry. 'It'll be like the old days at Cannes.'

Mrs Spottsworth was a shrewd woman. She had not failed to observe Captain Biggar lurking in the background, and it seemed to her that an admirable opportunity had presented itself of rousing the fiend that slept in him . . . far too soundly, in her opinion. What it was that was slowing up the White Hunter in his capacity of wooer, she did not know: but what she did know was that there is nothing that so lights a fire under a laggard lover as the spectacle of the woman he loves treading the measure in the arms of another man, particularly another man as good-looking as William, Earl of Rowcester.

'Yes, won't it!' she said, all sparkle and enthusiasm. 'How well I remember those days! Lord Rowcester dances so wonderfully,' she added, addressing Captain Biggar and imparting to him a piece of first-hand information which, of course, he would have been sorry to have missed. 'I love dancing. The one unpunished rapture left on earth.'

'What ho!' said Bill, concurring. 'The old Charleston . . . do you remember it?'

'You bet I do.'

'Put a Charleston record on the gramophone, Jeeves.'

'Very good, m'lord.'

When Jill returned from depositing Pomona in Mrs Spottsworth's sleeping quarters, only Jeeves, Bill and Mrs Spottsworth were present in the living room, for at the very outset of the proceedings Captain Biggar, unable to bear the sight before him, had plunged through the french window into the silent night.

The fact that it was he himself who had suggested this distressing exhibition, recalling, as it did in his opinion the worst excesses of the Carmagnole of the French Revolution combined with some of the more risqué features of native dances he had seen in Equatorial Africa, did nothing to assuage the darkness of his mood. The frogs on the lawn, which he was now pacing with a black scowl on his face, were beginning to get the illusion that it was raining number eleven boots.

His opinion of the Charleston, as rendered by his host and the woman he loved, was one which Jill found herself sharing. As she stood watching from the doorway, she was conscious of much the same rising feeling of nausea which had afflicted the White Hunter when listening to the exchanges on the rustic seat. Possibly there was nothing in the way in which Bill was comporting himself that rendered him actually liable to arrest, but she felt very strongly that some form of action should have been taken by the police. It was her view that there ought to have been a law.

Nothing is more difficult than to describe in words a Charleston danced by, on the one hand, a woman who loves dancing Charlestons and throws herself right into the spirit of them, and, on the other hand, by a man desirous of leaving no stone unturned in order to dislodge from some part of his associate's anatomy a diamond pendant which has lodged there. It will be enough, perhaps, to say that if Major Frobisher had happened to walk into the room at this moment, he would instantly have been reminded of old days in Smyrna or Joppa or Stamboul or possibly Baghdad. Mrs Spottsworth he would have compared favourably with the wife of the Greek consul, while Bill he would have patted on the back, recognizing his work as fully equal, if not superior, to his own.

Rory and Monica, coming out of the library, were frankly amazed.

'Good heavens!' said Monica.

'The old boy cuts quite a rug, does he not?' said Rory. 'Come, girl, let us join the revels.'

He put his arm about Monica's waist, and the action became general. Jill, unable to bear the degrading spectacle any longer, turned and went out. As she made her way to her room, she was thinking unpleasant thoughts of her betrothed. It is never agreeable for an idealistic girl to discover that she has linked her lot with a libertine, and it was plain to her now that William, Earl of Rowcester, was a debauchee whose correspondence course might have been taken with advantage by Casanova, Don Juan and the rowdier Roman Emperors.

'When I dance,' said Mrs Spottsworth, cutting, like her partner, quite a rug, 'I don't know I've got feet.'

Monica winced.

'If you danced with Rory, you'd know you've got feet. It's the way he jumps on and off that gets you down.'

'Ouch!' said Mrs Spottsworth suddenly. Bill had just lifted her and brought her down with a bump which would have excited Tubby Frobisher's generous admiration, and she was now standing rubbing her leg. 'I've twisted something,' she said, hobbling to a chair.

'I'm not surprised,' said Monica, 'the way Bill was dancing.'

'Oh, gee, I hope it is just a twist and not my sciatica come back. I suffer so terribly from sciatica, especially if I'm in a place that's at all damp.'

Incredible as it may seem, Rory did not say 'Like Rowcester Abbey, what?' and go on to speak of the garden which, in the winter months, was at the bottom of the river. He was peering down at an object lying on the floor.

'Hullo,' he said. 'What's this? Isn't this pendant yours, Mrs Spottsworth?'

'Oh, thank you,' said Mrs Spottsworth. 'Yes, it's mine. It must have . . . Ouch!' she said, breaking off, and writhed in agony once more.

Monica was all concern.

'You must get straight to bed, Rosalinda.'

'I guess I should.'

'With a nice hot-water bottle.'

'Yes.'

'Rory will help you upstairs.'

'Charmed,' said Rory. 'But why do people always speak of a "nice" hot-water bottle? We at Harrige's say "nasty" hot-water bottle. Our electric pads have rendered the hot-water bottle obsolete. Three speeds . . . Autumn Glow, Spring Warmth and Mae West.'

They moved to the door, Mrs Spottsworth leaning heavily on his arm. They passed out, and Bill, who had followed them with a bulging eye, threw up his hands in a wide gesture of despair.

'Jeeves!'

'M'lord?'

'This is the end!'

'Yes, m'lord.'

'She's gone to ground.'

'Yes, m'lord.'

'Accompanied by the pendant.'

'Yes, m'lord.'

'So unless you have any suggestions for getting her out of that room, we're sunk. Have you any suggestions?'

'Not at the moment, m'lord.'

'I didn't think you would have. After all, you're human, and the problem is one which is not within . . . what, Jeeves?'

'The scope of human power, m'lord.'

'Exactly. Do you know what I am going to do?'

'No, m'lord?'

'Go to bed, Jeeves. Go to bed and try to sleep and forget. Not that I have the remotest chance of getting to sleep, with every nerve in my body sticking out a couple of inches and curling at the ends.'

'Possibly if your lordship were to count sheep –'

'You think that would work?'

'It is a widely recognized specific, m'lord.'

'H'm.' Bill considered. 'Well, no harm in trying it. Goodnight, Jeeves.'

'Goodnight, m'lord.'

Except for the squeaking of mice behind the wainscoting and an occasional rustling sound as one of the bats in the chimney stirred uneasily in its sleep, Rowcester Abbey lay hushed and still. 'Twas now the very witching time of night, and in the Blue Room Rory and Monica, pleasantly fatigued after the activities of the day, slumbered peacefully. In the Queen Elizabeth Room Mrs Spottsworth, Pomona in her basket at her side, had also dropped off. In the Anne Boleyn Room Captain Biggar, the good man taking his rest, was dreaming of old days on the Me Wang river, which, we need scarcely inform our public, is a tributary of the larger and more crocodile-infested Wang Me.

Jill, in the Clock Room, was still awake, staring at the ceiling with hot eyes, and Bill, counting sheep in the Henry VIII Room, had also failed to find oblivion. The specific recommended by Jeeves might be widely recognized but so far it had done nothing toward enabling him to knit up the ravelled sleeve of care.

'Eight hundred and twenty-two,' murmured Bill. 'Eight hundred and twenty-three. Eight hundred and –'

He broke off, leaving the eight hundred and twenty-fourth sheep, an animal with a more than usually vacuous expression on its face, suspended in the air into which it had been conjured up. Someone had knocked on the door, a knock so soft and deferential that it could have proceeded from the knuckle of only one man. It was consequently without surprise that a moment later he perceived Jeeves entering.

'Your lordship will excuse me,' said Jeeves courteously. 'I would not have disturbed your lordship, had I not, listening at the door, gathered from your lordship's remarks that the stratagem which I proposed had proved unsuccessful.'

'No, it hasn't worked yet,' said Bill, 'but come in, Jeeves, come in.' He would have been glad to see anything that was not a sheep. 'Don't tell me,' he said, starting as he noted the gleam of intelligence in his visitor's eye, 'that you've thought of something?'

'Yes, m'lord, I am happy to say that I fancy I have found a solution to the problem which confronted us.'

'Jeeves, you're a marvel!'

'Thank you very much, m'lord.'

'I remember Bertie Wooster saying to me once that there was no crisis which you were unable to handle.'

'Mr Wooster has always been far too flattering, m'lord.'

'Nonsense. Not nearly flattering enough. If you have really put your finger on a way of overcoming the superhuman difficulties in our path –'

'I feel convinced that I have, m'lord.'

Bill quivered inside his mauve pyjama jacket.

'Think well, Jeeves,' he urged. 'Somehow or other we have got to get Mrs Spottsworth out of her room for a lapse of time sufficient to enable me to bound in, find that pendant, scoop it up and bound out again, all this without a human eye resting upon me. Unless I have completely misinterpreted your words owing to having suffered a nervous breakdown from counting sheep, you seem to be suggesting that you can do this. How? That is the question that springs to the lips. With mirrors?'

Jeeves did not speak for a moment. A pained look had come into his finely-chiselled face. It was as though he had suddenly seen some sight which was occasioning him distress.

'Excuse me, m'lord. I am reluctant to take what is possibly a liberty on my part –'

'Carry on, Jeeves. You have our ear. What is biting you?'

'It is your pyjamas, m'lord. Had I been aware that your lordship was in the habit of sleeping in mauve pyjamas, I would have advised against it. Mauve does not become your lordship. I was once compelled, in his best interests, to speak in a similar vein to Mr Wooster, who at that time was also a mauve-pyjama addict.'

Bill found himself at a loss.

'How have we got on to the subject of pyjamas?' he asked wonderingly.

'They thrust themselves on the notice, m'lord. That very aggressive purple. If your lordship would be guided by me and substitute a quiet blue or possibly a light pistachio green –'

'Jeeves!'

'M'lord?'

'This is no time to be prattling of pyjamas.'

'Very good, m'lord.'

'As a matter of fact, I rather fancy myself in mauve. But that, as

I say, is neither here nor there. Let us postpone the discussion to a more suitable moment. I will, however, tell you this. If you really have something to suggest with reference to that pendant and that something brings home the bacon, you may take these mauve pyjamas and raze them to the ground and sow salt on the foundations.'

'Thank you very much, m'lord.'

'It will be a small price to pay for your services. Well, now that you've got me all worked up, tell me more. What's the good news? What is this scheme of yours?'

'A quite simple one, m'lord. It is based on –'

Bill uttered a cry.

'Don't tell me. Let me guess. The psychology of the individual?'

'Precisely, m'lord.'

Bill drew in his breath sharply.

'I thought as much. Something told me that was it. Many a time and oft, exchanging dry Martinis with Bertie Wooster in the bar of the Drones Club, I have listened to him, rapt, as he spoke of you and the psychology of the individual. He said that, once you get your teeth into the psychology of the individual, it's all over except chucking one's hat in the air and doing spring dances. Proceed, Jeeves. You interest me strangely. The individual whose psychology you have been brooding on at the present juncture is, I take it, Mrs Spottsworth? Am I right or wrong, Jeeves?'

'Perfectly correct, m'lord. Has it occurred to your lordship what is Mrs Spottsworth's principal interest, the thing uppermost in the lady's mind?'

Bill gaped.

'You haven't come here at two in the morning to suggest that I dance the Charleston with her again?'

'Oh, no, m'lord.'

'Well, when you spoke of her principal interest –'

'There is another facet of Mrs Spottsworth's character which you have overlooked, m'lord. I concede that she is an enthusiastic Charleston performer, but what principally occupies her thoughts is psychical research. Since her arrival at the abbey, she has not ceased to express a hope that she may be granted the experience of seeing the spectre of Lady Agatha. It was that that I had in mind when I informed your lordship that I had formulated a scheme for obtaining the pendant, based on the psychology of the individual.'

Bill sank back on the pillows, a disappointed man.

'No, Jeeves,' he said. 'I won't do it.'

'M'lord?'

'I see where you're heading. You want me to dress up in a farthingale and wimple and sneak into Mrs Spottsworth's room, your contention being that if she wakes and sees me, she will simply say "Ah, the ghost of Lady Agatha", and go to sleep again. It can't be done, Jeeves. Nothing will induce me to dress up in women's clothes, not even in such a deserving cause as this one. I might stretch a point and put on the old moustache and black patch.'

'I would not advocate it, m'lord. Even on the race-course I have observed clients, on seeing your lordship, start back with visible concern. A lady, discovering such an apparition in her room, might quite conceivably utter a piercing scream.'

Bill threw his hands up with a despondent groan.

'Well, there you are, then. The thing's off. Your scheme falls to the ground and becomes null and void.'

'No, m'lord. Your lordship has not, if I may say so, grasped the substance of the plan I am putting forward. The essential at which one aims is the inducing of Mrs Spottsworth to leave her room, thus rendering it possible for your lordship to enter and secure the pendant. I propose now, with your lordship's approval, to knock on Mrs Spottsworth's door and request the loan of a bottle of smelling salts.'

Bill clutched at his hair.

'You said, Jeeves?'

'Smelling salts, m'lord.'

Bill shook his head.

'Counting those sheep has done something to me,' he said. 'My hearing has become affected. It sounded to me just as if you had said "Smelling salts".'

'I did, m'lord. I would explain that I required them in order to restore your lordship to consciousness.'

'There again. I could have sworn that I heard you say "restore your lordship to consciousness".'

'Precisely, m'lord. Your lordship has sustained a severe shock. Happening to be in the vicinity of the ruined chapel at about the hour of midnight, your lordship observed the wraith of Lady Agatha and was much overcome. How your lordship contrived to totter back to your room, your lordship will never know, but I found your lordship there in what appeared to be a coma and immediately applied to Mrs Spottsworth for the loan of her smelling salts.'

Bill was still at a loss.

'I don't get the gist, Jeeves.'

'If I might elucidate my meaning still further, m'lord. The thought

I had in mind was that, learning that Lady Agatha was, if I may so term it, on the wing, Mrs Spottsworth's immediate reaction would be an intense desire to hasten to the ruined chapel in order to observe the manifestation for herself. I would offer to escort her thither, and during her absence ...'

It is never immediately that the ordinary man, stunned by some revelation of genius, is able to find words with which to express his emotion. When Alexander Graham Bell, meeting a friend one morning in the year 1876, said 'Oh, hullo, George, heard the latest? I invented the telephone yesterday', it is probable that the friend merely shuffled his feet in silence. It was the same with Bill now. He could not speak. He lay there dumbly, while remorse flooded over him that he could ever have doubted this man. It was just as Bertie Wooster had so often said. Let this fish-fed mastermind get his teeth into the psychology of the individual, and it was all over except chucking your hat in the air and doing spring dances.

'Jeeves,' he began, at length finding speech, but Jeeves was shimmering through the door.

'Your smelling salts, m'lord,' he said, turning his head on the threshold. 'If your lordship will excuse me.'

It was perhaps two minutes, though to Bill it seemed longer, before he returned, bearing a small bottle.

'Well?' said Bill eagerly.

'Everything has gone according to plan, m'lord. The lady's reactions were substantially as I had anticipated. Mrs Spottsworth, on receiving my communication, displayed immediate interest. Is your lordship familiar with the expression "Jiminy Christmas!"?'

'No, I don't think I ever heard it. You don't mean "Merry Christmas"?'

'No, m'lord. "Jiminy Christmas!" It was what Mrs Spottsworth observed on receiving the information that the phantasm of Lady Agatha was to be seen in the ruined chapel. The words, I gathered, were intended to convey surprise and elation. She assured me that it would take her but a brief time to hop into a dressing gown and that at the conclusion of that period she would be with me with, I understood her to say, her hair in a braid. I am to return in a moment and accompany her to the scene of the manifestation. I will leave the door open a few inches, so that your lordship, by applying your lordship's eye to the crack, may be able to see us depart. As soon as we have descended the staircase, I would advocate instant action, for I need scarcely remind your lordship that time is —'

'Of the essence? No, you certainly don't have to tell me that. You remember what you were saying about cheetahs?'

'With reference to their speed of foot, m'lord?'

'That's right. Half a mile in forty-five seconds, I think you said?'

'Yes, m'lord.'

'Well, the way I shall move would leave the nippiest cheetah standing at the post.'

'That will be highly satisfactory, m'lord. I, on my side, may mention that on the dressing table in Mrs Spottsworth's room I observed a small jewel case, which I have no doubt contains the pendant. The dressing table is immediately beneath the window. Your lordship will have no difficulty in locating it.'

He was right, as always. It was the first thing that Bill saw when, having watched the little procession of two out of sight down the stairs, he hastened along the corridor to the Queen Elizabeth Room. There, as Jeeves had stated, was the dressing table. On it was the small jewel case of which he had spoken. And in that jewel case, as he opened it with shaking hands, Bill saw the pendant. Hastily he slipped it into the pocket of his pyjamas, and was turning to leave, when the silence, which had been complete but for his heavy breathing, was shattered by a series of dreadful screams.

Reference has been made earlier to the practice of the dog Pomona of shrieking loudly to express the ecstasy she always felt on beholding a friend or even what looked to her like a congenial stranger. It was ecstasy that was animating her now. In the course of that session on the rustic seat, when Bill had done his cooing, she had taken an immediate fancy to her host, as all dogs did. Meeting him now in this informal fashion, just at a moment when she had been trying to reconcile herself to the solitude which she so disliked, she made no attempt to place any bounds on her self-expression.

Screams sufficient in number and volume to have equipped a dozen baronets stabbed in the back in libraries burst from her lips and their effect on Bill was devastating. The author of *The Hunting of the Snark* says of one of his protagonists in a powerful passage:

> So great was his fright
> That his waistcoat turned white

and the experience through which he was passing nearly caused Bill's mauve pyjamas to do the same.

Though fond of Pomona, he did not linger to fraternize. He shot out of the door at a speed which would have had the most athletic cheetah shrugging its shoulders helplessly, and arrived in the corridor just as Jill, roused from sleep by those awful cries, came out of the Clock Room. She watched him steal softly into the Henry VIII Room, and thought in bitter mood that a more suitable spot for him could scarcely have been found.

It was some quarter of an hour later, as Bill, lying in bed, was murmuring 'Nine hundred and ninety-eight . . . Nine hundred and ninety-nine . . . One thousand . . .' that Jeeves entered.

He was carrying a salver.

On that salver was a ring.

'I encountered Miss Wyvern in the corridor a few moments ago, m'lord,' he said. 'She desired me to give this to your lordship.'

16

Wyvern Hall, the residence of Colonel Aubrey Wyvern, father of Jill and Chief Constable of the county of Southmoltonshire, lay across the river from Rowcester Abbey, and on the following afternoon Colonel Wyvern, having worked his way scowlingly through a most inferior lunch, stumped out of the dining room and went to his study and rang for his butler. And in due course the butler entered, tripping over the rug with a muffled 'Whoops!', his invariable practice when crossing any threshold.

Colonel Wyvern was short and stout, and this annoyed him, for he would have preferred to be tall and slender. But if his personal appearance gave him pangs of discomfort from time to time, they were as nothing compared to the pangs the personal appearance of his butler gave him. In England today the householder in the country has to take what he can get in the way of domestic help, and all Colonel Wyvern had been able to get was the scrapings and scourings of the local parish school. Bulstrode, the major-domo of Wyvern Hall, was a skinny stripling of some sixteen summers, on whom Nature in her bounty had bestowed so many pimples that there was scarcely room on his face for the vacant grin which habitually adorned it.

He was grinning now, and once again, as always happened at these staff conferences, his overlord was struck by the closeness of the lad's resemblance to a half-witted goldfish peering out of a bowl.

'Bulstrode,' he said, with a parade-ground rasp in his voice.

'Yus?' replied the butler affably.

At another moment, Colonel Wyvern would have had something to say on the subject of this unconventional verbal approach but today he was after bigger game. His stomach was still sending up complaints to the front office about the lunch, and he wanted to see the cook.

'Bulstrode,' he said, 'bring the cook to me.'

The cook, conducted into the presence, proved also to be one of the younger set. Her age was fifteen. She bustled in, her pigtails swinging behind her, and Colonel Wyvern gave her an unpleasant look.

'Trelawny!' he said.

'Yus?' said the cook.

This time there was no reticence on the part of the chief constable. The Wyverns did not as a rule war upon women, but there are times when chivalry is impossible.

'Don't say "Yus?", you piefaced little excrescence,' he thundered. 'Say "Yes, sir?", and say it in a respectful and soldierly manner, coming smartly to attention with the thumbs on the seam of the trousers. Trelawny, that lunch you had the temerity to serve up today was an insult to me and a disgrace to anyone daring to call herself a cook, and I have sent for you to inform you that if there is any more of this spirit of slackness and *laissez faire* on your part . . .' Colonel Wyvern paused. The 'I'll tell your mother', with which he had been about to conclude his sentence, seemed to him to lack a certain something. 'You'll hear of it,' he said and, feeling that even this was not as good as he could have wished, infused such vigour and venom into his description of underdone chicken, watery brussels sprouts and potatoes you couldn't get a fork into that a weaker girl might well have wilted.

But the Trelawnys were made of tough stuff. They did not quail in the hour of peril. The child met his eye with iron resolution, and came back strongly.

'Hitler!' she said, putting out her tongue.

The chief constable started.

'Did you call me Hitler?'

'Yus, I did.'

'Well, don't do it again,' said Colonel Wyvern sternly. 'You may go, Trelawny.'

Trelawny went, with her nose in the air, and Colonel Wyvern addressed himself to Bulstrode.

A proud man is never left unruffled when worsted in a verbal duel with a cook, especially a cook aged fifteen with pigtails, and in the chief constable's manner as he turned on his butler there was more than a suggestion of a rogue elephant at the height of its fever. For some minutes he spoke well and forcefully, with particular reference to the other's habit of chewing his sweet ration while waiting at table, and when at length he was permitted to follow Evangeline Trelawny to the lower regions in which they had their being, Bulstrode, if not actually shaking in every limb, was at any rate subdued enough to omit to utter his customary 'Whoops!' when tripping over the rug.

He left the chief constable, though feeling a little better after having cleansed his bosom of the perilous stuff that weighs upon the soul, still definitely despondent. 'Ichabod,' he was saying to himself, and he meant it. In the golden age before the social revolution, he was thinking, a gaping, pimpled tripper over rugs like this Bulstrode would have been a lowly hall-boy, if that. It revolted a Tory of the old school's finer feelings to have to regard such a blot on the Southmoltonshire scene in the sacred light of a butler.

He thought nostalgically of his young manhood in London at the turn of the century and of the vintage butlers he had been wont to encounter in those brave days . . . butlers who weighed two hundred and fifty pounds on the hoof, butlers with three chins and bulging abdomens, butlers with large, gooseberry eyes and that austere, supercilious, butlerine manner which has passed away so completely from the degenerate world of the nineteen-fifties. Butlers had been butlers then in the deepest and holiest sense of the word. Now they were mere chinless boys who sucked toffee and said 'Yus?' when you spoke to them.

It was almost inevitable that a man living so near to Rowcester Abbey and starting to brood on butlers should find his thoughts turning in the direction of the abbey's principal ornament, and it was with a warm glow that Colonel Wyvern now began to think of Jeeves. Jeeves had made a profound impression on him. Jeeves, in his opinion, was the goods. Young Rowcester himself was a fellow the colonel, never very fond of his juniors, could take or leave alone, but this man of his, this Jeeves, he had recognized from their first meeting as something special. Out of the night that covered the chief constable, black as the pit – after that disturbing scene with Evangeline Trelawny – from pole to pole, there shone a sudden gleam of light. He himself might have his Bulstrode, but at least he could console himself with the thought that his daughter was marrying a man with a butler in the fine old tradition on his payroll. It put heart into him. It made him feel that this was not such a bad little old world, after all.

He mentioned this to Jill when she came in a moment later, looking cold and proud, and Jill tilted her chin and looked colder and prouder. She might have been a Snow Queen or something of that sort.

'I am not going to marry Lord Rowcester,' she said curtly.

It seemed to Colonel Wyvern that his child must be suffering from some form of amnesia, and he set himself to jog her memory.

'Yes, you are,' he reminded her. 'It was in *The Times*. I saw it with my own eyes. The engagement is announced between –'

'I have broken off the engagement.'

That little gleam of light of which we were speaking a moment ago, the one we showed illuminating Colonel Wyvern's darkness, went out with a pop, like a stage moon that has blown a fuse. He stared incredulously.

'Broken off the engagement?'

'I am never going to speak to Lord Rowcester again.'

'Don't be an ass,' said Colonel Wyvern. 'Of course you are. Not going to speak to him again? I never heard such nonsense. I suppose what's happened is that you've had one of these lovers' tiffs.'

Jill did not intend to allow without protest what was probably the world's greatest tragedy since the days of Romeo and Juliet to be described in this inadequate fashion. One really must take a little trouble to find the *mot juste*.

'It was not a lovers' tiff,' she said, all the woman in her flashing from her eyes. 'If you want to know why I broke off the engagement, it was because of the abominable way he has been behaving with Mrs Spottsworth.'

Colonel Wyvern put a finger to his brow.

'Spottsworth? Spottsworth? Ah, yes. That's the American woman you were telling me about.'

'The American trollop,' corrected Jill coldly.

'Trollop?' said Colonel Wyvern, intrigued.

'That was what I said.'

'Why do you call her that? Did you catch them – er – trolloping?'

'Yes, I did.'

'Good gracious!'

Jill swallowed once or twice, as if something jagged in her throat was troubling her.

'It all seems to have started,' she said, speaking in that toneless voice which had made such a painful impression on Bill, 'in Cannes some years ago. Apparently she and Lord Rowcester used to swim together at Eden Roc and go for long drives in the moonlight. And you know what that sort of thing leads to.'

'I do indeed,' said Colonel Wyvern with animation, and was about to embark on an anecdote of his interesting past, when Jill went on, still speaking in that same strange, toneless voice.

'She arrived at the abbey yesterday. The story that has been put out is that Monica Carmoyle met her in New York and invited her to stay, but I have no doubt that the whole thing was arranged between her and Lord Rowcester, because it was obvious how matters stood between them. No sooner had she appeared than he was all over her . . . making love to her in the garden, dancing with her like a cat on hot bricks, and,' said Jill nonchalantly, wearing the mask like the Mrs Fish who had so diverted Captain Biggar by doing the can-can in her step-ins in Kenya, 'coming out of her room at two o'clock in the morning in mauve pyjamas.'

Colonel Wyvern choked. He had been about to try to heal the rift by saying that it was quite possible for a man to exchange a few civil remarks with a woman in a garden and while away the long evening by partnering her in the dance and still not be in any way culpable, but this statement wiped the words from his lips.

'Coming out of her room in mauve pyjamas?'

'Yes.'

'*Mauve* pyjamas?'

'Bright mauve.'

'God bless my soul!'

A club acquaintance, annoyed by the eccentricity of the other's bridge game, had once told Colonel Wyvern that he looked like a retired member of Sanger's troupe of midgets who for years had been doing himself too well on the starchy foods, and this was in a measure true. He was, as we have said, short and stout. But when the call to action came, he could triumph over his brevity of stature and rotundity of waistcoat and become a figure of dignity and menace. It was an impressive chief constable who strode across the room and rang the bell for Bulstrode.

'Yus?' said Bulstrode.

Colonel Wyvern choked down the burning words he would have liked to utter. He told himself that he must conserve his energies.

'Bulstrode,' he said, 'bring me my horsewhip.'

Down in the forest of pimples on the butler's face something stirred. It was a look of guilt.

'It's gorn,' he mumbled.

Colonel Wyvern stared.

'Gone? What do you mean, gone? Gone where?'

Bulstrode choked. He had been hoping that this investigation might have been avoided. Something had told him that it would prove embarrassing.

'To the mender's. To be mended. It got cracked.'

'Cracked?'

'Yus,' said Bulstrode, in his emotion adding the unusual word 'Sir'. 'I was cracking it in the stableyard, and it cracked. So I took it to the mender's.'

Colonel Wyvern pointed an awful finger at the door.

'Get out, you foul blot,' he said. 'I'll talk to you later.' Seating himself at his desk, as he always did when he wished to think, he drummed his fingers on the arm of his chair. 'I'll have to borrow young Rowcester's,' he said at length, clicking his tongue in evident annoyance. 'Infernally awkward, calling on a fellow you're going to horsewhip and having to ask him for the loan of his horsewhip to do it with. Still, there it is,' said Colonel Wyvern philosophically. 'That's how it goes.'

He was a man who could always adjust himself to circumstances.

17

Lunch at Rowcester Abbey had been a much more agreeable function than lunch at Wyvern Hall, on a different plane altogether. Where Colonel Wyvern had been compelled to cope with the distressing efforts of a pigtailed incompetent apparently under the impression that she was catering for a covey of buzzards in the Gobi Desert, the revellers at the abbey had been ministered to by an expert. Earlier in this chronicle passing reference was made to the virtuosity of Bill's OC Kitchen, the richly gifted Mrs Piggott, and in dishing up the midday meal today she had in no way fallen short of her high ideals. Three of the four celebrants at the table had found the food melting in their mouths and had downed it with cries of appreciation.

The exception was the host himself, in whose mouth it had turned to ashes. What with one thing and another – the instability of his financial affairs, last night's burglarious interlude and its devastating sequel, the shattering of his romance – Bill was far from being the gayest of all that gay company. In happier days he had sometimes read novels in which characters were described as pushing their food away untasted, and had often wondered, being a man who enjoyed getting his calories, how they could have brought themselves to do it. But at the meal which was now coming to an end he had been doing it himself, and, as we say, what little nourishment he had contrived to take had turned to ashes in his mouth. He had filled in the time mostly by crumbling bread, staring wildly and jumping like a galvanized frog when spoken to. A cat in a strange alley would have been more at its ease.

Nor had the conversation at the table done anything to restore his equanimity. Mrs Spottsworth would keep bringing it round to the subject of Captain Biggar, regretting his absence from the feast, and each mention of the White Hunter's name had had a seismic effect on his sensitive conscience. She did it again now.

'Captain Biggar was telling me –' she began, and Rory uttered one of his jolly laughs.

'He was, was he?' he said in his tactful way. 'Well, I hope you didn't believe him.'

Mrs Spottsworth stiffened. She sensed a slur on the man she loved.

'I beg your pardon?'

'Awful liar, that chap.'

'Why do you say that, Sir Roderick?'

'I was thinking of those yarns of his at dinner last night.'

'They were perfectly true.'

'Not a bit of it,' said Rory buoyantly. 'Don't you let him pull your leg, my dear Mrs Dogsbody. All these fellows from out East are the most frightful liars. It's due, I believe, to the ultra-violet rays of the sun in those parts. They go out without their solar topees, and it does something to them. I have this from an authoritative source. One of them used to come to headquarters a lot when I was in the Guns, Pistols and Ammunition, and we became matey. And one night, when in his cups, he warned me not to swallow a single word any of them said. "Look at me," he reasoned. "Did you ever hear a chap tell the ghastly lies I do? Why, I haven't spoken the truth since I was so high. And so low are standards East of Suez that my nickname out there is George Washington."'

'Coffee is served in the living room, m'lord,' said Jeeves, intervening in his polished way and averting what promised, judging from the manner in which Mrs Spottsworth's eyes had begun to glitter, to develop into an ugly brawl.

Following his guests into the living room, Bill was conscious of a growing sense of uneasiness and alarm. He had not supposed that anything could have increased his mental discomfort, but Rory's words had done so a hundredfold. As he lowered himself into a chair, accepted a cup of coffee and spilled it over his trousers, one more vulture had added itself to the little group already gnawing at his bosom. For the first time he had begun to question the veracity of Captain Biggar's story of the pendant, and at the thought of what he had let himself in for if that story had not been true his imagination boggled.

Dimly he was aware that Rory and Monica had collected all the morning papers and were sitting surrounded by them, their faces grave and tense. The sands were running out. Less than an hour from now the Derby would be run, and soon, if ever, they must decide how their wagers were to be placed.

'*Racing News*,' said Monica, calling the meeting to order. 'What does the *Racing News* say, Rory?'

Rory studied that sheet in his slow, thorough way.

'Lot of stuff about the Guineas form. Perfect rot, all of it. You can't go by the Guineas. Too many unknowns. If you want my considered opinion, there's nothing in sight to beat Taj Mahal. The Aga has the mares, and that's what counts. The sires don't begin to matter compared with the mares.'

'I'm glad to hear you pay this belated tribute to my sex.'

'Yes, I think for my two quid it's Taj Mahal on the nose.'

'That settles Taj Mahal for me. Whenever you bet on them, they start running backwards. Remember that dog-race.'

Rory was obliged to yield this point.

'I admit my nominee let the side down on that occasion,' he said. 'But when a real rabbit gets loose on a dog track, it's bound to cause a bit of confusion. Taj Mahal gets my two o'goblins.'

'I thought your money was going on Oratory.'

'Oratory is my outsider bet, ten bob each way.'

'Well, here's another hunch for you. Escalator.'

'Escalator?'

'Wasn't H's the first store to have escalators?'

'By jove, yes. We've got the cup, you know. Our safety-landing device has enabled us to clip three seconds off the record. The Oxford Street boys are livid. I must look into this Escalator matter.'

'Lester Piggott is riding it.'

'That settles it. L. Piggott is the name of the chap stationed in the Trunks, Bags and Suitcases, as fine a man as ever punched a time-clock. I admit his L stands for Lancelot, but that's a good enough omen for me.'

Monica looked across at Mrs Spottsworth.

'I suppose you think we're crazy, Rosalinda?'

Mrs Spottsworth smiled indulgently.

'Of course not, dear. This brings back the old days with Mr Bessemer. Racing was all he ever thought of. We spent our honeymoon at Sheepshead Bay. It's the Derby, is it, you're so interested in?'

'Just our silly little annual flutter. We don't bet high. Can't afford to. We have to watch the pennies.'

'Rigidly,' said Rory. He chuckled amusedly, struck by a whimsical idea. 'I was just thinking,' he went on in explanation of his mirth, 'that the smart thing for me to have done would have been to stick to that pendant of yours I picked up last night and go off to London with it and pawn it, thus raising a bit of . . . Yes, old man?'

Bill swallowed.

'I didn't speak.'

'I thought you did.'

'No, just a hiccup.'

'To which,' Rory conceded, 'you were fully entitled. If a man can't hiccup in his own house, in whose house can he hiccup? Well, summing up, Taj Mahal two quid. Escalator ten bob each way. I'll go and send off my wire.' He paused. 'But wait. Is it not rash to commit oneself without consulting Jeeves?'

'Why Jeeves?'

'My dear Moke, what that man doesn't know about form isn't worth knowing. You should have heard him yesterday when I asked him if he had any views on the respective contestants in England's premier classic race. He just stood there rattling off horses and times and records as if he were the Archbishop of Canterbury.'

Monica was impressed.

'I didn't know he was as hot as that. Are there no limits to the powers of this wonder man? We'll go and confer with him at once.'

They hurried out, and Bill, having cleared his throat, said 'Er'.

Mrs Spottsworth looked up inquiringly.

'Er, Rosie. That pendant of yours. The one Rory was speaking of.'

'Yes?'

'I was admiring it last night.'

'It's nice, isn't it?'

'Beautiful. You didn't have it at Cannes, did you?'

'No. I hadn't met Mr Spottsworth then. It was a present from him.'

Bill leaped. His worst suspicions had been confirmed.

'A present from Mr Sp–?' he gasped.

Mrs Spottsworth laughed.

'It's too funny,' she said. 'I was talking to Captain Biggar about it last night, and I told him one of my husbands gave it to me, but I couldn't remember which. It was Mr Spottsworth, of course. So silly of me to have forgotten.'

Bill gulped.

'Are you sure?'

'Oh, quite.'

'It . . . it wasn't given to you by some fellow on one of those hunting expeditions . . . as a . . . as a sort of memento?'

Mrs Spottsworth stared.

'What *do* you mean?'

'Well, I thought . . . fellow grateful for kindnesses . . . saying goodbye ... might have said "Won't you accept this as a little memento ... and all that sort of thing".'

The suggestion plainly offended Mrs Spottsworth.

'Do you imagine that I accept diamond pendants from "fellows", as you call them?'

'Well, I –'

'I wouldn't dream of such a thing. Mr Spottsworth bought that pendant when we were in Bombay. I can remember it as if it were yesterday. A funny little shop with a very fat Chinaman behind the counter, and Mr Spottsworth would insist on trying to speak Chinese. And just as he was bargaining, there was an earthquake. Not a bad one, but everything was all red dust for about ten minutes, and when it cleared, Mr Spottsworth said "Let's get out of here!" and paid what the man was asking and grabbed the pendant and we raced out and never stopped running till we had got back to the hotel.'

A dull despair had Bill in its grip. He heaved himself painfully to his feet.

'I wonder if you would excuse me,' he said 'I have to see Jeeves about something.'

'Well, ring for Jeeves.'

Bill shook his head.

'No, I think, if you don't mind, I'll go and see him in his pantry.'

It had occurred to him that in Jeeves' pantry there would be a drop of port, and a drop of port or some similar restorative was what his stricken soul craved.

18

When Rory and Monica entered Jeeves' pantry, they found its proprietor reading a letter. His fine face, always grave, seemed a little
graver than usual, as if the letter's contents had disturbed him.

'Sorry to interrupt you, Jeeves,' said Monica.

'Not at all, m'lady.'

'Finish your reading.'

'I had already done so, m'lady. A communication from Mr Wooster.'

'Oh?' said Rory. 'Bertie Wooster, eh? How is the old bounder?
Robust?'

'Mr Wooster says nothing to indicate the contrary, sir.'

'Good. Rosy cheeks, eh? Eating his spinach, no doubt? Capital.
Couldn't be better. Still, be that as it may,' said Rory, 'what do you
think of Taj Mahal for this afternoon's beano at Epsom Downs? I
thought of slapping my two quid on its nose, with your approval.'

'And Moke the Second,' said Monica. 'That's my fancy.'

Jeeves considered.

'I see no objection to a small wager on the animal you have named
sir, nor on yours, m'lady. One must bear in mind, however, that the
Derby is always an extremely open race.'

'Don't I know it!'

'It would be advisable, therefore, if the funds are sufficient, to
endeavour to save your stake by means of a bet each way on some
other horse.'

'Rory thought of Escalator. I'm hesitating.'

Jeeves coughed.

'Has your ladyship considered the Irish horse, Ballymore?'

'Oh, Jeeves, for heaven's sake. None of the nibs even mention it.
No, not Ballymore, Jeeves. I'll have to think of something.'

'Very good, m'lady. Would there be anything further?'

'Yes,' said Rory. 'Now that we're all here together, cheek by jowl
as it were, a word from our sponsor on a personal matter, Jeeves.
What was all that that Mrs Dogsbody was saying at lunch about you
and her being out on the tiles last night?'

'Sir?'

'Weren't you in the room when she was talking about it?'

'No, m'lady.'

'She said you bowled off together in the small hours to the ruined chapel.'

'Ah, yes, m'lady. I apprehend Sir Roderick's meaning now. Mrs Spottsworth did desire me to escort her to the ruined chapel last night. She was hoping to see the wraith of Lady Agatha, she informed me.'

'Any luck?'

'No, m'lady.'

'She says Bill saw the old girl.'

'Yes, m'lady.'

Rory uttered the gratified exclamation of one who has solved a mystery.

'So that's why Bill's looking like a piece of cheese today. It must have scared him stiff.'

'I believe Lord Rowcester was somewhat moved by the experience, Sir Roderick. But I fancy that if, as you say, there is a resemblance between his lordship and a portion of cheese, it is occasioned more by the circumstance of his lordship's matrimonial plans having been cancelled than by any manifestation from the spirit world.'

Monica squeaked excitedly.

'You don't mean Bill's engagement is off?'

'That is what I was endeavouring to convey, m'lady. Miss Wyvern handed me the ring in person, to return to his lordship. "Am I to infer, miss," I ventured to inquire, "that there is a symbolical significance attached to this gesture?" and Miss Wyvern replied in the affirmative.'

'Well, I'll be blowed. Poor old Bill!'

'Yes, m'lady.'

'The heart bleeds.'

'Yes, Sir Roderick.'

It was at this moment that Bill came charging in. Seeing his sister and her husband, he stopped.

'Oh, hullo, Rory,' he said. 'Hullo, Moke. I'd forgotten you were here.'

Rory advanced with outstretched hand. The dullest eye could have seen that he was registering compassion. He clasped Bill's right hand in his own, and with his left hand kneaded Bill's shoulder. A man, he knew, wants sympathy at a time like this. It is in such a crisis in his affairs that he thanks heaven that he has an understanding brother-in-law, a brother-in-law who knows how to give a pep talk.

'We are not only here, old man,' he said, 'but we have just heard from Jeeves a bit of news that has frozen our blood. He says the girl Jill has returned you to store. Correct? I see it is. Too bad, too bad. But don't let it get you down, boy. You must . . . how would you put it, Jeeves?'

'Stiffen the sinews, summon up the blood, Sir Roderick.'

'Precisely. You want to take the big, broad, spacious view, Bill. You are a fiancée short, let's face it, and your immediate reaction is, no doubt, a disposition to rend the garments and scatter ashes on the head. But you've got to look at these things from every angle, Bill, old man. Remember what Shakespeare said: "A woman is only a woman, but a good cigar is a smoke."'

Jeeves winced.

'Kipling, Sir Roderick.'

'And here's another profound truth. I don't know who said this one. All cats are grey in the dark.'

Monica spoke. Her lips, as she listened, had been compressed. There was a strange light in her eyes.

'Splendid. Go on.'

Rory stopped kneading Bill's shoulder and patted it.

'At the moment,' he resumed, 'you are reeling from the shock, and very naturally, too. You feel you've lost something valuable, and of course I suppose one might say you have, for Jill's a nice enough kid, no disputing that. But don't be too depressed about it. Look for the silver lining, whenever clouds appear in the blue, as I have frequently sung in my bath and you, I imagine, in yours. Don't forget you're back in circulation again. Personally, I think it's an extremely nice slice of luck for you that this has happened. A bachelor's life is the only happy one, old man. When it comes to love, there's a lot to be said for the à la carte as opposed to the table d'hôte.'

'Jeeves,' said Monica.

'M'lady?'

'What was the name of the woman who drove a spike into her husband's head? It's in the Bible somewhere.'

'I fancy your ladyship is thinking of the story of Jael. But she and the gentleman into whose head she drove the spike were not married, merely good friends.'

'Still, her ideas were basically sound.'

'It was generally considered so in her circle of acquaintance, m'lady.'

'Have you a medium-sized spike, Jeeves? No? I must look in at the ironmonger's,' said Monica. 'Goodbye, Table d'hôte.'

She walked out, and Rory watched her go, concerned. His was not a very quick mind, but he seemed to sense something wrong.

'I say! She's miffed. Eh, Jeeves?'

'I received that impression, Sir Roderick.'

'Dash it all, I was only saying that stuff about marriage to cheer you up, Bill. Jeeves, where can I get some flowers? And don't say "At the flower shop", because I simply can't sweat all the way to the town. Would there be flowers in the garden?'

'In some profusion, Sir Roderick.'

'I'll go and pluck her a bouquet. That's a thing you'll find it useful to remember, Bill, if ever you get married, not that you're likely to, of course, the way things are shaping. Always remember that when the gentler sex get miffed, flowers will bring them round every time.'

The door closed. Jeeves turned to Bill.

'Your lordship wished to see me about something?' he said courteously.

Bill passed a hand over his throbbing brow.

'Jeeves,' he said, 'I hardly know how to begin. Have you an aspirin about you?'

'Certainly, m'lord. I have just been taking one myself.'

He produced a small tin box, and held it out.

'Thank you, Jeeves. Don't slam the lid.'

'No, m'lord.'

'And now,' said Bill, 'to tell you all.'

Jeeves listened with gratifyingly close attention while he poured out his tale. There was no need for Bill at its conclusion to ask him if he had got the gist. It was plain from the gravity of his 'Most disturbing, m'lord' that he had got it nicely. Jeeves always got gists.

'If ever a man was in the soup,' said Bill, summing up, 'I am. I have been played up and made a sucker of. What are those things people get used as, Jeeves?'

'Cat's-paws, m'lord?'

'That's right. Cat's-paws. This blighted Biggar has used me as a cat's-paw. He told me the tale. Like an ass, I believed him. I pinched the pendant, swallowing that whole story of his about it practically belonging to him and he only wanted to borrow it for a few hours, and off he went to London with it, and I don't suppose we shall ever see him again. Do you?'

'It would appear improbable, m'lord.'

'One of those remote contingencies, what?'

'Extremely remote, I fear, m'lord.'

'You wouldn't care to kick me, Jeeves?'

'No, m'lord.'

'I've been trying to kick myself, but it's so dashed difficult if you aren't a contortionist. All that stuff about stingahs and long bars and the chap Sycamore! We ought to have seen through it in an instant.'

'We ought, indeed, m'lord.'

'I suppose that when a man has a face as red as that, one tends to feel that he must be telling the truth.'

'Very possibly, m'lord.'

'And his eyes were so bright and blue. Well, there it is,' said Bill. 'Whether it was the red face or the blue eyes that did it, one cannot say, but the fact remains that as a result of the general colour scheme I allowed myself to be used as a cat's-paw and pinched an expensive pendant which the hellhound Biggar has gone off to London with, thus rendering myself liable to an extended sojourn in the cooler . . . unless –'

'M'lord?'

'I was going to say "Unless you have something to suggest." Silly of me,' said Bill, with a hollow laugh. 'How could you possibly have anything to suggest?'

'I have, m'lord.'

Bill stared.

'You wouldn't try to be funny at a time like this, Jeeves?'

'Certainly not, m'lord.'

'You really have a life-belt to throw me before the gumbo closes over my head?'

'Yes, m'lord. In the first place, I would point out to your lordship that there is little or no likelihood of your lordship becoming suspect of the theft of Mrs Spottsworth's ornament. It has disappeared. Captain Biggar has disappeared. The authorities will put two and two together, m'lord, and automatically credit him with the crime.'

'Something in that.'

'It would seem impossible, m'lord, for them to fall into any other train of thought.'

Bill brightened a little, but only a little.

'Well, that's all to the good, I agree, but it doesn't let me out. You've overlooked something, Jeeves.'

'M'lord?'

'The honour of the Rowcesters. That is the snag we come up against. I can't go through life feeling that under my own roof – leaky, but still a roof – I have swiped a valuable pendant from a guest filled to the eyebrows with my salt. How am I to reimburse La Spottsworth? That is the problem to which we have to bend our brains.'

'I was about to touch on that point, m'lord. Your lordship will recall that in speaking of suspicion falling upon Captain Biggar I said "In the first place". In the second place, I was about to add, restitution can readily be made to Mrs Spottsworth, possibly in the form of notes to the correct amount dispatched anonymously to her address, if the lady can be persuaded to purchase Rowcester Abbey.'

'Great Scott, Jeeves!'

'M'lord?'

'The reason I used the expression "Great Scott!"' said Bill, his emotion still causing him to quiver from head to foot, 'was that in the rush and swirl of recent events I had absolutely forgotten all about selling the house. Of course! That would fix up everything, wouldn't it?'

'Unquestionably, m'lord. Even a sale at a sacrifice price would enable your lordship to do –'

'The square thing?'

'Precisely, m'lord. I may add that while on our way to the ruined chapel last night, Mrs Spottsworth spoke in high terms of the charms of Rowcester Abbey and was equally cordial in her remarks as we were returning. All in all, m'lord, I would say that the prospects were distinctly favourable, and if I might offer the suggestion, I think that your lordship should now withdraw to the library and obtain material for what is termed a sales talk by skimming through the advertisements in *Country Life*, in which, as your lordship is possibly aware, virtually every large house which has been refused as a gift by the National Trust is offered for sale. The language is extremely persuasive.'

'Yes, I know the sort of thing. "This lordly demesne, with its avenues of historic oaks, its tumbling streams alive with trout and tench, its breath-taking vistas lined with flowering shrubs . . ." Yes, I'll bone up.'

'It might possibly assist your lordship if I were to bring a small bottle of champagne to the library.'

'You think of everything, Jeeves.'

'Your lordship is too kind.'

'Half a bot should do the trick.'

'I think so, m'lord, if adequately iced.'

It was some minutes later, as Jeeves was passing through the living room with the brain-restorer on a small tray, that Jill came in through the french window.

19

It is a characteristic of women as a sex, and one that does credit
to their gentle hearts, that – unless they are gangsters' molls or
something of that kind – they shrink from the thought of violence.
Even when love is dead, they dislike the idea of the man to whom
they were once betrothed receiving a series of juicy ones from a
horsewhip in the competent hands of an elderly, but still muscular,
chief constable of a county. When they hear such a chief constable
sketching out plans for an operation of this nature, their instinct is
to hurry to the prospective victim's residence and warn him of his
peril by outlining the shape of things to come.

It was to apprise Bill of her father's hopes and dreams that Jill
had come to Rowcester Abbey and, not being on speaking terms
with her former fiancé, she had been wondering a little how the
information she was bringing could be conveyed to him. The sight
of Jeeves cleared up this point. A few words of explanation to Jeeves,
coupled with the suggestion that he should advise Bill to lie low till
the old gentleman had blown over, would accomplish what she had
in mind, and she could then go home again, her duty done and the
whole unpleasant affair disposed of.

'Oh, Jeeves,' she said.

Jeeves had turned, and was regarding her with respectful benevolence.

'Good afternoon, miss. You will find his lordship in the library.'

Jill stiffened haughtily. There was not much of her, but what there
was she drew to its full height.

'No, I won't,' she replied in a voice straight from the frigidaire,
'because I'm jolly well not going there. I haven't the slightest wish
to speak to Lord Rowcester. I want you to give him a message.'

'Very good, miss.'

'Tell him my father is coming here to borrow his horsewhip to
horsewhip him with.'

'Miss?'

'It's quite simple, isn't it? You know my father?'

'Yes, miss.'

'And you know what a horsewhip is?'

'Yes, miss.'

'Well, tell Lord Rowcester the combination is on its way over.'

'And if his lordship should express curiosity as to the reason for Colonel Wyvern's annoyance?'

'You may say it's because I told him about what happened last night. Or this morning, to be absolutely accurate. At two o'clock this morning. He'll understand.'

'At two o'clock this morning, miss? That would have been at about the hour when I was escorting Mrs Spottsworth to the ruined chapel. The lady had expressed a wish to establish contact with the apparition of Lady Agatha. The wife of Sir Caradoc the Crusader, miss, who did well, I believe, at the Battle of Joppa. She is reputed to haunt the ruined chapel.'

Jill collapsed into a chair. A sudden wild hope, surging through the cracks in her broken heart, had shaken her from stem to stern, making her feel boneless.

'What . . . what did you say?'

Jeeves was a kindly man, and not only a kindly man but a man who could open a bottle of champagne as quick as a flash. It was in something of the spirit of the Sir Philip Sidney who gave the water to the stretcher case that he now whisked the cork from the bottle he was carrying. Jill's need, he felt, was greater than Bill's.

'Permit me, miss.'

Jill drank gratefully. Her eyes had widened, and the colour was returning to her face.

'Jeeves, this is a matter of life and death,' she said. 'At two o'clock this morning I saw Lord Rowcester coming out of Mrs Spottsworth's room looking perfectly frightful in mauve pyjamas. Are you telling me that Mrs Spottsworth was not there?'

'Precisely, miss. She was with me in the ruined chapel, holding me spellbound with her account of recent investigations of the Society of Psychical Research.'

'Then what was Lord Rowcester doing in her room?'

'Purloining the lady's pendant, miss.'

It was unfortunate that as he said these words Jill should have been taking a sip of champagne, for she choked. And as her companion would have considered it a liberty to slap her on the back, it was some moments before she was able to speak.

'Purloining Mrs Spottsworth's pendant?'

'Yes, miss. It is a long and somewhat intricate story, but if you would care for me to run through the salient points, I should be delighted to do so. Would it interest you to hear the inside history of his lordship's recent activities, culminating, as I have indicated, in the abstracting of Mrs Spottsworth's ornament?'

Jill drew in her breath with a hiss.

'Yes, Jeeves, it would.'

'Very good, miss. Then must I speak of one who loved not wisely but too well, of one whose subdued eyes, albeit unused to the melting mood, drop tears as fast as the Arabian trees their medicinal gum.'

'Jeeves!'

'Miss?'

'What on earth are you talking about?'

Jeeves looked a little hurt.

'I was endeavouring to explain that it was for love of you, miss, that his lordship became a Silver Ring bookmaker.'

'A *what?*'

'Having plighted his troth to you, miss, his lordship felt – rightly, in my opinion – that in order to support a wife he would require a considerably larger income than he had been enjoying up to that moment. After weighing and rejecting the claims of other professions, he decided to embark on the career of a bookmaker in the Silver Ring, trading under the name of Honest Patch Perkins. I officiated as his lordship's clerk. We wore false moustaches.'

Jill opened her mouth, then, as if feeling that any form of speech would be inadequate, closed it again.

'For a time the venture paid very handsomely. In three days at Doncaster we were so fortunate as to amass no less a sum than four hundred and twenty pounds, and it was in optimistic mood that we proceeded to Epsom for the Oaks. But disaster was lurking in wait for his lordship. To use the metaphor that the tide turned would be inaccurate. What smote his lordship was not so much the tide as a single tidal wave. Captain Biggar, miss. He won a double at his lordship's expense – five pounds on Lucy Glitters at a hundred to six, all to come on Whistler's Mother, SP.'

Jill spoke faintly.

'What was the SP.?'

'I deeply regret to say, miss, thirty-three to one. And as he had rashly refused to lay the wager off, this cataclysm left his lordship in the unfortunate position of owing Captain Biggar in excess of three thousand pounds, with no assets with which to meet his obligations.'

'Golly!'

'Yes, miss. His lordship was compelled to make a somewhat hurried departure from the course, followed by Captain Biggar shouting "Welsher!", but when we were able to shake off our pursuer's challenge some ten miles from the abbey, we were hoping that the episode was concluded and that to Captain Biggar his lordship would remain merely a vague, unidentified figure in a moustache by Clarkson. But it was not to be, miss. The captain tracked his lordship here, penetrated his incognito and demanded an immediate settlement.'

'But Bill had no money.'

'Precisely, miss. His lordship did not omit to stress that point. And it was then that Captain Biggar proposed that his lordship should secure possession of Mrs Spottsworth's pendant, asserting, when met with a *nolle prosequi* on his lordship's part, that the object in question had been given by him to the lady some years ago, so that he was morally entitled to borrow it. The story, on reflection, seems somewhat thin, but it was told with so great a wealth of corroborative detail that it convinced us at the time, and his lordship, who had been vowing that he would ne'er consent, consented. Do I make myself clear, miss?'

'Quite clear. You don't mind my head swimming?'

'Not at all, miss. The question then arose of how the operation was to be carried through, and eventually it was arranged that I should lure Mrs Spottsworth from her room on the pretext that Lady Agatha had been seen in the ruined chapel, and during her absence his lordship should enter and obtain the trinket. This ruse proved successful. The pendant was duly handed to Captain Biggar, who has taken it to London with the purpose of pawning it and investing the proceeds on the Irish horse, Ballymore, concerning whose chances he is extremely sanguine. As regards his lordship's mauve pyjamas, to which you made a derogatory allusion a short while back, I am hoping to convince his lordship that a quiet blue or a pistachio green –'

But Jill was not interested in the Rowcester pyjamas and the steps which were being taken to correct their mauveness. She was hammering on the library door.

'Bill! Bill!' she cried, like a woman wailing for her demon lover, and Bill, hearing that voice, came out with the promptitude of a cork extracted by Jeeves from a bottle.

'Oh, Bill!' said Jill, flinging herself into his arms. 'Jeeves has told me everything!'

Over the head that rested on his chest Bill shot an anxious glance at Jeeves.

'When you say everything, do you mean *everything*?'

'Yes, m'lord. I deemed it advisable.'

'I know all about Honest Patch Perkins and your moustache and Captain Biggar and Whistler's Mother and Mrs Spottsworth and the pendant,' said Jill, nestling closely.

It seemed so odd to Bill that a girl who knew all this should be nestling closely that he was obliged to release her for a moment and step across and take a sip of champagne.

'And you really mean,' he said, returning and folding her in his embrace once more, 'that you don't recoil from me in horror?'

'Of course I don't recoil from you in horror. Do I look as if I were recoiling from you in horror?'

'Well, no,' said Bill, having considered this. He kissed her lips, her forehead, her ears and the top of her head. 'But the trouble is that you might just as well recoil from me in horror, because I don't see how the dickens we're ever going to get married. I haven't a bean, and I've somehow got to raise a small fortune to pay Mrs Spottsworth for her pendant. *Noblesse oblige*, if you follow my drift. So if I don't sell her the house –'

'Of course you'll sell her the house.'

'Shall I? I wonder – I'll certainly try. Where on earth's she disappeared to? She was in here when I came through into the library just now. I wish she'd show up. I'm all full of that *Country Life* stuff, and if she doesn't come soon, it will evaporate.'

'Excuse me, m'lord,' said Jeeves, who during the recent exchanges had withdrawn discreetly to the window. 'Mrs Spottsworth and her ladyship are at this moment crossing the lawn.'

With a courteous gesture he stepped to one side, and Mrs Spottsworth entered, followed by Monica.

'Jill!' cried Monica, halting, amazed. 'Good heavens!'

'Oh, it's all right,' said Jill. 'There's been a change in the situation. Sweethearts still.'

'Well, that's fine. I've been showing Rosalinda round the place –'

'– with its avenues of historic oaks, its tumbling streams alive with trout and tench, and its breath-taking vistas lined with flowering shrubs . . . How did you like it?' said Bill.

Mrs Spottsworth clasped her hands and closed her eyes in an ecstasy.

'It's wonderful, wonderful!' she said. 'I can't understand how you can bring yourself to part with it, Billiken.'

Bill gulped. 'Am I going to part with it?'

'You certainly are,' said Mrs Spottsworth emphatically, 'if I have anything to say about it. This is the house of my dreams. How much do you want for it – lock, stock and barrel?'

'You've taken my breath away.'

'Well, that's me. I never could endure beating about the bush. If I want a thing, I say so and write a note. I'll tell you what let's do. Suppose I pay you a deposit of two thousand, and we can decide on the purchase price later?'

'You couldn't make it three thousand?'

'Sure.' Mrs Spottsworth unscrewed her fountain pen and having unscrewed it, paused. 'There's just one thing, though, before I sign on the dotted line. This place isn't damp, is it?'

'*Damp?*' said Monica. 'Why, of course not.'

'You're sure?'

'Dry as a bone.'

'That's swell. Damp is death to me. Fibrositis *and* sciatica.'

Rory came in through the french window, laden with roses.

'A nosegay for you, Moke, old girl, with comps of R. Carmoyle,' he said, pressing the blooms into Monica's hands. 'I say, Bill, it's starting to rain.'

'What of it?'

'What *of* it?' echoed Rory, surprised. 'My dear old boy, you know what happens in this house when it rains. Water through the roof, water through the walls, water, water everywhere. I was merely about to suggest in a kindly Boy Scout sort of spirit that you had better put buckets under the upstairs skylight. Very damp house, this,' he said, addressing Mrs Spottsworth in his genial, confidential way. 'So near the river, you know. I often say that whereas in the summer months the river is at the bottom of the garden, in the winter months the garden is at the bottom of the –'

'Excuse me, m'lady,' said the housemaid Ellen, appearing in the doorway. 'Could I speak to Mrs Spottsworth, m'lady?'

Mrs Spottsworth, who had been staring, aghast, at Rory, turned, pen in hand.

'Yes?'

'Moddom,' said Ellen, 'your pendant's been pinched.'

She had never been a girl for breaking things gently.

20

With considerable gratification Ellen found herself the centre of attraction. All eyes were focused upon her, and most of them were bulging. Bill's, in particular, struck her as being on the point of leaving their sockets.

'Yes,' she proceeded, far too refined to employ the Bulstrode-Trelawny 'Yus', 'I was laying out your clothes for the evening, moddom, and I said to myself that you'd probably be wishing to wear the pendant again tonight, so I ventured to look in the little box, and it wasn't there, moddom. It's been stolen.'

Mrs Spottsworth drew a quick breath. The trinket in question was of little intrinsic worth – it could not, as she had said to Captain Biggar, have cost more than ten thousand dollars – but, as she had also said to Captain Biggar, it had a sentimental value for her. She was about to express her concern in words, but Bill broke in.

'What do you mean, it's been stolen?' he demanded hotly. You could see that the suggestion outraged him. 'You probably didn't look properly.'

Ellen was respectful, but firm.

'It's gone, m'lord.'

'You may have dropped it somewhere, Mrs Spottsworth,' said Jill. 'Was the clasp loose?'

'Why, yes,' said Mrs Spottsworth. 'The clasp was loose. But I distinctly remember putting it in its case last night.'

'Not there now, moddom,' said Ellen, rubbing it in.

'Let's go up and have a thorough search,' said Monica.

'We will,' said Mrs Spottsworth. 'But I'm afraid . . . very much afraid –'

She followed Ellen out of the room. Monica, pausing at the door, eyed Rory balefully for an instant.

'Well, Bill,' she said, 'so you don't sell the house, after all. And if Big Mouth there hadn't come barging in prattling about water and buckets, that cheque would have been signed.'

She swept out, and Rory looked at Bill, surprised.

'I say, did I drop a brick?'

Bill laughed hackingly.

'If one followed you about for a month, one would have enough bricks to build a house.'

'*In re* this pendant. Anything I can do?'

'Yes, keep out of it.'

'I could nip off in the car and fetch some of the local constabulary.'

'Keep right out of it.' Bill looked at his watch. 'The Derby will be starting in a few minutes. Go in there and get the television working.'

'Right,' said Rory. 'But if I'm needed, give me a shout.'

He disappeared into the library, and Bill turned to Jeeves, who had once again effaced himself. In times of domestic crisis, Jeeves had the gift, possessed by all good butlers, of creating the illusion that he was not there. He was standing now at the extreme end of the room, looking stuffed.

'Jeeves!'

'M'lord?' said Jeeves, coming to life like a male Galatea.

'Any suggestions?'

'None of practical value, m'lord. But a thought has just occurred which enables me to take a somewhat brighter view of the situation. We were speaking not long since of Captain Biggar as a gentleman who had removed himself permanently from our midst. Does it not seem likely to your lordship that in the event of Ballymore emerging victorious the captain, finding himself in possession of ample funds, will carry out his original plan of redeeming the pendant, bringing it back and affecting to discover it on the premises?'

Bill chewed his lip.

'You think so?'

'It would be the prudent course for him to pursue, m'lord. Suspicion, as I say, must inevitably rest upon him, and failure to return the ornament would place him in the disagreeable position of becoming a hunted man in hourly danger of being apprehended by the authorities. I am convinced that if Ballymore wins, we shall see Captain Biggar again.'

'*If* Ballymore wins.'

'Precisely, m'lord.'

'Then one's whole future hangs on whether it does.'

'That is how matters stand, m'lord.'

Jill uttered a passionate cry.

'I'm going to start praying!'

'Yes, do,' said Bill. 'Pray that Ballymore will run as he has never run before. Pray like billy-o. Pray all over the house. Pray –'

Monica and Mrs Spottsworth came back.

'Well,' said Monica, 'it's gone. There's no doubt about that. I've just phoned for the police.'

Bill reeled.

'What!'

'Yes. Rosalinda didn't want me to, but I insisted. I told her you wouldn't dream of not doing everything you could to catch the thief.'

'You . . . You think the thing's been stolen?'

'It's the only possible explanation.'

Mrs Spottsworth sighed.

'Oh, dear! I really am sorry to have started all this trouble.'

'Nonsense, Rosalinda. Bill doesn't mind. All Bill wants is to see the crook caught and bunged into the cooler. Isn't it, Bill?'

'Yes, *sir!*' said Bill.

'For a good long stretch, too, let's hope.'

'We mustn't be vindictive.'

'No,' said Mrs Spottsworth. 'You're quite right. Justice, but not vengeance.'

'Well, one thing's certain,' said Monica. 'It's an inside job.'

Bill stirred uneasily.

'Oh, do you think so?'

'Yes, and I've got a pretty shrewd idea who the guilty party is.'

'Who?'

'Someone who was in a terrible state of nerves this morning.'

'Oh?'

'His cup and saucer were rattling like castanets.'

'When was this?'

'At breakfast. Do you want me to name names?'

'Go ahead.'

'Captain Biggar!'

Mrs Spottsworth started.

'What!'

'You weren't down, Rosalinda, or I'm sure you would have noticed it, too. He was as nervous as a treeful of elephants.'

'Oh, no, no! Captain Biggar? That I can't and won't believe. If Captain Biggar were guilty, I should lose my faith in human nature. And that would be a far worse blow than losing the pendant.'

'The pendant is gone, and he's gone. It adds up, don't you think? Oh, well,' said Monica, 'we shall soon know.'

'What makes you so sure of that?'

'Why, the jewel case, of course. The police will take it away and test it for fingerprints. What on earth's the matter, Bill?'

'Nothing's the matter,' said Bill, who had leaped some eighteen inches into the air but saw no reason for revealing the sudden agonized thought which had motivated this adagio exhibition. 'Er, Jeeves.'

'M'lord?'

'Lady Carmoyle is speaking of Mrs Spottsworth's jewel case.'

'Yes, m'lord?'

'She threw out the interesting suggestion that the miscreant might have forgotten to wear gloves, in which event the bally thing would be covered with his fingerprints. That would be lucky, wouldn't it?'

'Extremely fortunate, m'lord.'

'I'll bet he's wishing he hadn't been such an ass.'

'Yes, m'lord.'

'And that he could wipe them off.'

'Yes, m'lord.'

'You might go and get the thing, so as to have it ready for the police when they arrive.'

'Very good, m'lord.'

'Hold it by the edges, Jeeves. You don't want to disturb those fingerprints.'

'I will exercise the greatest care, m'lord,' said Jeeves, and went out, and almost simultaneously Colonel Wyvern came in through the french window.

At the moment of his entry Jill, knowing that when a man is in a state of extreme agitation there is nothing he needs more than a woman's gentle sympathy, had put her arms round Bill's neck and was kissing him tenderly. The spectacle brought the colonel to a halt. It confused him. With this sort of thing going on, it was difficult to lead up to the subject of horsewhips.

'Ha, hrr'mph!' he said, and Monica spun round, astounded.

'My goodness!' she said. 'You have been quick. It's only five minutes since I phoned.'

'Eh?'

'Hullo, father,' said Jill. 'We were just waiting for you to show up. Have you brought your bloodhounds and magnifying glass?'

'What the dickens are you talking about?'

Monica was perplexed.

'Didn't you come in answer to my phone call, Colonel?'

'You keep talking about a phone call. What phone call? I came to see Lord Rowcester on a personal matter. What's all this about a phone call?'

'Mrs Spottsworth's diamond pendant has been stolen, Father.'

'What? What? What?'

'This is Mrs Spottsworth,' said Monica. 'Colonel Wyvern, Rosalinda, our Chief Constable.'

'Charmed,' said Colonel Wyvern, bowing gallantly, but an instant later he was the keen, remorseless police officer again. 'Had your pendant stolen, eh? Bad show, bad show.' He took out a notebook and a pencil. 'An inside job, was it?'

'That's what we think.'

'Then I'll have to have a list of everybody in the house.'

Jill stepped forward, her hands extended.

'Wyvern, Jill,' she said. 'Slip on the bracelets, officer. I'll come quietly.'

'Oh, don't be an ass,' said Colonel Wyvern.

Something struck the door gently. It might have been a foot. Bill opened the door, revealing Jeeves. He was carrying the jewel case, a handkerchief at its extreme edges.

'Thank you, m'lord,' he said.

He advanced to the table and lowered the case on to it very carefully.

'Here is the case the pendant was in,' said Mrs Spottsworth.

'Good.' Colonel Wyvern eyed Jeeves with approval. 'Glad to see you were careful about handling it, my man.'

'Oh, trust Jeeves for that,' said Bill.

'And now,' said Colonel Wyvern, 'for the names.'

As he spoke, the library door burst open, and Rory came dashing out, horror written on his every feature.

21

'I say, chaps,' said Rory, 'the most appalling thing has happened!'
Monica moaned.

'Not something *more?*'

'This is the absolute frozen limit. The Derby is just starting –'

'Rory, the Chief Constable is here.'

'– and the television set has gone on the blink. Oh, it's my fault,
I suppose. I was trying to get a perfect adjustment, and I must have
twiddled the wrong thingummy.'

'Rory, this is Colonel Wyvern, the Chief Constable.'

'How are you, Chief C? Do you know anything about television?'
The colonel drew himself up.

'I do not!'

'You couldn't fix a set?' said Rory wistfully. 'Not that there's time,
of course. The race will be over. What about the radio?'

'In the corner, Sir Roderick,' said Jeeves.

'Oh, thank heaven!' cried Rory, galloping to it. 'Come on and give
me a hand, Jeeves.'

The chief constable spoke coldly.

'Who is this gentleman?'

'Such as he is,' said Monica apologetically, 'my husband, Sir
Roderick Carmoyle.'

Colonel Wyvern advanced on Rory as majestically as his lack of
inches permitted, and addressed the seat of his trousers, the only
portion of him visible as he bent over the radio.

'Sir Roderick, I am conducting an investigation.'

'But you'll hold it up to listen to the Derby?'

'When on duty, Sir Roderick, I allow nothing to interfere. I want
a list –'

The radio, suddenly blaring forth, gave him one.

'. . . Taj Mahal, Sweet William, Garniture, Moke the Second,
Voleur . . . Quite an impressive list, isn't it?' said the radio. 'There
goes Gordon Richards. Lots of people think this will be his lucky
day. I don't see Bellwether . . . Oh, yes, he's turning round now and

walking back to the gate . . . They should be off in just a moment . . .
Sorry, no. Two more have turned round. One of them is being *very*
temperamental. It looks like Simple Simon. No, it's the Irish outsider,
Ballymore.'

The chief constable frowned. 'Really, I must ask –'

'Okay. I'll turn it down,' said Rory, and immediately, being Rory,
turned it up.

'They're in line now,' yelled the radio, like a costermonger calling
attention to his blood oranges, 'all twenty-six of them . . . They're
OFF . . . Ballymore is left at the post.'

Jill screamed shrilly. 'Oh, *no!*'

'Vaurien,' proceeded the radio, now, owing to Rory's ministrations,
speaking in an almost inaudible whisper, like an invalid uttering a few
last words from a sickbed, 'is in front, the Boussac pacemaker.' Its
voice strengthened a little. 'Taj Mahal is just behind. I see Escalator.
Escalator's going very strong. I see Sweet William. I see Moke the
Second. I see . . .' Here the wasting sickness set in again, and the
rest was lost in a sort of mouselike squeak.

The chief constable drew a relieved breath.

'Ha! At last! Now then, Lord Rowcester. What servants have
you here?'

Bill did not answer. Like a mechanical figure he was moving toward
the radio, as if drawn by some invisible force.

'There's a cook,' said Monica.

'A widow, sir,' said Jeeves. 'Mary Jane Piggott.'

Rory looked round.

'Piggott? Who said Piggott?'

'A housemaid,' said Monica, as Jill, like Bill, was drawn toward the
radio as if in a trance. 'Her name's Ellen. Ellen what, Jeeves?'

'French, m'lady. Ellen Tallulah French.'

'The French horse,' bellowed the radio, suddenly acquiring a new
access of strength, 'is still in front, then Moke the Second, Escalator,
Taj Mahal . . .'

'What about the gardener?'

'No, not Gardener,' said Rory. 'You mean Garniture.'

'. . . Sweet William, Oratory . . . Vaurien's falling back, and Garniture –'

'You see?' said Rory.

'– and Moke the Second moving up.'

'That's mine,' said Monica, and with a strange, set look on her
face began to move toward the radio.

'Looks quite as though Gordon Richards might be going to win the

Derby at last. They're down the hill and turning Tattenham Corner, Moke the Second in front, with Gordon up. Only three and a half furlongs to go . . .'

'Yes, sir,' said Jeeves, completely unmoved, 'there is a gardener, an old man named Percy Wellbeloved.'

The radio suddenly broke into a frenzy of excitement.

'Oo! . . . Oo! . . . There's a horse coming up on the outside. It's coming like an express train. I can't identify . . .'

'Gee, this is exciting, isn't it!' said Mrs Spottsworth.

She went to the radio. Jeeves alone remained at the chief constable's side. Colonel Wyvern was writing laboriously in his notebook.

'It's Ballymore. The horse on the outside is Ballymore. He's challenging the Moke. Hear that crowd roaring "Come on, Gordon!"'

'Moke . . . The Moke . . . Gordon,' wrote Colonel Wyvern.

'Come on, Gordon!' shouted Monica.

The radio was now becoming incoherent.

'It's Ballymore . . . No, it's the Moke . . . No, Ballymore . . . No, the Moke . . . No . . .'

'Make up your mind,' advised Rory.

For some moments Colonel Wyvern had been standing motionless, his notebook frozen in his hand. Now a sort of shudder passed through him, and his eyes grew wide and wild. Brandishing his pencil, he leaped toward the radio.

'Come on, Gordon!' he roared. 'COME ON, GORDON!!!'

'Come on, Ballymore,' said Jeeves with quiet dignity.

The radio had now given up all thoughts of gentlemanly restraint. It was as though on honeydew it had fed and drunk the milk of Paradise.

'Photo finish!' it shrieked. 'Photo finish! Photo finish! First time in the history of the Derby. Photo finish. Escalator in third place.'

Rather sheepishly the chief constable turned away and came back to Jeeves.

'The gardener's name you said was what? Clarence Wilberforce, was it?'

'Percy Wellbeloved, sir.'

'Odd name.'

'Shropshire, I believe, sir.'

'Ah? Percy Wellbeloved. Does that complete the roster of the staff?'

'Yes, sir, except for myself.'

Rory came away from the radio, mopping his forehead.

'Well, that Taj Mahal let me down with a bang,' he said bitterly. 'Why is it one can never pick a winner in this bally race?'

'"The Moke" didn't suggest a winner to you?' said Monica.

'Eh? No. Why? Why should it?'

'God bless you, Roderick Carmoyle.'

Colonel Wyvern was himself again now.

'I would like,' he said, in a curt, official voice, 'to inspect the scene of the robbery.'

'I will take you there,' said Mrs Spottsworth. 'Will you come too, Monica?'

'Yes, yes, of course,' said Monica. 'Listen in, some of you, will you, and see what that photo shows.'

'And I'll send this down to the station,' said Colonel Wyvern, picking up the jewel case by one corner, 'and find out what *it* shows.'

They went out, and Rory moved to the door of the library.

'I'll go and see if I really have damaged that TV set,' he said. 'All I did was twiddle a thingummy.' He stretched himself with a yawn. 'Damn dull Derby,' he said. 'Even if Moke the Second wins, the old girl's only got ten bob on it at eights.'

The library door closed behind him.

'Jeeves,' said Bill, 'I've got to have a drink.'

'I will bring it immediately, m'lord.'

'No, don't bring it. I'll come to your pantry.'

'And I'll come with you,' said Jill. 'But we must wait to hear that result. Let's hope Ballymore had sense enough to stick out his tongue.'

'Ha!' cried Bill.

The radio had begun to speak.

'Hundreds of thousands of pounds hang on what that photograph decides,' it was saying in the rather subdued voice of a man recovering from a hangover. It seemed to be a little ashamed of its recent emotion. 'The number should be going up at any moment. Yes, here it is . . .'

'Come on, Ballymore!' cried Jill.

'Come on, Ballymore!' shouted Bill.

'Come on, Ballymore,' said Jeeves reservedly.

'Moke the Second wins,' said the radio. 'Hard luck on Ballymore. He ran a wonderful race. If it hadn't been for that bad start, he would have won in a canter. His defeat saves the bookies a tremendous loss. A huge sum was bet on the Irish horse ten minutes before starting time, obviously one of those SP jobs which are so . . .'

Dully, with something of the air of a man laying a wreath on the tomb of an old friend, Bill turned the radio off.

'Come on,' he said. 'After all, there's still champagne.'

22

Mrs Spottsworth came slowly down the stairs. Monica and the chief constable were still conducting their examination of the scene of the crime, but they had been speaking freely of Captain Biggar, and the trend of their remarks had been such as to make her feel that knives were being driven through her heart. When a woman loves a man with every fibre of a generous nature, it can never be pleasant for her to hear this man alluded to as a red-faced thug (Monica) and as a scoundrel who can't possibly get away but must inevitably ere long be caught and slapped into the jug (Colonel Wyvern). It was her intention to make for that rustic seat and there sit and think of what might have been.

The rustic seat stood at a junction of two moss-grown paths facing the river which lay – though only, as we have seen, during the summer months – at the bottom of the garden. Flowering bushes masked it from the eye of one approaching, and it was not till she had turned the last corner that Mrs Spottsworth was able to perceive that it already had an occupant. At the sight of that occupant she stood for a moment transfixed. Then there burst from her lips a cry so like that of a zebu calling to its mate that Captain Biggar, who had been sitting in a deep reverie, staring at a snail, had the momentary illusion that he was back in Africa. He sprang to his feet, and for a long instant they stood there motionless, gazing at each other wide-eyed while the various birds, bees, wasps, gnats and other insects operating in the vicinity went about their business as if nothing at all sensational had happened. The snail, in particular, seemed completely unmoved.

Mrs Spottsworth did not share its detached aloofness. She was stirred to her depths.

'You!' she cried. 'Oh, I knew you would come. They said you wouldn't, but I knew.'

Captain Biggar was hanging his head. The man seemed crushed, incapable of movement. A rhinoceros, seeing him now, would have plucked up heart and charged on him without a tremor, feeling that this was going to be easy.

'I couldn't do it,' he muttered. 'I got to thinking of you and of the chaps at the club, and I couldn't do it.'

'The club?'

'The old Anglo-Malay Club in Kuala Lumpur, where men are white and honesty goes for granted. Yes, I thought of the chaps. I thought of Tubby Frobisher. Would I ever be able to look him again in that one good eye of his? And then I thought that you had trusted me because . . . because I was an Englishman. And I said to myself, it isn't only the old Anglo-Malay and Tubby and the Subahdar and Doc and Squiffy, Cuthbert Biggar – you're letting down the whole British Empire.'

Mrs Spottsworth choked.

'Did . . . did you take it?'

Captain Biggar threw up his chin and squared his shoulders. He was so nearly himself again, now that he had spoken those brave words, that the rhinoceros, taking a look at him, would have changed its mind and decided to remember an appointment elsewhere.

'I took it, and I brought it back,' he said in a firm, resonant voice, producing the pendant from his hip pocket. 'The idea was merely to borrow it for the day, as security for a gamble. But I couldn't do it. It might have meant a fortune, but I couldn't do it.'

Mrs Spottsworth bent her head.

'Put it round my neck, Cuthbert,' she whispered.

Captain Biggar stared incredulously at her back hair.

'You want me to? You don't mind if I touch you?'

'Put it round my neck,' repeated Mrs Spottsworth.

Reverently the captain did so, and there was a pause.

'Yes,' said the captain, 'I might have made a fortune, and shall I tell you why I wanted a fortune? Don't run away with the idea that I'm a man who values money. Ask any of the chaps out East, and they'll say "Give Bwana Biggar his .505 Gibbs, his eland steak of a night, let him breathe God's clean air and turn his face up to God's good sun and he asks nothing more." But it was imperative that I should lay my hands on a bit of the stuff so that I might feel myself in a position to speak my love. Rosie . . . I heard them calling you that, and I must use that name . . . Rosie, I love you. I loved you from that first moment in Kenya when you stepped out of the car and I said "Ah, the memsahib". All these years I have dreamed of you, and on this very seat last night it was all I could do to keep myself from pouring out my heart. It doesn't matter now. I can speak now because we are parting for ever. Soon I shall be wandering out into the sunset . . . alone.'

He paused, and Mrs Spottsworth spoke. There was a certain sharpness in her voice.

'You won't be wandering out into any old sunset alone,' she said. 'Jiminy Christmas! What do you want to wander out into sunsets alone for?'

Captain Biggar smiled a faint, sad smile.

'I don't *want* to wander out into sunsets alone, dear lady. It's the code. The code that says a poor man must not propose marriage to a rich woman, for if he does, he loses his self-respect and ceases to play with a straight bat.'

'I never heard such nonsense in my life. Who started all this apple-sauce?'

Captain Biggar stiffened a little.

'I cannot say who started it, but it is the rule that guides the lives of men like Squiffy and Doc and the Subahdar and Augustus Frobisher.'

Mrs Spottsworth uttered an exclamation.

'*Augustus* Frobisher? For Pete's sake! I've been thinking all along that there was something familiar about that name Frobisher, and now you say Augustus ... This friend of yours, this Frobisher. Is he a fellow with a red face?'

'We all have red faces east of Suez.'

'And a small, bristly moustache?'

'Small, bristly moustaches, too.'

'Does he stammer slightly? Has he a small mole on the left cheek? Is one of his eyes green and the other glass?'

Captain Biggar was amazed.

'Good God! That's Tubby. You've met him?'

'Met him? You bet I've met him. It was only a week before I left the States that I was singing "Oh, perfect love" at his wedding.'

Captain Biggar's eyes widened.

'*Howki wa hoo!*' he exclaimed. 'Tubby is married?'

'He certainly is. And do you know who he's married to? Cora Rita Rockmetteller, widow of the late Sigsbee Rockmetteller, the Sardine King, a woman with a darned sight more money than I've got myself. Now you see how much your old code amounts to. When Augustus Frobisher met Cora and heard that she had fifty million smackers hidden away behind the brick in the fireplace, did he wander out into any sunset alone? No, sir! He bought a clean collar and a gardenia for his buttonhole and snapped into it.'

Captain Biggar had lowered himself on to the rustic seat and was breathing heavily through the nostrils.

'You have shaken me, Rosie!'

'And you needed shaking, talking all that malarkey. You and your old code!'

'I can't take it in.'

'You will, if you sit and think it over for a while. You stay here and get used to the idea of walking down the aisle with me, and I'll go in and phone the papers that a marriage has been arranged and will shortly take place between Cuthbert . . . have you any other names, my precious lamb?'

'Gervase,' said the captain in a low voice. 'And it's Brabazon-Biggar. With a hyphen.'

'. . . between Cuthbert Gervase Brabazon-Biggar and Rosalinda Bessemer Spottsworth. It's a pity it isn't Sir Cuthbert. Say!' said Mrs Spottsworth, struck with an idea. 'What's wrong with buying you a knighthood? I wonder how much they cost these days? I'll have to ask Sir Roderick. I might be able to get it at Harrige's. Well, goodbye for the moment, my wonder man. Don't go wandering off into any sunsets.'

Humming gaily, for her heart was light, Mrs Spottsworth tripped down the moss-grown path, tripped across the lawn and tripped through the french window into the living room. Jeeves was there. He had left Bill and Jill trying mournfully to console each other in his pantry, and had returned to the living room to collect the coffee cups. At the sight of the pendant encircling Mrs Spottsworth's neck, no fewer than three hairs of his left eyebrow quivered for an instant, showing how deeply he had been moved by the spectacle.

'You're looking at the pendant, I see,' said Mrs Spottsworth, beaming happily. 'I don't wonder you're surprised. Captain Biggar found it just now in the grass by that rustic seat where we were sitting last night.'

It would be too much to say that Jeeves stared, but his eyes enlarged, the merest fraction, a thing they did only on special occasions.

'Has Captain Biggar returned, madam?'

'He got back a few minutes ago. Oh, Jeeves, do you know the telephone number of *The Times*?'

'No, madam, but I could ascertain.'

'I want to announce my engagement to Captain Biggar.'

Four hairs of Jeeves's right eyebrow stirred slightly, as if a passing breeze had disturbed them.

'Indeed, madam? May I wish you every happiness?'

'Thank you, Jeeves.'

'Shall I telephone *The Times*, madam?'

'If you will, and the *Telegraph* and *Mail* and *Express*. Any others?'

'I think not, madam. Those you have mentioned should be quite sufficient for an announcement of this nature.'

'Perhaps you're right. Just those, then.'

'Very good, madam. Might I venture to ask, madam, if you and Captain Biggar will be taking up your residence at the abbey?'

Mrs Spottsworth sighed.

'No, Jeeves, I wish I could buy it . . . I love the place . . . but it's damp. This English climate!'

'Our English summers *are* severe.'

'And the winters worse.'

Jeeves coughed.

'I wonder if I might make a suggestion, madam, which I think should be satisfactory to all parties.'

'What's that?'

'Buy the house, madam, take it down stone by stone and ship it to California.'

'And put it up there?' Mrs Spottsworth beamed. 'Why, what a brilliant idea!'

'Thank you, madam.'

'William Randolph Hearst used to do it, didn't he? I remember visiting at San Simeon once, and there was a whole French abbey lying on the grass near the gates. I'll do it, Jeeves. You've solved everything. Oh, Lord Rowcester,' said Mrs Spottsworth. 'Just the man I wanted to see.'

Bill had come in with Jill, walking with slow, despondent steps. As he saw the pendant, despondency fell from him like a garment. Unable to speak, he stood pointing a trembling finger.

'It was discovered in the grass adjoining a rustic seat in the garden, m'lord, by Mrs Spottsworth's fiancé, Captain Biggar,' said Jeeves.

Bill found speech, though with difficulty.

'Biggar's back?'

'Yes, m'lord.'

'And he found the pendant?'

'Yes, m'lord.'

'And he's engaged to Mrs Spottsworth?'

'Yes, m'lord. And Mrs Spottsworth has decided to purchase the abbey.'

'What?'

'Yes, m'lord.'

'I do believe in fairies!' said Bill, and Jill said she did, too.

'Yes, Billiken,' said Mrs Spottsworth. 'I'm going to buy the abbey.

I don't care what you're asking for it. I want it, and I'll write you a cheque the moment I come back from apologizing to that nice chief constable. I left him very abruptly just now, and I'm afraid he may be feeling offended. Is he still up in my room, Jeeves?'

'I believe so, madam. He rang for me not long ago to ask if I would provide him with a magnifying glass.'

'I'll go and see him,' said Mrs Spottsworth. 'I'm taking the abbey with me to America, Billiken. It was Jeeves' idea.'

She went out, and Jill hurled herself into Bill's arms.

'Oh, Bill! Oh, Bill! Oh, Bill!' she cried. 'Though I don't know why I'm kissing you,' she said. 'I ought to be kissing Jeeves. Shall I kiss you, Jeeves?'

'No, miss.'

'Just think, Jeeves. You'll have to buy that fish slice after all.'

'It will be a pleasure and a privilege, miss.'

'Of course, Jeeves,' said Bill, 'you must never leave us, wherever we go, whatever we do.'

Jeeves sighed apologetically.

'I am very sorry, m'lord, but I fear I cannot avail myself of your kindness. Indeed, I fear I am compelled to hand in my notice.'

'Oh, Jeeves!'

'With the deepest regret, miss, I need scarcely say. But Mr Wooster needs me. I received a letter from him this morning.'

'Has he left that school of his, then?'

Jeeves sighed again. 'Expelled, m'lord.'

'Good heavens!'

'It is all most unfortunate, m'lord. Mr Wooster was awarded the prize for sock-darning. Two pairs of his socks were actually exhibited on Speech Day. It was then discovered that he had used a crib . . . an old woman whom he smuggled into his study at night.'

'Poor old Bertie!'

'Yes, m'lord. I gather from the tone of his communication that the scandal has affected him deeply. I feel that my place is at his side.'

Rory came in from the library, looking moody.

'I can't fix it,' he said.

'Rory,' said Bill, 'do you know what's happened?'

'Yes, old boy, I've bust the television set.'

'Mrs Spottsworth is going to marry Captain Biggar, and she's buying the abbey.'

'Oh?' said Rory. His manner was listless. 'Well, as I was saying, I can't fix the bally thing, and I don't believe any of the local yokels can, either, so the only thing to do is to go to the fountain head.'

He went to the telephone. 'Give me Square one two three four,' he said.

Captain Biggar came bustling through the french window humming a Swahili wedding march.

'Where's my Rosie?' he asked.

'Upstairs,' said Bill. 'She'll be down in a minute. She's just been telling us the news. Congratulations, Captain.'

'Thank you, thank you.'

'I say,' said Rory, the receiver at his ear, 'I've just remembered another one. Which is bigger, Captain Biggar or Mrs Biggar? Mrs Biggar, because she became Biggar. Ha, ha. Ha, ha, ha! Meanwhile, I'm trying to get –'

His number came through.

'Oh, hullo,' he said. 'Harrige's?'

THE MATING SEASON

1

While I would not go so far, perhaps, as to describe the heart as actually leaden, I must confess that on the eve of starting to do my bit of time at Deverill Hall I was definitely short on chirpiness. I shrank from the prospect of being decanted into a household on chummy terms with a thug like my Aunt Agatha, weakened as I already was by having had her son Thomas, one of our most prominent fiends in human shape, on my hands for three days.

I mentioned this to Jeeves, and he agreed that the set-up could have been juicier.

'Still,' I said, taking a pop, as always, at trying to focus the silver lining, 'it's flattering, of course.'

'Sir?'

'Being the People's Choice, Jeeves. Having these birds going around chanting "We Want Wooster".'

'Ah, yes, sir. Precisely. Most gratifying.'

But half a jiffy. I'm forgetting that you haven't the foggiest what all this is about. It so often pans out that way when you begin a story. You whizz off the mark all pep and ginger, like a mettlesome charger going into its routine, and the next thing you know, the customers are up on their hind legs, yelling for footnotes.

Let me get into reverse and put you abreast.

My Aunt Agatha, the one who chews broken bottles and kills rats with her teeth, arriving suddenly in London from her rural lair with her son Thomas, had instructed me in her authoritative way to put the latter up in my flat for three days while he visited dentists and Old Vics and things preparatory to leaving for his school at Bramley-on-Sea and, that done, to proceed to Deverill Hall, King's Deverill, Hants, the residence of some pals of hers, and lend my services to the village concert. Apparently they wanted to stiffen up the programme with a bit of metropolitan talent, and I had been recommended by the vicar's niece.

And that, of course, was that. It was no good telling her that I would prefer not to touch young Thos with a ten-foot pole and that I disliked taking on blind dates. When Aunt Agatha issues her orders, you fill them. But I was conscious, as I have indicated, of an uneasiness as to the shape of things to come, and it didn't make the outlook any brighter to know that Gussie Fink-Nottle would be among those present at Deverill Hall. When you get trapped in the den of the Secret Nine, you want something a lot better than Gussie to help you keep the upper lip stiff.

I mused a bit.

'I wish I had more data about these people, Jeeves,' I said. 'I like on these occasions to know what I'm up against. So far, all I've gathered is that I am to be the guest of a landed proprietor called Harris or Hacker or possibly Hassock.'

'Haddock, sir.'

'Haddock, eh?'

'Yes, sir. The gentleman who is to be your host is a Mr Esmond Haddock.'

'It's odd, but that name seems to strike a chord, as if I'd heard it before somewhere.'

'Mr Haddock is the son of the owner of a widely advertised patent remedy known as Haddock's Headache Hokies, sir. Possibly the specific is familiar to you.'

'Of course. I know it well. Not so sensationally good as those pick-me-ups of yours, but none the less a sound stand-by on the morning after. So he's one of those Haddocks, is he?'

'Yes, sir. Mr Esmond Haddock's late father married the late Miss Flora Deverill.'

'Before they were both late, of course?'

'The union was considered something of a *mésalliance* by the lady's sisters. The Deverills are a very old county family – like so many others in these days, impoverished.'

'I begin to get the scenario. Haddock, though not as posh as he might be on the father's side, foots the weekly bills?'

'Yes, sir.'

'Well, no doubt he can afford to. There's gold in them thar Hokies, Jeeves.'

'So I should be disposed to imagine, sir.'

A point struck me which often does strike me when chewing the fat with this honest fellow – viz. that he seemed to know a hell of a lot about it. I mentioned this, and he explained that it was one of those odd chances that had enabled him to get the inside story.

'My Uncle Charlie holds the post of butler at the Hall, sir. It is from him that I derive my information.'

'I didn't know you had an Uncle Charlie. Charlie Jeeves?'

'No, sir. Charlie Silversmith.'

I lit a rather pleased cigarette. Things were beginning to clarify.

'Well, this is a bit of a goose. You'll be able to give me all the salient facts, if salient is the word I want. What sort of a joint is this Deverill Hall? Nice place? Gravel soil? Spreading views?'

'Yes, sir.'

'Good catering?'

'Yes, sir.'

'And touching on the personnel. Would there be a Mrs Haddock?'

'No, sir. The young gentleman is unmarried. He resides at the hall with his five aunts.'

'*Five?*'

'Yes, sir. The Misses Charlotte, Emmeline, Harriet and Myrtle Deverill and Dame Daphne Winkworth, relict of the late P.B. Winkworth, the historian. Dame Daphne's daughter, Miss Gertrude Winkworth, is, I understand, also in residence.'

On the cue 'five aunts' I had given at the knees a trifle, for the thought of being confronted with such a solid gaggle of aunts, even if those of another, was an unnerving one. Reminding myself that in this life it is not aunts that matter but the courage which one brings to them, I pulled myself together.

'I see,' I said. 'No stint of female society.'

'No, sir.'

'I may find Gussie's company a relief.'

'Very possibly, sir.'

'Such as it is.'

'Yes, sir.'

I wonder, by the way, if you recall this Augustus, on whose activities I have had occasion to touch once or twice before now? Throw the mind back. Goofy to the gills, face like a fish, horn-rimmed spectacles, drank orange juice, collected newts, engaged to England's premier pill, a girl called Madeline Bassett ... Ah, you've got him? Fine.

'Tell me, Jeeves,' I said, 'how does Gussie come to be mixed up with these bacteria? Surely a bit of an inscrutable mystery that he, too, should be headed for Deverill Hall?'

'No, sir. It was Mr Fink-Nottle himself who informed me.'

'You've seen him, then?'

'Yes, sir. He called while you were out.'

'How did he seem?'

'Low-spirited, sir.'

'Like me, he shrinks from the prospect of visiting this ghastly shack?'

'Yes, sir. He had supposed that Miss Bassett would be accompanying him, but she has altered her arrangements at the last moment and gone to reside at The Larches, Wimbledon Common, with an old school friend who has recently suffered a disappointment in love. It was Miss Bassett's view that she needed cheering up.'

I was at a loss to comprehend how the society of Madeline Bassett could cheer anyone up, she being from topknot to shoe sole the woman whom God forgot, but I didn't say so. I merely threw out the opinion that this must have made Gussie froth a bit.

'Yes, sir. He expressed annoyance at the change of plan. Indeed, I gathered from his remarks, for he was kind enough to confide in me, that there has resulted a certain coolness between himself and Miss Bassett.'

'Gosh!' I said.

And I'll tell you why I goshed. If you remember Gussie Fink-Nottle, you will probably also remember the chain of circumstances which led up, if chains do lead up, to this frightful Bassett getting the impression firmly fixed in her woollen head that Bertram Wooster was pining away for love of her. I won't go into details now, but it was her conviction that if ever she felt like severing relations with Gussie, she had only to send out a hurry call for me and I would come racing round, all ready to buy the licence and start ordering the wedding cake.

So, knowing my view regarding this Bassett, M., you will readily understand why this stuff about coolnesses drew a startled 'Gosh!' from me. The thought of my peril had never left me, and I wasn't going to be really easy in my mind till these two were actually centre-aisling. Only when the clergyman had definitely pronounced sentence would Bertram start to breathe freely again.

'Ah, well,' I said, hoping for the best. 'Just a lovers' tiff, no doubt. Always happening, these lovers' tiffs. Probably by this time a complete reconciliation has been effected and the laughing Love God is sweating away at the old stand once more with knobs on. Ha!' I proceeded as the front-door bell tootled, 'someone waits without. If it's young Thos, tell him that I shall expect him to be in readiness, all clean and rosy, at seven forty-five tonight to accompany me to the performance of *King Lear* at the Old Vic, and it's no good him trying to do a sneak. His mother said he had got to go to the Old Vic, and he's jolly well going.'

'I think it is more probable that it is Mr Pirbright, sir.'

'Old Catsmeat? What makes you think that?'

'He also called during your absence and indicated that he would return later. He was accompanied by his sister, Miss Pirbright.'

'Good Lord, really? Corky? I thought she was in Hollywood.'

'I understand that she has returned to England for a vacation, sir.'

'Did you give her tea?'

'Yes, sir. Master Thomas played host. Miss Pirbright took the young gentleman off subsequently to see a picture.'

'I wish I hadn't missed her. I haven't seen Corky for ages. Was she all right?'

'Yes, sir.'

'And Catsmeat? How was he?'

'Low-spirited, sir.'

'You're mixing him up with Gussie. It was Gussie, if you recall, who was low-spirited.'

'Mr Pirbright also.'

'There seems to be a lot of low-spiritedness kicking about these days.'

'We live in difficult times, sir.'

'True. Well, bung him in.'

He oozed out, and a few moments later oozed in again.

'Mr Pirbright,' he announced.

He had called his shots correctly. A glance at the young visitor was enough to tell me that he was low-spirited.

2

And, mind you, it isn't often that you find the object under advisement in this condition. A singularly fizzy bird, as a rule. In fact, taking him by and large, I should say that of all the rollicking lads at the Drones Club, Claude Cattermole Pirbright is perhaps the most rollicking, both on the stage and off.

I say 'on the stage', for it is behind the footlights that he earns his weekly envelope. He comes of a prominent theatrical family. His father was the man who wrote the music of *The Blue Lady* and other substantial hits which I unfortunately missed owing to being in the cradle at the time. His mother was Elsie Cattermole, who was a star in New York for years. And his sister Corky has been wowing the customers with her oomph and *espièglerie*, if that's the word I want, since she was about sixteen.

It was almost inevitable, therefore, that, looking about him on coming down from Oxford for some walk in life which would ensure the three squares a day and give him time to play a bit of county cricket, he should have selected the sock and buskin. Today he is the fellow managers pick first when they have a Society comedy to present and want someone for 'Freddie', the lighthearted friend of the hero, carrying the second love interest. If at such a show you see a willowy figure come bounding on with a tennis racket, shouting 'Hallo, girls' shortly after the kick-off, don't bother to look at the programme. That'll be Catsmeat.

On such occasions he starts off sprightly and continues sprightly till closing time, and it is the same in private life. There, too, his sprightliness is a byword. Pongo Twistleton and Barmy Phipps, who do each year at the Drones smoker the knockabout Pat and Mike cross-talk act of which he is the author and producer, have told me that when rehearsing them in their lines and business, he is more like Groucho Marx than anything human.

Yet now, as I say, he was low-spirited. It stuck out a mile. His brow was sicklied o'er with the pale cast of thought and his air that of a man who, if he had said 'Hallo, girls', would have said it like someone in a Russian drama announcing that Grandpapa had hanged himself in the barn.

I greeted him cordially and said I was sorry I had been out when he had come seeking an audience before, especially as he had had Corky with him.

'I should have loved a chat with Corky,' I said. 'I had no idea she was back in England. Now I'm afraid I've missed her.'

'No, you haven't.'

'Yes, I have. I leave tomorrow for a place called Deverill Hall in Hampshire to help at the village concert. It seems that the vicar's niece insisted on having me in the troupe, and what's puzzling me is how this girl of God heard of me. One hadn't supposed one's reputation was so far flung.'

'You silly ass, she's Corky.'

'Corky?'

I was stunned. There are few better eggs in existence than Cora ('Corky') Pirbright, with whom I have been on the matiest of terms since the days when in our formative years we attended the same dancing class, but nothing in her deportment had ever given me the idea that she was related to the clergy.

'My Uncle Sidney is the vicar down there, and my aunt's away at Bournemouth. In her absence, Corky is keeping house for him.'

'My God! Poor old Sid! She tidies his study, no doubt?'

'Probably.'

'Straightens his tie?'

'I wouldn't be surprised.'

'And tells him he smokes too much, and every time he gets comfortably setted in an armchair boosts him out of it so that she can smooth the cushions. He must be feeling as if he were living in the book of Revelations. But doesn't she find a vicarage rather slow after Hollywood?'

'Not a bit. She loves it. Corky's different from me. I wouldn't be happy out of show business, but she was never really keen on it, though she's been such a success. I don't think she would have gone on the stage at all, if it hadn't been for Mother wanting her to so much. Her dream is to marry someone who lives in the country and spend the rest of her life knee-deep in cows and dogs and things. I suppose it's the old Farmer Giles strain in the Pirbrights coming out. My grandfather was a farmer. I can just remember him. Yards of whiskers, and always bellyaching about the weather. Messing about in the parish and getting up village concerts is her dish.'

'Any idea what she wants me to give the local yokels? Not the "Yeoman's Wedding Song", I trust?'

'No. You're billed to do the Pat part in that cross-talk act of mine.'

This came under the head of tidings of great joy. Too often at these binges the Brass Hats in charge tell you to render the 'Yeoman's Wedding Song', which for some reason always arouses the worst passions of the tough eggs who stand behind the back row. But no rustic standees have ever been known not to eat a knockabout cross-talk act. There is something about the spectacle of Performer A sloshing Performer B over the head with an umbrella and Performer B prodding Performer A in the midriff with a similar blunt instrument that seems to speak to their depths. Wearing a green beard and given adequate assistance by my supporting cast, I could confidently anticipate that I should have the clientele rolling in the aisles.

'Right. Fine. Splendid. I can now face the future with an uplifted heart. But if she wanted someone for Pat, why didn't she get you? You being a seasoned professional. Ah, I see what must have happened. She offered you the role and you drew yourself up haughtily, feeling that you were above this amateur stuff.'

Catsmeat shook the lemon sombrely.

'It wasn't that at all. Nothing would have pleased me more than to have performed at the King's Deverill concert, but the shot wasn't on the board. Those women at the hall hate my insides.'

'So you've met them? What are they like? A pretty stiffish nymphery, I suspect.'

'No, I haven't met them. But I'm engaged to their niece, Gertrude Winkworth, and the idea of her marrying me gives them the pip. If I showed myself within a mile of Deverill Hall, dogs would be set on me. Talking of dogs, Corky bought one this morning at the Battersea Home.'

'God bless her,' I said, speaking absently, for my thoughts were concentrated on this romance of his and I was trying to sort out his little ball of worsted from the mob of aunts and what-have-you of whom Jeeves had spoken. Then I got her placed. Gertrude, daughter of Dame Daphne Winkworth, relict of the late P.B. Winkworth, the historian.

'That's what I came to see you about.'

'Corky's dog?'

'No, this Gertrude business. I need your help. I'll tell you the whole story.'

On Catsmeat's entry I had provided him with a hospitable whisky and splash, and of this he had downed up to this point perhaps a couple of sips and a gulp. He now knocked back the residuum, and it seemed to touch the spot, for when it was down the hatch he spoke with animation and fluency.

'I should like to start by saying, Bertie, that since the first human crawled out of the primeval slime and life began on this planet nobody has ever loved anybody as I love Gertrude Winkworth. I mention this because I want you to realize that what you're sitting in on is not one of those light summer flirtations but the real West End stuff. I love her!'

'That's good. Where did you meet her?'

'At a house in Norfolk. They were doing some amateur theatricals and roped me in to produce. My God! Those twilight evenings in the old garden, with the birds singing sleepily in the shrubberies and the stars beginning to peep out in the –'

'Right ho. Carry on.'

'She's wonderful, Bertie. Why she loves me, I can't imagine.'

'But she does?'

'Oh yes, she does. We got engaged, and she returned to Deverill Hall to break the news to her mother. And when she did, what do you think happened?'

Well, of course, he had rather given away the punch of his story at the outset.

'The parent kicked?'

'She let out a yell you could have heard at Basingstoke.'

'Basingstoke being –'

'About twenty miles away as the crow flies.'

'I know Basingstoke. Bless my soul yes, know it well.'

'She –'

'I've stayed there as a boy. An old nurse of mine used to live at Basingstoke in a semi-detached villa called Balmoral. Her name was Hogg, oddly enough. Nurse Hogg. She suffered from hiccups.'

Catsmeat's manner became a bit tense. He looked like a village standee hearing the 'Yeoman's Wedding Song'.

'Listen, Bertie,' he said, 'suppose we don't talk about Basingstoke or about your nurse either. To hell with Basingstoke and to hell with your ruddy nurse, too. Where was I?'

'We broke off at the point where Dame Daphne Winkworth was letting out a yell.'

'That's right. Her sisters, when informed that Gertrude was proposing to marry the brother of the Miss Pirbright down at the

Vicarage and that this brother was an actor by profession, also let out yells.'

I toyed with the idea of asking if these, too, could have been heard at Basingstoke, but wiser counsels prevailed.

'They don't like Corky, and they don't like actors. In their young days, in the reign of Queen Elizabeth, actors were looked on as rogues and vagabonds, and they can't get it into their nuts that the modern actor is a substantial citizen who makes his sixty quid a week and salts most of it away in sound Government securities. Why, dash it, if I could think of some way of doing down the income-tax people, I should be a rich man. You don't know of a way of doing down the income-tax people do you, Bertie?'

'Sorry, no. I doubt if even Jeeves does. So you got the bird?'

'Yes. I had a sad letter from Gertrude saying no dice. You may ask why don't we elope?'

'I was just going to.'

'I couldn't swing it. She fears her mother's wrath.'

'A tough character, this mother?'

'Of the toughest. She used to be headmistress of a big girls' school. Gertrude was a member of the chain gang and has never got over it. No, elopements seem to be out. And here's the snag, Bertie. Corky has wangled a contract for me with her studio in Hollywood, and I may have to sail at any moment. It's a frightful situation.'

I was silent for a moment. I was trying to remember something I had read somewhere about something not quenching something, but I couldn't get at it. However, the general idea was that if a girl loves you and you are compelled to leave her in storage for a while, she will wait for you, so I put this point, and he said that was all very well but I didn't know all. The plot, he assured me, was about to thicken.

'We now come,' he said, 'to the hellhound Haddock. And this is where I want you to rally round, Bertie.'

I said I didn't get the gist, and he said of course I didn't get the damned gist, but couldn't I wait half a second, blast me, and give him a chance to explain, and I said Oh, rather, certainly.

'Haddock!' said Catsmeat, speaking between clenched teeth and exhibiting other signs of emotion. 'Haddock the Home Wrecker! Do you know anything about this Grade A louse, Bertie?'

'Only that his late father was the proprietor of those Headache Hokies.'

'And left him enough money to sink a ship. I'm not suggesting, of course, that Gertrude would marry him for his money. She would scorn such raw work. But in addition to having more cash than you could shake a stick at, he's a sort of Greek god in appearance and extremely magnetic. So Gertrude says. And, what is more, I gather from her letters that pressure is being brought to bear on her by the family. And you can imagine what the pressure of a mother and four aunts is like.'

I began to grasp the trend.

'You mean Haddock is trying to move in?'

'Gertrude writes that he is giving her the rush of a lifetime. And this will show you the sort of flitting and sipping butterfly the hound is. It's only a short while ago that he was giving Corky a similar rush. Ask her when you see her, but tactfully, because she's as sore as a gum-boil about it. I tell you, the man is a public menace. He ought to be kept on a chain in the interests of pure womanhood. But we'll fix him, won't we?'

'Will we?'

'You bet we will. Here's what I want you to do. You'll agree that even a fellow like Esmond Haddock, who appears to be the nearest thing yet discovered to South American Joe, couldn't press his foul suit in front of you?'

'You mean he would need privacy?'

'Exactly. So the moment you are inside Deverill Hall, start busting up his sinister game. Be always at Gertrude's side. Stick to her like glue. See that he doesn't get her alone in the rose garden. If a visit to the rose garden is mooted, include yourself in. You follow me, Bertie?'

'I follow you, yes,' I said, a little dubiously. 'What you have in mind is something on the lines of Mary's lamb. I don't know if you happen to know the poem – I used to recite it as a child – but, broadly, the nub was that Mary had a little lamb with fleece as white as snow, and everywhere that Mary went the lamb was sure to go. You want me to model my technique on that of Mary's lamb?'

'That's it. Be on the alert every second, for the peril is frightful. Well, to give you some idea, his most recent suggestion is that Gertrude and he shall take sandwiches one of these mornings and ride out to a place about fifteen miles away, where there are cliffs and things. And do you know what he plans to do when they get there? Show her the Lovers' Leap.'

'Oh, yes?'

'Don't say "Oh, yes?" in that casual way. Think, man. Fifteen miles there, then the Lovers' Leap, then fifteen miles back. The imagination reels at the thought of what excesses a fellow like Esmond Haddock may commit on a thirty-mile ride with a Lovers' Leap thrown in half-way. I don't know what day the expedition is planned for, but whenever it is, you must be with it from start to finish. If possible riding between them. And for God's sake don't take your eye off him for an instant at the Lovers' Leap. That will be the danger spot. If you notice the slightest disposition on his part, when at the Lovers' Leap, to lean towards her and whisper in her ear, break up the act like lightning. I'm relying on you, Bertie. My life's happiness depends on you.'

Well, of course, if a man you've been at private school, public school and Oxford with says he's relying on you, you have no option but to let yourself be relied on. To say that the assignment was one I liked would be over-stating the facts, but I right-hoed, and he grasped my hand and said that if there were more fellows like me in it the world would be a better place – a view which differed sharply from that of my Aunt Agatha, and one which I had a hunch was going to differ sharply from that of Esmond Haddock. There might be those at Deverill Hall who would come to love Bertram, but my bet was that E. Haddock's name would not be on the roster.

'Well, you've certainly eased my mind,' said Catsmeat, having released the hand and then re-grabbed and re-squeezed it. 'Knowing that you are on the spot, working like a beaver in my interests, will mean everything. I have been off my feed for some little time now, but I'm going to enjoy my dinner tonight. I only wish there was something I could do for you in return.'

'There is,' I said.

A thought had struck me, prompted no doubt by his mention of the word 'dinner'. Ever since Jeeves had told me about the coolness which existed between Gussie Fink-Nottle and Madeline Bassett I had been more than a bit worried at the thought of Gussie dining by himself that night.

I mean, you know how it is when you've had one of these lovers' tiffs and then go off to a solitary dinner. You start brooding over the girl with the soup and wonder if it wasn't a mug's game hitching up with her. With the fish this feeling deepens, and by the time you're through with the *poulet rôti au cresson* and are ordering the coffee you've probably come definitely to the conclusion that she's a rag and a bone and a hank of hair and that it would be madness to sign her on as a life partner.

What you need on these occasions is entertaining company, so that your dark thoughts may be diverted, and it seemed to me that here was the chance to provide Gussie with some.

'There is,' I said. 'You know Gussie Fink-Nottle? He's low-spirited, and there are reasons why I would prefer that he isn't alone tonight, brooding. Could you give him a spot of dinner?'

Catsmeat chewed his lip. I knew what was passing in his mind. He was thinking, as others have thought, that the first essential for an enjoyable dinner-party is for Gussie not to be at it.

'Give Gussie Fink-Nottle dinner?'

'That's right.'

'Why don't you?'

'My Aunt Agatha wants me to take her son Thomas to the Old Vic.'

'Give it a miss.'

'I can't. I should never hear the last of it.'

'Well, all right.'

'Heaven bless you, Catsmeat,' I said.

So Gussie was off my mind. It was with a light heart that I retired to rest that night. I little knew, as the expression is, what the morrow was to bring forth.

3

Though, as a matter of fact, in its early stages the morrow brought forth some pretty good stuff. As generally happens on these occasions when you are going to cop it in the quiet evenfall, the day started extremely well. Knowing that at 2.53 I was to shoot young Thos off to his seaside Borstal, I breakfasted with a song on my lips, and at lunch, I recall, I was in equally excellent fettle.

I took Thos to Victoria, bunged him into his train, slipped him a quid and stood waving a cousinly hand till he was out of sight. Then, after looking in at Queen's Club for a game or two of rackets, I went back to the flat, still chirpy.

Up till then everything had been fine. As I put hat on hat-peg and umbrella in umbrella-stand, I was thinking that if God wasn't in His heaven and all right with the world, these conditions prevailed as near as made no matter. Not the suspicion of an inkling, if you see what I mean, that round the corner lurked the bitter awakening, stuffed eelskin in hand, waiting to sock me on the occiput.

The first thing to which my attention was drawn on crossing the threshold was that there seemed to be a lot more noise going on than was suitable in a gentleman's home. Through the closed door of the sitting room the ear detected the sound of a female voice raised in what appeared to be cries of encouragement and, mingled with this female voice, a loud barking, as of hounds on the trail. It was as though my boudoir had been selected by the management of the Quorn or the Pytchley as the site for their most recent meet, and my first instinct, as that of any householder would have been, was to look into this. Nobody can call Bertram Wooster a fussy man, but there are moments when he feels he has to take a firm stand.

I opened the door, accordingly, and was immediately knocked base over apex by some solid body with a tongue like an anteater's. This tongue it proceeded to pass enthusiastically over my upper slopes and, the mists clearing away, I perceived that what I was tangled up with was a shaggy dog of mixed parentage. And standing beside us, looking down like a mother watching the gambols of her first-born, was Catsmeat's sister Corky.

'Isn't he a lamb?' she said. 'Isn't he an absolute seraph?'

I was not able wholly to subscribe to this view. The animal appeared to have an agreeable disposition and to have taken an immediate fancy to me, but physically it was no beauty-prize winner. It looked like Boris Karloff made up for something.

Corky, on the other hand, as always, distinctly took the eye. Two years in Hollywood had left her even easier to look at than when last seen around these parts.

This young prune is one of those lissom girls of medium height, constructed on the lines of Gertrude Lawrence, and her map had always been worth more than a passing glance. In repose, it has a sort of meditative expression, as if she were a pure white soul thinking beautiful thoughts, and, when animated, so dashed animated that it boosts the morale just to look at her. Her eyes are a kind of browny-hazel and her hair rather along the same lines. The general effect is of an angel who eats lots of yeast. In fine, if you were called upon to pick something to be cast on a desert island with, Hedy Lamarr might be your first choice, but Corky Pirbright would inevitably come high up in the list of Hon. Mentions.

'His name's Sam Goldwyn,' she proceeded, hauling the animal off the prostrate form. 'I bought him at the Battersea Home.'

I rose and dried the face.

'Yes, so Catsmeat told me.'

'Oh, you've seen Catsmeat? Good.'

At this point she seemed to become aware that we had skipped the customary pip-pippings, for she took time out to say how nice it was to see me again after all this time. I said how nice it was to see her again after all this time, and she asked me how I was, and I said I was fine. I asked her how she was, and she said she was fine. She enquired if I was still as big a chump as ever, and I satisfied her curiosity at this point.

'I looked in yesterday, hoping to see you,' she said, 'but you were out.'

'Yes, Jeeves told me.'

'A small boy with red hair entertained me. He said he was your cousin.'

'My Aunt Agatha's son and, oddly enough, the apple of her eye.'

'Why oddly enough?'

'He's the King of the Underworld. They call him The Shadow.'

'I liked him. I gave him fifty of my autographs. He's going to sell them to the boys at his school and expects to get sixpence apiece. He has long admired me on the screen, and we hit it off together like a couple of Yes-men. Catsmeat didn't seem to take to him so much.'

'He once put a drawing-pin on Catsmeat's chair.'

'Ah, that would account for the imperfect sympathy. Talking of Catsmeat, did he give you the Pat and Mike script?'

'Yes, I've got it. I was studying it in bed last night.'

'Good. It was sporting of you to rally round.'

I didn't tell her that my rallying round had been primarily due to *force majeure* on the part of an aunt who brooks, if that's the word, no back-chat. Instead, I asked who was to be my partner in the merry *mélange* of fun and topicality, sustaining the minor but exacting role of Mike, and she said an artiste of the name of Dobbs.

'Police Constable Dobbs, the local rozzer. And in this connection, Bertie, there is one thing I want to impress upon you with all the emphasis at my disposal. When socking Constable Dobbs with your umbrella at the points where the script calls for it, don't pull your punches. Let the blighter have it with every ounce of wrist and muscle. I want to see him come off that stage a mass of contusions.'

It seemed to me, for I am pretty quick, that she had it in for this Dobbs. I said so, and she concurred, a quick frown marring the alabaster purity of her brow.

'I have. I'm devoted to my poor old Uncle Sidney, and this uncouth bluebottle is a thorn in his flesh. He's the village atheist.'

'Oh, really? An atheist, is he? I never went in for that sort of thing much myself. In fact, at my private school I once won a prize for Scripture Knowledge.'

'He annoys Uncle Sidney by popping out at him from side streets and making offensive cracks about Jonah and the Whale. This cross-talk act has been sent from heaven. In ordinary life, I mean, you get so few opportunities of socking cops with umbrellas, and if ever a cop needed the treatment, it is Ernest Dobbs. When he isn't smirching Jonah and the Whale with his low sneers, he's asking Uncle Sidney where Cain got his wife. You can't say that sort of thing is pleasant for a sensitive vicar, so hew to the line, my poppet, and let the chips fall where they may.'

She had stirred the Wooster blood and aroused the Wooster chivalry. I assured her that by the time they struck up 'God Save The King' in the old village hall Constable Dobbs would know he had been in a fight, and she thanked me prettily.

'I can see you're going to be good, Bertie. And I don't mind telling you your public is expecting big things. For days the whole village has been talking of nothing else but the coming visit of Bertram Wooster, the great London comic. You will be the high spot of the programme. And goodness knows it can do with a high spot or two.'

'Who are the performers?'

'Just the scourings of the neighbourhood ... and Esmond Haddock. He's singing a song.'

The way she spoke that name, with a sort of frigid distaste as if it soiled her lips, told me that Catsmeat had not erred in saying that she was as sore as a gum-boil about E. Haddock's in-and-out running. Remembering that he had warned me to approach the subject tactfully, I picked my words with care.

'Ah, yes. Esmond Haddock. Catsmeat was telling me about Esmond Haddock.'

'What did he tell you?'

'Oh, this and that.'

'Featuring me?'

'Yes, to a certain extent featuring you.'

'What did he say?'

'Well, he seemed to hint, unless I misunderstood him, that the above Haddock hadn't, as it were, done right by our Nell. According to Catsmeat, you and this modern Casanova were at one time holding hands, but after flitting and sipping for a while he cast you aside like a worn-out glove and attached himself to Gertrude Winkworth. Quite incorrect, probably. I expect he got the whole story muddled up.'

She came clean. I suppose a girl who has been going about for some weeks as sore as a gum-boil, and with the heart cracked in two places gets to feel that maidenly pride is all very well but that what eases the soul is confession. And, of course, making me her confidant was not like spilling the inside stuff to a stranger. No doubt the thought crossed her mind that we had attended the same dancing class, and it may be that a vision of the child Wooster in a Little Lord Fauntleroy suit and pimples rose before her eyes.

'No, he didn't get the story muddled up. We were holding hands. But Esmond didn't cast me aside like a worn-out glove, I cast him aside like a worn-out glove. I told him I wouldn't have any more to do with him unless he asserted himself and stopped crawling to those aunts of his.'

'He crawls to his aunts, does he?'

'Yes, the worm.'

I could not pass this. Better men than Esmond Haddock have crawled to their aunts, and I said so, but she didn't seem to be listening. Girls seldom do listen to me, I've noticed. Her face was drawn and her eyes had a misty look. The lips, I observed, were a-quiver.

'I oughtn't to call him a worm. It's not his fault, really. They brought him up from the time he was six, oppressing him daily, and it's difficult for him to cast off the shackles, I suppose. I'm very sorry for him. But there's a limit. When it came to being scared to tell them we were engaged, I put my foot down. I said he'd got to tell them, and he turned green and said Oh, he couldn't, and I said All right, then, let's call the whole thing off. And I haven't spoken to him since, except to ask him to sing this song at the concert. And the unfortunate part of it all is, Bertie, that I'm crazier about him than ever. Just to think of him makes me want to howl and chew the carpet.'

At this point she buried her face in Sam Goldwyn's coat, ostensibly by way of showing a proprietress's affection, but really, I could see, being shrewd, in order to dry the starting tears. Personally, for the animal niffed to heaven, I would have preferred to use my cambric handkerchief, but girls will be girls.

'Oh, well,' she said, coming to the surface again.

It was a bit difficult to know how to carry on. A 'There, there, little woman' might have gone well, or it might not. After thinking it over for a moment, I too-badded.

'Oh, it's all right,' she said, stiffening the upper lip. 'Just one of those things. When do you go down to Deverill?'

'This evening.'

'How do you feel about it?'

'Not too good. A certain coolness in the feet. I'm never at my best in the society of aunts and, according to Jeeves, they assemble in gangs at Deverill Hall. There are five of them, he says.'

'That's right.'

'It's a lot.'

'Five too many. I don't think you'll like them, Bertie. One's deaf, one's dotty, and they're all bitches.'

'You use strong words, child.'

'Only because I can't think of any stronger. They're awful. They've lived all their lives at that mouldering old hall, and they're like something out of a three-volume novel. They judge everybody by the county standard. If you aren't county, you don't exist. I believe they swooned for weeks when their sister married Esmond's father.'

'Yes, Jeeves rather suggested that in their opinion he soiled the escutcheon.'

'Nothing to the way I would have soiled it. Being in pix, I'm the scarlet woman.'

'I've often wondered about that scarlet woman. Was she scarlet all over, or was it just that her face was red? However, that is not germane to the issue. So that's how it is, is it?'

'That's how it is.'

I was rather glad that at this juncture the hound Sam Goldwyn made another of his sudden dives at my abdomen with the slogan 'Back to Bertram' on his lips, for it enabled me to bridge over an emotional moment. I was considerably concerned. What was to be done about it, I didn't know, but there was no gainsaying that when it came to making matrimonial plans, the Pirbrights were not a lucky family.

Corky seemed to be feeling this, too.

'It would happen, wouldn't it,' she said, 'that the only one of all the millions of men I've met that I've ever wanted to marry can't marry me because his aunts won't let him.'

'It's tough on you,' I agreed.

'And just as tough on poor old Catsmeat. You wouldn't think, just seeing him around, that Catsmeat was the sort of man to break his heart over a girl, but he is. He's full of hidden depths, if you really know him. Gertrude means simply everything to him. And I doubt if she will be able to hold out against a combination of Esmond and her mother and the aunts.'

'Yes, he told me pressure was being applied.'

'How did you think he seemed?'

'Low-spirited.'

'Yes, he's taking it hard,' said Corky.

Her face clouded. Catsmeat has always been her ewe lamb, if you understand what I mean by ewe lamb. It was plain that she mourned for him in spirit, and no doubt at this point we should have settled down to a long talk about his spot of bother, examining it from every angle and trying to decide what was to be done for the best, had not the door opened and he blown in in person.

'Hallo, Catsmeat,' I said.

'Hallo, Catsmeat, darling,' said Corky.

'Hallo,' said Catsmeat.

I looked at Corky. She looked at me. I rather think we pursed our lips and, speaking for myself, I know I raised my eyebrows. For the demeanour of this Pirbright was that of a man who has abandoned hope, and the voice in which he had said 'Hallo' had been to all intents and purposes a voice from the tomb. The whole set-up, in short, such as to occasion pity and terror in the bosoms of those who wished him well.

He sank into a chair and closed his eyes, and for some moments remained motionless. Then, as if a bomb had suddenly exploded inside the bean, he shot up with a stifled cry, clasping his temples, and I began to see daylight. His deportment, so plainly that of a man aware that only prompt action in the nick of time has prevented his head splitting in half, told me that we had been mistaken in supposing that this living corpse had got that way purely through disappointed love. I touched the bell, and Jeeves appeared.

'One of your special morning-afters, if you please, Jeeves.'

'Very good, sir.'

He shimmered out, and I subjected Catsmeat to a keen glance. I am told by those who know that there are six varieties of hangover – the Broken Compass, the Sewing Machine, the Comet, the Atomic, the Cement Mixer and the Gremlin Boogie, and his manner suggested that he had got them all.

'So you were lathered last night?' I said.

'I was perhaps a mite polluted,' he admitted.

'Jeeves has gone for one of his revivers.'

'Thank you, Bertie, thank you,' said Catsmeat in a low, soft voice, and closed his eyes again.

His intention obviously was to restore his tissues with a short nap, and personally I would have left him alone and let him go to it. But Corky was of sterner stuff. She took his head in both hands and shook it, causing him to shoot ceilingwards, this time with a cry so little stifled that it rang through the room like the death rattle of a hundred expiring hyenas. The natural consequence was that Sam Goldwyn began splitting the welkin, and with the view of taking him off the air I steered him to the door and bunged him out. I returned to find Corky ticking Catsmeat off in no uncertain manner.

'You promised me faithfully you wouldn't get pie-eyed, you poor fish,' she was saying with sisterly vehemence. 'What price the word of the Pirbrights?'

'That's all right "What price the word of the Pirbrights?"' retorted Catsmeat with some spirit. 'When I gave the word of the Pirbrights that I wouldn't get pie-eyed, I didn't know I should be dining with Gussie Fink-Nottle. Bertie will bear me out that it is not humanly possible to get through an evening alone with Gussie without large quantities of stimulants.'

I nodded.

'He's quite right,' I said. 'Even at the peak of his form Gussie isn't everybody's dream-comrade, and last night I should imagine he was low-spirited.'

'Very low-spirited,' said Catsmeat. 'In my early touring days I have sometimes arrived at Southport on a rainy Sunday morning. Gussie gave me that same sense of hopeless desolation. He sat there with his lower jaw drooping, goggling at me like a codfish –'

'Gussie,' I explained to Corky, 'has had a lovers' tiff with his betrothed.'

'– until after a bit I saw that there was only one thing to be done, if I was to survive the ordeal. I told the waiter to bring a magnum and leave it at my elbow. After that, things seemed to get better.'

'Gussie, of course, drank orange juice?'

'Throughout,' said Catsmeat with a slight shudder.

I could see that even though he had made this manly, straightforward statement, Corky was still threatening to do the heavy sister and heap reproaches on a man who was in no condition to receive them, for even the best of women cannot refrain from saying their say the morning after, so I hastened to continue the conversation on a neutral note.

'Where did you dine?'

'At the Dorchester.'

'Go anywhere after dinner?'

'Oh, yes.'

'Where?'

'Oh, hither and thither. East Dulwich, Ponder's End, Limehouse –'

'Why Limehouse?'

'Well, I had always wanted to see it, and I may have had some idea of comparing its blues with mine. As to East Dulwich and Ponder's End, I am not sure. Perhaps I heard someone recommend them, or possibly I just felt that the thing to do was to get about and see fresh faces. I had chartered a taxi for the evening and we roamed around, taking in the sights. Eventually we fetched up in Trafalgar Square.'

'What time was this?'

'About five in the morning. Have you ever been in Trafalgar Square at five in the morning? Very picturesque, that fountain in the first early light of the dawn. It was as we stood on its brink with the sun just beginning to gild the house-tops that I got an idea which I can now see, though it seemed a good one at the time, was a mistake.'

'What was that?'

'It struck me as a possibility that there might be newts in the fountain, and knowing how keen Gussie is on newts I advised him to wade in and hunt around.'

'With all his clothes on?'

'Yes, he had his clothes on. I remember noticing.'

'But you can't go wading in the Trafalgar Square fountain with all your clothes on.'

'Yes, you can. Gussie did. My recollection of the thing is a trifle blurred, but I seem to recall that he took a bit of persuading. Yes, I've got it now,' said Catsmeat, brightening. 'I told him to wade, and he wouldn't wade, and I said if he didn't wade I would bean him with my magnum. So he waded.'

'You still had the magnum?'

'This was another one, which we had picked up in Limehouse.'

'And Gussie waded?'

'Yes, Gussie waded.'

'I wonder he wasn't pinched.'

'He was,' said Catsmeat. 'A cop came along and gaffed him, and this morning he was given fourteen days without the option at Bosher Street police court.'

The door opened. Sam Goldwyn came bounding in and flung himself on my chest as if we had been a couple of lovers meeting at journey's end.

He was followed by Jeeves, bearing a salver with a glass on it containing one of his dynamite specials.

4

When I was a piefaced lad of some twelve summers, doing my stretch at Malvern House, Bramley-on-Sea, the private school conducted by the Rev. Aubrey Upjohn, I remember hearing the Rev. Aubrey give the late Sir Philip Sidney a big build-up because, when wounded at the battle of somewhere and offered a quick one by a companion in arms, he told the chap who was setting them up to leave him out of that round and slip his spot to a nearby stretcher-case, whose need was greater than his. This spirit of selfless sacrifice, said the Rev. Aubrey, was what he would like to see in you boys – particularly you, Wooster, and how many times have I told you not to gape at me in that half-witted way? Close your mouth, boy, and sit up.

Well, if he had been one of our little circle, he would have seen it now. My primary impulse was to charge across and grab that glass from that salver and lower it at a gulp, for if ever I needed a bracer, it was then. But I stayed my hand. Even in that dreadful moment I was able to tell myself that Catsmeat's need was greater than mine. I stood back, shimmying in every limb, and he got the juice and drained it, and after going through the motions of a man struck by lighting, always the immediate reaction to these pick-me-ups of Jeeves's, said 'Ha!' and looked a lot better.

I passed a fevered hand across the brow.

'Jeeves!'

'Sir?'

'Do you know what?'

'No, sir.'

'Gussie Fink-Nottle is in stir.'

'Indeed, sir?'

I passed another hand across the brow, and the blood pressure rose several notches. I ought, I suppose, to have got it into my nut by this time that no news item, however front page, is going to make Jeeves roll his eyes and leap about, but that 'Indeed, sir?' stuff of his never fails to get the Wooster goat.

'Don't say "Indeed, sir?" I repeat. Wading in the Trafalgar Square fountain at five ack emma this morning, Augustus Fink-Nottle was apprehended by the police and is in the coop for fourteen days. And he's due at Deverill Hall this evening.'

Catsmeat, who had closed his eyes, opened them for a moment. 'Shall I tell you something?' he said. 'He won't be there.'

He reclosed the eyes, and I passed a third hand across the brow.

'You see the ghastly position, Jeeves? What is Miss Bassett going to say? What will her attitude be when she learns the facts? She opens tomorrow's paper. She sees that loved name in headlines in the police court section . . .'

'No, she doesn't,' said Catsmeat. 'Because Gussie, showing unexpected intelligence, gave his name as Alfred Duff Cooper.'

'Well, what's going to happen when he doesn't turn up at the Hall?'

'Yes, there's that,' said Catsmeat, and fell into a refreshing sleep.

'I'll tell you what Miss Bassett is going to say. She is going to say . . . Jeeves!'

'Sir?'

'You are letting your attention wander.'

'I beg your pardon, sir. I was observing the dog. If you notice, sir, he has commenced to eat the sofa cushion.'

'Never mind about the dog.'

'I think it would be advisable to remove the little fellow to the kitchen, sir,' he said with respectful firmness. Jeeves is a great stickler for having things just right. 'I will return as soon as he is safely immured.'

He withdrew, complete with dog, and Corky caught the speaker's eye. For some moments she had been hovering on the outskirts with the air of one not completely abreast of the continuity.

'But, Bertie,' she said, 'why all the excitement and agony? I could understand this Mr Fink-Nottle being a little upset, but why are you skipping like the high hills?'

I was glad that Jeeves had temporarily absented himself from the conference-table, as it would have been impossible for me to unbosom myself freely about Madeline Bassett in his presence. Naturally he knows all the circumstances *in re* the Bassett, and I know he knows them, but we do not discuss her. To do so would be bandying a woman's name. The Woosters do not bandy a woman's name. Nor, for the matter of that, do the Jeeveses.

'Hasn't Catsmeat told you about me and Madeline Bassett?'

'Not a word.'

'Well, I'll tell you why I'm skipping like the high hills,' I said, and proceeded to do so.

The Bassett-Wooster imbroglio or mix-up will, of course, be old stuff to those of my public who were hanging on my lips when I told of it before, but there are always new members coming along, and for the benefit of these new members I will give a brief what's-it-called of the facts.

The thing started at Brinkley Court, my Aunt Dahlia's place in Worcestershire, when Gussie and I and this blighted Bassett were putting in a spell there during the previous summer. It was one of those cases you so often read about where Bloke A loves a girl but fears to speak and a friend of his, Bloke B, out of the kindness of his heart, offers to pave the way for him with a few well-chosen words – completely overlooking, poor fathead, the fact that by doing so he will be sticking his neck out and simply asking for it. What I'm driving at is that Gussie, though very much under the influence, could not bring himself to start the necessary *pourparlers*, and like an ass I told him to leave this to me.

And so, steering the girl out into the twilight one evening, I pulled some most injudicious stuff about there being hearts at Brinkley Court that ached for love of her. And the first thing I knew, she was saying that of course she had guessed how I felt, for a girl always knows, doesn't she, but she was so, so sorry it could not be, for she was sold on Gussie. But, she went on, and it was this that had made peril lurk ever since, if there should come a time when she found that Gussie was not the rare, stainless soul she thought him, she would hand him his hat and make me happy.

And, as I have related elsewhere, there had been moments when it had been touch and go, notably on the occasion when Gussie got lit up like a candelabra and in that condition presented the prizes to the young scholars of Market Snodsbury Grammar School. She had scratched his nomination then, though subsequently relenting, and it could not but be that she would scratch it again, should she discover that the man on whom she looked as a purer, loftier spirit than other men had received an exemplary sentence for wading in the Trafalgar Square fountain. Nothing puts an idealistic girl off a fellow more than the news that he is doing fourteen days in the jug.

All this I explained to Corky, and she said Yes, she saw what I meant.

'I should think you do see what I mean. I shan't have a hope. Let Madeline Bassett become hep to what has occurred, and there can be but one result. Gussie will get the bum's rush, and the bowed figure you will see shambling down the aisle at her side, while the customers reach for their hats and the organ plays 'The Voice That Breathed O'er Eden', will be that of Bertram Wilberforce Wooster.'

'I didn't know your name was Wilberforce.'

I explained that except in moments of great emotion one hushed it up.

'But Bertie, I can't understand why you don't want to shamble down aisles at her side. I've seen a photograph of her at the Hall, and she's a pippin.'

This is a very common error into which people fall who have never met Madeline Bassett but have only seen her photograph. As far as the outer crust is concerned, there is little, I fully realize, to cavil at in this pre-eminent bit of bad news. The eyes are large and lustrous, the features delicately moulded, the hair, nose, teeth and ears well up to, if not above, the average standard. Judge her by the photograph alone, and you have something that would be widely accepted as a pin-up girl.

But there is a catch, and a very serious catch.

'You ask me why I do not wish to shamble down aisles at her side,' I said. 'I will tell you. It is because, though externally, as you say, a pippin, she is the sloppiest, mushiest, sentimentalest young Gawd-help-us who ever thought the stars were God's daisy chain and that every time a fairy hiccoughs a wee baby is born. She is squashy and soupy. Her favourite reading is Christopher Robin and Winnie the Pooh. I can perhaps best sum it up by saying that she is the ideal mate for Gussie Fink-Nottle.'

'I've never met Mr Fink-Nottle.'

'Well, ask the man who has.'

She stood pondering. It was plain that she appreciated the gravity of the situation.

'Then you think that, if she finds out, you will be in for it?'

'Definitely and indubitably. I shall have no option but to take the rap. If a girl thinks you love her, and comes and says she is returning her betrothed to store and is now prepared to sign up with you, what can you do except marry her? One must be civil.'

'Yes, I see. Difficult. But how are you going to keep her from finding out? When she hears that Mr Fink-Nottle hasn't arrived at the Hall, she's bound to make inquiries.'

'And those inquiries, once made, must infallibly lead her to the awful truth? Exactly. But there is always Jeeves.'

'You think he will be able to fix things?'

'He never fails. He wears a number fourteen hat, eats tons of fish, and moves in a mysterious way his wonders to perform See, here he comes, looking as intelligent as dammit. Well, Jeeves? Have you speared a solution?'

'Yes, sir. But –'

'You see,' I said to Corky. I paused, knitting the brow a bit. 'Did I hear you use the word "but", Jeeves? Why "but"?'

'It is merely that I entertained a certain misgiving as to whether the solution which I am about to put forward would meet with your approval, sir.'

'If it's a solution, that's all I want.'

'Well, sir, to obviate the inquiries which would inevitably be set on foot, should Mr Fink-Nottle not present himself at Deverill Hall this evening, it would appear to be essential that a substitute, purporting to be Mr Fink-Nottle, should take his place.'

I reeled.

'You aren't suggesting that I should check in at this leper colony as Gussie?'

'Unless you can persuade one of your friends to do so, sir.'

I laughed. One of those hollow, mirthless ones.

'You can't go about London asking people to pretend to be Gussie Fink-Nottle. At least, you can, I suppose, but what a hell of a life. Besides, there isn't time to . . .' I paused. 'Catsmeat!' I cried.

Catsmeat opened his eyes.

'Hallo, there,' he said, seeming much refreshed. 'How's it coming?'

'It's come. Jeeves has found the way.'

'I thought he would. What does he suggest?'

'He thinks . . . What was it, Jeeves?'

'To obviate the inquiries which would inevitably be set on foot should Mr Fink-Nottle not present himself at Deverill Hall this evening –'

'Follow this closely, Catsmeat.'

'– it would appear to be essential that a substitute, purporting to be Mr Fink-Nottle, should take his place.'

Catsmeat nodded, and said he considered that very sound.

'You mean Bertie, of course?'

I massaged his coat sleeve tenderly.

'We thought of you,' I said.

'Me?'

'Yes.'

'You want me to say I'm Gussie Fink-Nottle?'

'That's right.'

'No,' said Catsmeat. 'A thousand times no. What a revolting idea!'

The shuddering horror with which he spoke made me realize how deeply his experiences of the previous night must have affected him. And, mind you, I could understand his attitude. Gussie is a fellow you can take or leave alone, and anyone having him as a constant companion from eight at night till five on the following morning might well become a bit allergic to him. I began to see that a good deal of silver-tongued eloquence would be needed in order to obtain service and cooperation from C.C. Pirbright.

'It would enable you to be beneath the same roof as Gertrude Winkworth,' I urged.

'Yes,' said Corky, 'you would be at your Gertrude's side.'

'Even to be at my Gertrude's side,' said Catsmeat firmly, 'I won't have people going about thinking I'm Gussie Fink-Nottle. Besides, I couldn't get away with it. I shouldn't be even adequate in the role. I'm much too obviously a man of intelligence and brains and gifts and all that sort of thing, and Gussie must have been widely publicized as the fat-headedest ass in creation. After five minutes' conversation with me the old folks would penetrate the deception like a dose of salts. No, what you want if you are putting on an understudy for Gussie Fink-Nottle is someone *like* Gussie Fink-Nottle, so that the eye is deceived. You get the part, Bertie.'

A cry escaped me.

'You don't think I'm like Gussie?'

'You might be twins.'

'I still think you're a chump, Catsmeat,' said Corky. 'If you were at Deverill Hall you could protect Gertrude from Esmond Haddock's advances.'

'Bertie's attending to that. I agree that I would much enjoy a brief visit to Deverill Hall, and if only there were some other way . . . But I won't say I'm Gussie Fink-Nottle.'

I bowed to the inev.

'Right ho,' I said, with one of those sighs. 'In all human affairs there has got to be a goat or Patsy doing the dirty work, and in the present crisis I see it has got to be me. It generally happens that way. Whenever there is a job to be taken on of a kind calculated to make Humanity shudder, the cry goes up "Let Wooster do it." I'm not complaining, I'm just mentioning it. Very well. No need to argue. I'll be Gussie.'

'Smiling, the boy fell dead. That's the way I like to hear you talk,' said Catsmeat. 'On the way down be thinking out your business.'

'What do you mean – my business?'

'Well, for instance, would it or would it not be a good move to kiss Gussie's girl's godmother when you meet? Those are the little points you will have to give thought to. And now, Bertie, if you don't mind, I'll be pushing along to your bedroom and taking a short nap. Too many interruptions in here, and sleep is what I must have, if I am to face the world again. What was it I heard you call sleep the other day, Jeeves?'

'Tired Nature's sweet restorer, sir.'

'That was it. And you said a mouthful.'

He crawled off, and Corky said she would have to be going too. A hundred things to attend to.

'Well, it all looks pretty smooth now, thanks to your quick thinking, Jeeves,' she said. 'The only nuisance is that there will be disappointment in the village when they hear they're going to get a Road Company Number Four Fink-Nottle as Pat, and not the celebrated Bertram Wooster. I rather played you up, Bertie, in the advance billing and publicity. Still, it can't be helped. Goodbye. We shall meet at Philippi. Goodbye, Jeeves.'

'Goodbye, miss.'

'Here, half a second,' I said. 'You're forgetting your dog.'

She paused at the door.

'Oh, I had been meaning to tell you about that, Bertie. I want you to take him to the hall with you for a day or two, so as to give me time to prepare Uncle Sidney's mind. He's not too keen on dogs, and Sam will have to be broken to him gently.'

I put in an instant *nolle prosequi*.

'I'm not going to appear at the hall with a dog like that. It would ruin my prestige.'

'Mr Fink-Nottle's prestige, you mean. And I don't suppose he has any. As Catsmeat said, they have been told all about him, and will probably be relieved that you aren't rolling in with half a dozen bowls of newts. Well, goodbye again.'

'Hey!' I yipped, but she had gone.

I turned to Jeeves.

'So, Jeeves!'

'Yes, sir.'

'What do you mean, "Yes, sir"?'

'I was endeavouring to convey my appreciation of the fact that your position *is* in many respects somewhat difficult, sir. But I wonder if I might call your attention to an observation of the Emperor Marcus Aurelius. He said: "Does aught befall you? It is good. It is part of the destiny of the Universe ordained for you from the beginning. All that befalls you is part of the great web.""

I breathed a bit stertorously.

'He said that, did he?'

'Yes, sir.'

'Well, you can tell him from me he's an ass. Are my things packed?'

'Yes, sir.'

'The two-seater is at the door?'

'Yes, sir.'

'Then lead me to it, Jeeves. If I'm to get to this lazar-house before midnight, I'd better be starting.'

Well, I did get there before midnight, of course, but I was dashed late, all the same. As might have been expected on a day like this, the two-seater, usually as reliable as an Arab steed, developed some sort of pox or sickness half-way through the journey, with the result that the time schedule was shot to pieces and it was getting on for eight when I turned in at the main gates. A quick burst up the drive enabled me to punch the front-door bell at about twenty to.

I remember once when he and I arrived at a country house where the going threatened to be sticky, Jeeves, as we alighted, murmured in my ear the words 'Childe Roland to the Dark Tower came, sir', and at the time I could make nothing of the crack. Subsequent inquiry, however, revealed that this Roland was one of those knights of the Middle Ages who spent their time wandering to and fro, and that on fetching up one evening at a dump known as the Dark Tower he had scratched the chin a bit dubiously, not liking the look of things.

It was the same with me now. I admired Deverill Hall, I could appreciate that it was a fine old pile, with battlements and all the fixings, and if the Deverill who built it had been with me at the moment, I would have slapped him on the back and said 'Nice work, Deverill'. But I quailed at the thought of what lay within. Behind that massive front door lurked five aunts of early Victorian vintage and an Esmond Haddock who, when he got on to the fact that I was proposing to pull a Mary's lamb on him, was quite likely to forget the obligations of a host and break my neck. Considerations like these prevent one feasting the eye on Tudor architecture with genuine enjoyment and take from fifty to sixty per cent off the entertainment value of spreading lawns and gay flower-beds.

The door opened, revealing some sixteen stone of butler.

'Good evening, sir,' said this substantial specimen. 'Mr Wooster?'

'Fink-Nottle,' I said hastily, to correct this impression.

As a matter of fact, it was all I could do to speak at all, for the sudden impact of Charlie Silversmith had removed the breath almost totally. He took me right back to the days when I was starting out as a *flâneur* and man about town and used to tremble beneath butlers' eyes and generally feel very young and bulbous.

Older now and tougher, I am able to take most of these fauna in my stride. When they open front doors to me, I shoot my cuffs nonchalantly. 'Aha, there, butler,' I say. 'How's tricks?' But Jeeves's Uncle Charlie was something special. He looked like one of those steel engravings of nineteenth-century statesmen. He had a large, bald head and pale, protruding gooseberry eyes, and those eyes, resting on mine, heightened the Dark Tower feeling considerably. The thought crossed my mind that if something like this had popped out at Childe Roland, he would have clapped spurs to his charger and been off like a jack-rabbit.

Sam Goldwyn, attached by a stout cord to the windscreen, seemed to be thinking along much the same lines, for, after one startled glance at Uncle Charlie, he had thrown his head back and was now uttering a series of agitated howls. I sympathized with his distress. A South London dog belonging to the lower middle classes or, rather, definitely of the people, I don't suppose he had ever seen a butler before, and it was a dashed shame that he should have drawn something like Uncle Charlie first crack out of the box. With an apologetic jerk of the thumb I directed the latter's attention to him.

'A dog,' I said, this seeming about as good a way as any other of effecting the introductions, and Uncle Charlie gave him an austere look, as if he had found him using a fish fork for the entrée.

'I will have the animal removed to the stables, sir,' he said coldly, and I said Oh, thanks, that would be fine.

'And now,' I said, 'I'd better be nipping along and dressing, what? I don't want to be late for dinner.'

'Dinner has already commenced, sir. We dine at seven-thirty punctually. If you would care to wash your hands, sir,' he said, and indicated a door to the left.

In the circles in which I move it is pretty generally recognized that I am a resilient sort of bimbo, and in circumstances where others might crack beneath the strain, may frequently be seen rising on stepping-stones of my dead self to higher things. Look in at the Drones and ask the first fellow you meet 'Can the fine spirit of the Woosters be crushed?' and he will offer you attractive odds against such a contingency. However tough the going, he will say, and however numerous what are called the slings and arrows of outrageous fortune, you will still find Bertram in there swinging.

But I had never before been thrust into the position of having to say I was Gussie Fink-Nottle and slap on top of that of having to dine in a strange house without dressing, and I don't mind admitting that for an instant everything went black. It was a limp and tottering Bertram Wooster who soaped, rinsed and dried the outlying portions and followed Uncle Charlie to the dining room. And what with the agony of feeling like a tramp cyclist and the embarrassment of having to bolt my rations with everybody, or so it seemed to my inflamed imag, clicking their tongues and drumming on the table and saying to one another in undertones what a hell of a nuisance this hold-up was, because they wanted the next course to appear so that they could start digging in and getting theirs, it was not for some time that I was sufficiently restored to be able to glance around the board and take a dekko at the personnel. There had been introductions of a sort, of course – I seemed to recall Uncle Charlie saying 'Mr Fink-Nottle' in a reserved sort of voice, as if wishing to make it clear that it was no good blaming *him* – but they hadn't really registered.

As far as the eye could reach, I found myself gazing on a surging sea of aunts. There were tall aunts, short aunts, stout aunts, thin aunts, and an aunt who was carrying on a conversation in a low voice to which nobody seemed to be paying the slightest attention. I was to learn later that this was Miss Emmeline Deverill's habitual practice, she being the aunt of whom Corky had spoken as the dotty one. From start to finish of every meal she soliloquized. Shakespeare would have liked her.

At the top of the table was a youngish bloke in a well-cut dinner jacket which made me more than ever conscious of the travel-stained upholstery in which I had been forced to appear. E. Haddock, presumably. He was sitting next to a girl in white, so obviously the junior member of the bunch that I deduced that here we had Catsmeat's Gertrude.

Drinking her in, I could see how Catsmeat had got that way. The daughter of Dame Daphne, relict of the late P.B. Winkworth, was slim and blonde and fragile, in sharp contradistinction to her mother, whom I had now identified as the one on my left, a rugged light-heavyweight with a touch of Wallace Beery in her make-up. Her eyes were blue, her teeth pearly, and in other respects she had what it takes. I was quite able to follow Catsmeat's thought processes. According to his own statement, he had walked with this girl in an old garden on twilight evenings, with the birds singing sleepily in the shrubberies and the stars beginning to peep out, and no man of spirit could do that with a girl like this without going under the ether.

I was musing on these two young hearts in springtime and speculating with a not unmanly touch of sentiment on their chances of spearing the happy ending, when the subject of the concert came up.

The conversation at the table up to this point had been pretty technical stuff, not easy for the stranger within the gates to get a toe-hold on. You know the sort of thing I mean. One aunt saying that she had had a letter from Emily by the afternoon post, and another aunt saying Had she said anything about Fred and Alice, and the first aunt saying Yes, everything was all right about Fred and Alice, because Agnes had now told Edith what Jane had said to Eleanor. All rather mystic.

But now an aunt in spectacles said she had met the vicar that evening and the poor old gook was spitting blood because his niece, Miss Pirbright, insisted on introducing into the programme of the concert what she described as a knockabout cross-talk act by Police Constable Dobbs and Agatha Worplesdon's nephew, Mr Wooster. What a knockabout cross-talk act was, she had no idea. Perhaps you can tell us, Augustus?

I was only too glad to have the opportunity of saying a few words, for, except for a sort of simpering giggle at the outset, I hadn't uttered since joining the party, and I felt it was about time, for Gussie's sake, that I came out of the silence. Carry along on these lines much longer, and the whole gang would be at their desks writing letters to the Bassett entreating her to think twice before entrusting her happiness to a dumb brick who would probably dish the success of the honeymoon by dashing off in the middle of it to become a Trappist monk.

'Oh, rather,' I said. 'It's one of those Pat and Mike things. Two birds come on in green beards, armed with umbrellas, and one bird says to the other bird 'Who was that lady I saw you coming down the street with?' and the second bird says to the first bird 'Faith and begob, that was no lady, that was my wife.' And then the second bird busts the first bird over the bean with his umbrella, and the first bird, not to be behindhand, busts the second bird over the head with *his* umbrella. And so the long day wears on.'

It didn't go well. There was a sharp intake of breath from one and all.

'Very vulgar!' said one aunt.

'Terribly vulgar!' said another.

'Disgustingly vulgar,' said Dame Daphne Winkworth. 'But how typical of Miss Pirbright to suggest such a performance at a village concert.'

The rest of the aunts didn't say 'You betcher' or 'You've got something there, Daph', but their manner suggested these words. Lips were pursed and noses looked down. I began to get on to what Catsmeat had meant when he had said that these females did not approve of Corky. Her stock was plainly down in the cellar and the market sluggish.

'Well, I am glad,' said the aunt in spectacles, 'that it is this Mr Wooster and not you, Augustus, who is disgracing himself by taking part in this degrading horseplay. Imagine how Madeline would feel!'

'Madeline would never get over it,' said a thin aunt.

'Dear Madeline is so spiritual,' said Dame Daphne Winkworth.

A cold hand seemed to clutch at my heart. I felt like a Gadarene swine that has come within a toucher of doing a nose-dive over the precipice. You'll scarcely believe it, but it had never so much as crossed my mind that Madeline Bassett, on learning that her lover had been going about in a green beard socking policemen with umbrellas, would be revolted to the depths of her soul. Why, dash it, the engagement wouldn't go on functioning for a minute after the news had reached her. You can't be too careful how you stir up these romantic girls with high ideals. A Gussie in a green beard would be almost worse than a Gussie in the cooler.

It gave me a pang to hand in my portfolio, for I had been looking forward to a sensational triumph, but I know when I'm licked. I resolved that bright and early tomorrow morning word must be sent to Corky that Bertram was out and that she would have to enlist the services of another artist for the role of Pat.

'From all I have heard of Mr Wooster,' said an aunt with a beaky nose, continuing the theme, 'this kind of vulgar foolery will be quite congenial to him. By the way, where *is* Mr Wooster?'

'Yes,' chimed in the aunt with spectacles. 'He was to have arrived this afternoon, and he has not even sent a telegram.'

'He must be a most erratic young man,' said a third aunt, who would have been the better for a good facial.

Dame Daphne took command of the conversation like a headmistress at a conference of her subordinates.

'"Erratic",' she said, 'is a kindly term. He appears to be completely irresponsible. Agatha tells me that sometimes she despairs of him. She says she often wonders if the best thing would not be to put him in a home of some kind.'

You may picture the emotions of Bertram on learning that his flesh and blood was in the habit of roasting the pants off him in this manner. One doesn't demand much in the way of gratitude, of course, but when you have gone to the expense and inconvenience of taking an aunt's son to the Old Vic, you are justified, I think, in expecting her to behave like an aunt who has had her son taken to the Old Vic – in expecting her, in other words, to exhibit a little decent feeling and a modicum of the live-and-let-live spirit. How sharper than a serpent's tooth, I remember Jeeves saying once, it is to have a thankless child, and it isn't a dashed sight better having a thankless aunt.

I flushed darkly, and would have drained my glass if it had contained anything restorative. But it didn't. Champagne of a sound vintage was flowing like water elsewhere, Uncle Charlie getting a stiff wrist pouring the stuff, but I, in deference to Gussie's known tastes, had been served with that obscene beverage which is produced by putting half an orange on a squeezer and pushing.

'There seems,' proceeded Dame Daphne in the cold and disapproving voice which in the old days she would have employed when rebuking Maud or Beatrice for smoking gaspers in the shrubbery, 'to be no end to his escapades. It is not so long ago that he was arrested and fined for stealing a policeman's helmet in Piccadilly.'

I could put her straight there, and did so.

'That,' I explained, 'was due to an unfortunate oversight. In pinching a policeman's helmet, as of course I don't need to tell you, it is essential before lifting to give a forward shove in order to detach the strap from the officer's chin. This Wooster omitted to do, with the results you have described. But I think you ought to take into consideration the fact that the incident occurred pretty late on Boat Race night, when the best of men are not quite themselves. Still, be that as it may,' I said, quickly sensing that I had not got the sympathy of the audience and adroitly changing the subject, 'I wonder if you know the one about the strip-tease dancer and the performing flea. Or, rather, no, not that one,' I said, remembering that it was a *conte* scarcely designed for the gentler sex and the tots. 'The one about the two men in the train. It's old, of course, so stop me if you've heard it before.'

'Pray go on, Augustus.'

'It's about these two deaf men in the train.'

'My sister Charlotte has the misfortune to be deaf. It is a great affliction.'

The thin aunt bent forward.

'What is he saying?'

'Augustus is telling us a story, Charlotte. Please go on, Augustus.'

Well, of course, this had damped the fire a bit, for the last thing one desires is to be supposed to be giving a maiden lady the horse's laugh on account of her physical infirmities, but it was too late now to take a bow and get off, so I had a go at it.

'Well, there were these two deaf chaps in the train, don't you know, and it stopped at Wembley, and one of them looked out of the window and said "This is Wembley", and the other said, "I thought it was Thursday", and the first chap said "Yes, so am I".'

I hadn't had much hope. Right from the start something had seemed to whisper in my ear that I was about to lay an egg. I laughed heartily to myself, but I was the only one. At the point where the aunts should have rolled out of their seats like one aunt there occurred merely a rather ghastly silence as of mourners at a death-bed, which was broken by Aunt Charlotte asking what I had said.

I would have been just as pleased to let the whole thing drop, but the stout aunt spoke into her ear, spacing her syllables carefully.

'Augustus was telling us a story about two men in a train. One of them said "Today is Wednesday", and the other said "I thought it was Thursday", and the first man said "Yes, so did I".'

'Oh?' said Aunt Charlotte, and I suppose that about summed it up.

Shortly after this, the browsing and sluicing being concluded, the females rose and filed from the room. Dame Daphne told Esmond Haddock not to be too long over his port, and popped off. Uncle Charlie brought the decanter, and also popped off. And Esmond Haddock and I were alone together, self wondering how chances were for getting a couple of glassfuls.

I moved up to his end of the table, licking the lips.

Esmond Haddock, seen close to, fully bore out Catsmeat's description of him as a Greek god, and I could well understand the concern of a young lover who saw his girl in danger of being steered into rose gardens by such a one. He was a fine, upstanding – sitting at the moment, of course, but you know what I mean – broad-shouldered bozo of about thirty, with one of those faces which I believe, though I should have to check up with Jeeves, are known as Byronic. He looked like a combination of a poet and an all-in wrestler.

It would not have surprised you to learn that Esmond Haddock was the author of sonnet sequences of a fruity and emotional nature which had made him the toast of Bloomsbury, for his air was that of a man who could rhyme 'love' and 'dove' as well as the next chap. Nor would you have been astonished if informed that he had recently felled an ox with a single blow. You would simply have felt what an ass the ox must have been to get into an argument with a fellow with a chest like that.

No, what was extraordinary was that this superman was in the habit, as testified to by the witness Corky, of crawling to his aunts. But for Corky's evidence I would have said, looking at him, that there sat a nephew capable of facing the toughest aunt and making her say Uncle. Not that you can ever tell, of course, by the outward appearance. Many a fellow who looks like the dominant male and has himself photographed smoking a pipe curls up like carbon paper when confronted with one of these relatives.

He helped himself to port, and there was a momentary silence, as so often occurs when two strong men who have not been formally introduced sit face to face. He worked painstakingly through his snootful, while I continued to fix my bulging eyes on the decanter. It was one of those outsize decanters, full to the brim.

He swigged away for some little while before opening the conversation. His manner was absent, and I got the impression that he was thinking deeply. Presently he spoke.

'I say,' he said, in an odd, puzzled voice. 'That story of yours.'

'Oh, yes?'

'About the fellows in the train.'

'Quite.'

'I was a bit *distrait* when you were telling it, and I think I may possibly have missed the point. As I got it, there were two men in a train, and it stopped at a station.'

'That's right.'

'And one of them said "This is Woking", and the other chap said "I'm thirsty". Was that how it went?'

'Not quite. It was Wembley the train stopped at, and the fellow said he thought it was Thursday.'

'Was it Thursday?'

'No, no, these chaps were deaf, you see. So when the first chap said "This is Woking", the other chap, thinking he had said "Wednesday", said "So am I". I mean –'

'I see. Yes, most amusing,' said Esmond Haddock.

He refilled his glass, and I think that as he did so he must have noticed the tense, set expression on my face, rather like that of a starving wolf giving a Russian peasant the once-over, for he started, as if realizing that he had been remiss.

'I say, I suppose it's no good offering you any of this?'

I felt the table-talk could not have taken a more satisfactory turn.

'Well, do you know,' I said, 'I wouldn't mind trying it. It would be an experience. It's whisky, or claret or something, isn't it?'

'Port. You may not like it.'

'Oh, I think I shall.'

And a moment later I was in a position to state that I did. It was a very fine old port, full of buck and body, and though my better self told me that it should be sipped, I lowered a beakerful at a gulp.

'It's good,' I said.

'It's supposed to be rather special. More?'

'Thanks.'

'I'll have another myself,' he said. 'One needs a lot of bracing up these days, I find. Do you know the expression "These are the times that try men's souls"?'

'New to me. Your own?'

'No, I heard it somewhere.'

'It's very neat.'

'It is, rather. Another?'

'Thanks.'

'I'll join you. Shall I tell you something?'

'Do.'

I inclined the ear invitingly. Three goblets of the right stuff had left me with a very warm affection for this man. I couldn't remember when I had liked a fellow more at a first meeting, and if he wanted to tell me his troubles, I was prepared to listen as attentively as any barman to an old and valued customer.

'The reason I mentioned the times that try men's souls is that I am right up against those identical times at this very moment. My soul is on the rack. More port?'

'Thanks. I find this stuff rather grows on you. Why is your soul on the rack, Esmond? You don't mind me calling you Esmond?'

'I prefer it. I'll call you Gussie.'

This, of course, came as rather an unpleasant shock, Gussie being to my mind about the ultimate low in names. But I quickly saw that in the role I had undertaken I must be prepared to accept the rough with the smooth. We drained our glasses, and Esmond Haddock refilled them. A princely host, he struck me as.

'Esmond,' I said, 'you strike me as a princely host.'

'Thank you, Gussie,' he replied. 'And you're a princely guest. But you were asking me why my soul was on the rack. I will tell you, Gussie. I must begin by saying that I like your face.'

I said I liked his.

'It is an honest face.'

I said his was, too.

'A glance at it tells me that you are trustworthy. By that I mean that I can trust you.'

'Quite.'

'If I couldn't, I wouldn't, if you follow what I mean. Because what I am about to tell you must go no further, Gussie.'

'Not an inch, Esmond.'

'Well, then, the reason my soul is on the rack is that I love a girl with every fibre of my being, and she has given me the brush-off. Enough to put anyone's soul on the rack, what?'

'I should say so.'

'Her name . . . But naturally I can't mention names.'

'Of course not.'

'Not cricket.'

'Not at all.'

'So I will merely say that her name is Cora Pirbright. Corky to her pals. You don't know her, of course. I remember when I told her you were coming here she said she had heard from mutual friends that you were a freak of the first water and practically dotty, but she had never met you. But she is probably familiar to you on the screen. The name she goes by professionally is Cora Starr. You've seen her?'

'Oh, rather.'

'An angel in human shape, didn't you think?'

'Definitely.'

'That was my view, too, Gussie. I was in love with her long before I met her. I had frequently seen her pictures in Basingstoke. And when old Pirbright, the vicar here, mentioned that his niece was coming to keep house for him and that she was just back from Hollywood and I said "Oh really? Who is she?" and he said "Cora Starr", you could have knocked me down with a feather, Gussie.'

'I bet I could, Esmond. Proceed. You are interesting me strangely.'

'Well, she arrived. Old Pirbright introduced us. Our eyes met.'

'They would, of course.'

'And it wasn't more than about two days after that that we talked it over and agreed that we were twin souls.'

'And then she gave you the brusheroo?'

'And then she gave me the brusheroo. But mark this, Gussie. Even though she has given me the brusheroo, she is still the lodestar of my life. My aunts . . . More port?'

'Thanks.'

'My aunts, Gussie, will try to kid you that I love my cousin Gertrude. Don't believe a word of it. I'll tell you how that mistake arose. Shortly after Corky handed me my papers, I went to the pictures in Basingstoke, and in the thing they were showing there was a fellow who had been turned down by a girl, and in order to make her think a bit and change her mind he started surging around another girl.'

'To make her jealous?'

'Exactly. I thought it a clever idea.'

'Very clever.'

'And it occurred to me that if I started surging round Gertrude, it might make Corky change her mind. So I surged.'

'I see. A bit risky, wasn't it?'

'Risky?'

'Suppose you overdid it and got too fascinating. Broke her heart, I mean.'

'Corky's heart?'

'No, your cousin Gertrude's heart.'

'Oh, that's all right. She's in love with Corky's brother. No chance of breaking Gertrude's heart. We might drink to the success of my scheme, don't you think, Gussie?'

'An excellent idea, Esmond.'

I was, as you may imagine, profoundly bucked. What this meant what that the dark menace of Esmond Haddock had passed from Catsmeat's life. No more need for him to worry about that rose garden. You could unleash Esmond Haddock in the rose gardens with Gertrude Winkworth by the hour, and no business would result. I raised my glass and emptied it to Catsmeat's happiness. Whether or not a tear stole into my eye, I couldn't say, but I should think it very probable.

It was a pity, of course, that, being supposed never to have met Corky, I couldn't electrify Esmond Haddock and bring the sunshine breezing back into his life by telling him what she had told me – viz. that she loved him still. All I could do was to urge him not to lose hope, and he said he hadn't lost hope, not by a jugful.

'And I'll tell you why I haven't lost hope, Gussie. The other day a very significant thing happened. She came to me and asked me to sing a song at this ghastly concert she's getting up. Well, of course, it wasn't a thing I would have gone out of my way to do, had the circumstances been different. I've never sung at a village concert. Have you?'

'Oh, rather. Often.'

'A terrible ordeal, was it not?'

'Oh, no. I enjoyed it. I don't say it was all jam for the audience, but a good time was had by me. You feel nervous at the prospect, do you, Esmond?'

'There are moments, Gussie, when the thought of what is before me makes me break into a cold perspiration. But then I say to myself that I'm the young Squire and pretty popular around these parts, so I'll probably get by all right.'

'That's the attitude.'

'But you're wondering why I said it was significant that she should have come to me and asked me to sing a song at this foul concert. I'll tell you. I take it as definite evidence that the old affection still lingers. Well, I mean, if it didn't would she come asking me to sing at concerts? I am banking everything on that song, Gussie. Corky is an emotional girl, and when she hears that audience cheering me to the echo, it will do something to her. She will melt. She will relent. I wouldn't be surprised if she didn't say "Oh, Esmond!" and fling herself into my arms. Always provided, of course, that I don't get the bird.'

'You won't get the bird.'

'You think not?'

'Not a chance. You'll go like a breeze.'

'You're a great comfort, Gussie.'

'I try to be, Esmond. What are you going to sing? The "Yeoman's Wedding Song"?'

'No, it's a thing written by my Aunt Charlotte, with music by my Aunt Myrtle.'

I pursed the lips. This didn't sound too good. Nothing that I had seen of Aunt Charlotte had led me to suppose that the divine fire lurked within her. One didn't want to condemn her unheard, of course, but I was prepared to bet that anything proceeding from her pen would be well on the lousy side.

'I say,' said Esmond Haddock, struck by an idea, 'would you mind if I just ran through it for you now?'

'Nothing I'd like better.'

'Except perhaps another spot of port?'

'Except that, perhaps. Thanks.'

Esmond Haddock drained his glass.

'I won't sing the verse. It's just a lot of guff about the sun is high up in the sky and the morn is bright and fair, and so forth.'

'Quite.'

'The chorus is what brings home the bacon. It goes like this.'

He assumed the grave, intent expression of a stuffed frog, and let it rip.

'"Hallo, hallo, hallo, hallo . . ."'

I raised a hand.

'Just a second. What are you supposed to be doing? Telephoning?'

'No, it's a hunting song.'

'Oh, a hunting song? I see. I thought it might be one of those "I'm going to telephone ma baby" things. Right ho.'

He resumed.

'"Hallo, hallo, hallo, hallo!
A-hunting we will go, pom pom,
A-hunting we will go, Gussie."'

I raised the hand again.

'I don't like that.'

'What?'

'That "pom pom".'

'Oh, that's just in the accompaniment.'

'And I don't like that "Gussie". It lets the side down.'

'Did I say "Gussie"?'

'Yes. You said "A-hunting we will go, pom pom, a-hunting we will go, Gussie".'

'Just a slip of the tongue.'

'It isn't in the script?'

'No, it isn't in the script.'

'I'd leave it out on the night.'

'I will. Shall I continue?'

'Do.'

'Where was I?'

'Better start again at the beginning.'

'Right. Another drop of port?'

'Just a trickle, perhaps.'

'Well, then, starting again at the beginning and omitting, as before, all the-sun-is-high-up-in-the-sky stuff, "Hallo, hallo, hallo, hallo! A-hunting we will go, pom pom, a-hunting we will go. Today's the day, so come what may, a-hunting we will go".'

I began to see that I had been right about Charlotte. This wouldn't do at all. Young Squire or no young Squire, a songster singing this sort of thing at a village concert was merely asking for the raspberry.

'All wrong,' I said.

'All wrong?'

'Well, think it out for yourself. You start off "A-hunting we will go, a-hunting we will go", and then, just as the audience is all keyed up for a punch line, you repeat that a-hunting we will go. There will be a sense of disappointment.'

'You think so, Gussie?'

'I'm sure of it, Esmond.'

'Then what would you advise?'

I pondered a moment.

'Try this,' I said. '"Hallo, hallo, hallo, hallo! A-hunting we will go, my lads, a-hunting we will go, pull up our socks and chase the fox and lay the blighter low."'

'I say, that's good!'

'Stronger, I think?'

'Much stronger.'

'How do you go on from there?'

He switched on the stuffed-frog expression once more:

'"Oh, hearken to the merry horn!

Over brake and over thorn

Upon this jolly hunting morn

A-hunting we will go."'

I weighed this.

'I pass the first two lines,' I said. '"Merry horn." "Brake and thorn."

Not bad at all. At-a-girl, Charlotte, we always knew you had it in you! But not the finish.'

'You don't like it?'

'Weak. Very weak. I don't know what sort of standees you get at King's Deverill, but if they're like the unshaven thugs behind the back row at every village concert I've ever known, you're simply inviting them to chi-yike and make a noise like tearing calico. No, we must do better than that. Born . . . corn . . . pawn . . . torn . . . Ha!' I said, reaching out for the decanter, 'I think I have it. "Oh, hearken to the merry horn! Over brake and over thorn we'll ride although our bags get torn! What ho! What ho! What ho!"'

I had more or less expected it to knock him cold and it did. For an instant he was speechless with admiration, then he said it lifted the whole thing and he couldn't thank me enough.

'It's terrific!'

'I was hoping you would like it.'

'How do you think of these things?'

'Oh, they just come to one.'

'We might run through the authorized version, old man, shall we?'

'No time like the present, dear old chap.'

It's curious how, looking back, you can nearly always spot where you went wrong in any binge or enterprise. Take this little slab of community singing of ours, for instance. In order to give the thing zip, I stood on my chair and waved the decanter like a baton, and this, I see now, was a mistake. It helped the composition enormously, but it tended to create a false impression in the mind of the observer, conjuring up a picture of drunken revels.

And if you are going to say that on the present occasion there was no observer, I quietly reply that you are wrong. We had just worked through the 'brake and thorn' and were going all out for the rousing finish, when a voice spoke behind us.

It said:

'Well!'

There are, of course, many ways of saying 'Well!' The speaker who had the floor at the moment – Dame Daphne Winkworth – said it rather in the manner of the prudish Queen of a monarch of Babylon who has happened to wander into the banqueting hall just as the Babylonian orgy is beginning to go nicely.

'*Well!*' she said.

Of course, what Corky had told me about Esmond Haddock's aunt-fixation ought to have prepared me for it, but I must say I was shocked at his deportment at this juncture. It was the deportment of a craven and a worm. Possibly stimulated by my getting on a chair, he had climbed onto the table and was using a banana as a hunting-crop, and he now came down like an apologetic sack of coals, his whole demeanour so crushed and cringing that I could hardly bear to look at him.

'It's all right, Aunt Daphne!'

'All right!'

'We were rehearsing. For the concert, you know. With the concert so near, one doesn't want to lose a minute.'

'Oh? Well, we are expecting you in the drawing room.'

'Yes, Aunt Daphne.'

'Gertrude is waiting to play backgammon with you.'

'Yes, Aunt Daphne.'

'If you feel capable of playing backgammon.'

'Oh, yes, Aunt Daphne.'

He slunk from the room with bowed head, and I was about to follow, when the old geezer checked me with an imperious gesture. One noted a marked increase in the resemblance to Wallace Beery, and the thought crossed my mind that life for the unfortunate moppets who had drawn this Winkworth as a headmistress must have been like Six Weeks on Sunny Devil's Island. Previous to making her acquaintance, I had always supposed the Rev. Aubrey Upjohn to be the nearest thing to the late Captain Bligh of the *Bounty* which the scholastic world had provided to date, but I could see now that compared with old Battling Daphne he was a mere prelim boy.

'Augustus, did you bring a great, rough dog with you this evening?' she demanded.

It shows how the rush and swirl of events at Deverill Hall had affected me when I say that for an instant nothing stirred.

'Dog?'

'Silversmith says it belongs to you.'

'Oh, ah,' I said, memory returning to its throne. 'Yes, yes, yes, of course. Yes, to be sure. You mean Sam Goldwyn. But he's not mine. He belongs to Corky.'

'To *whom?*'

'Corky Pirbright. She asked me to put him up for a day or two.'

The mention of Corky's name, as had happened at the dinner table, caused her to draw in her breath and do a quick-take-um. There was no getting away from the fact that the girl's popularity at Deverill Hall was but slight.

'Is Miss Pirbright a great friend of yours?'

'Oh, rather,' I said, remembering too late that this scarcely squared with what Corky had told Esmond Haddock. I was glad that he was no longer with us. 'She was a trifle dubious about springing the animal on her uncle without a certain amount of preliminary spade-work, he being apparently not very dog-minded, so she turned it over to me. It's in the stables.'

'It is not in the stables.'

'Then Silversmith was pulling my leg. He said he would have it taken there!'

'He did have it taken there, but it broke loose and came rushing into the drawing room just now like a mad thing.'

I saw that here was where the soothing word was required.

'Sam Goldwyn isn't dotty,' I assured her. 'I wouldn't say he was one of our great minds, but he's perfectly compos. *In re* his rushing into the drawing room, that was because he thought I was there. He has conceived a burning passion for me and counts every minute lost when he is not in my society. No doubt his first act on being tied up in the stables was to start gnawing through the rope in order to be free to come and look for me. Rather touching.'

Her manner suggested that she did not think it in the least touching. Her eye was alight with anti-Sam sentiment.

'Well, it was most unpleasant. We had left the french windows open, as the night was so warm, and suddenly this disgusting brute came galloping in. My sister Charlotte received a nervous shock from which it will take her a long time to recover. The animal leaped upon her back and chased her all over the room.'

I did not give the thought utterance, for if there is one thing the Woosters are, it is tactful, but it did occur to me that this had come more or less as a judgment on Charlotte for writing all that Hallo-hallo-hallo-hallo, a-hunting-we-will-go stuff and would be a lesson to her next time she took pen in hand. She was now in a position to see the thing from the fox's point of view.

'And when we rang for Silversmith, the creature bit him.'

I must confess to feeling a thrill of admiration as I heard these words. 'You're a better man than I am, Gunga Din', I came within a toucher of saying. I wouldn't have bitten Silversmith myself to please a dying grandmother.

'I'm frightfully sorry,' I said. 'Is there anything I can do?'

'No, thank you.'

'I have considerable influence with this hound. I might be able to induce him to call it a day and go back to the stables and get his eight hours.'

'It will not be necessary. Silversmith succeeded in overpowering the animal and locking it in a cupboard. Now that you tell me its home is at the Vicarage, I will send it there at once.'

'I'll take him, shall I?'

'Pray do not trouble. I think it would be better if you were to go straight to bed.'

This seemed to me the most admirable suggestion. From the moment when the females had legged it from the dinner table, I had been musing somewhat apprehensively on the quiet home evening which would set in as soon as Esmond and I were through with the port. You know what these quiet home evenings are like at country houses were the personnel of the ensemble is mainly feminine. You get backed into corners and shown photograph albums. Folk songs are sung at you. You find the head drooping like a lily on its stem and have to keep jerking it back into position one with an effort that taxes the frail strength to the utmost. Far, far better to retire to my sleeping quarters now, especially as I was most anxious to get in touch with Jeeves, who long 'ere this must have arrived by train with the heavy luggage.

I am not saying that this woman's words, with their underlying suggestion that I was fried to the tonsils, had not wounded me. It was all too plainly her opinion that, if let loose in drawing rooms, I would immediately proceed to create an atmosphere reminiscent of a waterfront saloon when the Fleet is in. But the Woosters are essentially fair-minded, and I did not blame her for holding these views. I could quite see that when you come into a dining room and find a guest leaping about on a chair with a decanter in his hand, singing Hallo, hallo, hallo, hallo, a-hunting we will go, my lads, a-hunting we will go, you are pretty well bound to fall into a certain train of thought.

'I do feel a little fatigued after my journey,' I said.

'Silversmith will show you to your room,' she replied, and I perceived that Uncle Charlie was in our midst. I had not seen or heard him arrive. Like Jeeves, he had manifested himself silently out of the void. No doubt these things run in families.

'Silversmith.'

'Madam?'

'Show Mr Fink-Nottle to his room,' said Dame Daphne, though I could see that she was feeling that 'help' would have been more the *mot juste*.

'Very good, madam.'

I noticed that the man was limping slightly, seeming to suggest that

Sam Goldwyn had connected with his calf, but I forbore to probe and question, realizing that the subject, like the calf, might be a sore one. I followed him up the stairs to a well-appointed chamber and wished him a cheery good night.

'Oh, Silversmith,' I said.

'Sir?'

'Has my man arrived?'

'Yes, sir.'

'You might send him along.'

'Very good, sir.'

He withdrew, and a few minutes later there entered a familiar form.

But it wasn't the familiar form of Jeeves. It was the familiar form of Claude Cattermole Pirbright.

Well, I suppose if I had been a Seigneur of the Middle Ages –
somebody like Childe Roland, for instance – in the days when you
couldn't throw a brick without beaning a magician or a wizard or
a sorcerer and people were always getting changed into something
else, I wouldn't have given the thing a second thought. I would just
have said 'Ah, so Jeeves has had a spell cast on him and been turned
into Catsmeat, has he? Too bad. Still, that's life', and carried on
regardless, calling for my pipe and my bowl and my fiddlers three.

But nowadays you tend to lose this easy outlook, and it would be
wilfully deceiving my public to say that I did not take it big. I stared
at the man, my eyes coming out of the parent sockets like a snail's
and waving about on their stems.

'Catsmeat!' I yipped.

He waggled his head frowningly, like a conspirator when a fellow-
conspirator has said the wrong thing.

'Meadowes,' he corrected.

'What do you mean, Meadowes?'

'That is my name while I remain in your employment. I'm
your man.'

A solution occurred to me. I have already mentioned that the port
which I had swigged perhaps a little too freely in Esmond Haddock's
society was of a fine old vintage and full of body. It now struck me that
it must have had even more authority than I had supposed and that
Dame Daphne Winkworth had been perfectly correct in assuming
that I was scrooched. And I was about to turn my face to the wall
and try to sleep it off, when he proceeded.

'Your valet. Your attendant. Your gentleman's personal gentleman.
It's quite simple. Jeeves couldn't come.'

'What!'

'No.'

'You mean Jeeves isn't going to be at my side?'

'That's right. So I am taking his place. What are you doing?'

'Turning my face to the wall.'

'Why?'

'Well, wouldn't you turn your face to the wall if you were trapped in a place like this with everybody thinking you were Gussie Fink-Nottle and without Jeeves to comfort and advise? Oh, hell! Oh, blast! Oh, damn! Why couldn't Jeeves come? Is he ill?'

'I don't think so. I speak only as a layman, of course, not as a medical man, but the last I saw of him he seemed pretty full of vitamins. Sparkling eyes. Rosy cheeks. No, Jeeves isn't ill. What stopped him coming was the fact that his Uncle Charlie is the butler here.'

'Why the devil should that stop him?'

'My good Bertie, use your intelligence, if any. Uncle Charlie knows that Jeeves is your keeper. No doubt Jeeves writes him weekly letters, saying how happy he is with you and how nothing would ever induce him to switch elsewhere. Well, what would happen if he suddenly showed up in attendance on Gussie Fink-Nottle? I'll tell you what would happen. Uncle Charlie's suspicions would be aroused. "Something fishy here," he would say to himself. And before you knew where you were he would be tearing off your whiskers and denouncing you. Obviously Jeeves couldn't come.'

I was forced to admit that there was something in this. But I still chafed.

'Why didn't he tell me?'

'It only occurred to him after you had left.'

'And why couldn't he have squared Silversmith?'

'That point came up when we were discussing the thing, and Jeeves said his Uncle Charlie was one of those fellows who can't be squared. A man of very rigid principles.'

'Every man has his price.'

'Not Jeeves's Uncle Charlie. My gosh, Bertie, what a lad! He received me when I arrived, and my bones turned to water. Do you remember the effect King Solomon had on the Queen of Sheba at their first meeting? My reactions were somewhat similar. "The half was not told unto me," I said to myself. If it hadn't been for Queenie leading me from the presence and buoying me up with a quick cooking sherry, I might have swooned in my tracks.'

'Who's Queenie?'

'Haven't you met her? The parlourmaid. Delightful girl. Engaged to the village policeman, a fellow named Dobbs. Have you ever tasted cooking sherry, Bertie? Odd stuff.'

I felt that we were wandering from the nub. This was no time for desultory chit-chat about cooking sherry.

'But, look here, dash it, I can understand Jeeves's reasons for backing out, but I can't see why you had to come.'

He raised a couple of eyebrows.

'You can't see why I had to come? Didn't you yourself say with your own lips, when we were discussing the idea of me understudying Gussie, that this was the one place where I ought to be? It's vital that I should be on the spot, seeing Gertrude constantly, pleading with her, reasoning with her, trying to break down her sales resistance.' He paused, and gave me a penetrating look. 'You've nothing against my being here, have you?'

'Well . . .'

'So!' he said, and his voice was cold and hard, like a picnic egg. 'You have some far-fetched objection to the scheme, have you? You don't want me to win the girl I love?'

'Of course I want you to win the bally girl you love.'

'Well, I can't do it by mail.'

'But I don't see why you've got to be at the Hall. Why couldn't you have stayed at the Vicarage?'

'You couldn't expect Uncle Sidney to have Corky *and* me on the premises. The mixture would be too rich.'

'At the inn, then.'

'There isn't an inn. Only what they call beer-houses.'

'You could have got a bed at a cottage.'

'And shared it with the cottager? No, thanks. How many beds do you think these birds have?'

I relapsed into a baffled silence. But it is never any good repining on these occasions. When I next spoke, I doubt if Catsmeat spotted the suspicion of a tremor in the voice. We Woosters are like that. In moments of mental anguish we resemble those Red Indians who, while getting cooked to a crisp at the stake, never failed to be the life and soul of the party.

'Have you seen her?' I asked.

'Gertrude? Yes, just before I came up here. I was in the hall, and she suddenly appeared from the drawing room.'

'I suppose she was surprised.'

'Surprised is right. She swayed and tottered. Queenie said "Oh, miss, are you ill?" and rushed off to get sal volatile.'

'Oh, Queenie was there?'

'Yes, Queenie was there with her hair in a braid. She had just been telling me how worried she was about her betrothed's spiritual outlook. He's an atheist.'

'So Corky told me.'

'And every time she tries to make him see the light, he just twirls his moustache and talks Ingersoll at her. This upsets the poor girl.'

'She's very pretty.'

'Extraordinarily pretty. I don't remember ever having seen a prettier parlourmaid.'

'Gertrude. Not Queenie.'

'Oh, Gertrude. Well, dash it, you don't need to tell me that. She's the top. She begins where Helen of Troy left off.'

'Did you get a chance to talk to her?'

'Unfortunately no. A couple of aunts came out of the drawing room, and I had to leg it. That's the trouble about being a valet. You can't mix. By the way, Bertie, I've found out something of the utmost importance. That Lovers' Leap binge is fixed for next Thursday. Queenie told me. She's cutting the sandwiches. I hope you haven't weakened? You are still in your splendid, resolute frame of mind of yesterday? I can rely on you to foil and battle that foul blot, Esmond Haddock?'

'I like Esmond Haddock.'

'Then you ought to be ashamed of yourself.'

I smiled an indulgent smile.

'It's all right, Catsmeat. You can simmer down. Gertrude Winkworth means nothing to Esmond Haddock. He's not really pursuing her with his addresses.'

'Don't be an ass. How about the Lovers' Leap? What price the sandwiches?'

'All that stuff is just to make Corky jealous.'

'What!'

'He thinks it will bring her round. You see, he didn't give Corky the brush-off. You had your facts twisted. She gave him the brush-off, because they had differed on a point of policy, and she is still the lodestar of his life. I had this from his own lips. We got matey over the port. So you can cease to regard him as a menace.'

He gaped at me. You could see hope beginning to dawn.

'Is this official?'

'Absolutely.'

'You say Corky is the lodestar of his life?'

'That's what he told me.'

'And all this rushing Gertrude is just a ruse?'

'That's right.'

Catsmeat expelled a deep breath. It sounded like the final effort of a Dying Rooster.

'My gosh, you've taken a weight off my mind.'

'I thought you'd be pleased.'

'You bet I'm pleased. Well, good night.'

'You're off?'

'Yes, I shall leave you now, Bertie, much as I enjoy your society, because I have man's work to do elsewhere. When I was chatting with Queenie, she happened to mention that she knows where Uncle Charlie keeps the key of the cellar. So long. I shall hope to see more of you later.'

'Just a second. Will you be seeing Corky shortly?'

'First thing tomorrow morning. I must let her know I'm here and put her in touch with the general situation, so that she will be warned against making any floaters. Why?'

'Tell her from me that she has got to find somebody else for Pat.'

'You're walking out on the act?'

'Yes, I am,' I said, and put him abreast.

He listened intelligently, and said he quite understood.

'I see. Yes, I think you're right. I'll tell her.'

He withdrew, walking on the tips of his toes and conveying in his manner the suggestion that if he had had a hat and that hat had contained roses, he would have started strewing them from it, and for a while the thought that I had been instrumental in re-sunshining a pal's life bucked me up no little.

But it takes more than that to buck a fellow up permanently who is serving an indeterminate sentence in a place like Deverill Hall, and it was not long before I was in sombre mood again, trying to find the bluebird but missing it by a wide margin.

I have generally found on these occasions when the heart is heavy that the best thing to do is to curl up with a good goose-flesher and try to forget, and fortunately I had packed among my effects one called *Murder At Greystone Grange*. I started to turn its pages now, and found that I couldn't have made a sounder move. It was one of those works in which Baronets are constantly being discovered dead in libraries and the heroine can't turn in for a night without a Thing popping through a panel in the wall of her bedroom and starting to chuck its weight about, and it was not long before I was so soothed that I was able to switch off the light and fall into a refreshing sleep, which lasted, as my refreshing sleeps always do, till the coming of the morning cup of tea.

My last thought, just before the tired eyelids closed, was that I had had an idea that I had heard the front-door bell ring and a murmur of distant voices, seeming to indicate the blowing-in of another guest.

It was Silversmith who brought me my tea ration, and though his manner, on the chilly side, suggested that the overnight activities of Sam Goldwyn still rankled, I had a dash at setting the conversational ball rolling. I always like, if I can, to establish matey relations between tea bringer and tea recipient.

'Oh, good morning, Silversmith, good morning,' I said. 'What sort of a day is it, Silversmith? Fine?'

'Yes, sir.'

'The lark on the wing and the snail on the thorn and all that?'

'Yes, sir.'

'Splendid. Oh, Silversmith,' I said, 'I don't know if it was but a dream, but latish last night I fancied I heard the front-door bell doing its stuff and a good lot of off-stage talking going on. Was I right? Did someone arrive after closing time?'

'Yes, sir. Mr Wooster.'

He gave me a cold look, as if to remind me that he would prefer not to be drawn into conversation with the man responsible for introducing Sam Goldwyn into his life, and vanished, leaving not a wrack behind.

And it was, as you may well imagine, a pensive Bertram with a puzzled frown on his face who propped himself against the pillows and sipped from the teacup. I could make nothing of this.

'Mr Wooster', the man had said, and only two explanations seemed to offer themselves – (a) that, like the fellows in the train at Wembley, I had not heard correctly and (b) that I had recently been in the presence of a butler who had been having a couple.

Neither theory satisfied me. From boyhood up my hearing has always been of the keenest, and as for the possibility of Silversmith having had one over the eight, I dismissed that instanter. It is a very frivolous butler who gets a load before nine in the morning, and I have gone sadly astray in my delineation of character if I have given my public the impression that Jeeves's Uncle Charlie was frivolous. You could imagine Little Lord Fauntleroy getting a skinful, but not Silversmith.

And yet he had unquestionably said 'Mr Wooster'.

I was still pondering like billy-o and nowhere near spiking a plausible solution of the mystery, when the door opened and the ghost of Jeeves entered, carrying a breakfast tray.

8

I say 'the ghost of Jeeves' because in that first awful moment that was what I had the apparition docketed as. The words 'What ho! A spectre!' trembled on my lips, and I reacted rather like the heroine of *Murder At Greystone Grange* on discovering that the Thing had come to doss in her room. I don't know if you have ever seen a ghost, but the general effect is to give you quite a start.

Then the scent of bacon floated to the nostrils, and feeling that it was improbable that a wraith would be horsing about the place with dishes of eggs and b., I calmed down a bit. That is to say, I stopped upsetting the tea and was able to stutter. It is true that all I said was 'Jeeves!' but that wasn't such bad going for one whose tongue had so recently been tangled up with the uvula, besides cleaving to the roof of the mouth.

He dumped the tray on my lap.

'Good morning, sir,' he said. 'I fancied that you would possibly wish to enjoy your breakfast in the privacy of your apartment, rather than make one of the party in the dining room.'

Cognizant as I was of the fact that in that dining room there would be five aunts, one of them deaf, one of them dotty, one of them Dame Daphne Winkworth, and all of them totally unfit for human consumption on an empty stomach, I applauded the kindly gesture; all the more heartily because it had just occurred to me that in a house like this, where things were sure to be run on old-fashioned lines rather than in a manner of keeping with the trend of modern thought, the butler probably waited at the breakfast table.

'Does he?' I asked. 'Does Silversmith minister to the revellers at the morning meal?'

'Yes, sir.'

'My God!' I said, paling beneath the tan. 'What a man, Jeeves!'

'Sir?'

'Your Uncle Charlie.'

'Ah, yes, sir. A forceful personality.'

'Forceful is correct. What's that thing of Shakespeare's about someone having an eye like Mother's?'

'An eye like Mars, to threaten and command, is possibly the quotation for which you are groping, sir.'

'That's right. Uncle Charlie has an eye like that. You really call him Uncle Charlie?'

'Yes, sir.'

'Amazing. To me, to think of him as Uncle Charlie is like thinking of him as Jimmy or Reggie, or, for the matter of that, Bertie. Used he in your younger days to dandle you on his knee?'

'Quite frequently, sir.'

'And you didn't quail? You must have been a child of blood and iron.' I addressed myself to the platter once more. 'Extraordinarily good bacon, this, Jeeves.'

'Home cured, I understand, sir.'

'And made, no doubt, from contented pigs. Kippers, too, not to mention toast, marmalade and, unless my senses deceive me, an apple. Say what you will of Deverill Hall, its hospitality is lavish. I don't know if you have ever noticed it, Jeeves, but a good, spirited kipper first thing in the morning seems to put heart into you.'

'Very true, sir, though I myself am more partial to a slice of ham.'

For some moments we discussed the relative merits of ham and kippers as buckers-up of the morale, there being much, of course, to be said on both sides, and then I touched on something which I had been meaning to touch on earlier. I can't think how it came to slip my mind.

'Oh, Jeeves,' I said, 'I knew there was something I wanted to ask you. What in the name of everything bloodsome are you doing here?'

'I fancied that you might possibly be curious on that point, sir, and I was about to volunteer an explanation. I have come here in attendance on Mr Fink-Nottle. Permit me, sir.'

He retrieved the slab of kipper which a quick jerk of the wrist had caused me to send flying from the fork, and replaced it on the dish. I stared at him wide-eyed as the expression is.

'Mr Fink-Nottle?'

'Yes, sir.'

'But Gussie's not here?'

'Yes. sir. We arrived at a somewhat late hour last night.'

A sudden blinding light flashed upon me.

'You mean it was Gussie to whom Uncle Charlie was referring when he said that Mr Wooster had punched the time-clock? I'm here saying I'm Gussie, and now Gussie has blown in, saying he's me?'

'Precisely, sir. It is a curious and perhaps somewhat complex situation that has been precipitated –'

'You're telling me, Jeeves!'

Only the fact that by doing so I should have upset the tray prevented me turning my face to the wall. When Esmond Haddock in our exchanges over the port had spoken of the times that try men's souls, he hadn't had a notion of what the times that try men's souls can really be, if they spit on their hands and get right down to it. I levered up a forkful of kipper and passed it absently over the larynx, endeavouring to adjust the faculties to a set-up which even the most intrepid would have had to admit was a honey.

'But how did Gussie get out of stir?'

'The magistrate decided on second thoughts to substitute a fine for the prison sentence, sir.'

'What made him do that?'

'Possibly the reflection that the quality of mercy is not strained, sir.'

'You mean it droppeth as the gentle rain from heaven?'

'Precisely, sir. Upon the place beneath. His Worship would no doubt have taken into consideration the fact that it blesseth him that gives and him that takes and becomes the throned monarch better than his crown.'

I mused. Yes, there was something in that.

'What did he soak him? Five quid?'

'Yes, sir.'

'And Gussie brassed up and was free?'

'Yes, sir.'

I put my finger on the nub.

'Why?' I said.

I thought I had him there, but I hadn't. Where a lesser man would have shuffled his feet and twiddled his finger and mumbled 'Yes, I see what you mean, that is the problem, is it not?' he had his explanation all ready to serve and dished it up without batting an eyelid.

'It was the only course to pursue, sir. On the one hand, her ladyship, your aunt, was most emphatic in her desire that you should visit the hall, and on the other Miss Bassett was equally insistent on Mr Fink-Nottle doing so. In the event of either of you failing to arrive, inquiries would have been instituted, with disastrous results. To take but one aspect of the matter, Miss Bassett is expecting to receive daily letters from Mr Fink-Nottle, giving her all the gossip of the hall and describing in detail his life there. These will, of course, have to be written on the hall notepaper and postmarked "King's Deverill".'

'True. You speak sooth, Jeeves. I never thought of that.'

I swallowed a sombre chunk of toast and marmalade. I was thinking how easily all this complex stuff could have been avoided, if only the beak had had the sense to fine Gussie in the first place, instead of as an afterthought. I have said it before, and I will say it again, all magistrates are asses. Show me a magistrate and I will show you a fathead.

I started on the apple.

'So here we are.'

'Yes, sir.'

'I'm Gussie and Gussie's me.'

'Yes, sir.'

'And ceaseless vigilance will be required if we are not to gum the game. We shall be walking on eggshells.'

'A very trenchant figure, sir.'

I finished the apple, and lit a thoughtful cigarette.

'Well, I suppose it had to be,' I said. 'But lay off the Marcus Aurelius stuff, because I don't think I could stand it if you talk about it all being part of the great web. How's Gussie taking the thing?'

'Not blithely, sir. I should describe him as disgruntled. I learn from Mr Pirbright –'

'Oh, you've seen Catsmeat?'

'Yes, sir, in the servants' hall. He was helping Queenie, the parlourmaid, with her crossword puzzle. He informed me that he had contrived to obtain an interview with Miss Pirbright and had apprised her of your reluctance to play the part of Pat in the Hibernian entertainment at the concert, and that Miss Pirbright fully appreciated your position and said that now that Mr Fink-Nottle had arrived he would, of course, sustain the role. Mr Pirbright has seen Mr Fink-Nottle and informed him of the arrangement, and it is this that has caused Mr Fink-Nottle to become disgruntled.'

'He shrinks from the task?'

'Yes, sir. He is also somewhat exercised in his mind by what he had heard the ladies of the hall saying with regard to –'

'My doings?'

'Yes, sir.'

'The dog?'

'Yes, sir.'

'The port?'

'Yes, sir.'

'And the hallo, hallo, a-hunting we will go?'

'Yes, sir.'

I whooshed out a remorseful puff of smoke.

'Yes,' I said, 'I'm afraid I haven't given Gussie a very good send-off. Quite inadvertently I fear that I have established him in the eyes of mine hostesses as one of those whited sepulchres which try to kid the public that they drink nothing but orange juice and the moment that public's back is turned, start doing the *Lost Week-End* stuff with the port. Of course, I could put up a pretty good case for myself. Esmond Haddock thrust the decanter on me, and I was dying of thirst. You wouldn't blame a snowbound traveller in the Alps for accepting a drop of brandy at the hands of a St Bernard dog. Still, one hopes that they will keep it under their hats and not pass it along to Miss Bassett. One doesn't want spanners bunged into Gussie's romance.'

We were silent for a moment, musing on what the harvest would be, were anything to cause Madeline Bassett to become de-Gussied. Then I changed a distasteful subject.

'Talking of romances, I suppose Catsmeat confided in you about his?'

'Yes, sir.'

'I thought he would. Amazing, the way all these birds come to you and sob out their troubles on your chest.'

'I find it most gratifying, sir, and am always eager to lend such assistance as may lie within my power. One desires to give satisfaction. Shortly after your departure yesterday, Mr Pirbright devoted some little time to an exposition of the problem confronting him. It was after learning the facts that I ventured to suggest that he should take my place here as your attendant.'

'I wish one of you had thought to tip me off with a telegram. I should have been spared a nasty shock. The last thing one wants on top of what might be termed a drinking bout is to have a changeling ring himself in on you without warning. You'd look pretty silly yourself if you came into my room one morning with the cup of tea after a thick night and found Ernie Bevin or someone propped up in the bed. When you saw Catsmeat just now, did he tell you the Stop Press news?'

'Sir?'

'About Esmond Haddock and Corky.'

'Ah, yes, sir. He informed me of what you had said to him with reference to Mr Haddock's unswerving devotion to Miss Pirbright.

He appeared greatly relieved. He feels that the principal obstacle to his happiness has now been removed.'

'Yes, Catsmeat's sitting pretty. One wishes one could say the same of poor old Esmond.'

'You think that Miss Pirbright does not reciprocate Mr Haddock's sentiments, sir?'

'Oh, she reciprocates them, all right. She freely admits that he is the lodestar of her life, and you're probably saying to yourself that in these circs everything should be hunkadory. I mean, if she's the lodestar of his life and he's the lodestar of hers, the thing ought to be in the bag. But you're wrong, and so is Esmond Haddock. His view, poor deluded clam, is that he will make such a whale of a hit with this song he's singing at the concert that when she hears the audience cheering him to the echo she will say "Oh, Esmond!" and fling herself into his arms. Not a hope.'

'No, sir?'

'Not a hope, Jeeves. There's a snag. The trouble is that she refuses to consider the idea of hitching up with him unless he defies his aunts, and he very naturally gets the vapours at the mere idea. It is what I have sometimes heard described as an impasse.'

'Why does the young lady wish Mr Haddock to defy his aunts, sir?'

'She says he has allowed them to oppress him from childhood, and it's time he threw off the yoke. She wants him to show her that he is a man of intrepid courage. It's the old dragon gag. In the days when knights were bold, as you probably know, girls used to hound fellows into going out and fighting dragons. I expect your old pal Childe Roland had it happen to him a dozen times. But dragons are one thing, and aunts are another. I have no doubt that Esmond Haddock would spring to the task of taking on a fire-breathing dragon, but there isn't the remotest chance of him ever standing up to Dame Daphne Winkworth, and the Misses Charlotte, Emmeline, Harriet and Myrtle Deverill and making them play ball.'

'I wonder, sir?'

'What do you mean, you wonder, Jeeves?'

'It crossed my mind as a possibility, sir, that were Mr Haddock's performance at the concert to be the success he anticipates, his attitude might become more resolute. I have not myself had the opportunity of studying the young gentleman's psychology, but from what my Uncle Charlie tells me I am convinced that he is one of these gentlemen on whom popular acclamation might have sensational effects. Mr Haddock's has been, as you say, a repressed life, and he has, no doubt, a very marked inferiority complex. The cheers of the multitude frequently act like a powerful drug upon young gentlemen with inferiority complexes.'

I began to grasp the gist.

'You mean that if he makes a hit he will get it up his nose to such an extent that he will be able to look his aunts in the eye and make them wilt?'

'Precisely, sir. You will recall the case of Mr Little.'

'Golly, yes, that's right. Bingo became a changed man, didn't he? Jeeves, I believe you've got something.'

'At least the theory which I have advanced is a tenable one, sir.'

'It's more than tenable. It's a pip. Then what we've got to do is to strain every nerve to see that he makes a hit. What are those things people have?'

'Sir?'

'Opera singers and people like that.'

'You mean a claque, sir?'

'That's right. The word was on the tip of my tongue. He must be provided with a claque. It will be your task, Jeeves, to move about the village, dropping a word here, standing a beer there, till the whole community is impressed with the necessity of cheering Esmond Haddock's song till their eyes bubble. I can leave this to you?'

'Certainly, sir. I will attend to the matter.'

'Fine. And now I suppose I ought to be getting up and seeing Gussie. There are probably one or two points he will want to discuss. Is there a ruined mill around here?'

'Not to my knowledge, sir.'

'Well any landmark where you could tell him to meet me? I don't want to roam the house and grounds, looking for him. My aim is rather to sneak down the back stairs and skirt around the garden via the shrubberies. You follow me, Jeeves?'

'Perfectly, sir. I would suggest that I arrange with Mr Fink-Nottle to meet you in, say, an hour's time outside the local post office.'

'Right,' I said. 'Outside the post office in an hour or sixty minutes. And now, Jeeves, if you will be so good as to turn it on, the refreshing bath.'

9

What with one thing and another, singing a bit too much in the bath and so on, I was about five minutes behind scheduled time in reaching the post office, and when I got there I found Gussie already at the tryst.

Jeeves, in speaking of this Fink-Nottle, had, if you remember, described him as disgruntled, and it was plain at a glance that the passage of time had done nothing to gruntle him. The eyes behind their horn-rimmed spectacles were burning with fury and resentment and all that sort of thing. He looked like a peevish halibut. In moment of emotion Gussie's resemblance to some marine monster always becomes accentuated.

'Well,' he said, starting in without so much as a What-ho. 'This is a pretty state of things!'

It seemed to me that a cheery, pep-giving word would be in order. I proceeded, accordingly, to shoot it across. Assenting to his opinion that the state of things was pretty, I urged him to keep the tail up, pointing out that though the storm clouds might lower, he was better off at Deverill Hall than he would have been in a dark dungeon with dripping walls and a platoon of resident rats, if that's where they put fellows who have been given fourteen days without the option at Bosher Street police court.

He replied curtly that he entirely disagreed with me.

'I would greatly have preferred prison,' he said. 'When you're in prison, you don't have people calling you Mr Wooster. How do you suppose I feel, knowing that everybody thinks I'm you?'

This startled me, I confess. Of all the things I had to worry about, the one that was gashing me like a knife most was the thought that the populace, beholding Gussie, were under the impression that there stood Bertram Wooster. When I reflected that the little world of King's Deverill would go to its grave believing that Bertram Wooster was an undersized gargoyle who looked like Lester de Pester in that comic strip in one of the New York papers, the iron entered my soul. It was a bit of a jar to learn that Gussie was suffering the same spiritual agonies.

'I don't know if you are aware,' he proceeded, 'what your reputation is in these parts? In case you are under any illusions, let me inform you that your name is mud. Those women at breakfast were drawing their skirts away as I passed. They shivered when I spoke to them. From time to time I would catch them looking at me in a way that would have wounded a smash-and-grab man. And, as if that wasn't bad enough, you seem in a single evening to have made my name mud, too. What's all this I hear about you getting tight last night and singing hunting songs?'

'I didn't get tight, Gussie. Just pleasantly mellowed, as you might say. And I sang hunting songs because my host seemed to wish it. One has to humour one's host. So they mentioned that, did they?'

'They mentioned it, all right. It was the chief topic of conversation at the breakfast table. And what's going to happen if they mention it to Madeline?'

'I advise stout denial.'

'It wouldn't work.'

'It might,' I said, for I had been giving a good deal of thought to the matter and was feeling more optimistic than I had been. 'After all, what can they prove?'

'Madeline's godmother said she came into the dining-room and found you on a chair, waving a decanter and singing A-hunting we will go.'

'True. We concede that. But who is to say that that decanter was not emptied exclusively by Esmond Haddock, who, you must remember, was on the table, also singing A-hunting we will go and urging his horse on with a banana? I feel convinced that, should the affair come to Madeline's ears, you can get away with it with stout denial.'

He pondered.

'Perhaps you're right. But all the same I wish you'd be more careful. The whole thing has been most annoying and upsetting.'

'Still,' I said, feeling that it was worth trying, 'it's part of the great web, what?'

'Great web?'

'One of Marcus Aurelius's cracks. He said: "Does aught befall you? It is good. It is part of the destiny of the Universe ordained for you from the beginning. All that befalls you is part of the great web."'

From the brusque manner in which he damned and blasted Marcus Aurelius, I gathered that, just as had happened when Jeeves sprang it on me, the gag had failed to bring balm. I hadn't had much hope that it would. I doubt, as a matter of fact, if Marcus Aurelius's material is ever the stuff to give the troops at a moment when they have just stubbed their toe on the brick of Fate. You want to wait till the agony has abated.

To ease the strain, I changed the subject, asking him if he had been surprised to find Catsmeat in residence at the hall, and immediately became aware that I had but poured kerosene on the flames. Heated though his observations on Marcus Aurelius had been, they were mildness itself compared with what he had to say about Catsmeat.

It was understandable, of course. If a fellow has forced you against your better judgment to go wading in the Trafalgar Square fountain at five in the morning, ruining your trousers and causing you to be pinched and jugged and generally put through it by the machinery of the Law, no doubt you do find yourself coming round to the view that what he needs is disembowelling with a blunt bread-knife. This, among other things, was what Gussie hoped some day to be able to do to Catsmeat, if all went well, and, as I say, one could follow the train of thought.

Presently, having said all he could think of on the topic of Catsmeat, he turned, as I had rather been expecting he would, to that of the cross-talk act of which the other was the originator and producer.

'What's all this Pirbright was saying about something he called a cross-talk act?' he asked, and I saw that we had reached a point in the exchanges where suavity and the honeyed word would be needed.

'Ah, yes, he mentioned that to you did he not? It's an item on the programme of the concert which his sister is impresarioing at the village hall shortly. I was to have played Pat in it, but owing to the changed circumstances you will now sustain the role.'

'Will I! We'll see about that. What the devil is the damned thing?'

'Haven't you seen it? Pongo Twistleton and Barmy Phipps do it every year at the Drones smoker.'

'I never go to the Drones smoker.'

'Oh? Well, it's a . . . How shall I put it? . . . It's what is known as a cross-talk act. The principals are a couple of Irishmen named Pat and Mike, and they come on and . . . But I have the script here,' I said, producing it. 'If you glance through it, you'll get the idea.'

He took the script and studied it with a sullen frown. Watching him, I realized what a ghastly job it must be writing plays. I mean, having to hand over your little effort to a hardfaced manager and stand shuffling your feet while he glares at it as if it hurt him in a tender spot, preparatory to pushing it back at you with a curt 'It stinks'.

'Who wrote this?' asked Gussie, as he turned the final page, and when I told him that Catsmeat was the author he said he might have guessed it. Throughout his perusal, he had been snorting at intervals, and he snorted again, a good bit louder, as if he were amalgamating about six snorts into one snort.

'The thing is absolute drivel. It has no dramatic coherence. It lacks motivation and significant form. Who are these two men supposed to be?'

'I told you. A couple of Irishmen named Pat and Mike.'

'Well, perhaps you can explain what their social position is, for it is frankly beyond me. Pat, for instance, appears to move in the very highest circles, for he describes himself as dining at Buckingham Palace, and yet his wife takes in lodgers.'

'I see what you mean. Odd.'

'Inexplicable. Is it credible that a man of his class would be invited to dinner at Buckingham Palace, especially as he is apparently completely without social *savoir-faire?* At this dinner party to which he alludes he relates how the Queen asked him if he would like some mulligatawny and he, thinking that there was nothing else coming, had six helpings, with the result that, to quote his words, he spent the rest of the evening sitting in a corner full of soup. And in describing the incident he prefaces his remarks at several points with the expressions "Begorrah" and "faith and begob". Irishmen don't talk like that. Have you ever read Synge's *Riders to the Sea?* Well, get hold of it and study it, and if you can show me a single character in it who says "Faith and begob", I'll give you a shilling. Irishmen are poets. They talk about their souls and mist and so on. They say things like "An evening like this, it makes me wish I was back in County Clare, watchin' the cows in the tall grass".'

He turned the pages frowningly, his nose wrinkled as if it had detected some unpleasant smell. It brought back to me the old days at Malvern House, Bramley-on-Sea, when I used to take my English essay to be blue-pencilled by the Rev. Aubrey Upjohn.

'Here's another bit of incoherent raving. "My sister's in the ballet." "You say your sister's in the ballet?" "Yes, begorrah, my sister's in the ballet." "What does your sister do in the ballet?" "She comes rushing in, and then she goes rushing out." "What does she have to rush like that for?" "Faith and begob, because it's a Rushin' ballet." It simply doesn't make sense. And now we come to something else that is quite beyond me, the word "*bus*". After the line "Because it's a Rushin' ballet" and in other places throughout the script the word "*bus*" in brackets occurs. It conveys nothing to me. Can you explain it?'

'It's short for "*business*". That's where you hit Mike with your umbrella. To show the audience that there has been a joke.'

Gussie started.

'Are these things jokes?'

'Yes.'

'I see. I *see*. Well, of course, that throws a different light on . . .' He paused, and eyed me narrowly. 'Did you say that I am supposed to strike my colleague with an umbrella?'

'That's right.'

'And if I understood Pirbright correctly, the other performer in this extraordinary production is the local policeman?'

'That's right.'

'The whole thing is impossible and utterly out of the question,' said Gussie vehemently. 'Have you any idea what happens when you hit a policeman with an umbrella? I did so on emerging from the fountain in Trafalgar Square, and I certainly do not intend to do it again.' A sort of grey horror came into his face, as if he had been taking a quick look into a past which he had hoped to forget. 'Well, let me put you quite straight, Wooster, as to what my stand is in this matter. I shall not say "Begorrah". I shall not say "Faith and begob". I shall not assault policemen with an umbrella. In short, I absolutely and positively refuse to have the slightest association with this degraded buffoonery. Wait till I meet Miss Pirbright. I'll tell her a thing or two. I'll show her she can't play fast and loose with human dignity like this.'

He was about to speak further, but at this point his voice died away in a sort of gurgle and I saw his eyes bulge. Glancing around, I perceived Corky approaching. She was accompanied by Sam Goldwyn and was looking, as is her wont, like a million dollars, gowned in some clinging material which accentuated rather than hid her graceful outlines, if you know what I mean.

I was delighted to see her. With Gussie in this non-cooperative mood, digging his feet in and refusing to play ball, like Balaam's ass, it seemed to me that precisely what was needed was the woman's touch. To decide to introduce them and leave her to take on the job of melting his iron front was with me the work of a moment.

I had high hopes that she would be able to swing the deal. Though differing from my Aunt Agatha in almost every possible respect, Corky has this in common with that outstanding scourge: she is authoritative. When she wants you to do a thing, you find yourself doing it. This has been so from her earliest years. I remember her on one occasion at our mutual dancing class handing me an antique orange, a blue and yellow mass of pips and mildew, and bidding me bung it at our instructress, who had incurred her displeasure for some reason which has escaped my recollection. And I did it without a murmur, though knowing full well how bitter the reckoning would be.

'Hoy!' I said, eluding the cheesehound's attempts to place his front paws on my shoulders and strop his tongue on my face. I jerked a thumb. 'Gussie,' I said.

Corky's face lit up in a tickled-to-death manner. She proceeded immediately to turn on the charm.

'Oh, is *this* Mr Fink-Nottle? How do you do, Mr Fink-Nottle? I *am* so glad to see you, Mr Fink-Nottle. How lucky meeting you. I wanted to talk to you about the act.'

'We've just been having a word or two on that subject,' I said, 'and Gussie's kicking a bit at playing Pat.'

'Oh, *no?*'

'I thought you might like to reason with him. I'll leave you to it,' I said and biffed off. Looking around as I turned the corner, I saw that she had attached herself with one slim hand to the lapel of Gussie's coat and with the other was making wide, appealing gestures, indicating to the most vapid and irreflective observer that she was giving him Treatment A.

Well pleased, I made my way back to the hall, keeping an eye skinned for prowling aunts, and won through without disaster to my room. I was enjoying a thoughtful smoke there about half an hour later when Gussie came in, and I could see right away that this was not the morose, sullen Fink-Nottle who had so uncompromisingly panned the daylights out of Pat and Mike in the course of our recent get-together. His bearing was buoyant. His face glowed. He was wearing in his buttonhole a flower which had not been there before.

'Hallo, there, Bertie,' he said. 'I say, Bertie, why didn't you tell me that Miss Pirbright was Cora Starr, the film actress? I have long been one of her warmest admirers. What a delightful girl she is, is she not, and how unlike her brother, whom I consider and always shall consider England's leading louse. She has made me see this cross-talk act in an entirely new light.'

'I thought she might.'

'It's extraordinary that a girl as pretty as that should also have a razor-keen intelligence and that amazing way of putting her arguments with a crystal clarity which convinces you in an instant that she is right in every respect.'

'Yes, Corky's a persuasive young gum-boil.'

'I would prefer that you did not speak of her as a gum-boil. Corky, eh? That's what you call her, is it? A charming name.'

'What was the outcome of your conference? Are you going to do the act?'

'Oh, yes, it's all settled. She overcame my objections entirely. We ran through the script after you had left us, and she quite brought me round to her view that there is nothing in the least degrading in this simple, wholesome form of humour. Hokum, yes, but, as she pointed out good theatre. She is convinced that I shall go over big.'

'You'll knock 'em cold. I'm sorry I can't play Pat myself –'

'A good thing, probably. I doubt if you are the type.'

'Of course I'm the type,' I retorted hotly. 'I should have given a sensational performance.'

'Corky thinks not. She was telling me how thankful she was that you had stepped out and I had taken over. She said the part wants broad, robust treatment and you would have played it too far down. It's a part that calls for personality and the most precise timing, and she said that the moment she saw me she felt that here was the ideal Pat. Girls with her experience can tell in a second.'

I gave it up. You can't reason with hams, and twenty minutes of Corky's society seemed to have turned Augustus Fink-Nottle from a blameless newt-fancier into as pronounced a ham as ever drank small ports in Bodegas and called people 'laddie'. In another half jiffy, I felt, he would be addressing me as 'laddie'.

'Well, it's no use talking about it,' I said, 'because I could never have taken the thing on. Madeline wouldn't have approved of her affianced appearing in public in a green beard.'

'No, she's an odd girl.'

It seemed to me that I might wipe that silly smile off his face by reminding him of something he appeared to have forgotten.

'And how about Dobbs?'

'Eh?'

'When last heard from, you were a bit agitated at the prospect of having to slosh Police Constable Dobbs with your umbrella.'

'Oh, Dobbs? He's out. He's been given his notice. He came along when we were rehearsing and started to read Mike's lines, but he was hopeless. No technique. No personality. And he wouldn't take direction. Kept arguing every point with the management, until finally Corky got heated and began raising her voice, and he got heated and began raising his voice, and the upshot was that that dog of hers, excited no doubt by the uproar, bit him in the leg.'

'Good Lord!'

'Yes, it created an unpleasant atmosphere. Corky put the animal's case extremely well, pointing out that it had probably been pushed around by policemen since it was a slip of a puppy and so was merely fulfilling a legitimate aspiration if it took an occasional nip at one, but Dobbs refused to accept her view that the offence was one calling for a mere reprimand. He took the creature into custody and is keeping it at the police station until he has been able to ascertain whether this was its first bite. Apparently a dog that has had only one bite is in a strong position legally.'

'Sam Goldwyn bit Silversmith last night.'

'Did he? Well, if that comes out, I'm afraid counsel for the prosecution will have a talking-point. But, to go on with my story, Corky, incensed, and quite rightly, by Dobbs's intransigent attitude, threw him out of the act and is getting her brother to play the part. There is the risk, of course, that the vicar will recognize him, which would lead to an unfortunate situation, but she thinks the green beard will form a sufficient disguise. I am looking forward to having Pirbright as a partner. I can think of few men whom it would give me more genuine pleasure to hit with an umbrella,' said Gussie broodingly, adding that the first time his weapon connected with Catsmeat's head, the latter would think he had been struck by a thunderbolt. It was plain that Time, the great healer, would have to put in a lot of solid work before he forgot and forgave.

'But I can't stay here talking,' he went on. 'Corky has asked me to lunch at the Vicarage, and I must be getting along. I just looked in to give you those poems.'

'Those what?'

'Those Christopher Robin poems. Here they are.'

He handed me a slim volume of verse, and I gave it the perplexed eye.

'What's this for?'

'You recite them at the concert. The ones marked with a cross. I was to have recited them, Madeline making a great point of it – you know how fond she is of the Christopher Robin poems – but now, of course, we have switched acts. And I don't mind telling you that I feel extremely relieved. There's one about the little blighter going hoppity-hoppity-hop which . . . Well, as I say, I feel extremely relieved.'

The slim volume fell from my nerveless fingers, and I goggled at him.

'But, dash it!'

'It's no good saying "But, dash it!" Do you think I didn't say "But, dash it!" when she forced nauseous productions on me? You've got to do them. She insists. The first thing she will want to know is how they went.'

'But the tough eggs at the back of the row will rush the stage and lynch me.'

'I shouldn't wonder. Still, you've got one consolation.'

'What's that?'

'The thought that all that befalls you is part of the great web, ha, ha, ha,' said Gussie, and exited smiling.

And so the first day of my sojourn at Deverill Hall wore to a close, full to the brim of V-shaped depressions and unsettled outlooks.

10

And as the days went by, these unsettled outlooks became more unsettled, those V-shaped depressions even V-er. It was on Friday that I had clocked in at Deverill Hall. By the morning of Tuesday I could no longer conceal it from myself that I was losing the old pep and that, unless the clouds changed their act and started dishing out at an early date a considerably more substantial slab of silver lining than they were coming across with at the moment, I should soon be definitely down among the wines and spirits.

It is bad to be trapped in a den of slavering aunts, lashing their tails and glaring at you out of their red eyes. It is unnerving to know that in a couple of days you will be up on a platform in a village hall telling an audience, probably well provided with vegetables, that Christopher Robin goes hoppity-hoppity-hop. It degrades the spirit to have to answer to the name of Augustus, and there are juicier experiences than being in a position where you are constantly asking yourself if an Aunt Agatha or a Madeline Bassett won't suddenly arrive and subject you to shame and exposure. No argument about that. We can take that, I think, as read.

But it was not these chunks of the great web that were removing the stiffening from the Wooster upper lip. No, the root of the trouble, the thing that was giving me dizzy spells and night sweats and making me look like the poor bit of human wreckage in the 'before taking' pictures in the advertisements of Haddock's Headache Hokies, was the sinister behaviour of Gussie Fink-Nottle. Contemplating Gussie, I found my soul darkened by a nameless fear.

I don't know if you have ever had your soul darkened by a nameless fear. It's a most unpleasant feeling. I used to get it when I was one of the resident toads beneath the harrow at Malvern House, Bramley-on-Sea, on hearing the Rev. Aubrey Upjohn conclude a series of announcements with the curt crack that he would like to see Wooster in his study after evening prayers. On the present occasion I had felt it coming on during the conversation with Gussie which I have just related, and in the days that followed it had grown and grown until now I found myself what is known as a prey to the liveliest apprehension.

I wonder if you spotted anything in the conversation to which I refer? Did it, I mean, strike you as significant and start you saying 'What ho!' to yourself? It didn't? Then you missed the gist.

The first day I had had merely a vague suspicion. The second day this suspicion deepened. By nightfall on the third day suspicion had become a certainty. The evidence was all in, and there was no getting round it. Reckless of the fact that there existed at The Larches, Wimbledon Common, a girl to whom he had plighted his troth and who would be madder than a bull-pup entangled in a fly-paper were she to discover that he was moving in on another, Augustus Fink-Nottle had fallen for Corky Pirbright like a ton of bricks.

You may say 'Come, come, Bertram, you are imagining things' or 'Tush, Wooster, this is but an idle fancy', but let me tell you that I wasn't the only one who had noticed it. Five solid aunts had noticed it.

'Well, really,' Dame Daphne Winkworth had observed bitterly just before lunch, when Silversmith had blown in with the news that Gussie had once again telephoned to say he would be taking pot-luck at the Vicarage, 'Mr Wooster seems to live in Miss Pirbright's pocket. He appears to regard Deverill Hall as a hotel which he can drop into or stay away from as he feels inclined.'

And Aunt Charlotte, when the facts had been relayed to her through her ear-trumpet, for she was wired for sound, had said with a short, quick sniff that she supposed they ought to consider themselves highly honoured that the piefaced young bastard condescended to sleep in the bally place, or words to that effect.

Nor could one fairly blame them for blinding and stiffing. Nothing sticks the gaff into your chatelaine more than a guest being constantly AWOL, and it was only on the rarest occasions nowadays that Gussie saw fit to put on the nosebag at Deverill Hall. He lunched, tea-ed and dined with Corky. Since that first meeting outside the post office he had seldom left her side. The human poultice, nothing less.

You can readily understand, then, why there were dark circles beneath my eyes and why I had almost permanently now a fluttering sensation at the pit of the stomach, as if I had recently swallowed far more mice than I could have wished. It only needed a word from Dame Daphne Winkworth to Aunt Agatha to the effect that her nephew Bertram had fallen into the toils of a most undesirable girl – a Hollywood film actress, my dear – I could see her writing it as clearly as if I had been peeping over her shoulder – to bring the old relative racing down to Deverill Hall with her foot in her hand. And then what? Ruin, desolation and despair.

The obvious procedure, of course, when the morale is being given the sleeve across the windpipe like this, is to get in touch with Jeeves and see what he has to suggest. So, encountering the parlourmaid, Queenie, in the passage outside my room after lunch, I enquired as to his whereabouts.

'I say,' I said, 'I wonder if you happen to know where Jeeves is? Wooster's man, you know.'

She stood staring at me goofily. Her eyes, normally like twin stars, were dull and a bit reddish about the edges, and I should have described her face as drawn. The whole set-up, in short, seeming to indicate that here one had a parlourmaid who had either gone off her onion or was wrestling with a secret sorrow.

'Sir?' she said, in a tortured sort of voice.

I repeated my remarks, and this time they penetrated.

'Mr Jeeves isn't here, sir. Mr Wooster let him go to London. There was a lecture he wanted to be at.'

'Oh thanks,' I said, speaking dully, for this was a blow. 'You don't know when he'll be back?'

'No, sir.'

'I see. Thanks.'

I went on into my room and took a good, square look at the situation.

If you ask any of the nibs who move in diplomatic circles and are accustomed to handling tricky affairs of state, he will tell you that when matters have reached a deadlock, it is not a bit of good just sitting on the seat of the pants and rolling the eyes up to heaven – you have got to turn stones and explore avenues and take prompt steps through the proper channels. Only thus can you hope to find a formula. And it seemed to me, musing tensely, that in the present crisis something constructive might be accomplished by rounding up Corky and giving her a straight-from-the-shoulder talk, pointing out the frightful jeopardy in which she was placing an old friend and dancing-class buddy by allowing Gussie to spend his time frisking and bleating round her.

I left the room, accordingly, and a few minutes later might have been observed stealing through the sunlit grounds en route for the village. In fact, I was observed, and by Dame Daphne Winkworth. I was nearing the bottom of the drive and in another moment should have won through to safety, when somebody called my name – or, rather, Gussie's name – and I saw the formidable old egg standing in the rose garden. From the fact that she had a syringe in her hand I deduced that she was in the process of doing the local green-fly a bit of no good.

'Come here, Augustus,' she said.

It was the last thing I would have done, if given the choice, for even at the best of times this dangerous specimen put the wind up me pretty vertically, and she was now looking about ten degrees more forbidding than usual. Her voice was cold and her eye was cold, and I didn't like the way she was toying with that syringe. It was plain that for some reason I had fallen in her estimation to approximately the level of a green-fly, and her air was that of a woman who for two pins would press the trigger and let me have a fluid ounce of whatever the hell-brew was squarely in the mazzard.

'Oh, hallo,' I said, trying to be debonair but missing by a mile. 'Squirting the rose trees?'

'Don't talk to me about rose trees!'

'Oh, no, rather not,' I said. Well, I hadn't wanted to particularly. Just filling in with *ad lib* stuff.

'Augustus, what is this I hear?'

'I beg your pardon?'

'You would do better to beg Madeline's.'

Mystic stuff. I didn't get it. The impression I received was of a Dame of the British Empire talking through the back of her neck.

'When I was in the house just now,' she proceeded, 'a telegram arrived for you from Madeline. It was telephoned from the post office. Sometimes they telephone, and sometimes they deliver personally.'

'I see. According to the whim of the moment.'

'Please do not interrupt. This time it happened that the message was telephoned, and as I was passing through the hall when the bell rang, I took it down.'

'Frightfully white of you,' I said, feeling that I couldn't go wrong in giving her the old oil.

I had gone wrong, however. She didn't like it. She frowned, raised the syringe, then, as if remembering in time that she was a Deverill, lowered it again.

'I have already asked you not to interrupt. I took down the message, as I say, and I have it here. No,' she said, having searched through her costume, 'I must have left it on the hall table. But I can tell you its contents. Madeline says she has not received a single letter from you since you arrived at the hall, and she wishes to know why. She is greatly distressed at your abominable neglect, and I am not surprised. You know how sensitive she is. You ought to have been writing to her every day. I have no words to express what I think of your heartless behaviour. That is all, Augustus,' she said, and dismissed me with a gesture of loathing, as if I had been a green-fly that had fallen short of even the very moderate level of decency of the average run-of-the-mill green-fly. And I tottered off and groped my way to a rustic bench and sank onto it.

The information which she had sprung on me had, I need scarcely say, affected me like the impact behind the ear of a stocking full of wet sand. Only once in my career had I experienced an emotion equally intense, on the occasion when Freddie Widgeon at the Drones, having possessed himself of a motor horn, stole up behind me as I crossed Dover Street in what is known as a reverie and suddenly tooted the apparatus in my immediate ear.

It had never so much as occurred to me to suppose that Gussie was not writing daily letters to the Bassett. It was what he had come to this Edgar Allen Poe residence to do, and I had taken it for granted that he was doing it. I didn't need a diagram to show me what the run of events would be, if he persisted in this policy of ca'canny. A spot more silence on his part, and along would come La Bassett in person to investigate, and the thought of what would happen then froze the blood and made the toes curl.

I suppose it may have been for a matter of about ten minutes that I sat there inert, the jaw drooping, the eyes staring sightlessly at the surrounding scenery. Then I pulled myself together and resumed my journey. It has been well said of Bertram Wooster that though he may sink onto rustic benches and for a while give the impression of being licked to a custard, the old spirit will always come surging back sooner or later.

As I walked, I was thinking hard and bitter thoughts of Corky, the *fons et origo*, if you know what I mean by *fons et origo*, of all the trouble. It was she who, by shamelessly flirting with him, by persistently giving him the flashing smile and the quick sidelong look out of the corner of the eye, had taken Gussie's mind off his job and slowed him up as our correspondent on the spot. Oh, Woman, Woman, I said to myself, not for the first time, feeling that the sooner the sex was suppressed, the better it would be for all of us.

At the age of eight, in the old dancing-class days, incensed by some incisive remarks on her part about my pimples, of which I had a notable collection at that time, I once forgot myself to the extent of socking Corky Pirbright on the top-knot with a wooden dumb-bell, and until this moment I had always regretted the unpleasant affair, considering my action a blot on an otherwise stainless record and, no matter what the provocation, scarcely the behaviour of a *preux chevalier*. But now, as I brooded on the Delilah stuff she was pulling, I found myself wishing I could do it again.

I strode on, rehearsing in my mind some opening sentence to be employed when we should meet, and not far from the Vicarage came upon her seated at the wheel of her car by the side of the road.

But when I confronted her and said I wanted a word with her, she regretted that it couldn't be managed at the moment. It was, she explained, her busy afternoon. In pursuance of her policy of being the Little Mother to her uncle, the sainted Sidney, she was about to take a bowl of strengthening soup to one of his needy parishioners.

'A Mrs Clara Wellbeloved, if you want to keep the record straight,' she proceeded. 'She lives in one of those picturesque cottages of the High Street. And it's no good you waiting, because after delivering the bouillon I sit and talk to her about Hollywood. She's a great fan, and it takes hours. Some other time, my lamb.'

'Listen, Corky –'

'You are probably saying to yourself "Where's the soup?" I unfortunately forgot to bring it along, and Gussie has trotted back for it. What a delightful man he is, Bertie. So kind. So helpful. Always on hand to run errands, when required, and with a fund of good stories about newts. I've given him my autograph. Speaking of autographs, I heard from your cousin Thomas this morning.'

'Never mind about young Thos. What I want –'

She broke into speech again, as girls always do. I have had a good deal of experience of this tendency on the part of the female sex to refrain from listening when you talk to them, and it has always made me sympathize with those fellows who tried to charm the deaf adder and had it react like a Wednesday matinée audience.

'You remember I gave him fifty of my autographs, and he expected to sell them to his playmates at sixpence apiece? Well, he tells me that he got a bob, not sixpence, which will give you a rough idea of how I stand with the boys at Bramley-on-Sea. He says a genuine Ida Lupino only fetches ninepence.'

'Listen, Corky –'

'He wants to come and spend his midterm holiday at the Vicarage, and, of course, I've written to say that I shall be delighted. I don't think Uncle Sidney is too happy at the prospect, but it's good for a clergyman to have these trials. Makes him more spiritual, and consequently hotter at his job.'

'Listen, Corky. What I want to talk to you about –'

'Ah, here's Gussie,' she said, once more doing the deaf adder.

Gussie came bounding up with a look of reverent adoration on his face and a steaming can in his hands. Corky gave him a dazzling smile which seemed to go through him like a red-hot bullet through a pat of butter, and stowed the can away in the rumble seat.

'Thank you, Gussie darling,' she said. 'Well, goodbye all. I must rush.'

She drove off, Gussie standing gaping after her transfixed, like a goldfish staring at an ant's egg. He did not, however, remain transfixed long, because I got him between the third and fourth ribs with a forceful finger, causing him to come to life with a sharp 'Ouch!'

'Gussie,' I said, getting down to brass tacks and beating about no bushes. 'What's all this about you not writing to Madeline?'

'Madeline?'

'Madeline.'

'Oh, Madeline?'

'Yes, Madeline. You ought to have been writing to her every day.'

This seemed to annoy him.

'How on earth could I write to her every day? What chance do I get to write letters when my time is all taken up with memorizing my lines in this cross-talk act and thinking up effective business? I haven't a moment.'

'Well, you'll jolly well have to find a moment. Do you realize she's started sending telegrams about it? You must write today without fail.'

'What, to Madeline?'

'Yes, blast you, to Madeline.'

I was surprised to see that he was glowering sullenly through his windshields.

'I'll be blowed if I write to Madeline,' he said, and would have looked like a mule if he had not looked so like a fish. 'I'm teaching her a lesson.'

'You're what?'

'Teaching her a lesson. I'm not at all pleased with Madeline. She wanted me to come to this ghastly house, and I consented on the understanding that she would come, too, and give me moral support. It was a clear-cut gentlemen's agreement. And at the last moment she coolly backed out on the flimsy plea that some school friend of hers at Wimbledon needed her. I was extremely annoyed, and I let her see it. She must be made to realize that she can't do that sort of thing. So I'm not writing to her. It's a sort of system.'

I clutched at the brow. The mice in my interior had now got up an informal dance and were buck-and-winging all over the place like a bunch of Nijinskys.

Gussie,' I said, 'once and for all, will you or will you not go back to the house and compose an eight-page letter breathing love in every syllable?'

'No, I won't,' he said and left me flat.

Baffled and despondent, I returned to the Hall. And the first person I saw there was Catsmeat. He was in my room, lying on the bed with one of my cigarettes in his mouth.

There was a sort of dreamy look on his dial, as if he were thinking of Gertrude Winkworth.

11

Observing me, he switched off the dreamy look.

'Oh, hallo, Bertie,' he said. 'I wanted to see you.'

'Oh, yes?' I riposted, quick as a flash, and I meant it to sting, for I was feeling a bit fed up with Catsmeat.

I mean of his own free will he had taken on the job of valeting me, and in his capacity of my gentleman's personal gentleman should have been in and out all the time, brushing here a coat, pressing there a trouser and generally making himself useful, and I hadn't set eyes on him since the night we had arrived. One frowns on this absenteeism.

'I wanted to tell you the good news.'

I laughed hollowly.

'Good news? Is there such a thing?'

'You bet there's such a thing. Things are looking up. The sun is smiling through. I believe I'm going to swing this Gertrude deal. Owing to the footling social conventions which prevent visiting valets hobnobbing with the daughter of the house, I haven't seen her, of course, to speak to, but I've been sending her notes by Jeeves and she has been sending me notes by Jeeves, and in her latest she shows distinct signs of yielding to my prayers. I think about two more communications, if carefully worded, should do the trick. Don't actually buy the fish-slice yet, but be prepared.'

My pique vanished. As I have said before, the Woosters are fair-minded. I knew what a dickens of a sweat these love letters are, a whole-time job calling for incessant concentration. If Catsmeat had been tied up with a lot of correspondence of this type, he wouldn't have had much time for attending to my wardrobe, of course. You can't press your suit and another fellow's trousers simultaneously.

'Well, that's fine,' I said, pleased to learn that, though the general outlook was so scaly, someone was getting a break. 'I shall watch your future progress with considerable interest. But pigeon-holing your love life for the moment, Catsmeat, a most frightful thing has happened, and I should be glad if you could come across with anything in the aid-and-comfort line. That criminal lunatic Gussie –'

'What's he been doing?'

'It's what he's not been doing that's the trouble. You could have flattened me with a toothpick just now when I found out that he hasn't written a single line to Madeline Bassett since he got here. And, what's more, he says he isn't going to write to her. He says he's teaching her a lesson,' I said, and in a few brief words placed the facts before him.

He looked properly concerned. Catsmeat's is a kindly and feeling heart, readily moved by the spectacle of an old friend splashing about in the gumbo, and he knows how I stand with regard to Madeline Bassett, because she told him the whole story one day when they met at a bazaar and the subject of me happened to come up.

'This is rather serious,' he said.

'You bet it's serious. I'm shaking like a leaf.'

'Girls of the Madeline Bassett type attach such importance to the daily letter.'

'Exactly. And if it fails to arrive, they come and make inquiries on the spot.'

'And you say Gussie was not to be moved?'

'Not an inch. I pleaded with him, I may say passionately, but he put his ears back and refused to cooperate.'

Catsmeat pondered.

'I think I know what's behind all this. The trouble is that Gussie at the moment is slightly off his rocker.'

'What do you mean, at the moment? And why slightly?'

'He's infatuated with Corky. Sorry to use such long words. I mean he's got a crush on her.'

'I know he has. So does everybody else for miles around. His crush is the favourite topic of conversation when aunt meets aunt.'

'There has been comment in the servants' hall, too.'

'I'm not surprised. I'll bet they're discussing the thing in Basingstoke.'

'You can't blame him, of course.'

'Yes, I can.'

'I mean, it isn't his fault, really. This is spring-time, Bertie, the mating season, when, as you probably know, a livelier iris gleams upon the burnished dove and a young man's fancy lightly turns to thoughts of love. The sudden impact plumb span in the middle of spring, of a girl like Corky on a fathead like Gussie, weakened by constantly swilling orange juice, must have been terrific. Corky, when she's going nicely, bowls over the strongest. No one knows that better than you. You were making a colossal ass of yourself over her at one time.'

'No need to rake up the dead past.'

'I only raked it up to drive home my point, which is that he is more to be pitied than censured.'

'She's the one that wants censuring. Why does she encourage him?'

'I don't think she encourages him. He just adheres.'

'She does encourage him. I've seen her doing it. She deliberately turns on the charm and gives him the old personality. Don't tell me that a girl like Corky, accustomed to giving Hollywood glamour men the brusheroo, couldn't put Gussie on ice, if she wanted to.'

'But she doesn't.'

'That's what I'm beefing about.'

'And I'll tell you why she doesn't. I haven't actually asked her, but I'm pretty sure she's working this Gussie continuity with the idea of sticking the harpoon into Esmond Haddock. To show him that if he doesn't want her, there are others who do.'

'But he does want her.'

'She doesn't know that. Unless you've told her.'

'I haven't.'

'Why not?'

'I wasn't sure if it would be the correct procedure. You see, he dished out all that stuff about his inner feelings under the seal of the confessional, as you might say, and he said he didn't want it to go any further. "This must go no further," he said. On the other hand, a word in season might quite easily reunite a couple of sundered hearts. The whole thing is extraordinarily moot.'

'I'd go ahead and tell her. Bung in the word in season. I'm all for reuniting sundered hearts.'

'Me, too. But I think we've left it too late. Already the Bassett is burning up the wires with telegrams asking what it's all about. A hot one just arrived. I found it on the hall table when I came in. It was the telegram of a girl on the verge of becoming fed to the eye teeth. I tell you, Catsmeat, I see no ray of light. I'm sunk.'

'No, you're not.'

'I am. When I told Gussie about this telegram, urging upon him that now was the time for all good men to come to the aid of the party, he merely as I say, stuck his ears back and said he was teaching the girl a lesson and not a smell of a letter should she get from him till that lesson had been learned. The man's *non compos*, and I repeat that I see no ray of light.'

'It seems to me it's all quite simple.'

'You mean you have something to suggest?'

'Of course I've something to suggest. I always have something to suggest. The thing's obvious. If Gussie won't write to this girl, you must write to her yourself.'

'But she doesn't want to hear from me. She wants to hear from Gussie.'

'And so she will, bless her heart. Gussie has sprained his wrist, so had to dictate the letter to you.'

'Gussie hasn't sprained his wrist.'

'Pardon me. He gave it a nasty wrench while stopping a runaway horse and at great personal risk saving a little child from a hideous death. A golden-haired child, if you will allow yourself to be guided by me, with blue eyes, pink cheeks and a lisp. I think a lisp is good box-office?'

I gasped. I had got his drift.

'Catsmeat, this is terrific! You'll write the thing?'

'Of course. It'll be pie. I've been writing Gertrude that sort of letter since I was so high.'

He seated himself at the table, took pen and paper and immediately became immersed in composition, as the expression is. I could see that it had been no idle boast on his part that the thing would be pie. He didn't even seem to have to stop and think. In almost no time he was handing me the finished script and bidding me get a jerk on and copy it out.

'It ought to go off at once, every moment being vital. Trot down to the post office with it yourself. Then she'll get it first thing in the morning. And now, Bertie, I must leave you. I promised to play gin rummy with Queenie, and I am already late. She wants cheering up, poor child. You've heard about her tragedy? The severing of her engagement to the flatty Dobbs?'

'No, really? Is her engagement off? Then that's why she was looking like that, I suppose. I ran into her after lunch,' I explained, 'and I got the impression that the heart was heavy. What went wrong?'

'She didn't like him being an atheist, and he wouldn't stop being an atheist, and finally he said something about Jonah and the Whale which it was impossible for her to overlook. This morning, she returned the ring, his letters and a china ornament with "A Present From Blackpool" on it, which he bought her last summer while visiting relatives in the north. It's hit her pretty hard, I'm afraid.

She's passing through the furnace. She loves him madly and yearns to be his, but she can't take that stuff about Jonah and the Whale. One can only hope that gin rummy will do something to ease the pain. Right ho, Bertie, get on with that letter. It's not actually one of my best, perhaps, because I was working against time and couldn't prune and polish, but I think you'll like it.'

He was correct. I studied the communication carefully, and was enchanted with its virtuosity. If it wasn't one of his best, his best must have been pretty good, and I was not surprised that upon receipt of a series Gertrude Winkworth was weakening. There are letters which sow doubts as to whether this bit here couldn't have been rather more neatly phrased and that bit there gingered up a trifle, and other letters of which you say to yourself 'This is the goods. Don't alter a word'. This was one of the latter letters. He had got just the right modest touch into the passage about the runaway horse, and the lisping child was terrific. She stuck out like a sore thumb and hogged the show. As for the warmer portions about missing Madeline every minute and wishing she were here so that he could fold her in his arms and what not, they simply couldn't have been improved upon.

I copied the thing out, stuffed it in an envelope and took it down to the post office. And scarcely had it plopped into the box, when I was hailed from behind by a musical soprano and, turning, saw Corky heaving alongside.

12

I felt profoundly bucked. The very girl I wanted to see. I grabbed her by the arm, so that she couldn't do another of her sudden sneaks.

'Corky,' I said, 'I want a long, heart to heart talk with you.'

'Not about Hollywood?'

'No, not about Hollywood.'

'Thank God. I don't think I could have stood any more Hollywood chatter this afternoon. I wouldn't have believed,' she said, proceeding, as always, to collar the conversation, 'that anybody except Louella Parsons and Hedda Hopper could be such an authority on the film world as is Mrs Clara Wellbeloved. She knows much more about it than I do, and I'll have been moving in celluloid circles two years come Lammas Eve. She knows exactly how many times everybody's been divorced and why, how much every picture for the last twenty years has grossed, and how many Warner brothers there are. She even knows how many times Artie Shaw has been married, which I'll bet he couldn't tell you himself. She asked if I had ever married Artie Shaw, and when I said No, seemed to think I was pulling her leg or must have done it without noticing. I tried to explain that when a girl goes to Hollywood she doesn't *have* to marry Artie Shaw, it's optional, but I don't think I convinced her. A very remarkable old lady, but a bit exhausting after the first hour or two. Did you say you wanted to speak to me about something.'

'Yes, I did.'

'Well, why don't you?'

'Because you won't let me get a word in edgeways.'

'Oh, have I been talking? I'm sorry. What's on your mind, my king?'

'Gussie.'

'Fink-Nottle?'

'Fink-Nottle is correct.'

'The whitest man I know.'

'The fatheadest man you know. Listen, Corky, I've just been talking to Catsmeat –'

'Did he tell you that he expects shortly to persuade Gertrude Winkworth to elope with him?'

'Yes.'

She smiled in a steely sort of way, like one of those women in the Old Testament who used to go about driving spikes into people's heads.

'I'm just waiting for that to happen,' she said, 'so that I can get a good laugh out of seeing Esmond's face when he finds out that his Gertrude has gone off with another. Most amusing it will be. Ha, ha,' she added.

That 'Ha, ha', so like the expiring quack of a duck dying of a broken heart, told me all I wanted to know. I saw that Catsmeat had not erred in his diagnosis of his young shrimp's motives in giving Gussie the old treatment, and I had no option but to slip her the lowdown without further delay. I tapped her on the shoulder, and bunged in the word in season.

'Corky,' I said, 'you're a chump. You've got a completely wrong angle on this Haddock. So far from being enamoured of Gertrude Winkworth, I don't suppose he would care, except in a distant, cousinly way, if she choked on a fish-bone. You are the lodestar of his life.'

'What!'

'I had it from his own lips. He was a bit pickled at the time, which makes it all the more impressive, because *in vino* what's-the-word.'

Her eyes had lighted up. She gave a quick gulp.

'He said I was the lodestar of his life?'

'With a "still" in front of the "lodestar". "Mark this," he said, helping himself to port, of which he was already nearly full. "Though she has given me the brusheroo, she is still the lodestar of my life."'

'Bertie, if you're kidding –'

'Of course I'm not.'

'I hope you're not, because if you are I shall put the curse of the Pirbrights on you, and it's not at all the sort of curse you will enjoy. Tell me more.'

I told her more. In fact I told her all. When I had finished, she laughed like a hyaena and also, for girls never make sense, let fall a pearly tear or two.

'Isn't that just the sort of thing he would think up, bless him!' she said, alluding to the hot idea Esmond Haddock had brought back with him from the Basingstoke cinema. 'What a woolly lambkin that man is!'

I was not sure if 'woolly lambkin' was quite the phrase I would have used myself to describe Esmond Haddock, but I let it go, it being no affair of mine. If she elected to regard a fellow with a forty-six-inch chest and muscles like writhing snakes as a woolly lambkin, that was up to her. My task, having started a good thing, was to push it along.

'In these circs,' I said, 'you will probably be glad of a word of advice from a knowledgeable man of the world. Catsmeat appears to have obtained excellent results on the Gertrude front from pouring out his soul in the form of notes, and if you take my tip, you will do the same. Drop Esmond Haddock a civil line telling him you are aching for his presence, and he will lower the world's record racing round to the Vicarage to fold you in his arms. He's only waiting for the green light.'

She shook her head.

'No,' she said.

'Why no?'

'We should simply be where we were before.'

I saw what she was driving at, of course.

'I know what's in your mind,' I said. 'You are alluding to his civil disobedience *in re* defying his aunts. Well, let me assure you that that little difficulty will very shortly yield to treatment. Listen. Esmond Haddock is singing a hunting song at the concert, words by his Aunt Charlotte, music by his Aunt Myrtle. You don't dispute that.'

'All correct so far.'

'Well, suppose that hunting song is a smackerino.'

And in a few well-chosen words I informed her of Jeeves's tenable theory.

'You get the idea?' I concluded. 'The cheers of the multitude frequently act like a powerful drug on these birds with inferiority complexes. Rouse such birds, as, for instance, by whistling through your fingers and yelling "*Bis! Bis!*" when they sing hunting songs, and they become changed men. Their morale stiffens. Their tails shoot up like rockets. They find themselves regarding the tough eggs before whom they have always been accustomed to crawl as less than the dust beneath their chariot wheels. If Esmond Haddock goes with the bang I anticipate, it won't be long before those aunts of his will be climbing trees and pulling them up after them whenever he looks squiggle-eyed at them.'

My eloquence had not been wasted. She started considerably, and said something about 'Out of the mouths of babes and sucklings', going on to explain that the gag was not her own but one of her Uncle Sidney's. And in return I told her that the tenable theory I had been outlining was not mine, but Jeeves's. Each giving credit where credit was due.

'I believe he's right, Bertie.'

'Of course he's right. Jeeves is always right. It's happened before. Do you know Bingo Little?'

'Just to say Hallo to. He married some sort of female novelist, didn't he?'

'Rosie M. Banks, author of *Mervyn Keene, Clubman*, and *Only A Factory Girl*. And their union was blessed. In due season a bouncing baby was added to the strength. Keep your eye on that baby, for the plot centres round it. Well, since you last saw Bingo, Mrs Bingo, by using her substantial pull, secured for him the post of editor of *Wee Tots*, a journal for the nursery and the home, a very good job in most respects but with this flaw, that the salary attached to it was not all it might have been. His proprietor, P.P. Purkiss, being one of those parsimonious birds in whose pocket-books moths nest and raise large families. It was Bingo's constant endeavour, accordingly, to try to stick old Gaspard the Miser for a raise. All clear so far?'

'I've got it.'

'Week after week he would creep into P.P. Purkiss's presence and falter out apologetic sentences beginning "Oh, Mr Purkiss, I wonder if . . ." and "Oh, Mr Purkiss, do you think you could possibly . . ." only to have the blighter gaze at him with fishy eyes and talk about the tightness of money and the growing cost of pulp paper. And Bingo would say "Oh, quite, Mr Purkiss," and "I see, Mr Purkiss, yes I see," and creep out again. That's Act One.'

'But mark the sequel?'

'You're right, mark the sequel. Came a day when Bingo's bouncing baby, entered in a baby contest against some of the warmest competition in South Kensington, scooped in the first prize, a handsome all-day sucker, getting kissed in the process by the wife of a Cabinet Minister and generally fawned upon by all and sundry. And next morning Bingo, with a strange light on his face, strode into P.P. Purkiss's private office without knocking, banged the desk with his fist and said he wished to see an additional ten fish in his pay envelope from now on, and to suit everybody's convenience the new arrangement would come into effect on the following Saturday. And when P.P. Purkiss started to go into his act, he banged the desk again and said he hadn't come there to argue. "Yes or no, Purkiss!" he said, and P.P. Purkiss, sagging like a wet sock, said "Why, yes, yes, of course, most certainly, Mr Little", adding that he had been on the point of suggesting some such idea himself. Well, I mean, that shows you.'

It impressed her. No mistaking that. She uttered a meditative 'Golly!' and stood on one leg, looking like 'The Soul's Awakening'.

'And so,' I proceeded, 'we are going to strain every nerve to see that Esmond Haddock's hunting song is the high-spot of the evening. Jeeves is to go about the village, scattering beers, so as to assemble what is known as a claque and ensure the thunderous applause. You will be able to help in that direction, too.'

'Of course I will. My standing in the village is terrific. I have the place in my pocket. I must get after this right away. I can't wait. You don't mind me leaving you?'

'Not at all, not at all, or, rather, yes, I jolly well do. Before you go, we've got to get this Gussie thing straight.'

'What Gussie thing?'

I clicked my tongue.

'You know perfectly well what Gussie thing. For reasons into which we need not go, you have recently been making Augustus Fink-Nottle the plaything of an idle hour, and it has got to stop. I don't have to tell you again what will happen if you continue carrying on as of even date. In our conference at the flat I made the facts clear to the meanest intelligence. You are fully aware that should the evil spread, should sand be shoved into the gears of the Fink-Nottle-Bassett romance to such an extent that it ceases to tick over, Bertram Wooster will be faced with the fate that is worse than death – viz. marriage. I feel sure that, now that you have been reminded of the hideous peril that looms, your good heart will not allow you to go on encouraging the above Fink-Nottle as, according to the evidence of five aunts, you are doing now. Appalled by the thought of poor old Wooster pressing the wedding trousers and packing the trunks for a honeymoon with that ghastly Bassett, you will obey the dictates of your better self and cool him off.'

She saw my point.

'You want me to restore Gussie to circulation?'

'Exactly.'

'Switch off the fascination? Release him from my clutches?'

'That's right.'

'Why, of course. I'll attend to it immediately.'

And on these very satisfactory terms we parted. A great weight had been lifted from my mind.

Well, I don't know what your experience has been, but mine is that there is very little percentage in having a weight lifted off your mind, because the first thing you know another, probably a dashed sight heavier, is immediately shoved on. It would appear to be a game you can't beat.

I had scarcely got back to my room, all soothed and relaxed, when in blew Catsmeat, and there was that in his mere appearance that chilled my merry mood like a slap in the eye with a wet towel. His face was grave, and his deportment not at all the sprightly deportment of a man who has recently been playing gin rummy with parlourmaids.

'Bertie,' he said, 'hold on tight to something. A very serious situation has arisen.'

The floor seemed to heave beneath me like a stage sea. The mice, which since that latter sequence and the subsequent chat with Corky had been taking a breather, sprang into renewed activity, as if starting training for some athletic sports.

'Oh, my sainted aunt!' I moaned, and Catsmeat said I might well say 'My sainted aunt', because she was the spearhead of the trouble.

'Here comes the bruise,' he said. 'When I was in the servants' hall a moment ago, Silversmith rolled in. And do you know what he had just been told by the girls higher up? He had been told that your Aunt Agatha is coming here. I don't know when, but in the next day or so. Dame Daphne Winkworth had a letter from her by the afternoon post, and in it she announced her intention of shortly being a pleasant visitor at this ruddy hencoop. So now what?'

13

It was a Bertram Wooster with a pale, careworn face and a marked disposition to start at sudden noises who sat in his bedroom on the following afternoon, rising occasionally to pace the floor. Few, seeing him, would have recognized in this limp and shivering chunk of human flotsam the suave, dapper *boulevardier* of happier years. I was waiting for Catsmeat to return from the metropolis and make his report.

Threshing the thing out on the previous evening, we had not taken long in reaching the conclusion that it would be madness to attempt to cope with this major crisis ourselves, and that the whole conduct of the affair must at the earliest moment be handed over to Jeeves. And as Jeeves was in London and it might have looked odd for me to dash away from the Big House for the night, Catsmeat had gone up to confer with him. He had tooled off secretly in my two-seater, expecting to be back around lunch-time.

But lunch had come and gone, the duck and green peas turning to ashes in my mouth, and still no sign of him. It was past three when he finally showed up.

At the sight of him, my heart, throwing off its burden of care, did a quick soft-shoe dance. No fellow, I reasoned, unless he was bringing good news, could look so like the United States Marines. When last seen, driving off on his mission, his air had been sober and downcast, as if he feared that even Jeeves would have to confess himself snookered by this one. He was now gay, bobbish and boomps-a-daisy.

'Sorry I'm late,' he said. 'I had to wait for Jeeves's brain to gather momentum. He was a little slower off the mark than usual.'

I clutched his arm.

'Did he click?' I cried, quivering in every limb.

'Oh, yes, he clicked. Jeeves always clicks. But this time only after brooding for what seemed an eternity. I found him in the kitchen at your flat, sipping a cup of tea and reading Spinoza, and put our problem before him, bidding him set the little grey cells in operation without delay and think of some way of preventing your blasted aunt from fulfilling her evil purpose of coming to infest Deverill Hall. He said he would, and I went back to the sitting room, where I took a seat, put my feet on the mantelpiece and thought of Gertrude. From time to time I would rise and look in at the kitchen and ask him how it was coming, but he motioned me away with a silent wave of the hand and let the brain out another notch. Finally he emerged and announced that he had got it. He had been musing, as always, on the psychology of the individual.'

'What individual? My Aunt Agatha?'

'Naturally, your Aunt Agatha. What other individual's psychology would you have expected him to muse on? Sir Stafford Cripps's? He then proceeded to outline a scheme which I think you will agree was a ball of fire. Tell me, Bertie, have you ever stolen a cub from a tigress?'

I said no, for one reason and another I never had, and he asked me what, if I ever did, I supposed the reactions of the tigress would be, always assuming that she was a good wife and mother. And I said that, while I didn't set myself up as an authority on tigresses, I imagined that she would be as sick as mud.

'Exactly. And you would expect the animal, the loss of its child having been drawn to its attention, to drop everything and start looking for it, would you not? It would completely revise its social plans, don't you think? If, for instance, it had arranged to visit other tigresses in a nearby cave, it would cancel the date and begin hunting around for clues. You agree?'

I said Yes, I thought this probable.

'Well, that is what Jeeves feels will happen in the case of your Aunt Agatha when she learns that her son Thomas has vanished from his school at Bramley-on-Sea.'

I can't tell you offhand what I had been expecting, but it certainly wasn't this. Having recovered sufficient breath to enable me to put the question, I asked what it was that he had said, and he repeated his words at dictation speed, and I said, 'But dash it!' and he said 'Well?'

'You aren't telling me that Jeeves is going to kidnap young Thos?'

He t'chk-t'chked impatiently.

'You don't have to kidnap dyed-in-the-wool fans like your cousin Thomas, if you inform them that their favourite film star is hoping that they will be able to get away and come and spend a few days at the Vicarage where she is staying. That is the message which Jeeves has gone to Bramley-on-Sea to deliver, and I confidently expect it to work like a charm.'

'You mean he'll run away from school?'

'Of course he'll run away from school. Like lightning. However, to clinch the thing, I empowered Jeeves in your name to offer a fee of five quid in the event of any hesitation. I gather from Jeeves, in whom he confided, that young Thomas is more than ordinarily out for the stuff just now. He's saving up to buy a camera.'

I applauded the shrewd thought, but I didn't think that this introduction of the sordid note would really be necessary. Thos is a boy of volcanic passions, the sort of boy who, if he had but threepence in the world, would spend it on a stamp, writing to Dorothy Lamour for her autograph, and the message which Catsmeat had outlined would, I felt, be in itself amply sufficient to get him on the move.

'Yes,' Catsmeat agreed, 'I think we should shortly have the young fellow with us. But not your Aunt Agatha, who will be occupied elsewhere. It's a pity she has to be temporarily deprived of her cub, of course, and one sympathizes with a mother's anxiety. It would have been nice if the thing could have been arranged some other way, but that's how it goes. One has simply got to say to oneself that into each life some rain must fall.'

My own view was that Aunt Agatha wouldn't be anxious so much as hopping mad.

'Thos,' I said, 'makes rather a speciality of running away from school. He's done it twice before this, once to attend a cup final and once to go hunting for buried treasure in the Caribbees, and I don't remember Aunt Agatha on either occasion as the stricken mother. Thos was the one who got stricken. Six of the best on the old spot, he tells me. This, I should imagine, will probably occur again, and I think that even if he takes the assignment on for love alone, I will slip him that fiver as added money.'

'It would be a graceful act.'

'After all, what's money? You can't take it with you.'

'The right spirit.'

'But isn't Corky going to be a bit at a loss when he suddenly shows up?'

'That's all fixed. I met her in the village and told her.'

'And she approved?'

'Wholeheartedly. Corky always approves of anything that seems likely to tend to start something.'

'She's a wonderful girl.'

'A very admirable character. By the way, she tells me you put in that word in season.'

'Yes. I thought she seemed braced.'

'That's how she struck me, too. Odd that she should be so crazy about Esmond Haddock. I've only seen him from a distance, of course, but I should have imagined he would have been a bit on the stiff side for Corky.'

'He's not really stiff. You should see him relaxing over the port.'

'Perhaps you're right. And, anyway, love's a thing you can't argue about. I suppose it would perplex thousands that Gertrude, bless her, loves me. Yet she does. And look at poor little Queenie. Heartbroken over the loss of a rozzer I wouldn't be seen in a ditch with. And talking of Queenie, I was thinking of taking her to the pictures in Basingstoke this afternoon, if you'll lend me your car.'

'Of course. You feel it would cheer her up?'

'It might. And I should like to slap balm on that wounded spirit, if it can be managed. It's curious how, when you're in love, you yearn to go about doing acts of kindness to everybody. I am bursting with a sort of yeasty benevolence these days, like one of those chaps in Dickens. I very nearly bought you a tie in London. Gosh! Who's that?'

Someone had knocked on the door.

'Come in,' I said, and Catsmeat dashed at the wardrobe and dashed out festooned in trousers and things. Striking the professional note.

Silversmith came navigating over the threshold. This majestic man always had in his deportment a suggestion of the ambassador about to deliver important State papers to a reigning monarch, and now the resemblance was heightened by the fact that in front of his ample stomach he was bearing a salver with a couple of telegrams on it. I gathered them in, and he went navigating out again.

Catsmeat replaced the trousers. He was quivering a little.

'What effect does that bloke have on you, Bertie?' he asked in a hushed voice, as if he were speaking in a cathedral. 'He paralyses me. I don't know if you are familiar with the works of Joseph Conrad, but there's a chap in his *Lord Jim* of whom he says "Had you been the Emperor of the East and West, you could not have ignored your inferiority in his presence". That's Silversmith. He fills me with an awful humility. He shrivels my immortal soul to the size of a parched pea. He's the living image of some of those old time pros who used to give me such a hell of a time when I first went on the stage. Well, go on. Open them.'

'You mean these telegrams?'

'What did you think I meant?'

'They're addressed to Gussie.'

'Of course they're addressed to Gussie. But they're for you.'

'We don't know that.'

'They must be. One's probably from Jeeves, telling you that the balloon has gone up.'

'But the other? It may be a tender bob's-worth from Madeline.'

'Ah, go on.'

I was firm.

'No, Catsmeat. The code of the Woosters restrains me. The code of the Woosters is more rigid than the code of the Catsmeats. A Wooster cannot open a telegram addressed to another, even if for the moment he is that other, if you see what I mean. I'll have to submit them to Gussie.'

'All right, if you see it that way. I'll be off, then, to try to bring a little sunshine into Queenie's life.'

He legged it, and I took a seat and went on being firm. The hour was then three-forty-five.

I continued firm till about five minutes to four.

The catch about the code of the Woosters is that if you start examining it with a couple of telegrams staring you in the face, one of them almost certainly containing news of vital import, you find yourself after a while beginning to wonder if it's really so hot, after all. I mean to say, the thought creeps in that maybe, if one did but know, the Woosters are priceless asses to let themselves be ruled by a code like that. By four o'clock I wasn't quite so firm as I had been. By ten past my fingers were definitely twitching.

It was at four-fifteen sharp that I opened the first telegram. As Catsmeat had predicted, it was a cautiously worded communication from Jeeves, handed in at Bramley-on-Sea and signed Bodger's Stores, guardedly intimating that everything had gone according to plan. The goods, it said, were in transit and would be delivered in a plain van in the course of the evening. Highly satisfactory.

I put a match to it and reduced it to ashes, for you can't be too careful, and having done so was concerned to find, as I looked at the other envelope, that my fingers were still twitching. I took the thing and twiddled it thoughtfully.

I can guess what you're going to say. You're going to say that, having perused the first one and mastered its contents, there was no need whatever for me to open the other, and you are perfectly right. But you know how it is. Ask the first lion cub you meet, and it will tell you that, once you've tasted blood, there is no pulling up, and it's the same with opening telegrams. Conscience whispered that this one, addressed to Gussie and intended for Gussie, was for Gussie's eyes alone, and I agreed absolutely. But I could no more stop myself opening it than you can stop yourself eating another salted almond.

I ripped the envelope, and the quick blush of shame mantled the cheek as my eye caught the signature 'Madeline'.

Then my eye caught the rest of the bally thing.

It read as follows:

Fink-Nottle
Deverill Hall
King's Deverill
Hants

Letter received. Cannot understand why not had reassuring telegram. Sure you concealing accident terribly serious. Fever anxiety. Fear worst. Arriving Deverill Hall tomorrow afternoon. Love. Kisses. Madeline.

14

Yes, that was the torpedo that exploded under my bows, and I had the feeling you get sometimes that some practical joker has suddenly removed all the bones from your legs, substituting for them an unsatisfactory jelly. I re-read the thing, to make sure I had seen what I thought I had seen, and, finding I had, buried the face in the hands.

It was the being without advisers that made the situation so bleak. On these occasions when Fate, having biffed you in the eye, proceeds to kick you in the pants, you want to gather the boys about you and thresh things out, and there weren't any boys to gather. Jeeves was in London, Catsmeat in Basingstoke. It made me feel like a Prime Minister who starts to call an important Cabinet meeting and finds that the Home Secretary and the Lord President of the Council have nipped over to Paris and the Minister of Agriculture and Fisheries and the rest of the gang are at the dog races.

There seemed to be nothing to do but wait till Catsmeat, having sat through the news and the main feature and the two-reel Silly Symphony, wended homeward. And though Reason told me that he couldn't get back for another two hours or more and that even when he did get back it was about a hundred to eight against him having any constructive policy to put forward, I went down to the main gate and paced up and down, scanning the horizon like Sister what-was-her-name in that story one used to read.

The evening was well advanced, and the local birds had long since called it a day, when I spotted the two-seater coming down the road. I flagged it, and Catsmeat applied the brakes.

'Oh, hallo, Bertie,' he said in a subdued sort of voice, and when he had alighted and I had drawn him apart he explained the reason for his sober deportment.

'Most unfortunate,' he said, throwing a commiserating glance at the occupant of the other seat, who was staring before her with anguished eyes and from time to time taking a dab at them with her handkerchief. 'With these tough films so popular, I suppose I might have foreseen that something like this would happen. The picture was full of cops, scores of cops racing to and fro saying "Oh, so you won't talk?" and it was too much for poor little Queenie. Just twisted the knife in the wound, as you might say. She's better now, though still sniffing.'

I suppose if you went through the W1 postal district of London with a fine-tooth comb and a brace of bloodhounds, you wouldn't find more than about three men readier than Bertram Wooster to sympathize with a woman's distress, and in ordinary circumstances I would unquestionably have given a low, pitying whistle and said 'Too bad, too bad'. But I hadn't time now to mourn over stricken parlourmaids. All the mourning at my disposal was earmarked for Wooster, B.

'Read this,' I said.

He cocked an eye at me.

'Hallo!' he said, in what is known as a sardonic manner. 'So the code of the Woosters sprang a leak? I had an idea it would.'

I think he was about to develop the theme and be pretty dashed humorous at my expense, but at this moment he started to scan the document and the gist hit him in the eyeball.

'H'm!' he said. 'This will want a little management.'

'Yes,' I concurred.

'It calls for sophisticated handling. We shall have to think this over.'

'I've been thinking it over for hours.'

'Yes, but you've got one of those cheap substitute brains which are never any good. It will be different when a man like me starts giving it the cream of his intellect.'

'If only Jeeves were here!'

'Yes, we could use Jeeves. It's a pity he is not with us.'

'And it's a pity,' I couldn't help pointing out, though the man of sensibility dislikes rubbing these things in, 'that you started the whole trouble by making Gussie wade in the Trafalgar Square fountain.'

'True. One regrets that. Yet at the time it seemed so right, so inevitable. There he was, I mean, and there was the fountain. I felt very strongly that here was an opportunity which might not occur again. And while I would be the last to deny that the aftermath hasn't been too good, it was certainly value for money. A man who has seen Gussie Fink-Nottle chasing newts in the Trafalgar Square fountain in correct evening costume at five o'clock in the morning is a man who has lived. He has got something he can tell his grandchildren. But if we are apportioning the blame, we can go further back than that. Where the trouble started was when you insisted on me giving him dinner. Madness. You might have known something would crack.'

'Well, it's no good talking about it.'

'No. Action is what we want. Sharp, decisive action as dished out by Napoleon. I suppose you will shortly be going in and dressing for dinner?'

'I suppose so.'

'How soon after dinner will you be in your room?'

'As soon as I can jolly well manage it.'

'Expect me there, then, probably with a whole plan of campaign cut and dried. And now I really must be getting back to Queenie. She will be on duty before long and will want to powder her nose and remove the tear stains. Poor little soul! If you knew how my heart bleeds for that girl, Bertie, you would shudder.'

And, of course, it being so vital that we should get together with the minimum of delay, that night turned out to be the one night when it was impossible to take an early powder. Instead of the ordinary dinner, a regular binge had been arranged, with guests from all over the countryside. No fewer than ten of Hampshire's more prominent stiffs had been summoned to the trough, and they stuck on like limpets long after any competent chucker-out would have bounced them. No doubt, if you have gone to the sweat of driving twenty miles to a house to dine, you don't feel like just snatching a chop and dashing off. You hang on for the musical evening and the drinks at ten-thirty.

Be that as it may, it wasn't till close on midnight that the final car rolled away. And when I bounded to my room, off duty at last, there was no sign of Catsmeat.

There was, however, a note from him lying on the pillow, and I tore it open with a feverish flick of the finger.

It was dated eleven pm, and its tone was reproachful. He rebuked me for what he described as sitting gorging and swilling with my fine friends when I ought to have been at the conference table doing a bit of honest work. He asked me if I thought he was going to remain seated on his fanny in my damned room all night, and hoped that I would have a hangover next day, as well as indigestion from too much rich food. He couldn't wait any longer, he said, it being his intention to take my car and drive to London so as to be at Wimbledon Common bright and early tomorrow morning for an interview with Madeline Bassett. And at that interview, he went on, concluding on a cheerier note, he would fix everything up just the same as Mother makes it, for he had got the idea of a lifetime, an idea so superb that I could set my mind, if I called it a mind, completely at rest. He doubted, he said, whether Jeeves himself, even if full to the brim of fish, could have dug up a better *modus operandi*.

Well, this was comforting, of course, always provided that one could accept the theory that he was as good as he thought he was. You never know with Catsmeat. In one of his school reports, which I happened to see while prowling about the Rev. Aubrey Upjohn's study one night in search of biscuits, the Rev. Aubrey had described him as 'brilliant but unsound', and if ever a headmaster with a face like a cassowary rang the bell and entitled himself to receive a cigar or a coco-nut, this headmaster was that headmaster.

However, I will own that his communication distinctly eased the spirit. It is a pretty well established fact that the heart bowed down with weight of woe to weakest hope will cling, and that's what mine did. It was in quite an uplifted frame of mind that I shed the soup and fish and climbed into the slumberwear. I rather think, though I wouldn't swear to it, that I sang a bar or two of a recent song hit.

I had just donned the dressing-gown and was preparing for a final cigarette, when the door opened and Gussie came in.

Gussie was in peevish mood. He hadn't liked the stiffs, and he complained with a good deal of bitterness at having had to waste in their society an evening which might have been spent *chez* Corky.

'You couldn't oil out of a big dinner party,' I urged.

'No, that's what Corky said. She said it wouldn't do. *Noblesse oblige* was one of the expressions she used. Amazing what high principles she has. You don't often find a girl as pretty as that with such high principles. And how pretty she is, isn't she, Bertie? Or, rather, when I say pretty, I mean angelically lovely.'

I agreed that Corky's face wouldn't stop a clock, and he retorted warmly what did I mean it wouldn't stop a clock.

'She's divine. She's the most beautiful girl I've ever seen. It seems so extraordinary that she should be Pirbright's sister. You would think any sister of Pirbright's would be as repulsive as he is.'

'I'd call Catsmeat rather good-looking.'

'I disagree with you. He's a hellhound, and it comes out in his appearance. "There are newts in that fountain, Gussie," he said to me. "Get after them without a second's delay." And wouldn't take No for an answer. Urged me on with sharp hunting cries. "Yoicks!" he said, and 'Tallyho!" But what I came about, Bertie,' said Gussie, breaking off abruptly as if this dip into the past pained him, 'was to ask if you could lend me that tie of yours with the pink lozenges on the dove-grey background. I shall be dropping in at the Vicarage tomorrow morning, and I want to look my best.'

Apart from the fleeting thought that he was a bit of an optimist if he expected a tie with pink lozenges on a dove-grey background to undo Nature's handiwork to the extent of making him look anything but a fish-faced gargoyle, my reaction to these words was a feeling of profound relief that I had had that talk with Corky and obtained her promise that she would lose no time in choking Gussie off and putting him on the ice.

For it was plain that there was no time to be lost. Every word this super-heated newt-fancier uttered showed more clearly the extent to which he had got it up his nose. Chatting with Augustus Fink-Nottle about Corky was like getting the inside from Mark Antony on the topic of Cleopatra, and every second he spent out of the frigidaire was fraught with peril. It was only too plain that The Larches, Wimbledon Common, had ceased to mean a thing in his life and instead of being a holy shrine housing the girl of his dreams, had become just an address in the suburban telephone book.

I gave him the tie, and he thanked me and started out.

'Oh, by the way,' he said, pausing at the door, 'you remember pestering me to write to Madeline. Well, I've done it. I wrote to her this afternoon. Why are you looking like a dying duck?'

I was looking like a dying duck because I had, of course, instantly spotted the snag. What, I was asking myself, was Madeline Bassett going to think when on top of the letter about the sprained wrist she got one in Gussie's handwriting with no reference in it whatever to runaway horses and completely silent on the theme of golden-haired children with lisps?

I revealed to Gussie the recent activities of the Catsmeat-Wooster duo, and he frowned disapprovingly. Most officious, he said, writing people's love letters for them, and not in the best of taste.

'However,' he proceeded, 'it doesn't really matter, because what I said in my letter was that everything was off.'

I tottered and would have fallen, had I not clutched at a passing chest of drawers.

'*Off?*'

'I've broken the engagement. I've been feeling for some days now that Madeline, though a nice girl, won't do. My heart belongs to Corky. Good night again, Bertie. Thanks for the tie.'

He withdrew, humming a sentimental ballad.

The Larches, Wimbledon Common, was one of those eligible residences standing in commodious grounds with Company's own water
both h. and c. and the usual domestic offices and all that sort of
thing, which you pass on the left as you drive out of London by way
of Putney Hill. I don't know who own these joints, though obviously
citizens who have got the stuff in sackfuls, and I didn't know who
owned The Larches. All I knew was that Gussie's letter to Madeline
Bassett would be arriving at that address by the first postal delivery,
and it was my intention, should the feat prove to be within the scope
of human power, to intercept and destroy it.

In tampering with His Majesty's mails in this manner, I had an idea
that I was rendering myself liable to about forty years in the coop,
but the risk seemed to me well worth taking. After all, forty years
soon pass, and only by preventing that letter reaching its destination
could I secure the bit of breathing space so urgently needed in order
to enable me to turn round and think things over.

That was why on the following morning the commodious grounds
of The Larches, in addition to a lawn, a summer-house, a pond,
flower-beds, bushes and an assortment of trees, contained also one
Wooster, noticeably cold about the feet and inclined to rise from
twelve to eighteen inches skywards every time an early bird gave
a sudden *cheep* over its worm. This Wooster to whom I allude was
crouching in the interior of a bush not far from the french windows
of what, unless the architect had got the place all cockeyed, was
the dining room. He had run up from King's Deverill on the 2.54
milk train.

I say 'run', but perhaps 'sauntered' would be more the *mot juste*.
When milk moves from spot to spot, it takes its time, and it was not
until very near zero hour that I had sneaked in through the gates
and got into position one. By the time I had wedged myself into
my bush, the sun was high up in the sky, as Esmond Haddock's
Aunt Charlotte would have said, and I found myself musing, as
I have so often had occasion to do, on the callous way in which

Nature refuses to chip in and do its bit when the human heart is in the soup.

Though howling hurricanes and driving rainstorms would have been a more suitable accompaniment to the run of the action, the morning – or morn, if you prefer to string along with Aunt Charlotte – was bright and fair. My nervous system was seriously disordered, and one of God's less likeable creatures with about a hundred and fourteen legs had crawled down the back of my neck and was doing its daily dozen on the sensitive skin, but did Nature care? Not a hoot. The sky continued blue, and the fatheaded sun which I have mentioned shone smilingly throughout.

Beetles on the spine are admittedly bad, calling for all that a man has of fortitude and endurance, but when embarking on an enterprise which involved parking the carcass in bushes one more or less budgets for beetles. What was afflicting me much more than the activities of the undersigned was the reflection that I didn't know what was going to happen when the postman arrived. It might quite well be, I felt, that everybody at The Larches fed in bed of a morning, in which event a maid would take Gussie's bit of trinitrotoluol up to Madeline's room on a tray, thus rendering my schemes null and void.

It was just as this morale-lowering thought came into my mind that something suddenly bumped against my leg, causing the top of my head to part from its moorings. My initial impression that I had been set upon by a powerful group of enemies lasted, though it seemed a year, for perhaps two seconds. Then, the spots clearing from before my eyes and the world ceasing to do the adagio dance into which it had broken, I was able to perceive that all that had come into my life was a medium-sized ginger cat. Breathing anew, as the expression is, I bent down and tickled it behind the ear, such being my invariable policy when closeted with cats, and was still tickling when there was a bang and a rattle and somebody threw back the windows of the dining room.

Shortly afterwards, the front door opened and a housemaid came out onto the steps and started shaking a mat in a languid sort of way.

Able now to see into the dining room and observing that the table was laid for the morning meal, I found my thoughts taking a more optimistic turn. Madeline Bassett, I told myself, was not the girl to remain sluggishly in bed while others rose. If the gang took their chow downstairs she would be with them. One of those plates now under my inspection, therefore, was her plate, and beside it the fateful letter would soon be deposited. A swift dash, and I should be able to get my hooks on it before she came down. I limbered up the muscles, so as to be ready for instant action, and was on my toes and all set to go, when there was a whistle to the south-west and a voice said 'Oo-oo!' and I saw that the postman had arrived. He was standing at the foot of the steps, giving the housemaid the eye.

'Hallo, beautiful!' he said.

I didn't like it. My heart sank. Now that I could see this postman steadily and see him whole, he stood out without disguise as a jaunty young postman, lissom of limb and a mass of sex-appeal, the sort of postman who, when off duty, is a devil of a fellow at the local hops and, when engaged on his professional rounds, considers the day wasted that doesn't start with about ten minutes intensive flirtation with the nearest domestic handy. I had been hoping for something many years older and much less the Society playboy. With a fellow like this at the helm, the delivery of the first post was going to take time. And every moment that passed made more probable the arrival on the scene of Madeline Bassett and others.

My fears were well founded. The minutes went by and still this gay young postman stood rooted to the spot, dishing out the brilliant badinage as if he were some carefree gentleman of leisure who was just passing by in the course of an early morning stroll. It seemed to me monstrous that a public servant, whose salary I helped to pay, should be wasting the Government's time in this frivolous manner, and it wouldn't have taken much to make me write a strong letter to *The Times* about it.

Eventually, awakening to a sense of his obligations, he handed over a wad of correspondence and with a final sally went on his way, and the housemaid disappeared, to manifest herself a few moments later in the dining room. There, having read a couple of postcards in rather a bored way, as if she found little in them to grip and interest, she did what she ought to have done at least a quarter of an hour earlier – viz. placed them and the letters beside the various plates.

I perked up. Things, I felt, were moving. What would happen now, I assumed, was that she would pop off and go about her domestic duties, leaving the terrain unencumbered, and it was with something of the emotions of the war-horse that sayeth 'Ha!' among the trumpets that I once more braced the muscles. Ignoring the cat, which was weaving in and out between my legs with a camaraderie in its manner that suggested that it had now got me definitely taped as God's gift to the animal kingdom of Wimbledon, I made ready for the leap.

Picture, then, my chagrin and agony of spirit when, instead of hoofing it out of the door, this undisciplined housemaid came through the window, and having produced a gasper stood leaning against the wall, puffing luxuriously and gazing dreamily at the sky, as if thinking of postmen.

I don't know anything more sickening than being baffled by an unforeseen stymie at the eleventh hour, and it would not be overstating it to say that I writhed with impotent fury. As a rule, my relations with housemaids are cordial and sympathetic. If I meet a housemaid, I beam at her and say 'Good morning', and she beams at me and says 'Good morning', and all is joy and peace. But this one I would gladly have socked on the napper with a brick.

I stood there cursing. She stood there smoking. How long I cursed and she smoked I couldn't say, but I was just wondering if this degrading exhibition was going on for ever when she suddenly leaped, looked hastily over her shoulder and, hurling the gasper from her, legged it round the side of the house. The whole thing rather reminiscent of a nymph surprised while bathing.

And it wasn't long before I was able to spot what had caused her concern. I had thought for a moment that the voice of conscience must have whispered in her ear, but this was not so. Somebody was coming out of the front door, and my heart did a quick double somersault as I saw that it was Madeline Bassett.

And I was just saying 'This is the end', for it seemed inevitable that in another two ticks she would be inside the dining room absorbing the latest news from Deverill Hall, when my *joie de vivre*, which had hit a new low, was restored by the sight of her turning to the left instead of to the right, and I perceived, what had failed to register in that first awful moment, that she was carrying a basket and gardening scissors. One sprang to the conclusion that she was off for a bit of pre-breakfast nosegay gathering, and one was right. She disappeared, and I was alone once more with the cat.

There is, as Jeeves rather neatly put it once, a tide in the affairs of men which, taken at the flood, leads on to fortune, and I could see clearly enough that this was it. What is known as the crucial moment had unquestionably arrived, and any knowledgeable adviser, had such a one been present, would have urged me to make it snappy and get moving while the going was good.

But recent events had left me weak. The spectacle of Madeline Bassett so close to me that I could have tossed a pebble into her mouth – not that I would, of course – had had the effect of numbing the sinews. I was for the nonce a spent force, incapable even of kicking the cat, which, possibly under the impression that this rigid Bertram was a tree, had now started to sharpen its claws on my leg.

And it was lucky I was – a spent force, I mean, not a tree – for at the very moment when, had I had the horse-power, I would have been sailing through the dining room window, a girl came out of it carrying a white, woolly dog. And a nice ass I should have looked if I had taken at the flood the tide which leads on to fortune, because it wouldn't have led on to fortune or anything like it. It would have resulted in a nasty collision on the threshold.

She was a solid, hefty girl, of the type which plays five sets of tennis without turning a hair, and from the fact that her face was sombre and her movements on the listless side, I deduced that this must be Madeline Bassett's school friend, the one whose sex life had recently stubbed its toe. Too bad, of course, and one was sorry that she and the dream man hadn't been able to make a go of it, but at the moment I wasn't thinking very much about her troubles, my attention being riveted on the disturbing fact that I was dished. Thanks to the delay caused by the dilatory methods of that sprightly young postman, my plan of campaign was a total loss. I couldn't possibly start to function, with solid girls cluttering up the fairway.

There was but one hope. Her demeanour was that of a girl about to take the dog for a run, and it might be that she and friend would wander far enough afield to enable me to bring the thing off. I was just speculating on the odds for and against this, when she put the dog on the ground and with indescribable emotion I saw that it was heading straight for my bush and in another moment would be noting contents and barking its head off. For no dog, white or not white, woolly or not woolly, accepts with a mere raised eyebrow the presence of strangers in bushes. The thing, I felt, might quite possibly culminate not only in exposure, disgrace and shame, but in a quick nip on the ankle.

It was the cat who eased a tense situation. Possibly because it had not yet breakfasted and wished to do so, or it may be because the charm of Bertram Wooster's society had at last begun to pall, it selected this moment to leave me. It turned on its heel and emerged from the bush with its tail in the air, and the white, woolly dog, sighting it, broke into a canine version of Aunt Charlotte's a-hunting-we-will-go song and with a brief 'Hallo, hallo, hallo, hallo' went a-hunting. The pursuit rolled away over brake and over thorn, with Madeline Bassett's school friend bringing up the rear.

Position at the turn:

1. Cat
2. Dog
3. Madeline Basset's school friend.

The leaders were well up in a bunch. Several lengths separated 2 and 3.

I did not linger and dally. All a passer-by, had there been a passer-by, would have seen, was a sort of blur. Ten seconds later, I was standing beside the breakfast table, panting slightly, with Gussie's letter in my hand.

To trouser it was with me the work of an instant; to reach the window with a view to the quick getaway that of an instant more. And I was on the point of passing through in the same old bustling way, when I suddenly perceived the solid girl returning with the white, woolly dog in her arms, and I saw what must have happened. These white, woolly dogs lack staying power. All right for the quick sprint, but hopeless across country. This one must have lost the hallo-hallo spirit in the first fifty yards or so and, pausing for breath, allowed itself to be gathered in.

In moments of peril, the Woosters act swiftly. One way out being barred to me, I decided in a flash to take the other. I nipped through the door, nipped across the hall and, still nipping, reached the temporary safety of the room on the other side of it.

16

The room in which I found myself was bright and cheerful, in which respect it differed substantially from Bertram Wooster. It had the appearance of being the den or snuggery of some female interested in sports and pastimes and was, I assumed, the headquarters of Madeline Bassett's solid school friend. There was an oar over the mantelpiece, a squash racket over the book-shelf, and on the walls a large number of photographs which even at a cursory glance I was able to identify as tennis and hockey groups.

A cursory glance was all I was at leisure to bestow upon them at the moment, for the first thing to which my eye had been attracted on my entry was a serviceable french window, and I made for it like a man on a walking tour diving into a village pub two minutes before closing time. It opened on a sunken garden at the side of the house, and offered an admirable avenue of escape to one whose chief object in life was to detach himself from this stately home of Wimbledon and never set eyes on the bally place again.

When I say that it offered an admirable avenue of escape, it would be more correct to put it that it would have done, had there not been standing immediately outside it, leaning languidly on a spade, a short, stout gardener in corduroy trousers and a red and yellow cap which suggested – erroneously, I imagine – that he was a member of the Marylebone Cricket Club. His shirt was brown, his boots black, his face cerise and his whiskers grey.

I am able to supply this detailed record of the colour scheme because for some considerable time I stood submitting this son of toil to a close inspection. And the closer I inspected him, the less I found myself liking the fellow. Just as I had felt my spirit out of tune with the gasper-smoking housemaid of The Larches, so did I now look askance at the establishment's gardener, feeling very strongly that what he needed was a pound and a half of dynamite exploded under his fat trouser seat.

Presently, unable to stand the sight of him any longer, I turned away and began to pace the room like some caged creature of the wild, the only difference being that whereas a caged creature of the wild would not have bumped into and come within a toucher of upsetting a small table with a silver cup, a golf ball in a glass case and a large framed photograph on it, I did. It was only by an outstanding feat of legerdemain that I succeeded in catching the photograph as it fell, thereby averting a crash which would have brought every inmate of the house racing to the spot. And having caught it, I saw that it was a speaking likeness of Madeline Bassett.

It was one of those full-face speaking likenesses. She was staring straight out of the picture with large, sad, saucerlike eyes, and the lips seemed to quiver with a strange, reproachful appeal. And as I gazed at those sad eyes and took a square look at those quivery lips, something went off inside my bean like a spring. I had had an inspiration.

Events were to prove that my idea, like about ninety-four per cent of Catsmeat's, was just one of those that seem good at the time, but at the moment I was convinced that if I were to snitch this studio portrait and confront Gussie with it, bidding him drink it in and let conscience be his guide, all would be well. Remorse would creep in, his better self would get it up the nose, and all the old love and affection would come surging back. I believe this sort of thing frequently happens. Burglars, catching sight of photographs of their mothers, instantly turn in their tools and resolve to lead a new life, and the same is probably true of footpads, con men and fellows who have not paid their dog licence. I saw no reason to suppose that Gussie would be slower off the mark.

It was at this moment that I heard the sound of a Hoover being wheeled along the hall, and realized that the housemaid was on her way to do the room.

If there is anything that makes you feel more like a stag at bay than being in a room where you oughtn't to be and hearing housemaids coming to do it, I don't know what is. If you described Bertram Wooster at this juncture as all of a doodah, you would not be going far astray. I sprang to the window. The gardener was still there. I sprang back, and nearly knocked the table over again. Finally, thinking quick, I sprang sideways. My eye had been caught by a substantial sofa in the corner of the room, and I could have wished no more admirable cover. I was behind it with perhaps two seconds to spare.

To say that I now breathed freely again would be putting it perhaps too strongly. I was still far from being at my ease. But I did feel that in this little nook of mine I ought to be reasonably secure. One of the things you learn, when you have knocked about the world a bit, is that housemaids don't sweep behind sofas. Having run the Hoover over the exposed portions of the carpet, they consider the day well spent and go off and have a cup of tea and a slice of bread and jam.

On the present occasion even the exposed portions of the carpet did not get their doing, for scarcely had the girl begun to ply the apparatus when she was called off the job by orders from up top.

'Morning, Jane,' said a voice, which from the fact that it was accompanied by a shrill bark such as could have proceeded only from a white, woolly dog I took to be that of the solid school friend. 'Never mind about doing the room now.'

'No, miss,' said the housemaid, seeming well pleased with the idea, and pushed off, no doubt to have another gasper in the scullery. There followed a rustling of paper as the solid girl, seating herself on the sofa, skimmed through the morning journal. Then I heard her say 'Oh, hallo, Madeline', and was aware that the Bassett was with us.

'Good morning, Hilda,' said the Bassett in that soupy, treacly voice which had got her so disliked by all right-thinking men. 'What a lovely, lovely morning.'

The solid girl said she didn't see what was so particularly hot about it, adding that personally she found all mornings foul. She spoke morosely, and I could see that her disappointment in love had soured her, poor soul. I mourned for her distress, and had the circumstances been different, might have reached up and patted her on the head.

'I have been gathering flowers,' proceeded the Bassett. 'Beautiful smiling flowers, all wet with the morning dew. How *happy* flowers seem, Hilda.'

The solid girl said why shouldn't they, what had they got to beef about, and there was a pause. The solid girl said something about the prospects of the Surrey Cricket Club, but received no reply, and a moment later it was evident that Madeline Bassett's thoughts had been elsewhere.

'I have just been in the dining room,' she said, and one spotted the tremor in the voice. 'There was no letter from Gussie. I'm so worried, Hilda. I think I shall go down to Deverill by an earlier train.'

'Suit yourself.'

'I can't help having an awful feeling that he is seriously injured. He said he had only sprained his wrist, but has he? That is what I ask myself. Suppose the horse knocked him down and trampled on him?'

'He'd have mentioned it.'

'But he wouldn't. That's what I mean. Gussie is so unselfish and considerate. His first thought would be to spare me anxiety. Oh, Hilda, do you think his spine is fractured?'

'What rot! Spine fractured, my foot. If there isn't a letter, all it means is that this other fellow – what's his name – Wooster – has kicked at acting as an amanuensis. I don't blame him. He's dippy about you, isn't he?'

'He loves me very, very dearly. It's a tragedy. I can't describe to you, Hilda, the pathos of that look of dumb suffering in his eyes when we meet.'

'Well, then, the thing's obvious. If you're dippy about a girl, and another fellow has grabbed her, it can't be pleasant to sit at a writing table, probably with a rotten pen, sweating away while the other fellow dictates "My own comma precious darling period I worship you comma I adore you period How I wish comma my dearest comma that I could press you to my bosom and cover your lovely face with burning kisses exclamation mark". I don't wonder Wooster kicked.'

'You're very heartless, Hilda.'

'I've had enough to make me heartless. I've sometimes thought of ending it all. I've got a gun in that drawer there.'

'Hilda!'

'Oh, I don't suppose I shall. Lot of fuss and trouble. Have you seen the paper this morning? It says there's some talk of altering the leg-before-wicket rule again. Odd how your outlook changes when your heart's broken. I can remember a time when I'd have been all excited if they altered the leg-before-wicket rule. Now I don't give a damn. Let 'em alter it, and I hope they have a fine day for it. What sort of a fellow is this Wooster?'

'Oh, a dear.'

'He must be, if he writes Gussie's love letters for him. Either that or a perfect sap. If I were in your place, I'd give Gussie the air and sign up with him. Being a man, I presume he's a louse, like all other men, but he's rich, and money's the only thing that matters.'

From the way Madeline said, 'Oh, Hilda *darling*!' – the wealth of reproach in the voice, I mean, and all that sort of thing – I could tell that these cynical words had got in amongst her, shocking her and wounding her finer feelings, and I found myself in complete accord with her attitude. I thoroughly disapproved of this girl and her whole outlook, and wished she wouldn't say things like that. The position of affairs was black enough already, without having old school friends egging Madeline Bassett on to give Gussie the air and sign up with me.

I think that Madeline would have gone on to chide and rebuke, but at this point, instead of speaking, she suddenly uttered a squeal or wordless exclamation, and the solid girl said 'Now what?'

'My photograph!'

'What about it?'

'Where is it?'

'On the table.'

'But it's not. It's gone.'

'Then I suppose Jane has smashed it. She always does smash everything that isn't made of sheet-iron, and I see no reason why she should have made an exception in favour of your photograph. You'd better go and ask her.'

'I will,' said Madeline, and I heard her hurrying out.

A few moments passed, self inhaling fluff and the solid girl presumably scanning her paper for further facts about the leg-before-wicket rule, and then I heard her say 'Sit still', no doubt addressing the white, woolly dog, for shortly afterwards she said 'Oh, all right, blast you, buzz off if you want to', and there was a thud; not a dull, sickening thud but the sort of thud a white, woolly dog makes when landing on a carpet from a sofa of medium height. And it was almost immediately after this that there came a sound of sniffing in my vicinity, and with a considerable lowering of the already low morale I realized that the animal must have picked up the characteristic Wooster smell and was now in the process of tracking it to its source.

And so it proved. Glancing round, I suddenly found its face about six inches from mine, its demeanour that of a dog that can hardly believe its eyes. Backing away with a startled 'Ooops!' it retreated to the centre of the room and began barking.

'What's the matter, you silly ass?' said the solid girl, and then there was a silence. On her part, that is. The white, woolly dog continued to strain its vocal cords.

Madeline Bassett re-entered.

'Jane says –' she began, then broke off with a piercing scream. '*Hilda!* Oh, Hilda, *what* are you doing with that pistol?'

The solid girl calmed her fears, though leaving mine in *status quo*.

'Don't get excited. I'm not going to shoot myself. Though it would be a pretty good idea, at that. There's a man behind the sofa.'

'Hilda!'

'I've been wondering for some time where that curious, breathing sound was coming from. Percy spotted him. At-a-boy, Percy, nice work. Come on out of it, you.'

Rightly concluding that she meant me, I emerged, and Madeline uttered another of her piercing screams.

'A dressy criminal, though shopsoiled,' said the solid girl, scrutinizing me over the young cannon which she was levelling at my waistcoat. 'One of those Mayfair men you read about, I suppose. Hallo, I see he's got that photograph you were looking for. And probably half a dozen other things as well. I think the first move is to make him turn out his pockets.'

The thought that in one of those pockets lay Gussie's letter caused me to reel and utter a strangled cry, and the solid girl said if I was going to have a fit, that was all right with her, but she would be obliged if I would step through the window and have it outside.

It was at this point that Madeline Bassett most fortunately found speech. During the preceding exchanges, if you can call it exchanges when one person has taken the floor and is doing all the talking, she had been leaning against the wall with a hand to her heart, giving an impersonation, and not at all a bad one either, of a cat with a herring-bone in its throat. She now made her first contribution to the dialogue.

'Bertie!' she cried.

The solid girl seemed puzzled.

'Bertie?'

'This is Bertie Wooster.'

'The complete letter-writer? Well, what's he doing here? And why has he swiped your photograph?'

Madeline's voice sank to a tremulous whisper.

'I think I know.'

'Then you're smarter than I am. Goofy, the whole proceeding strikes me as.'

'Will you leave us, Hilda? I want to speak to Bertie . . . alone.'

'Right ho. I'll be shifting along to the dining room. I don't suppose, feeling the way I do, there's a dog's chance of my being able to swallow a mouthful, but I can be counting the spoons.'

The solid girl pushed off, accompanied by the white, woolly dog, leaving us all set for a *tête-à-tête* which I for one would willingly have avoided. In fact, though it would, of course, have been a near thing with not much in it either way, I think I would have preferred a *tête-à-tête* with Dame Daphne Winkworth.

17

The proceedings opened with one of those long, sticky silences which give you the same unpleasant feeling you get when you let them rope you in to play 'Bulstrode, a butler' in amateur theatricals and you go on and find you have forgotten your opening lines. She was standing gazing at me as if I had been a photographer about to squeeze the bulb and take a studio portrait in sepia and silver-grey wash, and after a while it seemed to me that it was about time one of us said something. The great thing on these occasions is to get the conversation going.

'Nice day,' I said. 'I thought I'd look in.'

She enlarged the eyes a bit, but did not utter, so I proceeded.

'It occurred to me that you might be glad to have the latest bulletin about Gussie, so I popped up on the milk train. Gussie, I am glad to say, is getting along fine. The wrist is still stiff, but the swelling is subsiding and there is no pain. He sends his best.'

She remained *sotto voce* as the silent tomb, and I carried on. I thought a word or two touching upon my recent activities might now be in order. I mean, you can't just come bounding up from behind the furniture and let it go at that. You have to explain and clarify your motives. Girls like to know these things.

'You are probably asking yourself,' I said, 'what I was doing behind that sofa. I parked myself there on a sudden whim. You know how one gets these sudden whims. And you may be thinking it a bit odd that I should be going around with this studio portrait in my possession. Well, I'll tell you. I happened to see it on the table there, and I took it to give to Gussie. I thought he would like to have it, to buck him up in your absence. He misses you sorely, of course, and it occurred to me that it would be nice for him to shove it on the dressing table and study it from time to time. No doubt he already has several of these speaking likenesses, but a fellow can always do with one more.'

Not too bad, it seemed to me, considering that the material had had to be thrown together rather against time, and I was hoping for the bright smile and the cordial 'Why, yes, to be sure, a capital idea'.

Instead of which, she waggled her head in a slow, mournful sort of way, and a teardrop stood in her eye.

'Oh, Bertie!' she said.

I have always found it difficult to think of just the right come-back when people say 'Oh, Bertie!' to me. My Aunt Agatha is always doing it, and she has me stymied every time. I found myself stymied now. It is true that this 'Oh, Bertie!' of the Bassett's differed in many respects from Aunt Agatha's 'Oh, Bertie!' its tone being one of soupiness rather than asperity, but the effect was the same. I stood there at a loss.

'Oh, Bertie!' she said again. 'Do you read Rosie M. Banks's novels?' she asked.

I was a bit surprised at her changing the subject like this, but equally relieved. A talk about current literature, I felt, might ease the strain. These booksy chats often do.

'Not very frequently,' I said. 'They sell like hot cakes, Bingo tells me.'

'You have not read *Mervyn Keene, Clubman?*'

'No, I missed that. Good stuff?'

'It is very, very beautiful.'

'I must put it on my library list.'

'You are sure you have not read it?'

'Oh, quite. As a matter of fact, I've always steered rather clear of Mrs Bingo's stuff. Why?'

'It seemed such an extraordinary coincidence . . . Shall I tell you the story of Mervyn Keene?'

'Do.'

She took time out to gulp a bit. Then she carried on in a low voice with a goodish amount of throb to it.

'He was young and rich and handsome, an officer in the Coldstream Guards and the idol of all who knew him. Everybody envied him.'

'I don't wonder, the lucky stiff.'

'But he was not really to be envied. There was a tragedy in his life. He loved Cynthia Grey, the most beautiful girl in London, but just as he was about to speak his love, he found that she was engaged to Sir Hector Mauleverer, the explorer.'

'Dangerous devils, these explorers. You want to watch them like hawks. In these circs, of course, he would have refrained from speaking his love? Kept it under his hat, I suppose, what?'

'Yes, he spoke no word of love. But he went on worshipping her, outwardly gay and cheerful, inwardly gnawed by a ceaseless pain. And then one night her brother Lionel, a wild young man who had unfortunately got into bad company, came to his rooms and told him that he had committed a very serious crime and was going to be arrested, and he asked Mervyn to save him by taking the blame himself. And, of course, Mervyn said he would.'

'The silly ass! Why?'

'For Cynthia's sake. To save her brother from imprisonment and shame.'

'But it meant going to chokey himself. I suppose he overlooked that?'

'No. Mervyn fully realized what must happen. But he confessed to the crime and went to prison. When he came out, grey and broken, he found that Cynthia had married Sir Hector and he went out to the South Sea Islands and became a beachcomber. And time passed. And then one day Cynthia and her husband arrived at the island on their travels and stayed at Government House, and Mervyn saw her drive by, and she was just as beautiful as ever, and their eyes met, but she didn't recognize him, because of course he had a beard and his face was changed because he had been living the pace that kills, trying to forget.'

I remembered a good one I had read somewhere about the pace that kills nowadays being the slow, casual walk across a busy street, but I felt that this was not the moment to spring it.

'He found out that she was leaving next morning, and he had nothing to remember her by, so he broke into Government House in the night and took from her dressing table the rose she had been wearing in her hair. And Cynthia found him taking it, and, of course, she was very upset when she recognized him.'

'Oh, she recognized him this time? He'd shaved, had he?'

'No, he still wore his beard, but she knew him when he spoke her name, and there was a very powerful scene in which he told her how he had always loved her and had come to steal her rose, and she told him that her brother had died and confessed on his death-bed that it was he who had been guilty of the crime for which Mervyn had gone to prison. And then Sir Hector came in.'

'Good situation. Strong.'

'And, of course, he thought Mervyn was a burglar, and he shot him, and Mervyn died with the rose in his hand. And, of course, the sound of the shot roused the house, and the Governor came running in and said: "Is anything missing?" And Cynthia in a low, almost inaudible voice said: "Only a rose." That is the story of Mervyn Keene, Clubman.'

Well, it was difficult, of course, to know quite what comment to make. I said 'Oh, ah!' but I felt at the time that it could have been improved on. The fact is, I was feeling a bit stunned. I had always known in a sort of vague, general way that Mrs Bingo wrote the world's worst tripe – Bingo generally changes the subject nervously if anyone mentions the little woman's output – but I had never supposed her capable of bilge like this.

But the Bassett speedily took my mind off literary criticism. She had resumed her saucerlike stare, and the teardrop in the eye was now more noticeable than ever.

'Oh, Bertie,' she said, and her voice, like Cynthia's, was low and almost inaudible, 'I ought to have given you my photograph long ago. I blame myself. But I thought it would be too painful for you, too sad a reminder of all that you had lost. I see now that I was wrong. You found the strain too great to bear. At all costs you had to have it. So you stole into the house, like Mervyn Keene, and took it.'

'What!'

'Yes, Bertie. There need be no pretences between you and me. And don't think I am angry. I am touched, more deeply touched than I can say, and oh, so, so sorry. How sad life is!'

I was with her there.

'You betcher,' I said.

'You saw my friend Hilda Gudgeon. There is another tragedy. Her whole happiness has been ruined by a wretched quarrel with the man she loves, a man called Harold Anstruther. They were playing in the Mixed Doubles in a tennis tournament not long ago and – according to her – I don't understand tennis very well – he insisted on hogging the game, as she calls it. I think she means that when the ball came near her and she was going to strike it, he rushed across and struck it himself, and this annoyed her very much. She complained to him, and he was very rude and said she was a rabbit and had better leave everything to him, and she broke off the engagement directly the game was finished. And now she is broken-hearted.'

I must say she didn't sound very broken-hearted. Just as the Bassett said these words, there came from without the uproar of someone singing, and I identified the voice as that of the solid school friend. She was rendering that old number 'Give yourself a pat on the back', and the general effect was of an exhilarated foghorn. The next moment, she came leaping into the room, and I have never seen anything more radiant. If she hadn't had the white, woolly dog in her arms, I wouldn't have recognized the sombre female of so short a while ago.

'Hi, Madeline,' she cried. 'What do you think I found on the breakfast table? A grovelling letter from the boy friend, no less. He's surrendered unconditionally. He says he must have been mad to call me a rabbit. He says he can never forgive himself, but can I forgive him. Well, I can answer that one. I'm going to forgive him the day after tomorrow. Not earlier, because we must have discipline.'

'Oh, Hilda! How glad I am!'

'I'm pretty pleased about it myself. Good old Harold! A king among men, but, of course, needs keeping in his place from time to time and has to be taught what's what. But I mustn't run on about Harold. What I came to tell you was that there's a fellow outside in a car who says he wants to see you.'

'To see me?'

'So he says. Name of Pirbright.'

Madeline turned to me.

'Why, it must be your friend Claude Pirbright, Bertie. I wonder what he wants. I'd better go and see.' She threw a quick glance at the solid girl, and seeing that she had stepped through the french window, no doubt to give the gardener the devil about something, came to me and pressed my hand. 'You must be brave, Bertie,' she said in a low, roopy voice. 'Some day another girl will come into your life and you will be happy. When we are both old and grey, we shall laugh together over all this . . . laugh, but I think with a tear behind the smile.'

She popped off, leaving me feeling sick. The solid girl, whom I had dimly heard telling the gardener he needn't be afraid of breaking that spade by leaning on it, came back and immediately proceeded, in which I considered an offensively familiar manner, to give me a hearty slap on the back.

'Well, Wooster, old bloke,' she said.

'Well, Gudgeon, old bird,' I replied courteously.

'Do you know, Wooster, I keep feeling there's something familiar about your name? I must have heard Harold mention it. Do you know Harold Anstruther?'

I had recognized the name directly I heard Madeline Bassett utter it. Beefy Anstruther had been my partner at Rackets my last year at Oxford, when I had represented the establishment at that sport. I revealed this to the solid girl, and she slapped my back again.

'I thought I wasn't wrong. Harold speaks very highly of you, Wooster, old-timer, and I'll tell you something. I have a lot of influence with Madeline, and I'll exert it on your behalf. I'll talk to her like a mother. Dash it all, we can't have her marrying a pill like Gussie Fink-Nottle, when there's a Rackets Blue on her waiting list. Courage, Wooster, old cock. Courage and patience. Come and have a bit of breakfast.'

'Thanks awfully, no,' I said, though I needed it sorely. 'I must be getting along.'

'Well, if you won't, you won't. But I will. I'm going to have the breakfast of a lifetime. I haven't felt so roaring fit since I won the tennis singles at Roedean.'

I had braced myself for another slap on the back, but with a swift change of policy she prodded me in the ribs, depriving me of what little breath her frightful words had left inside me. At the thought of what might result from a girl of her dominating personality talking to Madeline Bassett like a mother, I had wilted where I stood. It was with what are called leaden steps that I passed through the french window and made my way to the road. I was anxious to intercept Catsmeat when he drove out, so that I might learn from him the result of his interview.

And, of course, when he did drive out, he was hareing along at such a pace that it was impossible to draw myself to his attention. He vanished over the skyline as if he had been competing in some event at Brooklands, leaving me standing.

In sombre mood, bowed down with dark forebodings, I went off to get a bit of breakfast and catch a train back to King's Deverill.

18

The blokes who run the railway don't make it easy for you to get from Wimbledon to King's Deverill, feeling no doubt – and I suppose it's a kindly thought – that that abode of thugs and ghouls is a place you're better away from. You change twice before you get to Basingstoke and then change again and take the branch line. And once you're on the branch line, it's quicker to walk.

The first person I saw when I finally tottered out at journey's end, feeling as if I had been glued to the cushioned seat since early boyhood and a bit surprised that I hadn't put out tendrils like a Virginia creeper, was my cousin Thomas. He was buying motion-picture magazines at the bookstall.

'Oh, hallo,' I said. 'So you got here all right?'

He eyed me coldly and said 'Crumbs!' a word of which he is far too fond. This Thos is one of those tough, hardboiled striplings, a sort of juvenile James Cagney with a touch of Edward G. Robinson. He has carroty hair and a cynical expression, and his manner is supercilious. You would think that anyone conscious of having a mother like my Aunt Agatha and knowing it could be proved against him, would be crushed and apologetic, but this is not the case. He swanks about the place as if he'd bought it, and in conversation with a cousin lacks tact and is apt to verge on the personal.

He became personal now, on the subject of my appearance, which I must confess was not spruce. Night travel in milk trains always tends to remove the gloss, and you can't hobnob with beetles in bushes and remain dapper.

'Crumbs!' he said. 'You look like something the cat brought in.'

You see what I mean? The wrong note. In no frame of mind to bandy words, I clouted the child moodily on the head and passed on. And as I emerged into the station yard, somebody yoo-hooed and I saw Corky sitting in her car.

'Hallo, Bertie,' she said. 'Where did you spring from, moon of my delight?' She looked about her in a wary and conspiratorial manner, as if she had been registering snakiness in a spy film. 'Did you see what was in the station?' she asked, lowering the voice.

'I did.'

'Jeeves delivered him as per memo last night. Uncle Sidney looked a little taken aback for a moment, and seemed as if he were on the point of saying some of the things he gave up saying when he took Orders, but everything has turned out for the best. He loves his game of chess, and it seems that Thomas is the undisputed champion of his school, brimming over with gambits and openings and things, so they get along fine. And I love him. What a sympathetic, sweet-natured boy he is, Bertie.'

I blinked.

'You are speaking of my cousin Thomas?'

'He's so *loyal*. When I told him about the heel Dobbs arresting Sam Goldwyn, he simply boiled with generous indignation. He says he's going to cosh him.'

'To what him?'

'It's something people do to people in detective stories. You use a small but serviceable rubber bludgeon.'

'He hasn't got a small but serviceable rubber bludgeon.'

'Yes, he has. He bought it in Seven Dials when he was staying at your flat. His original idea was to employ it on a boy called Stinker at Bramley-on-Sea, but it is now earmarked for Dobbs.'

'Oh, my God!'

'It will do Dobbs all the good in the world to be coshed. It may prove a turning-point in his life. I have a feeling that things are breaking just right these days and that very shortly an era of universal happiness will set in. Look at Catsmeat, if you want Exhibit A. Have you seen him?'

'Not to speak to,' I said, speaking in a *distrait* manner, for my mind was still occupied with Thos and his plans. The last thing you want, when the nervous system is in a state of hash, are your first cousins socking policemen with rubber bludgeons. 'What about Catsmeat?'

'I met him just now, and he was singing like a linnet all over the place. He had a note from Gertrude last night, and she says that, if and when she can elude her mother's eye, she will elope with him. His cup of joy is full.'

'I'm glad someone's is.'

The sombreness of my tone caused her to look sharply at me, and her eyes widened as she saw the disorder of my outer crust.

'Bertie! My lamb!' she cried, visibly moved. 'What have you been doing to yourself? You look like —'

'Something the cat brought in?'

'I was going to say something excavated from Tutankhamen's tomb, but your guess is as good as mine. What's been happening?'

I passed a weary hand over the brow.

'Corky,' I said, 'I've been through hell.'

'About the only place I thought you didn't have to go through to get to King's Deverill. And how were they all?'

'I have a frightful story to relate.'

'Did somebody cosh you?'

'I've just come from Wimbledon.'

'From Wimbledon? But Catsmeat was attending to the Wimbledon end. He told me all about it.'

'He didn't tell you all about it, because all about it is precisely what he doesn't know. If you've only heard Catsmeat's reminiscences, you simply aren't within a million miles of being in possession of the facts. He barely scratched the surface of Wimbledon, whereas I . . . Would you care to have the ghastly details?'

She said she would love to, and I slipped them to her, and for once she listened attentively from start to finish, an agreeable deviation from her customary deaf-adder tactics. I found her a good audience. She was properly impressed when I spoke of Gussie's letter, nor did she omit to draw the breath in sharply as I touched on the Gudgeon and the sinister affair of the studio portrait. The facts in connection with the white, woolly dog also went over big.

'Golly!' she said, as I wore to a close. 'You do live, don't you, Bertie?'

I agreed that I lived, but expressed a doubt as to whether, the circumstances being what they were it was worthwhile continuing to do so. One was rather inclined, I said, to murmur 'Death, where is thy sting?' and turn the toes up.

'The best one can say,' I concluded, 'is that one has obtained a brief respite, if respite is the word. And that only if Catsmeat was successful in dissuading the Bassett from her awful purpose. For all I know, she may be coming on the next train.'

'No, she's not. He headed her off.'

'You had that straight from the horse's mouth?'

'Direct from his personal lips.'

I drew a deep breath. This certainly put a brighter aspect on the cloud wreck. In fact, it seemed to me that 'Hallelujah!' about summed it up, and I mentioned this.

I was concerned to note that she appeared a bit dubious.

'Yes, I suppose "Hallelujah!" sums it up . . . to a certain extent. I mean you can make your mind easy about her coming here. She isn't coming. But in the light of what you tell me about Mervyn Keene, Clubman, and the studio portrait, it's a pity Catsmeat didn't hit on some other method of heading her off. I do feel that.'

My heart stood still. I clutched at the windscreen for support, and what-whatted.

'The great thing to remember, the thing to bear in mind and keep the attention fixed on, is that he meant well.'

My heart stood stiller. In your walks about London you will sometimes see bent, haggard figures that look as if they had recently been caught in some powerful machinery. They are those of fellows who got mixed up with Catsmeat when he was meaning well.

'What he told Miss Bassett was this. He said that on hearing that she was coming to the hall you betrayed agitation and concern, and finally he got it out of you what the trouble was. Loving her hopelessly as you do, you shrank from the agony of having to see her day after day in Gussie's society.'

My heart, ceasing to stand still, gave a leap and tried to get out through my front teeth.

'He told Madeline Bassett that?' I quavered, shaking on my stem.

'Yes, and implored her to stay away and not subject you to this anguish. He says he was terrific and wished one or two managers had been there to catch his work, and I think he must have been pretty good, because Miss Bassett cried buckets and said she quite understood and, of course, would cancel her visit, adding something in a low voice about the desire of the moth for the star and how sad life was. What did you say?'

I explained that I had not spoken, merely uttered one of those hollow groans, and she agreed that in the circs hollow groans were perhaps in order.

'But, of course, it wasn't easy for the poor angel to think of a good way of stopping her coming,' she argued. 'And the great thing was to stop her somehow.'

'True.'

'So, if I were you, I would try to look on the bright side. Count your blessings one by one, if you know what I mean.'

This is an appeal which, when addressed to Bertram Wooster, rarely falls on deaf ears. The stunned sensation which her words had induced did not actually leave me, but it diminished somewhat in intensity. I saw her point.

'There is much in what you say,' I agreed, rising on stepping-stones of my dead self to higher things, as I have mentioned is my custom.

'The great thing, as you justly remark, was to stop the Bassett blowing in, and, if that has been accomplished, one does wrong to be fussy about the actual mechanism. And, after all, she was already firmly convinced of my unswerving devotion, so Catsmeat hasn't really plunged me so very much deeper in the broth than I was before.'

'That's my brave little man. That's the way to talk.'

'We now have a respite, and all depends on how quickly you can put Gussie on ice. The moment that is done, the whole situation will clarify. Released from your fatal spell, he will automatically return to the old love, feeling that the cagey thing is to go where he is appreciated. When do you expect to cool him off?'

'Very soon.'

'Why not instanter?'

'Well, I'll tell you, Bertie. There's a little job I want him to do for me first.'

'What job?'

'Ah, here's Thomas at last. He seems to have bought every fan magazine in existence. To read at the concert, if he's sensible. You haven't forgotten the concert is this evening? Well, mind you don't. And when you see Jeeves, ask him how that claque of Esmond's has come out. Hop in, Thomas.'

Thos hopped in, giving me another of his supercilious looks, and when in, leaned across and slipped a penny into my hand, saying 'Here, my poor man' and urging me not to spend it on drink. At any other moment this coarse ribaldry would have woken the fiend that sleeps in Bertram Wooster and led to the young pot of poison receiving another clout on the head, but I had no time now for attending to Thoses. I fixed Corky with a burning eye.

'What job?' I repeated.

'Oh, it wouldn't interest you,' she said. 'Just a trivial little job about the place.'

And she drove off, leaving me a prey to a nameless fear.

I was hoofing along the road that led to the hall, speculating dully as to what precisely she had meant by the expression 'trivial little job', when, as I rounded a corner, something large and Norfolk-coated hove in sight, and I identified it as Esmond Haddock.

19

Owing to the fact that on the instructions of Dame Daphne ('Safety First') Winkworth port was no longer served after dinner and the male and female members of the gang now left the table in a body at the conclusion of the evening repast, I had not enjoyed a *tête-à-tête* with Esmond Haddock since the night of my arrival. I had seen him around the place, of course, but always in the company of a brace of assorted aunts or that of his cousin Gertrude, in each case looking Byronic. (Checking up with Jeeves, I find that that is the word all right. Apparently it means looking like the late Lord Byron, who was a gloomy sort of bird, taking things the hard way.)

We came together, he approaching from the nor'-nor'-east and self approaching from the sou'-sou'-west, and he greeted mc with a moody twitch of the cheek muscles, as if he had thought of smiling and then thought again and said 'Oh, to hell with it'.

'Hallo,' he said.

'Hallo,' I said.

'Nice day,' he said.

'Yes,' I said. 'Out for a walk?'

'Yes,' he said. 'You out for a walk?'

Prudence compelled me to descend to subterfuge.

'Yes,' I said. 'I'm out for a walk. I just ran into Miss Pirbright.'

At the mention of that name, he winced as if troubled by an old wound.

'Oh?' he said. 'Miss Pirbright, eh?'

He swallowed a couple of times. I could see a question trembling on his lips, but it was plainly one that nauseated him, for after uttering the word 'Was' he kept right along swallowing. I was just about to touch on the situation in the Balkans in order to keep the conversation going, when he got it out.

'Was Wooster with her?'

'No, she was alone.'

'You're sure?'

'Certain.'

'He may have been lurking in the background. Behind a tree or something.'

'The meeting occurred in the station yard.'

'He wasn't skulking in a doorway?'

'Oh, no.'

'Strange. You don't often see her without Wooster these days,' he said, and ground his teeth a trifle.

I had a shot at trying to mitigate his anguish, which I could see was considerable. He, too, had obviously noted Gussie's spotty work, and it was plain that what is technically known as the green-eyed monster had been slipping it across him properly.

'They're old friends, of course,' I said.

'Are they?'

'Oh, rather. We – I should say they – have known each other since childhood. They went to the same dancing class.'

The moment I had mentioned that, I was wishing I hadn't, for it seemed to affect him as though some hidden hand had given him the hotfoot. You couldn't say his brow darkened because it had been dark to start with, but he writhed visibly. Like Lord Byron reading a review of his last slim volume of verse and finding it a stinker. I wasn't surprised. A man in love and viewing with concern the competition of a rival does not like to think of the adored object and that rival pirouetting about together at dancing classes and probably splitting a sociable milk and biscuit in the eleven o'clock interval.

'Oh?' he said, and gave a sort of whistling sigh like the last whoosh of a dying soda-water syphon. 'The same dancing class? The same dancing class, eh?'

He brooded a while. When he spoke again, his voice was hoarse and rumbling.

'Tell me about this fellow Wooster, Gussie. He is a friend of yours?'

'Oh, yes.'

'Known him long?'

'We were at school together.'

'I suppose he was a pretty loathsome boy? The pariah of the establishment?'

'Oh, no.'

'Changed after he grew up, eh? Well, he certainly made up leeway all right, because of all the slinking snakes it has ever been my misfortune to encounter, he is the slimiest.'

'Would you call him a slinking snake?'

'I did call him a slinking snake, and I'll do it again as often as you wish. The fishfaced trailing arbutus!'

'He's not a bad chap.'

'That may be your opinion. It is not mine, nor, I should imagine, that of most decent-minded people. Hell is full of men like Wooster. What the devil does she see in him?'

'I don't know.'

'Nor anyone else. I've studied the fellow carefully and without bias, and he seems to me entirely lacking in charm. Have you ever turned over a flat stone?'

'From time to time.'

'And what came crawling out? A lot of obscene creatures that might have been his brothers. I tell you, Gussie, if you were to put a bit of gorgonzola cheese on the slide of a microscope and tell me to take a look, the first thing I'd say on getting it focused would be: "Why, hallo, Wooster!"'

He brooded Byronically for a moment.

'I know the specious argument you are going to put forward, Gussie,' he proceeded. 'You are going to say that it is not Wooster's fault that he looks like a slightly enlarged cheesemite. Very true. One strives to be fair. But it is not only the man's revolting appearance that distresses the better element. He is a menace to the community.'

'Oh, come.'

'What do you mean, "Oh, come"? You heard what my Aunt Daphne was telling us at dinner the night you arrived. About this ghastly Wooster perpetually stealing policemen's helmets.'

'Not perpetually. Just as a treat on Boat Race night.'

He frowned.

'I don't like the way you stick up for the fellow, Gussie. You probably consider that you are being broad-minded, but you want to be careful how you let that so-called broad-mindedness grow on you. It is apt to become mere moral myopia. The facts are well documented. Whenever Wooster has a spare moment, he goes about London persecuting unfortunate policemen, assaulting them, hampering them in their duties, making their lives a hell on earth. That's the kind of man Wooster is.'

He paused, and became for a moment lost in thought. Then there flitted across his map another of those quick twitches which he seemed to be using nowadays, on the just-as-good principle, as a substitute for smiles.

'Well, I'll tell you one thing, Gussie. I only hope he intends to start something on those lines here, because we're ready for him.'

'Eh?'

'Ready and waiting. You know Dobbs?'

'The flatty?'

'Our village constable, yes. A splendid fellow, tireless in the performance of his duties.'

'I've not met him. I hear his engagement is broken off.'

'So much the better, for it will remove the last trace of pity and weakness from his heart. I have told Dobbs all about Wooster and warned him to be on the alert. And he is on the alert. He is straining at the leash. Let Wooster so much as lift a finger in the direction of Dobbs's helmet, and he's for it. You might not think so at a casual glance, Gussie, but I'm a Justice of the Peace. I sit on the Bench at our local Sessions and put it across the criminal classes when they start getting above themselves. It is my earnest hope that the criminal streak in Wooster will come to the surface and cause him to break out, because in that event Dobbs will be on him like a leopard and he will come up before me and I shall give him thirty days without the option, regardless of his age or sex.'

I didn't like the sound of this.

'You wouldn't do that, Esmond?'

'I would. I'm looking forward to it. Let Wooster stray one inch from the straight and narrow path – just one inch – and you can kiss him goodbye for thirty days. Well, I'll be moving along, Gussie. I find it helps a little to keep walking.'

He disappeared over the horizon at five mph, and I stood there aghast. The sense of impending peril was stronger on the wing than ever. 'Oh, that Jeeves were here!' I said to myself.

I found he was. For some little time past I had been conscious of some substance in the offing that was saying 'Good morning, sir', and, turning to see where the noise was coming from, I beheld him at my side, looking bronzed and fit, as if his visit to Bramley-on-Sea had done him good.

20

'Good morning, sir,' he said. 'May I make a remark?'

'Certainly, Jeeves. Carry on. Make several.'

'It is with reference to your appearance, sir. If I might take the liberty of suggesting –'

'Go on. Say it. I look like something the cat found in Tutankhamen's tomb, do I not?'

'I would not go so far as that, sir, but I have unquestionably seen you more *soigné*.'

It crossed my mind for an instant that with a little thought one might throw together something rather clever about 'Way down upon the *soigné* river', but I was too listless to follow it up.

'If you will allow me, sir, I will take the suit which you are wearing and give it my attention.'

'Thank you, Jeeves.'

'I will sponge and press it.'

'Thank you, Jeeves.'

'Very good, sir. A beautiful morning, is it not, sir?'

'Thank you, Jeeves.'

He raised an eyebrow.

'You appear *distrait*, sir.'

'I am *distrait*, Jeeves. About as *distrait* as I can stick. And there's enough to make me *distrait*.'

'But surely, sir, matters are proceeding most satisfactorily. I delivered Master Thomas at the Vicarage. And I learn from my Uncle Charlie that her ladyship, your aunt, has postponed her visit to the hall.'

'Quite. But these things are mere side issues. I don't say they aren't silver linings in their limited way, but take a look at the clouds that lower elsewhere. First and foremost, that man is in again.'

'Sir?'

I pulled myself together with a strong effort, for I saw that I was being obscure.

'Sorry to speak in riddles, Jeeves,' I said. 'What I meant was that Gussie had once more become a menace of the first water.'

'Indeed, sir? In what way?'

'I will tell you. What started all this rannygazoo?'

'The circumstances of Mr Fink-Nottle being sent to prison, sir.'

'Exactly. Well, it's an odds-on bet that he's going to be sent to prison again.'

'Indeed, sir?'

'I wish you wouldn't say "Indeed, sir?" Yes, the shadow of the Pen is once more closing in on Augustus Fink-Nottle. The Law is flexing its muscles and waiting to pounce. One false step – and he's bound to make at least a dozen in the first minute – and into the coop he goes for thirty days. And we know what'll happen then, don't we?'

'We do indeed, sir.'

'I don't mind you saying "Indeed, sir" if you tack it on to something else like that. Yes, we know what will happen, and the flesh creeps, what?'

'Distinctly, sir.'

I forced myself to a sort of calm. Only a frozen calm, but frozen calms are better than nothing.

'Of course, it may be, Jeeves, that I am mistaken in supposing that this old lag is about to resume his life of crime, but I don't think so. Here are the facts. Just now I encountered Miss Pirbright in the station yard. We naturally fell into conversation, and after a while the subject of Gussie came up. And we had been speaking of him for some moments when she let fall an observation that filled me with a nameless fear. She said there was a little job she was getting him to do for her. And when I said "What job?" she replied "Oh, just a trivial little job about the place". And her manner was evasive. Or shall I say furtive?'

'Whichever you prefer, sir.'

'It was the manner of a girl guiltily conscious of being in the process of starting something. "What ho!" I said to myself. "Hallo, hallo, hallo, hallo!"'

'If I might interrupt for a moment, sir, I am happy to inform you that my efforts to secure a claque for Mr Esmond Haddock at the concert have been crowned with gratifying success. The back of the hall will be thronged with his supporters and well-wishers.'

I frowned.

'This is excellent news, Jeeves, but I'm dashed if I can see what it's got to do with the *res* under discussion.'

'No, sir. I am sorry. It was your observing "Hallo, hallo, hallo,

hallo", that put the matter into my mind. Pardon me, sir. You were saying –'

'Well, what *was* I saying? I've forgotten.'

'You were commenting on Miss Pirbright's furtive and evasive manner, sir.'

'Ah, yes. It suggested that she was in the process of starting something. And the thought that smote me like a blow was this. If Corky is starting something, it's a hundred to eight it's something in the nature of reprisals against Constable Dobbs. Am I right or wrong, Jeeves?'

'The probability certainly lies in that direction, sir.'

'I know Corky. Her psychology is an open book to me. Even in the distant days when she wore rompers and had a tooth missing in front, hers was always a fiery and impulsive nature, quick to resent anything in the shape of oompus-boompus. And it is inevitably as oompus-boompus that she will have classed the zealous officer's recent arrest of her dog. And if she had it in for him merely on account of their theological differences, how much more will she have it in for him now. The unfortunate hound is languishing in a dungeon with gyves upon his wrists, and a girl of her spirit is not likely to accept such a state of things supinely.'

'No, sir.'

'You're right, No, sir. The facts are hideous, but we must face them. Corky is planning direct action against Constable Dobbs, taking we cannot say what form, and it seems only too sickeningly certain that Gussie, whom it is so imperative to keep from getting embroiled again with the Force, is going to lend himself as an instrument to her sinister designs. And here's something that'll make you say "Indeed, sir?" I've just been talking to Esmond Haddock, and he turns out to be a JP. He has the powers of the High, the Middle and the Low Justice in King's Deverill, and is consequently in a position to give anyone thirty days without the option as soon as look at them. And what's more, he has taken a violent dislike to Gussie and told me in so many words that it is his dearest wish to see the darbies clapped on him. Try that one on your pianola, Jeeves.'

He seemed about to speak, but I raised a restraining hand.

'I know what you're going to say, and I quite agree. Left to himself, with Conscience as his guide, Gussie is the last person likely to commit a tort or malfeasance and start JPs ladling out exemplary sentences. Quite true. From boyhood up, his whole policy, instilled into him, no doubt, at his mother's knee, has been to give the primrose path a solid miss and sedulously avoid those rash acts which put wilder spirits in line for thirty days in the jug. But one knows that he is easily swayed. Catsmeat, for instance, swayed him in Trafalgar Square by threatening to bean him with a bottle. I shall be vastly surprised if Corky doesn't sway him, too. And I know from personal experience,' I said, thinking of that orange at the dancing school, 'that when Corky sways people, the sky is the limit.'

'You think that Mr Fink-Nottle will lend a willing ear to the young lady's suggestions?'

'Her word is law to him. He will be wax in her hands. I tell you, Jeeves, the spirits are low. I don't know if you have ever been tied hand and foot to a chair in front of a barrel of gunpowder with an inch of lighted candle on top of it?'

'No, sir, I have not had that experience.'

'Well, that's how I am feeling. I'm just clenching the teeth and waiting for the bang.'

'Would you wish me to speak a word to Mr Fink-Nottle, sir, warning him of the inadvisability of doing anything rash?'

'There's nothing I'd like better. He might listen to you.'

'I will make a point of doing so at the earliest opportunity, sir.'

'Thank you, Jeeves. It's a black business, isn't it?'

'Extremely, sir.'

'I don't know when I've come across a blacker. Very, very murky everything is.'

'With perhaps the exception of the affairs of Mr Pirbright, sir?'

'Ah, yes, Catsmeat. I was informed of his lucky strike. His hat is on the side of his head, they tell me.'

'It was distinctly in that position when I last saw him, sir.'

'Well, that's something. Yes, that cheers the heart a bit,' I said, for even when preoccupied with the stickiness of their own concerns, the Woosters can always take time out to rejoice over a buddy's bliss. 'One may certainly chalk up Catsmeat's happy ending as a ray of light. And you say that the village toughs are going to rally round Mr Haddock this evening?'

'In impressive numbers, sir.'

'Well, dash it, that's two rays of light. And if you can talk Gussie out of making an ass of himself, that'll be three. We're getting on. All right, Jeeves, push off and see what you can do with him. I should imagine you will find him at the Vicarage.'

'Very good, sir.'

'Oh, and, Jeeves, most important. When at the Vicarage, get in touch with young Thos and remove from his possession a blunt instrument known as a cosh, which he has managed to acquire.

It's a species of rubber bludgeon, and you know as well as I do how reluctantly one would trust him with such a thing. You could go through the telephone book from A to Z without hitting on the name of anyone one wouldn't prefer to see with his hooks on a rubber bludgeon. You will get an idea of what I mean when I tell you that he speaks freely of beaning Constable Dobbs with the weapon. So choke it out of him without fail. I shan't be easy in my mind till I know you've got it.'

'Very good, sir. I will give the matter my attention,' he said and we parted with mutual civilities, he to do his day's good deed at the Vicarage, I to resume my hoofing in the opposite direction.

And I had hoofed perhaps a matter of two hundred yards, when I was jerked out of the reverie into which I had fallen by a sight which froze the blood and caused the two eyes, like stars, to start from their spheres. I had seen Gussie coming out of a gate of a picturesque cottage standing back from the road behind a neat garden.

King's Deverill was one of those villages where picturesque cottages breed like rabbits, but what distinguished this picturesque cottage from the others was that over its door were the Royal Arms and the words

POLICE STATION

And evidence that the above legend was not just a gag was supplied by the fact that accompanying Gussie, not actually with a hand on his collar and another gripping the seat of his trousers but so nearly so that the casual observer might have been excused for supposing that this was a pinch, was a stalwart figure in a blue uniform and a helmet, who could be no other than Constable Ernest Dobbs.

21

It was the first time I had been privileged to see this celebrated rozzer, of whom I had heard so much, and I think that even had the circumstances been less tense I would have paused to get an eyeful, for his, like Silversmith's, was a forceful personality, arresting the attention and causing the passer-by to draw the breath in quite a bit.

The sleepless guardian of the peace of King's Deverill was one of those chunky, nobbly officers. It was as though Nature, setting out to assemble him, had said to herself 'I will not skimp'. Nor had she done so, except possibly in the matter of height. I believe that in order to become a member of the Force you have to stand five feet nine inches in your socks, and Ernest Dobbs can only just have got his nose under the wire. But this slight perpendicular shortage had the effect of rendering his bulk all the more impressive. He was plainly a man who, had he felt disposed, could have understudied the village blacksmith and no questions asked, for it could be seen at a glance that the muscles of his brawny arms were strong as iron bands.

To increase the similarity, his brow at the moment was wet with honest sweat. He had the look of a man who has recently passed through some testing emotional experience. His eyes were aglow, his moustache a-bristle and his nose a-wiggle.

'Grrh!' he said and spat. Only that and nothing more. A man of few words, apparently, but a good spitter.

Gussie, having reached the great open spaces, smiled weakly. He, too, appeared to be in the grip of some strong emotion. And as I was, also, that made three of us.

'Well, good day, officer,' he said.

'Good day, sir,' said the constable shortly.

He went back into the cottage and banged the door, and I sprang at Gussie like a jumping bean.

'What's all this?' I quavered.

The door of the cottage opened, and Constable Dobbs re-appeared. He had a shovel in his hand, and in this shovel one noted what seemed to be frogs. Yes, on a closer inspection, definitely frogs. He gave the shovel a jerk, shooting the dumb chums through the air as if he had been scattering confetti. They landed on the grass and went about their business. The officer paused, directed a hard look at Gussie, spat once more with all the old force and precision and withdrew, and Gussie, removing his hat, wiped his forehead.

'Let's get out of this,' he urged, and it was not until we were some quarter of a mile distant that he regained a certain measure of calm. He removed his glasses, polished them, replaced them on his nose and seemed the better for it. His breathing became more regular.

'That was Constable Dobbs,' he said.

'So I deduced.'

'From the uniform, no doubt?'

'That and the helmet.'

'Quite,' said Gussie. 'I see. Quite. I see. Quite. I see.'

It seemed possible that he would go rambling on like this for a goodish while, but after saying 'Quite' about another six times and 'I see' about another seven he snapped out of it.

'Bertie,' he said, 'you have frequently been in the hands of the police, haven't you?'

'Not frequently. Once.'

'It is a ghastly experience, is it not? Your whole life seems to rise before you. By Jove, I could do with a drink of orange juice!'

I paused for a moment, to allow a dizzy feeling to pass.

'What was happening?' I asked, when I felt stronger.

'Eh?'

'What had you been doing?'

'Who, me?'

'Yes, you.'

'Oh,' said Gussie in an offhand way, as if it were only what might have been expected of an English gentleman, 'I had been strewing frogs.'

I goggled.

'Doing *what*?'

'Strewing frogs. In Constable Dobbs's boudoir. The Vicar suggested it.'

'The Vicar?'

'I mean it was he who gave Corky the idea. She had been brooding a lot, poor girl, on Dobbs's high-handed behaviour in connection with her dog, and last night the Vicar happened to speak of Pharaoh and all those Plagues he got when he wouldn't let the Children of Israel go. You probably recall the incident? His words started a train of thought.

It occurred to Corky that if Dobbs were visited by a Plague of Frogs, it might quite possibly change his heart and make him let Sam Goldwyn go. So she asked me to look in at his cottage and attend to the matter. She said it would please her and be good for Dobbs and would only take a few minutes of my time. She felt that the Plague of Lice might be even more effective, but she is a practical, clear-thinking girl and realized that lice are hard to come by, whereas you can find frogs in any hedgerow.'

Every mouse in my interior sprang into renewed life. With a strong effort I managed to refrain from howling like a lost soul. It seemed incredible to me that this super-goof should have gone through life all this while without fetching up in some loony bin. You would have thought that some such establishment as Colney Hatch, with its talent scouts out all over the place, would have snapped him up years ago.

'Tell me exactly what happened. He caught you?'

'Fortunately, no. He came in about half a minute too late. I had bided my time, and having ascertained that the cottage was empty I went in and distributed my frogs.'

'And he was somewhere round the corner?'

'Exactly. In a sort of shed place by the back door, where I think he must have been potting geraniums or something, for his hands were all covered with mould. I suppose he had come in to wash them. It was a most embarrassing moment. One didn't quite know how to begin the conversation. Eventually I said "Oh, hallo, there you are!" and he stared at the frogs for some time, and then he said, "What's all this?" They were hopping about a bit. You know how frogs hop.'

'Hither and thither, you mean?'

'That's right. Hither and thither. Well, I kept my presence of mind. I said "What's all what, officer?" And he said "All these frogs". And I said "Ah, yes, there do seem to be quite a few frogs in here. You are fond of them?" He then asked if these frogs were my doing. And I said "In what sense do you use the word 'doing', officer?" and he said "Did you bring these frogs in here?" Well, then, I'm afraid, I wilfully misled him, for I said No. It went against the grain to tell a deliberate falsehood, of course, but I do think there are times when one is justified in –'

'Get on!'

'You bustle me so, Bertie. Where was I? Ah, yes. I said No, I couldn't account for their presence in any way. I said it was just one of those things we should never be able to understand. Probably, I said, we were not meant to understand. And, of course, he could prove nothing. I mean, anyone could wander innocently into a room where there happened to be some frogs hopping about – the Archbishop of Canterbury or anyone. I think he must have appreciated this, for all he did was mutter something about it being a very serious offence to bring frogs into a police station and I said I supposed it was and what a pity one could never hope to catch the fellow who had done it. And then he asked me what I was doing there, and I said I had come to ask him to release Sam Goldwyn, and he said he wouldn't because he had now established that the bite Sam had given him was his second bite and that the animal was in a very serious position. So I said "Oh, well, then, I think I'll be going", and I went. He came with me, as you saw, growling under his breath. I can't say I liked the man. His manner is bad. Brusque. Abrupt. Not at all the sort of chap likely to win friends and influence people. Well, I suppose I had better be getting along and reporting to Corky. That stuff about the second bite will worry her, I'm afraid.'

Repeating his remark about being in the vein for a drink of orange juice, he set a course for the Vicarage and pushed off, and I resumed my progress to the Deverilleries, speculating dully as to what would be the next horror to come into my life. It only needed a meeting with Dame Daphne Winkworth, I felt sombrely, to put the tin hat on this dark day.

My aim was to sneak in unobserved, and it seemed at first as though luck were with me. From time to time, as I slunk through the grounds, keeping in the shelter of the bushes and trying not to let a twig snap beneath my feet, I could hear the distant baying of aunts, but I wasn't spotted. With something approaching a 'Tra-la' on my lips I passed through the front door into the hall, and – *bing* – right in the middle of the fairway, arranging flowers at a table, Dame Daphne Winkworth.

Well, I suppose Napoleon or Attila the Hun or one of those fellows would just have waved a hand and said 'Aha, there!' and hurried on, but the feat was beyond me. Her eye, swivelling round, stopped me like a bullet. The Wedding Guest, if you remember, had the same trouble with the Ancient Mariner.

'Ah, there you are, Augustus.'

It was fruitless to deny it. I stood on one leg and dashed a bead of persp from the brow.

'I had no time to ask you last night. Have you written to Madeline?'

'Oh, yes, rather.'

'I hope you were properly apologetic.'

'Oh, rather, yes.'

'And why are you looking as if you had slept in your clothes?' she asked, giving the upholstery a look of distaste.

The thing about the Woosters is that they know when to speak out and when not to speak out. Something told me that here was where manly frankness might pay dividends.

'Well, as a matter of fact,' I said, 'I did. I ran up to Wimbledon last night on the milk train. To see Madeline, don't you know. You know how it is. You can't say all you want to in letters, and I thought . . . well, the personal touch, if you see what I mean.'

It couldn't have gone better. I have never actually seen a shepherd welcoming a strayed lamb back into the fold, but I should imagine that his manner on such an occasion would closely parallel that of this female twenty-minute egg as she heard my words. The eyes softened. The face split in a pleased smile. That wrinkling of the nose which had been so noticeable a moment before, as if I had been an escape of gas or a not-quite-up-to-sample egg, disappeared totally. It would not be putting it too strongly to say that she beamed.

'Augustus!'

'I think it was a good move.'

'It was, indeed. It is just the sort of thing that would appeal to Madeline's romantic nature. Why, you are quite a Romeo, Augustus. In the *milk* train? You must have been travelling all night.'

'Pretty well.'

'You poor boy! I can see you're worn out. I will ring for Silversmith to bring you some orange juice.'

She pressed the bell. There was a stage wait. She pressed it again, and there was another stage wait. She was on the point of giving it a third prod, when the hour produced the man. Uncle Charlie entered left, and I was amazed to see that there was an indulgent smile on his face. It is true that he switched it off immediately and resumed his customary aspect of a respectful chunk of dough, but the facial contortion had unquestionably been there.

'I must apologize for my delay in answering the bell, m'lady,' he said. 'When your ladyship rang, I was in the act of making a speech, and it was not until some moments had elapsed that I became aware of the summons.'

Dame Daphne blinked. Me, too.

'Making a speech?'

'In honour of the happy event, m'lady. My daughter Queenie has become affianced, m'lady.'

Dame Daphne oh-really-ed, and I very nearly said 'Indeed, sir?'

for the information had come as a complete surprise. For one thing I hadn't suspected for an instant that ties of blood linked this bulging butler and that lissom parlourmaid, and for another, it seemed to me that she had got over her spot of Dobbs trouble pretty snappily. So this is what Woman's constancy amounts to, is it, I remember saying to myself, and I'm not at all sure I didn't add the word 'Faugh!'

'And who is the happy man, Silversmith?'

'A nice steady young fellow, m'lady. A young fellow called Meadowes.'

I had a feeling I had heard the name before somewhere, but I couldn't place it. Meadowes? Meadowes? No, it eluded me.

'Indeed? From the village?'

'No, m'lady. Meadowes is Mr Fink-Nottle's personal attendant,' said Silversmith, now definitely unshipping a smile and directing it at me. He seemed to be trying to indicate that after this he looked on me as one of the boys and practically a relation by marriage and that, on his side at least, no more would be said of my weakness for singing hunting songs over the port and introducing into country houses dogs that bit like serpents.

I suppose the gasp that had escaped my lips sounded to Dame Daphne like the gurgle of a man dying of thirst, for she instantly put in her order for orange juice.

'Silversmith had better take it to your room. You will be wanting to change your clothes.'

'He might tell Meadowes to bring it,' I said faintly.

'Why, of course. You will want to wish him happiness.'

'That's right,' I said.

It was not immediately that Catsmeat presented himself. No doubt if you have made all your plans for marrying the daughter of the house and then suddenly find yourself engaged to the parlourmaid you need a little time to adjust the faculties. When he finally did appear, it seemed to me from his dazed expression that he had still a longish way to go in that direction. His air was that of a man who has recently been coshed by a small but serviceable rubber bludgeon.

'Bertie,' he said, 'a rather unfortunate thing has happened.'

'I know.'

'Oh, you know, do you? Then what do you advise?'

There could be but one answer to this.

'You'd better place the whole matter before Jeeves.'

'I will. That great brain may find a formula. I'll lay the facts before Jeeves and bid him brood on them.'

'But what are the facts? How did it happen?'

'I'll tell you. Do you want this orange juice?'

'No.'

'Then I'll have it. It may help a little.'

He drank deeply, and mopped the forehead.

'It all comes of letting that Dickens spirit creep over you, Bertie. The advice I give to every young man starting life is Never get Dickensy. You remember I told you that for some days I have been bursting with a sort of yeasty benevolence? This morning it came to a head. I had had Gertrude's note saying that she would elope with me, and I was just a solid chunk of sweetness and light. In ecstasies myself, I wanted to see happiness all around me. I loved my species and yearned to do it a bit of good. And with these sentiments fizzing about inside me, with the milk of human kindness sloshing up against my back teeth, I wandered into the servants' hall and found Queenie there in tears.'

'Your heart bled?'

'Profusely. I said "There, there". I took her hand and patted it. And then, as I didn't seem to be making any headway, almost unconsciously I drew her on to my knee and put my arm around her waist and started kissing her. Like a brother.'

'H'm.'

'Don't say "H'm", Bertie. It was only what Sir Galahad or someone like that would have done in my place. Dash it, there's nothing wrong, is there, in acting like a sympathetic elder brother when a girl is in distress? Pretty square behaviour, I should have thought. But don't run away with the idea that I don't wish I hadn't yielded to the kindly impulse. I regret it sincerely, because at that moment Silversmith came in. And what do you think? He's her father.'

'I know.'

'You seem to know everything.'

'I do.'

'Well, there's one thing you don't know, and that is that he was accompanied by Gertrude.'

'Gosh!'

'Yes. Her manner on beholding me was a bit reserved. Silversmith's, on the other hand, wasn't. He looked like a minor prophet without a beard suddenly confronted with the sins of the people, and started in immediately to thunder denunciations. There are fathers who know how to set about an erring daughter, and fathers who do not. Silversmith is one of the former. And then, in a sort of dream, I heard Queenie telling him that we were engaged. She has since informed me that it seemed to her the only way out. It did, of course, momentarily ease the strain.'

'How did Gertrude appear to take it?'

'Not very blithely. I've just had a brief note from her, cancelling our arrangements.'

He groaned the sort of hollow groan I had been groaning so much of late.

'You see before you, Bertie, a spent egg, a man in whom hope is dead. You don't happen to have any cyanide on you?' He groaned another hollow one. 'And on top of all this,' he said, 'I've got to put on a green beard and play Mike in a knockabout cross-talk act!'

I was sorry for the unhappy young blister, of course, but it piqued me somewhat that he seemed to consider that he was the only one who had any troubles.

'Well, I've got to recite Christopher Robin poems.'

'Pah!' he said. 'It might have been Winnie the Pooh.'

Well, there was that, of course.

22

The village hall stood in the middle of the High Street, just abaft the duck-pond. Erected in the year 1881 by Sir Quintin Deverill, Bart, a man who didn't know much about architecture but knew what he liked, it was one of those mid-Victorian jobs in glazed red brick which always seem to bob up in these olde-worlde hamlets and do so much to encourage the drift to the towns. Its interior, like those of all the joints of its kind I've ever come across, was dingy and fuggy and smelled in about equal proportions of apples, chalk, damp plaster, Boy Scouts and the sturdy English peasantry.

The concert was slated to begin at eight-fifteen, and a few minutes before the kick-off, my own little effort not being billed till after the intermission, I wandered in and took my place among the standees at the back, noting dully that I should be playing to absolute capacity. The populace had rolled up in droves, though I could have warned them that they were asking for it. I had seen the programme, and I knew the worst.

The moment I scanned the bill of fare, I was able to understand why Corky, that afternoon at my flat, had spoken so disgruntedly of the talent at her disposal, like a girl who has been thwarted and frustrated and kept from fulfilling herself and what not. I knew what had happened. Starting out to arrange this binge with high hopes and burning ideals and all that sort of thing, poor child, she had stubbed her toe on the fatal snag which always lurks in the path of the impresario of this type of entertainment. I allude to the fact that at every village concert there are certain powerful vested interests which have to be considered. There are, that is to say, divers local nibs who, having always done their bit, are going to be pretty cold and sniffy if not invited to do it again this time. What Corky had come up against was the Kegley-Bassington clan.

To a man of my wide experience, such items as 'Solo: Miss Muriel Kegley-Bassington' and 'Duologue (A Pair of Lunatics): Colonel and Mrs R.P. Kegley-Bassington' told their own story; and the same thing applied to 'Imitations: Watkyn Kegley-Bassington';

'Card Tricks: Percival Kegley-Bassington' and 'Rhythmic Dance: Miss Poppy Kegley-Bassington'. Master George Kegley-Bassington, who was down for a recitation, I absolved from blame. I strongly suspected that he, like me, had been thrust into his painful position by *force majeure* and would have been equally willing to make a cash settlement.

In the intervals of feeling a brotherly sympathy for Master George and wishing I could run across him and stand him a commiserating gingerbeer, I devoted my time to studying the faces of my neighbours, hoping to detect in them some traces of ruth and pity and what is known as kind indulgence. But not a glimmer. Like all rustic standees, these were stern, implacable men, utterly incapable of taking the broad, charitable view and realizing that a fellow who comes on a platform and starts reciting about Christopher Robin going hoppity-hoppity-hop (or, alternatively, saying his prayers) does not do so from sheer wantonness but because he is a helpless victim of circumstances beyond his control.

I was gazing with considerable apprehension at a particularly dangerous specimen on my left, a pleasure-seeker with hair oil on his head and those mobile lips to which the raspberry springs automatically, when a mild splatter of applause from the two-bob seats showed that we were off. The vicar was opening the proceedings with a short address.

Apart from the fact that I was aware that he played chess and shared with Catsmeat's current *fiancée* a dislike for hearing policemen make cracks about Jonah and the Whale, the Rev. Sidney Pirbright had hitherto been a sealed book to me, and this was, of course, the first time I had seen him in action. A tall, drooping man, looking as if he had been stuffed in a hurry by an incompetent taxidermist, it became apparent immediately that he was not one of those boisterous vicars who, when opening a village concert, bound on the stage with a whoop and a holler, give the parishioners a huge Hallo, slam across a couple of travelling-salesman-and-farmer's-daughter stories and bound off, beaming. He seemed low-spirited, as I suppose he had every right to be. With Corky permanently on the premises, doing the little Mother, and Gussie rolling up for practically every meal, and on top of that a gorilla like young Thos coming and parking himself in the spare bedroom, you could scarcely expect him to bubble over with *joie de vivre*. These things take their toll.

At any rate, he didn't. His theme was the Church Organ, in aid of which these grim doings had been set afoot, and it was in a vein of pessimism that he spoke of its prospects. The Church Organ, he told us frankly was in a hell of a bad way. For years it had been going around with holes in its socks, doing the Brother-can-you-spare-a-dime stuff, and now it was about due to hand in its dinner pail. There had been a time when he had hoped that the pull-together spirit might have given it a shot in the arm, but the way it looked to him at the moment, things had gone too far and he was prepared to bet his shirt on the bally contrivance going down the drain and staying there.

He concluded by announcing sombrely that the first item on the programme would be a Violin Solo by Miss Eustacia Pulbrook, managing to convey the suggestion that, while he knew as well as we did that Eustacia was going to be about as corny as they come, he advised us to make the most of her, because after that we should have the Kegley-Bassington family at our throats.

Except for knowing that when you've heard one, you've heard them all, I'm not really an authority on violin solos, so cannot state definitely whether La Pulbrook's was or was not a credit to the accomplices who had taught her the use of the instrument. It was loud in spots and less loud in other spots, and it had that quality which I have noticed in all violin solos, of seeming to last much longer than it actually did. When it eventually blew over, one saw what the sainted Sidney had meant about the Kegley-Bassingtons. A minion came on the stage carrying a table. On this table he placed a framed photograph, and I knew that we were for it. Show Bertram Wooster a table and a framed photograph, and you don't have to tell him what the upshot is going to be. Muriel Kegley-Bassington stood revealed as a 'My Hero' from *The Chocolate Soldier* addict.

I thought the boys behind the back row behaved with extraordinary dignity and restraint, and their suavity gave me the first faint hope I had had that when my turn came to face the firing-squad I might be spared the excesses which I had been anticipating. I would rank 'My Hero' next after 'The Yeoman's Wedding Song' as a standee-rouser, and when a large blonde appeared and took up the photograph and gave it a soulful look and rubbed her hands in the rosin and inflated her lungs, I was expecting big things. But these splendid fellows apparently did not war on women. Not only did they refrain from making uncouth noises with the tongue between the lips, one or two actually clapped – an imprudent move, of course, because, taken in conjunction with the applause of the two-bobbers, who applaud everything, it led to 'Oh, who will o'er the downs with me' as an encore.

Inflamed by this promising start, Muriel would, I think, willingly have continued, probably with 'The Indian Love Call', but something in our manner must have shown her that she couldn't do that here, for she shrank back and withdrew. There was a brief stage wait, and then a small, bullet-headed boy in an Eton jacket came staggering on like Christopher Robin going hoppity-hoppity-hop, in a manner that suggested that blood relations in the background had overcome his reluctance to appear by putting a hand between his shoulder-blades and shoving. Master George Kegley-Bassington, and no other. My heart went out to the little fellow. I knew just how he was feeling.

One could picture so clearly all that must have led up to this rash act. The first fatal suggestion by his mother that it would please the vicar if George gave that recitation which he did so nicely. The agonized 'Hoy!' The attempted rebuttal. The family pressure. The sullen scowl. The calling in of Father to exercise his authority. The reluctant acquiescence. The dash for freedom at the eleventh hour, foiled, as we have seen, by that quick thrust between the shoulder-blades.

And here he was, out in the middle.

He gave us an unpleasant look, and said:

'"Ben Battle."'

I pursed the lips and shook the head. I knew this 'Ben Battle', for it had been in my own repertoire in my early days. One of those gruesome antiques with a pun in every other line, the last thing to which any right-minded boy would wish to lend himself, and quite unsuited to this artiste's style. If I had had the ear of Colonel and Mrs R.P. Kegley-Bassington, I would have said to them: 'Colonel, Mrs Kegley-Bassington, be advised by an old friend. Keep George away from comedy, and stick to good sound "Dangerous Dan McGrews". His forte is grimness.'

Having said 'Ben Battle', he paused and repeated the unpleasant look. I could see what was passing through his mind. He wished to know if anybody out front wanted to make anything of this. The pause was a belligerent pause. But it was evident that it had been misinterpreted by his nearest and dearest, for two voices, both loud and carrying, spoke simultaneously from the wings. One had a parade-ground rasp, the other was that of the songstress who had so recently My-Heroed.

'Ben Battle was a soldier bold . . .'

'All *right*!' said George, transferring the unpleasant look in that direction. '*I* know. Ben-Battle-was-a-soldier-bold-and-used-to-war's-alarms, A-cannon-ball-took-off-his-legs-so-he-laid-down-his-arms,' he added, crowding the thing into a single word. He then proceeded.

Well, really, come, come, I felt, as he did so, this is most encouraging. Can it be, I asked myself, that these rugged exteriors around me hide hearts of gold? It certainly seemed so, for despite the fact that it would have been difficult, nay impossible, to imagine anything lousier than Master George Kegley-Bassington's performance, it was producing nothing in the nature of a demonstration from the standees. They had not warred on women, and they did not war on children. Might it not quite easily happen, I mused, that they would not war on Woosters? Tails up, Bertram, I said to myself, and it was with almost a light heart that I watched George forget the last three stanzas and shamble off, giving us that unpleasant look again over his shoulder, and in the exuberance with which I greeted the small man with the face like an anxious marmoset – Adrian Higgins, I gathered from my programme; by profession, I subsequently learned, King's Deverill's courteous and popular grave-digger – there was something that came very close to being carefree.

Adrian Higgins solicited our kind attention for Impressions of Woodland Songsters Which Are Familiar To You All, and while these did not go with any particular bang, the farmyard imitations which followed were cordially received, and the drawing of a cork and pouring out a bottle of beer which took him off made a solid hit, leaving the customers in excellent mood. With the conclusion of George's recitation, they were feeling that the worst was behind them and a few clenched teeth would see them through the remainder of the Kegley-Bassington offensive. There was a general sense of relaxation, and Gussie and Catsmeat could not have had a better spot. When they came on, festooned in green beards, they got a big hand.

It was the last time they did. The act died standing up. Right from the start I saw that it was going to be a turkey, and so it proved. It was listless. It lacked fire and oomph. The very opening words struck a chill.

'Hallo, Pat,' said Catsmeat in a dull, toneless voice.

'Hallo, Mike,' said Gussie, with equal moodiness. 'How's your father?'

'He's not enjoying himself just now.'

'What's he doing?'

'Seven years,' said Catsmeat glumly, and went on in the same depressed way to speak of his brother Jim, who, having obtained employment as a swimming teacher, was now often in low water.

Well, I couldn't see what Gussie could have on his mind, unless he was brooding on the Church Organ, but Catsmeat's despondency was, of course, susceptible of a ready explanation. From where he stood he had an excellent view of Gertrude Winkworth in row one of the two-bob seats, and the sight of her, looking pale and proud in something which I should say at a venture was *mousseline*, must have been like a sword-thrust through the bosom. Just as you allow a vicar a wide latitude in the way of gloom when his private life has become cluttered up with Corkies and Gussies and Thoses, so should you, if a fair-minded man, permit a tortured lover, confronted with the girl he has lost, to sink into the depths a bit.

Well, that's all right. I'm not saying you shouldn't, and, as a matter of fact, I did. If you had come along and asked me, 'Has Claude Cattermole Pirbright your heartfelt sympathy, Wooster?' I would have replied, 'You betcher he has my heartfelt sympathy. I mourn in spirit.' All I do say is that this Byronic outlook doesn't help you bang across your points in a Pat and Mike knockabout cross-talk act.

The whole performance gave one a sort of grey, hopeless feeling, like listening to the rain at three o'clock on a Sunday afternoon in November. Even the standees, tough, rugged men who would not have recognized the finer feelings if you had served them up on a plate with watercress round them, obviously felt the pathos of it all. They listened in dejected silence, shuffling their feet, and I didn't blame them. There should be nothing so frightfully heartrending in one fellow asking another fellow who that lady was he saw him coming down the street with and the other fellow replying that there was no lady, that was his wife. An amusing little misunderstanding, you would say. But when Gussie and Catsmeat spoke the lines, they seemed to bring home to you all the underlying sadness of life.

At first, I couldn't think what the thing reminded me of. Then I got it. At the time when I was engaged to Florence Craye and she was trying to jack up my soul, one of the methods she employed to this end was to take me on Sunday nights to see Russian plays; the sort of things where the old home is being sold up and people stand around saying how sad it all is. If I had to make a criticism of Catsmeat and Gussie, I should say that they got too much of the Russian spirit into their work. It was a relief to one and all when the poignant slice of life drew to a close.

'My sister's in the ballet,' said Catsmeat despondently.

There was a pause here, because Gussie had fallen into a sort of trance and was standing staring silently before him as if the Church Organ had really got him down at last, and Catsmeat, realizing that only moral support, if that, was to be expected from this quarter, was obliged to carry on the conversation by himself, a thing which I always think spoils the effect on these occasions. The essence of a cross-talk act is that there should be wholesome give and take, and you never get the same snappy zip when one fellow is asking the questions and answering them himself.

'You say your sister's in the ballet?' said Catsmeat with a catch in his voice. 'Yes, begorrah, my sister's in the ballet. What does your sister do in the ballet?' he went on, taking a look at Gertrude Winkworth and quivering in agony. 'She comes rushin' in and she goes rushin' out. What does she have to rush like that for?' asked Catsmeat with a stifled sob. 'Faith and begob, because it's a Rushin' ballet.'

And, too broken in spirit to hit Gussie with his umbrella, he took him by the elbow and directed him to the exit. They moved slowly off with bowed heads, like a couple of pallbearers who have forgotten their coffin and had to go back for it, and to the rousing strains of 'Hallo, hallo, hallo, hallo, a-hunting we will go, pom pom', Esmond Haddock strode masterfully onto the stage.

Esmond looked terrific. Anxious to omit no word or act which would assist him in socking the clientele on the button, he had put on full hunting costume, pink coat and everything, and the effect was sensational. He seemed to bring into that sombre hall a note of joy and hope. After all, you felt, there was still happiness in the world. Life, you told yourself, was not all men in green beards saying 'Faith' and 'Begorrah'.

To the practised eye like mine it was apparent that in the interval since the conclusion of the scratch meal which had taken the place of dinner the young Squire had been having a couple, but, as I often say, why not? There is no occasion on which a man of retiring disposition with an inferiority complex and all the trimmings needs the old fluid more than when he is about to perform at a village concert, and with so much at stake it would have been madness on his part not to get moderately ginned.

It is to the series of quick ones which he had absorbed that I attribute the confident manner of his entry, but the attitude of the audience must speedily have convinced him that he could really have got by perfectly well on limejuice. Any doubt lingering in his mind as to his being the popular pet must have been dispelled instantly by the thunders of applause from all parts of the house. I noted twelve distinct standees who were whistling through their fingers, and those who were not whistling were stamping on the floor. The fellow with the hair oil on my left was doing both.

And now, of course, came the danger spot. A feeble piping at this point, like gas escaping from a pipe, or let us say a failure to remember more than an odd word or two of the subject matter, and a favourable first impression might well be undone. True, the tougher portion of the audience had been sedulously stood beers over a period of days and in return had entered into a gentleman's agreement to be indulgent, but nevertheless it was unquestionably up to Esmond Haddock to deliver the goods.

He did so abundantly and in heaping measure. That first night over the port, when we had been having our run-through, my thoughts at the outset had been centred on the lyric and I had been too busy polishing up Aunt Charlotte's material to give much attention to the quality of his voice. And later on, of course, I had been singing myself, which always demands complete concentration. When I was on the chair, waving my decanter, I had been aware in a vague sort of way of some kind of disturbance in progress on the table, but if Dame Daphne Winkworth on her entry had asked me my opinion of Esmond Haddock's timbre and brio, I should have had to reply that I really hadn't noticed them much.

He now stood forth as the possessor of a charming baritone – full of life and feeling and, above all, loud. And volume of sound is what you want at a village concert. Make the lights flicker and bring plaster down from the ceiling, and you are home. Esmond Haddock did not cater simply for those who had paid the price of admission, he took in strollers along the High Street and even those who had remained at their residences, curled up with a good book. Catsmeat, you may recall, in speaking of the yells which Dame Daphne and the Misses Deverill had uttered on learning of his betrothal to Gertrude Winkworth, had hazarded the opinion that they could have been heard at Basingstoke. I should say that Basingstoke got Esmond Haddock's hunting song nicely.

If so, it got a genuine treat and one of some duration, for he took three encores, a couple of bows, a fourth encore, some more bows and then the chorus once over again by way of one for the road. And even then his well-wishers seemed reluctant to let him go.

This reluctance made itself manifest during the next item on the programme – Glee (Oh, come unto these yellow sands) by the Church Choir, conducted by the school-mistress – in murmurs at the back and an occasional 'Hallo', but it was not until Miss Poppy Kegley-Bassington was performing her rhythmic dance that it found full expression.

Unlike her sister Muriel, who had resembled a Criterion barmaid of the old school, Poppy Kegley-Bassington was long and dark and supple, with a sinuous figure suggestive of a snake with hips; one of those girls who do rhythmic dances at the drop of a hat and can be dissuaded from doing them only with a meat-axe. The music that accompanied her act was Oriental in nature, and I should be disposed to think that the thing had started out in life as a straight Vision of Salome but had been toned down and had the whistle blown on it in spots in deference to the sensibilities of the Women's Institute. It consisted of a series of slitherings and writhings, punctuated with occasional pauses when, having got herself tied in a clove-hitch, she seemed to be waiting for someone who remembered the combination to come along and disentangle her.

It was during one of these pauses that the plug-ugly with the hair oil made an observation. Since Esmond's departure he had been standing with a rather morose expression on his face, like an elephant that has had its bun taken from it, and you could see how deeply he was regretting that the young Squire was no longer with us. From time to time he would mutter in a peevish undertone, and I seemed to catch Esmond's name. He now spoke, and I found that my hearing had not been at fault.

'We want Haddock,' he said. 'We want Haddock, we want Haddock, we want Haddock, we want HADDOCK!'

He uttered the words in a loud, clear, penetrating voice, not unlike that of a costermonger informing the public that he has blood oranges for sale, and the sentiment expressed evidently chimed in with the views of those standing near him. It was not long before perhaps twenty or more discriminating concert-goers were also chanting:

'We want Haddock, we want Haddock, we want Haddock, we want Haddock, we want HADDOCK!'

And it just shows you how catching this sort of thing is. It wasn't more than about five seconds later that I heard another voice intoning.

'We want Haddock, we want Haddock, we want Haddock, we want Haddock, we want HADDOCK!' and discovered with a mild surprise that it was mine. And as the remainder of the standees, some thirty in number, also adopted the slogan, this made us unanimous.

To sum up, then, the fellow with the hair oil, fifty other fellows, also with hair oil, and I had begun to speak simultaneously and what we said was:

'We want Haddock, we want Haddock, we want Haddock, we want Haddock, we want HADDOCK!'

There was some shushing from the two-bobbers, but we were firm, and though Miss Kegley-Bassington pluckily continued to slither for a few moments longer, the contest of wills could have but one ending. She withdrew, getting a nice hand, for we were generous in victory, and Esmond came on, all boots and pink coat. And what with him going a-hunting at one end of the hall and our group of thinkers going a-hunting at the other, the thing might have occupied the rest of the evening quite agreeably, had not some quick-thinking person dropped the curtain for the intermission.

You might have supposed that my mood, as I strolled from the building to enjoy a smoke, would have been one of elation. And so, for some moments, it was. The whole aim of my foreign policy had been to ensure the making of a socko by Esmond, and he had made a socko. He had slain them and stopped the show. For perhaps the space of a quarter of a cigarette I rejoiced unstintedly.

Then my uplifted mood suddenly left me. The cigarette fell from my nerveless fingers, and I stood rooted to the spot, the lower jaw resting negligently on the shirt front. I had just realized that, what with one thing and another – my disturbed night, my taxing day, the various burdens weighing on my mind and so forth – every word of those Christopher Robin poems had been expunged from my memory.

And I was billed next but two after intermission.

23

How long I stood there, rooted to the s., I cannot say. A goodish while, no doubt, for this wholly unforeseen development had unmanned me completely. I was roused from my reverie by the sound of rustic voices singing 'Hallo, hallo, hallo, hallo, a-hunting we will go, my lads, a-hunting we will go' and discovered that the strains were proceeding from the premises of the Goose and Cowslip on the other side of the road. And it suddenly struck me – I can't think why it hadn't before – that here might possibly be the mental tonic of which I was in need. It might be that all that was wrong with me was that I was faint for lack of nourishment. Hitching up the lower jaw, I hurried across and plunged into the saloon bar.

The revellers who were singing the gem of the night's Hit Parade were doing so in the public bar. The only occupant of the more posh saloon bar was a godlike man in a bowler hat with grave, finely chiselled features and a head that stuck out at the back, indicating great brain power. To cut a long story short, Jeeves. He was having a meditative beer at the table by the wall.

'Good evening, sir,' he said, rising with his customary polish. 'I am happy to inform you that I was successful in obtaining the cosh from Master Thomas. I have it in my pocket.'

I raised a hand.

'This is no time for talking about coshes.'

'No, sir. I merely mentioned it in passing. Mr Haddock's was an extremely gratifying triumph, did you not think, sir?'

'Nor is it a time for talking about Esmond Haddock, Jeeves,' I said, 'I'm sunk.'

'Indeed, sir?'

'Jeeves!'

'I beg your pardon, sir. I should have said "Really, sir?"'

'"Really, sir?" is just as bad. What the crisis calls for is a "Gosh!" or a "Gorblimey!" There have been occasions, numerous occasions, when you have beheld Bertram Wooster in the bouillon, but never so deeply immersed in it as now. You know those damned poems I was to recite? I've forgotten every word of them. I need scarcely stress the gravity of the situation. Half an hour from now I shall be up on that platform with the Union Jack behind me and before me an expectant audience, waiting to see what I've got. And I haven't got anything. I shan't have a word to say. And while an audience at a village concert justifiably resents having Christopher Robin poems recited at it, its resentment becomes heightened if the reciter merely stands there opening and shutting his mouth in silence like a goldfish.'

'Very true, sir. You cannot jog your memory?'

'It was in the hope of jogging it that I came in here. Is there brandy in this joint?'

'Yes, sir. I will procure you a double.'

'Make it two doubles.'

'Very good, sir.'

He moved obligingly to the little hatch thing in the wall and conveyed his desire to the unseen provider on the other side, and presently a hand came through with a brimming glass and he brought it to the table.

'Let's see what this does,' I said. 'Skin off your nose, Jeeves.'

'Mud in your eye, sir, if I may use the expression.'

I drained the glass and laid it down.

'The ironical thing,' I said, while waiting for the stuff to work, 'is that though, except for remembering in a broad, general way that he went hoppity-hoppity-hop, I am a spent force as regards Christopher Robin, I could do them "Ben Battle" without a hitch. Did you hear Master George Kegley-Bassington on the subject of "Ben Battle"?'

'Yes, sir. A barely adequate performance, I thought.'

'That is not the point, Jeeves. What I'm trying to tell you is that listening to him has had the effect of turning back time in its flight, if you know what I mean, so that from the reciting angle I am once more the old Bertram Wooster of bygone days and can remember every word of "Ben Battle" as clearly as in the epoch when it was constantly on my lips. I could do the whole thing without fluffing a syllable. But does that profit me?'

'No, sir.'

'No, sir, is correct. Thanks to George, saturation point has been reached with this particular audience as far as "Ben Battle" is concerned. If I started to give it them, too, I shouldn't get beyond the first stanza. There would be an ugly rush for the platform, and I should be roughly handled. So what do you suggest?'

'You have obtained no access of mental vigour from the refreshment which you have been consuming, sir?'

'Not a scrap. The stuff might have been water.'

'In that case, I think you would be well advised to refrain from attempting to entertain the audience, sir. It would be best to hand the whole conduct of the affair over to Mr Haddock.'

'Eh?'

'I am confident that Mr Haddock would gladly deputize for you. In the uplifted frame of mind in which he now is, he would welcome an opportunity to appear again before his public.'

'But he couldn't learn the stuff in a quarter of an hour.'

'No, sir, but he could read it from the book. I have a copy of the book on my person, for I had been intending to station myself at the side of the stage in order to prompt you, as I believe the technical expression is, should you have need of my services.'

'Dashed good of you, Jeeves. Very white. Very feudal.'

'Not at all, sir. Shall I step across and explain the position of affairs to Mr Haddock and hand him the book?'

I mused. The more I examined his suggestion, the better I liked it. When you are slated to go over Niagara Falls in a barrel, the idea of getting a kindly friend to take your place is always an attractive one; the only thing that restrains you, as a rule, from making the switch being the thought that it is a bit tough on the kindly f. But in the present case this objection did not apply. On this night of nights Esmond Haddock could get away with anything. There was, I seemed to remember dimly, a poem in the book about Christopher Robin having ten little toes. Even that, dished out by the idol of King's Deverill, would not provoke mob violence.

'Yes, buzz straight over and fix up the deal, Jeeves,' I said hesitating no longer. 'As always, you have found the way.'

He adjusted the bowler hat which he had courteously doffed at my entry, and went off on his errand of mercy. And I, too agitated to remain sitting, wandered out into the street and began to pace up and down outside the hostelry. And I had paused for a moment to look at the stars, wondering, as I always did when I saw stars, why Jeeves had once described them to me as quiring to the young-eyed Cherubim, when a tapping on my arm and a bleating voice saying 'I say, Bertie' told me that some creature of the night was trying to arrest my attention. I turned and beheld something in a green beard and a check suit of loud pattern which, as it was not tall enough to be Catsmeat, the only other person likely to be going about in that striking get-up, I took correctly to be Gussie.

'I say, Bertie,' said Gussie, speaking with obvious emotion, 'do you think you could get me some brandy?'

'You mean orange juice?'

'No, I do not mean orange juice. I mean brandy. About a bucketful.'

Puzzled, but full of the St-Bernard-dog spirit, I returned to the saloon bar and came back with the snifter. He accepted it gratefully and downed about half of it at a gulp, gasping in a struck-by-lightning manner, as I have seen men gasp after taking one of Jeeves's special pick-me-ups.

'Thanks,' he said, when he had recovered. 'I needed that. And I didn't like to go in myself with this beard on.'

'Why don't you take it off?'

'I can't get it off. I stuck it on with spirit gum, and it hurts like sin when I pull at it. I shall have to get Jeeves to see what he can do about it later. Is this stuff brandy?'

'That's what they told me.'

'What appalling muck. Like vitriol. How on earth can you and your fellow topers drink it for pleasure?'

'What are you drinking it for? Because you promised your mother you would?'

'I am drinking it, Bertie, to nerve myself for a frightful ordeal.'

I gave his shoulder a kindly pat. It seemed to me that the man's mind was wandering.

'You're forgetting, Gussie. Your ordeal is over. You've done your act. And pretty lousy it was,' I said, unable to check the note of censure. 'What was the matter with you?'

He blinked like a chidden codfish.

'Wasn't I good?'

'No, you were not good. You were cheesy. Your work lacked fire and snap.'

'Well, so would your work lack fire and snap, if you had to play in a knockabout cross-talk act and knew that directly the thing was over, you were going to break into a police station and steal a dog.'

The stars, ceasing for a moment to quire to the young-eyed Cherubim, did a quick buck-and-wing.

'Say that again!'

'What's the point of saying it again? You heard. I've promised Corky I'll go to Dobbs's cottage and extract that dog of hers. She will be waiting in her car near at hand and will gather the animal in and whisk it off to the house of some friends of hers who live about twenty miles along the London road, well out of Dobbs's sphere of influence. So now you know why I wanted brandy.'

I wanted brandy, too. Either that or something equally restorative.

Oh, I was saying to myself, for a beaker full of the warm south, full of the true, the blushful Hippocrene. I have spoken earlier of the tendency of the spirit of the Woosters to rise when crushed to earth, but there is a limit, and this limit had now been reached. At these frightful words, the spirit of the Woosters felt as if it had been sat on by an elephant. And not one of your streamlined, schoolgirl-figured elephants, either. A big, fat one.

'Gussie! You mustn't!'

'What do you mean, I mustn't? Of course I must. Corky wishes it.'

'But you don't realize the peril. Dobbs is laying for you. Esmond Haddock is laying for you. They're just waiting to spring.'

'How do you know that?'

'Esmond Haddock told me so himself. He dislikes you intensely and it is his dearest hope some day to catch you bending and put you behind the bars. And he's a JP, so is in a strong position to bring about the happy ending. You'll look pretty silly when you find yourself doing thirty days in the jug.'

'For Corky's sake I'd do a year. As a matter of fact,' said Gussie in a burst of confidence, 'though you might not think it from the way I've been calling for brandy, there's no chance of my being caught. Dobbs is watching the concert.'

This, of course, improved the outlook. I don't say I breathed freely, but I breathed more freely than I had been breathing.

'You're sure of that?'

'I saw him myself.'

'You couldn't have been mistaken?'

'My dear Bertie, when Dobbs has come into a room in which you have been strewing frogs and stood face to face with you for an eternity, chewing his moustache and grinding his teeth at you, you know him when you see him again.'

'But all the same –'

'It's no good saying "All the same". Corky wants me to extract her dog, and I'm going to do it. "Gussie", she said to me, "you're such a *help*", and I intend to be worthy of those words.'

And, having spoken thus, he gave his beard a hitch and vanished into the silent night, leaving me to pay for the brandy.

I had just finished doing so when Jeeves returned.

'Everything has been satisfactorily arranged, sir,' he said. 'I have seen Mr Haddock, and, as I anticipated, he is more than willing to deputize for you.'

A great weight seemed to roll off my mind.

'Then God bless Mr Haddock!' I said. 'There is splendid stuff in these young English landowners, Jeeves, is there not?'

'Unquestionably, sir.'

'The backbone of the country, I sometimes call them. But I gather from the fact that you have been gone the dickens of a time that you had to do some heavy persuading.'

'No, sir. Mr Haddock consented immediately and with enthusiasm. My delay in returning was due to the fact that I was detained in conversation by Police Constable Dobbs. There were a number of questions of a theological nature on which he was anxious to canvas my views. He appears particularly interested in Jonah and the Whale.'

'Is he enjoying the concert?'

'No, sir. He spoke in disparaging terms of the quality of the entertainment provided.'

'He didn't like George Kegley-Bassington much?'

'No, sir. On the subject of Master Kegley-Bassington he expressed himself strongly, and was almost equally caustic when commenting upon Miss Kegley-Bassington's rhythmic dance. It is in order to avoid witnessing the efforts of the remaining members of the family that he has returned to his cottage, where he plans to pass what is left of the evening with a pipe and the works of Colonel Robert G. Ingersoll.'

24

So that was that. You get the picture. Above, in the serene sky, the stars quiring to the Cherubim. Off-stage, in the public bar, the local toughies quiring to the potboy. And down centre Jeeves, having exploded his bombshell, regarding me with the eye of concern, as if he feared that all was not well with the young master, in which conjecture he was one hundred per cent right. The young master was feeling as if his soul had just received the Cornish Riviera express on the seat of its pants.

I gulped perhaps half a dozen times before I was able to utter.

'Jeeves, you didn't really say that, did you?'

'Sir?'

'About Constable Dobbs going back to his cottage.'

'Yes, sir. He informed me that it was his intention to do so. He said he desired solitude.'

'Solitude!' I said. 'Ha!'

And in a dull, toneless voice, like George Kegley-Bassington reciting 'Ben Battle', I gave him the lowdown.

'That is the situation in what is sometimes called a nutshell, Jeeves,' I concluded. 'And, not that it matters, for nothing matters now, I wonder if you have spotted how extraordinarily closely the present set-up resembles that of Alfred, Lord Tennyson's well-known poem, "The Charge of the Light Brigade", which is another of the things I used to recite in happier days. I mean to say, someone has blundered and Gussie, like the Six Hundred, is riding into the Valley of Death. His not to reason why, his but to do or —'

'Pardon me, sir, for interrupting you —'

'Not at all, Jeeves. I had nearly finished.'

'— but would it not be advisable to take some form of action?' I gave him the lacklustre eye.

'Action, Jeeves? How can that help us now? And what form of it would you suggest? I should have said the thing had got beyond the scope of human power.'

'It might be possible to overtake Mr Fink-Nottle, sir, and apprise him of his peril.'

I shrugged the shoulders.

'We can try, if you like. I see little percentage in it, but I suppose one should leave no stone unturned. Can you find your way to *chez* Dobbs?'

'Yes, sir.'

'Then shift ho,' I said listlessly.

As we made our way out of the High Street into the dark regions beyond, we chatted in desultory vein.

'I noticed, Jeeves, that when I started telling you the bad news just now, one of your eyebrows flickered.'

'Yes, sir. I was much exercised.'

'Don't you ever get exercised enough to say "Coo!"?'

'No, sir.'

'Or "Crumbs!"?'

'No, sir.'

'Strange. I should have thought you might have done so at a moment like that. I would say this was the end, wouldn't you?'

'While there is life, there is hope, sir.'

'Neatly put, but I disagree with you. I see no reason for even two-pennorth of hope. We shan't overtake Gussie. He must have got there long ago. About now, Dobbs is sitting on his chest and slipping the handcuffs on him.'

'The officer may not have proceeded directly to his home, sir.'

'You think there is a possibility that he paused at a pub for a gargle? It may be so, of course, but I am not sanguine. It would mean that Fate was handing out lucky breaks, and my experience of Fate –'

I would have spoken further and probably been pretty deepish, for the subject of Fate and its consistent tendency to give good men the elbow was one to which I had devoted considerable thought, but at this moment I was accosted by another creature of the night, a soprano one this time, and I perceived a car drawn up at the side of the road.

'Yoo-hoo, Bertie,' said a silvery voice. 'Hi-ya, Jeeves.'

'Good evening, miss,' said Jeeves in his suave way. 'Miss Pirbright, sir,' he added, giving me the office in an undertone.

I had already recognized the silvery v.

'Hallo, Corky,' I said moodily. 'You are waiting for Gussie?'

'Yes, he went by just now. What did you say?'

'Oh, nothing,' I replied, for I had merely remarked by way of a passing comment that cannons to left of him, cannons to right of him volleyed and thundered. 'I suppose you know that you have lured him on to a doom so hideous that the brain reels, contemplating it?'

'What do you mean?'

'He will find Dobbs at journey's end reading Robert G. Ingersoll. How long the officer will continue reading Robert G. Ingersoll after discovering that Gussie has broken in and is de-dogging the premises, one cannot –'

'Don't be an ass. Dobbs is at the concert.'

'He *was* at the concert. But he left early and is now –'

Once more I was interrupted when about to speak further. From down the road there had begun to make itself heard in the silent night a distant barking. It grew in volume, indicating that the barker was heading our way, and Corky sprang from the car and established herself as a committee of welcome in the middle of the fairway.

'What a chump you are, Bertie,' she said with some heat, 'pulling a girl's leg and trying to scare her stiff. Everything has gone according to plan. Here comes Sam. I'd know his voice anywhere. At-a-boy, Sam! This way. Come to Mother.'

What ensued was rather like the big scene in *The Hound of the Baskervilles*. The baying and the patter of feet grew louder, and suddenly out of the darkness Sam Goldwyn clocked in, coming along at a high rate of speed and showing plainly in his manner how keenly he appreciated the termination of the sedentary life he had been leading these last days. He looked good for about another fifty miles at the same pace, but the sight of us gave him pause. He stopped, looked and listened. Then, as our familiar odour reached his nostrils, he threw his whole soul into a cry of ecstasy. He bounded at Jeeves as if contemplating licking his face, but was checked by the latter's quiet dignity. Jeeves views the animal kingdom with a benevolent eye and is the first to pat its head and offer it a slice of whatever is going, but he does not permit it to lick his face.

'Inside, Sam,' said Corky, when the rapture of reunion had had the first keen edge taken off it and we had all simmered down a bit. She boosted him into the car, and resumed her place at the wheel. 'Time to be leaving,' she said. 'The quick fade-out is what the director would suggest here, I think. I'll be seeing you at the hall later, Bertie. Uncle Sidney has been asked to look in for coffee and sandwiches after the show, and I was included in the invitation, I don't think. Still, I shall assume I was.'

She clapped spurs to her two-seater and vanished into the darkness. Sam Goldwyn's vocal solo died away, and all was still once more.

No, not all, to be absolutely accurate, for at this moment there
came to the ear-drum an odd sort of hammering noise in the distance
which at first I couldn't classify. It sounded as if someone was doing
a tap-dance, but it seemed improbable that people would be doing
tap-dances out of doors at this hour. Then I got it. Somebody – no,
two people – was – or I should say were – haring towards us along
the road, and I was turning to cock an enquiring eyebrow at Jeeves,
when he drew me into the shadows.

'I fear the worst, sir,' he said in a hushed voice, and, sure enough,
along it came.

In addition to the stars quiring to the young-eyed Cherubim, there
was now in the serene sky a fair-sized moon, and as always happens
under these conditions the visibility was improved. By its light one
could see what was in progress.

Gussie and Constable Dobbs were in progress, in the order named.
Not having been present at the outset of the proceedings, I can only
guess at what had occurred in the early stages, but anyone entering
a police station to steal a dog and finding Constable Dobbs on the
premises would have lost little time in picking up the feet, and I think
we can assume that Gussie had got off to a good start. At any rate, at
the moment when the runners came into view he had established a
nice lead and appeared to be increasing it.

It is curious how you can be intimate with a fellow from early
boyhood and yet remain unacquainted with one side of him. Mixing
constantly with Gussie through the years, I had come to know him
as a newt-fancier, a lover and a fathead, but I had never suspected
him of possessing outstanding qualities as a sprinter on the flat, and I
was amazed at the high order of ability he was exhibiting in this very
specialized form of activity. He was coming along like a jack-rabbit
of the western prairie, his head back and his green beard floating in
the breeze. I liked his ankle work.

Dobbs, on the other hand, was more laboured in his movements
and to an eye like mine, trained in the watching of point-to-point
races, had all the look of an also-ran. One noted symptoms of roaring,
and I am convinced that had Gussie had the intelligence to stick to his
job and make a straight race of it, he would soon have out-distanced
the field and come home on a tight rein. Police constables are not
built for speed. Where you catch them at their best is standing on
street corners saying 'Pass along there'.

But, as I was stressing a moment ago, Augustus Fink-Nottle, in
addition to being a flat racer of marked ability, was also a fathead,
and now, when he had victory in his grasp, the fatheaded streak in

him came uppermost. There was a tree standing at the roadside and, suddenly swerving off the course, he made for it and hoisted himself into its branches. And what he supposed that was going to get him, only his diseased mind knew. Ernest Dobbs may not have been one of Hampshire's brightest thinkers, but he was smart enough to stand under a tree.

And this he proceeded to do. Determination to fight it out on these lines if it took all summer was written on every inch of his powerful frame. His back being towards me, I couldn't see his face, but I have no doubt it was registering an equal amount of resolution, and nothing could have been firmer than his voice as he urged upon the rooster above the advisability of coming down without further waste of time. It was a fair cop, said Ernest Dobbs, and I agreed with him. To shut out the painful scene which must inevitably ensue, I closed my eyes.

It was an odd, chunky sound, like some solid substance striking another solid substance, that made me open them. And when they were opened, I could hardly believe them. Ernest Dobbs, who a moment before had been standing with his feet apart and his thumbs in his belt like a statue of Justice Putting It Across the Evil-Doer, had now assumed what I have heard described as a recumbent position. To make what I am driving at clear to the meanest intelligence, he was lying in the road with his face to the stars, while Jeeves, like a warrior sheathing his sword, replaced in his pocket some object which instinct told me was small but serviceable and constructed of india-rubber.

I tottered across, and drew the breath in sharply as I viewed the remains. The best you could have said of Constable Ernest Dobbs was that he looked peaceful.

'Good Lord, Jeeves!' I said.

'I took the liberty of coshing the officer, sir,' he explained respectfully. 'I considered it advisable in the circumstances as the simplest method of averting unpleasantness. You will find it safe to descend now, sir,' he proceeded, addressing Gussie. 'If I might offer the suggestion, speed is of the essence. One cannot guarantee that the constable will remain indefinitely immobile.'

This opened up a new line of thought.

'You don't mean he'll recover?'

'Why, yes, sir, almost immediately.'

'I'd have said that all he wanted was a lily in the right hand, and he'd be set.'

'Oh, no, sir. The cosh produces merely a passing malaise. Permit me, sir,' he said, assisting Gussie to alight. 'I anticipate that Dobbs, on coming to his senses, will experience a somewhat severe headache, but –'

'Into each life some rain must fall?'

'Precisely, sir. I think it would be prudent of Mr Fink-Nottle to remove his beard. It presents too striking a means of identification.'

'But he can't. It's stuck on with spirit gum.'

'If Mr Fink-Nottle will permit me to escort him to his room, sir, I shall be able to adjust that without difficulty.'

'You will? Then get on with it, Gussie.'

'Eh?' said Gussie, being just the sort of chap who would stand about saying 'Eh?' at a moment like this. He had a dazed air, as if he, too, had stopped one.

'Push off.'

'Eh?'

I gave a weary gesture.

'Remove him, Jeeves,' I said.

'Very good, sir.'

'I would come along with you, but I shall be occupied elsewhere. I need about six more of those brandies, and I need them quick. You're sure about this living corpse?'

'Sir?'

'I mean, "living" really is the *mot juste*?'

'Oh, yes, sir. If you will notice, the officer is already commencing to regain consciousness.'

I did notice it. Ernest Dobbs was plainly about to report for duty. He moved, he stirred, he seemed to feel the rush of life along his keel. And, this being so, I deemed it best to withdraw. I had no desire to be found standing at the sick-bed when a fellow of his muscular development and uncertain temper came to and started looking about for responsible parties. I returned to the Goose and Cowslip at a good speed, and proceeded to put big business in the way of the hand that came through the hatch. Then, feeling somewhat restored, I went back to the Hall and dug in in my room.

I had, as you will readily understand, much food for thought. The revelation of this deeper, coshing side to Jeeves's character had come as something of a shock to me. One found oneself wondering how far the thing would spread. He and I had had our differences in the past, failing to see eye to eye on such matters as purple socks and white dinner jackets, and it was inevitable, both of us being men of high spirit, that similar differences would arise in the future. It was a disquieting thought that in the heat of an argument about, say, soft-bosomed shirts for evening wear he might forget the decencies of debate and elect to apply the closure by hauling off and socking me on the frontal bone with something solid. One could but trust that the feudal spirit would serve to keep the impulse in check.

I was still trying to adjust the faculties to the idea that I had been nursing in my bosom all these years something that would be gratefully accepted as a muscle guy by any gang on the look out for new blood, when Gussie appeared, minus the shrubbery. He had changed the check suit for a dinner jacket, and with a start I realized that I ought to be dressing, too. I had forgotten that Corky had said that a big coffee-and-sandwiches binge was scheduled to take place in the drawing room at the conclusion of the concert, which must by now be nearing the 'God Save The King' stage.

There seemed to be something on Gussie's mind. His manner was nervous. As I hurriedly socked, shirted and evening shoe-ed myself, he wandered about the room, fiddling with the *objets d'art* on the mantelpiece, and as I slid into the form-fitting trousers there came to my ears the familiar sound of a hollow groan – whether hollower than those recently uttered by self and Catsmeat I couldn't say, but definitely hollow. He had been staring for some moments at a picture on the wall of a girl in a poke bonnet cooing to a pigeon with a fellow in a cocked hat and tight trousers watching her from the background, such as you will always find in great profusion in places like Deverill Hall, and he now turned and spoke.

'Bertie, do you know what it is to have the scales fall from your eyes?'

'Why, yes. Scales have frequently fallen from my eyes.'

'They have fallen from mine,' said Gussie. 'And I'll tell you the exact moment when it happened. It was when I was up in that tree gazing down at Constable Dobbs and hearing him describe the situation as a fair cop. That was when the scales fell from my eyes.'

I ventured to interrupt.

'Half a second,' I said. 'Just to keep the record straight, what are you talking about?'

'I'm telling you. The scales fell from my eyes. Something happened to me. In a flash, with no warning, love died.'

'Whose love?'

'Mine, you ass. For Corky. I felt that a girl who could subject a man to such an ordeal was not the wife for me. Mind you, I still admire her enormously, and I think she would make an excellent helpmeet for somebody of the Ernest Hemingway type who likes living dangerously, but after what has occurred tonight, I am quite clear in my mind that what I require as a life partner is someone slightly less impulsive. If you could have seen Constable Dobb's eyes glittering in the moonlight!' he said, and broke off with a strong shudder.

A silence ensued, for my ecstasy at this sensational news item was so profound that for an instant I was unable to utter. Then I said 'Whoopee!' and in doing so may possibly have raised my voice a little, for he leaped somewhat and said he wished I wouldn't suddenly yell 'Whoopee!' like that, because I had made him bite his tongue.

'I'm sorry,' I said, 'but I stick to it. I said "Whoopee!" and I meant "Whoopee!" "Whoopee!" with the possible exception of "Hallelujah!" is the only word that meets the case, and if I yelled it, it was merely because I was deeply stirred. I don't mind telling you now, Gussie, that I have viewed your passion for young Corky with concern, pursing the lips and asking myself dubiously if you were on the right lines. Corky is fine and, as you say, admirably fitted to be the bride of the sort of man who won't object to her landing him on the whim of the moment in a cell in one of our popular prisons, but the girl for you is obviously Madeline Bassett. Now you can go back to her and live happily ever after. It will be a genuine pleasure to me to weigh in with the silver egg-boiler or whatever you may suggest as a wedding gift, and during the ceremony you can rely on me to be in a ringside pew, singing "Now the labourer's task is o'er" like nobody's business.'

I paused at this point, for I noticed that he was writhing rather freely. I asked him why he writhed, and he said, Well, wouldn't anybody writhe who had got himself into the jam he had, and he wished I wouldn't stand there talking rot about going back to Madeline.

'How can I go back to Madeline, dearly as I would like to, after writing that letter telling her it was all off?'

I saw that the time had come to slip him the good news.

'Gussie,' I said, 'all is well. No need for concern. Others have worked while you slept.'

And without further preamble I ran through the Wimbledon continuity.

At the outset he listened dumbly, his eyes bulging, his lips moving like those of a salmon in the spawning season.

Then, as the gist penetrated, his face lit up, his horn-rimmed spectacles flashed fire and he clasped my hand, saying rather handsomely that while as a general rule he yielded to none in considering me the world's premier half-wit, he was bound to own that on this occasion I had displayed courage, resource, enterprise and an almost human intelligence.

'You've saved my life, Bertie!'

'Quite all right, old man.'

'But for you –'

'Don't mention it. Just the Wooster service.'

'I'll go and telephone her.'

'A sound move.'

He mused for a moment.

'No, I won't, by Jove. I'll pop right off and see her. I'll get my car and drive to Wimbledon.'

'She'll be in bed.'

'Well, I'll sleep in London and go out there first thing in the morning.'

'You'll find her up and about shortly after eight. Don't forget your sprained wrist.'

'By Jove, no. I'm glad you reminded me. What sort of a child was it you told her I had saved?'

'Small, blue-eyed, golden-haired and lisping.'

'Small, blue-eyed, golden-haired and lisping. Right.'

He clasped my hand once more and bounded off, pausing at the door to tell me to tell Jeeves to send on his luggage, and I, having completed the toilet, sank into a chair to enjoy a quick cigarette before leaving for the drawing room.

I suppose in this moment of *bien être*, with the heart singing within me and the good old blood coursing through my veins, as I believe the expression is, I ought to have been saying to myself, 'Go easy on the rejoicing, cocky. Don't forget that the tangled love-lives of Catsmeat, Esmond Haddock, Gertrude Winkworth, Constable Dobbs and Queenie the parlourmaid remain still unstraightened out', but you know how it is. There come times in a man's life when he rather tends to think only of self, and I must confess that the anguish of the above tortured souls was almost completely thrust into the background of my consciousness by the reflection that Fate after a rocky start had at last done the square thing by Bertram Wooster.

My mental attitude, in short, was about that of an African explorer who by prompt shinning up a tree has just contrived to elude a quick-tempered crocodile and gathers from a series of shrieks below that his faithful native bearer had not been so fortunate. I mean to say he mourns, no doubt, as he listens to the doings, but though his heart may bleed, he cannot help his primary emotion being one of sober relief that, however, sticky life may have become for native bearers, he, personally, is sitting on top of the world.

I was crushing out the cigarette and preparing to leave, feeling just ripe for a cheery sandwich and an invigorating cup of coffee, when there was a flash of pink in the doorway, and Esmond Haddock came in.

25

In dishing up this narrative for family consumption, it has been my constant aim throughout to get the right word in the right place and to avoid fobbing the customers off with something weak and inexpressive when they have a right to expect the telling phrase. It means a bit of extra work, but one has one's code.

We will therefore expunge that 'came' at the conclusion of the previous spasm and substitute for it 'curvetted'. There was a flash of pink, and Esmond Haddock curvetted in. I don't know if you have ever seen a fellow curvet, but war-horses used to do it rather freely in the old days, and Esmond Haddock was doing it now. His booted feet spurned the carpet in a sort of rhythmic dance something on the lines of that of the recent Poppy Kegley-Bassington, and it scarcely needed the ringing hunting cries which he uttered to tell me that here stood a bird who was about as full of beans and buck as a bird could be.

I Hallo-Esmonded and invited him to take a seat, and he stared at me in an incredulous sort of way.

'You don't seriously think that on this night of nights I can *sit down*?' he said. 'I don't suppose I shall sit down again for months and months and months. It's only by the exercise of the greatest will-power that I'm keeping myself from floating up to the ceiling. Yoicks!' he proceeded, changing the subject. 'Hard for'ard! Tally ho! Loo-loo-loo-loo-loo-loo!'

It had become pretty plain by now that Jeeves and I, while budgeting for a certain uplift of the spirit as the result of the success on the concert platform, had underestimated the heady results of a popular triumph. Watching this Haddock as he curvetted and listening to his animal cries, I felt that it was lucky for him that my old buddy Sir Roderick Glossop did not happen to be among those present. That zealous loony doctor would long ere this have been on the telephone summoning horny-handed assistants to rally round with the straight waistcoat and dust off the padded cell.

'Well, be that as it may,' I said, after he had loo-loo-looed for perhaps another minute and a quarter, 'I should like, before going any further, to express my gratitude to you for your gallant conduct in taking on those poems of mine. Was everything all right?'

'Terrific.'

'No mob violence?'

'Not a scrap. They ate 'em.'

'That's good. One felt that you were so solidly established with the many-headed that you would be in no real danger. Still, you were taking a chance, and thank Heaven that all has ended well. I don't wonder you're bucked,' I said, interrupting him in a fresh outbreak of loo-loo-looing. 'Anyone would be after making the sort of hit you did. You certainly wowed them.'

He paused in his curvetting to give me another incredulous look.

'My good Gussie,' he said, 'you don't think I'm floating about like this just because my song got over?'

'Aren't you?'

'Certainly not.'

'Then why do you float?'

'Because of Corky, of course. Good Lord!' he said, smiting his brow and seeming a moment later to wish he hadn't, for he had caught it a rather juicy wallop. 'Good Lord! I haven't told you, have I? And that'll give you a rough idea of the sort of doodah I'm in, because it was simply in order to tell you that I came here. You aren't abreast, Gussie. You haven't heard the big news. The most amazing front-page stuff has been happening, and you know nothing about it. Let me tell you the whole story.'

'Do,' I said, adding that I was agog.

He simmered down a bit, not sufficiently to enable him to take a seat but enough to make him cheese the curvetting for a while.

'I wonder, Gussie, if you remember a conversation we had the first night you were here? To refresh your memory, it was the last time we were allowed to get at the port; the occasion when you touched up that lyric of my Aunt Charlotte's in such a masterly way, strengthening the weak spots and making it box-office. If you recall?'

I said I recalled.

'In the course of that conversation I told you that Corky had given me the brusheroo. If you recollect?'

I said I recollected.

'Well, tonight – You know, Gussie,' he said, breaking off, 'it's the most extraordinary sensation, swaying a vast audience . . .'

'Would you call it a vast audience?'

The question seemed to ruffle him.

'Well, the two-bob, shilling and eightpenny seats were all sold out and there must have been fully fifty threepenny standees at the back,' he said, a bit stiffly. 'Still, call it a fairly vast audience, if you prefer. It makes no difference to the argument. It's the most extraordinary sensation, swaying a fairly vast audience. It does something to you. It fills you with a sense of power. It makes you feel that you're a pretty hot number and that you aren't going to stand any nonsense from anyone. And under the head of nonsense you find yourself classing girls giving you the brusheroo. I mention this so that you will be able to understand what follows.'

I smiled one of my subtle smiles.

'I know what follows. You got hold of Corky and took a strong line.'

'Why, yes,' he said, seeming a little flattened. 'As a matter of fact that was what I was leading up to. How did you guess?'

I smiled another subtle one.

'I foresaw what would happen if you slew that fairly vast audience. I knew you were one of those birds on whom popular acclamation has sensational effects. Yours has been a repressed life, and you have, no doubt, a marked inferiority complex. The cheers of the multitude frequently act like a powerful drug upon bimbos with inferiority complexes.'

I had rather expected this to impress him, and it did. His lower jaw fell a notch, and he gazed at me in a reverent sort of way.

'You're a deep thinker, Gussie.'

'I always have been. From a child.'

'One wouldn't suspect it, just to look at you.'

'It doesn't show on the surface. Yes,' I said, getting back to the *res*, 'matters have taken precisely the course which I anticipated. With the cheers of the multitude ringing in your ears, you came off that platform a changed man, full of yeast and breathing flame through the nostrils. You found Corky. You backed her into a corner. You pulled a dominant male on her and fixed everything up. Right?'

'Yes, that was just what happened. Amazing how you got it all taped out.'

'Oh, well, one studies the psychology of the individual, you know.'

'Only I didn't back her into a corner. She was in her car, just driving off somewhere, and I shoved my head in at the window.'

'And –?'

'Oh, we kidded back and forth,' he said a little awkwardly, as if reluctant to reveal what had passed at that sacred scene. 'I told her she was the lodestar of my life and all that sort of thing, adding that

I intended to have no more rot about her not marrying me, and after a bit of pressing she came clean and admitted that I was the tree on which the fruit of her life hung.'

Those who know Bertram Wooster best are aware that he is not an indiscriminate back-slapper. He picks and chooses. But there was no question in my mind that here before me stood a back which it would be churlish not to slap. So I slapped it.

'Nice work,' I said. 'Then everything's all right?'

'Yes,' he assented. 'Everything's fine ... except for one small detail.'

'What is that in round numbers?'

'Well, it's a thing I don't know if you will quite understand. To make it clear I shall have to go back to that time when we were engaged before. She severed relations then because she considered that I was a bit too much under the domination of my aunts, and she didn't like it.'

Well, of course, I knew this, having had it from her personal lips, but I wore the mask and weighed in with a surprised 'Really?'

'Yes. And unfortunately she hasn't changed her mind. Nothing doing in the orange-blossom and wedding-cake line, she says, until I have defied my aunts.'

'Well, go ahead. Defy them.'

My words seemed to displease him. With a certain show of annoyance he picked up a statuette of a shepherdess on the mantelpiece and hurled it into the fireplace, reducing it to hash and removing it from the active list.

'It's all very well to say that. It's a thing that presents all sorts of technical difficulties. You can't just walk up to an aunt and say "I defy you". You need a cue of some sort. I'm dashed if I know how to set about it.'

I mused.

'I'll tell you what,' I said. 'It seems to me that here is a matter on which you would do well to seek advice from Jeeves.'

'Jeeves?'

'My man.'

'I thought your man's name was Meadowes.'

'A slip of the tongue,' I said hastily. 'I meant to say Wooster's man. He is a bird of extraordinary sagacity and never fails to deliver the goods.'

He frowned a bit.

'Doesn't one rather want to keep visiting valets out of this?'

'No, one does not want to keep visiting valets out of this,' I said firmly. 'Not when they're Jeeves. If you didn't live all the year round in this rural morgue, you'd know that Jeeves isn't so much a valet as a Mayfair consultant. The highest in the land bring their problems to him. I shouldn't wonder if they didn't give him jewelled snuff-boxes.'

'And you think he would have something to suggest?'

'He always has something to suggest.'

'In that case,' said Esmond Haddock, brightening, 'I'll go and find him.'

With a brief 'Loo-loo-loo' he pushed off, clicking his spurs, and I settled down to another cigarette and a pleasant reverie.

Really, I told myself, things were beginning to straighten out. Deverill Hall still housed, no doubt, its quota of tortured souls, but the figures showed a distinct downward trend. I was all right. Gussie was all right. It was only on the Catsmeat front that the outlook was still unsettled and the blue bird a bit slow in picking up its cues.

I pondered on Catsmeat's affairs for a while, then turned to the more agreeable theme of my own, and I was still doing so, feeling more braced every moment, when the door opened.

There was no flash of pink this time, because it wasn't Esmond home from the hunt. It was Jeeves.

'I have extricated Mr Fink-Nottle from his beard, sir,' he said, looking modestly pleased with himself, like a man who has fought the good fight, and I said Yes, Gussie had been paying me a neighbourly call and I had noticed the absence of the fungoid growth.

'He told me to tell you to pack his things and send them on. He's gone back to London.'

'Yes, sir. I saw Mr Fink-Nottle and received his instructions in person.'

'Did he tell you why he was going to London?'

'No, sir.'

I hesitated. I yearned to share the good news with him, but I was asking myself if it wouldn't involve bandying a woman's name. And, as I have explained earlier, Jeeves and I do not bandy women's names.

I put out a feeler.

'You've been seeing a good deal of Gussie recently, Jeeves?'

'Yes, sir.'

'Constantly together, swapping ideas, what?'

'Yes, sir.'

'I wonder if by any chance ... in some moment of expansiveness, if that's the word ... he ever happened to let fall anything that gave you the impression that his heart, instead of sticking like glue to Wimbledon, had skidded a bit in another direction?'

'Yes, sir. Mr Fink-Nottle was good enough to confide in me regarding the emotions which Miss Pirbright had aroused in his bosom. He spoke freely on the subject.'

'Good. Then I can speak freely, too. All that's off.'

'Indeed, sir?'

'Yes. He came down from that tree feeling that Corky was not the dream mate he had supposed her to be. The scales fell from his eyes. He still admires her many fine qualities and considers that she would make a good wife for Sinclair Lewis, but –'

'Precisely, sir. I must confess that I had rather anticipated some such contingency. Mr Fink-Nottle is of the quiet, domestic type that enjoys a calm, regular life, and Miss Pirbright is perhaps somewhat –'

'More than somewhat. Considerably more. He sees that now. He realizes that association with young Corky, though having much to be said for it, must inevitably lead in the end to a five-year stretch in Wormwood Scrubs or somewhere, and his object in going to London tonight is to get a good flying start for an early morning trip to Wimbledon Common tomorrow. He is very anxious to see Miss Bassett as soon as possible. No doubt they will breakfast together, and having downed a couple of rashers and a pot of coffee, saunter side by side through the sunlit grounds.'

'Most gratifying, sir.'

'Most. And I'll tell you something else that's gratifying. Esmond Haddock and Corky are engaged.'

'Indeed, sir?'

'Provisionally, perhaps I ought to say.'

And I sketched out for him the set-up at the moment of going to press.

'I advised him to consult you,' I said, 'and he went off to find you. You see the posish, Jeeves? As he rightly says, however much you may want to defy a bunch of aunts, you can't get started unless they give you something to defy them about. What we want is some situation where they're saying "Go", like the chap in the Bible, and instead of going he cometh. If you see what I mean?'

'I interpret your meaning exactly, sir, and I will devote my best thought to the problem. Meanwhile, I fear I must be leaving you, sir. I promised to help my Uncle Charlie serve the refreshments in the drawing room.'

'Scarcely your job, Jeeves?'

'No, sir. But one is glad to stretch a point to oblige a relative.'

'Blood is thicker than water, you mean?'

'Precisely, sir.'

He withdrew, and about a minute later Esmond blew in again, looking baffled, like a Master of Hounds who has failed to locate the fox.

'I can't find the blighter,' he said.

'He has just this moment left. He's gone to the drawing room to help push around the sandwiches.'

'And that's where we ought to be, my lad,' said Esmond. 'We're a bit late.'

He was right. Silversmith, whom we encountered in the hall, informed us that he had just shown out the last batch of alien guests, the Kegley-Bassington gang, and that apart from members of the family only the vicar, Miss Pirbright and what he called 'the young gentleman', a very loose way of describing my cousin Thomas, remained on the burning deck. Esmond exhibited pleasure at the news, saying that now we should have a bit of elbow room.

'Smooth work, missing those stiffs, Gussie. What England needs is fewer and better Kegley-Bassingtons. You agree with me, Silversmith?'

'I fear I have not formulated an opinion on the subject, sir.'

'Silversmith,' said Esmond, 'you're a pompous old ass,' and, incredible as it may seem, he poised a finger and with a cheery 'Yoicks!' drove it into the other's well-covered ribs.

And it was as the stricken butler reeled back and tottered off with an incredulous stare of horror in his gooseberry eyes, no doubt to restore himself with a quick one in the pantry, that Dame Daphne came out of the drawing room.

'Esmond!' she said in the voice which in days gone by had reduced so many Janes and Myrtles and Gladyses to tearful pulp in the old study. 'Where have you been?'

It was a situation which in the pre-Hallo-hallo epoch would have had Esmond Haddock tying himself in apologetic knots and perspiring at every pore: and no better evidence of the changed conditions prevailing in the soul of King's Deverill's Bing Crosby could have been afforded than by the fact that his brow remained unmoistened and he met her eye with a pleasant smile.

'Oh, hallo, Aunt Daphne,' he said. 'Where are you off to?'

'I am going to bed. I have a headache. Why are you so late, Esmond?'

'Well, if you ask me,' said Esmond cheerily, 'I'd say it was because I didn't arrive sooner.'

'Colonel and Mrs Kegley-Bassington were most surprised. They could not understand why you were not here.'

Esmond uttered a ringing laugh.

'Then they must be the most priceless fatheads,' he said. 'You'd think a child would have realized that the solution was that I was somewhere else. Come along, Gussie. Loo-loo-loo-loo-loo,' he added in a dispassionate sort of way, and led me into the drawing room.

Even though the drawing room had been cleansed of Kegley-Bassingtons, it still gave the impression of being fairly well filled up. Four aunts, Corky, young Thos, Gertrude Winkworth and the Rev. Sidney Pirbright might not be absolute capacity, but it was not at all what you would call a poor house. Add Esmond and self and Jeeves and Queenie moving to and fro with the refreshments, and you had quite a quorum.

I had taken a couple of sandwiches (sardine) off Jeeves and was lolling back in my chair, feeling how jolly this all was, when Silversmith appeared in the doorway, still pale after his recent ordeal.

He stood to attention and inflated his chest.

'Constable Dobbs,' he announced.

26

The reactions of a gaggle of coffee and sandwich chewers in the drawing room of an aristocratic home who, just as they are getting down to it, observe the local flatty muscling in through the door, vary according to what Jeeves calls the psychology of the individual. Thus, while Esmond Haddock welcomed the newcomer with a genial 'Loo-loo-loo', the aunts raised their eyebrows with a good deal of To-what-are-we-indebted-for-the-honour-of-this-visitness and the vicar drew himself up austerely, suggesting in his manner that one crack out of the zealous officer about Jonah and the Whale and he would know what to do about it. Gertrude Winkworth, who had been listless, continued listless, Silversmith preserved the detached air which butlers wear on all occasions, and the parlourmaid Queenie turned pale and uttered a stifled 'Oo-er!' giving the impression of a woman on the point of wailing for her demon lover. I, personally, put in a bit of quick gulping. The mood of *bien être* left me, and I was conscious of a coolness about the feet. When the run of events has precipitated, as Jeeves would say, a situation of such delicacy as existed at Deverill Hall, it jars you to find the place filling up with rozzers.

It was to Esmond Haddock that the constable directed his opening remark.

'I've come on an unpleasant errand, sir,' he said, and the chill in the Wooster feet became accentuated. 'But before I go into that there,' he proceeded, now addressing himself to the Rev. Sidney Pirbright, 'there's this here. I wonder if I might have a word with you, sir, on a spiritual subject?'

I saw the sainted Sidney stiffen, and knew that he was saying to himself 'Here it comes'.

'It's with ref to my having seen the light, sir.'

Somebody gave a choking gasp, like a Pekingese that has taken on a chump chop too large for its frail strength, and looking around I saw that it was Queenie. She was staring at Constable Dobbs wide-eyed and parted-lipped.

This choking gasp might have attracted more attention had it not dead-heated with another, equally choking, which proceeded from the thorax of the Rev. Sidney. He, too, was staring wide-eyed. He looked like a vicar who has just seen the outsider on whom he has placed his surplice nose its way through the throng of runners and flash in the lead past the judge's box.

'Dobbs! What did you say? You have seen the light?'

I could have told the officer he was a chump to nod so soon after taking that juicy one on the napper from the serviceable rubber instrument, but he did so, and the next thing he said was 'Ouch!' But the English policeman is made of splendid stuff, and after behaving for a moment like a man who has just swallowed one of Jeeves's morning specials he resumed his normal air, which was that of a stuffed gorilla.

'R,' he said. 'And I'll tell you how it come about, sir. On the evening of the twenty-third inst . . . well, tonight, as a matter of fact . . . I was proceeding about my duties, chasing a marauder up a tree, when I was unexpectedly struck by a thunderbolt.'

That, as might have been expected, went big. The vicar said 'A thunderbolt', two of the aunts said 'A *thunderbolt?*' and Esmond Haddock said 'Yoicks'.

'Yes, sir,' proceeded the officer, 'a thunderbolt. Caught me on the back of the head, it did, and hasn't half raised a lump.'

The vicar said 'Most extraordinary', the other two aunts said 'Tch, tch' and Esmond said 'Tally ho'.

'Well, sir, I'm no fool,' continued Ernest Dobbs. 'I can take a hint. "Dobbs," I said to myself, "no use kidding yourself about what *this* is, Dobbs. It's a warning from above, Dobbs," I said to myself, "it's time you made a drawstic revision of your spiritual outlook, Dobbs," I said to myself. So, if you follow my meaning, sir, I've seen the light, and what I wanted to ask you, sir, was Do I have to join the Infants' Bible Class or can I start singing in the choir right away?'

I mentioned earlier in this narrative that I had never actually seen a shepherd welcoming a strayed lamb back into the fold, but watching Dame Daphne Winkworth on the occasion to which I allude I had picked up a pointer or two about the technique, so was able to recognize that this was what was going to happen now. You could see from his glowing eyes and benevolent smile, not to mention the hand raised as if about to bestow a blessing, that this totally unexpected reversal of form on the part of the local backslider had taken the Rev. Sidney's mind right off the church organ. I think that in about another couple of ticks he would have come across with something pretty impressive in the way of simple, manly words, but, as it so happened, he hadn't time to get set. Even as his lips parted, there was a noise like a rising pheasant from the outskirts and some solid object left the ranks and hurled itself on Constable Dobbs's chest.

Closer inspection showed this to be Queenie. She was clinging to the representative of the Law like a poultice, and from the fact that she was saying 'Oh, Ernie!' and bedewing his uniform with happy tears I deduced, being pretty shrewd, that what she was trying to convey was that all was forgiven and forgotten and that she was expecting the prompt return of the ring, the letters and the china ornament with 'A Present From Blackpool' on it. And as it did not escape my notice that he, on his side, was covering her upturned face with burning kisses and saying 'Oh, Queenie!' I gathered that Tortured Souls Preferred had taken another upward trend and that one could chalk up on the slate two more sundered hearts reunited in the springtime.

These tender scenes affect different people in different ways. I myself, realizing Catsmeat's honourable obligations to this girl might now be considered cancelled, was definitely bucked by the spectacle. But the emotion aroused in Silversmith was plainly a shuddering horror that such goings-on should be going on in the drawing room of Deverill Hall. Pulling a quick Stern Father, he waddled up to the happy pair and with a powerful jerk of the wrist detached his child and led her from the room.

Constable Dobbs, though still dazed, recovered himself sufficiently to apologize for his display of naked emotion, and the Rev. Sidney said he quite, quite understood.

'Come and see me tomorrow, Dobbs,' he said benevolently, 'and we will have a long talk.'

'Very good, sir.'

'And now,' said the Rev. Sidney, 'I think I will be wending my way homeward. Will you accompany me, Cora?'

Corky said she thought she would stick on for a bit, and Thos, keenly alive to the fact that there were still stacks of sandwiches on tap, also declined to shift, so he beamed his way out of the room by himself, and it was only after the door had closed that I realized that Constable Dobbs was still standing there and remembered that his opening words had been that he had come upon an unpleasant errand. Once more the temperature of the feet fell, and I eyed him askance.

He was not long in getting down to the agenda. These flatties are trained to snap into it.

'Sir,' he said, addressing Esmond.

Esmond interrupted to ask him if he would like a sardine sandwich, and he said 'No, sir, I thank you', and when Esmond said that he did not insist on sardine but would be equally gratified if the other would wade into the ham, tongue, cucumber or potted meat, explained that he would prefer to take no nourishment of any kind, because of this unpleasant errand he had come on. Apparently, when policemen come on unpleasant errands, they lay off the vitamins.

'I'm looking for Mr Wooster, sir,' he said.

In the ecstasy of this recent reunion with the woman he loved I imagine that Esmond had temporarily forgotten how much he disliked Gussie, but at these words it was plain that all the old distaste for one who had made passes at the adored object had come flooding back, for his eyes gleamed, his face darkened and he did a spot of brow-knitting. The sweet singer of King's Deverill had vanished, leaving in his place the stern, remorseless Justice of the Peace.

'Wooster, eh?' he said, and I saw him lick his lips. 'You wish to see him officially?'

'Yes, sir.'

'What has he been doing?'

'Effecting burglarious entries, sir.'

'Has he, by Jove!'

'Yes, sir. On the twenty . . . This evening, sir a burglarious entry was effected by the accused into my police station and certain property of the Crown abstracted – to wit, one dog, what was in custody for having effected two bites. I copped him in the very act, sir,' said Constable Dobbs, simplifying his narrative style. 'He was the marauder I was chasing up trees at the moment when I was inadvertently struck by that thunderbolt.'

Esmond continued to knit his brow. It was evident that he took a serious view of the matter. And when Justices of the Peace take serious views of matters, you want to get out from under.

'You actually found him abstracting this to wit one dog?' he said keenly, looking like Judge Jeffreys about to do his stuff.

'Yes, sir. I come into my police station and he was in the act of unloosing it and encouraging it to buzz off. It proceeded to buzz off, and I proceeded to say "Ho!" whereupon, becoming cognizant of my presence, he also proceeded to buzz off, with me after him lickerty-split. I proceeded to pursue him up a tree and was about to effect an arrest, when along come this here thunderbolt, stunning me and depriving me of my senses. When I come to, the accused had departed.'

'And what makes you think it was Wooster?'

'He was wearing a green beard, sir, and a check suit. This rendered him conspicuous.'

'I see. He had not changed after his performance.'

'No, sir.'

Esmond licked his lips again.

'Then the first thing to do,' he said, 'is to find Wooster. Has anybody seen him?'

'Yes, sir. Mr Wooster has gone to London in his car.'

It was Jeeves who spoke, and Esmond gave him a rather surprised look.

'Who are you?' he asked.

'My name is Jeeves, sir. I am Mr Wooster's personal attendant.'

Esmond eyed him with interest.

'Oh, you're Jeeves? I'd like a word with you, Jeeves, some time.'

'Very good, sir.'

'Not now. Later on. So Wooster has gone to London, has he?'

'Yes, sir.'

'Fleeing from justice, eh?'

'No, sir. Might I make a remark, sir?'

'Carry on, Jeeves.'

'Thank you, sir. I merely wished to say that the officer is mistaken in supposing that the miscreant responsible for the outrage was Mr Wooster. I was continuously in Mr Wooster's society from the time he left the concert hall. I accompanied him to his room, and we remained together until he took his departure for London. I was assisting him to remove his beard, sir.'

'You mean you give him an alibi?'

'A complete alibi, sir.'

'Oh?' said Esmond, looking baffled, like the villain in a melodrama. One could sense that the realization that he was not to be able to dish out a sharp sentence on Gussie had cut him to the quick.

'Ho!' said Constable Dobbs, not, probably, with an idea of contributing anything vital to the debate but just because policemen never lose a chance of saying 'Ho!' Then suddenly a strange light came into his face and he said 'Ho!' again, this time packing a lot of meaning into the word.

'Ho!' he said. 'Then if it wasn't the accused Wooster, it must have been the other chap. That fellow Meadowes, who was doing Mike. He was wearing a green beard, too.'

'Ah!' said Esmond.

'Ha!' said the aunts.

'Oh!' said Gertrude Winkworth, starting visibly.

'Hoy!' said Corky, also starting visibly.

I must say I felt like saying 'Hoy!' too. It astonished me that Jeeves had not spotted what must inevitably ensue if he gave Gussie that alibi. Just throwing Catsmeat to the wolves, I mean to say. It was not like him to overlook a snag like that.

I caught Corky's eye. It was the eye of a girl seeing a loved brother going down for the third time in the soup. And then my gaze, swivelling round, picked up Gertrude Winkworth.

Gertrude Winkworth was plainly wrestling with some strong emotion. Her face was drawn, her bosom heaved. Her fragile handkerchief, torn by a sudden movement of the fingers, came apart in her hands.

Esmond was being very Justice-of-the-Peace-y.

'Bring Meadowes here,' he said curtly.

'Very good, sir,' said Jeeves, and pushed off.

When he had gone, the aunts started to question Constable Dobbs, demanding more details, and when it had been brought home to them that the dog in question was none other than the one which had barged into the drawing room on the night of my arrival and chased Aunt Charlotte to and fro, they were solidly in favour of Esmond sentencing this Meadowes to the worst the tariff would allow, Aunt Charlotte being particularly vehement.

They were still urging Esmond to display no weakness, when Jeeves returned, ushering in Catsmeat. Esmond gave him the bleak eye.

'Meadowes?'

'Yes, sir. You wished to speak to me?'

'I not only wished to speak to you,' said Esmond nastily, 'I wished to give you thirty days without the option.'

I heard Constable Dobbs snort briefly, and recognized his snort as a snort of ecstasy. The impression I received was that a weaker man, not trained in the iron discipline of the Force, would have said 'Whoopee!' For, just as Esmond Haddock had got it in for Gussie for endeavouring to move in on Corky, so had Constable Dobbs got it in for Catsmeat for endeavouring to move in on the parlourmaid, Queenie. Both were strong men, who believed in treating rivals rough.

Catsmeat seemed puzzled.

'I beg your pardon, sir?'

'You heard,' said Esmond. He intensified the bleakness of his eye. 'Let me ask you a few simple questions. You sustained the role of Pat in the Pat-and-Mike entertainment this evening?'

'Yes, sir.'

'You wore a green beard?'

'Yes, sir.'

'And a check suit?'

'Yes, sir.'

'Then you're for it,' said Esmond crisply, and the four aunts said So they should think, indeed, Aunt Charlotte going on to ask Esmond rather pathetically if thirty days was really all that the book of rules permitted. She had been reading a story about life in the United States, she said, and there, it seemed, even comparatively trivial offences rated ninety.

She was going on to say that the whole trend of modern life in England was towards a planned Americanization and that she, for one, approved of this, feeling that we had much to learn from our cousins across the sea, when there was a brusque repetition of that rising pheasant effect which had preceded the Hobbs-Queenie one-act sketch and the eye noted that Gertrude Winkworth had risen from her seat and precipitated herself into Catsmeat's arms. No doubt she had picked up a hint or two from watching Queenie's work for in its broad lines her performance was modelled on that of the recent parlourmaid. The main distinction was that whereas Silversmith's ewe lamb had said 'Oh, Ernie!' she was saying 'Oh, Claude!'

Esmond Haddock stared.

'Hallo!' he said, adding another three hallos from force of habit.

You might have thought that a fellow in Catsmeat's position, faced with the prospect of going up the river for a calendar month, would have been too perturbed to have time for hugging girls, and it would scarcely have surprised me if he had extricated himself from Gertrude Winkworth's embrace with a 'Yes, yes, quite, but some other time, what?' Not so, however. To clasp her to his bosom was with him the work of a moment, and you could see that he was regarding this as the important part of the evening's proceedings, giving him little scope for attending to Justices of the Peace.

'Oh, Gertrude!' he said. 'Be with you in a minute,' he added to Esmond. 'Oh, Gertrude!' he proceeded, once more addressing his remarks to the lovely burden. And, precisely as Constable Dobbs had done in a similar situation, he covered her upturned face with burning kisses.

'Eeek!' said the aunts, speaking as one aunt.

I didn't blame them for being fogged and unable to follow the run of the scenario. It is unusual for a niece to behave towards a visiting valet as their niece Gertrude was behaving as of even date, and if they

squeaked like mice, I maintain they had every right to do so. Theirs
had been a sheltered life, and this was all new stuff to them.

Esmond, too, seemed a bit not abreast.

'What's all this?' he said, a remark which would have proceeded
more fittingly from the lips of Constable Dobbs. In fact, I saw the
officer shoot a sharp look at him, as if stung by this infringement of
copyright.

Corky came forward and slipped her arm through his. It was plain
that she felt the time had come for a frank, manly explanation.

'It's my brother Catsmeat, Esmond.'

'What is?'

'This is.'

'What, that?'

'Yes. He came here as a valet for love of Gertrude, and a darned
good third-reel situation, if you ask me.'

Esmond wrinkled his brow. He looked rather as he had done when
discussing that story of mine with me on the night of my arrival.

'Let's go into this,' he said. 'Let's thresh it out. This character is
not Meadowes?'

'No.'

'He's not a valet?'

'No.'

'But he *is* your brother Catsmeat?'

'Yes.'

Esmond's face cleared.

'Now I've got it,' he said. 'Now it's all straight. How are you,
Catsmeat?'

'I'm fine,' said Catsmeat.

'That's good,' said Esmond heartily. 'That's splendid.'

He paused, and started. I suppose the baying that arose at this
point from the pack of aunts, together with the fact that he had just
tripped over his spurs, had given him the momentary illusion that he
was in the hunting field, for a 'Yoicks' trembled on his lips and he
raised an arm as if about to give his horse one on the spot where it
would do most good.

The aunts were a bit on the incoherent side, but gradually what you
might call a message emerged from their utterances. They were trying
to impress on Esmond that the fact that the accused was Corky's
brother Catsmeat merely deepened the blackness of his crime and
that he was to carry on and administer the sentence as planned.

Their observations would have gone stronger with Esmond if he
had been listening to them. But he wasn't. His attention was riveted on

Catsmeat and Gertrude, who had seized the opportunity afforded by the lull in the proceedings to exchange a series of burning kisses.

'Are you and Gertrude going to get married?' he asked.

'Yes,' said Catsmeat.

'Yes,' said Gertrude.

'No,' said the aunts.

'Please,' said Esmond, raising a hand. 'What's the procedure?' he asked, once more addressing himself to Catsmeat.

Catsmeat said he thought the best scheme would be for them to nip up to London right away and put the thing through on the morrow. He had the licence all ready and waiting, he explained, and he saw no difficulties ahead that a good registry office couldn't solve. Esmond said he agreed with him, and suggested that they should borrow his car, and Catsmeat said that was awfully good of him, and Esmond said Not at all. 'Please,' he added to the aunts, who were now shrieking like Banshees.

It was at this point that Constable Dobbs thrust himself forward.

'Hoy,' said Constable Dobbs.

Esmond proved fully equal to the situation.

'I see what you're driving at, Dobbs. You very naturally wish to make a pinch. But consider, Dobbs, how slender is the evidence which you can bring forward to support your charge. You say you chased a man in a green beard and a check suit up a tree. But the visibility was very poor, and you admit yourself that you were being struck by thunderbolts all the time, which must have distracted your attention, so it is more than probable that you were mistaken. I put it to you, Dobbs, that when you thought you saw a man in a green beard and a check suit, it may quite easily have been a clean-shaven man in something quiet and blue?'

He paused for a reply, and one could divine that the officer was thinking it over.

The thing that poisons life for a country policeman, the thing that makes him pick at the coverlet and brings him out in rashes, is the ever-present fear that one of these days he may talk out of turn and get in wrong with a Justice of the Peace. He knows what happens when you get in wrong with Justices of the Peace. They lay for you. They bide their time. And sooner or later they catch you bending, and the next thing you know you've drawn a strong rebuke from the Bench. And if there is one experience the young copper wishes to avoid, it is being in the witness-box and having the Bench look coldly at him and say something beginning with 'Then are we to understand, officer . . .?' and culminating in the legal equivalent of the raspberry or Bronx cheer. And it was evident to him that defiance of Esmond on the present occasion must inevitably lead to that.

'I put it to you, Dobbs,' said Esmond.

Constable Dobbs sighed. There is, I suppose, no spiritual agony so keen as that of the rozzer who has made a cop and seen it turn blue on him. But he bowed to the inev.

'Perhaps you're right, sir.'

'Of course I'm right,' said Esmond heartily. 'I knew you would see it when it was pointed out to you. We don't want any miscarriages of justice, what?'

'No, sir.'

'I should say not. If there's one thing that gives me the pip, it's a miscarriage of justice. Catsmeat, you are dismissed without a stain on your character.'

Catsmeat said that was fine, and Esmond said he thought he would be pleased.

'I suppose you and Gertrude aren't going to hang around, spending a lot of time packing?'

'No, we thought we'd leg it instanter.'

'Exactly what I would suggest.'

'If Gertrude wants clothes,' said Corky, 'she can get them at my apartment.'

'Splendid,' said Esmond. 'Then the quickest way to the garage is along there.'

He indicated the french windows, which, the night being balmy, had been left open. He slapped Catsmeat on the back, and shook Gertrude by the hand, and they trickled out.

Constable Dobbs, watching them recede, heaved another sigh, and Esmond slapped his back, too.

'I know just how you're feeling, Dobbsy,' he said. 'But when you think it over, I'm sure that you'll be glad you haven't been instrumental in throwing a spanner into the happiness of two young hearts in springtime. If I were you, I'd pop off to the kitchen and have a word with Queenie. There must be much that you want to discuss.'

Constable Dobbs's was not a face that lent itself readily to any great display of emotion. It looked as if it had been carved out of some hard kind of wood by a sculptor who had studied at a Correspondence School and had got to about Lesson Three. But at this suggestion it definitely brightened.

'You're right, sir,' he said, and with a brief 'Good night, all' vanished in the direction indicated, his air that of a policeman who is feeling that life, while greyish in spots, is not without its compensations.

'So that's that,' said Esmond.

'That's that,' said Corky. 'I think your aunts are trying to attract your attention, angel.'

All through the preceding scene, though pressure of other matter prevented me mentioning it, the aunts had been extremely vocal. Indeed, it would not be putting it too strongly to say that they had been kicking up the hell of a row. And this row must have penetrated to the upper regions of the house, for at this moment the door suddenly opened, revealing Dame Daphne Winkworth. She wore a pink dressing-gown, and had the appearance of a woman who has been taking aspirins and bathing her temples with eau-de-Cologne.

'Really!' she said. She spoke with a goodish bit of asperity, and one couldn't fairly blame her. When you go up to your bedroom with a headache, you don't want to be dragged down again half an hour later by disturbances from below. 'Will someone be so kind as to tell me what is the reason for this uproar?'

Four simultaneous aunts were so kind. The fact that they all spoke together might have rendered their remarks hard to follow, had not the subject matter been identical. Gertrude, they said, had just eloped with Miss Pirbright's brother, and Esmond had not only expressed his approval of the move but had actually offered the young couple his car.

'There!' they said, as the sound of an engine gathering speed and the cheery toot-toot of a klaxon made themselves heard in the silent night, pointing up their statement.

Dame Daphne blinked as if she had been struck on the mazard with a wet dishcloth. She turned on the young squire menacingly, and one could understand her peevishness. There are few things more sickening for a mother than to learn that her only child has eloped with a man whom she has always regarded as a blot on the species. Not surprising if it spoils her day.

'Esmond! Is this true?'

The voice in which she spoke would have had me clambering up the wall and seeking refuge on the chandelier, had she been addressing me, but Esmond Haddock did not wilt. The man seemed fearless. He was like the central figure in one of those circus posters which show an intrepid bozo in a military uniform facing with death-defying determination twelve murderous, man-eating monarchs of the jungle.

'Quite true,' he replied. 'And I really cannot have any discussion and argument about it. I acted as I deemed best, and the subject is closed. Silence, Aunt Daphne. Less of it, Aunt Emmeline. Quiet, Aunt Charlotte. Desist, Aunt Harriet. Aunty Myrtle, put a sock in it. Really, the way you're going on, one would scarcely suppose that I was the master of the house and the head of the family and that my word was law. I don't know if you happen to know it, but in Turkey all this insubordinate stuff, these attempts to dictate to the master of the house and the head of the family, would have led long before this to you being strangled with bowstrings and bunged into the Bosporus. Aunt Daphne, you have been warned. One more yip out of you, Aunt Myrtle, and I stop your pocket-money. Now, then,' said Esmond Haddock, having obtained silence, 'let me give you the strength of this. The reason I abetted young Gertrude in her matrimonial plans was that the man she loves is a good egg. I have this on the authority of his sister Corky, who speaks extremely well of him. And, by the way, before I forget, his sister Corky and I are going to be married ourselves. Correct?'

'In every detail,' said Corky.

She was gazing at him with shining eyes. One got the feeling that if she had had a table with a photograph on it, she would have been singing 'My Hero'.

'Come, come,' said Esmond kindly, as the yells of the personnel died away, 'no need to be upset about it. It won't affect you dear old souls. You will go on living here, if you call it living, just as you have always done. All that'll happen is that you will be short one Haddock. I propose to accompany my wife to Hollywood. And when she's through with her contract there, we shall set up a shack in some rural spot and grow pigs and cows and things. I think that covers everything, doesn't it?'

Corky said she thought it did.

'Right,' said Esmond. 'Then how about a short stroll in the moonlight?'

He led her lovingly through the french windows, kissing her en route and I edged to the door and made my way upstairs to my room. I could have stayed on and chatted with the aunts, if I had wanted to, but I didn't feel in the mood.

27

My first act on reaching the sleeping quarters was to take pencil and paper and sit down and make out a balance sheet. As follows:

Sundered Hearts	Reunited Hearts
(1) Esmond	(1) Esmond
(2) Corky	(2) Corky
(3) Gussic	(3) Gussie
(4) Madeline	(4) Madeline
(5) Officer Dobbs	(5) Officer Dobbs
(6) Queenie	(6) Queenie
(7) Catsmeat	(7) Catsmeat
(8) Gertrude	(8) Gertrude

It came out exactly square. Not a single loose end left over. With a not unmanly sigh, for if there is one thing that is the dish of the decent-minded man, it is seeing misunderstanding between loving hearts cleared up, especially in the springtime, I laid down the writing materials and was preparing to turn in for the night, when Jeeves came shimmering in.

'Oh, hallo, Jeeves,' I said, greeting him cordially. 'I was rather wondering if you would show up. A big night, what?'

'Extremely, sir.'

I showed him the balance sheet.

'No flaws in that, I think?'

'None, sir.'

'Gratifying, what?'

'Most gratifying, sir.'

'And, as always, due to your unremitting efforts.'

'It is very kind of you to say so, sir.'

'Not at all, Jeeves. We chalk up one more of your triumphs on the slate. I will admit that for an instant during the proceedings, when you gave Gussie that alibi, I experienced a momentary doubt as to whether you were on the right lines, feeling that you were but landing Catsmeat in the bouillon. But calmer reflection told me what you were up to. You felt that if Catsmeat stood in peril of receiving an exemplary sentence, Gertrude Winkworth would forget all that had passed and would cluster round him, her gentle heart melted by his distress. Am I right?'

'Quite right, sir. The poet Scott –'

'Pigeon-hole the poet Scott for a moment, or I shall be losing the thread of my remarks.'

'Very good, sir.'

'But I know what you mean. Oh, Woman in our hours of ease, what?'

'Precisely, sir. Uncertain, coy and hard to please. When –'

'– pain and anguish wring the brow, a ministering angel thou and so on and so forth. You can't stump me on the poet Scott. That is one more of the things I used to recite in the old days. First "Charge of Light Brigade" or "Ben Battle": then, in response to gales of applause, the poet Scott as an encore. But to return to what I was saying . . . There, as I suspected would be the case, Jeeves, I can't remember what I was saying. I warned you what would happen if you steered the conversation to the poet Scott.'

'You were speaking of the reconciliation between Miss Winkworth and Mr Pirbright, sir.'

'Of course. Well, I was about to say that having studied the psychology of the individual you foresaw what would occur. And you knew that Catsmeat wouldn't be in any real peril. Esmond Haddock was not going to jug the brother of the woman he loved.'

'Exactly, sir.'

'You can't get engaged to a girl with one hand and send her brother up for thirty days with the other.'

'No, sir.'

'And your subtle mind also spotted that this would lead to Esmond Haddock defying his aunts. I thought the intrepid Haddock was splendidly firm, didn't you?'

'Unquestionably, sir.'

'It's nice to think that he and Corky are now headed for the centre aisle.' I paused, and looked at him sharply. 'You sighed, Jeeves.'

'Yes, sir.'

'Why did you sigh?'

'I was thinking of Master Thomas, sir. The announcement of Miss Pirbright's betrothal came as a severe blow to him.'

I refused to allow my spirits to be lowered by any such side issues.

'Waste no time commiserating with young Thos, Jeeves. His is a resilient nature, and the agony will pass. He may have lost Corky, but there's always Betty Grable and Dorothy Lamour and Jennifer Jones.'

'I understand those ladies are married, sir.'

'That won't affect Thos. He'll be getting their autographs, just the same. I see a bright future ahead of him. Or, rather,' I said, correcting myself, 'fairly bright. There is that interview with his mother to be got over first.'

'It has already occurred, sir.'

I goggled at the man.

'What do you mean?'

'My primary motive in intruding upon you at this late hour, sir, was to inform you that her ladyship is downstairs.'

I quivered from brilliantine to shoe sole.

'Aunt Agatha?'

'Yes, sir.'

'Downstairs?'

'Yes, sir. In the drawing room. Her ladyship arrived some few moments ago. It appears that Master Thomas, unwilling to occasion her anxiety, wrote her a letter informing her that he was safe and well, and unfortunately the postmark "King's Deverill" on the envelope –'

'Oh, my gosh! She came racing down?'

'Yes, sir.'

'And –?'

'A somewhat painful scene took place between mother and son, in the course of which Master Thomas happened to –'

'Mention me?'

'Yes, sir.'

'He blew the gaff?'

'Yes, sir. And I was wondering whether in these circumstances you might not consider it advisable to take an immediate departure down the waterpipe. I understand there is an excellent milk train at two fifty-four. Her ladyship is expressing a desire to see you, sir.'

It would be deceiving my public to say that for an instant I did not quail. I quailed, as a matter of fact, like billy-o. And then, suddenly, it was as if strength had descended upon me.

'Jeeves,' I said, 'this is grave news, but it comes at a moment when I am well fitted to receive it. I have just witnessed Esmond Haddock pound the stuffing out of five aunts, and I feel that after an exhibition like that it would ill beseem a Wooster to curl up before a single aunt. I feel strong and resolute, Jeeves. I shall now go downstairs and pull an Esmond Haddock on Aunt Agatha. And if things look like becoming too sticky, I can always borrow that cosh of yours, what?'

I squared the shoulders and strode to the door, like Childe Roland about to fight the paynim.

VERY GOOD, JEEVES

To
E. Phillips Oppenheim

PREFACE

(to the original edition of Very Good, Jeeves, *which appeared in 1930)*

The question of how long an author is to be allowed to go on recording the adventures of any given character or characters is one that has frequently engaged the attention of thinking men. The publication of this book brings it once again into the foreground of national affairs.

It is now some fourteen summers since, an eager lad in my early thirties, I started to write Jeeves stories: and many people think this nuisance should now cease. Carpers say that enough is enough. Cavillers say the same. They look down the vista of the years and see these chronicles multiplying like rabbits, and the prospect appals them. But against this must be set the fact that writing Jeeves stories gives me a great deal of pleasure and keeps me out of the public houses.

At what conclusion, then, do we arrive? The whole thing is undoubtedly very moot.

From the welter of recrimination and argument one fact emerges – that we have here the third volume of a series. And what I do feel very strongly is that, if a thing is worth doing, it is worth doing well and thoroughly. It is perfectly possible, no doubt, to read *Very Good, Jeeves!* as a detached effort – or, indeed, not to read it at all: but I like to think that this country contains men of spirit who will not rest content till they have dug down into the old oak chest and fetched up the sum necessary for the purchase of its two predecessors – *The Inimitable Jeeves* and *Carry On, Jeeves!* Only so can the best results be obtained. Only so will allusions in the present volume to incidents occurring in the previous volumes become intelligible, instead of mystifying and befogging.

We do you these two books at the laughable price of half-a-crown apiece, and the method of acquiring them is simplicity itself.

All you have to do is to go to the nearest bookseller, when the following dialogue will take place:

YOURSELF: Good morning, Mr Bookseller.
BOOKSELLER: Good morning, Mr Everyman.
YOURSELF: I want *The Inimitable Jeeves* and *Carry on, Jeeves!*
BOOKSELLER: Certainly, Mr Everyman. You make the easy payment of five shillings, and they will be delivered to your door in a plain van.
YOURSELF: Good morning, Mr Bookseller.
BOOKSELLER: Good morning, Mr Everyman.

Or take the case of a French visitor to London, whom, for want of a better name, we will call Jules St Xavier Popinot. In this instance the little scene will run on these lines:

AU COIN DE LIVRES

POPINOT: Bon jour, Monsieur le marchand de livres.
MARCHAND: Bon jour, Monsieur. Quel beau temps aujourd'hui, n'est-ce-pas?
POPINOT: Absolument. Eskervous avez le *Jeeves Inimitable* et le *Continuez, Jeeves!* du maître Vodeouse?
MARCHAND: Mais certainement, Monsieur.
POPINOT: Donnez-moi les deux, s'il vous plaît.
MARCHAND: Oui, par exemple, morbleu. Et aussi la plume, l'encre, et la tante du jardinière?
POPINOT: Je m'en fiche de cela. Je désire seulement le Vodeouse.
MARCHAND: Pas de chemises, de cravates, ou le tonic pour les cheveux?
POPINOT: Seulement le Vodeouse, je vous assure.
MARCHAND: Parfaitement, Monsieur. Deux-et-six pour chaque bibelot – exactement cinq roberts.
POPINOT: Bon jour, Monsieur.
MARCHAND: Bon jour, Monsieur.

As simple as that.
See that the name 'Wodehouse' is on every label.

P.G.W.

1

JEEVES AND THE IMPENDING DOOM

It was the morning of the day on which I was slated to pop down to my Aunt Agatha's place at Woollam Chersey in the county of Herts for a visit of three solid weeks; and, as I seated myself at the breakfast table, I don't mind confessing that the heart was singularly heavy. We Woosters are men of iron, but beneath my intrepid exterior at that moment there lurked a nameless dread.

'Jeeves,' I said, 'I am not the old merry self this morning.'

'Indeed, sir?'

'No, Jeeves. Far from the old merry self.'

'I am sorry to hear that, sir.'

He uncovered the fragrant eggs and b., and I pronged a moody forkful.

'Why – this is what I keep asking myself, Jeeves – why has my Aunt Agatha invited me to her country seat?'

'I could not say, sir.'

'Not because she is fond of me.'

'No, sir.'

'It is a well-established fact that I give her a pain in the neck. How it happens I cannot say, but every time our paths cross, so to speak, it seems to be a mere matter of time before I perpetrate some ghastly floater and have her hopping after me with her hatchet. The result being that she regards me as a worm and an outcast. Am I right or wrong, Jeeves?'

'Perfectly correct, sir.'

'And yet now she has absolutely insisted on my scratching all previous engagements and buzzing down to Woollam Chersey. She must have some sinister reason of which we know nothing. Can you blame me, Jeeves, if the heart is heavy?'

'No, sir. Excuse me, sir, I fancy I heard the front-door bell.'

He shimmered out, and I took another listless stab at the e. and bacon.

'A telegram, sir,' said Jeeves, re-entering the presence.

'Open it, Jeeves, and read contents. Who is it from?'

'It is unsigned, sir.'

'You mean there's no name at the end of it?'

'That is precisely what I was endeavouring to convey, sir.'

'Let's have a look.'

I scanned the thing. It was a rummy communication. Rummy. No other word.

As follows:

Remember when you come here absolutely vital meet perfect strangers.

We Woosters are not very strong in the head, particularly at breakfast-time; and I was conscious of a dull ache between the eyebrows.

'What does it mean, Jeeves?'

'I could not say, sir.'

'It says "come here". Where's here?'

'You will notice the message was handed in at Woollam Chersey, sir.'

'You're absolutely right. At Woollam, as you very cleverly spotted, Chersey. This tells us something, Jeeves.'

'What, sir?'

'I don't know. It couldn't be from my Aunt Agatha, do you think?'

'Hardly, sir.'

'No; you're right again. Then all we can say is that some person unknown, resident at Woollam Chersey, considers it absolutely vital for me to meet perfect strangers. But why should I meet perfect strangers, Jeeves?'

'I could not say, sir.'

'And yet, looking at it from another angle, why shouldn't I?'

'Precisely, sir.'

'Then what it comes to is that the thing is a mystery which time alone can solve. We must wait and see, Jeeves.'

'The very expression I was about to employ, sir.'

I hit Woollam Chersey at about four o'clock, and found Aunt Agatha in her lair, writing letters. And, from what I know of her, probably offensive letters, with nasty postscripts. She regarded me with not a fearful lot of joy.

'Oh, there you are, Bertie.'

'Yes, here I am.'

'There's a smut on your nose.'

I plied the handkerchief.

'I am glad you have arrived so early. I want to have a word with you before you meet Mr Filmer.'

'Who?'

'Mr Filmer, the Cabinet Minister. He is staying in the house. Surely even you must have heard of Mr Filmer?'

'Oh, rather,' I said, though as a matter of fact the bird was completely unknown to me. What with one thing and another, I'm not frightfully up in the personnel of the political world.

'I particularly wish you to make a good impression on Mr Filmer.'

'Right-ho.'

'Don't speak in that casual way, as if you supposed that it was perfectly natural that you would make a good impression upon him. Mr Filmer is a serious-minded man of high character and purpose, and you are just the type of vapid and frivolous wastrel against which he is most likely to be prejudiced.'

Hard words, of course, from one's own flesh and blood, but well in keeping with past form.

'You will endeavour, therefore, while you are here not to display yourself in the *rôle* of a vapid and frivolous wastrel. In the first place, you will give up smoking during your visit.'

'Oh, I say!'

'Mr Filmer is president of the Anti-Tobacco League. Nor will you drink alcoholic stimulants.'

'Oh, dash it!'

'And you will kindly exclude from your conversation all that is suggestive of the bar, the billiardroom, and the stage door. Mr Filmer will judge you largely by your conversation.'

I rose to a point of order.

'Yes, but why have I got to make an impression on this – on Mr Filmer?'

'Because,' said the old relative, giving me the eye, 'I particularly wish it.'

Not, perhaps, a notably snappy come-back as come-backs go; but it was enough to show me that that was more or less that; and I beetled out with an aching heart.

I headed for the garden, and I'm dashed if the first person I saw wasn't young Bingo Little.

Bingo Little and I have been pals practically from birth. Born in the same village within a couple of days of one another, we went through kindergarten, Eton, and Oxford together; and, grown to riper years we have enjoyed in the old metrop. full many a first-class binge in each other's society. If there was one fellow in the world, I felt, who could alleviate the horrors of this blighted visit of mine, that bloke was young Bingo Little.

But how he came to be there was more than I could understand. Some time before, you see, he had married the celebrated authoress, Rosie M. Banks; and the last I had seen of him he had been on the point of accompanying her to America on a lecture tour. I distinctly remembered him cursing rather freely because the trip would mean his missing Ascot.

Still, rummy as it might seem, here he was. And aching for the sight of a friendly face, I gave tongue like a bloodhound.

'Bingo!'

He spun round; and, by Jove, his face wasn't friendly after all. It was what they call contorted. He waved his arms at me like a semaphore.

'Sh!' he hissed. 'Would you ruin me?'

'Eh?'

'Didn't you get my telegram?'

'Was that *your* telegram?'

'Of course it was my telegram.'

'Then why didn't you sign it?'

'I did sign it.'

'No, you didn't. I couldn't make out what it was all about.'

'Well, you got my letter.'

'What letter?'

'My letter.'

'I didn't get any letter.'

'Then I must have forgotten to post it. It was to tell you that I was down here tutoring your Cousin Thomas, and that it was essential that, when we met, you should treat me as a perfect stranger.'

'But why?'

'Because, if your aunt supposed that I was a pal of yours, she would naturally sack me on the spot.'

'Why?'

Bingo raised his eyebrows.

'Why? Be reasonable, Bertie. If you were your aunt, and you knew the sort of chap you were, would you let a fellow you knew to be your best pal tutor your son?'

This made the old head swim a bit, but I got his meaning after awhile, and I had to admit that there was much rugged good sense in what he said. Still, he hadn't explained what you might call the nub or gist of the mystery.

'I thought you were in America,' I said.

'Well, I'm not.'

'Why not?'

'Never mind why not. I'm not.'

'But why have you taken a tutoring job?'

'Never mind why, I have my reasons. And I want you to get it into your head, Bertie – to get it right through the concrete – that you and I must not be seen hobnobbing. Your foul cousin was caught smoking in the shrubbery the day before yesterday, and that has made my position pretty tottery, because your aunt said that, if I had exercised an adequate surveillance over him, it couldn't have happened. If, after that, she finds out I'm a friend of yours, nothing can save me from being shot out. And it is vital that I am not shot out.'

'Why?'

'Never mind why.'

At this point he seemed to think he heard somebody coming, for he suddenly leaped with incredible agility into a laurel bush. And I toddled along to consult Jeeves about these rummy happenings.

'Jeeves,' I said, repairing to the bedroom, where he was unpacking my things, 'you remember that telegram?'

'Yes, sir.'

'It was from Mr Little. He's here, tutoring my young Cousin Thomas.'

'Indeed, sir?'

'I can't understand it. He appears to be a free agent, if you know what I mean; and yet would any man who was a free agent wantonly came to a house which contained my Aunt Agatha?'

'It seems peculiar, sir.'

'Moreover, would anybody of his own free will and as a mere pleasure-seeker tutor my Cousin Thomas, who is notoriously a tough egg and a fiend in human shape?'

'Most improbable, sir.'

'These are deep waters, Jeeves.'

'Precisely, sir.'

'And the ghastly part of it all is that he seems to consider it necessary, in order to keep his job, to treat me like a long-lost leper. Thus killing my only chance of having anything approaching a decent time in this abode of desolation. For do you realize, Jeeves, that my aunt says I mustn't smoke while I'm here?'

'Indeed, sir?'

'Nor drink.'

'Why is this, sir?'

'Because she wants me – for some dark and furtive reason which she will not explain – to impress a fellow named Filmer.'

'Too bad, sir. However, many doctors, I understand, advocate such abstinence as the secret of health. They say it promotes a freer circulation of the blood and insures the arteries against premature hardening.'

'Oh, do they? Well, you can tell them next time you see them that they are silly asses.'

'Very good, sir.'

And so began what, looking back along a fairly eventful career, I think I can confidently say was the scaliest visit I have ever experienced in the course of my life. What with the agony of missing the lifegiving cocktail before dinner; the painful necessity of being obliged, every time I wanted a quiet cigarette, to lie on the floor in my bedroom and puff the smoke up the chimney; the constant discomfort of meeting Aunt Agatha round unexpected corners; and the fearful strain on the morale of having to chum with the Right Hon. A. B. Filmer, it was not long before Bertram was up against it to an extent hitherto undreamed of.

I played golf with the Right Hon. every day, and it was only by biting the Wooster lip and clenching the fists till the knuckles stood out white under the strain that I managed to pull through. The Right Hon. punctuated some of the ghastliest golf I have ever seen with a flow of conversation which, as far as I was concerned, went completely over the top; and, all in all, I was beginning to feel pretty sorry for myself when, one night as I was in my room listlessly donning the soup-and-fish in preparation for the evening meal, in trickled young Bingo and took my mind off my own troubles.

For when it is a question of a pal being in the soup, we Woosters no longer think of self; and that poor old Bingo was knee-deep in the bisque was made plain by his mere appearance – which was that of a cat which has just been struck by a half-brick and is expecting another shortly.

'Bertie,' said Bingo, having sat down on the bed and diffused silent gloom for a moment, 'how is Jeeves's brain these days?'

'Fairly strong on the wing, I fancy. How is the grey matter, Jeeves? Surging about pretty freely?'

'Yes, sir.'

'Thank Heaven for that,' said young Bingo, 'for I require your

soundest counsel. Unless right-thinking people take strong steps
through the proper channels, my name will be mud.'

'What's wrong, old thing?' I asked, sympathetically.

Bingo plucked at the coverlet.

'I will tell you,' he said. 'I will also now reveal why I am staying
in this pest-house, tutoring a kid who requires not education in the
Greek and Latin languages but a swift slosh on the base of the skull
with a black-jack. I came here, Bertie, because it was the only thing
I could do. At the last moment before she sailed to America, Rosie
decided that I had better stay behind and look after the Peke. She
left me a couple of hundred quid to see me through till her return.
This sum, judiciously expended over the period of her absence, would
have been enough to keep Peke and self in moderate affluence. But
you know how it is.'

'How what is?'

'When someone comes slinking up to you in the club and tells you
that some cripple of a horse can't help winning even if it develops
lumbago and the botts ten yards from the starting-post. I tell you,
I regarded the thing as a cautious and conservative investment.'

'You mean you planked the entire capital on a horse?'

Bingo laughed bitterly.

'If you could call the thing a horse. If it hadn't shown a flash of
speed in the straight, it would have got mixed up with the next race.
It came in last, putting me in a dashed delicate position. Somehow
or other I had to find the funds to keep me going, so that I could win
through till Rosie's return without her knowing what had occurred.
Rosie is the dearest girl in the world; but if you were a married man,
Bertie, you would be aware that the best of wives is apt to cut up rough
if she finds that her husband has dropped six weeks' housekeeping
money on a single race. Isn't that so, Jeeves?'

'Yes, sir. Women are odd in that respect.'

'It was a moment for swift thinking. There was enough left from
the wreck to board the Peke out at a comfortable home. I signed him
up for six weeks at the Kosy Komfort Kennels at Kingsbridge, Kent,
and tottered out, a broken man, to get a tutoring job. I landed the kid
Thomas. And here I am.'

It was a sad story, of course, but it seemed to me that, awful as
it might be to be in constant association with my Aunt Agatha and
young Thos, he had got rather well out of a tight place.

'All you have to do,' I said, 'is to carry on here for a few weeks
more, and everything will be oojah-cum-spiff.'

Bingo barked bleakly.

'A few weeks more! I shall be lucky if I stay two days. You remember I told you that your aunt's faith in me as a guardian of her blighted son was shaken a few days ago by the fact that he was caught smoking. I now find that the person who caught him smoking was the man Filmer. And ten minutes ago young Thomas told me that he was proposing to inflict some hideous revenge on Filmer for having reported him to your aunt. I don't know what he is going to do, but if he does it, out I inevitably go on my left ear. Your aunt thinks the world of Filmer, and would sack me on the spot. And three weeks before Rosie gets back!'

I saw all.

'Jeeves,' I said.

'Sir?'

'I see all. Do you see all?'

'Yes, sir.'

'Then flock round.'

'I fear, sir –'

Bingo gave a low moan.

'Don't tell me, Jeeves,' he said, brokenly, 'that nothing suggests itself.'

'Nothing at the moment, I regret to say sir.'

Bingo uttered a stricken woofle like a bull-dog that has been refused cake.

'Well, then, the only thing I can do, I suppose,' he said sombrely, 'is not to let the pie-faced little thing out of my sight for a second.'

'Absolutely,' I said. 'Ceaseless vigilance, eh, Jeeves?'

'Precisely, sir.'

'But meanwhile, Jeeves,' said Bingo in a low, earnest voice, 'you will be devoting your best thought to the matter, won't you?'

'Most certainly, sir.'

'Thank you, Jeeves.'

'Not at all, sir.'

I will say for young Bingo that, once the need for action arrived, he behaved with an energy and determination which compelled respect. I suppose there was not a minute during the next two days when the kid Thos was able to say to himself, 'Alone at last!' But on the evening of the second day Aunt Agatha announced that some people were coming over on the morrow for a spot of tennis, and I feared that the worst must now befall.

Young Bingo, you see, is one of those fellows who, once their fingers close over the handle of a tennis racket, fall into a sort of trance in which nothing outside the radius of the lawn exists for them. If you came up to Bingo in the middle of a set and told him that panthers were devouring his best friend in the kitchen garden, he would look at you and say, 'Oh, ah?' or words to that effect. I knew that he would not give a thought to young Thomas and the Right Hon. till the last ball had bounced, and, as I dressed for dinner that night, I was conscious of an impending doom.

'Jeeves,' I said, 'have you ever pondered on Life?'

'From time to time, sir, in my leisure moments.'

'Grim, isn't it, what?'

'Grim, sir?'

'I mean to say, the difference between things as they look and things as they are.'

'The trousers perhaps a half-inch higher, sir. A very slight adjustment of the braces will effect the necessary alteration. You were saying, sir?'

'I mean, here at Woollam Chersey we have apparently a happy, care-free country-house party. But beneath the glittering surface, Jeeves, dark currents are running. One gazes at the Right Hon. wrapping himself round the salmon mayonnaise at lunch, and he seems a man without a care in the world. Yet all the while a dreadful fate is hanging over him, creeping nearer and nearer. What exact steps do you think the kid Thomas intends to take?'

'In the course of an informal conversation which I had with the young gentleman this afternoon, sir, he informed me that he had been reading a romance entitled *Treasure Island*, and had been much struck by the character and actions of a certain Captain Flint. I gathered that he was weighing the advisability of modelling his own conduct on that of the Captain.'

'But, good heavens, Jeeves! If I remember *Treasure Island*, Flint was the bird who went about hitting people with a cutlass. You don't think young Thomas would bean Mr Filmer with a cutlass?'

'Possibly he does not possess a cutlass, sir.'

'Well, with anything.'

'We can but wait and see, sir. The tie, if I might suggest it, sir, a shade more tightly knotted. One aims at the perfect butterfly effect. If you will permit me –'

'What do ties matter, Jeeves, at a time like this? Do you realize that Mr Little's domestic happiness is hanging in the scale?'

'There is no time, sir, at which ties do not matter.'

I could see the man was pained, but I did not try to heal the wound. What's the word I want? Preoccupied. I was too preoccupied, don't you know. And *distrait*. Not to say careworn. I was still careworn when, next day at half-past two, the revels commenced on the tennis lawn. It was one of those close, baking days, with thunder rumbling just round the corner; and it seemed to me that there was a brooding menace in the air.

'Bingo,' I said, as we pushed forth to do our bit in the first doubles, 'I wonder what young Thos will be up to this afternoon, with the eye of authority no longer on him?'

'Eh?' said Bingo, absently. Already the tennis look had come into his face, and his eye was glazed. He swung his racket and snorted a little.

'I don't see him anywhere,' I said.

'You don't what?'

'See him.'

'Who?'

'Young Thos.'

'What about him?'

I let it go.

The only consolation I had in the black period of the opening of the tourney was the fact that the Right Hon. had taken a seat among the spectators and was wedged in between a couple of females with parasols. Reason told me that even a kid so steeped in sin as young Thomas would hardly perpetrate any outrage on a man in such a strong strategic position. Considerably relieved, I gave myself up to the game; and was in the act of putting it across the local curate with a good deal of vim when there was a roll of thunder and the rain started to come down in buckets.

We all stampeded for the house, and had gathered in the drawing room for tea, when suddenly Aunt Agatha, looking up from a cucumber sandwich, said:

'Has anybody seen Mr Filmer?'

It was one of the nastiest jars I have ever experienced. What with my fast serve zipping sweetly over the net and the man of God utterly unable to cope with my slow bending return down the centre-line, I had for some little time been living, as it were, in another world. I now came down to earth with a bang: and my slice of cake, slipping from my nerveless fingers, fell to the ground and was wolfed by Aunt Agatha's spaniel, Robert. Once more I seemed to become conscious of an impending doom.

For this man Filmer, you must understand, was not one of those men who are lightly kept from the tea table. A hearty trencherman, and particularly fond of his five o'clock couple of cups and bite of muffin, he had until this afternoon always been well up among the leaders in the race for the food-trough. If one thing was certain, it was that only the machinations of some enemy could be keeping him from being in the drawing room now, complete with nose-bag.

'He must have got caught in the rain and be sheltering somewhere in the grounds,' said Aunt Agatha. 'Bertie, go out and find him. Take a raincoat to him.'

'Right-ho!' I said. My only desire in life now was to find the Right Hon. And I hoped it wouldn't be merely his body.

I put on a raincoat and tucked another under my arm, and was sallying forth, when in the hall I ran into Jeeves.

'Jeeves,' I said, 'I fear the worst. Mr Filmer is missing.'

'Yes, sir.'

'I am about to scour the grounds in search of him.'

'I can save you the trouble, sir. Mr Filmer is on the island in the middle of the lake.'

'In this rain? Why doesn't the chump row back?'

'He has no boat, sir.'

'Then how can he be on the island?'

'He rowed there, sir. But Master Thomas rowed after him and set his boat adrift. He was informing me of the circumstances a moment ago, sir. It appears that Captain Flint was in the habit of marooning people on islands, and Master Thomas felt that he could pursue no more judicious course than to follow his example.'

'But, good Lord, Jeeves! The man must be getting soaked.'

'Yes, sir. Master Thomas commented upon that aspect of the matter.'

It was a time for action.

'Come with me, Jeeves!'

'Very good, sir.'

I buzzed for the boathouse.

My Aunt Agatha's husband, Spenser Gregson, who is on the Stock Exchange, had recently cleaned up to an amazing extent in Sumatra Rubber; and Aunt Agatha, in selecting a country estate, had lashed out on an impressive scale. There were miles of what they call rolling parkland, trees in considerable profusion well provided with doves and what not cooing in no uncertain voice, gardens full of roses, and also stables, out-houses, and messuages, the whole forming a rather fruity *tout ensemble*. But the feature of the place was the lake.

It stood to the east of the house, beyond the rose garden, and covered several acres. In the middle of it was an island. In the middle of the island was a building known as the Octagon. And in the middle of the Octagon, seated on the roof and spouting water like a public fountain, was the Right Hon. A. B. Filmer. As we drew nearer, striking a fast clip with self at oars and Jeeves handling the tiller-ropes, we heard cries of gradually increasing volume, if that's the expression I want; and presently, up aloft, looking from a distance as if he were perched on top of the bushes, I located the Right Hon. It seemed to me that even a Cabinet Minister ought to have had more sense than to stay right out in the open like that when there were trees to shelter under.

'A little more to the right, Jeeves.'

'Very good, sir.'

I made a neat landing.

'Wait here, Jeeves.'

'Very good, sir. The head gardener was informing me this morning, sir, that one of the swans had recently nested on this island.'

'This is no time for natural history gossip, Jeeves,' I said, a little severely, for the rain was coming down harder than ever and the Wooster trouser-legs were already considerably moistened.

'Very good, sir.'

I pushed my way through the bushes. The going was sticky and took about eight and elevenpence off the value of my Sure-Grip tennis shoes in the first two yards: but I persevered, and presently came out in the open and found myself in a sort of clearing facing the Octagon.

This building was run up somewhere in the last century, I have been told, to enable the grandfather of the late owner to have some quiet place out of earshot of the house where he could practise the fiddle. From what I know of fiddlers, I should imagine that he had produced some fairly frightful sounds there in his time, but they can have been nothing to the ones that were coming from the roof of the place now. The Right Hon., not having spotted the arrival of the rescue-party, was apparently trying to make his voice carry across the waste of waters to the house; and I'm not saying it was not a good sporting effort. He had one of those highish tenors, and his yowls seemed to screech over my head like shells.

I thought it about time to slip him the glad news that assistance had arrived, before he strained a vocal cord.

'Hi!' I shouted, waiting for a lull.

He poked his head over the edge.

'Hi' he bellowed, looking in every direction but the right one, of course.

'Hi!'

'Hi!'

'Hi!'

'Hi!'

'Oh!' he said, spotting me at last.

'What-ho!' I replied, sort of clinching the thing.

I suppose the conversation can't be said to have touched a frightfully high level up to this moment; but probably we should have got a good deal brainier very shortly – only just then, at the very instant when I was getting ready to say something good, there was a hissing noise like a tyre bursting in a nest of cobras, and out of the bushes to my left there popped something so large and white and active that, thinking quicker than I have ever done in my puff, I rose like a rocketing pheasant, and, before I knew what I was doing, had begun to climb for life. Something slapped against the wall about an inch below my right ankle, and any doubts I may have had about remaining below vanished. The lad who bore 'mid snow and ice the banner with the strange device 'Excelsior!' was the model for Bertram.

'Be careful!' yipped the Right Hon.

I was.

Whoever built the Octagon might have constructed it especially for this sort of crisis. Its walls had grooves at regular intervals which were just right for the hands and feet, and it wasn't very long before I was parked up on the roof beside the Right Hon., gazing down at one of the largest and shortest-tempered swans I had ever seen. It was standing below, stretching up a neck like a hosepipe, just where a bit of brick, judiciously bunged, would catch it amidships.

I bunged the brick and scored a bull's-eye.

The Right Hon. didn't seem any too well pleased.

'Don't tease it!' he said.

'It teased me,' I said.

The swan extended another eight feet of neck and gave an imitation of steam escaping from a leaky pipe. The rain continued to lash down with what you might call indescribable fury, and I was sorry that in the agitation inseparable from shinning up a stone wall at practically a second's notice I had dropped the raincoat which I had been bringing with me for my fellow-rooster. For a moment I thought of offering him mine, but wiser counsels prevailed.

'How near did it come to getting you?' I asked.

'Within an ace,' replied my companion, gazing down with a look of marked dislike. 'I had to make a very rapid spring.'

The Right Hon. was a tubby little chap who looked as if he had been poured into his clothes and had forgotten to say 'When!' and the picture he conjured up, if you know what I mean, was rather pleasing.

'It is no laughing matter,' he said, shifting the look of dislike to me.

'Sorry.'

'I might have been seriously injured.'

'Would you consider bunging another brick at the bird?'

'Do nothing of the sort. It will only annoy him.'

'Well, why not annoy him? He hasn't shown such a dashed lot of consideration for our feelings.'

The Right Hon. now turned to another aspect of the matter.

'I cannot understand how my boat, which I fastened securely to the stump of a willow-tree, can have drifted away.'

'Dashed mysterious.'

'I begin to suspect that it was deliberately set loose by some mischievous person.'

'Oh, I say, no, hardly likely, that. You'd have seen them doing it.'

'No, Mr Wooster. For the bushes form an effective screen. Moreover, rendered drowsy by the unusual warmth of the afternoon, I dozed off for some little time almost immediately I reached the island.'

This wasn't the sort of thing I wanted his mind dwelling on, so I changed the subject.

'Wet, isn't it, what?' I said.

'I had already observed it,' said the Right Hon. in one of those nasty, bitter voices. 'I thank you, however, for drawing the matter to my attention.'

Chit-chat about the weather hadn't gone with much of a bang, I perceived. I had a shot at Bird Life in the Home Counties.

'Have you ever noticed,' I said, 'how a swan's eyebrows sort of meet in the middle?'

'I have had every opportunity of observing all that there is to observe about swans.'

'Gives them a sort of peevish look, what?'

'The look to which you allude has not escaped me.'

'Rummy,' I said, rather warming to my subject, 'how bad an effect family life has on a swan's disposition.'

'I wish you would select some other topic of conversation than swans.'

'No, but, really, it's rather interesting. I mean to say, our old pal down there is probably a perfect ray of sunshine in normal circumstances. Quite the domestic pet, don't you know. But purely and simply because the little woman happens to be nesting –'

I paused. You will scarcely believe me, but until this moment, what with all the recent bustle and activity, I had clean forgotten that, while we were treed up on the roof like this, there lurked all the time in the background one whose giant brain, if notified of the emergency and requested to flock round, would probably be able to think up half-a-dozen schemes for solving our little difficulties in a couple of minutes.

'Jeeves!' I shouted.

'Sir?' came a faint respectful voice from the great open spaces.

'My man,' I explained to the Right Hon. 'A fellow of infinite resource and sagacity. He'll have us out of this in a minute. Jeeves!'

'Sir?'

'I'm sitting on the roof.'

'Very good, sir.'

'Don't say "Very good". Come and help us. Mr Filmer and I are treed, Jeeves.'

'Very good, sir.'

'Don't keep saying "Very good". It's nothing of the kind. The place is alive with swans.'

'I will attend to the matter immediately, sir.'

I turned to the Right Hon. I even went so far as to pat him on the back. It was like slapping a wet sponge.

'All is well,' I said. 'Jeeves is coming.'

'What can he do?'

I frowned a trifle. The man's tone had been peevish, and I didn't like it.

'That,' I replied with a touch of stiffness, 'we cannot say until we see him in action. He may pursue one course, or he may pursue another. But on one thing you can rely with the utmost confidence – Jeeves will find a way. See, here he comes stealing through the undergrowth, his face shining with the light of pure intelligence. There are no limits to Jeeves's brain-power. He virtually lives on fish.'

I bent over the edge and peered into the abyss.

'Look out for the swan, Jeeves.'

'I have the bird under close observation, sir.'

The swan had been uncoiling a further supply of neck in our direction; but now he whipped round. The sound of a voice speaking in his rear seemed to affect him powerfully. He subjected Jeeves to a short, keen scrutiny; and then, taking in some breath for hissing purposes, gave a sort of jump and charged ahead.

'Look out, Jeeves!'

'Very good, sir.'

Well, I could have told that swan it was no use. As swans go, he may have been well up in the ranks of the intelligentsia; but, when it came to pitting his brains against Jeeves, he was simply wasting his time. He might just as well have gone home at once.

Every young man starting life ought to know how to cope with an angry swan, so I will briefly relate the proper procedure. You begin by picking up the raincoat which somebody has dropped; and then, judging the distance to a nicety, you simply shove the raincoat over the bird's head; and, taking the boat-hook which you have prudently brought with you, you insert it underneath the swan and heave. The swan goes into a bush and starts trying to unscramble itself; and you saunter back to your boat, taking with you any friends who may happen at the moment to be sitting on roofs in the vicinity. That was Jeeves's method, and I cannot see how it could have been improved upon.

The Right Hon. showing a turn of speed of which I would not have believed him capable, we were in the boat in considerably under two ticks.

'You behaved very intelligently, my man,' said the Right Hon. as we pushed away from the shore.

'I endeavour to give satisfaction, sir.'

The Right Hon. appeared to have said his say for the time being. From that moment he seemed to sort of huddle up and meditate. Dashed absorbed he was. Even when I caught a crab and shot about a pint of water down his neck he didn't seem to notice it.

It was only when we were landing that he came to life again.

'Mr Wooster.'

'Oh, ah?'

'I have been thinking of that matter of which I spoke to you some time back – the problem of how my boat can have got adrift.'

I didn't like this.

'The dickens of a problem,' I said. 'Better not bother about it any more. You'll never solve it.'

'On the contrary, I have arrived at a solution, and one which I think is the only feasible solution. I am convinced that my boat was set adrift by the boy Thomas, my hostess's son.'

'Oh, I say, no! Why?'

'He had a grudge against me. And it is the sort of thing only a boy, or one who is practically an imbecile, would have thought of doing.'

He legged it for the house; and I turned to Jeeves, aghast. Yes, you might say aghast.

'You heard, Jeeves?'

'Yes, sir.'

'What's to be done?'

'Perhaps Mr Filmer, on thinking the matter over, will decide that his suspicions are unjust.'

'But they aren't unjust.'

'No, sir.'

'Then what's to be done?'

'I could not say, sir.'

I pushed off rather smartly to the house and reported to Aunt Agatha that the Right Hon. had been salved; and then I toddled upstairs to have a hot bath, being considerably soaked from stem to stern as the result of my rambles. While I was enjoying the grateful warmth, a knock came at the door.

It was Purvis, Aunt Agatha's butler.

'Mrs Gregson desires me to say, sir, that she would be glad to see you as soon as you are ready.'

'But she has seen me.'

'I gather that she wishes to see you again, sir.'

'Oh, right-ho.'

I lay beneath the surface for another few minutes; then, having dried the frame, went along the corridor to my room. Jeeves was there, fiddling about with underclothing.

'Oh, Jeeves,' I said, 'I've just been thinking. Oughtn't somebody to go and give Mr Filmer a spot of quinine or something? Errand of mercy, what?'

'I have already done so, sir.'

'Good. I wouldn't say I like the man frightfully, but I don't want him to get a cold in the head.' I shoved on a sock. 'Jeeves,' I said, 'I suppose you know that we've got to think of something pretty quick? I mean to say, you realize the position? Mr Filmer suspects young Thomas of doing exactly what he did do, and if he brings home the charge Aunt Agatha will undoubtedly fire Mr Little, and then Mrs Little will find out what Mr Little has been up to, and what will be the upshot and outcome, Jeeves? I will tell you. It will mean that Mrs Little will get the goods on Mr Little to an extent to which, though only a bachelor myself, I should say that no wife ought to get the goods on her husband if the proper give and take of married life – what you might call the essential balance, as it were – is to be preserved. Women bring these things up, Jeeves. They do not forget and forgive.'

'Very true, sir.'

'Then how about it?'

'I have already attended to the matter, sir.'

'You have?'

'Yes, sir. I had scarcely left you when the solution of the affair presented itself to me. It was a remark of Mr Filmer's that gave me the idea.'

'Jeeves, you're a marvel!'

'Thank you very much, sir.'

'What was the solution?'

'I conceived the notion of going to Mr Filmer and saying that it was you who had stolen his boat, sir.'

The man flickered before me. I clutched a sock in a feverish grip.

'Saying – what?'

'At first Mr Filmer was reluctant to credit my statement. But I pointed out to him that you had certainly known that he was on the island – a fact which he agreed was highly significant. I pointed out, furthermore, that you were a light-hearted young gentleman, sir, who might well do such a thing as a practical joke. I left him quite convinced, and there is now no danger of his attributing the action to Master Thomas.'

I gazed at the blighter spellbound.

'And that's what you consider a neat solution?' I said.

'Yes, sir. Mr Little will now retain his position as desired.'

'And what about me?'

'You are also benefited, sir.'

'Oh, I am, am I?'

'Yes, sir. I have ascertained that Mrs Gregson's motive in inviting you to this house was that she might present you to Mr Filmer with a view to your becoming his private secretary.'

'What!'

'Yes, sir. Purvis, the butler, chanced to overhear Mrs Gregson in conversation with Mr Filmer on the matter.'

'Secretary to that superfatted bore! Jeeves, I could never have survived it.'

'No, sir. I fancy you would not have found it agreeable. Mr Filmer is scarcely a congenial companion for you. Yet, had Mrs Gregson secured the position for you, you might have found it embarrassing to decline to accept it.'

'Embarrassing is right!'

'Yes, sir.'

'But I say, Jeeves, there's just one point which you seem to have overlooked. Where exactly do I get off?'

'Sir?'

'I mean to say, Aunt Agatha sent word by Purvis just now that she wanted to see me. Probably she's polishing up her hatchet at this very moment.'

'It might be the most judicious plan not to meet her, sir.'

'But how can I help it?'

'There is a good, stout waterpipe running down the wall immediately outside this window, sir. And I could have the two-seater waiting outside the park gates in twenty minutes.'

I eyed him with reverence.

'Jeeves,' I said, 'you are always right. You couldn't make it five, could you?'

'Let us say ten, sir.'

'Ten it is. Lay out some raiment suitable for travel, and leave the rest to me. Where is this waterpipe of which you speak so highly?'

2

THE INFERIORITY COMPLEX OF OLD SIPPY

I checked the man with one of my glances. I was astounded and shocked.

'Not another word, Jeeves,' I said. 'You have gone too far. Hats, yes. Socks, yes. Coats, trousers, shirts, ties, and spats, absolutely. On all these things I defer to your judgment. But when it comes to vases, no.'

'Very good, sir.'

'You say that this vase is not in harmony with the appointments of the room – whatever that means, if anything. I deny this, Jeeves, *in toto*. I like this vase. I call it decorative, striking, and all in all, an exceedingly good fifteen bob's worth.'

'Very good, sir.'

'That's that, then. If anybody rings up, I shall be closeted during the next hour with Mr Sipperley at the offices of *The Mayfair Gazette*.'

I beetled off with a fairish amount of restrained hauteur, for I was displeased with the man. On the previous afternoon, while sauntering along the Strand, I had found myself wedged into one of those sort of alcove places where fellows with voices like foghorns stand all day selling things by auction. And, though I was still vague as to how exactly it had happened, I had somehow become the possessor of a large china vase with crimson dragons on it. And not only dragons, but birds, dogs, snakes, and a thing that looked like a leopard. This menagerie was now stationed on a bracket over the door of my sitting room.

I liked the thing. It was bright and cheerful. It caught the eye. And that was why, when Jeeves, wincing a bit, had weighed in with some perfectly gratuitous art-criticism, I ticked him off with no little vim. *Ne sutor ultra* whatever-it-is, I would have said to him, if I'd thought of it. I mean to say, where does a valet get off, censoring vases? Does it fall within his province to knock the young master's chinaware? Absolutely not, and so I told him.

I was still pretty heartily hipped when I reached the office of *The Mayfair Gazette*, and it would have been a relief to my feelings to have decanted my troubles on to old Sippy, who, being a very dear old pal of mine, would no doubt have understood and sympathized. But when the office-boy had slipped me through into the inner cubbyhole where the old lad performed his editorial duties, he seemed so preoccupied that I hadn't the heart.

All these editor blokes, I understand, get pretty careworn after they've been at the job for awhile. Six months before, Sippy had been a cheery cove, full of happy laughter; but at that time he was what they call a freelance, bunging in a short story here and a set of verses there and generally enjoying himself. Ever since he had become editor of this rag, I had sensed a change, so to speak.

Today he looked more editorial than ever; so, shelving my own worries for the nonce, I endeavoured to cheer him up by telling him how much I had enjoyed his last issue. As a matter of fact, I hadn't read it, but we Woosters do not shrink from subterfuge when it is a question of bracing up a buddy.

The treatment was effective. He showed animation and verve.

'You really liked it?'

'Red-hot, old thing.'

'Full of good stuff, eh?'

'Packed.'

'That poem – "Solitude"?'

'What a gem!'

'A genuine masterpiece.'

'Pure tabasco. Who wrote it?'

'It was signed,' said Sippy, a little coldly.

'I keep forgetting names.'

'It was written,' said Sippy, 'by Miss Gwendolen Moon. Have you ever met Miss Moon, Bertie?'

'Not to my knowledge. Nice girl?'

'My God!' said Sippy.

I looked at him keenly. If you ask my Aunt Agatha she will tell you – in fact, she is quite likely to tell you even if you don't ask her – that I am a vapid and irreflective chump. Barely sentient, was the way she once described me: and I'm not saying that in a broad, general sense she isn't right. But there is one department of life in which I am Hawkshaw the detective in person. I can recognize Love's Young Dream more quickly than any other bloke of my weight and age in the Metropolis. So many of my pals have copped it in the past few years that now I can spot it a mile off on a foggy day. Sippy was leaning back in his chair, chewing a piece of india-rubber with a far-off look in his eyes, and I formed my diagnosis instantly.

'Tell me all, laddie,' I said.

'Bertie, I love her.'

'Have you told her so?'

'How can I?'

'I don't see why not. Quite easy to bring into the general conversation.'

Sippy groaned hollowly.

'Do you know what it is, Bertie, to feel the humility of a worm?'

'Rather! I do sometimes with Jeeves. But today he went too far. You will scarcely credit it, old man, but he had the crust to criticize a vase which –'

'She is so far above me.'

'Tall girl?'

'Spiritually. She is all soul. And what am I? Earthy.'

'Would you say that?'

'I would. Have you forgotten that a year ago I did thirty days without the option for punching a policeman in the stomach on Boat Race night?'

'But you were whiffed at the time.'

'Exactly. What right has an inebriated jail-bird to aspire to a goddess?'

My heart bled for the poor old chap.

'Aren't you exaggerating things a trifle, old lad?' I said. 'Everybody who has had a gentle upbringing gets a bit sozzled on Boat Race night, and the better element nearly always have trouble with the gendarmes.'

He shook his head.

'It's no good, Bertie. You mean well, but words are useless. No, I can but worship from afar. When I am in her presence a strange dumbness comes over me. My tongue seems to get entangled with my tonsils. I could no more muster up the nerve to propose to her than . . . Come in!' he shouted.

For, just as he was beginning to go nicely and display a bit of eloquence, a knock had sounded on the door. In fact, not so much a knock as a bang – or even a slosh. And there now entered a large, important-looking bird with penetrating eyes, a Roman nose, and high cheek-bones. Authoritative. That's the word I want. I didn't like his collar, and Jeeves would have had a thing or two to say about the sit of his trousers; but, nevertheless, he was authoritative. There was something compelling about the man. He looked like a traffic-policeman.

'Ah, Sipperley!' he said.

Old Sippy displayed a good deal of agitation. He had leaped from his chair, and was now standing in a constrained attitude, with a sort of pop-eyed expression on his face.

'Pray be seated, Sipperley,' said the cove. He took no notice of me. After one keen glance and a brief waggle of the nose in my direction, he had washed Bertram out of his life. 'I have brought you another little offering – ha! Look it over at your leisure, my dear fellow.'

'Yes, sir,' said Sippy.

'I think you will enjoy it. But there is just one thing. I should be glad, Sipperley, if you would give it a leetle better display, a rather more prominent position in the paper than you accorded to my "Landmarks of Old Tuscany". I am quite aware that in a weekly journal space is a desideratum, but one does not like one's efforts to be – I can only say pushed away in a back corner among advertisements of bespoke tailors and places of amusement.' He paused, and a nasty gleam came into his eyes. 'You will bear this in mind, Sipperley?'

'Yes, sir,' said Sippy.

'I am greatly obliged, my dear fellow,' said the cove, becoming genial again. 'You must forgive my mentioning it. I would be the last person to attempt to dictate the – ha! – editorial policy, but – Well, good afternoon, Sipperley. I will call for your decision at three o'clock tomorrow.'

He withdrew, leaving a gap in the atmosphere about ten feet by six. When this had closed in, I sat up.

'What was it?' I said.

I was startled to observe poor old Sippy apparently go off his onion. He raised his hands over his head, clutched his hair, wrenched it about for a while, kicked a table with great violence, and then flung himself into his chair.

'Curse him!' said Sippy. 'May he tread on a banana-skin on his way to chapel and sprain both ankles!'

'Who was he?'

'May he get a frog-in-the-throat and be unable to deliver the end-of-term sermon!'

'Yes, but who was he?'

'My old headmaster, Bertie,' said Sippy.

'Yes, but, my dear old soul –'

'Headmaster of my old school.' He gazed at me in a distraught sort of way. 'Good Lord! Can't you understand the position?'

'Not by a jugful, laddie.'

Sippy sprang from his chair and took a turn or two up and down the carpet.

'How do you feel,' he said, 'when you meet the headmaster of your old school?'

'I never do. He's dead.'

'Well, I'll tell you how I feel. I feel as if I were in the Lower Fourth again, and had been sent up by my form-master for creating a disturbance in school. That happened once, Bertie, and the memory still lingers. I can recall as if it were yesterday knocking at old Waterbury's door and hearing him say, "Come in!" like a lion roaring at an early Christian, and going in and shuffling my feet on the mat and him looking at me and me explaining – and then, after what seemed a lifetime, bending over and receiving six of the juiciest on the old spot with a cane that bit like an adder. And whenever he comes into my office now the old wound begins to trouble me, and I just say, "Yes, sir," and "No, sir," and feel like a kid of fourteen.'

I began to grasp the posish. The whole trouble with these fellows like Sippy, who go in for writing, is that they develop the artistic temperament, and you never know when it is going to break out.

'He comes in here with his pockets full of articles on "The Old School Cloisters" and "Some Little-Known Aspects of Tacitus", and muck like that, and I haven't the nerve to refuse them. And this is supposed to be a paper devoted to the lighter interests of Society.'

'You must be firm, Sippy. Firm, old thing.'

'How can I, when the sight of him makes me feel like a piece of chewed blotting-paper? When he looks at me over that nose, my morale goes blue at the roots and I am back at school again. It's persecution, Bertie. And the next thing that'll happen is that my proprietor will spot one of those articles, assume with perfect justice that, if I can print that sort of thing, I must be going off my chump, and fire me.'

I pondered. It was a tough problem.

'How would it be –?' I said.

'That's no good.'

'Only a suggestion,' I said.

'Jeeves,' I said, when I got home, 'surge round!'

'Sir?'

'Burnish the old bean. I have a case that calls for one of your best efforts. Have you ever heard of a Miss Gwendolen Moon?'

'Authoress of "Autumn Leaves", " 'Twas on an English June", and other works. Yes, sir.'

'Great Scott, Jeeves, you seem to know everything.'

'Thank you very much, sir.'

'Well, Mr Sipperley is in love with Miss Moon.'

'Yes, sir.'

'But fears to speak.'

'It is often the way, sir.'

'Deeming himself unworthy.'

'Precisely, sir.'

'Right! But that is not all. Tuck that away in a corner of the mind, Jeeves, and absorb the rest of the facts. Mr Sipperley, as you are aware, is the editor of a weekly paper devoted to the interests of the lighter Society. And now the headmaster of his old school has started calling at the office and unloading on him junk entirely unsuited to the lighter Society. All clear?'

'I follow you perfectly, sir.'

'And this drip Mr Sipperley is compelled to publish, much against his own wishes, purely because he lacks the nerve to tell the man to go to blazes. The whole trouble being, Jeeves, that he has got one of those things that fellows do get – it's on the tip of my tongue.'

'An inferiority complex, sir?'

'Exactly. An inferiority complex. I have one myself with regard to my Aunt Agatha. You know me, Jeeves. You know that if it were a question of volunteers to man the lifeboat, I would spring to the task. If anyone said, "Don't go down the coal-mine, daddy," it would have not the slightest effect on my resolution –'

'Undoubtedly, sir.'

'And yet – and this is where I want you to follow me very closely, Jeeves – when I hear that my Aunt Agatha is out with her hatchet and moving in my direction, I run like a rabbit. Why? Because she gives me an inferiority complex. And so it is with Mr Sipperley. He would, if called upon, mount the deadly breach, and do it without a tremor; but he cannot bring himself to propose to Miss Moon, and he cannot kick his old headmaster in the stomach and tell him to take his beastly essays on "The Old School Cloisters" elsewhere, because he has an inferiority complex. So what about it, Jeeves?'

'I fear I have no plan which I could advance with any confidence on the spur of the moment, sir.'

'You want time to think, eh?'

'Yes, sir.'

'Take it, Jeeves, take it. You may feel brainier after a night's sleep. What is it Shakespeare calls sleep, Jeeves?'

'Tired Nature's sweet restorer, sir.'

'Exactly. Well, there you are, then.'

You know, there's nothing like sleeping on a thing. Scarcely had I woken up next morning when I discovered that, while I slept, I had got the whole binge neatly into order and worked out a plan Foch might have been proud of. I rang the bell for Jeeves to bring me my tea.

I rang again. But it must have been five minutes before the man showed up with the steaming.

'I beg your pardon, sir,' he said, when I reproached him. 'I did not hear the bell. I was in the sitting room, sir.'

'Ah?' I said, sucking down a spot of the mixture. 'Doing this and that, no doubt?'

'Dusting your new vase, sir.'

My heart warmed to the fellow. If there's one person I like, it's the chap who is not too proud to admit it when he's in the wrong. No actual statement to that effect has passed his lips, of course, but we Woosters can read between the lines. I could see that he was learning to love the vase.

'How does it look?'

'Yes, sir.'

A bit cryptic, but I let it go.

'Jeeves,' I said.

'Sir?'

'That matter we were in conference about yestereen.'

'The matter of Mr Sipperley, sir?'

'Precisely. Don't worry yourself any further. Stop the brain working. I shall not require your service. I have found the solution. It came on me like a flash.'

'Indeed, sir?'

'Just like a flash. In a matter of this kind, Jeeves, the first thing to do is to study – what's the word I want?'

'I could not say, sir.'

'Quite a common word – though long.'

'Psychology, sir?'

'The exact noun. It is a noun?'

'Yes, sir.'

'Spoken like a man! Well, Jeeves, direct your attention to the psychology of old Sippy. Mr Sipperley, if you follow me, is in the position of a man from whose eyes the scales have not fallen. The task that faced me, Jeeves, was to discover some scheme which would cause those scales to fall. You get me?'

'Not entirely, sir.'

'Well, what I'm driving at is this. At present this headmaster bloke, this Waterbury, is tramping all over Mr Sipperley because he is hedged about with dignity, if you understand what I mean. Years have passed; Mr Sipperley now shaves daily and is in an important editorial position; but he can never forget that this bird once gave him six of the juiciest. Result: an inferiority complex. The only way to remove that complex, Jeeves, is to arrange that Mr Sipperley shall see this Waterbury in a thoroughly undignified position. This done, the scales will fall from his eyes. You must see that for yourself, Jeeves. Take your own case. No doubt there are a number of your friends and relations who look up to you and respect you greatly. But suppose one night they were to see you, in an advanced state of intoxication, dancing the Charleston in your underwear in the middle of Piccadilly Circus?'

'The contingency is remote, sir.'

'Ah, but suppose they did. The scales would fall from their eyes, what?'

'Very possibly, sir.'

'Take another case. Do you remember a year or so ago the occasion when my Aunt Agatha accused the maid at that French hotel of pinching her pearls, only to discover that they were in her drawer?'

'Yes, sir.'

'Whereupon she looked the most priceless ass. You'll admit that.'

'Certainly I have seen Mrs Spenser Gregson appear to greater advantage than at that moment, sir.'

'Exactly. Now follow me like a leopard. Observing my Aunt Agatha in her downfall; watching her turn bright mauve and listening to her being told off in liquid French by a whiskered hotel proprietor without coming back with so much as a single lift of the eyebrows, I felt as if the scales had fallen from my eyes. For the first time in my life, Jeeves, the awe with which this woman had inspired me from childhood's days left me. It came back later, I'll admit; but at the moment I saw my Aunt Agatha for what she was – not, as I had long imagined, a sort of man-eating fish at the very mention of whose name strong men quivered like aspens, but a poor goop who had just dropped a very serious brick. At that moment, Jeeves, I could have told her precisely where she got off; and only a too chivalrous regard for the sex kept me from doing so. You won't dispute that?'

'No, sir.'

'Well, then, my firm conviction is that the scales will fall from Mr Sipperley's eyes when he sees this Waterbury, this old headmaster, stagger into his office covered from head to foot with flour.'

'Flour, sir?'

'Flour, Jeeves.'

'But why should he pursue such a course, sir?'

'Because he won't be able to help it. The stuff will be balanced on top of the door, and the force of gravity will do the rest. I propose to set a booby-trap for this Waterbury, Jeeves.'

'Really, sir, I would scarcely advocate –'

I raised my hand.

'Peace, Jeeves! There is more to come. You have not forgotten that Mr Sipperley loves Miss Gwendolen Moon, but fears to speak. I bet you'd forgotten that.'

'No, sir.'

'Well, then, my belief is that, once he finds he has lost his awe of this Waterbury, he will be so supremely braced that there will be no holding him. He will rush right off and bung his heart at her feet, Jeeves.'

'Well, sir –'

'Jeeves,' I said a little severely, 'whenever I suggest a plan or scheme or course of action, you are too apt to say "Well, sir," in a nasty tone of voice. I do not like it, and it is a habit you should check. The plan or scheme or course of action which I have outlined contains no flaw. If it does, I should like to hear it.'

'Well, sir –'

'Jeeves!'

'I beg your pardon, sir. I was about to remark that, in my opinion, you are approaching Mr Sipperley's problems in the wrong order.'

'How do you mean, the wrong order?'

'Well, I fancy, sir, that better results would be obtained by first inducing Mr Sipperley to offer marriage to Miss Moon. In the event of the young lady proving agreeable, I think that Mr Sipperley would be in such an elevated frame of mind that he would have no difficulty in asserting himself with Mr Waterbury.'

'Ah, but you are then stymied by the question – How is he to be induced?'

'It had occurred to me, sir, that, as Miss Moon is a poetess and of a romantic nature, it might have weight with her if she heard that Mr Sipperley had met with a serious injury and was mentioning her name.'

'Calling for her brokenly, you mean?'

'Calling for her, as you say, sir, brokenly.'

I sat up in bed, and pointed at him rather coldly with the teaspoon.

'Jeeves,' I said, 'I would be the last man to accuse you of dithering, but this is not like you. It is not the old form, Jeeves. You are losing your grip. It might be years before Mr Sipperley had a serious injury.'

'There is that to be considered, sir.'

'I cannot believe that it is you, Jeeves, who are meekly suggesting that we should suspend all activities in this matter year after year, on the chance that some day Mr Sipperley may fall under a truck or something. No! The programme will be as I have sketched it out, Jeeves. After breakfast, kindly step out, and purchase about a pound and a half of the best flour. The rest you may leave to me.'

'Very good, sir.'

The first thing you need in matters of this kind, as every general knows, is a thorough knowledge of the terrain. Not know the terrain, and where are you? Look at Napoleon and that sunken road at Waterloo. Silly ass!

I had a thorough knowledge of the terrain of Sippy's office, and it ran as follows. I won't draw a plan, because my experience is that, when you're reading one of those detective stories and come to the bit where the author draws a plan of the Manor, showing room where body was found, stairs leading to passage-way, and all the rest of it, one just skips. I'll simply explain in a few brief words.

The offices of *The Mayfair Gazette* were on the first floor of a mouldy old building off Covent Garden. You went in at a front door and ahead of you was a passage leading to the premises of Bellamy Bros, dealers in seeds and garden produce. Ignoring the Bros Bellamy, you proceeded upstairs and found two doors opposite you. One, marked Private, opened into Sippy's editorial sanctum. The other – sub-title: Inquiries – shot you into a small room where an office-boy sat, eating peppermints and reading the adventures of Tarzan. If you got past the office-boy, you went through another door and there you were in Sippy's room, just as if you had nipped through the door marked Private. Perfectly simple.

It was over the door marked Inquiries that I proposed to suspend the flour.

Now, setting a booby-trap for a respectable citizen like a headmaster (even of an inferior school to your own) is not a matter to be approached lightly and without careful preparation. I don't suppose I've ever selected a lunch with more thought than I did that day. And after a nicely-balanced meal, preceded by a couple of dry Martinis, washed down with half a bot, of a nice light, dry champagne, and followed by a spot of brandy, I could have set a booby-trap for a bishop.

The only really difficult part of the campaign was to get rid of the office-boy; for naturally you don't want witnesses when you're shoving bags of flour on doors. Fortunately, every man has his price, and it wasn't long before I contrived to persuade the lad that there was sickness at home and he was needed at Cricklewood. This done, I mounted a chair and got to work.

It was many, many years since I had tackled this kind of job, but the old skill came back as good as ever. Having got the bag so nicely poised that a touch on the door would do all that was necessary, I skipped down from my chair, popped off through Sippy's room, and went into the street. Sippy had not shown up yet, which was all to the good, but I knew he usually trickled in at about five to three. I hung about in the street, and presently round the corner came the bloke Waterbury. He went in at the front door, and I started off for a short stroll. It was no part of my policy to be in the offing when things began to happen.

It seemed to me that, allowing for wind and weather, the scales should have fallen from old Sippy's eyes by about three-fifteen, Greenwich mean time; so, having prowled around Covent Garden among the spuds and cabbages for twenty minutes or so, I retraced my steps and pushed up the stairs. I went in at the door marked Private, fully expecting to see old Sippy, and conceive of my astonishment and chagrin when I found on entering only the bloke Waterbury. He was seated at Sippy's desk, reading a paper, as if the place belonged to him.

And, moreover, there was of flour on his person not a trace.

'Great Scott!' I said.

It was a case of the sunken road, after all. But, dash it, how could I have been expected to take into consideration the possibility that this cove, headmaster though he was, would have had the cold nerve to walk into Sippy's private office instead of pushing in a normal and orderly manner through the public door?

He raised the nose, and focused me over it.

'Yes?'

'I was looking for old Sippy.'

'Mr Sipperley has not yet arrived.'

He spoke with a good deal of pique, seeming to be a man who was not used to being kept waiting.

'Well, how is everything?' I said, to ease things along.

He started reading again. He looked up as if he found me pretty superfluous.

'I beg your pardon?'

'Oh, nothing.'

'You spoke.'

'I only said "How is everything?" don't you know.'

'How is what?'

'Everything.'

'I fail to understand you.'

'Let it go,' I said.

I found a certain difficulty in boosting along the chit-chat. He was not a responsive cove.

'Nice day,' I said.

'Quite.'

'But they say the crops need rain.'

He had buried himself in his paper once more, and seemed peeved this time on being lugged to the surface.

'What?'

'The crops.'

'The crops?'

'Crops.'

'What crops?'

'Oh, just crops.'

He laid down his paper.

'You appear to be desirous of giving me some information about crops. What is it?'

'I hear they need rain.'

'Indeed?'

That concluded the small-talk. He went on reading, and I found a chair and sat down and sucked the handle of my stick. And so the long day wore on.

It may have been some two hours later, or it may have been about five minutes, when there became audible in the passage outside a strange wailing sound, as of some creature in pain. The bloke Waterbury looked up. I looked up.

The wailing came closer. It came into the room. It was Sippy, singing.

'– I love you. That's all I can say. I love you, I lo-o-ve you. The same old –'

He suspended the chant, not too soon for me.

'Oh, hullo!' he said.

I was amazed. The last time I had seen old Sippy, you must remember, he had had all the appearance of a man who didn't know it was loaded. Haggard. Drawn face. Circles under the eyes. All that sort of thing. And now, not much more than twenty-four hours later, he was simply radiant. His eyes sparkled. His mobile lips were curved in a happy smile. He looked as if he had been taking as much as will cover a sixpence every morning before breakfast for years.

'Hullo, Bertie!' he said. 'Hullo, Waterbury old man! Sorry I'm late.'

The bloke Waterbury seemed by no means pleased at this cordial form of address. He froze visibly.

'You are exceedingly late. I may mention that I have been waiting for upwards of half an hour, and my time is not without its value.'

'Sorry, sorry, sorry, sorry, sorry,' said Sippy, jovially. 'You wanted to see me about that article on the Elizabethan dramatists you left here yesterday, didn't you? Well, I've read it, and I'm sorry to say, Waterbury, my dear chap, that it's NG.'

'I beg your pardon?'

'No earthly use to us. Quite the wrong sort of stuff. This paper is supposed to be all light Society interest. What the *débutante* will wear for Goodwood, you know, and I saw Lady Betty Bootle in the Park yesterday – she is, of course, the sister-in-law of the Duchess of Peebles, "Cuckoo" to her intimates – all that kind of rot. My readers don't want stuff about Elizabethan dramatists.'

'Sipperley –!'

Old Sippy reached out and patted him in a paternal manner on the back.

'Now listen, Waterbury,' he said, kindly. 'You know as well as I do that I hate to turn down an old pal. But I have my duty to the paper. Still, don't be discouraged. Keep trying, and you'll do fine. There is a lot of promise in your stuff, but you want to study your market. Keep your eyes open and see what editors need. Now just as a suggestion, why not have a dash at a light, breezy article on pet dogs. You've probably noticed that the pug, once so fashionable, has been superseded by the Peke, the griffon, and the Sealyham. Work on that line and –'

The bloke Waterbury navigated towards the door.

'I have no desire to work on that line, as you put it,' he said, stiffly. 'If you do not require my paper on the Elizabethan dramatists I shall no doubt be able to find another editor whose tastes are more in accord with my work.'

'The right spirit absolutely, Waterbury,' said Sippy, cordially. 'Never give in. Perseverance brings home the gravy. If you get an article accepted, send another article to that editor. If you get an article refused, send that article to another editor. Carry on, Waterbury. I shall watch your future progress with considerable interest.'

'Thank you,' said the bloke Waterbury, bitterly. 'This expert advice should prove most useful.'

He biffed off, banging the door behind him, and I turned to Sippy, who was swerving about the room like an exuberant snipe.

'Sippy –'

'Eh? What? Can't stop, Bertie, can't stop. Only looked in to tell you the news. I'm taking Gwendolen to tea at the Carlton. I'm the happiest man in the world, Bertie. Engaged, you know. Betrothed. All washed up and signed on the dotted line. Wedding, June the first, at eleven am sharp, at St Peter's Eaton Square. Presents should be delivered before the end of May.'

'But, Sippy! Come to roost for a second. How did this happen? I thought –'

'Well, it's a long story. Much too long to tell you now. Ask Jeeves. He came along with me, and is waiting outside. But when I found her bending over me, weeping, I knew that a word from me was all that was needed. I took her little hand in mine and –'

'What do you mean, bending over you? Where?'

'In your sitting room.'

'Why?'

'Why what?'

'Why was she bending over you?'

'Because I was on the floor, ass. Naturally a girl would bend over a fellow who was on the floor. Goodbye, Bertie. I must rush.'

He was out of the room before I knew he had started. I followed at a high rate of speed, but he was down the stairs before I reached the passage. I legged it after him, but when I got into the street it was empty.

No, not absolutely empty. Jeeves was standing on the pavement, gazing dreamily at a brussels sprout which lay in the fairway.

'Mr Sipperley has this moment gone, sir,' he said, as I came charging out.

I halted and mopped the brow.

'Jeeves,' I said, 'what has been happening?'

'As far as Mr Sipperley's romance is concerned, sir, all, I am happy to report, is well. He and Miss Moon have arrived at a satisfactory settlement.'

'I know. They're engaged. But how did it happen?'

'I took the liberty of telephoning to Mr Sipperley in your name, asking him to come immediately to the flat, sir.'

'Oh, that's how he came to be at the flat? Well?'

'I then took the liberty of telephoning to Miss Moon and informing her that Mr Sipperley had met with a nasty accident. As I anticipated, the young lady was strongly moved and announced her intention of coming to see Mr Sipperley immediately. When she arrived, it required only a few moments to arrange the matter. It seems that Miss Moon has long loved Mr Sipperley, sir, and –'

'I should have thought that, when she turned up and found he hadn't had a nasty accident, she would have been thoroughly pipped at being fooled.'

'Mr Sipperley had had a nasty accident, sir.'

'He had?'

'Yes, sir.'

'Rummy coincidence. I mean, after what you were saying this morning.'

'Not altogether, sir. Before telephoning to Miss Moon, I took the further liberty of striking Mr Sipperley a sharp blow on the head with one of your golf-clubs, which was fortunately lying in a corner of the room. The putter, I believe, sir. If you will recollect, you were practising with it this morning before you left.'

I gaped at the blighter. I had always known Jeeves for a man of infinite sagacity, sound beyond belief on any question of ties or spats; but never before had I suspected him capable of strong-arm work like this. It seemed to open up an entirely new aspect of the fellow. I can't put it better than by saying that, as I gazed at him, the scales seemed to fall from my eyes.

'Good heavens, Jeeves!'

'I did it with the utmost regret, sir. It appeared to me the only course.'

'But look here, Jeeves. I don't get this. Wasn't Mr Sipperley pretty shirty when he came to and found that you had been socking him with putters?'

'He was not aware that I had done so, sir. I took the precaution of waiting until his back was momentarily turned.'

'But how did you explain the bump on his head?'

'I informed him that your new vase had fallen on him, sir.'

'Why on earth would he believe that? The vase would have been smashed.'

'The vase was smashed, sir.'

'What!'

'In order to achieve verisimilitude, I was reluctantly compelled to break it, sir. And in my excitement, sir, I am sorry to say I broke it beyond repair.'

I drew myself up.

'Jeeves!' I said.

'Pardon me, sir, but would it not be wiser to wear a hat? There is a keen wind.'

I blinked.

'Aren't I wearing a hat?'

'No, sir.'

I put up a hand and felt the lemon. He was perfectly right.

'Nor I am! I must have left it in Sippy's office. Wait here, Jeeves, while I fetch it.'

'Very good, sir.'

'I have much to say to you.'

'Thank you, sir.'

I galloped up the stairs and dashed in at the door. And something squashy fell on my neck, and the next minute the whole world was a solid mass of flour. In the agitation of the moment I had gone in at the wrong door; and what it all boils down to is that, if any more of my pals gets inferiority complexes, they can jolly well get rid of them for themselves. Bertram is through.

3

JEEVES AND THE YULE-TIDE SPIRIT

The letter arrived on the morning of the sixteenth. I was pushing a bit of breakfast into the Wooster face at the moment and, feeling fairly well-fortified with coffee and kippers, I decided to break the news to Jeeves without delay. As Shakespeare says, if you're going to do a thing you might just as well pop right at it and get it over. The man would be disappointed, of course, and possibly even chagrined: but, dash it all, a splash of disappointment here and there does a fellow good. Makes him realize that life is stern and life is earnest.

'Oh, Jeeves,' I said.

'Sir?'

'We have here a communication from Lady Wickham. She has written inviting me to Skeldings for the festives. So you will see about bunging the necessaries together. We repair thither on the twenty-third. Plenty of white ties, Jeeves, also a few hearty country suits for use in the daytime. We shall be there some little time, I expect.'

There was a pause. I could feel he was directing a frosty gaze at me, but I dug into the marmalade and refused to meet it.

'I thought I understood you to say, sir, that you proposed to visit Monte Carlo immediately after Christmas.'

'I know. But that's all off. Plans changed.'

'Very good, sir.'

At this point the telephone bell rang, tiding over very nicely what had threatened to be an awkward moment. Jeeves unhooked the receiver.

'Yes? . . . Yes, madam . . . Very good, madam. Here is Mr Wooster.' He handed me the instrument. 'Mrs Spenser Gregson, sir.'

You know, every now and then I can't help feeling that Jeeves is losing his grip. In his prime it would have been with him the work of a moment to have told Aunt Agatha that I was not at home. I gave him one of those reproachful glances, and took the machine.

'Hullo?' I said. 'Yes? Hullo? Hullo? Bertie speaking. Hullo? Hullo? Hullo?'

'Don't keep on saying Hullo,' yipped the old relative in her customary curt manner. 'You're not a parrot. Sometimes I wish you were, because then you might have a little sense.'

Quite the wrong sort of tone to adopt towards a fellow in the early morning, of course, but what can one do?

'Bertie, Lady Wickham tells me she has invited you to Skeldings for Christmas. Are you going?'

'Rather!'

'Well, mind you behave yourself. Lady Wickham is an old friend of mine.'

I was in no mood for this sort of thing over the telephone. Face to face, I'm not saying, but at the end of a wire, no.

'I shall naturally endeavour, Aunt Agatha,' I replied stiffly, 'to conduct myself in a manner befitting an English gentleman paying a visit –'

'What did you say? Speak up. I can't hear.'

'I said Right-ho.'

'Oh? Well, mind you do. And there's another reason why I particularly wish you to be as little of an imbecile as you can manage while at Skeldings. Sir Roderick Glossop will be there.'

'What!'

'Don't bellow like that. You nearly deafened me.'

'Did you say Sir Roderick Glossop?'

'I did.'

'You don't mean Tuppy Glossop?'

'I mean Sir Roderick Glossop. Which was my reason for saying Sir Roderick Glossop. Now, Bertie, I want you to listen to me attentively. Are you there?'

'Yes, still here.'

'Well, then, listen. I have at last succeeded, after incredible difficulty, and in face of all the evidence, in almost persuading Sir Roderick that you are not actually insane. He is prepared to suspend judgment until he has seen you once more. On your behaviour at Skeldings, therefore –'

But I had hung up the receiver. Shaken. That's what I was. S to the core.

Stop me if I've told you this before: but, in case you don't know, let me just mention the facts in the matter of this Glossop. He was a formidable old bird with a bald head and out-size eyebrows, by profession a loony-doctor. How it happened, I couldn't tell you to this day, but I once got engaged to his daughter, Honoria, a ghastly dynamic exhibit who read Nietzsche and had a laugh like waves breaking on a stern and rock-bound coast. The fixture was scratched owing to events occurring which convinced the old boy that I was off my napper; and since then he has always had my name at the top of his list of 'Loonies I have Lunched With'.

It seemed to me that even at Christmas time, with all the peace on earth and goodwill towards men that there is knocking about at that season, a reunion with this bloke was likely to be tough going. If I hadn't had more than one particularly good reason for wanting to go to Skeldings, I'd have called the thing off.

'Jeeves,' I said, all of a twitter, 'Do you know what? Sir Roderick Glossop is going to be at Lady Wickham's.'

'Very good, sir. If you have finished breakfast, I will clear away.'

Cold and haughty. No symp. None of the rallying-round spirit which one likes to see. As I had anticipated, the information that we were not going to Monte Carlo had got in amongst him. There is a keen sporting streak in Jeeves, and I knew he had been looking forward to a little flutter at the tables.

We Woosters can wear the mask. I ignored his lack of decent feeling.

'Do so, Jeeves,' I said proudly, 'and with all convenient speed.'

Relations continued pretty fairly strained all through the rest of the week. There was a frigid detachment in the way the man brought me my dollop of tea in the mornings. Going down to Skeldings in the car on the afternoon of the twenty-third, he was aloof and reserved. And before dinner on the first night of my visit he put the studs in my dress-shirt in what I can only call a marked manner. The whole thing was extremely painful, and it seemed to me, as I lay in bed on the morning of the twenty-fourth, that the only step to take was to put the whole facts of the case before him and trust to his native good sense to effect an understanding.

I was feeling considerably in the pink that morning. Everything had gone like a breeze. My hostess, Lady Wickham, was a beaky female built far too closely on the lines of my Aunt Agatha for comfort, but she had seemed matey enough on my arrival. Her daughter, Roberta, had welcomed me with a warmth which, I'm bound to say, had set the old heart-strings fluttering a bit. And Sir Roderick, in the brief moment we had had together, appeared to have let the Yule-Tide Spirit soak into him to the most amazing extent. When he saw me, his mouth sort of flickered at one corner, which I took to be his idea of smiling, and he said 'Ha, young man!' Not particularly chummily, but he said it: and my view was that it practically amounted to the lion lying down with the lamb.

So, all in all, life at this juncture seemed pretty well all to the mustard, and I decided to tell Jeeves exactly how matters stood.

'Jeeves,' I said, as he appeared with the steaming.

'Sir?'

'Touching on this business of our being here, I would like to say a few words of explanation. I consider that you have a right to the facts.'

'Sir?'

'I'm afraid scratching that Monte Carlo trip has been a bit of a jar for you, Jeeves.'

'Not at all, sir.'

'Oh, yes, it has. The heart was set on wintering in the world's good old Plague Spot, I know. I saw your eye light up when I said we were due for a visit there. You snorted a bit and your fingers twitched. I know, I know. And now that there has been a change of programme the iron has entered into your soul.'

'Not at all, sir.'

'Oh, yes, it has. I've seen it. Very well, then, what I wish to impress upon you, Jeeves, is that I have not been actuated in this matter by any mere idle whim. It was through no light and airy caprice that I accepted this invitation to Lady Wickham's. I have been angling for it for weeks, prompted by many considerations. In the first place, does one get the Yule-Tide Spirit at a spot like Monte Carlo?'

'Does one desire the Yule-Tide Spirit, sir?'

'Certainly one does. I am all for it. Well, that's one thing. Now here's another. It was imperative that I should come to Skeldings for Christmas, Jeeves, because I knew that young Tuppy Glossop was going to be here.'

'Sir Roderick Glossop, sir?'

'His nephew. You may have observed hanging about the place a fellow with light hair and a Cheshire-cat grin. That is Tuppy, and I have been anxious for some time to get to grips with him, I have it in for that man of wrath. Listen to the facts, Jeeves, and tell me if I am not justified in planning a hideous vengeance.' I took a sip of tea, for the mere memory of my wrongs had shaken me. 'In spite of the fact that young Tuppy is the nephew of Sir Roderick Glossop, at whose hands, Jeeves, as you are aware, I have suffered much, I fraternized with him freely, both at the Drones Club and elsewhere. I said to myself that a man is not to be blamed for his relations, and that I would hate to have my pals hold my Aunt Agatha, for instance, against me. Broad-minded, Jeeves, I think?'

'Extremely, sir.'

'Well, then, as I say, I sought this Tuppy out, Jeeves, and hob-nobbed, and what do you think he did?'

'I could not say, sir.'

'I will tell you. One night after dinner at the Drones he betted me I wouldn't swing myself across the swimming-bath by the ropes and rings. I took him on and was buzzing along in great style until I came to the last ring. And then I found that this fiend in human shape had looped it back against the rail, thus leaving me hanging in the void with no means of getting ashore to my home and loved ones. There was nothing for it but to drop into the water. He told me that he had often caught fellows that way: and what I maintain, Jeeves, is that, if I can't get back at him somehow at Skeldings – with all the vast resources which a country-house affords at my disposal – I am not the man I was.'

'I see, sir.'

There was still something in his manner which told me that even now he lacked complete sympathy and understanding, so, delicate though the subject was, I decided to put all my cards on the table.

'And now, Jeeves, we come to the most important reason why I had to spend Christmas at Skeldings. Jeeves,' I said, diving into the old cup once more for a moment and bringing myself out wreathed in blushes, 'the fact of the matter is, I'm in love.'

'Indeed, sir?'

'You've seen Miss Roberta Wickham?'

'Yes, sir.'

'Very well, then.'

There was a pause, while I let it sink in.

'During your stay here, Jeeves,' I said, 'you will, no doubt, be thrown a good deal together with Miss Wickham's maid. On such occasions, pitch it strong.'

'Sir?'

'You know what I mean. Tell her I'm rather a good chap. Mention my hidden depths. These things get round. Dwell on the fact that I have a kind heart and was runner-up in the Squash Handicap at the Drones this year. A boost is never wasted, Jeeves.'

'Very good, sir. But –'

'But what?'

'Well, sir –'

'I wish you wouldn't say "Well, sir" in that soupy tone of voice. I have had to speak of this before. The habit is one that is growing upon you. Check it. What's on your mind?'

'I hardly like to take the liberty –'

'Carry on, Jeeves. We are always glad to hear from you, always.'

'What I was about to remark, if you will excuse me, sir, was that I would scarcely have thought Miss Wickham a suitable –'

'Jeeves,' I said coldly, 'if you have anything to say against that lady, it had better not be said in my presence.'

'Very good, sir.'

'Or anywhere else, for that matter. What is your kick against Miss Wickham?'

'Oh, really, sir!'

'Jeeves, I insist. This is a time for plain speaking. You have beefed about Miss Wickham. I wish to know why.'

'It merely crossed my mind, sir, that for a gentleman of your description Miss Wickham is not a suitable mate.'

'What do you mean by a gentleman of my description?'

'Well, sir –'

'Jeeves!'

'I beg your pardon, sir. The expression escaped me inadvertently. I was about to observe that I can only asseverate –'

'Only what?'

'I can only say that, as you have invited my opinion –'

'But I didn't.'

'I was under the impression that you desired to canvass my views on the matter, sir.'

'Oh? Well, let's have them, anyway.'

'Very good, sir. Then briefly, if I may say so, sir, though Miss Wickham is a charming young lady –'

'There, Jeeves, you spoke an imperial quart. What eyes!'

'Yes, sir.'

'What hair!'

'Very true, sir.'

'And what *espièglerie*, if that's the word I want.'

'The exact word, sir.'

'All right, then. Carry on.'

'I grant Miss Wickham the possession of all these desirable qualities, sir. Nevertheless, considered as a matrimonial prospect for a gentleman of your description, I cannot look upon her as suitable. In my opinion Miss Wickham lacks seriousness, sir. She is too volatile and frivolous. To qualify as Miss Wickham's husband, a gentleman would need to possess a commanding personality and considerable strength of character.'

'Exactly!'

'I would always hesitate to recommend as a life's companion a young lady with quite such a vivid shade of red hair. Red hair, sir, in my opinion, is dangerous.'

I eyed the blighter squarely.

'Jeeves,' I said, 'you're talking rot.'

'Very good, sir.'

'Absolute drivel.'

'Very good, sir.'

'Pure mashed potatoes.'

'Very good, sir.'

'Very good, sir – I mean very good, Jeeves, that will be all,' I said.

And I drank a modicum of tea, with a good deal of hauteur.

It isn't often that I find myself able to prove Jeeves in the wrong, but by dinner-time that night I was in a position to do so, and I did it without delay.

'Touching on that matter we were touching on, Jeeves,' I said, coming in from the bath and tackling him as he studied the shirt, 'I should be glad if you would give me your careful attention for a moment. I warn you that what I am about to say is going to make you look pretty silly.'

'Indeed, sir?'

'Yes, Jeeves. Pretty dashed silly it's going to make you look. It may lead you to be rather more careful in future about broadcasting these estimates of yours of people's characters. This morning, if I remember rightly, you stated that Miss Wickham was volatile, frivolous and lacking in seriousness. Am I correct?'

'Quite correct, sir.'

'Then what I have to tell you may cause you to alter that opinion. I went for a walk with Miss Wickham this afternoon: and, as we walked, I told her about what young Tuppy Glossop did to me in the swimming-bath at the Drones. She hung upon my words, Jeeves, and was full of sympathy.'

'Indeed, sir?'

'Dripping with it. And that's not all. Almost before I had finished, she was suggesting the ripest, fruitiest, brainiest scheme for bringing young Tuppy's grey hairs in sorrow to the grave that anyone could possibly imagine.'

'That is very gratifying, sir.'

'Gratifying is the word. It appears that at the girls' school where Miss Wickham was educated, Jeeves, it used to become necessary from time to time for the right-thinking element of the community to slip it across certain of the baser sort. Do you know what they did, Jeeves?'

'No, sir.'

'They took a long stick, Jeeves, and – follow me closely here – they tied a darning-needle to the end of it. Then at dead of night, it appears, they sneaked privily into the party of the second part's cubicle and shoved the needle through the bed-clothes and punctured her hot-water bottle. Girls are much subtler in these matters than boys, Jeeves. At my old school one would occasionally heave a jug of water over another bloke during the night-watches, but we never thought of effecting the same result in this particularly neat and scientific manner. Well, Jeeves, that was the scheme which Miss Wickham suggested I should work on young Tuppy, and this is the girl you call frivolous and lacking in seriousness. Any girl who can think up a wheeze like that is my idea of a helpmeet. I shall be glad, Jeeves, if by the time I come to bed tonight you have for me in this room a stout stick with a good sharp darning needle attached.'

'Well, sir –'

I raised my hand.

'Jeeves,' I said. 'Not another word. Stick, one, and needle, darning, good, sharp, one, without fail in this room at eleven-thirty tonight.'

'Very good, sir.'

'Have you any idea where young Tuppy sleeps?'

'I could ascertain, sir.'

'Do so, Jeeves.'

In a few minutes he was back with the necessary informash.

'Mr Glossop is established in the Moat Room, sir.'

'Where's that?'

'The second door on the floor below this, sir.'

'Right ho, Jeeves. Are the studs in my shirt?'

'Yes, sir.'

'And the link also?'

'Yes, sir.'

'Then push me into it.'

The more I thought about this enterprise which a sense of duty and good citizenship had thrust upon me, the better it seemed to me. I am not a vindictive man, but I felt, as anybody would have felt in my place, that if fellows like young Tuppy are allowed to get away with it the whole fabric of Society and Civilization must inevitably crumble. The task to which I had set myself was one that involved hardship and discomfort, for it meant sitting up till well into the small hours and then padding down a cold corridor, but I did not shrink from it. After all, there is a lot to be said for family tradition. We Woosters did our bit in the Crusades.

It being Christmas Eve, there was, as I had foreseen, a good deal of revelry and what not. First, the village choir surged round and sang carols outside the front door, and then somebody suggested a dance, and after that we hung around chatting of this and that, so that it wasn't till past one that I got to my room. Allowing for everything, it didn't seem that it was going to be safe to start my little expedition till half-past two at the earliest: and I'm bound to say that it was only the utmost resolution that kept me from snuggling into the sheets and calling it a day. I'm not much of a lad now for late hours.

However, by half-past two everything appeared to be quiet. I shook off the mists of sleep, grabbed the good old stick-and-needle and off along the corridor. And presently, pausing outside the Moat Room, I turned the handle, found the door wasn't locked, and went in.

I suppose a burglar – I mean a real professional who works at the job six nights a week all the year round – gets so that finding himself standing in the dark in somebody else's bedroom means absolutely nothing to him. But for a bird like me, who has had no previous experience, there's a lot to be said in favour of washing the whole thing out and closing the door gently and popping back to bed again. It was only by summoning up all the old bulldog courage of the Woosters, and reminding myself that, if I let this opportunity slip another might never occur, that I managed to stick out what you might call the initial minute of the binge. Then the weakness passed, and Bertram was himself again.

At first when I beetled in, the room had seemed as black as a coal-cellar: but after a bit things began to lighten. The curtains weren't quite drawn over the window and I could see a trifle of the scenery here and there. The bed was opposite the window, with the head against the wall and the end where the feet were jutting out towards where I stood, thus rendering it possible after one had sown the seed, so to speak, to make a quick getaway. There only remained now the rather tricky problem of locating the old hot-water bottle. I mean to say, the one thing you can't do if you want to carry a job like this through with secrecy and dispatch is to stand at the end of a fellow's bed, jabbing the blankets at random with a darning-needle.

Before proceeding to anything in the nature of definite steps, it is imperative that you locate the bot.

I was a good deal cheered at this juncture to hear a fruity snore from the direction of the pillows. Reason told me that a bloke who could snore like that wasn't going to be awakened by a trifle. I edged forward and ran a hand in a gingerly sort of way over the coverlet. A moment later I had found the bulge. I steered the good old darning-needle on to it, gripped the stick, and shoved. Then, pulling out the weapon, I sidled towards the door, and in another moment would have been outside, buzzing for home and the good night's rest, when suddenly there was a crash that sent my spine shooting up through the top of my head and the contents of the bed sat up like a jack-in-the-box and said:

'Who's that?'

It just shows how your most careful strategic moves can be the very ones that dish your campaign. In order to facilitate the orderly retreat according to plan I had left the door open, and the beastly thing had slammed like a bomb.

But I wasn't giving much thought to the causes of the explosion, having other things to occupy my mind. What was disturbing me was the discovery that, whoever else the bloke in the bed might be, he was not young Tuppy. Tuppy has one of those high, squeaky voices that sound like the tenor of the village choir failing to hit a high note. This one was something in between the last Trump and a tiger calling for breakfast after being on a diet for a day or two. It was the sort of nasty, rasping voice you hear shouting 'Fore!' when you're one of a slow foursome on the links and are holding up a couple of retired colonels. Among the qualities it lacked were kindliness, suavity and that sort of dove-like cooing note which makes a fellow feel he has found a friend.

I did not linger. Getting swiftly off the mark, I dived for the door-handle and was off and away, banging the door behind me. I may be a chump in many ways, as my Aunt Agatha will freely attest, but I know when and when not to be among those present.

And I was just about to do the stretch of corridor leading to the stairs in a split second under the record time for the course, when something brought me up with a sudden jerk. One moment, I was all dash and fire and speed; the next, an irresistible force had checked me in my stride and was holding me straining at the leash, as it were.

You know, sometimes it seems to me as if Fate were going out of its way to such an extent to snooter you that you wonder if it's worth while continuing to struggle. The night being a trifle chillier than the dickens, I had donned for this expedition a dressing-gown. It was the tail of this infernal garment that had caught in the door and pipped me at the eleventh hour.

The next moment the door had opened, light was streaming through it, and the bloke with the voice had grabbed me by the arm.

It was Sir Roderick Glossop.

The next thing that happened was a bit of a lull in the proceedings. For about three and a quarter seconds or possibly more we just stood there, drinking each other in, so to speak, the old boy still attached with a limpet-like grip to my elbow. If I hadn't been in a dressing-gown and he in pink pyjamas with a blue stripe, and if he hadn't been glaring quite so much as if he were shortly going to commit a murder, the tableau would have looked rather like one of those advertisements you see in the magazines, where the experienced elder is patting the young man's arm, and saying to him, 'My boy, if you subscribe to the Mutt-Jeff Correspondence School of Oswego, Kan, as I did, you may some day, like me, become Third Assistant Vice-President of the Schenectady Consolidated Nail-File and Eyebrow Tweezer Corporation.'

'You!' said Sir Roderick finally. And in this connection I want to state that it's all rot to say you can't hiss a word that hasn't an 's' in it. The way he pushed out that 'You!' sounded like an angry cobra, and I am betraying no secrets when I mention that it did me no good whatsoever.

By rights, I suppose, at this point I ought to have said something. The best I could manage, however, was a faint, soft bleating sound. Even on ordinary social occasions, when meeting this bloke as man to man and with a clear conscience, I could never be completely at my ease: and now those eyebrows seemed to pierce me like a knife.

'Come in here,' he said, lugging me into the room. 'We don't want to wake the whole house. 'Now,' he said, depositing me on the carpet and closing the door and doing a bit of eyebrow work, 'kindly inform me what is this latest manifestation of insanity?'

It seemed to me that a light and cheery laugh might help the thing along. So I had a pop at one.

'Don't gibber!' said my genial host. And I'm bound to admit that the light and cheery hadn't come out quite as I'd intended.

I pulled myself together with a strong effort.

'Awfully sorry about all this,' I said in a hearty sort of voice. 'The fact is, I thought you were Tuppy.'

'Kindly refrain from inflicting your idiotic slang on me. What do you mean by the adjective "tuppy"?'

'It isn't so much an adjective, don't you know. More of a noun, I should think, if you examine it squarely. What I mean to say is, I thought you were your nephew.'

'You thought I was my nephew? Why should I be my nephew?'

'What I'm driving at is, I thought this was his room.'

'My nephew and I changed rooms. I have a great dislike for sleeping on an upper floor. I am nervous about fire.'

For the first time since this interview had started, I braced up a trifle. The injustice of the whole thing stirred me to such an extent that for a moment I lost that sense of being a toad under the harrow which had been cramping my style up till now. I even went so far as to eye this pink-pyjamed poltroon with a good deal of contempt and loathing. Just because he had this craven fear of fire and this selfish preference for letting Tuppy be cooked instead of himself should the emergency occur, my nice-reasoned plans had gone up the spout. I gave him a look, and I think I may even have snorted a bit.

'I should have thought that your man-servant would have informed you,' said Sir Roderick, 'that we contemplated making this change. I met him shortly before luncheon and told him to tell you.'

I reeled. Yes, it is not too much to say that I reeled. This extraordinary statement had taken me amidships without any preparation, and it staggered me. That Jeeves had been aware all along that this old crumb would be the occupant of the bed which I was proposing to prod with darning-needles and had let me rush upon my doom without a word of warning was almost beyond belief. You might say I was aghast. Yes, practically aghast.

'You told Jeeves that you were going to sleep in this room?' I gasped.

'I did. I was aware that you and my nephew were on terms of intimacy, and I wished to spare myself the possibility of a visit from you. I confess that it never occurred to me that such a visit was to be anticipated at three o'clock in the morning. What the devil do you mean,' he barked, suddenly hotting up, 'by prowling about the house at this hour? And what is that thing in your hand?'

I looked down, and found that I was still grasping the stick. I give you my honest word that, what with the maelstrom of emotions into which his revelation about Jeeves had cast me, the discovery came as an absolute surprise.

'This?' I said. 'Oh, yes.'

'What do you mean, Oh yes? What is it?'

'Well, it's a long story –'

'We have the night before us.'

'It's this way. I will ask you to picture me some weeks ago, perfectly peaceful and inoffensive, after dinner at the Drones, smoking a thoughtful cigarette and –'

I broke off. The man wasn't listening. He was goggling in a rapt sort of way at the end of the bed, from which there had now begun to drip onto the carpet a series of drops.

'Good heavens!'

'– thoughtful cigarette and chatting pleasantly of this and that –'

I broke off again. He had lifted the sheets and was gazing at the corpse of the hot-water bottle.

'Did you do this?' he said in a low, strangled sort of voice.

'Er – yes. As a matter of fact, yes. I was just going to tell you –'

'And your aunt tried to persuade me that you were not insane!'

'I'm not. Absolutely not. If you'll just let me explain.'

'I will do nothing of the kind.'

'It all began –'

'Silence!'

'Right-ho.'

He did some deep-breathing exercises through the nose.

'My bed is drenched!'

'The way it all began –'

'Be quiet!' He heaved somewhat for awhile. 'You wretched, miserable idiot,' he said, 'kindly inform me which bedroom you are supposed to be occupying?'

'It's on the floor above. The Clock Room.'

'Thank you. I will find it.'

'Eh?'

He gave me the eyebrow.

'I propose,' he said, 'to pass the remainder of the night in your room, where, I presume, there is a bed in a condition to be slept in. You may bestow yourself as comfortably as you can here. I will wish you good-night.'

He buzzed off, leaving me flat.

Well, we Woosters are old campaigners. We can take the rough with the smooth. But to say that I liked the prospect now before me would be paltering with the truth. One glance at the bed told me that any idea of sleeping there was out. A goldfish could have done it, but not Bertram. After a bit of a look round, I decided that the best chance of getting a sort of night's rest was to doss as well as I could in the arm-chair. I pinched a couple of pillows off the bed, shoved the hearth-rug over my knees, and sat down and started counting sheep.

But it wasn't any good. The old lemon was sizzling much too much to admit of anything in the nature of slumber. This hideous revelation of the blackness of Jeeves's treachery kept coming back to me every time I nearly succeeded in dropping off: and, what's more, it seemed to get colder and colder as the long night wore on. I was just wondering if I would ever get to sleep again in this world when a voice at my elbow said 'Good-morning, sir' and I sat up with a jerk.

I could have sworn I hadn't so much as dozed off for even a minute, but apparently I had. For the curtains were drawn back and daylight was coming in through the window and there was Jeeves standing beside me with a cup of tea on a tray.

'Merry Christmas, sir!'

I reached out a feeble hand for the restoring brew. I swallowed a mouthful or two, and felt a little better. I was aching in every limb and the dome felt like lead, but I was now able to think with a certain amount of clearness, and I fixed the man with a stony eye and prepared to let him have it.

'You think so, do you?' I said. 'Much, let me tell you, depends on what you mean by the adjective "merry". If, moreover, you suppose that it is going to be merry for you, correct that impression, Jeeves,' I said, taking another half-oz of tea and speaking in a cold, measured voice, 'I wish to ask you one question. Did you or did you not know that Sir Roderick Glossop was sleeping in this room last night?'

'Yes, sir.'

'You admit it!'

'Yes, sir.'

'And you didn't tell me!'

'No, sir. I thought it would be more judicious not to do so.'

'Jeeves —'

'If you will allow me to explain, sir.'

'Explain!'

'I was aware that my silence might lead to something in the nature of an embarrassing contretemps, sir —'

'You thought that, did you?'

'Yes, sir.'

'You were a good guesser,' I said, sucking down further Bohea.

'But it seemed to me, sir, that whatever might occur was all for the best.'

I would have put in a crisp word or two here, but he carried on without giving me the opp.

'I thought that possibly, on reflection, sir, your views being what they are, you would prefer your relations with Sir Roderick Glossop and his family to be distant rather than cordial.'

'My views? What do you mean, my views?'

'As regards a matrimonial alliance with Miss Honoria Glossop, sir.'

Something like an electric shock seemed to zip through me. The man had opened up a new line of thought. I suddenly saw what he was driving at, and realized all in a flash that I had been wronging this faithful fellow. All the while I supposed he had been landing me in the soup, he had really been steering me away from it. It was like those stories one used to read as a kid about the traveller going along on a dark night and his dog grabs him by the leg of his trousers and he says 'Down, sir! What are you doing, Rover?' and the dog hangs on and he gets rather hot under the collar and curses a bit but the dog won't let him go and then suddenly the moon shines through the clouds and he finds he's been standing on the edge of a precipice and one more step would have – well, anyway, you get the idea: and what I'm driving at is that much the same sort of thing seemed to have been happening now.

It's perfectly amazing how a fellow will let himself get off his guard and ignore the perils which surround him. I give you my honest word, it had never struck me till this moment that my Aunt Agatha had been scheming to get me in right with Sir Roderick so that I should eventually be received back into the fold, if you see what I mean, and subsequently pushed off on Honoria.

'My God, Jeeves!' I said, paling.

'Precisely, sir.'

'You think there was a risk?'

'I do, sir. A very grave risk.'

A disturbing thought struck me.

'But, Jeeves, on calm reflection won't Sir Roderick have gathered by now that my objective was young Tuppy and that puncturing his hot-water bottle was just one of those things that occur when the Yule-Tide Spirit is abroad – one of those things that have to be overlooked and taken with the indulgent smile and the fatherly shake of the head? I mean to say, Young Blood and all that sort of thing? What I mean is he'll realize that I wasn't trying to snooter him, and then all the good work will have been wasted.'

'No, sir. I fancy not. That might possibly have been Sir Roderick's mental reaction, had it not been for the second incident.'

'The second incident?'

'During the night, sir, while Sir Roderick was occupying your bed, somebody entered the room, pierced his hot-water bottle with some sharp instrument, and vanished in the darkness.'

I could make nothing of this.

'What! Do you think I walked in my sleep?'

'No, sir. It was young Mr Glossop who did it. I encountered him this morning, sir, shortly before I came here. He was in cheerful spirits and enquired of me how you were feeling about the incident. Not being aware that his victim had been Sir Roderick.'

'But, Jeeves, what an amazing coincidence!'

'Sir?'

'Why, young Tuppy getting exactly the same idea as I did. Or, rather, as Miss Wickham did. You can't say that's not rummy. A miracle, I call it.'

'Not altogether, sir. It appears that he received the suggestion from the young lady.'

'From Miss Wickham?'

'Yes, sir.'

'You mean to say that, after she had put me up to the scheme of puncturing Tuppy's hot-water bottle, she went away and tipped Tuppy off to puncturing mine?'

'Precisely, sir. She is a young lady with a keen sense of humour, sir.'

I sat there, you might say stunned. When I thought how near I had come to offering the heart and hand to a girl capable of double-crossing a strong man's honest love like that, I shivered.

'Are you cold, sir?'

'No, Jeeves. Just shuddering.'

'The occurrence, if I may take the liberty of saying so, sir, will perhaps lend colour to the view which I put forward yesterday that Miss Wickham, though in many respects a charming young lady –'

I raised a hand.

'Say no more, Jeeves,' I replied. 'Love is dead.'

'Very good, sir.'

I brooded for a while.

'You've seen Sir Roderick this morning, then?'

'Yes, sir.'

'How did he seem?'

'A trifle feverish, sir.'

'Feverish?'

'A little emotional, sir. He expressed a strong desire to meet you, sir.'

'What would you advise?'

'If you were to slip out by the back entrance as soon as you are dressed, sir, it would be possible for you to make your way across the field without being observed and reach the village, where you could hire an automobile to take you to London. I could bring on your effects later in your own car.'

'But London, Jeeves? Is any man safe? My Aunt Agatha is in London.'

'Yes, sir.'

'Well, then?'

He regarded me for a moment with a fathomless eye.

'I think the best plan, sir, would be for you to leave England, which is not pleasant at this time of the year, for some little while. I would not take the liberty of dictating your movements, sir, but as you already have accommodation engaged on the Blue Train for Monte Carlo for the day after tomorrow –'

'But you cancelled the booking?'

'No, sir.'

'I thought you had.'

'No, sir.'

'I told you to.'

'Yes, sir. It was remiss of me, but the matter slipped my mind.'

'Oh?'

'Yes, sir.'

'All right, Jeeves. Monte Carlo ho, then.'

'Very good, sir.'

'It's lucky, as things have turned out, that you forgot to cancel that booking.'

'Very fortunate indeed, sir. If you will wait here, sir, I will return to your room and procure a suit of clothes.'

4

JEEVES AND THE SONG OF SONGS

Another day had dawned all hot and fresh and, in pursuance of my unswerving policy at that time, I was singing 'Sonny Boy' in my bath, when there was a soft step without and Jeeves's voice came filtering through the woodwork.

'I beg your pardon, sir.'

I had just got to that bit about the Angels being lonely, where you need every ounce of concentration in order to make the spectacular finish, but I signed off courteously.

'Yes, Jeeves? Say on.'

'Mr Glossop, sir.'

'What about him?'

'He is in the sitting room, sir.'

'Young Tuppy Glossop?'

'Yes, sir.'

'In the sitting room?'

'Yes, sir.'

'Desiring speech with me?'

'Yes, sir.'

'H'm!'

'Sir?'

'I only said H'm.'

And I'll tell you why I said H'm. It was because the man's story had interested me strangely. The news that Tuppy was visiting me at my flat, at an hour when he must have known that I would be in my bath and consequently in a strong strategic position to heave a wet sponge at him, surprised me considerably.

I hopped out with some briskness and, slipping a couple of towels about the limbs and torso, made for the sitting room. I found young Tuppy at the piano, playing 'Sonny Boy' with one finger.

'What ho!' I said, not without a certain hauteur.

'Oh, hullo, Bertie,' said young Tuppy. 'I say, Bertie, I want to see you about something important.'

It seemed to me that the bloke was embarrassed. He had moved to the mantelpiece, and now he broke a vase in rather a constrained way.

'The fact is, Bertie, I'm engaged.'

'Engaged?'

'Engaged,' said young Tuppy, coyly dropping a photograph frame into the fender. 'Practically, that is.'

'Practically?'

'Yes. You'll like her, Bertie. Her name is Cora Bellinger. She's studying for Opera. Wonderful voice she has. Also dark, flashing eyes and a great soul.'

'How do you mean, practically?'

'Well, it's this way. Before ordering the trousseau, there is one little point she wants cleared up. You see, what with her great soul and all that, she has a rather serious outlook on life: and the one thing she absolutely bars is anything in the shape of hearty humour. You know, practical joking and so forth. She said if she thought I was a practical joker she would never speak to me again. And unfortunately she appears to have heard about that little affair at the Drones – I expect you have forgotten all about that, Bertie?'

'I have not!'

'No, no, not forgotten exactly. What I mean is, nobody laughs more heartily at the recollection than you. And what I want you to do, old man, is to seize an early opportunity of taking Cora aside and categorically denying that there is any truth in the story. My happiness, Bertie, is in your hands, if you know what I mean.'

Well, of course, if he put it like that, what could I do? We Woosters have our code.

'Oh, all right,' I said, but far from brightly.

'Splendid fellow!'

'When do I meet this blighted female?'

'Don't call her "this blighted female", Bertie, old man. I have planned all that out. I will bring her round here today for a spot of lunch.'

'What!'

'At one-thirty. Right. Good. Fine. Thanks. I knew I could rely on you.'

He pushed off, and I turned to Jeeves, who had shimmered in with the morning meal.

'Lunch for three today, Jeeves,' I said.

'Very good, sir.'

'You know, Jeeves, it's a bit thick. You remember my telling you about what Mr Glossop did to me that night at the Drones?'

'Yes, sir.'

'For months I have been cherishing dreams of getting a bit of my own back. And now, so far from crushing him into the dust, I've got to fill him and fiancée with rich food and generally rally round and be the good angel.'

'Life is like that, sir.'

'True, Jeeves. What have we here?' I asked, inspecting the tray.

'Kippered herrings, sir.'

'And I shouldn't wonder,' I said, for I was in thoughtful mood, 'if even herrings haven't troubles of their own.'

'Quite possibly, sir.'

'I mean, apart from getting kippered.'

'Yes, sir.'

'And so it goes on, Jeeves, so it goes on.'

I can't say I exactly saw eye to eye with young Tuppy in his admiration for the Bellinger female. Delivered on the mat at one-twenty-five, she proved to be an upstanding light-heavyweight of some thirty summers, with a commanding eye and a square chin which I, personally, would have steered clear of. She seemed to me a good deal like what Cleopatra would have been after going in too freely for the starches and cereals. I don't know why it is, but women who have anything to do with Opera, even if they're only studying for it, always appear to run to surplus poundage.

Tuppy, however, was obviously all for her. His whole demeanour, both before and during lunch, was that of one striving to be worthy of a noble soul. When Jeeves offered him a cocktail, he practically recoiled as from a serpent. It was terrible to see the change which love had effected in the man. The spectacle put me off my food.

At half-past two, the Bellinger left to go to a singing lesson. Tuppy trotted after her to the door, bleating and frisking a goodish bit, and then came back and looked at me in a goofy sort of way.

'Well, Bertie?'

'Well, what?'

'I mean, isn't she?'

'Oh, rather,' I said, humouring the poor fish.

'Wonderful eyes?'

'Oh, rather.'

'Wonderful figure?'

'Oh, quite.'

'Wonderful voice?'

Here I was able to intone the response with a little more heartiness. The Bellinger, at Tuppy's request, had sung us a few songs before digging in at the trough, and nobody could have denied that her pipes were in great shape. Plaster was still falling from the ceiling.

'Terrific,' I said.

Tuppy sighed, and, having helped himself to about four inches of whisky and one of soda, took a deep, refreshing draught.

'Ah!' he said. 'I needed that.'

'Why didn't you have it at lunch?'

'Well, it's this way,' said Tuppy. 'I have not actually ascertained what Cora's opinions are on the subject of taking of slight snorts from time to time, but I thought it more prudent to lay off. The view I took was that laying off would seem to indicate the serious mind. It is touch-and-go, as you might say, at the moment, and the smallest thing may turn the scale.'

'What beats me is how on earth you expect to make her think you've got a mind at all – let alone a serious one.'

'I have my methods.'

'I bet they're rotten.'

'You do, do you?' said Tuppy warmly. 'Well, let me tell you, my lad, that that's exactly what they're anything but. I am handling this affair with consummate generalship. Do you remember Beefy Bingham who was at Oxford with us?'

'I ran into him only the other day. He's a parson now.'

'Yes. Down in the East End. Well, he runs a Lads' Club for the local toughs – you know the sort of thing – cocoa and backgammon in the reading room and occasional clean, bright entertainments in the Oddfellows' Hall: and I've been helping him. I don't suppose I've passed an evening away from the backgammon board for weeks. Cora is extremely pleased. I've got her to promise to sing on Tuesday at Beefy's next clean, bright entertainment.'

'You have?'

'I absolutely have. And now mark my devilish ingenuity, Bertie. I'm going to sing, too.'

'Why do you suppose that's going to get you anywhere?'

'Because the way I intend to sing the song I intend to sing will prove to her that there are great deeps in my nature, whose existence she has not suspected. She will see that rough, unlettered audience wiping the tears out of its bally eyes and she will say to herself 'What ho! The old egg really has a soul!' For it is not one of your mouldy comic songs, Bertie. No low buffoonery of that sort for me. It is all about Angela being lonely and what not –'

I uttered a sharp cry.

'You don't mean you're going to sing "Sonny Boy"?'

'I jolly well do.'

I was shocked. Yes, dash it, I was shocked. You see, I held strong views on 'Sonny Boy'. I considered it a song only to be attempted by a few of the elect in the privacy of the bathroom. And the thought of it being murdered in open Oddfellows Hall by a man who could treat a pal as young Tuppy had treated me that night at the Drones sickened me. Yes, sickened me.

I hadn't time, however, to express my horror and disgust, for at this juncture Jeeves came in.

'Mrs Travers has just rung up on the telephone, sir. She desired me to say that she will be calling to see you in a few minutes.'

'Contents noted, Jeeves,' I said. 'Now listen, Tuppy –'

I stopped. The fellow wasn't there.

'What have you done with him, Jeeves?' I asked.

'Mr Glossop has left, sir.'

'Left? How can he have left? He was sitting there –'

'That is the front door closing now, sir.'

'But what made him shoot off like that?'

'Possibly Mr Glossop did not wish to meet Mrs Travers, sir.'

'Why not?'

'I could not say, sir. But undoubtedly at the mention of Mrs Travers' name he rose very swiftly.'

'Strange, Jeeves.'

'Yes, sir.'

I turned to a subject of more moment.

'Jeeves,' I said. 'Mr Glossop proposes to sing "Sonny Boy" at an entertainment down in the East End next Tuesday.'

'Indeed, sir?'

'Before an audience consisting mainly of costermongers, with a sprinkling of whelk-stall owners, purveyors of blood-oranges, and minor pugilists.'

'Indeed, sir?'

'Make a note to remind me to be there. He will infallibly get the bird, and I want to witness his downfall.'

'Very good, sir.'

'And when Mrs Travers arrives, I shall be in the sitting room.'

Those who know Bertram Wooster best are aware that in his journey through life he is impeded and generally snootered by about as scaly a platoon of aunts as was ever assembled. But there is one exception to the general ghastliness – viz., my Aunt Dahlia. She married old Tom Travers the year Blue-bottle won the Cambridgeshire, and is one of the best. It is always a pleasure to me to chat with her, and it was with a courtly geniality that I rose to receive her as she sailed over the threshold at about two fifty-five.

She seemed somewhat perturbed, and snapped into the agenda without delay. Aunt Dahlia is one of those big, hearty women. She used to go in a lot for hunting, and she generally speaks as if she had just sighted a fox on a hillside half a mile away.

'Bertie,' she cried, in a manner of one encouraging a bevy of hounds to renewed efforts. 'I want your help.'

'And you shall have it, Aunt Dahlia,' I replied suavely. 'I can honestly say that there is no one to whom I would more readily do a good turn than yourself; no one to whom I am more delighted to be –'

'Less of it,' she begged, 'less of it. You know that friend of yours, young Glossop?'

'He's just been lunching here.'

'He has, has he? Well, I wish you'd poisoned his soup.'

'We didn't have soup. And, when you describe him as a friend of mine, I wouldn't quite say the term absolutely squared with the facts. Some time ago, one night when we had been dining together at the Drones –'

At this point Aunt Dahlia – a little brusquely, it seemed to me – said that she would rather wait for the story of my life till she could get it in book-form. I could see now that she was definitely not her usual sunny self, so I shelved my personal grievances and asked what was biting her.

'It's that young hound Glossop,' she said.

'What's he been doing?'

'Breaking Angela's heart.' (Angela. Daughter of above. My cousin. Quite a good egg.)

'Breaking Angela's heart?'

'Yes . . . Breaking . . . Angela's HEART!'

'You say he's breaking Angela's heart?'

She begged me in rather a feverish way to suspend the vaudeville cross-talk stuff.

'How's he doing that?' I asked.

'With his neglect. With his low, callous, double-crossing duplicity.'

'Duplicity is the word, Aunt Dahlia,' I said. 'In treating of young

Tuppy Glossop, it springs naturally to the lips. Let me just tell you what he did to me one night at the Drones. We had finished dinner –'

'Ever since the beginning of the season, up till about three weeks ago, he was all over Angela. The sort of thing which, when I was a girl, we should have described as courting –'

'Or wooing?'

'Wooing or courting, whichever you like.'

'Whichever *you* like, Aunt Dahlia,' I said courteously.

'Well, anyway, he haunted the house, lapped up daily lunches, danced with her half the night, and so on, till naturally the poor kid, who's quite off her oats about him, took it for granted that it was only a question of time before he suggested that they should feed for life out of the same crib. And now he's gone and dropped her like a hot brick, and I hear he's infatuated with some girl he met at a Chelsea tea-party – a girl named – now, what was it?'

'Cora Bellinger.'

'How do you know?'

'She was lunching here today.'

'He brought her?'

'Yes.'

'What's she like?'

'Pretty massive. In shape, a bit on the lines of the Albert Hall.'

'Did he seem very fond of her?'

'Couldn't take his eyes off the chassis.'

'The modern young man,' said Aunt Dahlia, 'is a congenital idiot and wants a nurse to lead him by the hand and some strong attendant to kick him regularly at intervals of a quarter of an hour.'

I tried to point out the silver lining.

'If you ask me, Aunt Dahlia,' I said, 'I think Angela is well out of it. This Glossop is a tough baby. One of London's toughest. I was trying to tell you just now what he did to me one night at the Drones. First having got me in a sporting mood with a bottle of the ripest, he betted I wouldn't swing myself across the swimming-bath by the ropes and rings. I knew I could do it on my head, so I took him on, exulting in the fun, so to speak. And when I'd done half the trip and was going as strong as dammit, I found he had looped the last rope back against the rail, leaving me no alternative but to drop into the depths and swim ashore in correct evening costume.'

'He did?'

'He certainly did. It was months ago, and I haven't got really dry yet. You wouldn't want your daughter to marry a man capable of a thing like that?'

'On the contrary, you restore my faith in the young hound. I see that there must be lots of good in him, after all. And I want this Bellinger business broken up, Bertie.'

'How?'

'I don't care how. Any way you please.'

'But what can I do?'

'Do? Why, put the whole thing before your man Jeeves. Jeeves will find a way. One of the most capable fellers I ever met. Put the thing squarely up to Jeeves and tell him to let his mind play round the topic.'

'There may be something in what you say, Aunt Dahlia,' I said thoughtfully.

'Of course there is,' said Aunt Dahlia. 'A little thing like this will be child's play to Jeeves. Get him working on it, and I'll look in tomorrow to hear the result.'

With which, she biffed off, and I summoned Jeeves to the presence.

'Jeeves,' I said, 'you have heard all?'

'Yes, sir.'

'I thought you would. My Aunt Dahlia has what you might call a carrying voice. Has it ever occurred to you that, if all other sources of income failed, she could make a good living calling the cattle home across the Sands of Dee?'

'I had not considered the point, sir, but no doubt you are right.'

'Well, how do we go? What is your reaction? I think we should do our best to help and assist.'

'Yes, sir.'

'I am fond of my Aunt Dahlia and I am fond of my cousin Angela. Fond of them both, if you get my drift. What the misguided girl finds to attract her in young Tuppy, I cannot say, Jeeves, and you cannot say. But apparently she loves the man – which shows it can be done, a thing I wouldn't have believed myself – and is pining away like –'

'Patience on a monument, sir.'

'Like Patience, as you very shrewdly remark, on a monument. So we must cluster round. Bend your brain to the problem, Jeeves. It is one that will tax you to the uttermost.'

Aunt Dahlia blew in on the morrow, and I rang the bell for Jeeves. He appeared looking brainier than one could have believed possible

– sheer intellect shining from every feature – and I could see at once that the engine had been turning over.

'Speak, Jeeves,' I said.

'Very good, sir.'

'You have brooded?'

'Yes, sir.'

'With what success?'

'I have a plan, sir, which I fancy may produce satisfactory results.'

'Let's have it,' said Aunt Dahlia.

'In affairs of this description, madam, the first essential is to study the psychology of the individual.'

'The what of the individual?'

'The psychology, madam.'

'He means the psychology,' I said. 'And by psychology, Jeeves, you imply –?'

'The natures and dispositions of the principals in the matter, sir.'

'You mean, what they're like?'

'Precisely, sir.'

'Does he talk like this to you when you're alone, Bertie?' asked Aunt Dahlia.

'Sometimes. Occasionally. And, on the other hand, sometimes not. Proceed, Jeeves.'

'Well, sir, if I may say so, the thing that struck me most forcibly about Miss Bellinger when she was under my observation was that hers was a somewhat hard and intolerant nature. I could envisage Miss Bellinger applauding success. I could not so easily see her pitying and sympathizing with failure. Possibly you will recall, sir, her attitude when Mr Glossop endeavoured to light her cigarette with his automatic lighter? I thought I detected a certain impatience at his inability to produce the necessary flame.'

'True, Jeeves. She ticked him off.'

'Precisely, sir.'

'Let me get this straight,' said Aunt Dahlia, looking a bit fogged. 'You think that, if he goes on trying to light her cigarettes with his automatic lighter long enough, she will eventually get fed up and hand him the mitten? Is that the idea?'

'I merely mentioned the episode, madam, as an indication of Miss Bellinger's somewhat ruthless nature.'

'Ruthless,' I said, 'is right. The Bellinger is hard-boiled. Those eyes. That chin. I could read them. A woman of blood and iron, if ever there was one.'

'Precisely, sir. I think, therefore, that, should Miss Bellinger be a witness of Mr Glossop appearing to disadvantage in public, she would cease to entertain affection for him. In the event, for instance, of his failing to please the audience on Tuesday with his singing –'

I saw daylight.

'By Jove, Jeeves! You mean if he gets the bird, all will be off?'

'I shall be greatly surprised if such is not the case, sir.'

I shook my head.

'We cannot leave this thing to chance, Jeeves. Young Tuppy, singing "Sonny Boy", is the likeliest prospect for the bird that I can think of – but, no – you must see for yourself that we can't simply trust to luck.'

'We need not trust to luck, sir. I would suggest that you approach your friend, Mr Bingham, and volunteer your services as a performer at his forthcoming entertainment. It could readily be arranged that you sang immediately before Mr Glossop. I fancy, sir, that, if Mr Glossop were to sing "Sonny Boy" directly after you, too, had sung "Sonny Boy", the audience would respond satisfactorily. By the time Mr Glossop began to sing, they would have lost their taste for that particular song and would express their feelings warmly.'

'Jeeves,' said Aunt Dahlia, 'you're a marvel!'

'Thank you, madam.'

'Jeeves,' I said, 'you're an ass!'

'What do you mean, he's an ass?' said Aunt Dahlia hotly. 'I think it's the greatest scheme I ever heard.'

'Me sing "Sonny Boy" at Beefy Bingham's clean, bright entertainment? I can see myself!'

'You sing it daily in your bath, sir. Mr Wooster,' said Jeeves, turning to Aunt Dahlia, 'has a pleasant, light baritone –'

'I bet he has,' said Aunt Dahlia.

I froze the man with a look.

'Between singing "Sonny Boy" in one's bath, Jeeves, and singing it before a hall full of assorted blood-orange merchants and their young, there is a substantial difference.'

'Bertie,' said Aunt Dahlia, 'you'll sing, and like it!'

'I will not.'

'Bertie!'

'Nothing will induce –'

'Bertie,' said Aunt Dahlia firmly, 'you will sing "Sonny Boy" on Tuesday, the third *prox*, and sing it like a lark at sunrise, or may an aunt's curse –'

'I won't.'

'Think of Angela!'

'Dash Angela!'

'Bertie!'

'No, I mean, hang it all!'

'You won't?'

'No, I won't.'

'That is your last word, is it?'

'It is. Once and for all, Aunt Dahlia, nothing will induce me to let out so much as a single note.'

And so that afternoon I sent a pre-paid wire to Beefy Bingham, offering my services in the cause, and by nightfall the thing was fixed up. I was billed to perform next but one after the intermission. Following me, came Tuppy. And, immediately after him, Miss Cora Bellinger, the well-known operatic soprano.

'Jeeves,' I said that evening – and I said it coldly – 'I shall be obliged if you will pop round to the nearest music-shop and procure me a copy of "Sonny Boy". It will now be necessary for me to learn both verse and refrain. Of the trouble and nervous strain which this will involve, I say nothing.'

'Very good, sir.'

'But this I do say –'

'I had better be starting immediately, sir, or the shop will be closed.'

'Ha!' I said.

And I meant it to sting.

Although I had steeled myself to the ordeal before me and had set out full of the calm, quiet courage which makes men do desperate deeds with careless smiles, I must admit that there was a moment, just after I had entered the Oddfellows' Hall at Bermondsey East and run an eye over the assembled pleasure-seekers, when it needed all the bulldog pluck of the Woosters to keep me from calling it a day and taking a cab back to civilization. The clean, bright entertainment was in full swing when I arrived, and somebody who looked as if he might be the local undertaker was reciting 'Gunga Din'. And the audience, though not actually chi-yiking in the full technical sense of the term, had a grim look which I didn't like at all. The mere sight of them gave me the sort of feeling Shadrach, Meshach and Abednego must have had when preparing to enter the burning, fiery furnace.

Scanning the multitude, it seemed to me that they were for the nonce suspending judgment. Did you ever tap on the door of one of those New York speakeasy places and see the grille snap back and a Face appear? There is one long, silent moment when its eyes are fixed on yours and all your past life seems to rise up before you. Then you say that you are a friend of Mr Zinzinheimer and he told you they would treat you right if you mentioned his name, and the strain relaxes. Well, these costermongers and whelkstallers appeared to me to be looking just like that Face. Start something, they seemed to say, and they would know what to do about it. And I couldn't help feeling that my singing 'Sonny Boy' would come, in their opinion, under the head of starting something.

'A nice, full house, sir,' said a voice at my elbow. It was Jeeves, watching the proceedings with an indulgent eye.

'You here, Jeeves?' I said, coldly.

'Yes, sir. I have been present since the commencement.'

'Oh?' I said. 'Any casualties yet?'

'Sir?'

'You know what I mean, Jeeves,' I said sternly, 'and don't pretend you don't. Anybody got the bird yet?'

'Oh, no, sir.'

'I shall be the first, you think?'

'No, sir. I see no reason to expect such a misfortune. I anticipate that you will be well received.'

A sudden thought struck me.

'And you think everything will go according to plan?'

'Yes, sir.'

'Well, I don't,' I said. 'And I'll tell you why I don't. I've spotted a flaw in your beastly scheme.'

'A flaw, sir?'

'Yes. Do you suppose for a moment that, if when Mr Glossop hears me singing that dashed song, he'll come calmly on a minute after me and sing it too? Use your intelligence, Jeeves. He will perceive the chasm in his path and pause in time. He will back out and refuse to go on at all.'

'Mr Glossop will not hear you sing, sir. At my advice, he has stepped across the road to the Jug and Bottle, an establishment immediately opposite the hall, and he intends to remain there until it is time for him to appear on the platform.'

'Oh?' I said.

'If I might suggest it, sir, there is another house named the Goat and Grapes only a short distance down the street. I think it might be a judicious move –'

'If I were to put a bit of custom in their way?'

'It would ease the nervous strain of waiting, sir.'

I had not been feeling any too pleased with the man for having let me in for this ghastly binge, but at these words, I'm bound to say, my austerity softened a trifle. He was undoubtedly right. He had studied the psychology of the individual, and it had not led him astray. A quiet ten minutes at the Goat and Grapes was exactly what my system required. To buzz off there and inhale a couple of swift whisky-and-sodas was with Bertram Wooster the work of a moment.

The treatment worked like magic. What they had put into the stuff, besides vitriol, I could not have said; but it completely altered my outlook on life. That curious, gulpy feeling passed. I was no longer conscious of the sagging sensation at the knees. The limbs ceased to quiver gently, the tongue became loosened in its socket, and the backbone stiffened. Pausing merely to order and swallow another of the same, I bade the barmaid a cheery good night, nodded affably to one or two fellows in the bar whose faces I liked, and came prancing back to the hall, ready for anything.

And shortly afterwards I was on the platform with about a million bulging eyes goggling up at me. There was a rummy sort of buzzing in my ears, and then through the buzzing I heard the sound of a piano starting to tinkle: and, commending my soul to God, I took a good, long breath and charged in.

Well, it was a close thing. The whole incident is a bit blurred, but I seem to recollect a kind of murmur as I hit the refrain. I thought at the time it was an attempt on the part of the many-headed to join in the chorus, and at the moment it rather encouraged me. I passed the thing over the larynx with all the vim at my disposal, hit the high note, and off gracefully into the wings. I didn't come on again to take a bow. I just receded and oiled round to where Jeeves awaited me among the standees at the back.

'Well, Jeeves,' I said, anchoring myself at his side and brushing the honest sweat from the brow, 'they didn't rush the platform.'

'No, sir.'

'But you can spread it about that that's the last time I perform outside my bath. My swan-song, Jeeves. Anybody who wants to hear me in future must present himself at the bathroom door and shove his ear against the keyhole. I may be wrong, but it seemed to me that towards the end they were hotting up a trifle. The bird was hovering in the air. I could hear the beating of its wings.'

'I did detect a certain restlessness, sir, in the audience. I fancy they has lost their taste for that particular melody.'

'Eh?'

'I should have informed you earlier, sir, that the song had already been sung twice before you arrived.'

'What!'

'Yes, sir. Once by a lady and once by a gentleman. It is a very popular song, sir.'

I gaped at the man. That, with this knowledge, he could calmly have allowed the young master to step straight into the jaws of death, so to speak, paralysed me. It seemed to show that the old feudal spirit had passed away altogether. I was about to give him my views on the matter in no uncertain fashion, when I was stopped by the spectacle of young Tuppy lurching on to the platform.

Young Tuppy had the unmistakable air of a man who has recently been round to the Jug and Bottle. A few cheery cries of welcome, presumably from some of his backgammon-playing pals who felt that blood was thicker than water, had the effect of causing the genial smile on his face to widen till it nearly met at the back. He was plainly feeling about as good as a man can feel and still remain on his feet. He waved a kindly hand to his supporters, and bowed in a regal sort of manner, rather like an Eastern monarch acknowledging the plaudits of the mob.

Then the female at the piano struck up the opening bars of 'Sonny Boy', and Tuppy swelled like a balloon, clasped his hands together, rolled his eyes up at the ceiling in a manner denoting Soul, and began. I think the populace was too stunned for the moment to take immediate steps. It may seem incredible, but I give you my word that young Tuppy got right through the verse without so much as a murmur. Then they all seemed to pull themselves together.

A costermonger, roused, is a terrible thing. I had never seen the proletariat really stirred before, and I'm bound to say it rather awed me. I mean, it gave you some idea of what it must have been like during the French Revolution. From every corner of the hall there proceeded simultaneously the sort of noise which you hear, they tell me, at one of those East End boxing places when the referee disqualifies the popular favourite and makes the quick dash for life. And then they passed beyond mere words and began to introduce the vegetable motive.

I don't know why, but somehow I had got it into my head that the first thing thrown at Tuppy would be a potato. One gets these fancies. It was, however, as a matter of fact, a banana, and I saw in an instant that the choice had been made by wiser heads than mine. These blokes who have grown up from childhood in the knowledge of how to treat a dramatic entertainment that doesn't please them are aware by a sort of instinct just what to do for the best, and the moment I saw the banana splash on Tuppy's shirt-front I realized how infinitely more effective and artistic it was than any potato could have been.

Not that the potato school of thought had not also its supporters. As the proceedings warmed up, I noticed several intelligent-looking fellows who threw nothing else.

The effect on young Tuppy was rather remarkable. His eyes bulged and his hair seemed to stand up, and yet his mouth went on opening and shutting, and you could see that in a dazed, automatic way he was still singing 'Sonny Boy'. Then, coming out of his trance, he began to pull for the shore with some rapidity. The last seen of him, he was beating a tomato to the exit by a short head.

Presently the tumult and the shouting died. I turned to Jeeves.

'Painful, Jeeves,' I said. 'But what would you?'

'Yes, sir.'

'The surgeon's knife, what?'

'Precisely, sir.'

'Well, with this happening beneath her eyes, I think we may definitely consider the Glossop-Bellinger romance off.'

'Yes, sir.'

At this point old Beefy Bingham came out on to the platform.

'Ladies and gentlemen,' said old Beefy.

I supposed that he was about to rebuke his flock for the recent expression of feeling. But such was not the case. No doubt he was accustomed by now to the wholesome give-and-take of these clean, bright entertainments and had ceased to think it worth while to make any comment when there was a certain liveliness.

'Ladies and gentlemen,' said old Beefy, 'the next item on the programme was to have been Songs by Miss Cora Bellinger, the well-known operatic soprano. I have just received a telephone-message from Miss Bellinger, saying that her car has broken down. She is, however, on her way here in a cab and will arrive shortly. Meanwhile, our friend Mr Enoch Simpson will recite "Dangerous Dan McGrew".'

I clutched at Jeeves.

'Jeeves! You heard?'

'Yes, sir.'

'She wasn't there!'

'No, sir.'

'She saw nothing of Tuppy's Waterloo.'

'No, sir.'

'The whole bally scheme has blown a fuse.'

'Yes, sir.'

'Come, Jeeves,' I said, and those standing by wondered, no doubt, what had caused that clean-cut face to grow so pale and set. 'I have been subjected to a nervous strain unparalleled since the days of the early Martyrs. I have lost pounds in weight and permanently injured my entire system. I have gone through an ordeal, the recollection of which will make me wake up screaming in the night for months to come. And all for nothing. Let us go.'

'If you have no objection, sir, I would like to witness the remainder of the entertainment.'

'Suit yourself, Jeeves,' I said moodily. 'Personally, my heart is dead and I am going to look in at the Goat and Grapes for another of their cyanide specials and then home.'

It must have been about half-past ten, and I was in the old sitting room sombrely sucking down a more or less final restorative, when the front-door bell rang, and there on the mat was young Tuppy. He looked like a man who has passed through some great experience and stood face to face with his soul. He had the beginnings of a black eye.

'Oh, hullo, Bertie,' said young Tuppy.

He came in and hovered about the mantelpiece as if he were looking for things to fiddle with and break.

'I've just been singing at Beefy Bingham's entertainment,' he said after a pause.

'Oh?' I said. 'How did you go?'

'Like a breeze,' said young Tuppy. 'Held them spellbound.'

'Knocked 'em, eh?'

'Cold,' said young Tuppy. 'Not a dry eye.'

And this, mark you, a man who had had a good upbringing and had, no doubt, spent years at his mother's knee being taught to tell the truth.

'I suppose Miss Bellinger is pleased?'

'Oh, yes. Delighted.'

'So now everything's all right?'

'Oh, quite.'

Tuppy paused.

'On the other hand, Bertie –'

'Yes?'

'Well, I've been thinking things over. Somehow I don't believe Miss Bellinger is the mate for me after all.'

'You don't?'

'No, I don't.'

'Why don't you?'

'Oh, I don't know. These things sort of flash on you. I respect Miss Bellinger, Bertie. I admire her. But – er – well, I can't help feeling now that a sweet, gentle girl – er – like your cousin Angela, for instance, Bertie, – would – er – in fact – well, what I came round for was to ask if you would 'phone Angela and find out how she reacts to the idea of coming out with me tonight to the Berkeley for a segment of supper and a spot of dancing.'

'Go ahead. There's the phone.'

'No, I'd rather you asked her, Bertie. What with one thing and another, if you paved the way – You see, there's just a chance that she may be – I mean, you know how misunderstandings occur – and – well, what I'm driving at, Bertie, old man, is that I'd rather you surged round and did a bit of paving, if you don't mind.'

I went to the 'phone and called up Aunt Dahlia's.

'She says come right along,' I said.

'Tell her,' said Tuppy in a devout sort of voice, 'that I will be with her in something under a couple of ticks.'

He had barely biffed, when I heard a click in the keyhole and a soft padding in the passage without.

'Jeeves,' I called.

'Sir?' said Jeeves, manifesting himself.

'Jeeves, a remarkably rummy thing has happened. Mr Glossop has just been here. He tells me that it is all off between him and Miss Bellinger.'

'Yes, sir.'

'You don't seem surprised.'

'No, sir. I confess I had anticipated some such eventuality.'

'Eh? What gave you that idea?'

'It came to me, sir, when I observed Miss Bellinger strike Mr Glossop in the eye.'

'Strike him!'

'Yes, sir.'

'In the eye?'

'The right eye, sir.'

I clutched the brow.

'What on earth made her do that?'

'I fancy she was a little upset, sir, at the reception accorded to her singing.'

'Great Scott! Don't tell me she got the bird, too?'

'Yes, sir.'

'But why? She's got a red-hot voice.'

'Yes, sir. But I think the audience resented her choice of a song.'

'Jeeves!' Reason was beginning to do a bit of tottering on its throne. 'You aren't going to stand there and tell me that Miss Bellinger sang "Sonny Boy" too!'

'Yes, sir. And – rashly, in my opinion – brought a large doll on to the platform to sing it to. The audience affected to mistake it for a ventriloquist's dummy, and there was some little disturbance.'

'But, Jeeves, what a coincidence!'

'Not altogether, sir. I ventured to take the liberty of accosting Miss Bellinger on her arrival at the hall and recalling myself to her recollection. I then said that Mr Glossop had asked me to request her that as a particular favour to him – the song being a favourite of his – she would sing "Sonny Boy". And when she found that you and Mr Glossop had also sung the song immediately before her, I rather fancy that she supposed that she had been made the victim of a practical pleasantry by Mr Glossop. Will there be anything further, sir?'

'No, thanks.'

'Good night, sir.'

'Good night, Jeeves,' I said reverently.

5

EPISODE OF THE DOG MCINTOSH

I was jerked from the dreamless by a sound like the rolling of distant thunder; and, in the mists of sleep clearing away, was enabled to diagnose this and trace it to its source. It was my Aunt Agatha's dog, McIntosh, scratching at the door. The above, an Aberdeen terrier of weak intellect, had been left in my charge by the old relative while she went off to Aix-les-Bains to take the cure, and I had never been able to make it see eye to eye with me on the subject of early rising. Although a glance at my watch informed me that it was barely ten, here was the animal absolutely up and about.

I pressed the bell, and presently in shimmered Jeeves, complete with tea-tray and preceded by dog, which leaped upon the bed, licked me smartly in the right eye, and immediately curled up and fell into a deep slumber. And where the sense is in getting up at some ungodly hour of the morning and coming scratching at people's doors, when you intend at the first opportunity to go to sleep again, beats me. Nevertheless, every day for the last five weeks this loony hound had pursued the same policy, and I confess I was getting a bit fed.

There were one or two letters on the tray; and, having slipped a refreshing half-cupful into the abyss, I felt equal to dealing with them. The one on top was from my Aunt Agatha.

'Ha!' I said.

'Sir?'

'I said "Ha!" Jeeves. And I meant "Ha!" I was registering relief. My Aunt Agatha returns this evening. She will be at her town residence between the hours of six and seven, and she expects to find McIntosh waiting for her on the mat.'

'Indeed, sir? I shall miss the little fellow.'

'I, too, Jeeves. Despite his habit of rising with the milk and being hearty before breakfast, there is sterling stuff in McIntosh. Nevertheless, I cannot but feel relieved at the prospect of shooting him back to the old home. It has been a guardianship fraught with anxiety. You know what my Aunt Agatha is. She lavishes on that dog a love which might better be bestowed on a nephew: and if the slightest thing had gone wrong with him while I was *in loco parentis*; if, while in my charge, he had developed rabies or staggers or the botts, I should have been blamed.'

'Very true, sir.'

'And, as you are aware, London is not big enough to hold Aunt Agatha and anybody she happens to be blaming.'

I had opened the second letter, and was giving it the eye.

'Ha!' I said.

'Sir?'

'Once again "Ha!" Jeeves, but this time signifying mild surprise. This letter is from Miss Wickham.'

'Indeed, sir?'

I sensed – if that is the word I want – the note of concern in the man's voice, and I knew he was saying to himself 'Is the young master about to slip?' You see, there was a time when the Wooster heart was to some extent what you might call ensnared by this Roberta Wickham, and Jeeves had never approved of her. He considered her volatile and frivolous and more or less of a menace to man and beast. And events, I'm bound to say, had rather borne out his view.

'She wants me to give her lunch today.'

'Indeed, sir?'

'And two friends of hers.'

'Indeed, sir?'

'Here. At one-thirty.'

'Indeed, sir?'

I was piqued.

'Correct this parrot-complex, Jeeves,' I said, waving a slice of bread-and-butter rather sternly at the man. 'There is no need for you to stand there saying "Indeed, sir?" I know what you're thinking, and you're wrong. As far as Miss Wickham is concerned, Bertram Wooster is chilled steel. I see no earthly reason why I should not comply with this request. A Wooster may have ceased to love, but he can still be civil.'

'Very good, sir.'

'Employ the rest of the morning, then, in buzzing to and fro and collecting provender. The old King Wenceslas touch, Jeeves. You remember? Bring me fish and bring me fowl –'

'Bring me flesh and bring me wine, sir.'

'Just as you say. You know best. Oh, and roly-poly pudding, Jeeves.'

'Sir?'

'Roly-poly pudding with lots of jam in it. Miss Wickham specifically mentions this. Mysterious, what?'

'Extremely, sir.'

'Also oysters, ice-cream, and plenty of chocolates with that goo-ey, slithery stuff in the middle. Makes you sick to think of it, eh?'

'Yes, sir.'

'Me, too. But that's what she says. I think she must be on some kind of diet. Well, be that as it may, see to it, Jeeves, will you?'

'Yes, sir.'

'At one-thirty of the clock.'

'Very good, sir.'

'Very good, Jeeves.'

At half past twelve I took the dog McIntosh for his morning saunter in the Park; and, returning at about one-ten, found young Bobbie Wickham in the sitting room, smoking a cigarette and chatting to Jeeves, who seemed a bit distant, I thought.

I have an idea I've told you about this Bobbie Wickham. She was the red-haired girl who let me down so disgracefully in the sinister affair of Tuppy Glossop and the hot-water bottle, that Christmas when I went to stay at Skeldings Hall, her mother's place in Hertfordshire. Her mother is Lady Wickham, who writes novels which, I believe, command a ready sale among those who like their literature pretty sloppy. A formidable old bird, rather like my Aunt Agatha in appearance. Bobbie does not resemble her, being constructed more on the lines of Clara Bow. She greeted me cordially as I entered – in fact, so cordially that I saw Jeeves pause at the door before biffing off to mix the cocktails and shoot me the sort of grave, warning look a wise old father might pass out to the effervescent son on seeing him going fairly strong with the local vamp. I nodded back, as much as to say 'Chilled steel!' and he oozed out, leaving me to play the sparkling host.

'It was awfully sporting of you to give us this lunch, Bertie,' said Bobbie.

'Don't mention it, my dear old thing,' I said. 'Always a pleasure.'

'You got all the stuff I told you about?'

'The garbage, as specified, is in the kitchen. But since when have you become a roly-poly pudding addict?'

'That isn't for me. There's a small boy coming.'

'What!'

'I'm awfully sorry,' she said, noting my agitation. 'I know just how you feel, and I'm not going to pretend that this child isn't pretty near the edge. In fact, he has to be seen to be believed. But it's simply vital that he be cosseted and sucked up to and generally treated as the guest of honour, because everything depends on him.'

'How do you mean?'

'I'll tell you. You know mother?'

'Whose mother?'

'My mother.'

'Oh, yes. I thought you meant the kid's mother.'

'He hasn't got a mother. Only a father, who is a big theatrical manager in America. I met him at a party the other night.'

'The father?'

'Yes, the father.'

'Not the kid?'

'No, not the kid.'

'Right. All clear so far. Proceed.'

'Well, mother – my mother – has dramatized one of her novels and when I met this father, this theatrical manager father, and, between ourselves, made rather a hit with him, I said to myself, "Why not?"'

'Why not what?'

'Why not plant mother's play on him.'

'Your mother's play?'

'Yes, not his mother's play. He is like his son, he hasn't got a mother, either.'

'These things run in families, don't they?'

'You see, Bertie, what with one thing and another, my stock isn't very high with mother just now. There was that matter of my smashing up the car – oh, and several things. So I thought, here is where I get a chance to put myself right. I cooed to old Blumenfeld –'

'Name sounds familiar.'

'Oh, yes, he's a big man over in America. He has come to London to see if there's anything in the play line worth buying. So I cooed to him a goodish bit and then asked him if he would listen to mother's play. He said he would, so I asked him to come to lunch and I'd read it to him.'

'You're going to read your mother's play – here?' I said, paling.

'Yes.'

'My God!'

'I know what you mean,' she said. 'I admit it's pretty sticky stuff. But I have an idea that I shall put it over. It all depends on how the kid likes it. You see, old Blumenfeld, for some reason, always banks on his verdict. I suppose he thinks the child's intelligence is exactly the same as an average audience's and –'

I uttered a slight yelp, causing Jeeves, who had entered with cocktails, to look at me in a pained sort of way. I had remembered.

'Jeeves!'

'Sir?'

'Do you recollect, when we were in New York, a dish-faced kid of the name of Blumenfeld who on a memorable occasion snootered Cyril Bassington-Bassington when the latter tried to go on the stage?'

'Very vividly, sir.'

'Well, prepare yourself for a shock. He's coming to lunch.'

'Indeed, sir?'

'I'm glad you can speak in that light, careless way. I only met the young stoup of arsenic for a few brief minutes, but I don't mind telling you the prospect of hob-nobbing with him again makes me tremble like a leaf.'

'Indeed, sir?'

'Don't keep saying "Indeed, sir?" You have seen this kid in action and you know what he's like. He told Cyril Bassington-Bassington, a fellow to whom he had never been formally introduced, that he had a face like a fish. And this not thirty seconds after their meeting. I give you fair warning that, if he tells me I have a face like a fish, I shall clump his head.'

'Bertie!' cried the Wickham, contorted with anguish and apprehension and what not.

'Yes, I shall.'

'Then you'll simply ruin the whole thing.'

'I don't care. We Woosters have our pride.'

'Perhaps the young gentleman will not notice that you have a face like a fish, sir,' suggested Jeeves.

'Ah! There's that, of course.'

'But we can't just trust to luck,' said Bobbie. 'It's probably the first thing he will notice.'

'In that case, miss,' said Jeeves, 'it might be the best plan if Mr Wooster did not attend the luncheon.'

I beamed on the man. As always, he had found the way.

'But Mr Blumenfeld will think it so odd.'

'Well, tell him I'm eccentric. Tell him I have these moods, which come upon me quite suddenly, when I can't stand the sight of people. Tell him what you like.'

'He'll be offended.'

'Not half so offended as if I socked his son on the upper maxillary bone.'

'I really think it would be the best plan, miss.'

'Oh, all right,' said Bobbie. 'Push off, then. But I wanted you to be here to listen to the play and laugh in the proper places.'

'I don't suppose there are any proper places,' I said. And with these words I reached the hall in two bounds, grabbed a hat, and made for the street. A cab was just pulling up at the door as I reached it, and inside it were Pop Blumenfeld and his foul son. With a slight sinking of the old heart, I saw that the kid had recognized me.

'Hullo!' he said.

'Hullo!' I said.

'Where are you off to?' said the kid.

'Ha, ha!' I said, and legged it for the great open spaces.

I lunched at the Drones, doing myself fairly well and lingering pretty considerably over coffee and cigarettes. At four o'clock I thought it would be safe to think about getting back; but, not wishing to take any chances, I went to the 'phone and rang up the flat.

'All clear, Jeeves?'

'Yes, sir.'

'Blumenfeld junior nowhere about?'

'No, sir.'

'Not hiding in any nook or cranny, what?'

'No, sir.'

'How did everything go off?'

'Quite satisfactorily, I fancy, sir.'

'Was I missed?'

'I think Mr Blumenfeld and young Master Blumenfeld were somewhat surprised at your absence, sir. Apparently they encountered you as you were leaving the building.'

'They did. An awkward moment, Jeeves. The kid appeared to desire speech with me, but I laughed hollowly and passed on. Did they comment on this at all?'

'Yes, sir. Indeed, young Master Blumenfeld was somewhat outspoken.'

'What did he say?'

'I cannot recall his exact words, sir, but he drew a comparison between your mentality and that of a cuckoo.'

'A cuckoo, eh?'

'Yes, sir. To the bird's advantage.'

'He did, did he? Now you see how right I was to come away. Just one crack like that out of him face to face, and I should infallibly have done his upper maxillary a bit of no good. It was wise of you to suggest that I should lunch out.'

'Thank you, sir.'

'Well, the coast being clear, I will now return home.'

'Before you start, sir, perhaps you would ring Miss Wickham up. She instructed me to desire you to do so.'

'You mean she asked you to ask me?'

'Precisely, sir.'

'Right ho. And the number?'

'Sloane 8090. I fancy it is the residence of Miss Wickham's aunt, in Eaton Square.'

I got the number. And presently young Bobbie's voice came floating over the wire. From the *timbre* I gathered that she was extremely bucked.

'Hullo? Is that you, Bertie?'

'In person. What's the news?'

'Wonderful. Everything went off splendidly. The lunch was just right. The child stuffed himself to the eyebrows and got more and more amiable, till by the time he had had his third go of ice-cream he was ready to say that any play – even one of mother's – was the goods. I fired it at him before he could come out from under the influence, and he sat there absorbing it in a sort of gorged way, and at the end old Blumenfeld said "Well, sonny, how about it?" and the child gave a sort of faint smile, as if he was thinking about roly-poly pudding, and said "OK, pop," and that's all there was to it. Old Blumenfeld has taken him off to the movies, and I'm to look in at the Savoy at five-thirty to sign the contract. I've just been talking to mother on the 'phone, and she's quite consumedly braced.'

'Terrific!'

'I knew you'd be pleased. Oh, Bertie, there's just one other thing. You remember saying to me once that there wasn't anything in the world you wouldn't do for me?'

I paused a trifle warily. It is true that I had expressed myself in some such terms as she had indicated, but that was before the affair of Tuppy and the hot-water bottle, and in the calmer frame of mind induced by that episode I wasn't feeling quite so spacious. You know how it is. Love's flame flickers and dies, Reason returns to her throne, and you aren't nearly as ready to hop about and jump through hoops as in the first pristine glow of the divine passion.

'What do you want me to do?'

'Well, it's nothing I actually want you to do. It's something I've done that I hope you won't be sticky about. Just before I began reading the play, that dog of yours, the Aberdeen terrier, came into the room. The child Blumenfeld was very much taken with it and said he wished he had a dog like that, looking at me in a meaning sort of way. So naturally, I had to say "Oh, I'll give you this one!"'

I swayed somewhat.

'You . . . You . . . What was that?'

'I gave him the dog. I knew you wouldn't mind. You see, it was vital to keep cosseting him. If I'd refused, he would have cut up rough and all that roly-poly pudding and stuff would have been thrown away. You see –'

I hung up. The jaw had fallen, the eyes were protruding. I tottered from the booth and, reeling out of the club, hailed a taxi. I got to the flat and yelled for Jeeves.

'Jeeves!'

'Sir?'

'Do you know what?'

'No, sir.'

'The dog . . . my Aunt Agatha's dog . . . McIntosh . . .'

'I have not seen him for some little while, sir. He left me after the conclusion of luncheon. Possibly he's in your bedroom.'

'Yes, and possibly he jolly dashed well isn't. If you want to know where he is, he's in a suite at the Savoy.'

'Sir?'

'Miss Wickham has just told me she gave him to Blumenfeld junior.'

'Sir?'

'Gave him to Jumenfeld blunior, I tell you. As a present. As a gift. With warm personal regards.'

'What was her motive in doing that, sir?'

I explained the circs. Jeeves did a bit of respectful tongue-clicking.

'I have always maintained, if you will remember, sir,' he said, when I had finished, 'that Miss Wickham, though a charming young lady –'

'Yes, yes, never mind about that. What are we going to do? That's the point. Aunt Agatha is due back between the hours of six and seven. She will find herself short one Aberdeen terrier. And, as she will probably have been considerably sea-sick all the way over, you will readily perceive, Jeeves, that, when I break the news that her dog has been given away to a total stranger, I shall find her in no mood of gentle charity.'

'I see, sir, most disturbing.'

'What did you say it was?'

'Most disturbing, sir.'

I snorted a trifle.

'Oh?' I said. 'And I suppose, if you had been in San Francisco when the earthquake started, you would just have lifted up your finger and said "Tweet, tweet! Shush, shush! Now, now! Come, come!" The English language, they used to tell me at school, is the richest in the world, crammed full from end to end with about a million red-hot adjectives. Yet the only one you can find to describe this ghastly business is the adjective "disturbing". It is not disturbing, Jeeves. It is . . . what's the word I want?'

'Cataclysmal, sir.'

'I shouldn't wonder. Well, what's to be done?'

'I will bring you a whisky-and-soda, sir.'

'What's the good of that?'

'It will refresh you, sir. And in the meantime, if it is your wish, I will give the matter consideration.'

'Carry on.'

'Very good, sir. I assume that it is not your desire to do anything that may in any way jeopardize the cordial relations which now exist between Miss Wickham and Mr and Master Blumenfeld?'

'Eh?'

'You would not, for example, contemplate proceeding to the Savoy Hotel and demanding the return of the dog?'

It was a tempting thought, but I shook the old onion firmly. There are things which a Wooster can do and things which, if you follow me, a Wooster cannot do. The procedure which he had indicated would undoubtedly have brought home the bacon, but the thwarted kid would have been bound to turn nasty and change his mind about the play. And, while I didn't think that any drama written by Bobbie's mother was likely to do the theatre-going public much good, I couldn't dash the cup of happiness, so to speak, from the blighted girl's lips, as it were. *Noblesse oblige* about sums the thing up.

'No, Jeeves,' I said. 'But if you can think of some way by which I can oil privily into the suite and sneak the animal out of it without causing any hard feelings, spill it.'

'I will endeavour to do so, sir.'

'Snap into it, then, without delay. They say fish are good for the brain. Have a go at the sardines and come back and report.'

'Very good, sir.'

It was about ten minutes later that he entered the presence once more.

'I fancy, sir –'

'Yes, Jeeves?'

'I rather fancy, sir, that I have discovered a plan of action.'

'Or scheme.'

'Or scheme, sir. A plan of action or scheme which will meet the situation. If I understood you rightly, sir, Mr and Master Blumenfeld have attended a motion-picture performance?'

'Correct.'

'In which case, they should not return to the hotel before five-fifteen?'

'Correct once more. Miss Wickham is scheduled to blow in at five-thirty to sign the contract.'

'The suite, therefore, is presently unoccupied.'

'Except for McIntosh.'

'Except for McIntosh, sir. Everything, accordingly, must depend on whether Mr Blumenfeld left instructions that, in the event of her arriving before he did, Miss Wickham was to be shown straight up to the suite, to await his return.'

'Why does everything depend on that?'

'Should he have done so, the matter becomes quite simple. All that is necessary is that Miss Wickham shall present herself at the hotel at five o'clock. She will go up to the suite. You will also have arrived at the hotel at five, sir, and will have made your way to the corridor outside the suite. If Mr and Master Blumenfeld have not returned, Miss Wickham will open the door and come out and you will go in, secure the dog, and take your departure.'

I stared at the man.

'How many tins of sardines did you eat, Jeeves?'

'None, sir. I am not fond of sardines.'

'You mean, you thought of this great, this ripe, this amazing scheme entirely without the impetus given to the brain by fish?'

'Yes, sir.'

'You stand alone, Jeeves.'

'Thank you, sir.'

'But I say!'

'Sir?'

'Suppose the dog won't come away with me? You know how meagre his intelligence is. By this time, especially when he's got used to a new place, he may have forgotten me completely and will look on me as a perfect stranger.'

'I had thought of that, sir. The most judicious move will be for you to sprinkle your trousers with aniseed.'

'Aniseed?'

'Yes, sir. It is extensively used in the dog-stealing industry.'

'But, Jeeves . . . dash it . . . aniseed?'

'I consider it essential, sir.'

'But where do you get the stuff?'

'At any chemist's, sir. If you will go out now and procure a small bottle, I will be telephoning to Miss Wickham to apprise her of the contemplated arrangements and ascertain whether she is to be admitted to the suite.'

I don't know what the record is for popping out and buying aniseed, but I should think I hold it. The thought of Aunt Agatha getting nearer and nearer to the Metropolis every minute induced a rare burst of speed. I was back at the flat so quick that I nearly met myself coming out.

Jeeves had good news.

'Everything is perfectly satisfactory, sir. Mr Blumenfeld did leave instructions that Miss Wickham was to be admitted to his suite. The young lady is now on her way to the hotel. By the time you reach it, you will find her there.'

You know, whatever you may say about old Jeeves – and I, for one, have never wavered in my opinion that his views on shirts for evening wear are hidebound and reactionary to a degree – you've got to admit that the man can plan a campaign. Napoleon could have taken his correspondence course. When he sketches out a scheme, all you have to do is to follow it in every detail, and there you are.

On the present occasion everything went absolutely according to plan, I had never realized before that dog-stealing could be so simple, having always regarded it rather as something that called for the ice-cool brain and the nerve of steel. I see now that a child can do it, if directed by Jeeves. I got to the hotel, sneaked up the stairs, hung about in the corridor trying to look like a potted palm in case anybody came along, and presently the door of the suite opened and Bobbie appeared, and suddenly, as I approached, out shot McIntosh, sniffing passionately, and the next moment his nose was up against my Spring trouserings, and he was drinking me in with every evidence of enjoyment. If I had been a bird that had been dead about five days, he could not have nuzzled me more heartily. Aniseed isn't a scent that I care for particularly myself, but it seemed to speak straight to the deeps of McIntosh's soul.

The connection, as it were, having been established in this manner, the rest was simple. I merely withdrew, followed by the animal in the order named. We passed down the stairs in good shape, self reeking to heaven and animal inhaling the bouquet, and after a few anxious moments were safe in a cab, homeward bound. As smooth a bit of work as London had seen that day.

Arrived at the flat, I handed McIntosh to Jeeves and instructed him to shut him up in the bathroom or somewhere where the spell cast by my trousers would cease to operate. This done, I again paid the man a marked tribute.

'Jeeves,' I said, 'I have had occasion to express the view before, and I now express it again fearlessly – you stand in a class of your own.'

'Thank you very much, sir. I am glad that everything proceeded satisfactorily.'

'The festivities went like a breeze from start to finish. Tell me, were you always like this, or did it come on suddenly?'

'Sir?'

'The brain. The grey matter. Were you an outstandingly brilliant boy?'

'My mother thought me intelligent, sir.'

'You can't go by that. My mother thought *me* intelligent. Anyway, setting that aside for the moment, would a fiver be any use to you?'

'Thank you very much, sir.'

'Not that a fiver begins to cover it. Figure to yourself, Jeeves – try to envisage, if you follow what I mean, the probable behaviour of my Aunt Agatha if I had gone to her between the hours of six and seven and told her that McIntosh had passed out of the picture. I should have had to leave London and grow a beard.'

'I can readily imagine, sir, that she would have been somewhat perturbed.'

'She would. And on the occasions when my Aunt Agatha is perturbed heroes dive down drain-pipes to get out of her way. However, as it is, all has ended happily . . . Oh, great Scott!'

'Sir?'

I hesitated. It seemed a shame to cast a damper on the man just when he had extended himself so notably in the cause, but it had to be done.

'You've overlooked something, Jeeves.'

'Surely not, sir?'

'Yes, Jeeves, I regret to say that the late scheme or plan of action, while gilt-edged as far as I am concerned, has rather landed Miss Wickham in the cart.'

'In what way, sir?'

'Why, don't you see that, if they know that she was in the suite at the time of the outrage, the Blumenfelds, father and son, will instantly assume that she was mixed up in McIntosh's disappearance, with the result that in their pique and chagrin they will call off the deal about the play? I'm surprised at you not spotting that, Jeeves. You'd have done much better to eat those sardines, as I advised.'

I waggled my head rather sadly, and at this moment there was a ring at the front-door bell. And not an ordinary ring, mind you, but one of those resounding peals that suggest that somebody with a high blood-pressure and a grievance stands without. I leaped in my tracks. My busy afternoon had left the old nervous system not quite in mid-season form.

'Good Lord, Jeeves!'

'Somebody at the door, sir.'

'Yes.'

'Probably Mr Blumenfeld, senior, sir.'

'What!'

'He rang up on the telephone, sir, shortly before you returned, to say that he was about to pay you a call.'

'You don't mean that?'

'Yes, sir.'

'Advise me, Jeeves.'

'I fancy the most judicious procedure would be for you to conceal yourself behind the settee, sir.'

I saw that his advice was good. I have never met this Blumenfeld socially, but I had seen him from afar on the occasion when he and Cyril Bassington-Bassington had had their falling out, and he hadn't struck me then as a bloke with whom, if in one of his emotional moods, it would be at all agreeable to be shut up in a small room. A large, round, flat, overflowing bird, who might quite easily, if stirred, fall on a fellow and flatten him to the carpet.

So I nestled behind the settee, and in about five seconds there was a sound like a mighty, rushing wind and something extraordinarily substantial bounded into the sitting room.

'This guy, Wooster,' bellowed a voice that had been strengthened by a lifetime of ticking actors off at dress-rehearsals from the back of the theatre.

'Where is he?'

Jeeves continued suave.

'I could not say, sir.'

'He's sneaked my son's dog.'

'Indeed, sir?'

'Walked into my suite as cool as dammit and took the animal away.'

'Most disturbing, sir.'

'And you don't know where he is?'

'Mr Wooster may be anywhere, sir. He is uncertain in his movements.'

The bloke Blumenfeld gave a loud sniff.

'Odd smell here!'

'Yes, sir?'

'What is it?'

'Aniseed, sir.'

'Aniseed?'

'Yes, sir. Mr Wooster sprinkles it on his trousers.'

'Sprinkles it on his trousers?'

'Yes, sir.'

'What on earth does he do that for?'

'I could not say, sir. Mr Wooster's motives are always somewhat hard to follow. He is eccentric.'

'Eccentric? He must be a loony.'

'Yes, sir.'

'You mean he is?'

'Yes, sir!'

There was a pause. A long one.

'Oh?' said old Blumenfeld, and it seemed to me that a good deal of what you might call the vim had gone out of his voice.

He paused again.

'Not *dangerous?*'

'Yes, sir, when roused.'

'Er – what rouses him chiefly?'

'One of Mr Wooster's peculiarities is that he does not like the sight of gentlemen of full habit, sir. They seem to infuriate him.'

'You mean, fat men?'

'Yes, sir.'

'Why?'

'One cannot say, sir.'

There was another pause.

'*I'm* fat!' said old Blumenfeld in a rather pensive sort of voice.

'I would not venture to suggest it myself, sir, but as you say so . . . You may recollect that, on being informed that you were to be a member of the luncheon party, Mr Wooster, doubting his power of self-control, refused to be present.'

'That's right. He went rushing out just as I arrived. I thought it odd at the time. My son thought it odd. We both thought it odd.'

'Yes, sir. Mr Wooster, I imagine, wished to avoid any possible unpleasantness, such as has occurred before ... With regard to the smell of aniseed, sir, I fancy I have now located it. Unless I am mistaken it proceeds from behind the settee. No doubt Mr Wooster is sleeping there.'

'Doing what?'

'Sleeping, sir.'

'Does he often sleep on the floor?'

'Most afternoons, sir. Would you desire me to wake him?'

'No!'

'I thought you had something that you wished to say to Mr Wooster, sir.'

Old Blumenfeld drew a deep breath. 'So did I,' he said. 'But I find I haven't. Just get me alive out of here, that's all I ask.'

I heard the door close, and a little while later the front door banged. I crawled out. It hadn't been any too cosy behind the settee, and I was glad to be elsewhere. Jeeves came trickling back.

'Gone, Jeeves?'

'Yes, sir.'

I bestowed an approving look on him.

'One of your best efforts, Jeeves.'

'Thank you, sir.'

'But what beats me is why he ever came here. What made him think that I had sneaked McIntosh away?'

'I took the liberty of recommending Miss Wickham to tell Mr Blumenfeld that she had observed you removing the animal from his suite, sir. The point which you raised regarding the possibility of her being suspected of complicity in the affair had not escaped me. It seemed to me that this would establish her solidly in Mr Blumenfeld's good opinion.'

'I see. Risky, of course, but possibly justified. Yes, on the whole, justified. What's that you've got there?'

'A five pound note, sir.'

'Ah, the one I gave you?'

'No, sir. The one Mr Blumenfeld gave me.'

'Eh? Why did he give you a fiver?'

'He very kindly presented it to me on my handing him the dog, sir.'

I gaped at the man.

'You don't mean to say —?'

'Not McIntosh, sir. McIntosh is at present in my bedroom. This was another animal of the same species which I purchased at the shop in Bond Street during your absence. Except to the eye of love, one Aberdeen terrier looks very much like another Aberdeen terrier, sir. Mr Blumenfeld, I am happy to say, did not detect the innocent subterfuge.'

'Jeeves,' I said – and I am not ashamed to confess that there was a spot of chokiness in the voice – 'there is none like you, none.'

'Thank you very much, sir.'

'Owing solely to the fact that your head bulges in unexpected spots, thus enabling you to do about twice as much bright thinking in any given time as any other two men in existence, happiness, you might say, reigns supreme. Aunt Agatha is on velvet, I am on velvet, the Wickhams, mother and daughter, are on velvet, the Blumenfelds, father and son, are on velvet. As far as the eye can reach, a solid mass of humanity, owing to you, all on velvet. A fiver is not sufficient, Jeeves. If I thought the world thought that Bertram Wooster thought a measly five pounds an adequate reward for such services as yours, I should never hold my head up again. Have another?'

'Thank you, sir.'

'And one more?'

'Thank you very much, sir.'

'And a third for luck?'

'Really, sir, I am exceedingly obliged. Excuse me, sir, I fancy I heard the telephone.'

He pushed out into the hall, and I heard him doing a good deal of the 'Yes, madam', 'Certainly, madam!' stuff. Then he came back.

'Mrs Spenser Gregson on the telephone, sir.'

'Aunt Agatha?'

'Yes, sir. Speaking from Victoria Station. She desires to communicate with you with reference to the dog McIntosh. I gather that she wishes to hear from your own lips that all is well with the little fellow, sir.'

I straightened the tie. I pulled down the waistcoat. I shot the cuffs. I felt absolutely all-righto.

'Lead me to her,' I said.

THE SPOT OF ART

I was lunching at my Aunt Dahlia's, and despite the fact that Anatole, her outstanding cook, had rather excelled himself in the matter of the bill-of-fare, I'm bound to say the food was more or less turning to ashes in my mouth. You see, I had some bad news to break to her – always a prospect that takes the edge off the appetite. She wouldn't be pleased, I knew, and when not pleased Aunt Dahlia, having spent most of her youth in the hunting-field, has a crispish way of expressing herself.

However, I supposed I had better have a dash at it and get it over.

'Aunt Dahlia,' I said, facing the issue squarely.

'Hullo?'

'You know that cruise of yours?'

'Yes.'

'That yachting-cruise you arc planning?'

'Yes.'

'That jolly cruise in your yacht in the Mediterranean to which you so kindly invited me and to which I have been looking forward with such keen anticipation?'

'Get on, fathead, what about it?'

I swallowed a chunk of *côtelette-suprème-aux-choux-fleurs* and slipped her the distressing info.

'I'm frightfully sorry, Aunt Dahlia,' I said, 'but I shan't be able to come.'

As I had foreseen, she goggled.

'What!'

'I'm afraid not.'

'You poor, miserable hell-hound, what do you mean, you won't be able to come?'

'Well, I won't.'

'Why not?'

'Matters of the most extreme urgency render my presence in the Metropolis imperative.'

She sniffed.

'I suppose what you really mean is that you're hanging round some unfortunate girl again?'

I didn't like the way she put it, but I admit I was stunned by her penetration, if that's the word I want. I mean the sort of thing detectives have.

'Yes, Aunt Dahlia,' I said, 'you have guessed my secret. I do indeed love.'

'Who is she?'

'A Miss Pendlebury. Christian name, Gwladys. She spells it with a "w".'

'With a "g", you mean.'

'With a "w" *and* a "g".'

'Not Gwladys?'

'That's it.'

The relative uttered a yowl.

'You sit there and tell me you haven't enough sense to steer clear of a girl who calls herself Gwladys? Listen, Bertie,' said Aunt Dahlia earnestly, 'I'm an older woman than you are – well, you know what I mean – and I can tell you a thing or two. And one of them is that no good can come of association with anything labelled Gwladys or Ysobel or Ethyl or Mabelle or Kathryn. But particularly Gwladys. What sort of girl is she?'

'Slightly divine.'

'She isn't that female I saw driving you at sixty miles ph in the Park the other day. In a red two-seater?'

'She did drive me in the Park the other day. I thought it rather a hopeful sign. And her Widgeon Seven is red.'

Aunt Dahlia looked relieved.

'Oh well, then, she'll probably break your silly fat neck before she can get you to the altar. That's some consolation. Where did you meet her?'

'At a party in Chelsea. She's an artist.'

'Ye gods!'

'And swings a jolly fine brush, let me tell you. She's painted a portrait of me. Jeeves and I hung it up in the flat this morning. I have an idea Jeeves doesn't like it.'

'Well, if it's anything like you I don't see why he should. An artist! Calls herself Gwladys! And drives a car in the sort of way Segrave would if he were pressed for time.' She brooded awhile. 'Well, it's all very sad, but I can't see why you won't come on the yacht.'

I explained.

'It would be madness to leave the metrop at this juncture,' I said. 'You know what girls are. They forget the absent face. And I'm not at all easy in my mind about a certain cove of the name of Lucius Pim. Apart from the fact that he's an artist, too, which forms a bond, his hair waves. One must never discount wavy hair, Aunt Dahlia. Moreover, this bloke is one of those strong, masterful men. He treats Gwladys as if she were less than the dust beneath his taxi wheels. He criticizes her hats and says nasty things about her chiaroscuro. For some reason, I've often noticed, this always seems to fascinate girls, and it has sometimes occurred to me that, being myself more the parfait gentle knight, if you know what I mean, I am in grave danger of getting the short end. Taking all these things into consideration, then, I cannot breeze off to the Mediterranean, leaving this Pim a clear field. You must see that?'

Aunt Dahlia laughed. Rather a nasty laugh. Scorn in its *timbre*, or so it seemed to me.

'I shouldn't worry,' she said. 'You don't suppose for a moment that Jeeves will sanction the match?'

I was stung.

'Do you imply, Aunt Dahlia,' I said – and I can't remember if I rapped the table with the handle of my fork or not, but I rather think I did – 'that I allow Jeeves to boss me to the extent of stopping me marrying somebody I want to marry?'

'Well, he stopped you wearing a moustache, didn't he? And purple socks. And soft-fronted shirts with dress-clothes.'

'That is a different matter altogether.'

'Well, I'm prepared to make a small bet with you, Bertie. Jeeves will stop this match.'

'What absolute rot!'

'And if he doesn't like that portrait, he will get rid of it.'

'I never heard such dashed nonsense in my life.'

'And, finally, you wretched, pie-faced wambler, he will present you on board my yacht at the appointed hour. I don't know how he will do it, but you will be there, all complete with yachting-cap and spare pair of socks.'

'Let us change the subject, Aunt Dahlia,' I said coldly.

Being a good deal stirred up by the attitude of the flesh-and-blood at the luncheon-table, I had to go for a bit of a walk in the Park after leaving, to soothe the nervous system. By about four-thirty the ganglions had ceased to vibrate, and I returned to the flat. Jeeves was in the sitting room, looking at the portrait.

I felt a trifle embarrassed in the man's presence, because just before leaving I had informed him of my intention to scratch the yacht-trip, and he had taken it on the chin a bit. You see, he had been looking forward to it rather. From the moment I had accepted the invitation, there had been a sort of nautical glitter in his eye, and I'm not sure I hadn't heard him trolling Chanties in the kitchen. I think some ancestor of his must have been one of Nelson's tars or something, for he has always had the urge of the salt sea in his blood. I have noticed him on liners, when we were going to America, striding the deck with a sailorly roll and giving the distinct impression of being just about to heave the main-brace or splice the binnacle.

So, though I had explained my reasons, taking the man fully into my confidence and concealing nothing, I knew that he was distinctly peeved; and my first act, on entering, was to do the cheery a bit. I joined him in front of the portrait.

'Looks good, Jeeves, what?'

'Yes, sir.'

'Nothing like a spot of art for brightening the home.'

'No, sir.'

'Seems to lend the room a certain – what shall I say –'

'Yes, sir.'

The responses were all right, but his manner was far from hearty, and I decided to tackle him squarely. I mean, dash it. I mean, I don't know if you have ever had your portrait painted, but if you have you will understand my feelings. The spectacle of one's portrait hanging on the wall creates in one a sort of paternal fondness for the thing: and what you demand from the outside public is approval and enthusiasm – not the curling lip, the twitching nostril, and the kind of supercilious look which you see in the eye of a dead mackerel. Especially is this so when the artist is a girl for whom you have conceived sentiments deeper and warmer than those of ordinary friendship.

'Jeeves,' I said, 'you don't like this spot of art.'

'Oh, yes, sir.'

'No. Subterfuge is useless. I can read you like a book. For some reason this spot of art fails to appeal to you. What do you object to about it?'

'Is not the colour-scheme a trifle bright, sir?'

'I had not observed it, Jeeves. Anything else?'

'Well, in my opinion, sir, Miss Pendlebury has given you a some-what too hungry expression.'

'Hungry?'

'A little like that of a dog regarding a distant bone, sir.'

I checked the fellow.

'There is no resemblance whatever, Jeeves, to a dog regarding a distant bone. The look to which you allude is wistful and denotes Soul.'

'I see, sir.'

I proceeded to another subject.

'Miss Pendlebury said she might look in this afternoon to inspect the portrait. Did she turn up?'

'Yes, sir.'

'But has left?'

'Yes, sir.'

'You mean she's gone, what?'

'Precisely, sir.'

'She didn't say anything about coming back, I suppose?'

'No, sir. I received the impression that it was not Miss Pendlebury's intention to return. She was a little upset, sir, and expressed a desire to go to her studio and rest.'

'Upset? What was she upset about?'

'The accident, sir.'

I didn't actually clutch the brow, but I did a bit of mental brow-clutching, as it were.

'Don't tell me she had an accident!'

'Yes, sir.'

'What sort of accident?'

'Automobile, sir.'

'Was she hurt?'

'No, sir. Only the gentleman.'

'What gentleman?'

'Miss Pendlebury had the misfortune to run over a gentleman in her car almost immediately opposite this building. He sustained a slight fracture of the leg.'

'Too bad! But Miss Pendlebury is all right?'

'Physically, sir, her condition appeared to be satisfactory. She was suffering a certain distress of mind.'

'Of course, with her beautiful, sympathetic nature. Naturally. It's a hard world for a girl, Jeeves, with fellows flinging themselves under the wheels of her car in one long, unending stream. It must have been a great shock to her. What became of the chump?'

'The gentleman, sir?'

'Yes.'

'He is in your spare bedroom, sir.'

'What!'

'Yes, sir.'

'In my spare bedroom?'

'Yes, sir. It was Miss Pendlebury's desire that he should be taken there. She instructed me to telegraph to the gentleman's sister, sir, who is in Paris, advising her of the accident. I also summoned a medical man, who gave it as his opinion that the patient should remain for the time being *in statu quo.*'

'You mean, the corpse is on the premises for an indefinite visit?'

'Yes, sir.'

'Jeeves, this is a bit thick!'

'Yes, sir.'

And I meant it, dash it. I mean to say, a girl can be pretty heftily divine and ensnare the heart and what not, but she's no right to turn a fellow's flat into a morgue. I'm bound to say that for a moment passion ebbed a trifle.

'Well, I suppose I'd better go and introduce myself to the blighter. After all, I am his host. Has he a name?'

'Mr Pim, sir.'

'Pim!'

'Yes, sir. And the young lady addressed him as Lucius. It was owing to the fact that he was on his way here to examine the portrait which she had painted that Mr Pim happened to be in the roadway at the moment when Miss Pendlebury turned the corner.'

I headed for the spare bedroom. I was perturbed to a degree. I don't know if you have ever loved and been handicapped in your wooing by a wavy-haired rival, but one of the things you don't want in such circs is the rival parking himself on the premises with a broken leg. Apart from anything else, the advantage the position gives him is obviously terrific. There he is, sitting up and toying with a grape and looking pale and interesting, the object of the girl's pity and concern, and where do you get off, bounding about the place in morning costume and spats and with the rude flush of health on the cheek? It seemed to me that things were beginning to look pretty mouldy.

I found Lucius Pim lying in bed, draped in a suit of my pyjamas, smoking one of my cigarettes, and reading a detective story. He waved the cigarette at me in what I considered a dashed patronizing manner.

'Ah, Wooster!' he said.

'Not so much of the "Ah, Wooster!"' I replied brusquely. 'How soon can you be moved?'

'In a week or so, I fancy.'

'In a week!'

'Or so. For the moment, the doctor insists on perfect quiet and repose. So forgive me, old man, for asking you not to raise your voice. A hushed whisper is the stuff to give the troops. And now, Wooster, about this accident. We must come to an understanding.'

'Are you sure you can't be moved?'

'Quite. The doctor said so.'

'I think we ought to get a second opinion.'

'Useless, my dear fellow. He was most emphatic, and evidently a man who knew his job. Don't worry about my not being comfortable here. I shall be quite all right. I like this bed. And now, to return to the subject of this accident. My sister will be arriving tomorrow. She will be greatly upset. I am her favourite brother.'

'You are?'

'I am.'

'How many of you are there?'

'Six.'

'And you're her favourite?'

'I am.'

It seemed to me that the other five must be pretty fairly subhuman, but I didn't say so. We Woosters can curb the tongue.

'She married a bird named Slingsby. Slingsby's Superb Soups. He rolls in money. But do you think I can get him to lend a trifle from time to time to a needy brother-in-law?' said Lucius Pim bitterly. 'No, sir! However, that is neither here nor there. The point is that my sister loves me devotedly: and, this being the case, she might try to prosecute and persecute and generally bite pieces out of poor little Gwladys if she knew that it was she who was driving the car that laid me out. She must never know, Wooster. I appeal to you as a man of honour to keep your mouth shut.'

'Naturally.'

'I'm glad you grasp the point so readily, Wooster. You are not the fool people take you for.'

'Who takes me for a fool?'

The Pim raised his eyebrows slightly.

'Don't people?' he said. 'Well, well. Anyway, that's settled. Unless I can think of something better I shall tell my sister that I was knocked down by a car which drove on without stopping and I didn't get its number. And now perhaps you had better leave me. The doctor made a point of quiet and repose. Moreover, I want to go on with this story. The villain has just dropped a cobra down the heroine's chimney, and I must be at her side. It is impossible not to be thrilled by Edgar Wallace. I'll ring if I want anything.'

I headed for the sitting room. I found Jeeves there, staring at the portrait in rather a marked manner, as if it hurt him.

'Jeeves,' I said, 'Mr Pim appears to be a fixture.'

'Yes, sir.'

'For the nonce, at any rate. And tomorrow we shall have his sister, Mrs Slingsby, of Slingsby's Superb Soups, in our midst.'

'Yes, sir. I telegraphed to Mrs Slingsby shortly before four. Assuming her to have been at her hotel in Paris at the moment of the telegram's delivery, she will no doubt take a boat early tomorrow afternoon, reaching Dover – or, should she prefer the alternative route, Folkestone – in time to begin the railway journey at an hour which will enable her to arrive in London at about seven. She will possibly proceed first to her London residence –'

'Yes, Jeeves,' I said, 'Yes. A gripping story, full of action and human interest. You must have it set to music some time and sing it. Meanwhile, get this into your head. It is imperative that Mrs Slingsby does not learn that it was Miss Pendlebury who broke her brother in two places. I shall require you, therefore, to approach Mr Pim before she arrives, ascertain exactly what tale he intends to tell, and be prepared to back it up in every particular.'

'Very good, sir.'

'And now, Jeeves, what of Miss Pendlebury?'

'Sir?'

'She's sure to call to make enquiries.'

'Yes, sir.'

'Well, she mustn't find me here. You know all about women, Jeeves?'

'Yes, sir.'

'Then tell me this. Am I not right in supposing that if Miss Pendlebury is in a position to go into the sick-room, take a long look at the interesting invalid, and then pop out, with the memory of that look fresh in her mind, and get a square sight of me lounging about in sponge-bag trousers, she will draw damaging comparisons? You see what I mean? Look on this picture and on that – the one romantic, the other not . . . Eh?'

'Very true, sir. It is a point which I had intended to bring to your attention. An invalid undoubtedly exercises a powerful appeal to the motherliness which exists in every woman's heart, sir. Invalids seem to stir their deepest feelings. The poet Scott has put the matter neatly in the lines – 'Oh, Woman in our hours of ease uncertain, coy, and hard to please . . . When pain and anguish rack the brow –'

I held up a hand.

'At some other time, Jeeves,' I said, 'I shall be delighted to hear your piece, but just now I am not in the mood. The position being as I have outlined, I propose to clear out early tomorrow morning and not to reappear until nightfall. I shall take the car and dash down to Brighton for the day.'

'Very good, sir.'

'It is better so, is it not, Jeeves?'

'Indubitably, sir.'

'I think so, too. The sea breezes will tone up my system, which sadly needs a dollop of toning. I leave you in charge of the old home.'

'Very good, sir.'

'Convey my regrets and sympathy to Miss Pendlebury and tell her I have been called away on business.'

'Yes, sir.'

'Should the Slingsby require refreshment, feed her in moderation.'

'Very good, sir.'

'And, in poisoning Mr Pim's soup, don't use arsenic which is readily detected. Go to a good chemist and get something that leaves no traces.'

I sighed, and cocked an eye at the portrait.

'All this is very wonky, Jeeves.'

'Yes, sir.'

'When the portrait was painted, I was a happy man.'

'Yes, sir.'

'Ah, well, Jeeves!'

'Very true, sir.'

And we left it at that.

It was latish when I got back on the following evening. What with a bit of ozone-sniffing, a good dinner, and a nice run home in the moonlight with the old car going as sweet as a nut, I was feeling in pretty good shape once more. In fact, coming through Purley, I went so far as to sing a trifle. The spirit of the Woosters is a buoyant spirit, and optimism had begun to reign again, in the W bosom.

The way I looked at it was, I saw I had been mistaken in assuming that a girl must necessarily love a fellow just because he had broken a leg. At first, no doubt, Gwladys Pendlebury would feel strangely drawn to the Pim when she saw him lying there a more or less total loss. But it would not be long before other reflections crept in. She would ask herself if she were wise in trusting her life's happiness to a man who hadn't enough sense to leap out of the way when he saw a car coming. She would tell herself that, if this sort of thing had happened once, who knew that it might not go on happening again and again all down the long years. And she would recoil from a married life which consisted entirely of going to hospitals and taking her husband fruit. She would realize how much better off she would be, teamed up with a fellow like Bertram Wooster, who, whatever his faults, at least walked on the pavement and looked up and down a street before he crossed it.

It was in excellent spirits, accordingly, that I put the car in the garage, and it was with a merry Tra-la on my lips that I let myself into the flat as Big Ben began to strike eleven. I rang the bell and presently, as if he had divined my wishes, Jeeves came in with siphon and decanter.

'Home again, Jeeves,' I said, mixing a spot.

'Yes, sir.'

'What has been happening in my absence? Did Miss Pendlebury call?'

'Yes, sir. At about two o'clock.'

'And left?'

'At about six, sir.'

I didn't like this so much. A four-hour visit struck me as a bit sinister. However, there was nothing to be done about it.

'And Mrs Slingsby?'

'She arrived shortly after eight and left at ten, sir.'

'Ah? Agitated?'

'Yes, sir. Particularly when she left. She was very desirous of seeing you, sir.'

'Seeing me?'

'Yes, sir.'

'Wanted to thank me brokenly, I suppose, for so courteously allowing her favourite brother a place to have his game legs in. Eh?'

'Possibly, sir. On the other hand, she alluded to you in terms suggestive of disapprobation, sir.'

'She – what?'

'"Feckless idiot" was one of the expressions she employed, sir.'

'Feckless idiot?'

'Yes, sir.'

I couldn't make it out. I simply couldn't see what the woman had based her judgment on. My Aunt Agatha has frequently said that sort of thing about me, but she has known me from a boy.

'I must look into this, Jeeves. Is Mr Pim asleep?'

'No, sir. He rang the bell a moment ago to enquire if we had not a better brand of cigarette in the flat.'

'He did, did he?'

'Yes, sir.'

'The accident doesn't seem to have affected his nerve.'

'No, sir.'

I found Lucius Pim sitting propped up among the pillows, reading his detective story.

'Ah, Wooster,' he said. 'Welcome home. I say, in case you were worrying, it's all right about that cobra. The hero had got at it without the villain's knowledge and extracted its poison-fangs. With the result that when it fell down the chimney and started trying to bite the heroine its efforts were null and void. I doubt if a cobra has ever felt so silly.'

'Never mind about cobras.'

'It's no good saying Never mind about cobras,' said Lucius Pim in a gentle, rebuking sort of voice. 'You've jolly well *got* to mind about cobras, if they haven't had their poison-fangs extracted. Ask anyone. By the way, my sister looked in. She wants to have a word with you.'

'And I want to have a word with her.'

'"Two minds with but a single thought." What she wants to talk to you about is this accident of mine. You remember that story I was to tell her? About the car driving on? Well the understanding was, if you recollect, that I was only to tell it if I couldn't think of something better. Fortunately, I thought of something much better. It came to me in a flash as I lay in bed looking at the ceiling. You see, that driving-on story was thin. People don't knock fellows down and break their legs and go driving on. The thing wouldn't have held water for a minute. So I told her you did it.'

'What!'

'I said it was you who did it in your car. Much more likely. Makes the whole thing neat and well-rounded. I knew you would approve. At all costs we have got to keep it from her that I was outed by Gwladys. I made it as easy for you as I could, saying that you were a bit pickled at the time and so not to be blamed for what you did. Some fellows wouldn't have thought of that. Still,' said Lucius Pim with a sigh, 'I'm afraid she's not any too pleased with you.'

'She isn't, isn't she?'

'No, she is not. And I strongly recommend you, if you want anything like a pleasant interview tomorrow, to sweeten her a bit overnight.'

'How do you mean, sweeten her?'

'I'd suggest you sent her some flowers. It would be a graceful gesture. Roses are her favourites. Shoot her in a few roses – Number Three, Hill Street is the address – and it may make all the difference. I think it my duty to inform you, old man, that my sister Beatrice is rather a tough egg, when roused. My brother-in-law is due back from New York at any moment, and the danger, as I see it, is that Beatrice, unless sweetened, will get at him and make him bring actions against you for torts and malfeasances and what not and get thumping damages. He isn't overfond of me and, left to himself, would rather approve than otherwise of people who broke my legs; but he's crazy about Beatrice and will do anything she asks him to. So my advice, is Gather ye rose-buds while ye may and bung them in to Number Three, Hill Street. Otherwise, the case of Slingsby v Wooster will be on the calendar before you can say What-ho.'

I gave the fellow a look. Lost on him, of course.

'It's a pity you didn't think of all that before,' I said. And it wasn't so much the actual words, if you know what I mean, as the way I said it.

'I thought of it all right,' said Lucius Pim. 'But as we were both agreed that at all costs –'

'Oh, all right,' I said. 'All right, all right.'

'You aren't annoyed?' said Lucius Pim, looking at me with a touch of surprise.

'Oh, no!'

'Splendid,' said Lucius Pim, relieved. 'I knew you would feel that I had done the only possible thing. It would have been awful if Beatrice had found out about Gwladys. I daresay you have noticed, Wooster, that when women find themselves in a position to take a running kick at one of their own sex they are twice as rough on her as they would be on a man. Now, you, being of the male persuasion, will find everything made nice and smooth for you. A quart of assorted roses, a few smiles, a tactful word or two, and she'll have melted before you know where you are. Play your cards properly, and you and Beatrice will be laughing merrily and having a game of Round and Round the Mulberry Bush together in about five minutes. Better not let Slingsby's Soups catch you at it, however. He's very jealous where Beatrice is concerned. And now you'll forgive me, old chap, if I send you away. The doctor says I ought not to talk too much for a day or two. Besides, it's time for bye-bye.'

The more I thought it over, the better that idea of sending those roses looked. Lucius Pim was not a man I was fond of – in fact, if I had had to choose between him and a cockroach as a companion for a walking-tour, the cockroach would have had it by a short head – but there was no doubt that he had outlined the right policy. His advice was good, and I decided to follow it. Rising next morning at ten-fifteen, I swallowed a strengthening breakfast and legged it off to that flower-shop in Piccadilly. I couldn't leave the thing to Jeeves. It was essentially a mission that demanded the personal touch. I laid out a couple of quid on a sizeable bouquet, sent it with my card to Hill Street, and then looked in at the Drones for a brief refresher. It is a thing I don't often do in the morning, but this threatened to be rather a special morning.

It was about noon when I got back to the flat. I went into the sitting room and tried to adjust the mind to the coming interview. It had to be faced, of course, but it wasn't any good my telling myself that it was going to be one of those jolly scenes the memory of which cheer you up as you sit toasting your toes at the fire in your old age. I stood or fell by the roses. If they sweetened the Slingsby, all would be well. If they failed to sweeten her, Bertram was undoubtedly for it.

The clock ticked on, but she did not come. A late riser, I took it, and was slightly encouraged by the reflection. My experience of women has been that the earlier they leave the hay the more vicious specimens they are apt to be. My Aunt Agatha, for instance, is always up with the lark, and look at her.

Still, you couldn't be sure that this rule always worked, and after a while the suspense began to get in amongst me a bit. To divert the mind, I fetched the old putter out of its bag and began to practise putts into a glass. After all, even if the Slingsby turned out to be all that I had pictured her in my gloomier moments, I should have improved my close-to-the-hole work on the green and be that much up, at any rate.

It was while I was shaping for a rather tricky shot that the front-door bell went.

I picked up the glass and shoved the putter behind the settee. It struck me that if the woman found me engaged on what you might call a frivolous pursuit she might take it to indicate lack of remorse and proper feeling. I straightened the collar, pulled down the waistcoat, and managed to fasten on the face a sort of sad half-smile which was welcoming without being actually jovial. It looked all right in the mirror, and I held it as the door opened.

'Mr Slingsby,' announced Jeeves.

And, having spoken these words, he closed the door and left us alone together.

For quite a time there wasn't anything in the way of chit-chat. The shock of expecting Mrs Slingsby and finding myself confronted by something entirely different – in fact, not the same thing at all – seemed to have affected the vocal chords. And the visitor didn't appear to be disposed to make light conversation himself. He stood there looking strong and silent. I suppose you have to be like that if you want to manufacture anything in the nature of a really convincing soup.

Slingsby's Superb Soups was a Roman Emperor-looking sort of bird, with keen, penetrating eyes and one of those jutting chins. The eyes seemed to be fixed on me in a dashed unpleasant stare and, unless I was mistaken, he was grinding his teeth a trifle. For some reason he appeared to have taken a strong dislike to me at sight, and I'm bound to say this rather puzzled me. I don't pretend to have one of those Fascinating Personalities which you get from studying the booklets advertized in the back pages of the magazines, but I couldn't recall another case in the whole of my career where a single glimpse of the old map had been enough to make anyone look as if he wanted to foam at the mouth. Usually, when people meet me for the first time, they don't seem to know I'm there.

However, I exerted myself to play the host.

'Mr Slingsby?'

'That is my name.'

'Just got back from America?'

'I landed this morning.'

'Sooner than you were expected, what?'

'So I imagine.'

'Very glad to see you.'

'You will not be for long.'

I took time off to do a bit of gulping. I saw now what had happened. This bloke had been home, seen his wife, heard the story of the accident, and had hastened round to the flat to slip it across me. Evidently those roses had not sweetened the female of the species. The only thing to do now seemed to be to take a stab at sweetening the male.

'Have a drink?' I said.

'No!'

'A cigarette?'

'No!'

'A chair?'

'No!'

I went into the silence once more. These non-drinking, non-smoking, non-sitters are hard birds to handle.

'Don't grin at me, sir!'

I shot a glance at myself in the mirror, and saw what he meant. The sad half-smile *had* slopped over a bit. I adjusted it, and there was another pause.

'Now, sir,' said the Superb Souper. 'To business. I think I need scarcely tell you why I am here.'

'No. Of course. Absolutely. It's about that little matter –'

He gave a snort which nearly upset a vase on the mantelpiece.

'Little matter? So you consider it a little matter, do you?'

'Well –'

'Let me tell you, sir, that when I find that during my absence from the country a man has been annoying my wife with his importunities I regard it as anything but a little matter. And I shall endeavour,' said the Souper, the eyes gleaming a trifle brighter as he rubbed his hands together in a hideous, menacing way, 'to make you see the thing in the same light.'

I couldn't make head or tail of this. I simply couldn't follow him. The lemon began to swim.

'Eh?' I said. 'Your wife?'

'You heard me.'

'There must be some mistake.'

'There is. You made it.'

'But I don't know your wife.'

'Ha!'

'I've never even met her.'

'Tchah!'

'Honestly, I haven't.'

'Bah!'

He drank me in for a moment.

'Do you deny you sent her flowers?'

I felt the heart turn a double somersault. I began to catch his drift.

'Flowers!' he proceeded. 'Roses, sir. Great, fat, beastly roses. Enough of them to sink a ship. Your card was attached to them by a small pin –'

His voice died away in a sort of gurgle, and I saw that he was staring at something behind me. I spun round, and there, in the doorway – I hadn't seen it open, because during the last spasm of dialogue I had been backing cautiously towards it – there in the doorway stood a female. One glance was enough to tell me who she was. No woman could look so like Lucius Pim who hadn't the misfortune to be related to him. It was Sister Beatrice, the tough egg. I saw all. She had left home before the flowers had arrived; she had sneaked, unsweetened, into the flat, while I was fortifying the system at the Drones; and here she was.

'Er –' I said.

'Alexander!' said the female.

'Goo!' said the Souper. Or it may have been 'Coo!'

Whatever it was, it was in the nature of a battle-cry or slogan of war. The Souper's worst suspicions had obviously been confirmed. His eyes shone with a strange light. His chin pushed itself out another couple of inches. He clenched and unclenched his fingers once or twice, as if to make sure that they were working properly and could be relied on to do a good, clean job of strangling. Then, once more observing 'Coo!' (or 'Goo!'), he sprang forward, trod on the golf-ball I had been practising putting with, and took one of the finest tosses I have ever witnessed. The purler of a lifetime. For a moment the air seemed to be full of arms and legs, and then, with a thud that nearly dislocated the flat, he made a forced landing against the wall.

And, feeling I had had about all I wanted, I oiled from the room and was in the act of grabbing my hat from the rack in the hall, when Jeeves appeared.

'I fancied I heard a noise, sir,' said Jeeves.

'Quite possibly,' I said. 'It was Mr Slingsby.'

'Sir?'

'Mr Slingsby practising Russian dances,' I explained. 'I rather think he has fractured an assortment of limbs. Better go in and see.'

'Very good, sir.'

'If he is the wreck I imagine, put him in my room and send for the doctor. The flat is filling up nicely with the various units of the Pim family and its connections, eh, Jeeves?'

'Yes, sir.'

'I think the supply is about exhausted, but should any aunts or uncles by marriage come along and break their limbs, bed them out on the Chesterfield.'

'Very good, sir.'

'I, personally, Jeeves,' I said, opening the front door and pausing on the threshold, 'am off to Paris. I will wire you the address. Notify me in due course when the place is free from Pims and completely purged of Slingsbys, and I will return. Oh, and Jeeves.'

'Sir?'

'Spare no effort to mollify these birds. They think – at least, Slingsby (female) thinks, and what she thinks today he will think tomorrow – that it was I who ran over Mr Pim in my care. Endeavour during my absence to sweeten them.'

'Very good, sir.'

'And now perhaps you had better be going in and viewing the body. I shall proceed to the Drones, where I shall lunch, subsequently catching the two o'clock train at Charing Cross. Meet me there with an assortment of luggage.'

It was a matter of three weeks or so before Jeeves sent me the 'All clear' signal. I spent the time pottering pretty perturbedly about Paris and environs. It is a city I am fairly fond of, but I was glad to be able to return to the old home. I hopped on to a passing aeroplane and a couple of hours later was bowling through Croydon on my way to the centre of things. It was somewhere down in the Sloane Square neighbourhood that I first caught sight of the posters.

A traffic block had occurred, and I was glancing idly this way and that, when suddenly my eye was caught by something that looked familiar. And then I saw what it was.

Pasted on a blank wall and measuring about a hundred feet each way was an enormous poster, mostly red and blue. At the top of it were the words:

SLINGSBY'S SUPERB SOUPS

and at the bottom:

SUCCULENT AND STRENGTHENING

And, in between, me. Yes, dash it, Bertram Wooster in person. A reproduction of the Pendlebury portrait, perfect in every detail.

It was the sort of thing to make a fellow's eyes flicker, and mine flickered. You might say a mist seemed to roll before them. Then it lifted, and I was able to get a good long look before the traffic moved on.

Of all the absolutely foul sights I have ever seen, this took the biscuit with ridiculous ease. The thing was a bally libel on the Wooster face, and yet it was as unmistakable as if it had had my name under it. I saw now what Jeeves had meant when he said that the portrait had given me a hungry look. In the poster this look had become one of bestial greed. There I sat absolutely slavering through a monocle about six inches in circumference at a plateful of soup, looking as if I hadn't had a meal for weeks. The whole thing seemed to take one straight away into a different and a dreadful world.

I woke from a species of trance or coma to find myself at the door of the block of flats. To buzz upstairs and charge into the home was with me the work of a moment.

Jeeves came shimmering down the hall, the respectful beam of welcome on his face.

'I am glad to see you back, sir.'

'Never mind about that,' I yipped. 'What about –?'

'The posters, sir? I was wondering if you might have observed them.'

'I observed them!'

'Striking, sir?'

'Very striking. Now, perhaps you'll kindly explain –'

'You instructed me, if you recollect, sir, to spare no effort to mollify Mr Slingsby.'

'Yes, but –'

'It proved a somewhat difficult task, sir. For some time Mr Slingsby, on the advice and owing to the persuasion of Mrs Slingsby, appeared to be resolved to institute an action in law against you – a procedure which I knew you would find most distasteful.'

'Yes, but –'

'And then, the first day he was able to leave his bed, he observed the portrait, and it seemed to me judicious to point out to him its possibilities as an advertising medium. He readily fell in with the suggestion and, on my assurance that, should he abandon the projected action in law, you would willingly permit the use of the portrait, he entered into negotiations with Miss Pendlebury for the purchase of the copyright.'

'Oh? Well, I hope she's got something out of it, at any rate?'

'Yes, sir. Mr Pim, acting as Miss Pendlebury's agent, drove, I understand, an extremely satisfactory bargain.'

'He acted as her agent, eh?'

'Yes, sir. In his capacity as fiancé to the young lady, sir.'

'Fiancé!'

'Yes, sir.'

It shows how the sight of that poster had got into my ribs when I state that, instead of being laid out cold by this announcement, I merely said 'Ha!' or 'Ho!' or it may have been 'H'm.' After the poster, nothing seemed to matter.

'After that poster, Jeeves,' I said, 'nothing seems to matter.'

'No, sir?'

'No, Jeeves. A woman has tossed my heart lightly away, but what of it?'

'Exactly, sir.'

'The voice of Love seemed to call to me, but it was a wrong number. Is that going to crush me?'

'No, sir.'

'No, Jeeves. It is not. But what does matter is this ghastly business of my face being spread from end to end of the Metropolis with the eyes fixed on a plate of Slingsby's Superb Soup. I must leave London. The lads at the Drones will kid me without ceasing.'

'Yes, sir. And Mrs Spenser Gregson —'

I paled visibly. I hadn't thought of Aunt Agatha and what she might have to say about letting down the family prestige.

'You don't mean to say she has been ringing up?'

'Several times daily, sir.'

'Jeeves, flight is the only resource.'

'Yes, sir.'

'Back to Paris, what?'

'I should not recommend the move, sir. The posters are, I understand, shortly to appear in that city also, advertising the *Bouillon Suprême*. Mr Slingsby's products command a large sale in France. The sight would be painful for you, sir.'

'Then where?'

'If I might make a suggestion, sir, why not adhere to your original intention of cruising in Mrs Travers' yacht in the Mediterrancan? On the yacht you would be free from the annoyance of these advertising displays.'

The man seemed to me to be drivelling.

'But the yacht started weeks ago. It may be anywhere by now.'

'No, sir. The cruise was postponed for a month owing to the illness of Mrs Travers' chef, Anatole, who contracted influenza. Mrs Travers refused to sail without him.'

'You mean they haven't started?'

'Not yet, sir. The yacht sails from Southampton on Tuesday next.'

'Why, then, dash it, nothing could be sweeter.'

'No, sir.'

'Ring up Aunt Dahlia and tell her we'll be there.'

'I ventured to take the liberty of doing so a few moments before you arrived, sir.'

'You did?'

'Yes, sir. I thought it probable that the plan would meet with your approval.'

'It does! I've wished all along I was going on that cruise.'

'I, too, sir. It should be extremely pleasant.'

'The tang of the salt breezes, Jeeves!'

'Yes, sir.'

'The moonlight on the water!'

'Precisely, sir.'

'The gentle heaving of the waves!'

'Exactly, sir.'

I felt absolutely in the pink. Gwladys – pah! The posters – bah! That was the way I looked at it.

'Yo-ho-ho, Jeeves!' I said, giving the trousers a bit of a hitch.

'Yes, sir.'

'In fact, I will go further. Yo-ho-ho and a bottle of rum!'

'Very good, sir. I will bring it immediately.'

JEEVES AND THE KID CLEMENTINA

It has been well said of Bertram Wooster by those who know him best that, whatever other sporting functions he may see fit to oil out of, you will always find him battling to his sixteen handicap at the annual golf tournament of the Drones Club. Nevertheless, when I heard that this year they were holding it at Bingley-on-Sea, I confess I hesitated. As I stood gazing out of the window of my suite at the Splendide on the morning of the opening day, I was not exactly a-twitter, if you understand me, but I couldn't help feeling I might have been rather rash.

'Jeeves,' I said, 'Now that we have actually arrived, I find myself wondering if it was quite prudent to come here.'

'It is a pleasant spot, sir.'

'Where every prospect pleases,' I agreed. 'But though the spicy breezes blow fair o'er Bingley-on-Sea, we must never forget that this is where my Aunt Agatha's old friend, Miss Mapleton, runs a girls' school. If the relative knew I was here, she would expect me to call on Miss Mapleton.'

'Very true, sir.'

I shivered somewhat.

'I met her once, Jeeves. 'Twas on a summer's evening in my tent, the day I overcame the Nervii. Or, rather, at lunch at Aunt Agatha's a year ago come Lammas Eve. It is not an experience I would willingly undergo again.'

'Indeed, sir?'

'Besides, you remember what happened last time I got into a girls' school?'

'Yes, sir.'

'Secrecy and silence, then. My visit here must be strictly incog. If Aunt Agatha happens to ask you where I spent this week, say I went to Harrogate for the cure.'

'Very good, sir. Pardon me, sir, are you proposing to appear in those garments in public?'

Up to this point our conversation had been friendly and cordial, but I now perceived that the jarring note had been struck. I had been wondering when my new plus-fours would come under discussion, and I was prepared to battle for them like a tigress for her young.

'Certainly, Jeeves,' I said. 'Why? Don't you like them?'

'No, sir.'

'You think them on the bright side?'

'Yes, sir.'

'A little vivid, they strike you as?'

'Yes, sir.'

'Well, I think highly of them, Jeeves,' I said firmly.

There already being a certain amount of chilliness in the air, it seemed to me a suitable moment for springing another item of information which I had been keeping from him for some time.

'Er – Jeeves,' I said.

'Sir?'

'I ran into Miss Wickham the other day. After chatting of this and that, she invited me to join a party she is getting up to go to the Antibes this summer.'

'Indeed, sir?'

He now looked definitely squiggle-eyed. Jeeves, as I think I have mentioned before, does not approve of Bobbie Wickham.

There was what you might call a tense silence. I braced myself for an exhibition of the good old Wooster determination. I mean to say, one has got to take a firm stand from time to time. The trouble with Jeeves is that he tends occasionally to get above himself. Just because he has surged round and – I admit it freely – done the young master a bit of good in one or two crises, he has a nasty way of conveying the impression that he looks on Bertram Wooster as a sort of idiot child who, but for him, would conk in the first chukka. I resent this.

'I have accepted, Jeeves,' I said in a quiet, level voice, lighting a cigarette with a careless flick of the wrist.

'Indeed, sir?'

'You will like Antibes.'

'Yes, sir?'

'So shall I.'

'Yes, sir?'

'That's settled, then.'

'Yes, sir.'

I was pleased. The firm stand, I saw, had done its work. It was plain that the man was crushed beneath the iron heel – cowed, if you know what I mean.

'Right-ho, then, Jeeves.'

'Very good, sir.'

I had not expected to return from the arena until well on in the evening, but circumstances so arranged themselves that it was barely three o'clock when I found myself back again. I was wandering moodily to and fro on the pier, when I observed Jeeves shimmering towards me.

'Good afternoon, sir,' he said. 'I had not supposed that you would be returning quite so soon, or I would have remained at the hotel.'

'I had not supposed that I would be returning quite so soon myself, Jeeves,' I said, sighing somewhat. 'I was outed in the first round, I regret to say.'

'Indeed, sir? I am sorry to hear that.'

'And, to increase the mortification of defeat, Jeeves, by a blighter who had not spared himself at the luncheon table and was quite noticeably sozzled. I couldn't seem to do anything right.'

'Possibly you omitted to keep your eye on the ball with sufficient assiduity, sir?'

'Something of that nature, no doubt. Anyway, here I am, a game and popular loser and . . .' I paused, and scanned the horizon with some interest. 'Great Scott, Jeeves! Look at that girl just coming on to the pier. I never saw anybody so extraordinarily like Miss Wickham. How do you account for these resemblances?'

'In the present instance, sir, I attribute the similarity to the fact that the young lady *is* Miss Wickham.'

'Eh?'

'Yes, sir. If you notice, she is waving to you now.'

'But what on earth is she doing down here?'

'I am unable to say, sir.'

His voice was chilly and seemed to suggest that whatever had brought Bobbie Wickham to Bingley-on-Sea, it could not, in his opinion, be anything good. He dropped back into the offing, registering alarm and despondency, and I removed the old Homburg and waggled it genially.

'What-ho!' I said.

Bobbie came to anchor alongside.

'Hullo, Bertie,' she said. 'I didn't know you were here.'

'I am,' I assured her.

'In mourning?' she asked, eyeing the trouserings.

'Rather natty, aren't they?' I said, following her gaze. 'Jeeves doesn't like them, but then he's notoriously hidebound in the matter of leg-wear. What are you doing in Bingley?'

'My cousin Clementina is at school here. It's her birthday and I thought I would come down and see her. I'm just off there now. Are you staying here tonight?'

'Yes. At the Splendide.'

'You can give me dinner there if you like.'

Jeeves was behind me, and I couldn't see him, but at these words I felt his eye slap warningly against the back of my neck. I knew what it was that he was trying to broadcast – viz. that it would be tempting Providence to mix with Bobbie Wickham even to the extent of giving her a bite to eat. Dashed absurd, was my verdict. Get entangled with young Bobbie in the intricate lie of a country-house, where almost anything can happen, and I'm not saying. But how any doom or disaster could lurk behind the simple pronging of a spot of dinner together, I failed to see. I ignored the man.

'Of course. Certainly. Rather. Absolutely,' I said.

'That'll be fine. I've got to get back to London tonight for revelry of sorts at the Berkeley, but it doesn't matter if I'm a bit late. We'll turn up at about seven-thirty, and you can take us to the movies afterwards.'

'We? Us?'

'Clementina and me.'

'You don't mean you intend to bring your ghastly cousin?'

'Of course I do. Don't you want the child to have a little pleasure on her birthday? And she isn't ghastly. She's a dear. She won't be any trouble. All you'll have to do is take her back to the school afterwards. You can manage that without straining a sinew can't you?'

I eyed her keenly.

'What does it involve?'

'How do you mean, what does it involve?'

'The last time I was lured into a girls' school, a headmistress with an eye like a gimlet insisted on my addressing the chain-gang on Ideals and the Life To Come. This will not happen tonight?'

'Of course not. You just go to the front door, ring the bell and bung her in.'

I mused.

'That would appear to be well within our scope. Eh, Jeeves?'

'I should be disposed to imagine so, sir.'

The man's tone was cold and soupy: and, scanning his face, I observed on it an 'If-you-would-only-be-guided-by-me' expression which annoyed me intensely. There are moments when Jeeves looks just like an aunt.

'Right,' I said, ignoring him once more – and rather pointedly, at that. 'Then I'll expect you at seven-thirty. Don't be late. And see,' I added, just to show the girl that beneath the smiling exterior I was a man of iron, 'that the kid has her hands washed and does not sniff.'

I had not, I confess, looked forward with any great keenness to hobnobbing with Bobbie Wickham's cousin Clementina, but I'm bound to admit that she might have been considerably worse. Small girls as a rule, I have noticed, are inclined, when confronted with me, to giggle a good deal. They snigger and they stare. I look up and find their eyes glued on me in an incredulous manner, as if they were reluctant to believe that I was really true. I suspect them of being in the process of memorizing any little peculiarities of deportment that I may possess, in order to reproduce them later for the entertainment of their fellow-inmates.

With the kid Clementina there was nothing of this description. She was a quiet, saintlike child of about thirteen – in fact, seeing that this was her birthday, exactly thirteen – and her gaze revealed only silent admiration. Her hands were spotless; she had not a cold in the head; and at dinner, during which her behaviour was unexceptionable, she proved a sympathetic listener, hanging on my lips, so to speak, when with the aid of a fork and two peas I explained to her how my opponent that afternoon had stymied me on the tenth.

She was equally above criticism at the movies, and at the conclusion of the proceedings thanked me for the treat with visible emotion. I was pleased with the child, and said as much to Bobbie while assisting her into her two-seater.

'Yes, I told you she was a dear,' said Bobbie, treading on the self-starter in preparation for the dash to London. 'I always insist that they misjudge her at that school. They're always misjudging people. They misjudged me when I was there.'

'Misjudged her? How?'

'Oh, in various ways. But, then, what can you expect of a dump like St Monica's?'

I started.

'St Monica's?'

'That's the name of the place.'

'You don't mean the kid is at Miss Mapleton's school?'

'Why shouldn't she be?'

'But Miss Mapleton is my Aunt Agatha's oldest friend.'

'I know. It was your Aunt Agatha who got mother to send me there when I was a kid.'

'I say,' I said earnestly, 'when you were there this afternoon you didn't mention having met me down here?'

'No.'

'That's all right.' I was relieved. 'You see, if Miss Mapleton knew I was in Bingley, she would expect me to call. I shall be leaving tomorrow morning, so all will be well. But, dash it,' I said, spotting the snag, 'how about tonight?'

'What about tonight?'

'Well, shan't I have to see her? I can't just ring the front-door bell, sling the kid in, and leg it. I should never hear the last of it from Aunt Agatha.'

Bobbie looked at me in an odd, meditative sort of way.

'As a matter of fact, Bertie,' she said, 'I had been meaning to touch on that point. I think, if I were you, I wouldn't ring the front-door bell.'

'Eh? Why not?'

'Well, it's like this, you see. Clementina is supposed to be in bed. They sent her there just as I was leaving this afternoon. Think of it! On her birthday – right plumb spang in the middle of her birthday – and all for putting sherbet in the ink to make it fizz!'

I reeled.

'You aren't telling me that this foul kid came out without leave?'

'Yes, I am. That's exactly it. She got up and sneaked out when nobody was looking. She had set her heart on getting a square meal. I suppose I really ought to have told you right at the start, but I didn't want to spoil your evening.'

As a general rule, in my dealings with the delicately-nurtured, I am the soul of knightly chivalry – suave, genial and polished. But I can on occasion say the bitter, cutting thing, and I said it now.

'Oh?' I said.

'But it's all right.'

'Yes,' I said, speaking, if I recollect, between my clenched teeth, 'nothing could be sweeter, could it? The situation is one which it would be impossible to view with concern, what? I shall turn up with the kid, get looked at through steel-rimmed spectacles by the Mapleton, and after an agreeable five minutes shall back out, leaving the Mapleton to go to her escritoire and write a full account of the proceedings to my Aunt Agatha. And, contemplating what will happen after that, the imagination totters. I confidently expect my Aunt Agatha to beat all previous records.'

The girl clicked her tongue chidingly.

'Don't make such heavy weather, Bertie. You must learn not to fuss so.'

'I must, must I?'

'Everything's going to be all right. I'm not saying it won't be necessary to exercise a little strategy in getting Clem into the house, but it will be perfectly simple, if you'll only listen carefully to what I'm going to tell you. First, you will need a good long piece of string.'

'String?'

'String. Surely even you know what string is?'

I stiffened rather haughtily.

'Certainly,' I replied. 'You mean string.'

'That's right. String. You take this with you –'

'And soften the Mapleton's heart by doing tricks with it, I suppose?'

Bitter, I know. But I was deeply stirred.

'You take this string with you,' proceeded Bobbie patiently, 'and when you get into the garden you go through it till you come to a conservatory near the house. Inside it you will find a lot of flower-pots. How are you on recognizing a flower-pot when you see one, Bertie?'

'I am thoroughly familiar with flower-pots. If, as I suppose, you mean those sort of pot things they put flowers in.'

'That's exactly what I do mean. All right, then. Grab an armful of these flower-pots and go round the conservatory till you come to a tree. Climb this, tie a string to one of the pots, balance it on a handy branch which you will find overhangs the conservatory, and then, having stationed Clem near the front door, retire into the middle distance and jerk the string. The flower-pot will fall and smash the glass, someone in the house will hear the noise and come out to investigate, and while the door is open and nobody near, Clem will sneak in and go up to bed.'

'But suppose no one comes out?'

'Then you repeat the process with another pot.'

It seemed sound enough.

'You're sure it will work?'

'It's never failed yet. That's the way I always used to get in after lock-up when I was at St Monica's. Now, you're sure you've got it clear, Bertie? Let's have a quick run-through to make certain, and then I really must be off. String.'

'String.'

'Conservatory.'

'Or greenhouse.'

'Flower-pot.'

'Flower-pot.'

'Tree. Climb. Branch. Climb down. Jerk. Smash. And then off to beddy-bye. Got it?'

'I've got it. But,' I said sternly, 'let me tell you just one thing –'

'I haven't time. I must rush. Write to me about it, using one side of the paper only. Goodbye.'

She rolled off, and after following her with burning eyes for a moment I returned to Jeeves, who was in the background showing the kid Clementina how to make a rabbit with a pocket handkerchief. I drew him aside. I was feeling a little better now, for I perceived that an admirable opportunity had presented itself for putting the man in his place and correcting his view that he is the only member of our establishment with brains and resource.

'Jeeves,' I said, 'You will doubtless be surprised to learn that something in the nature of a hitch has occurred.'

'Not at all, sir.'

'No?'

'No, sir. In matters where Miss Wickham is involved, I am, if I may take the liberty of saying so, always on the alert for hitches. If you recollect sir, I have frequently observed that Miss Wickham, while a charming young lady, is apt –'

'Yes, yes, Jeeves. I know.'

'What would the precise nature of the trouble be this time, sir?'

I explained the circs.

'The kid is AWOL. They sent her to bed for putting sherbet in the ink, and in bed they imagine her to have spent the evening. Instead of which, she was out with me, wolfing the eight-course table d'hôte dinner at seven and six, and then going on to the Marine Plaza to enjoy an entertainment on the silver screen. It is our task to get her back into the house without anyone knowing. I may mention, Jeeves, that the school in which this young excrescence is serving her sentence is the one run by my Aunt Agatha's old friend, Miss Mapleton.'

'Indeed, sir?'

'A problem, Jeeves, what?'

'Yes, sir.'

'In fact, one might say a pretty problem?'

'Undoubtedly, sir. If I might suggest –'

I was expecting this. I raised the hand.

'I do not require any suggestions, Jeeves. I can handle this matter myself.'

'I was merely about to propose –'

I raised the hand again.

'Peace, Jeeves. I have the situation well under control. I have had one of my ideas. It may interest you to hear how my brain worked. It occurred to me, thinking the thing over, that a house like St Monica's would be likely to have near it a conservatory containing flower-pots. Then, like a flash, the whole thing came to me. I propose to procure some string, to tie it to a flower-pot, to balance the pot on a branch – there will, no doubt, be a tree near the conservatory with a branch overhanging it – and to retire to a distance, holding the string. You will station yourself with the kid near the front door, taking care to keep carefully concealed. I shall then jerk the string, the pot will smash the glass, the noise will bring someone out, and while the front door is open you will shoot the kid in and leave the rest to her personal judgment. Your share in the proceedings, you will notice, is simplicity itself – mere routine-work – and should not tax you unduly. How about it?'

'Well, sir –'

'Jeeves, I have had occasion before to comment on this habit of yours of saying "Well, sir" whenever I suggest anything in the nature of a ruse or piece of strategy. I dislike it more every time you do it. But I shall be glad to hear what possible criticism you can find to make.'

'I was merely about to express the opinion, sir, that the plan seems a trifle elaborate.'

'In a place as tight as this you have got to be elaborate.'

'Not necessarily, sir. The alternative scheme which I was about to propose –'

I shushed the man.

'There will be no need for alternative schemes, Jeeves. We will carry on along the lines I have indicated. I will give you ten minutes' start. That will enable you to take up your position near the front door and self to collect the string. At the conclusion of that period I will come along and do all the difficult part. So no more discussion. Snap into it, Jeeves.'

'Very good, sir.'

I felt pretty bucked as I tooled up the hill to St Monica's and equally bucked as I pushed open the front gate and stepped into the dark garden. But, just as I started to cross the lawn, there suddenly came upon me a rummy sensation as if all my bones had been removed and spaghetti substituted, and I paused.

I don't know if you have ever had the experience of starting off on a binge filled with a sort of glow of exhilaration, if that's the word I want, and then, without a moment's warning, having it disappear as if somebody had pressed a switch. That is what happened to me at this juncture, and a most unpleasant feeling it was – rather like when you take one of those express elevators in New York at the top of the building and discover, on reaching the twenty-seventh floor, that you have carelessly left all your insides up on the thirty-second, and too late now to stop and fetch them back.

The truth came to me like a bit of ice down the neck. I perceived that I had been a dashed sight too impulsive. Purely in order to score off Jeeves, I had gone and let myself in for what promised to be the mouldiest ordeal of a lifetime. And the nearer I got to the house, the more I wished that I had been a bit less haughty with the man when he had tried to outline that alternative scheme of his. An alternative scheme was just what I felt I could have done with, and the more alternative it was the better I would have liked it.

At this point I found myself at the conservatory door, and a few moments later I was inside, scooping up the pots.

Then ho, for the tree, bearing 'mid snow and ice the banner with the strange device 'Excelsior!'

I will say for that tree that it might have been placed there for the purpose. My views on the broad, general principle of leaping from branch to branch in a garden belonging to Aunt Agatha's closest friend remained unaltered; but I had to admit that, if it was to be done, this was undoubtedly the tree to do it on. It was a cedar of sorts; and almost before I knew where I was, I was sitting on top of the world with the conservatory roof gleaming below me. I balanced the flower-pot on my knee and began to tie the string round it.

And, as I tied, my thoughts turned in a moody sort of way to the subject of Woman.

I was suffering from a considerable strain of the old nerves at the moment, of course, and, looking back, it may be that I was too harsh; but the way I felt in that dark, roosting hour was that you can say what you like, but the more a thoughtful man has to do with women, the more extraordinary it seems to him that such a sex should be allowed to clutter up the earth.

Women, the way I looked at it, simply wouldn't do. Take the females who were mixed up in this present business. Aunt Agatha, to start with, better known as the Pest of Pont Street, the human snapping-turtle. Aunt Agatha's closest friend, Miss Mapleton, of whom I can only say that on the single occasion on which I had met her she had struck me as just the sort of person who would be Aunt Agatha's closest friend. Bobbie Wickham, a girl who went about the place letting the pure in heart in for the sort of thing I was doing now. And Bobbie Wickham's cousin Clementina, who, instead of sticking sedulously to her studies and learning to be a good wife and mother, spent the springtime of her life filling ink-pots with sherbet –

What a crew! What a crew!

I mean to say, what a *crew!*

I had just worked myself up into rather an impressive state of moral indignation, and was preparing to go even further, when a sudden bright light shone upon me from below and a voice spoke.

'Ho!' it said.

It was a policeman. Apart from the fact of his having a lantern, I knew it was a policeman because he had said 'Ho!' I don't know if you recollect my telling you of the time I broke into Bingo Little's house to pinch the dictaphone record of the mushy article his wife had written about him and sailed out of the study window right into the arms of the Force? On that occasion the guardian of the Law had said 'Ho!' and kept on saying it, so evidently policemen are taught this as part of their training. And after all, it's not a bad way of opening conversation in the sort of circs in which they generally have to chat with people.

'You come on down out of that,' he said.

I came down. I had just got the flower-pot balanced on its branch, and I left it there, feeling rather as if I had touched off the time-fuse of a bomb. Much seemed to me to depend on its stability and poise, as it were. If it continued to balance, an easy nonchalance might still get me out of this delicate position. If it fell, I saw things being a bit hard to explain. In fact, even as it was, I couldn't see my way to any explanation which would be really convincing.

However, I had a stab at it.

'Ah, officer,' I said.

It sounded weak. I said it again, this time with the emphasis on the 'Ah!' It sounded weaker than ever. I saw that Bertram would have to do better than this.

'It's all right, officer,' I said.

'All right, is it?'

'Oh, yes. Oh, yes.'

'What you doing up there?'

'Me, officer?'

'Yes, you.'

'Nothing, sergeant.'

'Ho!'

We eased into the silence, but it wasn't one of those restful silences that occur in talks between old friends. Embarrassing. Awkward.

'You'd better come along with me,' said the gendarme.

The last time I had heard those words from a similar source had been in Leicester Square one Boat Race night when, on my advice, my old pal Oliver Randolph Sipperley had endeavoured to steal a policeman's helmet at a moment when the policeman was inside it. On that occasion they had been addressed to young Sippy, and they hadn't sounded any too good, even so. Addressed to me, they more or less froze the marrow.

'No, I say, dash it!' I said.

And it was at this crisis, when Bertram had frankly shot his bolt and could only have been described as nonplussed, that a soft step sounded beside us and a soft voice broke the silence.

'Have you got them, officer? No, I see. It is Mr Wooster.'

The policeman switched the lantern round.

'Who are you?'

'I am Mr Wooster's personal gentleman's gentleman.'

'Whose?'

'Mr Wooster's.'

'Is this man's name Wooster?'

'This gentleman's name is Mr Wooster. I am in his employment as gentleman's personal gentleman.

I think the cop was awed by the man's majesty of demeanour, but he came back strongly.

'Ho!' he said. 'Not in Miss Mapleton's employment?'

'Miss Mapleton does not employ a gentleman's personal gentleman.'

'Then what are you doing in her garden?'

'I was in conference with Miss Mapleton inside the house, and she desired me to step out and ascertain whether Mr Wooster had been successful in apprehending the intruders.'

'What intruders?'

'The suspicious characters whom Mr Wooster and I had observed passing through the garden as we entered it.'

'And what were you doing entering it?'

'Mr Wooster had come to pay a call on Miss Mapleton, who is a close friend of his family. We noticed suspicious characters crossing the lawn. On perceiving these suspicious characters, Mr Wooster dispatched me to warn and reassure Miss Mapleton, he himself remaining to investigate.'

'I found him up a tree.'

'If Mr Wooster was up a tree, I have no doubt he was actuated by excellent motives and had only Miss Mapleton's best interests at heart.'

The policeman brooded.

'Ho!' he said. 'Well, if you want to know, I don't believe a word of it. We had a telephone call at the station saying there was somebody in Miss Mapleton's garden, and I found this fellow up a tree. It's my belief you're both in this, and I'm going to take you in to the lady for identification.'

Jeeves inclined his head gracefully.

'I shall be delighted to accompany you, officer, if such is your wish. And I feel sure that in this connection I may speak for Mr Wooster also. He too, I am confident, will interpose no obstacle in the way of your plans. If you consider that circumstances have placed Mr Wooster in a position that may be termed equivocal, or even compromising, it will naturally be his wish to exculpate himself at the earliest possible –'

'Here! said the policeman, slightly rattled.

'Officer?'

'Less of it.'

'Just as you say, officer.'

'Switch it off and come along.'

'Very good, officer.'

I must say that I have enjoyed functions more than that walk to the front door. It seemed to me that the doom had come upon me, so to speak, and I thought it hard that a gallant effort like Jeeves's, well reasoned and nicely planned, should have failed to click. Even to me his story had rung almost true in spots, and it was a great blow that the man behind the lantern had not sucked it in without question. There's no doubt about it, being a policeman warps a man's mind and ruins that sunny faith in his fellow human beings which is the foundation of a lovable character. There seems no way of avoiding this.

I could see no gleam of light in the situation. True, the Mapleton would identify me as the nephew of her old friend, thus putting the stopper on the stroll to the police station and the night in the prison cell, but, when you came right down to it, a fat lot of use that was. The kid Clementina was presumably still out in the night somewhere, and she would be lugged in and the full facts revealed, and then the burning glance, the few cold words and the long letter to Aunt Agatha. I wasn't sure that a good straight term of penal servitude wouldn't have been a happier ending.

So, what with one consideration and another, the heart, as I toddled in through the front door, was more or less bowed down with weight of woe. We went along the passage and into the study, and there, standing behind a desk with the steel-rimmed spectacles glittering as nastily as on the day when I had seen them across Aunt Agatha's luncheon-table, was the boss in person. I gave her one swift look, then shut my eyes.

'Ah!' said Miss Mapleton.

Now, uttered in a certain way – dragged out, if you know what I mean, and starting high up and going down into the lower register – the word 'Ah!' can be as sinister and devastating as the word 'Ho!' In fact, it is a very moot question which is the scalier. But what stunned me was that this wasn't the way she had said it. It had been, or my ears deceived me, a genial 'Ah!' A matey 'Ah!' The 'Ah!' of one old buddy to another. And this startled me so much that, forgetting the dictates of prudence, I actually ventured to look at her again. And a stifled exclamation burst from Bertram's lips.

The breath-taking exhibit before me was in person a bit on the short side. I mean to say, she didn't tower above one, or anything like that. But, to compensate for this lack of inches, she possessed to a remarkable degree that sort of quiet air of being unwilling to stand any rannygazoo which females who run schools always have. I had noticed the same thing when *in statu pupillari*, in my old headmaster, one glance from whose eye had invariably been sufficient to make me confess all. Sergeant-majors are like that, too. Also traffic-cops and some post office girls. It's something in the way they purse up their lips and look through you.

In short, through years of disciplining the young – ticking off Isabel and speaking with quiet severity to Gertrude and that sort of thing – Miss Mapleton had acquired in the process of time rather the air of a female lion-tamer; and it was this air which had caused me after the first swift look to shut my eyes and utter a short prayer. But now, though she still resembled a lion-tamer, her bearing had most surprisingly become that of a chummy lion-tamer – a tamer who, after tucking the lions in for the night, relaxes in the society of the boys.

'So you did not find them, Mr Wooster?' she said. 'I am sorry. But I am none the less grateful for the trouble you have taken, nor lacking in appreciation of your courage. I consider that you have behaved splendidly.'

I felt the mouth opening feebly and the vocal chords twitching but I couldn't manage to say anything. I was simply unable to follow her train of thought. I was astonished. Amazed. In fact, dumbfounded about sums it up.

The hell-hound of the Law gave a sort of yelp, rather like a wolf that sees its Russian peasant getting away.

'You identify this man, ma'am?'

'Identify him? In what way identify him?'

Jeeves joined the symposium.

'I fancy the officer is under the impression, madam, that Mr Wooster was in your garden for some unlawful purpose. I informed him that Mr Wooster was the nephew of your friend, Mrs Spenser Gregson, but he refused to credit me.'

There was a pause. Miss Mapleton eyed the constable for an instant as if she had caught him sucking acid-drops during the Scripture lesson.

'Do you mean to tell me, officer,' she said, in a voice that hit him just under the third button of the tunic and went straight through to the spinal column, 'that you have had the imbecility to bungle this whole affair by mistaking Mr Wooster for a burglar?'

'He was up a tree, ma'am.'

'And why should he not be up a tree? No doubt you had climbed the tree in order to watch the better, Mr Wooster?'

I could answer that. The first shock over, the old sang-froid was beginning to return.

'Yes. Rather. That's it. Of course. Certainly. Absolutely,' I said. 'Watch the better. That's it in a nutshell.'

'I took the liberty of suggesting that to the officer, madam, but he declined to accept the theory as tenable.'

'The officer is a fool,' said Miss Mapleton. It seemed a close thing for a moment whether or not she would rap him on the knuckles with a ruler. 'By this time, no doubt, owing to this idiocy, the miscreants have made good their escape. And it is for this,' said Miss Mapleton, 'that we pay rates and taxes!'

'Awful!' I said.

'Iniquitous.'

'A bally shame.'

'A crying scandal,' said Miss Mapleton.

'A grim show,' I agreed.

In fact, we were just becoming more like a couple of love-birds than anything, when through the open window there suddenly breezed a noise.

I'm never at my best at describing things. At school, when we used to do essays and English composition, my report generally read 'Has little or no ability, but does his best,' or words to that effect. True, in the course of years I have picked up a vocabulary of sorts from Jeeves, but even so I'm not nearly hot enough to draw a word-picture that would do justice to that extraordinarily hefty crash. Try to imagine the Albert Hall falling on the Crystal Palace, and you will have got the rough idea.

All four of us, even Jeeves, sprang several inches from the floor. The policeman uttered a startled 'Ho!'

Miss Mapleton was her calm masterful self again in a second.

'One of the men appears to have fallen through the conservatory roof,' she said. 'Perhaps you will endeavour at the eleventh hour to justify your existence, officer, by proceeding there and making investigations.'

'Yes, ma'am.'

'And try not to bungle matters this time.'

'No, ma'am.'

'Please hurry, then. Do you intend to stand there gaping all night?'

'Yes, ma'am. No, ma'am. Yes, ma'am.'

It was pretty to hear him.

'It is an odd coincidence, Mr Wooster,' said Miss Mapleton, becoming instantly matey once more as the outcast removed himself. 'I had just finished writing a letter to your aunt when you arrived. I shall certainly reopen it to tell her how gallantly you have behaved tonight. I have not in the past entertained a very high opinion of the modern young man, but you have caused me to alter it. To track these men unarmed through a dark garden argues courage of a high order. And it was most courteous of you to think of calling upon me. I appreciate it. Are you making a long stay in Bingley?'

This was another one I could answer.

'No,' I said. 'Afraid not. Must be in London tomorrow.'

'Perhaps you could lunch before your departure?'

'Afraid not. Thanks most awfully. Very important engagement that I can't get out of. Eh, Jeeves?'

'Yes, sir.'

'Have to catch the ten-thirty train, what?'

'Without fail, sir.'

'I am sorry,' said Miss Mapleton. 'I had hoped that you would be able to say a few words to my girls. Some other time perhaps?'

'Absolutely.'

'You must let me know when you are coming to Bingley again.'

'When I come to Bingley again,' I said, 'I will certainly let you know.'

'If I remember your plans correctly, sir, you are not likely to be in Bingley for some little time, sir.'

'Not for some considerable time, Jeeves,' I said.

The front door closed. I passed a hand across the brow.

'Tell me all, Jeeves,' I said.

'Sir?'

'I say, tell me all. I am fogged.'

'It is quite simple, sir. I ventured to take the liberty, on my own responsibility, of putting into operation the alternative scheme which, if you remember, I wished to outline to you.'

'What was it?'

'It occurred to me, sir, that it would be most judicious for me to call at the back door and desire an interview with Miss Mapleton. This, I fancied, would enable me, while the maid had gone to convey my request to Miss Mapleton, to introduce the young lady into the house unobserved.'

'And did you?'

'Yes, sir. She proceeded up the back stairs and is now safely in bed.'

I frowned. The thought of the kid Clementina jarred upon me.

'She is, is she?' I said. 'A murrain on her, Jeeves, and may she be stood in the corner next Sunday for not knowing her Collect. And then you saw Miss Mapleton?'

'Yes, sir.'

'And told her that I was out in the garden, chivvying burglars with my bare hands?'

'Yes, sir.'

'And had been on my way to call upon her?'

'Yes, sir.'

'And now she's busy adding a postscript to her letter to Aunt Agatha, speaking of me in terms of unstinted praise.'

'Yes, sir.'

I drew in a deep breath. It was too dark for me to see the super-human intelligence which must have been sloshing about all over the surface of the man's features. I tried to, but couldn't make it.

'Jeeves,' I said, 'I should have been guided by you from the first.'

'It might have spared you some temporary unpleasantness, sir.'

'Unpleasantness is right. When that lantern shone up at me in the silent night, Jeeves, just as I had finished poising the pot, I thought I had unshipped a rib. Jeeves!'

'Sir?'

'That Antibes expedition is off.'

'I am glad to hear it, sir.'

'If young Bobbie Wickham can get me into a mess like this in a quiet spot like Bingley-on-Sea, what might she not be able to accomplish at a really lively resort like Antibes?'

'Precisely, sir. Miss Wickham, as I have sometimes said, though a charming –'

'Yes, yes, Jeeves. There is no necessity to stress the point. The Wooster eyes are definitely opened.'

I hesitated.

'Jeeves.'

'Sir?'

'Those plus-fours.'

'Yes, sir?'

'You may give them to the poor.'

'Thank you very much, sir.'

I sighed.

'It is my heart's blood, Jeeves.'

'I appreciate the sacrifice, sir. But, once the first pang of separation is over, you will feel much easier without them.'

'You think so?'

'I am convinced of it, sir.'

'So be it, then, Jeeves,' I said, 'so be it.'

8

THE LOVE THAT PURIFIES

There is a ghastly moment in the year, generally about the beginning of August, when Jeeves insists on taking a holiday, the slacker, and legs it off to some seaside resort for a couple of weeks, leaving me stranded. This moment had now arrived, and we were discussing what was to be done with the young master.

'I had gathered the impression, sir,' said Jeeves, 'that you were proposing to accept Mr Sipperley's invitation to join him at his Hampshire residence.'

I laughed. One of those bitter, rasping ones.

'Correct, Jeeves. I was. But mercifully I was enabled to discover young Sippy's foul plot in time. Do you know what?'

'No, sir.'

'My spies informed me that Sippy's fiancée, Miss Moon, was to be there. Also his fiancée's mother, Mrs Moon, and his fiancée's small brother, Master Moon. You see the hideous treachery lurking behind the invitation? You see the man's loathsome design? Obviously my job was to be the task of keeping Mrs Moon and little Sebastian Moon interested and amused while Sippy and his blighted girl went off for the day, roaming the pleasant woodlands and talking of this and that. I doubt if anyone has ever had a narrower escape. You remember little Sebastian?'

'Yes, sir.'

'His goggle eyes? His golden curls?'

'Yes, sir.'

'I don't know why it is, but I've never been able to bear with fortitude anything in the shape of a kid with golden curls. Confronted with one, I feel the urge to step on him or drop things on him from a height.'

'Many strong natures are affected in the same way, sir.'

'So no *chez* Sippy for me. Was that the front-door bell ringing?'

'Yes, sir.'

'Somebody stands without.'

'Yes, sir.'

'Better go and see who it is.'

'Yes, sir.'

He oozed off, to return a moment later bearing a telegram. I opened it, and a soft smile played about the lips.

'Amazing how often things happen as if on a cue, Jeeves. This is from my Aunt Dahlia, inviting me down to her place in Worcestershire.'

'Most satisfactory, sir.'

'Yes. How I came to overlook her when searching for a haven, I can't think. The ideal home from home. Picturesque surroundings. Company's own water, and the best cook in England. You have not forgotten Anatole?'

'No, sir.'

'And above all, Jeeves, at Aunt Dahlia's there should be an almost total shortage of blasted kids. True, there is her son Bonzo, who, I take it, will be home for the holidays, but I don't mind Bonzo. Buzz off and send a wire, accepting.'

'Yes, sir.'

'And then shove a few necessaries together, including golf clubs and tennis racquet.'

'Very good, sir. I am glad that matters have been so happily adjusted.'

I think I have mentioned before that my Aunt Dahlia stands alone in the grim regiment of my aunts as a real good sort and a chirpy sportsman. She is the one, if you remember, who married old Tom Travers and, with the assistance of Jeeves, lured Mrs Bingo Little's French cook, Anatole, away from Mrs BL and into her own employment. To visit her is always a pleasure. She generally has some cheery birds staying with her, and there is none of that rot about getting up for breakfast which one is sadly apt to find at country-houses.

It was, accordingly, with unalloyed lightness of heart that I edged the two-seater into the garage at Brinkley Court, Worc., and strolled round to the house by way of the shrubbery and the tennis-lawn, to report arrival. I had just got across the lawn when a head poked itself out of the smoking room window and beamed at me in an amiable sort of way.

'Ah, Mr Wooster,' it said. 'Ha, ha!'

'Ho, ho!' I replied, not to be outdone in the courtesies.

It had taken me a couple of seconds to place this head. I now perceived that it belonged to a rather moth-eaten septuagenarian of

the name of Anstruther, an old friend of Aunt Dahlia's late father.
I had met him at her house in London once or twice. An agreeable
cove but somewhat given to nervous breakdowns.

'Just arrived?' he asked, beaming as before.

'This minute,' I said, also beaming.

'I fancy you will find our good hostess in the drawing room.'

'Right,' I said, and after a bit more beaming to and fro I
pushed on.

Aunt Dahlia was in the drawing room, and welcomed me with
gratifying enthusiasm. She beamed, too. It was one of those big days
for beamers.

'Hullo, ugly,' she said. 'So here you are. Thank heaven you were
able to come.'

It was the right tone, and one I should be glad to hear in others
of the family circle, notably my Aunt Agatha.

'Always a pleasure to enjoy your hosp, Aunt Dahlia,' I said
cordially. 'I anticipate a delightful and restful visit. I see you've got
Mr Anstruther staying here. Anybody else?'

'Do you know Lord Snettisham?'

'I've met him, racing.'

'He's here, and Lady Snettisham.'

'And Bonzo, of course?'

'Yes. And Thomas?'

'Uncle Thomas?'

'No, he's in Scotland. Your cousin Thomas.'

'You don't mean Aunt Agatha's loathly son?'

'Of course I do. How many cousin Thomases do you think you've
got, fathead? Agatha has gone to Homburg and planted the child
on me.'

I was visibly agitated.

'But, Aunt Dahlia! Do you realize what you've taken on? Have you
an inkling of the sort of scourge you've introduced into your home?
In the society of young Thos, strong men quail. He is England's
premier fiend in human shape. There is no devilry beyond his
scope.'

'That's what I have always gathered from the form book,' agreed
the relative. 'But just now, curse him, he's behaving like something
out of a Sunday School story. You see, poor old Mr Anstruther is
very frail these days, and when he found he was in a house containing
two small boys he acted promptly. He offered a prize of five pounds
to whichever behaved best during his stay. The consequence is that,
ever since, Thomas has had large white wings sprouting out of his

shoulders.' A shadow seemed to pass across her face. She appeared embittered. 'Mercenary little brute!' she said. 'I never saw such a sickeningly well-behaved kid in my life. It's enough to make one despair of human nature.'

I couldn't follow her.

'But isn't that all to the good?'

'No, it's not.'

'I can't see why. Surely a smug, oily Thos about the house is better than a Thos, raging hither and thither and being a menace to society? Stands to reason.'

'It doesn't stand to anything of the kind. You see, Bertie, this Good Conduct prize has made matters a bit complex. There are wheels within wheels. The thing stirred Jane Snettisham's sporting blood to such an extent that she insisted on having a bet on the result.'

A great light shone upon me. I got what she was driving at.

'Ah!' I said. 'Now I follow. Now I see. Now I comprehend. She's betting on Thos, is she?'

'Yes. And naturally, knowing him, I thought the thing was in the bag.'

'Of course.'

'I couldn't see myself losing. Heaven knows I have no illusions about my darling Bonzo. Bonzo is, and has been from the cradle, a pest. But to back him to win a Good Conduct contest with Thomas seemed to me simply money for jam.'

'Absolutely.'

'When it comes to devilry, Bonzo is just a good, ordinary selling-plater. Whereas Thomas is a classic yearling.'

'Exactly. I don't see that you have any cause to worry, Aunt Dahlia. Thos can't last. He's bound to crack.'

'Yes. But before that the mischief may be done.'

'Mischief?'

'Yes. There is dirty work afoot, Bertie,' said Aunt Dahlia gravely. 'When I booked this bet, I reckoned without the hideous blackness of the Snettishams' souls. Only yesterday it came to my knowledge that Jack Snettisham had been urging Bonzo to climb on the roof and boo down Mr Anstruther's chimney.'

'No!'

'Yes. Mr Anstruther is very frail, poor old fellow, and it would have frightened him into a fit. On coming out of which, his first action would have been to disqualify Bonzo and declare Thomas the winner by default.'

'But Bonzo did not boo?'

'No,' said Aunt Dahlia, and a mother's pride rang in her voice. 'He firmly refused to boo. Mercifully, he is in love at the moment and it has quite altered his nature. He scorned the tempter.'

'In love? Who with?'

'Lilian Gish. We had an old film of hers at the Bijou Dream in the village a week ago, and Bonzo saw her for the first time. He came out with a pale, set face, and ever since has been trying to lead a finer, better life. So the peril was averted.'

'That's good.'

'Yes. But now it's my turn. You don't suppose I am going to take a thing like that lying down, do you? Treat me right, and I am fairness itself; but try any of this nobbling of starters, and I can play that game, too. If this Good Conduct contest is to be run on rough lines, I can do my bit as well as anyone. Far too much hangs on the issue for me to handicap myself by remembering the lessons I learned at my mother's knee.'

'Lot of money involved?'

'Much more than mere money. I've betted Anatole against Jane Snettisham's kitchen-maid.'

'Great Scott! Uncle Thomas will have something to say if he comes back and finds Anatole gone.'

'And won't he say it!'

'Pretty long odds you gave her, didn't you? I mean, Anatole is famed far and wide as a hash-slinger without peer.'

'Well, Jane Snettisham's kitchen-maid is not to be sneezed at. She is very hot stuff, they tell me, and good kitchen-maids nowadays are about as rare as original Holbeins. Besides, I had to give her a shade the best of the odds. She stood out for it. Well, anyway, to get back to what I was saying, if the opposition are going to place temptations in Bonzo's path, they shall jolly well be placed in Thomas's path, too, and plenty of them. So ring for Jeeves and let him get his brain working.'

'But I haven't brought Jeeves.'

'You haven't brought Jeeves?'

'No. He always takes his holiday at this time of year. He's down at Bognor for the shrimping.'

Aunt Dahlia registered deep concern.

'Then send for him at once! What earthly use do you suppose you are without Jeeves, you poor ditherer?'

I drew myself up a trifle – in fact, to my full height. Nobody has a greater respect for Jeeves than I have, but the Wooster pride was stung.

'Jeeves isn't the only one with brains,' I said coldly. 'Leave this thing to me, Aunt Dahlia. By dinner-time tonight I shall hope to have a fully matured scheme to submit for your approval. If I can't thoroughly encompass this Thos, I'll eat my hat.'

'About all you'll get to eat if Anatole leaves,' said Aunt Dahlia in a pessimistic manner which I did not like to see.

I was brooding pretty tensely as I left the presence. I have always had a suspicion that Aunt Dahlia, while invariably matey and bonhomous and seeming to take pleasure in my society, has a lower opinion of my intelligence than I quite like. Too often it is her practice to address me as 'fathead', and if I put forward any little thought or idea or fancy in her hearing it is apt to be greeted with the affectionate but jarring guffaw. In our recent interview she had hinted quite plainly that she considered me negligible in a crisis which, like the present one, called for initiative and resource. It was my intention to show her how greatly she had underestimated me.

To let you see the sort of fellow I really am, I got a ripe, excellent idea before I had gone half-way down the corridor. I examined it for the space of one and a half cigarettes, and could see no flaw in it, provided – I say, provided – old Mr Anstruther's notion of what constituted bad conduct squared with mine.

The great thing on these occasions, as Jeeves will tell you, is to get a toe-hold on the psychology of the individual. Study the individual, and you will bring home the bacon. Now, I had been studying young Thos for years, and I knew his psychology from caviare to nuts. He is one of those kids who never let the sun go down on their wrath, if you know what I mean. I mean to say, do something to annoy or offend or upset this juvenile thug, and he will proceed at the earliest possible opp. to wreak a hideous vengeance upon you. Only the previous summer, for instance, it having been drawn to his attention that the latter had reported him for smoking, he had marooned a Cabinet Minister on an island in the lake at Aunt Agatha's place in Hertfordshire – in the rain, mark you, and with no company but that of one of the nastiest-minded swans I have ever encountered. Well, I mean!

So now it seemed to me that a few well-chosen taunts, or jibes, directed at his more sensitive points, must infallibly induce in this Thos a frame of mind which would lead to his working some sensational violence upon me. And, if you wonder that I was willing to sacrifice myself to this frightful extent in order to do Aunt Dahlia a bit of good, I can only say that we Woosters are like that.

The one point that seemed to me to want a spot of clearing up was this: viz., would old Mr Anstruther consider an outrage perpetrated on the person of Bertram Wooster a crime sufficiently black to cause him to rule Thos out of the race? Or would he just give a senile chuckle and mumble something about boys being boys? Because, if the latter, the thing was off. I decided to have a word with the old boy and make sure.

He was still in the smoking room, looking very frail over the morning *Times*. I got to the point at once.

'Oh, Mr Anstruther,' I said. 'What ho!'

'I don't like the way the American market is shaping,' he said. 'I don't like this strong Bear movement.'

'No?' I said. 'Well, be that as it may, about this Good Conduct prize of yours?'

'Ah, you have heard of that, eh?'

'I don't quite understand how you are doing the judging.'

'No? It is very simple. I have a system of daily marks. At the beginning of each day I accord the two lads twenty marks apiece. These are subject to withdrawal either in small or large quantities according to the magnitude of the offence. To take a simple example, shouting outside my bedroom in the early morning would involve a loss of three marks – whistling two. The penalty for a more serious lapse would be correspondingly greater. Before retiring to rest at night I record the day's marks in my little book. Simple, but, I think, ingenious, Mr Wooster?'

'Absolutely.'

'So far the result has been extremely gratifying. Neither of the little fellows has lost a single mark, and my nervous system is acquiring a tone which, when I learned that two lads of immature years would be staying in the house during my visit, I confess I had not dared to anticipate.'

'I see,' I said. 'Great work. And how do you react to what I might call general moral turpitude?'

'I beg your pardon?'

'Well, I mean when the thing doesn't affect you personally. Suppose one of them did something to me, for instance? Set a booby-trap or something? Or, shall we say, put a toad or so in my bed?'

He seemed shocked at the very idea.

'I would certainly in such circumstances deprive the culprit of a full ten marks.'

'Only ten?'

'Fifteen, then.'

'Twenty is a nice, round number.'

'Well, possibly even twenty. I have a peculiar horror of practical joking.'

'Me, too.'

'You will not fail to advise me, Mr Wooster, should such an outrage occur?'

'You shall have the news before anyone,' I assured him.

And so out into the garden, ranging to and fro in quest of young Thos. I knew where I was now. Bertram's feet were on solid ground.

I hadn't been hunting long before I found him in the summer-house, reading an improving book.

'Hullo,' he said, smiling a saintlike smile.

This scourge of humanity was a chunky kid whom a too indulgent public had allowed to infest the country for a matter of fourteen years. His nose was snub, his eyes green, his general aspect that of one studying to be a gangster. I had never liked his looks much, and with a saintlike smile added to them they became ghastly to a degree.

I ran over in my mind a few assorted taunts.

'Well, young Thos,' I said. 'So there you are. You're getting as fat as a pig.'

It seemed as good an opening as any other. Experience had taught me that if there was a subject on which he was unlikely to accept persiflage in a spirit of amused geniality it was this matter of his bulging tum. On the last occasion when I made a remark of this nature, he had replied to me, child though he was, in terms which I would have been proud to have had in my own vocabulary. But now, though a sort of wistful gleam did flit for a moment into his eyes, he merely smiled in a more saintlike manner than ever.

'Yes, I think I have been putting on a little weight,' he said gently. 'I must try and exercise a lot while I'm here. Won't you sit down, Bertie?' he asked, rising. 'You must be tired after your journey. I'll get you a cushion. Have you cigarettes? And matches? I could bring you some from the smoking room. Would you like me to fetch you something to drink?'

It is not too much to say that I felt baffled. In spite of what Aunt Dahlia had told me, I don't think that until this moment I had really believed there could have been anything in the nature of a genuinely sensational change in this young plugugly's attitude towards his fellows. But now, hearing him talk as if he were a combination of

Boy Scout and delivery wagon, I felt definitely baffled. However, I stuck at it in the old bull-dog way.

'Are you still at that rotten kids' school of yours?' I asked.

He might have been proof against jibes at his *embonpoint*, but it seemed to me incredible that he could have sold himself for gold so completely as to lie down under taunts directed at his school. I was wrong. The money-lust evidently held him in its grip. He merely shook his head.

'I left this term. I'm going to Pevenhurst next term.'

'They wear mortar-boards there, don't they?'

'Yes.'

'With pink tassels?'

'Yes.'

'What a priceless ass you'll look!' I said, but without much hope. And I laughed heartily.

'I expect I shall,' he said, and laughed still more heartily.

'Mortar-boards!'

'Ha, ha!'

'Pink tassels!'

'Ha, ha!'

I gave the thing up.

'Well, teuf-teuf,' I said moodily, and withdrew.

A couple of days later I realized that the virus had gone even deeper than I had thought. The kid was irredeemably sordid.

It was old Mr Anstruther who sprang the bad news.

'Oh, Mr Wooster,' he said, meeting me on the stairs as I came down after a refreshing breakfast. 'You were good enough to express an interest in this little prize for Good Conduct which I am offering.'

'Oh, ah?'

'I explained to you my system of marking, I believe. Well, this morning I was impelled to vary it somewhat. The circumstances seemed to me to demand it. I happened to encounter our hostess's nephew, the boy Thomas, returning to the house, his aspect somewhat weary, it appeared to me, and travel-stained. I inquired of him where he had been at that early hour – it was not yet breakfast-time – and he replied that he had heard you mention overnight a regret that you had omitted to order the *Sporting Times* to be sent to you before leaving London, and he had actually walked all the way to the railway-station, a distance of more than three miles, to procure it for you.'

The old boy swam before my eyes. He looked like two old Mr Anstruthers, both flickering at the edges.

'What!'

'I can understand your emotion, Mr Wooster. I can appreciate it. It is indeed rarely that one encounters such unselfish kindliness in a lad of his age. So genuinely touched was I by the goodness of heart which the episode showed that I have deviated from my original system and awarded the little fellow a bonus of fifteen marks.'

'Fifteen!'

'On second thoughts, I shall make it twenty. That, as you yourself suggested, is a nice, round number.'

He doddered away, and I bounded off to find Aunt Dahlia.

'Aunt Dahlia,' I said, 'matters have taken a sinister turn.'

'You bet your Sunday spats they have,' agreed Aunt Dahlia emphatically. 'Do you know what happened just now? That crook Snettisham, who ought to be warned off the turf and hounded out of his club, offered Bonzo ten shillings if he would burst a paper bag behind Mr Anstruther's chair at breakfast. Thank heaven the love of a good woman triumphed again. My sweet Bonzo merely looked at him and walked away in a marked manner. But it just shows you what we are up against.'

'We are up against worse than that, Aunt Dahlia,' I said. And I told her what had happened.

She was stunned. Aghast, you might call it.

'*Thomas* did that?'

'Thos in person.'

'Walked six miles to get you a paper?'

'Six miles and a bit.'

'The young hound! Good heavens, Bertie, do you realize that he may go on doing these Acts of Kindness daily – perhaps twice a day? Is there no way of stopping him?'

'None that I can think of. No, Aunt Dahlia, I must confess it. I am baffled. There is only one thing to do. We must send for Jeeves.'

'And about time,' said the relative churlishly. 'He ought to have been here from the start. Wire him this morning.'

There is good stuff in Jeeves. His heart is in the right place. The acid test does not find him wanting. Many men in his position, summoned back by telegram in the middle of their annual vacation, might have cut up rough a bit. But not Jeeves. On the following afternoon in he blew, looking bronzed and fit, and I gave him the scenario without delay.

'So there you have it, Jeeves,' I said, having sketched out the facts. 'The problem is one that will exercise your intelligence to the utmost.

Rest now, and tonight, after a light repast, withdraw to some solitary place and get down to it. Is there any particularly stimulating food or beverage you would like for dinner? Anything that you feel would give the old brain just that extra fillip? If so, name it.'

'Thank you very much, sir, but I have already hit upon a plan which should, I fancy, prove effective.'

I gazed at the man with some awe.

'Already?'

'Yes, sir.'

'Not *already?*'

'Yes, sir.'

'Something to do with the psychology of the individual?'

'Precisely, sir.'

I shook my head, a bit discouraged. Doubts had begun to creep in.

'Well, spring it, Jeeves,' I said. 'But I have not much hope. Having only just arrived, you cannot possibly be aware of the frightful change that has taken place in young Thos. You are probably building on your knowledge of him, when last seen. Useless, Jeeves. Stirred by the prospect of getting his hooks on five of the best, this blighted boy has become so dashed virtuous that his armour seems to contain no chink. I mocked at his waistline and sneered at his school and he merely smiled in a pale, dying-duck sort of way. Well, that'll show you. However, let us hear what you have to suggest.'

'It occurred to me, sir, that the most judicious plan in the circumstances would be for you to request Mrs Travers to invite Master Sebastian Moon here for a short visit.'

I shook the onion again. The scheme sounded to me like apple sauce, and Grade A apple sauce, at that.

'What earthly good would that do?' I asked, not without a touch of asperity. 'Why Sebastian Moon?'

'He has golden curls, sir.'

'What of it?'

'The strongest natures are sometimes not proof against long golden curls.'

Well, it was a thought, of course. But I can't say I was leaping about to any great extent. It might be that the sight of Sebastian Moon would break down Thos's iron self-control to the extent of causing him to inflict mayhem on the person, but I wasn't any too hopeful.

'It may be so, Jeeves.'

'I do not think I am too sanguine, sir. You must remember that

Master Moon, apart from his curls, has a personality which is not uniformly pleasing. He is apt to express himself with a breezy candour which I fancy Master Thomas might feel inclined to resent in one some years his junior.'

I had had a feeling all along that there was a flaw somewhere, and now it seemed to me that I had spotted it.

'But, Jeeves. Granted that little Sebastian is the pot of poison you indicate, why won't he act just as forcibly on young Bonzo as on Thos? Pretty silly we should look if our nominee started putting it across him. Never forget that already Bonzo is twenty marks down and falling back in the betting.'

'I do not anticipate any such contingency, sir. Master Travers is in love, and love is a very powerful restraining influence at the age of thirteen.'

'H'm.' I mused. 'Well, we can but try, Jeeves.'

'Yes, sir.'

'I'll get Aunt Dahlia to write to Sippy tonight.'

I'm bound to say that the spectacle of little Sebastian when he arrived two days later did much to remove pessimism from my outlook. If ever there was a kid whose whole appearance seemed to call aloud to any right-minded boy to lure him into a quiet spot and inflict violence upon him, that kid was undeniably Sebastian Moon. He reminded me strongly of Little Lord Fauntleroy. I marked young Thos's demeanour closely at the moment of their meeting and, unless I was much mistaken, there came into his eyes the sort of look which would come into those of an Indian chief – Chingachgook, let us say, or Sitting Bull – just before he started reaching for his scalping-knife. He had the air of one who is about ready to begin.

True, his manner as he shook hands was guarded. Only a keen observer could have detected that he was stirred to his depths. But I had seen, and I summoned Jeeves forthwith.

'Jeeves,' I said, 'if I appeared to think poorly of that scheme of yours, I now withdraw my remarks. I believe you have found the way. I was noticing Thos at the moment of impact. His eyes had a strange gleam.'

'Indeed, sir?'

'He shifted uneasily on his feet and his ears wiggled. He had, in short, the appearance of a boy who was holding himself in with an effort almost too great for his frail body.'

'Yes, sir?'

'Yes, Jeeves. I received a distinct impression of something being on the point of exploding. Tomorrow I shall ask Aunt Dahlia to take the two warts for a country ramble, to lose them in some sequestered spot, and to leave the rest to Nature.'

'It is a good idea, sir.'

'It is more than a good idea, Jeeves,' I said. 'It is a pip.'

You know, the older I get the more firmly do I become convinced that there is no such thing as a pip in existence. Again and again have I seen the apparently sure thing go phut, and now it is rarely indeed that I can be lured from my aloof scepticism. Fellows come sidling up to me at the Drones and elsewhere, urging me to invest on some horse that can't lose even if it gets struck by lightning at the starting-post, but Bertram Wooster shakes his head. He has seen too much of life to be certain of anything.

If anyone had told me that my Cousin Thos, left alone for an extended period of time with a kid of the superlative foulness of Sebastian Moon, would not only refrain from cutting off his curls with a pocket-knife and chasing him across country into a muddy pond but would actually return home carrying the gruesome kid on his back because he had got a blister on his foot, I would have laughed scornfully. I knew Thos. I knew his work. I had seen him in action. And I was convinced that not even the prospect of collecting five pounds would be enough to give him pause.

And yet what happened? In the quiet evenfall, when the little birds were singing their sweetest and all Nature seemed to whisper of hope and happiness, the blow fell. I was chatting with old Mr Anstruther on the terrace when suddenly round a bend in the drive the two kids hove in view. Sebastian, seated on Thos's back, his hat off and his golden curls floating on the breeze, was singing as much as he could remember of a comic song, and Thos, bowed down by the burden but carrying on gamely, was trudging along, smiling that bally saintlike smile of his. He parked the kid on the front steps and came across to us.

'Sebastian got a nail in his shoe,' he said in a low, virtuous voice. 'It hurt him to walk, so I gave him a piggy-back.'

I heard old Mr Anstruther draw in his breath sharply.

'All the way home?'

'Yes, sir.'

'In this hot sunshine?'

'Yes, sir.'

'But was he not very heavy?'

'He was a little, sir,' said Thos, uncorking the saintlike once more. 'But it would have hurt him awfully to walk.'

I pushed off. I had had enough. If ever a septuagenarian looked on the point of handing out another bonus, that septuagenarian was old Mr Anstruther. He had the unmistakable bonus glitter in his eye. I withdrew, and found Jeeves in my bedroom messing about with ties and things.

He pursed the lips a bit on hearing the news.

'Serious, sir.'

'Very serious, Jeeves.'

'I had feared this, sir.'

'Had you? I hadn't. I was convinced Thos would have massacred young Sebastian. I banked on it. It just shows what the greed for money will do. This is a commercial age, Jeeves. When I was a boy, I would cheerfully have forfeited five quid in order to deal faithfully with a kid like Sebastian. I would have considered it money well spent.'

'You are mistaken, sir, in your estimate of the motives actuating Master Thomas. It was not a mere desire to win five pounds that caused him to curb his natural impulses.'

'Eh?'

'I have ascertained the true reason for his change of heart, sir.'

I felt fogged.

'Religion, Jeeves?'

'No, sir. Love.'

'Love?'

'Yes, sir. The young gentleman confided in me during a brief conversation in the hall shortly after luncheon. We had been speaking for a while on neutral subjects, when he suddenly turned a deeper shade of pink and after some slight hesitation inquired of me if I did not think Miss Greta Garbo the most beautiful woman at present in existence.'

I clutched the brow.

'Jeeves! Don't tell me Thos is in love with Greta Garbo?'

'Yes, sir. Unfortunately such is the case. He gave me to understand that it had been coming on for some time, and her last picture settled the issue. His voice shook with an emotion which it was impossible to misread. I gathered from his observations, sir, that he proposes to spend the remainder of his life trying to make himself worthy of her.'

It was a knock-out. This was the end.

'This is the end, Jeeves,' I said. 'Bonzo must be a good forty marks behind by now. Only some sensational and spectacular outrage upon the public weal on the part of young Thos could have enabled him to wipe out the lead. And of that there is now, apparently, no chance.'

'The eventuality does appear remote, sir.'

I brooded.

'Uncle Thomas will have a fit when he comes back and finds Anatole gone.'

'Yes, sir.'

'Aunt Dahlia will drain the bitter cup to the dregs.'

'Yes, sir.'

'And speaking from a purely selfish point of view, the finest cooking I have ever bitten will pass out of my life for ever, unless the Snettishams invite me in some night to take pot luck. And that eventuality is also remote.'

'Yes, sir.'

'Then the only thing I can do is square the shoulders and face the inevitable.'

'Yes, sir.'

'Like some aristocrat of the French Revolution popping into the tumbril, what? The brave smile. The stiff upper lip.'

'Yes, sir.'

'Right ho, then. Is the shirt studded?'

'Yes, sir.'

'The tie chosen?'

'Yes, sir.'

'The collar and evening underwear all in order?'

'Yes, sir.'

'Then I'll have a bath and be with you in two ticks.'

It is all very well to talk about the brave smile and the stiff upper lip, but my experience – and I daresay others have found the same – is that they are a dashed sight easier to talk about than actually to fix on the face. For the next few days, I'm bound to admit, I found myself, in spite of every effort, registering gloom pretty consistently. For, as if to make things tougher than they might have been, Anatole at this juncture suddenly developed a cooking streak which put all his previous efforts in the shade.

Night after night we sat at the dinner table, the food melting in our mouths, and Aunt Dahlia would look at me and I would look at Aunt Dahlia, and the male Snettisham would ask the female Snettisham in a ghastly, gloating sort of way if she had ever tasted such cooking and the female Snettisham would smirk at the male Snettisham and say she never had in all her puff, and I would look at Aunt Dahlia and

Aunt Dahlia would look at me and our eyes would be full of unshed tears, if you know what I mean.

And all the time old Mr Anstruther's visit drawing to a close.

The sands running out, so to speak.

And then, on the very last afternoon of his stay, the thing happened.

It was one of those warm, drowsy, peaceful afternoons. I was up in my bedroom, getting off a spot of correspondence which I had neglected of late, and from where I sat I looked down on the shady lawn, fringed with its gay flower-beds. There was a bird or two hopping about, a butterfly or so fluttering to and fro, and an assortment of bees buzzing hither and thither. In a garden chair sat old Mr Anstruther, getting his eight hours. It was a sight which, had I had less on my mind, would no doubt have soothed the old soul a bit. The only blot on the landscape was Lady Snettisham, walking among the flower-beds and probably sketching out future menus, curse her.

And so for a time everything carried on. The birds hopped, the butterflies fluttered, the bees buzzed, and old Mr Anstruther snored – all in accordance with the programme. And I worked through a letter to my tailor to the point where I proposed to say something pretty strong about the way the right sleeve of my last coat bagged.

There was a tap on the door, and Jeeves entered, bringing the second post. I laid the letters listlessly on the table beside me.

'Well, Jeeves,' I said sombrely.

'Sir?'

'Mr Anstruther leaves tomorrow.'

'Yes, sir.'

I gazed down at the sleeping septuagenarian.

'In my young days, Jeeves,' I said, 'however much I might have been in love, I could never have resisted the spectacle of an old gentleman asleep like that in a deck-chair. I would have done *something* to him, no matter what the cost.'

'Indeed, sir?'

'Yes. Probably with a pea-shooter. But the modern boy is degenerate. He has lost his vim. I suppose Thos is indoors on this lovely afternoon, showing Sebastian his stamp-album or something. Ha!' I said, and I said it rather nastily.

'I fancy Master Thomas and Master Sebastian are playing in the stable-yard, sir. I encountered Master Sebastian not long back and he informed me he was on his way thither.'

'The motion pictures, Jeeves,' I said, 'are the curse of the age. But for them, if Thos had found himself alone in a stable-yard with a kid like Sebastian –'

I broke off. From some point to the south-west, out of my line of vision, there had proceeded a piercing squeal.

It cut through the air like a knife, and old Mr Anstruther leaped up as if it had run into the fleshy part of his leg. And the next moment little Sebastian appeared, going well and followed at a short interval by Thos, who was going even better. In spite of the fact that he was hampered in his movements by a large stable-bucket which he bore in his right hand, Thos was running a great race. He had almost come up with Sebastian, when the latter, with great presence of mind, dodged behind Mr Anstruther, and there for a moment the matter rested.

But only for a moment. Thos, for some reason plainly stirred to the depths of his being, moved adroitly to one side and, poising the bucket for an instant, discharged its contents. And Mr Anstruther, who had just moved to the same side, received, as far as I could gather from a distance, the entire consignment. In one second, without any previous training or upbringing, he had become the wettest man in Worcestershire.

'Jeeves!' I cried.

'Yes, indeed, sir,' said Jeeves, and seemed to me to put the whole thing in a nutshell.

Down below, things were hotting up nicely. Old Mr Anstruther may have been frail, but he undoubtedly had his moments. I have rarely seen a man of his years conduct himself with such a lissom abandon. There was a stick lying beside the chair, and with this in hand he went into action like a two-year-old. A moment later, he and Thos had passed out of the picture round the side of the house, Thos cutting out a rare pace but, judging from the sounds of anguish, not quite good enough to distance the field.

The tumult and the shouting died; and, after gazing for a while with considerable satisfaction at the Snettisham, who was standing there with a sand-bagged look watching her nominee pass right out of the betting, I turned to Jeeves. I felt quietly triumphant. It is not often that I score off him, but now I had scored in no uncertain manner.

'You see, Jeeves,' I said, 'I was right and you were wrong. Blood will tell. Once a Thos, always a Thos. Can the leopard change his spots or the Ethiopian his what-not? What was that thing they used to teach us at school about expelling Nature?'

'You may expel Nature with a pitchfork, sir, but she will always return? In the original Latin –'

'Never mind about the original Latin. The point is that I told you Thos could not resist those curls, and he couldn't. You would have it that he could.'

'I do not fancy it was the curls that caused the upheaval, sir.'

'Must have been.'

'No, sir. I think Master Sebastian had been speaking disparagingly of Miss Garbo.'

'Eh? Why would he do that?'

'I suggested that he should do so, sir, not long ago when I encountered him on his way to the stable-yard. It was a move which he was very willing to take, as he informed me that in his opinion Miss Garbo was definitely inferior both in beauty and talent to Miss Clara Bow, for whom he has long nourished a deep regard. From what we have just witnessed, sir, I imagine that Master Sebastian must have introduced the topic into the conversation at an early point.'

I sank into a chair. The Wooster system can stand just so much.

'Jeeves!'

'Sir?'

'You tell me that Sebastian Moon, a stripling of such tender years that he can go about the place with long curls without causing mob violence, is in love with Clara Bow?'

'And has been for some little time, he gave me to understand, sir.'

'Jeeves, this Younger Generation is hot stuff.'

'Yes, sir.'

'Were you like that in your day?'

'No, sir.'

'Nor I, Jeeves. At the age of fourteen I once wrote to Marie Lloyd for her autograph, but apart from that my private life could bear the strictest investigation. However, that is not the point. The point is, Jeeves, that once more I must pay you a marked tribute.'

'Thank you very much, sir.'

'Once more you have stepped forward like the great man you are and spread sweetness and light in no uncertain measure.'

'I am glad to have given satisfaction, sir. Would you be requiring my services any further?'

'You mean you wish to return to Bognor and its shrimps? Do so, Jeeves, and stay there another fortnight, if you wish. And may success attend your net.'

'Thank you very much, sir.'

I eyed the man fixedly. His head stuck out at the back, and his eyes sparkled with the light of pure intelligence.

'I am sorry for the shrimp that tries to pit its feeble cunning against you, Jeeves,' I said.

And I meant it.

9

JEEVES AND THE OLD SCHOOL CHUM

In the autumn of the year in which Yorkshire Pudding won the Manchester November Handicap, the fortunes of my old pal Richard ('Bingo') Little seemed to have reached their – what's the word I want? He was, to all appearances, absolutely on plush. He ate well, slept well, was happily married; and, his Uncle Wilberforce having at last handed in his dinner-pail, respected by all, had come into possession of a large income and a fine old place in the country about thirty miles from Norwich. Buzzing down there for a brief visit, I came away convinced that, if ever a bird was sitting on top of the world, that bird was Bingo.

I had to come away because the family were shooting me off to Harrogate to chaperone my Uncle George, whose liver had been giving him the elbow again. But, as we sat pushing down the morning meal on the day of my departure, I readily agreed to play a return date as soon as ever I could fight my way back to civilization.

'Come in time for the Lakenham races,' urged young Bingo. He took aboard a second cargo of sausages and bacon, for he had always been a good trencherman and the country air seemed to improve his appetite. 'We're going to motor over with a luncheon basket, and more or less revel.'

I was just about to say that I would make a point of it, when Mrs Bingo, who was opening letters behind the coffee-apparatus, suddenly uttered a pleased yowl.

'Oh, sweetie-lambkin!' she cried.

Mrs B., if you remember, before her marriage, was the celebrated female novelist, Rosie M. Banks, and it is in some such ghastly fashion that she habitually addresses the other half of the sketch. She has got that way, I take it, from a life-time of writing heart-throb fiction for the masses. Bingo doesn't seem to mind. I suppose, seeing that the little woman is the author of such outstanding bilge as *Mervyn*

Keene, Clubman and *Only A Factory Girl*, he is thankful it isn't anything worse.

'Oh, sweetie-lambkin, isn't that lovely?'

'What?'

'Laura Pyke wants to come here.'

'Who?'

'You must have heard me speak of Laura Pyke. She was my dearest friend at school. I simply worshipped her. She always had such a wonderful mind. She wants us to put her up for a week or two.'

'Right ho. Bung her in.'

'You're sure you don't mind?'

'Of course not. Any pal of yours –'

'Darling!' said Mrs Bingo, blowing him a kiss.

'Angel!' said Bingo, going on with the sausages.

All very charming, in fact. Pleasant domestic scene, I mean. Cheery give-and-take in the home and all that. I said as much to Jeeves as we drove off.

'In these days of unrest, Jeeves,' I said, 'with wives yearning to fulfil themselves and husbands slipping round the corner to do what they shouldn't, and the home, generally speaking, in the melting-pot, as it were, it is nice to find a thoroughly united couple.'

'Decidedly agreeable, sir.'

'I allude to the Bingos – Mr and Mrs.'

'Exactly, sir.'

'What was it the poet said of couples like the Bingeese?'

'"Two minds but with a single thought, two hearts that beat as one," sir.'

'A dashed good description, Jeeves.'

'It has, I believe, given uniform satisfaction, sir.'

And yet, if I had only known, what I had been listening to that am was the first faint rumble of the coming storm. Unseen, in the background, Fate was quietly slipping the lead into the boxing-glove.

I managed to give Uncle George a miss at a fairly early date and, leaving him wallowing in the waters, sent a wire to the Bingos, announcing my return. It was a longish drive and I fetched up at my destination only just in time to dress for dinner. I had done a quick dash into the soup and fish and was feeling pretty good at the prospect of a cocktail and the well-cooked, when the door opened and Bingo appeared.

'Hello, Bertie,' he said. 'Ah, Jeeves.'

He spoke in one of those toneless voices: and, catching Jeeves's eye as I adjusted the old cravat, I exchanged a questioning glance with it. From its expression I gathered that the same thing had struck him that had struck me – viz., that our host, the young Squire, was none too chirpy. The brow was furrowed, the eye lacked that hearty sparkle, and the general bearing and demeanour were those of a body discovered after being several days in the water.

'Anything up, Bingo?' I asked, with the natural anxiety of a boyhood friend. 'You have a mouldy look. Are you sickening for some sort of plague?'

'I've got it.'

'Got what?'

'The plague.'

'How do you mean?'

'She's on the premises now,' said Bingo, and laughed in an unpleasant, hacking manner, as if he were missing on one tonsil.

I couldn't follow him. The old egg seemed to me to speak in riddles.

'You seem to me, old egg,' I said, 'to speak in riddles. Don't you think he speaks in riddles, Jeeves?'

'Yes, sir.'

'I'm talking about the Pyke,' said Bingo.

'What pike?'

'Laura Pyke. Don't you remember –?'

'Oh, ah. Of course. The school chum. The seminary crony. Is she still here?'

'Yes, and looks like staying for ever. Rosie's absolutely potty about her. Hangs on her lips'

'The glamour of the old days still persists, eh?'

'I should say it does,' said young Bingo 'This business of schoolgirl friendships beats me. Hypnotic is the only word. I can't understand it. Men aren't like that. You and I were at school together, Bertie, but, my gosh, I don't look on you as a sort of mastermind.'

'You don't?'

'I don't treat your lightest utterance as a pearl of wisdom.'

'Why not?'

'Yet Rosie does with this Pyke. In the hands of the Pyke she is mere putty. If you want to see what was once a first-class Garden of Eden becoming utterly ruined as a desirable residence by the machinations of a Serpent, take a look round this place.'

'Why, what's the trouble?'

'Laura Pyke,' said young Bingo with intense bitterness, 'is a food crank, curse her. She says we all eat too much and eat it too quickly and, anyway, ought not to be eating it at all but living on parsnips and similar muck. And Rosie, instead of telling the woman not to be a fathead, gazes at her in wide-eyed admiration, taking it in through the pores. The result is that the cuisine of this house has been shot to pieces, and I am starving on my feet. Well, when I tell you that it's weeks since a beefsteak pudding raised its head in the home, you'll understand what I mean.'

At this point the gong went. Bingo listened with a moody frown.

'I don't know why they still bang that damned thing,' he said. 'There's nothing to bang it for. By the way, Bertie, would you like a cocktail?'

'I would.'

'Well, you won't get one. We don't have cocktails anymore. The girl friend says they corrode the stomach tissues.'

I was appalled. I had had no idea that the evil had spread as far as this.

'No cocktails!'

'No. And you'll be dashed lucky if it isn't a vegetarian dinner.'

'Bingo,' I cried, deeply moved, 'you must act. You must assert yourself. You must put your foot down. You must take a strong stand. You must be master in the home.'

He looked at me, a long, strange look.

'You aren't married, are you, Bertie?'

'You know I'm not.'

'I should have guessed it, anyway. Come on.'

Well, the dinner wasn't absolutely vegetarian, but when you had said that you had said everything. It was sparse, meagre, not at all the jolly, chunky repast for which the old tum was standing up and clamouring after its long motor ride. And what there was of it was turned to ashes in the mouth by the conversation of Miss Laura Pyke.

In happier circs, and if I had not been informed in advance of the warped nature of her soul, I might have been favourably impressed by this female at the moment of our meeting. She was really rather a good-looking girl, a bit strong in the face but nevertheless quite reasonably attractive. But had she been a thing of radiant beauty, she could never have clicked with Bertram Wooster. Her conversation was of a kind which would have queered Helen of Troy with any right-thinking man.

During dinner she talked all the time, and it did not take me long to see why the iron had entered into Bingo's soul. Practically all she said

was about food and Bingo's tendency to shovel it down in excessive
quantities, thereby handing the lemon to his stomachic tissues. She
didn't seem particularly interested in my stomachic tissues, rather
giving the impression that if Bertram burst it would be all right with
her. It was on young Bingo that she concentrated as the brand to be
saved from the burning. Gazing at him like a high priestess at the
favourite, though erring, disciple, she told him all the things that
were happening to his insides because he would insist on eating
stuff lacking in fat-soluble vitamins. She spoke freely of proteins,
carbohydrates, and the physiological requirements of the average
individual. She was not a girl who believed in mincing her words,
and a racy little anecdote she told about a man who refused to eat
prunes had the effect of causing me to be a non-starter for the last
two courses.

'Jeeves,' I said, on reaching the sleeping-chamber that night, 'I
don't like the look of things.'

'No, sir?'

'No, Jeeves, I do not. I view the situation with concern. Things are
worse than I thought they were. Mr Little's remarks before dinner
may have given you the impression that the Pyke merely lectured
on food-reform in a general sort of way. Such, I now find, is not
the case. By way of illustrating her theme, she points to Mr Little
as the awful example. She criticises him, Jeeves.'

'Indeed, sir?'

'Yes. Openly. Keeps telling him he eats too much, drinks too much,
and gobbles his food. I wish you could have heard a comparison she
drew between him and the late Mr Gladstone, considering them in
the capacity of food chewers. It left young Bingo very much with
the short end of the stick. And the sinister thing is that Mrs Bingo
approves. Are wives often like that? Welcoming criticism of the lord
and master, I mean?'

'They are generally open to suggestion from the outside public
with regard to the improvement of their husbands, sir.'

'That is why married men are wan, what?'

'Yes, sir.'

I had had the foresight to send the man downstairs for a plate of
biscuits. I bit a representative specimen thoughtfully.

'Do you know what I think, Jeeves?'

'No, sir.'

'I think Mr Little doesn't realize the full extent of the peril
which threatens his domestic happiness. I'm beginning to understand this business of matrimony. I'm beginning to see how

the thing works. Would you care to hear how I figure it out, Jeeves?'

'Extremely, sir.'

'Well, it's like this. Take a couple of birds. These birds get married, and for a while all is gas and gaiters. The female regards her mate as about the best thing that ever came a girl's way. He is her king, if you know what I mean. She looks up to him and respects him. Joy, as you might say, reigns supreme. Eh?'

'Very true, sir.'

'Then gradually, by degrees – little by little, if I may use the expression – disillusionment sets in. She sees him eating a poached egg, and the glamour starts to fade. She watches him mangling a chop, and it continues to fade. And so on and so on, if you follow me, and so forth.'

'I follow you perfectly, sir.'

'But mark this Jeeves. This is the point. Here we approach the nub. Usually it is all right, because, as I say, the disillusionment comes gradually and the female has time to adjust herself. But in the case of young Bingo, owing to the indecent outspokenness of the Pyke, it's coming in a rush. Absolutely in a flash, without any previous preparation, Mrs Bingo is having Bingo presented to her as a sort of human boa-constrictor full of unpleasantly jumbled interior organs. The picture which the Pyke is building up for her in her mind is that of one of those men you see in restaurants with three chins, bulging eyes, and the veins starting out on the forehead. A little more of this, and love must wither.'

'You think so, sir?'

'I'm sure of it. No affection can stand the strain. Twice during dinner tonight the Pyke said things about your Bingo's intestinal canal which I shouldn't have thought would have been possible in mixed company even in this lax post-war era. Well, you see what I mean. You can't go on knocking a man's intestinal canal indefinitely without causing his wife to stop and ponder. The danger, as I see it, is that after a bit more of this, Mrs Little will decide that tinkering is no use and the only thing to do is to scrap Bingo and get a newer model.'

'Most disturbing, sir.'

'Something must be done, Jeeves. You must act. Unless you can find some way of getting this Pyke out of the woodwork, and that right speedily, the home's number is up. You see, what makes matters worse is that Mrs Bingo is romantic. Women like her, who consider the day illspent if they have not churned out five thousand words of superfatted fiction, are apt even at the best of times to yearn a trifle. The ink gets into their heads. I mean to say, I shouldn't wonder if right from the start Mrs Bingo hasn't had a sort of sneaking regret that Bingo isn't one of those strong, curt, Empire-building kind of Englishmen she puts into her books, with sad, unfathomable eyes, lean sensitive hands, and riding-boots. You see what I mean?'

'Precisely, sir. You imply that Miss Pyke's criticisms will have been instrumental in moving the hitherto unformulated dissatisfaction from the subconscious to the conscious mind.'

'Once again, Jeeves?' I said, trying to grab it as it came off the bat, but missing it by several yards.

He repeated the dose.

'Well, I daresay you're right,' I said. 'Anyway, the point is, P.M.G. Pyke must go. How do you propose to set about it?'

'I fear I have nothing to suggest at the moment, sir.'

'Come, come, Jeeves.'

'I fear not, sir. Possibly after I have seen the lady —'

'You mean, you want to study the psychology of the individual and what not?'

'Precisely, sir.'

'Well, I don't know how you're going to do it. After all, I mean you can hardly cluster round the dinner table and drink in the Pyke's small talk.'

'There is that difficulty, sir.'

'Your best chance, it seems to me, will be when we go to the Lakenham races on Thursday. We shall feed out of a luncheon-basket in God's air, and there's nothing to stop you hanging about and passing the sandwiches. Prick the ears and be at your most observant then, is my advice.'

'Very good, sir.'

'Very good, Jeeves. Be there, then, with the eyes popping. And, meanwhile, dash downstairs and see if you can dig up another instalment of these biscuits. I need them sorely.'

The morning of the Lakenham races dawned bright and juicy. A casual observer would have said that God was in His Heaven and all right with the world. It was one of those days you sometimes get latish in the autumn when the sun beams, the birds toot, and there is a bracing tang in the air that sends the blood beetling briskly through the veins.

Personally, however, I wasn't any too keen on the bracing tang. It made me feel so exceptionally fit that almost immediately after breakfast I found myself beginning to wonder what there would be for lunch. And the thought of what there probably would be for lunch, if the Pyke's influence made itself felt, lowered my spirits considerably.

'I fear the worst, Jeeves,' I said. 'Last night at dinner Miss Pyke threw out the remark that the carrot was the best of all vegetables, having an astonishing effect on the blood and beautifying the complexion. Now, I am all for anything that bucks up the Wooster blood. Also, I would like to give the natives a treat by letting them take a look at my rosy, glowing cheeks. But not at the expense of lunching on raw carrots. To avoid any rannygazoo, therefore, I think it will be best if you add a bit for the young master to your personal packet of sandwiches. I don't want to be caught short.'

'Very good, sir.'

At this point, young Bingo came up. I hadn't seen him look so jaunty for days.

'I've just been superintending the packing of the lunch-basket, Bertie,' he said. 'I stood over the butler and saw that there was no nonsense.'

'All pretty sound?' I asked, relieved.

'All indubitably sound.'

'No carrots?'

'No carrots,' said young Bingo. 'There's ham sandwiches,' he proceeded, a strange, soft light in his eyes, 'and tongue sandwiches and potted meat sandwiches and game sandwiches and hard-boiled eggs and lobster and a cold chicken and sardines and a cake and a couple of bottles of Bollinger and some old brandy —'

'It has the right ring,' I said. 'And if we want a bite to eat after that, of course we can go to the pub.'

'What pub?'

'Isn't there a pub on the course?'

'There's not a pub for miles. That's why I was so particularly careful that there should be no funny work about the basket. The common where these races are held is a desert without an oasis. Practically a death-trap. I met a fellow the other day who told me he got there last year and unpacked his basket and found that the champagne had burst and, together with the salad dressing, had soaked into the ham, which in its turn had got mixed up with the gorgonzola cheese, forming a sort of paste. He had had rather a bumpy bit of road to travel over.'

'What did he do?'

'Oh, he ate the mixture. It was the only course. But he said he could still taste it sometimes, even now.'

In ordinary circs I can't say I should have been any too braced at the news that we were going to split up for the journey in the following order – Bingo and Mrs Bingo in their car and the Pyke in mine, with Jeeves sitting behind in the dickey. But, things being as they were, the arrangement had its points. It meant that Jeeves would be able to study the back of her head and draw his deductions, while I could engage her in conversation and let him see for himself what manner of female she was.

I started, accordingly, directly we had rolled off and all through the journey until we fetched up at the course she gave of her best. It was with considerable satisfaction that I parked the car beside a tree and hopped out.

'You were listening, Jeeves?' I said gravely.

'Yes, sir.'

'A tough baby?'

'Undeniably, sir.'

Bingo and Mrs Bingo came up.

'The first race won't be for half an hour,' said Bingo. 'We'd better lunch now. Fish the basket out, Jeeves, would you mind?'

'Sir?'

'The luncheon-basket,' said Bingo in a devout sort of voice, licking his lips slightly.

'The basket is not in Mr Wooster's car, sir.'

'What!'

'I assumed that you were bringing it in your own, sir.'

I have never seen the sunshine fade out of anybody's face as quickly as it did out of Bingo's. He uttered a sharp, wailing cry.

'Rosie!'

'Yes, sweetie-pie?'

'The bunch! The lasket!'

'What, darling?'

'The luncheon-basket!'

'What about it, precious?'

'It's been left behind!'

'Oh, has it?' said Mrs Bingo.

I confess she had never fallen lower in my estimation. I had always known her as a woman with as healthy an appreciation of her meals as any of my acquaintance. A few years previously, when my Aunt Dahlia had stolen her French cook, Anatole, she had called Aunt Dahlia some names in my presence which had impressed me profoundly. Yet now, when informed that she was marooned on a bally prairie without bite or sup, all she could find to say was, 'Oh, has it?' I had never fully realised before the extent to which she had allowed herself to be dominated by the deleterious influence of the Pyke.

The Pyke, for her part, touched an even lower level.

'It is just as well,' she said, and her voice seemed to cut Bingo like a knife. 'Luncheon is a meal better omitted. If taken, it should consist merely of a few muscatels, bananas and grated carrots. It is a well-known fact –'

And she went on to speak at some length of the gastric juices in a vein far from suited to any gathering at which gentlemen were present.

'So, you see, darling,' said Mrs Bingo, 'you will really feel ever so much better and brighter for not having eaten a lot of indigestible food. It is much the best thing that could have happened.'

Bingo gave her a long, lingering look.

'I see,' he said. 'Well, if you will excuse me, I'll just go off somewhere where I can cheer a bit without exciting comment.'

I perceived Jeeves withdrawing in a meaning manner, and I followed him, hoping for the best. My trust was not misplaced. He had brought enough sandwiches for two. In fact, enough for three, I whistled to Bingo, and he came slinking up, and we restored the tissues in a makeshift sort of way behind a hedge. Then Bingo went off to interview bookies about the first race, and Jeeves gave a cough.

'Swallowed a crumb the wrong way?' I said.

'No, sir, I thank you. It is merely that I desired to express a hope that I had not been guilty of taking a liberty, sir.'

'How?'

'In removing the luncheon-basket from the car before we started, sir.'

I quivered like an aspen. I stared at the man. Aghast. Shocked to the core.

'You, Jeeves?' I said, and I should rather think Caesar spoke in the same sort of voice on finding Brutus puncturing him with the sharp instrument. 'You mean to tell me it was you who deliberately, if that's the word I want –'

'Yes, sir. It seemed to me the most judicious course to pursue. It would not have been prudent, in my opinion, to have allowed Mrs Little, in her present frame of mind, to witness Mr Little eating a meal on the scale which he outlined in his remarks this morning.'

I saw his point.

'True, Jeeves,' I said thoughtfully. 'I see what you mean. If young Bingo has a fault, it is that, when in the society of a sandwich, he is apt to get a bit rough. I've picnicked with him before, many a time and oft, and his method of approach to the ordinary tongue or ham sandwich rather resembles that of the lion, the king of beasts, tucking into an antelope. Add lobster and cold chicken, and I admit the spectacle might have been something of a jar for the consort ... Still ... all the same ... nevertheless –'

'And there is anther aspect of the matter, sir.'

'What's that?'

'A day spent without nourishment in the keen autumnal air may induce in Mrs Little a frame of mind not altogether in sympathy with Miss Pyke's view on diet.'

'You mean, hunger will gnaw and she'll be apt to bite at the Pyke when she talks about how jolly it is for the gastric juices to get a day off?'

'Exactly, sir.'

I shook the head. I hated to damp the man's pretty enthusiasm, but it had to be done.

'Abandon the idea, Jeeves,' I said. 'I fear you have not studied the sex as I have. Missing her lunch means little or nothing to the female of the species. The feminine attitude towards lunch is notoriously airy and casual. Where you have made your bloomer is in confusing lunch with tea. Hell, it is well known, has no fury like a woman who wants her tea and can't get it. At such times the most amiable of the sex become mere bombs which a spark may ignite. But lunch, Jeeves, no. I should have thought you would have known that – a bird of your established intelligence.'

'No doubt you are right, sir.'

'If you could somehow arrange for Mrs Little to miss her tea ... but these are idle dreams, Jeeves. By tea-time she will be back at the old home, in the midst of plenty. It only takes an hour to do the trip. The last race is over shortly after four. By five o'clock Mrs Little will have her feet tucked under the table and will be revelling in buttered toast. I am sorry, Jeeves, but your scheme was a wash-out from the start. No earthly. A dud.'

'I appreciate the point you have raised, sir. What you say is extremely true.'

'Unfortunately. Well, there it is. The only thing to do seems to be to get back to the course and try to skin a bookie or two and forget.'

Well, the long day wore on, so to speak. I can't say I enjoyed myself much. I was distrait, if you know what I mean. Preoccupied. From time to time assorted clusters of spavined local horses clumped down the course with farmers on top of them, but I watched them with a languid eye. To get them into the spirit of one of these rural meetings it is essential that the subject have a good, fat lunch inside him. Subtract the lunch, and what ensues? Ennui. Not once but many times during the afternoon I found myself thinking hard thoughts about Jeeves. The man seemed to me to be losing his grip. A child could have told him that that footling scheme of his would not have got him anywhere.

I mean to say, when you reflect that the average woman considers she has lunched luxuriously if she swallows a couple of macaroons, half a chocolate éclair and a raspberry vinegar, is she going to be peevish because you do her out of a midday sandwich? Of course not. Perfectly ridiculous. Too silly for words. All that Jeeves had accomplished by his bally trying to be clever was to give me a feeling as if foxes were gnawing my vitals and a strong desire for home.

It was a relief, therefore, when, as the shades of evening were beginning to fall, Mrs Bingo announced her intention of calling it a day and shifting.

'Would you mind very much missing the last race, Mr Wooster?' she asked.

'I am all for it,' I replied cordially. 'The last race means little or nothing in my life. Besides, I am a shilling and sixpence ahead of the game, and the time to leave off is when you're winning.'

'Laura and I thought we would go home. I feel I should like an early cup of tea. Bingo says he will stay on. So I thought you could drive our car, and he would follow later in yours, with Jeeves.'

'Right ho.'

'You know the way?'

'Oh yes. Main road as far as that turning by the pond, and then across country.'

'I can direct you from there.'

I sent Jeeves to fetch the car, and presently we were bowling off in good shape. The short afternoon had turned into a rather chilly, misty sort of evening, the kind of evening that sends a fellow's thoughts straying off in the direction of hot Scotch-and-water with a spot of lemon in it. I put the foot firmly on the accelerator, and we did the five or six miles of main road in quick time.

Turning eastwards at the pond, I had to go a bit slower, for we had struck a wildish stretch of country where the going wasn't so good. I don't know any part of England where you feel so off the map as on the by-roads of Norfolk. Occasionally we would meet a cow or two, but otherwise we had the world pretty much to ourselves.

I began to think about that drink again, and the more I thought the better it looked. It's rummy how people differ in this matter of selecting the beverage that is to touch the spot. It's what Jeeves would call the psychology of the individual. Some fellows in my position might have voted for a tankard of ale, and the Pyke's idea of a refreshing snort was, as I knew from what she had told me on the journey out, a cupful of tepid pip-and-peel water or, failing that, what she called the fruit-liquor. You make this, apparently, by soaking raisins in cold water and adding the juice of a lemon. After which, I suppose, you invite a couple of old friends in and have an orgy, burying the bodies in the morning.

Personally, I had no doubts. I never wavered. Hot Scotch-and-water was the stuff for me – stressing the Scotch, if you know what I mean, and going fairly easy on the H_2O. I seemed to see the beaker smiling at me across the misty fields, beckoning me on, as it were, and saying 'Courage, Bertram! It will not be long now!' And with renewed energy I bunged the old foot down on the accelerator and tried to send the needle up to sixty.

Instead of which, if you follow my drift, the bally thing flickered for a moment to thirty-five and then gave the business up as a bad job. Quite suddenly and unexpectedly, no one more surprised than myself, the car let out a faint gurgle like a sick moose and stopped in its tracks. And there we were, somewhere in Norfolk, with darkness coming on and a cold wind that smelled of guano and dead mangel-wurzels playing searchingly about the spinal column.

The back-seat drivers gave tongue.

'What's the matter? What has happened? Why don't you go on? What are you stopping for?'

I explained.

'I'm not stopping. It's the car.'

'Why has the car stopped?'

'Ah!' I said, with a manly frankness that became me well. 'There you have me.'

You see, I'm one of those birds who drive a lot but don't know the first thing about the works. The policy I pursue is to get aboard, prod the self-starter, and leave the rest to Nature. If anything goes wrong, I scream for an AA scout. It's a system that answers admirably as a rule, but on the present occasion it blew a fuse owing to the fact that there wasn't an AA scout within miles. I explained as much to the fair cargo and received in return a 'Tchah!' from the Pyke that nearly lifted the top of my head off. What with having a covey of female relations who have regarded me from childhood as about ten degrees short of a half-wit, I have become rather a connoisseur of 'Tchahs', and the Pyke's seemed to me well up in Class A, possessing much of the *timbre* and *brio* of my Aunt Agatha's.

'Perhaps I can find out what the trouble is,' she said, becoming calmer. 'I understand cars.'

She got out and began peering into the thing's vitals. I thought for a moment of suggesting that its gastric juices might have taken a turn for the worse owing to lack of fat-soluble vitamins, but decided on the whole not. I'm a pretty close observer, and it didn't seem to me that she was in the mood.

And yet, as a matter of fact, I should have been about right, at that. For after fiddling with the engine for a while in a discontented sort of way the female was suddenly struck with an idea. She tested it, and it was proved correct. There was not a drop of petrol in the tank. No gas. In other words, a complete lack of fat-soluble vitamins. What it amounted to was that the job now before us was to get the old bus home purely by will-power.

Feeling that, from whatever angle they regarded the regrettable occurrence, they could hardly blame me, I braced up a trifle in fact, to the extent of a hearty 'Well, well, well!'

'No petrol,' I said. 'Fancy that.'

'But Bingo told me he was going to fill the tank this morning,' said Mrs Bingo.

'I suppose he forgot,' said the Pyke. 'He would!'

'What do you mean by that?' said Mrs Bingo, and I noted in her voice a touch of what-is-it.

'I mean he is just the sort of man who would forget to fill the tank,' replied the Pyke, who also appeared somewhat moved.

'I should be very much obliged, Laura,' said Mrs Bingo, doing the heavy loyal-little-woman stuff, 'if you would refrain from criticizing my husband.'

'Tchah!' said the Pyke.

'And don't say "Tchah!"' said Mrs Bingo.

'I shall say whatever I please,' said the Pyke.

'Ladies, ladies!' I said. 'Ladies, ladies, ladies!'

It was rash. Looking back, I can see that. One of the first lessons life teaches us is that on these occasions of back-chat between the delicately-nurtured, a man should retire into the offing, curl up in a ball, and imitate the prudent tactics of the opossum, which, when danger is in the air, pretends to be dead, frequently going to the length of hanging out crêpe and instructing its friends to stand round and say what a pity it all is. The only result of my dash at the soothing intervention was that the Pyke turned on me like a wounded leopardess.

'Well!' she said. 'Aren't you proposing to do anything, Mr Wooster?'

'What can I do?'

'There's a house over there. I should have thought it would be well within even your powers to go and borrow a tin of petrol.'

I looked. There was a house. And one of the lower windows was lighted, indicating to the trained mind of the presence of a ratepayer.

'A very sound and brainy scheme,' I said ingratiatingly. 'I will first honk a little on the horn to show we're here, and then rapid action.'

I honked, with the most gratifying results. Almost immediately a human form appeared in the window. It seemed to be waving its arms in a matey and welcoming sort of way. Stimulated and encouraged, I hastened to the front door and gave it a breezy bang with the knocker. Things, I felt, were moving.

The first bang produced no result. I had just lifted the knocker for the encore, when it was wrenched out of my hand. The door flew open, and there was a bloke with spectacles on his face and all round the spectacles an expression of strained anguish. A bloke with a secret sorrow.

I was sorry he had troubles, of course, but, having some of my own, I came right down to the agenda without delay.

'I say . . .' I began.

The bloke's hair was standing up in a kind of tousled mass, and at this juncture, as if afraid it would not stay like that without assistance, he ran a hand through it. And for the first time I noted that the spectacles had a hostile gleam.

'Was that you making that infernal noise?' he asked.

'Er – yes,' I said. 'I did toot.'

'Toot once more – just once,' said the bloke, speaking in a low, strangled voice, 'and I'll shred you up into little bits with my bare hands. My wife's gone out for the evening and after hours of ceaseless toil I've at last managed to get the baby to sleep, and you come along making that hideous din with your damned horn. What do you mean by it, blast you?'

'Er –'

'Well, that's how matters stand,' said the bloke, summing up. 'One more toot – just one single, solitary suggestion of the faintest shadow or suspicion of anything remotely approaching a toot – and may the Lord have mercy on your soul.'

'What I want,' I said, 'is petrol.'

'What you'll get,' said the bloke, 'is a thick ear.'

And, closing the door with the delicate caution of one brushing flies off a sleeping Venus, he passed out of my life.

Women as a sex are always apt to be a trifle down on the defeated warrior. Returning to the car, I was not well received. The impression seemed to be that Bertram had not acquitted himself in a fashion worthy of his Crusading ancestors. I did my best to smooth matters over, but you know how it is. When you've broken down on a chilly autumn evening miles from anywhere and have missed lunch and look like missing tea as well, mere charm of manner can never be a really satisfactory substitute for a tinful of the juice.

Things got so noticeably unpleasant, in fact, that after a while, mumbling something about getting help, I sidled off down the road. And, by Jove, I hadn't gone half a mile before I saw lights in the distance and there, in the middle of this forsaken desert, was a car.

I stood in the road and whooped as I had never whooped before.

'Hi!' I shouted. 'I say! Hi! Half a minute! Hi! Ho! I say! Ho! Hi! Just a second if you don't mind.'

The car reached me and slowed up. A voice spoke.

'Is that you, Bertie?'

'Hullo, Bingo! Is that you? I say, Bingo, we've broken down.'

Bingo hopped out.

'Give us five minutes, Jeeves,' he said, 'and then drive slowly on.'

'Very good, sir.'

Bingo joined me.

'We aren't going to walk, are we?' I asked. 'Where's the sense?'

'Yes, walk, laddie,' said Bingo, 'and warily withal. I want to make sure of something. Bertie, how were things when you left? Hotting up?'

'A trifle.'

'You observed symptoms of a row, a quarrel, a parting of brass rags between Rosie and the Pyke?'

'There did seem a certain liveliness.'

'Tell me.'

I related what had occurred. He listened intently.

'Bertie,' he said as we walked along, 'you are present at a crisis in your old friend's life. It may be that this vigil in a broken-down car will cause Rosie to see what you'd have thought she ought to have seen years ago – viz: that the Pyke is entirely unfit for human consumption and must be cast into outer darkness where there is wailing and gnashing of teeth. I am not betting on it, but stranger things have happened. Rosie is the sweetest girl in the world, but, like all women, she gets edgy towards tea-time. And today, having missed lunch . . . Hark!'

He grabbed my arm, and we paused. Tense. Agog. From down the road came the sound of voices, and a mere instant was enough to tell us that it was Mrs Bingo and the Pyke talking things over.

I had never listened in on a real, genuine female row before, and I'm bound to say it was pretty impressive. During my absence, matters appeared to have developed on rather a spacious scale. They had reached the stage now where the combatants had begun to dig into the past and rake up old scores. Mrs Bingo was saying that the Pyke would never have got into the hockey team at St Adela's if she hadn't flattered and fawned upon the captain in a way that it made Mrs Bingo, even after all these years, sick to think of. The Pyke replied that she had refrained from mentioning it until now, having always felt it better to let bygones be bygones, but that if Mrs Bingo supposed her to be unaware that Mrs Bingo had won the Scripture prize by taking a list of the Kings of Judah into the examination room, tucked into her middy-blouse, Mrs Bingo was vastly mistaken.

Furthermore, the Pyke proceeded, Mrs Bingo was also labouring under an error if she imagined that the Pyke proposed to remain a night longer under her roof. It had been in a moment of weakness, a moment of mistaken kindliness, supposing her to be lonely and in need of intellectual society, that the Pyke had decided to pay her a visit at all. Her intention now was, if ever Providence sent them aid and enabled her to get out of this beastly car and back to her trunks, to pack those trunks and leave by the next train, even if that train was a milk-train, stopping at every station. Indeed, rather than endure another night at Mrs Bingo's, the Pyke was quite willing to walk to London.

To this, Mrs Bingo's reply was long and eloquent and touched on the fact that in her last term at St Adela's a girl named Simpson had told her (Mrs Bingo) that a girl named Waddesley had told her (the Simpson) that the Pyke, while pretending to be a friend of hers (the

Bingo's), had told her (the Waddesley) that she (the Bingo) couldn't eat strawberries and cream without coming out in spots, and, in addition, had spoken in the most catty manner about the shape of her nose. It could all have been condensed, however, into the words 'Right ho'.

It was when the Pyke had begun to say that she had never had such a hearty laugh in her life as when she read the scene in Mrs Bingo's last novel where the heroine's little boy dies of croup that we felt it best to call the meeting to order before bloodshed set in. Jeeves had come up in the car, and Bingo, removing a tin of petrol from the dickey, placed it in the shadows at the side of the road. Then we hopped on and made the spectacular entry.

'Hullo, hullo, hullo,' said Bingo brightly. 'Bertie tells me you've had a breakdown.'

'Oh, Bingo!' cried Mrs Bingo, wifely love thrilling in every syllable. 'Thank goodness you've come.'

'Now, perhaps,' said the Pyke, 'I can get home and do my packing. If Mr Wooster will allow me to use his car, his man can drive me back to the house in time to catch the six-fifteen.'

'You aren't leaving us?' said Bingo.

'I am,' said the Pyke.

'Too bad,' said Bingo.

She climbed in beside Jeeves and they popped off. There was a short silence after they had gone. It was too dark to see her, but I could feel Mrs Bingo struggling between love of her mate and the natural urge to say something crisp about his forgetting to fill the petrol tank that morning. Eventually nature took its course.

'I must say, sweetie-pie,' she said, 'it was a little careless of you to leave the tank almost empty when we started today. You promised me you would fill it, darling.'

'But I did fill it, darling.'

'But, darling, it's empty.'

'It can't be, darling.'

'Laura said it was.'

'The woman's an ass,' said Bingo. 'There's plenty of petrol. What's wrong is probably that the sprockets aren't running true with the differential gear. It happens that way sometimes. I'll fix it in a second. But I don't want you to sit freezing out here while I'm doing it. Why not go to that house over there and ask them if you can't come in and sit down for ten minutes? They might give you a cup of tea, too.'

A soft moan escaped Mrs Bingo.

'Tea!' I heard her whisper.

I had to bust Bingo's daydream.

'I'm sorry, old man,' I said, 'but I fear the old English hospitality which you outline is off. That house is inhabited by a sort of bandit. As unfriendly a bird as I ever met. His wife's out and he's just got the baby to sleep, and this has darkened his outlook. Tap even lightly on his front door and you take your life into your hands.'

'Nonsense,' said Bingo. 'Come along.'

He banged the knocker, and produced an immediate reaction.

'Hell!' said the Bandit, appearing as if out of a trap.

'I say,' said young Bingo, 'I'm just fixing our car outside. Would you object to my wife coming in out of the cold for a few minutes?'

'Yes,' said the Bandit, 'I would.'

'And you might give her a cup of tea.'

'I might,' said the Bandit, 'but I won't.'

'You won't?'

'No. And for heaven's sake don't talk so loud. I know that baby. A whisper sometimes does it.'

'Let us get this straight,' said Bingo. 'You refuse to give my wife tea?'

'Yes.'

'You would see a woman starve?'

'Yes.'

'Well, you jolly well aren't going to,' said young Bingo. 'Unless you go straight to your kitchen, put the kettle on, and start slicing bread for the buttered toast, I'll yell and wake the baby.'

The Bandit turned ashen.

'You wouldn't do that?'

'I would.'

'Have you no heart?'

'No.'

'No human feeling?'

'No.'

The Bandit turned to Mrs Bingo. You could see his spirit was broken.

'Do your shoes squeak?' he asked humbly.

'No.'

'Then come on in.'

'Thank you,' said Mrs Bingo.

She turned for an instant to Bingo, and there was a look in her eyes that one of those damsels in distress might have given the knight as he shot his cuffs and turned away from the dead dragon. It was a look of adoration, of almost reverent respect. Just the sort of look, in fact, that a husband likes to see.

'Darling!' she said.

'Darling!' said Bingo.

'Angel!' said Mrs Bingo.

'Precious!' said Bingo. 'Come along, Bertie, let's get at that car.'

He was silent till he had fetched the tin of petrol and filled the tank and screwed the cap on again. Then he drew a deep breath.

'Bertie,' he said, 'I am ashamed to admit it, but occasionally in the course of a lengthy acquaintance there have been moments when I have temporarily lost faith in Jeeves.'

'My dear chap!' I said, shocked.

'Yes, Bertie, there have. Sometimes my belief in him has wobbled. I have said to myself, "Has he the old speed, the ancient vim?" I shall never say it again. From now on, childlike trust. It was his idea, Bertie, that if a couple of women headed for tea suddenly found the cup snatched from their lips, so to speak, they would turn and rend one another. Observe the result.'

'But, dash it, Jeeves couldn't have known that the car would break down.'

'On the contrary. He let all the petrol out of the tank when you sent him to fetch the machine – all except just enough to carry it well into the wilds beyond the reach of human aid. He foresaw what would happen. I tell you, Bertie, Jeeves stands alone.'

'Absolutely.'

'He's a marvel.'

'A wonder.'

'A wizard.'

'A stout fellow,' I agreed. 'Full of fat-soluble vitamins.'

'The exact expression,' said young Bingo. 'And now let's go and tell Rosie the car is fixed, and then home to the tankard of ale.'

'Not the tankard of ale, old man,' I said firmly. 'The hot Scotch-and-water with a spot of lemon in it.'

'You're absolutely right,' said Bingo. 'What a flair you have in these matters, Bertie. Hot Scotch-and-water it is.'

10

INDIAN SUMMER OF AN UNCLE

Ask anyone at the Drones, and they will tell you that Bertram Wooster is a fellow whom it is dashed difficult to deceive. Old Lynx-Eye is about what it amounts to. I observe and deduce. I weigh the evidence and draw my conclusions. And that is why Uncle George had not been in my midst more than about two minutes before I, so to speak, saw all. To my trained eye the thing stuck out a mile.

And yet it seemed so dashed absurd. Consider the facts, if you know what I mean.

I mean to say, for years, right back to the time when I first went to school, this bulging relative had been one of the recognized eyesores of London. He was fat then, and day by day in every way has been getting fatter ever since, till now tailors measure him just for the sake of the exercise. He is what they call a prominent London clubman – one of those birds in tight morning-coats and grey toppers whom you see toddling along St James's Street on fine afternoons, puffing a bit as they make the grade. Slip a ferret into any good club between Piccadilly and Pall Mall, and you would start half a dozen Uncle Georges.

He spends his time lunching and dining at the Buffers and, between meals, sucking down spots in the smoking room and talking to anyone who will listen about the lining of his stomach. About twice a year his liver lodges a formal protest and he goes off to Harrogate or Carlsbad to get planed down. Then back again and on with the programme. The last bloke in the world, in short, who you would think would ever fall a victim to the divine pash. And yet, if you will believe me, that was absolutely the strength of it.

This old pestilence blew in on me one morning at about the hour of the after-breakfast cigarette.

'Oh, Bertie,' he said.

'Hullo?'

'You know those ties you've been wearing. Where did you get them?'

'Blucher's, in the Burlington Arcade.'

'Thanks.'

He walked across to the mirror and stood in front of it, gazing at himself in an earnest manner.

'Smut on your nose?' I asked courteously.

Then I suddenly perceived that he was wearing a sort of horrible simper, and I confess it chilled the blood to no little extent. Uncle George, with face in repose, is hard enough on the eye. Simpering, he goes right above the odds.

'Ha!' he said.

He heaved a long sigh, and turned away. Not too soon, for the mirror was on the point of cracking.

'I'm not so old,' he said, in a musing sort of voice.

'So old as what?'

'Properly considered, I'm in my prime. Besides, what a young and inexperienced girl needs is a man of weight and years to lean on. The sturdy oak, not the sapling.'

It was at this point that, as I said above, I saw all.

'Great Scott, Uncle George!' I said. 'You aren't thinking of getting married?'

'Who isn't?' he said.

'You aren't,' I said.

'Yes, I am. Why not?'

'Oh, well –'

'Marriage is an honourable state.'

'Oh, absolutely.'

'It might make you a better man, Bertie.'

'Who says so?'

'I say so. Marriage might turn you from frivolous young scallywag into – er – a non-scallywag. Yes, confound you, I *am* thinking of getting married, and if Agatha comes sticking her oar in I'll – I'll – well, I shall know what to do about it.'

He exited on the big line, and I rang the bell for Jeeves. The situation seemed to me one that called for a cosy talk.

'Jeeves,' I said.

'Sir?'

'You know my Uncle George?'

'Yes, sir. His lordship has been familiar to me for some years.'

'I don't mean do you know my Uncle George. I mean do you know what my Uncle George is thinking of doing?'

'Contracting a matrimonial alliance, sir.'

'Good Lord! Did he tell you?'

'No, sir. Oddly enough, I chance to be acquainted with the other party in the matter.'

'The girl?'

'The young person, yes, sir. It was from her aunt, with whom she resides, that I received the information that his lordship was contemplating matrimony.'

'Who is she?'

'A Miss Platt, sir. Miss Rhoda Platt. Of Wistaria Lodge, Kitchener Road, East Dulwich.'

'Young?'

'Yes, sir.'

'The old fathead!'

'Yes, sir. The expression is one which I would, of course, not have ventured to employ myself, but I confess to thinking his lordship somewhat ill-advised. One must remember, however, that it is not unusual to find gentlemen of a certain age yielding to what might be described as a sentimental urge. They appear to experience what I may term a sort of Indian summer, a kind of temporarily renewed youth. The phenomenon is particularly noticeable, I am given to understand, in the United States of America among the wealthier inhabitants of the city of Pittsburgh. It is notorious, I am told, that sooner or later, unless restrained, they always endeavour to marry chorus-girls. Why this should be so, I am at a loss to say, but –'

I saw that this was going to take some time. I tuned out.

'From something in Uncle George's manner, Jeeves, as he referred to my Aunt Agatha's probable reception of the news, I gather that this Miss Platt is not of the *noblesse*.'

'No, sir. She is a waitress at his lordship's club.'

'My God! The proletariat!'

'The lower middle classes, sir.'

'Well, yes, by stretching it a bit, perhaps. Still, you know what I mean.'

'Yes, sir.'

'Rummy thing, Jeeves,' I said thoughtfully, 'this modern tendency to marry waitresses. If you remember, before he settled down, young Bingo Little was repeatedly trying to do it.'

'Yes, sir.'

'Odd!'

'Yes, sir.'

'Still, there it is, of course. The point to be considered now is, what will Aunt Agatha do about this? You know her, Jeeves. She is not like me. I'm broad-minded. If Uncle George wants to marry waitresses, let him, say I. I hold that the rank is but the penny stamp –'

'Guinea stamp, sir.'

'All right, guinea stamp. Though I don't believe there is such a thing. I shouldn't have thought they came higher than five bob. Well, as I was saying, I maintain that the rank is but the guinea stamp and a girl's a girl for all that.'

'"For *a*' that," sir. The poet Burns wrote in the North British dialect.'

'Well, "a' that," then, if you prefer it.'

'I have no preference in the matter, sir. It is simply that the poet Burns –'

'Never mind about the poet Burns.'

'No, sir.'

'Forget the poet Burns.'

'Very good, sir.'

'Expunge the poet Burns from your mind.'

'I will do so immediately, sir.'

'What we have to consider is not the poet Burns but the Aunt Agatha. She will kick, Jeeves.'

'Very probably, sir.'

'And, what's worse, she will lug me into the mess. There is only one thing to be done. Pack the toothbrush and let us escape while we may, leaving no address.'

'Very good, sir.'

At this moment the bell rang.

'Ha!' I said. 'Someone at the door.'

'Yes, sir.'

'Probably Uncle George back again. I'll answer it. You go and get ahead with the packing.'

'Very good, sir.'

I sauntered along the passage, whistling carelessly, and there on the mat was Aunt Agatha. Herself. Not a picture.

A nasty jar.

'Oh, hullo!' I said, it seeming but little good to tell her I was out of town and not expected back for some weeks.

'I wish to speak to you, Bertie,' said the Family Curse. 'I am greatly upset.'

She legged it into the sitting room and volplaned into a chair. I followed, thinking wistfully of Jeeves packing in the bedroom. That suitcase would not be needed now. I knew what she must have come about.

'I've just seen Uncle George,' I said, giving her a lead.

'So have I,' said Aunt Agatha, shivering in a marked manner. 'He called on me while I was still in bed to inform me of his intention of marrying some impossible girl from South Norwood.'

'East Dulwich, the *cognoscenti* informed me.'

'Well, East Dulwich, then. It is the same thing. But who told you?'

'Jeeves.'

'And how, pray, does Jeeves come to know all about it?'

'There are very few things in this world, Aunt Agatha,' I said gravely, 'that Jeeves doesn't know all about. He's met the girl.'

'Who is she?'

'One of the waitresses at the Buffers.'

I had expected this to register and it did. The relative let out a screech rather like the Cornish Express going through a junction.

'I take it from your manner, Aunt Agatha,' I said, 'that you want this thing stopped.'

'Of course it must be stopped.'

'Then there is but one policy to pursue. Let me ring for Jeeves and ask his advice.'

Aunt Agatha stiffened visibly. Very much the *grande dame* of the old *régime*.

'Are you seriously suggesting that we should discuss this intimate family matter with your man-servant?'

'Absolutely. Jeeves will find the way.'

'I have always known that you were an imbecile, Bertie,' said the flesh-and-blood, now down at about three degrees Fahrenheit, 'but I did suppose that you had some proper feeling, some pride, some respect for your position.'

'Well, you know what the poet Burns says.'

She squelched me with a glance.

'Obviously the only thing to do,' she said, 'is to offer this girl money.'

'Money?'

'Certainly. It will not be the first time your uncle has made such a course necessary.'

We sat for a bit, brooding. The family always sits brooding when the subject of Uncle George's early romance comes up. I was too young to be actually in on it at the time, but I've had the details frequently from many sources, including Uncle George. Let him get even the slightest bit pickled, and he will tell you the whole story, sometimes twice in an evening. It was a barmaid at the Criterion, just before he came into the title. Her name was Maudie and he loved her dearly, but the family would have none of it. They dug down into the sock and paid her off. Just one of those human-interest stories, if you know what I mean.

I wasn't so sold on this money-offering scheme.

'Well, just as you like, of course,' I said, 'but you're taking an awful chance. I mean, whenever people do it in novels and plays, they always get the dickens of a welt. The girl gets the sympathy of the audience every time. She just draws herself up and looks at them with clear, steady eyes, causing them to feel not a little cheesy. If I were you, I would sit tight and let Nature take its course.'

'I don't understand you.'

'Well, consider for a moment what Uncle George looks like. No Greta Garbo, believe me. I should simply let the girl go on looking at him. Take it from me, Aunt Agatha, I've studied human nature and I don't believe there's a female in the world who could see Uncle George fairly often in those waistcoats he wears without feeling that it was due to her better self to give him the gate. Besides, this girl sees him at meal-times, and Uncle George with his head down among the food-stuffs is a spectacle which –'

'If it is not troubling you too much, Bertie, I should be greatly obliged if you would stop drivelling.'

'Just as you say. All the same, I think you're going to find it dashed embarrassing, offering this girl money.'

'I am not proposing to do so. *You* will undertake the negotiations.'

'Me?'

'Certainly. I should think a hundred pounds would be ample. But I will give you a blank cheque, and you are at liberty to fill it in for a higher sum if it becomes necessary. The essential point is that, cost what it may, your uncle must be released from this entanglement.'

'So you're going to shove this off on me?'

'It is quite time you did something for the family.'

'And when she draws herself up and looks at me with clear, steady eyes, what do I do for an encore?'

'There is no need to discuss the matter any further. You can get down to East Dulwich in half an hour. There is a frequent service of trains. I will remain here to await your report.'

'But, listen!'

'Bertie, you will go and see this woman immediately.'

'Yes, but dash it!'
'Bertie!'
I threw in the towel.
'Oh, right ho, if you say so.'
'I do say so.'
'Oh, well, in that case, right ho.'

I don't know if you have ever tooled off to East Dulwich to offer a strange female a hundred smackers to release your Uncle George. In case you haven't, I may tell you that there are plenty of things that are lots better fun. I didn't feel any too good driving to the station. I didn't feel any too good in the train. And I didn't feel any too good as I walked to Kitchener Road. But the moment when I felt least good was when I had actually pressed the front-door bell and a rather grubby-looking maid had let me in and shown me down a passage and into a room with pink paper on the walls, a piano in the corner and a lot of photographs on the mantelpiece.

Barring a dentist's waiting-room, which it rather resembles, there isn't anything that quells the spirit much more than one of these suburban parlours. They are extremely apt to have stuffed birds in glass cases standing about on small tables, and if there is one thing which gives the man of sensibility that sinking feeling it is the cold, accusing eye of a ptarmigan or whatever it may be that has had its interior organs removed and sawdust substituted.

There were three of these cases in the parlour of Wistaria Lodge, so that, wherever you looked, you were sure to connect. Two were singletons, the third a family group, consisting of a father bullfinch, a mother bullfinch, and little Master Bullfinch, the last-named of whom wore an expression that was definitely that of a thug, and did more to damp my *joie de vivre* than all the rest of them put together.

I had moved to the window and was examining the aspidistra in order to avoid this creature's gaze, when I heard the door open and, turning, found myself confronted by something which, since it could hardly be the girl, I took to be the aunt.

'Oh, what ho,' I said. 'Good morning.'

The words came out rather roopily, for I was feeling a bit on the stunned side. I mean to say, the room being so small and this exhibit so large, I had got that sensation of wanting air. There are some people who don't seem to be intended to be seen close to, and this aunt was one of them. Billowy curves, if you know what I mean. I should think that in her day she must have been a very handsome girl, though even then on the substantial side. By the time she came into my life, she had taken on a good deal of excess weight. She looked like a photograph of an opera singer of the 'eighties. Also the orange hair and the magenta dress.

However, she was a friendly soul. She seemed glad to see Bertram. She smiled broadly.

'So here you are at last!' she said.

I couldn't make anything of this.

'Eh?'

'But I don't think you had better see my niece just yet. She's just having a nap.'

'Oh, in that case –'

'Seems a pity to wake her, doesn't it?'

'Oh, absolutely,' I said, relieved.

'When you get the influenza, you don't sleep at night, and then if you doze off in the morning – well, it seems a pity to wake someone, doesn't it?'

'Miss Platt has influenza?'

'That's what we think it is. But, of course, you'll be able to say. But we needn't waste time. Since you're here, you can be taking a look at my knee.'

'Your knee?'

I am all for knees at their proper time and, as you might say, in their proper place, but somehow this didn't seem the moment. However, she carried on according to plan.

'What do you think of that knee?' she asked, lifting the seven veils.

Well, of course, one has to be polite.

'Terrific!' I said.

'You wouldn't believe how it hurts me sometimes.'

'Really?'

'A sort of shooting pain. It just comes and goes. And I'll tell you a funny thing.'

'What's that?' I said, feeling I could do with a good laugh.

'Lately I've been having the same pain just here, at the end of the spine.'

'You don't mean it!'

'I do. Like red-hot needles. I wish you'd have a look at it.'

'At your spine?'

'Yes.'

I shook my head. Nobody is fonder of a bit of fun than myself, and I am all for Bohemian camaraderie and making a party go, and all that. But there is a line, and we Woosters know when to draw it.

'It can't be done,' I said austerely. 'Not spines. Knees, yes. Spines, no,' I said.

She seemed surprised.

'Well,' she said, 'you're a funny sort of doctor, I must say.'

I'm pretty quick, as I said before, and I began to see that something in the nature of a misunderstanding must have arisen.

'Doctor?'

'Well, you call yourself a doctor, don't you?'

'Did you think I was a doctor?'

'Aren't you a doctor?'

'No. Not a doctor.'

We had got it straightened out. The scales had fallen from our eyes. We knew where we were.

I had suspected that she was a genial soul. She now endorsed this view. I don't think I have ever heard a woman laugh so heartily.

'Well, that's the best thing!' she said, borrowing my handkerchief to wipe her eyes. 'Did you ever! But, if you aren't the doctor, who are you?'

'Wooster's the name. I came to see Miss Platt.'

'What about?'

This was the moment, of course, when I should have come out with the cheque and sprung the big effort. But somehow I couldn't make it. You know how it is. Offering people money to release your uncle is a scaly enough job at best, and when the atmosphere's not right the shot simply isn't on the board.

'Oh, just came to see her, you know.' I had rather a bright idea. 'My uncle heard she was seedy, don't you know, and asked me to look in and make enquiries,' I said.

'Your uncle?'

'Lord Yaxley.'

'Oh! So you are Lord Yaxley's nephew?'

'That's right. I suppose he's always popping in and out here, what?'

'No. I've never met him.'

'You haven't?'

'No. Rhoda talks a lot about him, of course, but for some reason she's never so much as asked him to look in for a cup of tea.'

I began to see that this Rhoda knew her business. If I'd been a girl with someone wanting to marry me and knew that there was an exhibit like this aunt hanging around the home, I, too, should have thought twice about inviting him to call until the ceremony was over and he had actually signed on the dotted line. I mean to say, a thoroughly good soul – heart of gold beyond a doubt – but not the sort of thing you wanted to spring on Romeo before the time was ripe.

'I suppose you were all very surprised when you heard about it?' she said.

'Surprised is right.'

'Of course, nothing is definitely settled yet.'

'You don't mean that? I thought –'

'Oh, no. She's thinking it over.'

'I see.'

'Of course, she feels it's a great compliment. But then sometimes she wonders if he isn't too old.'

'My Aunt Agatha has rather the same idea.'

'Of course, a title *is* a title.'

'Yes, there's that. What do you think about it yourself?'

'Oh, it doesn't matter what I think. There's no doing anything with girls these days, is there?'

'Not much.'

'What I often say is, I wonder what girls are coming to. Still, there it is.'

'Absolutely.'

There didn't seem much reason why the conversation shouldn't go on for ever. She had the air of a woman who had settled down for the day. But at this point the maid came in and said the doctor had arrived.

I got up.

'I'll be tooling off, then.'

'If you must.'

'I think I'd better.'

'Well, pip pip.'

'Toodle-oo,' I said, and out into the fresh air.

Knowing what was waiting for me at home, I would have preferred to have gone to the club and spent the rest of the day there. But the thing had to be faced.

'Well?' said Aunt Agatha, as I trickled into the sitting room.

'Well, yes and no,' I replied.

'What do you mean? Did she refuse the money?'

'Not exactly.'

'She accepted it?'

'Well, there again, not precisely.'

I explained what had happened. I wasn't expecting her to be any too frightfully pleased, and it's as well that I wasn't, because she wasn't. In fact, as the story unfolded, her comments became fruitier and fruitier, and when I had finished she uttered an exclamation that nearly broke a window. It sounded something like 'Gor!' as if she had started to say 'Gorblimey!' and had remembered her ancient lineage just in time.

'I'm sorry,' I said. 'And can a man say more? I lost my nerve. The old morale suddenly turned blue on me. It's the sort of thing that might have happened to anyone.'

'I never heard of anything so spineless in my life.'

I shivered, like a warrior whose old wound hurts him.

'I'd be most awfully obliged, Aunt Agatha,' I said, 'if you would not use that word spine. It awakens memories.'

The door opened. Jeeves appeared.

'Sir?'

'Yes, Jeeves?'

'I thought you called, sir.'

'No, Jeeves.'

'Very good, sir.'

There are moments when, even under the eye of Aunt Agatha, I can take the firm line. And now, seeing Jeeves standing there with the light of intelligence simply fizzing in every feature, I suddenly felt how perfectly footling it was to give this pre-eminent source of balm and comfort the go-by simply because Aunt Agatha had prejudices against discussing family affairs with the staff. It might make her say 'Gor!' again, but I decided to do as we ought to have done right from the start – put the case in his hands.

'Jeeves,' I said, 'this matter of Uncle George.'

'Yes, sir.'

'You know the circs?'

'Yes, sir.'

'You know what we want.'

'Yes, sir.'

'Then advise us. And make it snappy. Think on your feet.'

I heard Aunt Agatha rumble like a volcano just before it starts to set about the neighbours, but I did not wilt. I had seen the sparkle in Jeeves's eye which indicated that an idea was on the way.

'I understand that you have been visiting the young person's home, sir?'

'Just got back.'

'Then you no doubt encountered the young person's aunt?'

'Jeeves, I encountered nothing else but.'

'Then the suggestion which I am about to make will, I feel sure, appeal to you, sir. I would recommend that you confront his lordship with this woman. It has always been her intention to continue residing with her niece after the latter's marriage. Should he meet her, this reflection might give his lordship pause. As you are aware, sir, she is a kind-hearted woman, but definitely of the people.'

'Jeeves, you are right! Apart from anything else, that orange hair!'

'Exactly, sir.'

'Not to mention the magenta dress.'

'Precisely, sir.'

'I'll ask her to lunch tomorrow, to meet him. You see,' I said to Aunt Agatha, who was still fermenting in the background, 'a ripe suggestion first crack out of the box. Did I or did I not tell you –'

'That will do, Jeeves,' said Aunt Agatha.

'Very good, madam.'

For some minutes after he had gone, Aunt Agatha strayed from the point a bit, confining her remarks to what she thought of a Wooster who could lower the prestige of the clan by allowing menials to get above themselves. Then she returned to what you might call the main issue.

'Bertie,' she said, 'you will go and see this girl again tomorrow and this time you will do as I told you.'

'But, dash it! With this excellent alternative scheme, based firmly on the psychology of the individual –'

'That is quite enough, Bertie. You heard what I said. I am going. Goodbye.'

She buzzed off, little knowing of what stuff Bertram Wooster was made. The door had hardly closed before I was shouting for Jeeves.

'Jeeves,' I said, 'the recent aunt will have none of your excellent alternative schemes, but none the less I propose to go through with it unswervingly. I consider it a ball of fire. Can you get hold of this female and bring her here for lunch tomorrow?'

'Yes, sir.'

'Good. Meanwhile, I will be 'phoning Uncle George. We will do Aunt Agatha good despite herself. What is it the poet says, Jeeves?'

'The poet Burns, sir?'

'Not the poet Burns. Some other poet. About doing good by stealth.'

'"These little acts of unremembered kindness," sir?'

'That's it in a nutshell, Jeeves.'

I suppose doing good by stealth ought to give one a glow, but I can't say I found myself exactly looking forward to the binge in prospect. Uncle George by himself is a mouldy enough luncheon companion, being extremely apt to collar the conversation and confine it to a description of his symptoms, he being one of those birds who can never be brought to believe that the general public isn't agog to hear all about the lining of his stomach. Add the aunt, and you have a little gathering which might well dismay the stoutest. The moment I woke, I felt conscious of some impending doom, and the cloud, if you know what I mean, grew darker all the morning. By the time Jeeves came in with the cocktails, I was feeling pretty low.

'For two pins, Jeeves,' I said, 'I would turn the whole thing up and leg it to the Drones.'

'I can readily imagine that this will prove something of an ordeal, sir.'

'How did you get to know these people, Jeeves?'

'It was through a young fellow of my acquaintance, sir, Colonel Mainwaring-Smith's personal gentleman's gentleman. He and the young person had an understanding at the time, and he desired me to accompany him to Wistaria Lodge and meet her.'

'They were engaged?'

'Not precisely engaged, sir. An understanding.'

'What did they quarrel about?'

'They did not quarrel, sir. When his lordship began to pay his addresses, the young person, naturally flattered, began to waver between love and ambition. But even now she has not formally rescinded the understanding.'

'Then, if your scheme works and Uncle George edges out, it will do your pal a bit of good?'

'Yes, sir. Smethurst – his name is Smethurst – would consider it a consummation devoutly to be wished.'

'Rather well put, that Jeeves. Your own?'

'No, sir. The Swan of Avon, sir.'

An unseen hand without tootled on the bell, and I braced myself to play the host. The binge was on.

'Mrs Wilberforce, sir,' announced Jeeves.

'And how I'm to keep a straight face with you standing behind and saying "Madam, can I tempt you with a potato?" is more than I know,' said the aunt, sailing in, looking larger and pinker and matier than ever. 'I know him, you know,' she said, jerking a thumb after Jeeves. 'He's been round and taken tea with us.'

'So he told me.'

She gave the sitting room the once-over.

'You've got a nice place here,' she said. 'Though I like more pink about. It's so cheerful. What's that you've got there? Cocktails?'

'Martini with a spot of absinthe,' I said, beginning to pour.

She gave a girlish squeal.

'Don't you try to make me drink that stuff! Do you know what would happen if I touched one of those things? I'd be racked with pain. What they do to the lining of your stomach!'

'Oh, I don't know.'

'I do. If you had been a barmaid as long as I was, you'd know, too.'

'Oh – er – were you a barmaid?'

'For years, when I was younger than I am. At the Criterion.'

I dropped the shaker.

'There!' she said, pointing the moral. 'That's through drinking that stuff. Makes your hand woböle. What I always used to say to the boys was, "Port, if you like. Port's wholesome. I appreciate a drop of port myself. But these new-fangled messes from America, no." But they would never listen to me.'

I was eyeing her warily. Of course, there must have been thousands of barmaids at the Criterion in its time, but still it gave one a bit of a start. It was years ago that Uncle George's dash at a *mésalliance* had occurred – long before he came into the title – but the Wooster clan still quivered at the name of the Criterion.

'Er – when you were at the Cri,' I said, 'did you ever happen to run into a fellow of my name?'

'I've forgotten what it is. I'm always silly about names.'

'Wooster.'

'Wooster! When you were there yesterday I thought you said Foster. Wooster! Did I run into a fellow named Wooster? Well! Why, George Wooster and me – Piggy, I used to call him – were going off to the registrar's, only his family heard of it and interfered. They offered me a lot of money to give him up, and, like a silly girl, I let them persuade me. If I've wondered once what became of him, I've wondered a thousand times. Is he a relation of yours?'

'Excuse me,' I said. 'I just want a word with Jeeves.'

I legged it for the pantry.

'Jeeves!'

'Sir?'

'Do you know what's happened?'

'No, sir.'

'This female –'

'Sir?'

'She's Uncle George's barmaid!'

'Sir?'

'Oh, dash it, you must have heard of Uncle George's barmaid. You know all the family history. The barmaid he wanted to marry years ago.'

'Ah, yes, sir.'

'She's the only woman he ever loved. He's told me so a million times. Every time he gets to the fourth whisky-and-potash, he always becomes maudlin about this female. What a dashed bit of bad luck! The first thing we know, the call of the past will be echoing in his heart. I can feel it, Jeeves. She's just his sort. The first thing she did when she came in was to start talking about the lining of her stomach. You see the hideous significance of that, Jeeves? The lining of his stomach is Uncle George's favourite topic of conversation. It means that he and she are kindred souls. This woman and he will be like –'

'Deep calling to deep, sir?'

'Exactly.'

'Most disturbing, sir.'

'What's to be done?'

'I could not say, sir.'

'I'll tell you what I'm going to do – 'phone him and say the lunch is off.'

'Scarcely feasible, sir. I fancy that is his lordship at the door now.'

And so it was. Jeeves let him in, and I followed him as he navigated down the passage to the sitting room. There was a stunned silence as he went in, and then a couple of the startled yelps you hear when old buddies get together after long separation.

'Piggy!'

'Maudie!'

'Well, I never!'

'Well, I'm dashed!'

'Did you ever!'

'Well, bless my soul!'

'Fancy you being Lord Yaxley!'

'Came into the title soon after we parted.'

'Just to think!'

'You could have knocked me down with a feather!'

I hung about in the offing, now on this leg, now on that. For all the notice they took of me, I might just as well have been the late Bertram Wooster, disembodied.

'Maudie, you don't look a day older, dash it!'

'Nor do you, Piggy.'

'How have you been all these years?'

'Pretty well. The lining of my stomach isn't all it should be.'

'Good Gad! You don't say so? I have trouble with the lining of *my* stomach.'

'It's a sort of heavy feeling after meals.'

'*I* get a sort of heavy feeling after meals. What are you trying for it?'

'I've been taking Perkins' Digestine.'

'My dear girl, no use! No use at all. Tried it myself for years and got no relief. Now, if you really want something that is some good –'

I slid away. The last I saw of them, Uncle George was down beside her on the Chesterfield, buzzing hard.

'Jeeves,' I said, tottering into the pantry.

'Sir?'

'There will only be two for lunch. Count me out. If they notice I'm not there, tell them I was called away by an urgent 'phone message. The situation has got beyond Bertram, Jeeves. You will find me at the Drones.'

'Very good, sir.'

It was latish in the evening when one of the waiters came to me as I played a distrait game of snooker pool and informed me that Aunt Agatha was on the 'phone.

'Bertie!'

'Hullo?'

I was amazed to note that her voice was that of an aunt who feels that things are breaking right. It had the birdlike trill.

'Bertie, have you that cheque I gave you?'

'Yes.'

'Then tear it up. It will not be needed.'

'Eh?'

'I say it will not be needed. Your uncle has been speaking to me on the telephone. He is not going to marry that girl.'

'Not?'

'No. Apparently he has been thinking it over and sees how

unsuitable it would have been. But what is astonishing is that he *is* going to be married!'

'He is?'

'Yes, to an old friend of his, a Mrs Wilberforce. A woman of a sensible age, he gave me to understand. I wonder which Wilberforces that would be. There are two main branches of the family – the Essex Wilberforces and the Cumberland Wilberforces. I believe there is also a cadet branch somewhere in Shropshire.'

'And one in East Dulwich.'

'What did you say?'

'Nothing,' I said. 'Nothing.'

I hung up. Then back to the old flat, feeling a trifle sandbagged.

'Well, Jeeves,' I said, and there was censure in the eyes. 'So I gather everything is nicely settled?'

'Yes, sir. His lordship formally announced the engagement between the sweet and cheese courses, sir.'

'He did, did he?'

'Yes, sir.'

I eyed the man sternly.

'You do not appear to be aware of it, Jeeves,' I said, in a cold, level voice, 'but this binge has depreciated your stock very considerably. I have always been accustomed to look upon you as a counsellor without equal. I have, so to speak, hung upon your lips. And now see what you have done. All this is the direct consequence of your scheme, based on the psychology of the individual. I should have thought, Jeeves, that, knowing the woman – meeting her socially, as you might say, over the afternoon cup of tea – you might have ascertained that she was Uncle George's barmaid.'

'I did, sir.'

'What!'

'I was aware of the fact, sir.'

'Then you must have known what would happen if she came to lunch and met him.'

'Yes, sir.'

'Well, I'm dashed!'

'If I might explain, sir. The young man Smethurst, who is greatly attached to the young person, is an intimate friend of mine. He applied to me some little while back in the hope that I might be able to do something to ensure that the young person followed the dictates of her heart and refrained from permitting herself to be lured by gold and the glamour of his lordship's position. There will now be no obstacle to their union.'

'I see. "Little acts of unremembered kindness," what?'

'Precisely, sir.'

'And how about Uncle George? You've landed him pretty nicely in the cart.'

'No, sir, if I may take the liberty of opposing your view. I fancy that Mrs Wilberforce should make an ideal mate for his lordship. If there was a defect in his lordship's mode of life, it was that he was a little unduly attached to the pleasures of the table –'

'Ate like a pig, you mean?'

'I would not have ventured to put it in quite that way, sir, but the expression does meet the facts of the case. He was also inclined to drink rather more than his medical adviser would have approved of. Elderly bachelors who are wealthy and without occupation tend somewhat frequently to fall into this error, sir. The future Lady Yaxley will check this. Indeed, I overheard her ladyship saying as much as I brought in the fish. She was commenting on a certain puffiness of the face which had been absent in his lordship's appearance in the earlier days of their acquaintanceship, and she observed that his lordship needed looking after. I fancy, sir, that you will find the union will turn out an extremely satisfactory one.'

It was – what's the word I want? – it was plausible, of course, but still I shook the onion.

'But, Jeeves!'

'Sir?'

'She *is*, as you remarked not long ago, definitely of the people.'

He looked at me in a reproachful sort of way.

'Sturdy lower-middle-class stock, sir.'

'H'm!'

'Sir?'

'I said "H'm!" Jeeves.'

'Besides, sir, remembering what the poet Tennyson said: "Kind hearts are more than coronets".'

'And which of us is going to tell Aunt Agatha that?'

'If I might make the suggestion, sir, I would advise that we omitted to communicate with Mrs Spenser Gregson in any way. I have your suitcase practically packed. It would be a matter of but a few minutes to bring the car round from the garage –'

'And off over the horizon to where men are men?'

'Precisely, sir.'

'Jeeves,' I said. 'I'm not sure that even now I can altogether see eye to eye with you regarding your recent activities. You think you have scattered light and sweetness on every side. I am not so sure.

However, with this latest suggestion you have rung the bell. I examine it narrowly and I find no flaw in it. It is the goods. I'll get the car at once.'

'Very good, sir.

'Remember what the poet Shakespeare said, Jeeves.'

'What was that, sir?'

'"Exit hurriedly, pursued by a bear." You'll find it in one of his plays. I remember drawing a picture of it on the side of the page, when I was at school.'

11

THE ORDEAL OF YOUNG TUPPY

'What-Ho, Jeeves!' I said, entering the room where he waded knee-deep in suitcases and shirts and winter suitings, like a sea-beast among rocks. 'Packing?'

'Yes, sir,' replied the honest fellow, for there are no secrets between us.

'Pack on!' I said approvingly. 'Pack, Jeeves, pack with care. Pack in the presence of the passenjare.' And I rather fancy I added the words 'Tra-la!' for I was in merry mood.

Every year, starting about the middle of November, there is a good deal of anxiety and apprehension among owners of the better-class of country-house throughout England as to who will get Bertram Wooster's patronage for Christmas holidays. It may be one or it may be another. As my Aunt Dahlia says, you never know where the blow will fall.

This year, however, I had decided early. It couldn't have been later than Nov. 10 when a sigh of relief went up from a dozen stately homes as it became known that the short straw had been drawn by Sir Reginald Witherspoon, Bart, of Bleaching Court, Upper Bleaching, Hants.

In coming to the decision to give this Witherspoon my custom, I had been actuated by several reasons, not counting the fact that, having married Aunt Dahlia's husband's younger sister Katherine, he is by way of being a sort of uncle of mine. In the first place, the Bart does one extraordinarily well, both browsing and sluicing being above criticism. Then, again, his stables always contain something worth riding, which is a consideration. And, thirdly, there is no danger of getting lugged into a party of amateur Waits and having to tramp the countryside in the rain, singing, 'When Shepherds Watched Their Flocks By Night.' Or for the matter of that, 'Noel! Noel!'

All these things counted with me, but what really drew me to

Bleaching Court like a magnet was the knowledge that young Tuppy Glossop would be among those present.

I feel sure I have told you before about this black-hearted bird, but I will give you the strength of it once again, just to keep the records straight. He was the fellow, if you remember, who, ignoring a lifelong friendship in the course of which he had frequently eaten my bread and salt, betted me one night at the Drones that I wouldn't swing myself across the swimming-bath by the ropes and rings and then, with almost inconceivable treachery, went and looped back the last ring, causing me to drop into the fluid and ruin one of the nattiest suits of dress-clothes in London.

To execute a fitting vengeance on this bloke had been the ruling passion of my life ever since.

'You are bearing in mind, Jeeves,' I said, 'the fact that Mr Glossop will be at Bleaching?'

'Yes, sir.'

'And, consequently, are not forgetting to put in the Giant Squirt?'

'No, sir.'

'Nor the Luminous Rabbit?'

'No, sir.'

'Good! I am rather pinning my faith on the Luminous Rabbit, Jeeves. I hear excellent reports of it on all sides. You wind it up and put it in somebody's room in the night watches, and it shines in the dark and jumps about, making odd, squeaking noises the while. The whole performance being, I should imagine, well calculated to scare young Tuppy into a decline.'

'Very possibly, sir.'

'Should that fail, there is always the Giant Squirt. We must leave no stone unturned to put it across the man somehow,' I said. 'The Wooster honour is at stake.'

I would have spoken further on this subject, but just then the front-door bell buzzed.

'I'll answer it,' I said. 'I expect it's Aunt Dahlia. She 'phoned that she would be calling this morning.'

It was not Aunt Dahlia. It was a telegraph-boy with telegram. I opened it, read it, and carried it back to the bedroom, the brow a bit knitted.

'Jeeves,' I said. 'A rummy communication has arrived. From Mr Glossop.'

'Indeed, sir?'

'I will read it to you. Handed in at Upper Bleaching. Message runs as follows:

When you come tomorrow, bring my football boots. Also, if humanly possible, Irish water-spaniel. Urgent. Regards. Tuppy.

'What do you make of that, Jeeves?'

'As I interpret the document, sir, Mr Glossop wishes you, when you come tomorrow, to bring his football boots. Also, if humanly possible, an Irish water-spaniel. He hints that the matter is urgent, and sends his regards.'

'Yes, that's how I read it, too. But why football boots?'

'Perhaps Mr Glossop wishes to play football, sir.'

I considered this.

'Yes,' I said. 'That may be the solution. But why would a man, staying peacefully at a country-house, suddenly develop a craving to play football?'

'I could not say, sir.'

'And why an Irish water-spaniel?'

'There again I fear I can hazard no conjecture, sir.'

'What *is* an Irish water-spaniel?'

'A water-spaniel of a variety bred in Ireland, sir.'

'You think so?'

'Yes, sir.'

'Well, perhaps you're right. But why should I sweat about the place collecting dogs – of whatever nationality – for young Tuppy? Does he think I'm Santa Claus? Is he under the impression that my feelings towards him, after that Drones Club incident, are those of kindly benevolence? Irish water-spaniels, indeed! Tchah!'

'Sir?'

'Tchah, Jeeves.'

'Very good, sir.'

The front-door bell buzzed again.

'A busy morning, Jeeves.'

'Yes, sir.'

'All right. I'll go.'

This time it was Aunt Dahlia. She charged in with the air of a woman with something on her mind – giving tongue, in fact, while actually on the very doormat.

'Bertie,' she boomed, in that ringing voice of hers which cracks window-panes and upsets vases, 'I've come about that young hound, Glossop.'

'It's quite all right, Aunt Dahlia,' I replied soothingly. 'I have the situation well in hand. The Giant Squirt and the Luminous Rabbit are even now being packed.'

'I don't know what you're talking about, and I don't for a moment suppose you do, either,' said the relative somewhat brusquely, 'but, if you'll kindly stop gibbering, I'll tell you what I mean. I have had a most disturbing letter from Katherine. About this reptile. Of course, I haven't breathed a word to Angela. She'd hit the ceiling.'

This Angela is Aunt Dahlia's daughter. She and young Tuppy are generally supposed to be more or less engaged, though nothing definitely 'Morning Posted' yet.

'Why?' I said.

'Why what?'

'Why would Angela hit the ceiling?'

'Well, wouldn't you, if you were practically engaged to a fiend in human shape and somebody told you he had gone off to the country and was flirting with a dog-girl?'

'With a what was that, once again?'

'A dog-girl. One of these dashed open-air flappers in thick boots and tailor-made tweeds who infest the rural districts and go about the place followed by packs of assorted dogs. I used to be one of them myself in my younger days, so I know how dangerous they are. Her name is Dalgleish. Old Colonel Dalgleish's daughter. They live near Bleaching.'

I saw a gleam of daylight.

'Then that must be what his telegram was about. He's just wired, asking me to bring down an Irish water-spaniel. A Christmas present for this girl, no doubt.'

'Probably. Katherine tells me he seems to be infatuated with her. She says he follows her about like one of her dogs, looking like a tame cat and bleating like a sheep.'

'Quite the private zoo, what?'

'Bertie,' said Aunt Dahlia – and I could see her generous nature was stirred to its depths – 'one more crack like that out of you, and I shall forget that I am an aunt and hand you one.'

I became soothing. I gave her the old oil.

'I shouldn't worry,' I said. 'There's probably nothing in it. Whole thing no doubt much exaggerated.'

'You think so, eh? Well, you know what he's like. You remember the trouble we had when he ran after that singing-woman.'

I recollected the case. You will find it elsewhere in the archives. Cora Bellinger was the female's name. She was studying for Opera, and young Tuppy thought highly of her. Fortunately, however, she punched him in the eye during Beefy Bingham's clean, bright entertainment in Bermondsey East, and love died.

'Besides,' said Aunt Dahlia, 'There's something I haven't told you. Just before he went to Bleaching, he and Angela quarrelled.'

'They did?'

'Yes. I got it out of Angela this morning. She was crying her eyes out, poor angel. It was something about her last hat. As far as I could gather, he told her it made her look like a Pekingese, and she told him she never wanted to see him again in this world or the next. And he said "Right ho!" and breezed off. I can see what has happened. This dog-girl has caught him on the rebound and, unless something is done quick, anything may happen. So place the facts before Jeeves, and tell him to take action the moment you get down there.'

I am always a little piqued, if you know what I mean, at this assumption on the relative's part that Jeeves is so dashed essential on these occasions. My manner, therefore, as I replied, was a bit on the crisp side.

'Jeeve's services will not be required,' I said. 'I can handle this business. The programme which I have laid out will be quite sufficient to take young Tuppy's mind off love-making. It is my intention to insert the Luminous Rabbit in his room at the first opportunity that presents itself. The Luminous Rabbit shines in the dark and jumps about, making odd, squeaking noises. It will sound to young Tuppy like the Voice of Conscience, and I anticipate that a single treatment will make him retire into a nursing-home for a couple of weeks or so. At the end of which period he will have forgotten all about the bally girl.'

'Bertie,' said Aunt Dahlia, with a sort of frozen calm, 'You are the Abysmal Chump. Listen to me. It's simply because I am fond of you and have influence with the Lunacy Commissioners that you weren't put in a padded cell years ago. Bungle this business, and I withdraw my protection. Can't you understand that this thing is far too serious for any fooling about? Angela's whole happiness is at stake. Do as I tell you, and put it up to Jeeves.'

'Just as you say, Aunt Dahlia,' I said stiffly.

'All right, then. Do it now.'

I went back to the bedroom.

'Jeeves,' I said, and I did not trouble to conceal my chagrin, 'you need not pack the Luminous Rabbit.'

'Very good, sir.'

'Nor the Giant Squirt.'

'Very good, sir.'

'They have been subjected to destructive criticism, and the zest has gone. Oh, and, Jeeves.'

'Sir?'

'Mrs Travers wishes you, on arriving at Bleaching Court, to disentangle Mr Glossop from a dog-girl.'

'Very good, sir. I will attend to the matter and will do my best to give satisfaction.'

That Aunt Dahlia had not exaggerated the perilous nature of the situation was made clear to me on the following afternoon. Jeeves and I drove down to Bleaching in the two-seater, and we were tooling along about half-way between the village and the Court when suddenly there appeared ahead of us a sea of dogs and in the middle of it young Tuppy frisking round one of those largish, corn-fed girls. He was bending towards her in a devout sort of way, and even at a considerable distance I could see that his ears were pink. His attitude, in short, was unmistakably that of a man endeavouring to push a good thing along; and when I came closer and noted that the girl wore tailor-made tweeds and thick boots, I had no further doubts.

'You observe, Jeeves?' I said in a low, significant voice.

'Yes, sir.'

'The girl, what?'

'Yes, sir.'

I tooted amiably on the horn and yodelled a bit. They turned – Tuppy, I fancied, not any too pleased.

'Oh, hullo, Bertie,' he said.

'Hullo,' I said.

'My friend, Bertie Wooster,' said Tuppy to the girl, in what seemed to me rather an apologetic manner. You know – as if he would have preferred to hush me up.

'Hullo,' said the girl.

'Hullo,' I said.

'Hullo, Jeeves,' said Tuppy.

'Good afternoon, sir,' said Jeeves.

There was a somewhat constrained silence.

'Well, goodbye, Bertie,' said young Tuppy. 'You'll be wanting to push along, I expect.'

We Woosters can take a hint as well as the next man.

'See you later,' I said.

'Oh, rather,' said Tuppy.

I set the machinery in motion again, and we rolled off.

'Sinister, Jeeves,' I said. 'You noticed that the subject was looking like a stuffed frog?'

'Yes, sir.'

'And gave no indication of wanting us to stop and join the party?'

'No, sir.'

'I think Aunt Dahlia's fears are justified. The thing seems serious.'

'Yes, sir.'

'Well, strain the brain, Jeeves.'

'Very good, sir.'

It wasn't till I was dressing for dinner that night that I saw young Tuppy again. He trickled in just as I was arranging the tie.

'Hullo!' I said.

'Hullo!' said Tuppy.

'Who was the girl?' I asked, in that casual, snaky way of mine – off-hand, I mean.

'A Miss Dalgleish,' said Tuppy, and I noticed that he blushed a spot.

'Staying here?'

'No. She lives in that house just before you come to the gates of this place. Did you bring my football boots?'

'Yes. Jeeves has got them somewhere.'

'And the water-spaniel?'

'Sorry. No water-spaniel.'

'Dashed nuisance. She's set her heart on an Irish water-spaniel.'

'Well, what do you care?'

'I wanted to give her one.'

'Why?'

Tuppy became a trifle haughty. Frigid. The rebuking eye.

'Colonel and Mrs Dalgleish,' he said, 'have been extremely kind to me since I got here. They have entertained me. I naturally wish to make some return for their hospitality. I don't want them to look upon me as one of those ill-mannered modern young men you read about in the papers who grab everything they can lay their hooks on and never buy back. If people ask you to lunch and tea and what not, they appreciate it if you make them some little present in return.'

'Well, give them your football boots. In passing, why did you want the bally things?'

'I'm playing in a match next Thursday.'

'Down here?'

'Yes. Upper Bleaching versus Hockley-cum-Meston. Apparently it's the big game of the year.'

'How did you get roped in?'

'I happened to mention in the course of conversation the other day that, when in London, I generally turn out on Saturdays for the Old Austinians, and Miss Dalgleish seemed rather keen that I should help the village.'

'Which village?'

'Upper Bleaching, of course.'

'Ah, then you're going to play for Hockley?'

'You needn't be funny, Bertie. You may not know it, but I'm pretty hot stuff on the football field. Oh, Jeeves.'

'Sir?' said Jeeves, entering right centre.

'Mr Wooster tells me you have my football boots.'

'Yes, sir. I have placed them in your room.'

'Thanks. Jeeves, do you want to make a bit of money?'

'Yes, sir.'

'Then put a trifle on Upper Bleaching for the annual encounter with Hockley-cum-Meston next Thursday,' said Tuppy, exiting with swelling bosom.

'Mr Glossop is going to play on Thursday,' I explained as the door closed.

'So I was informed in the Servants' Hall, sir.'

'Oh? And what's the general feeling there about it?'

'The impression I gathered, sir, was that the Servants' Hall considers Mr Glossop ill-advised.'

'Why's that?'

'I am informed by Mr Mulready, Sir Reginald's butler, sir, that this contest differs in some respects from the ordinary football game. Owing to the fact that there has existed for many years considerable animus between the two villages, the struggle is conducted, it appears, on somewhat looser and more primitive lines than is usually the case when two teams meet in friendly rivalry. The primary object of the players, I am given to understand, is not so much to score points as to inflict violence.'

'Good Lord, Jeeves!'

'Such appears to be the case, sir. The game is one that would have a great interest for the antiquarian. It was played first in the reign of King Henry VIII, when it lasted from noon till sundown over an area covering several square miles. Seven deaths resulted on that occasion.'

'Seven!'

'Not inclusive of two of the spectators, sir. In recent years, however, the casualties appear to have been confined to broken limbs and other minor injuries. The opinion of the Servants' Hall is that it would be more judicious on Mr Glossop's part, were he to refrain from mixing himself up in the affair.'

I was more or less aghast. I mean to say, while I had made it my mission in life to get back at young Tuppy for that business at the Drones, there still remained certain faint vestiges, if vestiges is the word I want, of the old friendship and esteem. Besides, there are limits to one's thirst for vengeance. Deep as my resentment was for the ghastly outrage he had perpetrated on me, I had no wish to see him toddle unsuspiciously into the arena and get all chewed up by wild villagers. A Tuppy scared stiff by a Luminous Rabbit – yes. Excellent business. The happy ending, in fact. But a Tuppy carried off on a stretcher in half a dozen pieces – no. Quite a different matter. All wrong. Not to be considered for a moment.

Obviously, then, a kindly word of warning while there was yet time, was indicated. I buzzed off to his room forthwith, and found him toying dreamily with the football boots.

I put him in possession of the facts.

'What you had better do – and the Servants' Hall thinks the same,' I said, 'is fake a sprained ankle on the eve of the match.'

He looked at me in an odd sort of way.

'You suggest that, when Miss Dalgleish is trusting me, relying on me, looking forward with eager, girlish enthusiasm to seeing me help her village on to victory, I should let her down with a thud?'

I was pleased with his ready intelligence.

'That's the idea,' I said.

'Faugh!' said Tuppy – the only time I've ever heard the word.

'How do you mean, "Faugh"?' I asked.

'Bertie,' said Tuppy, 'what you tell me merely makes me all the keener for the fray. A warm game is what I want. I welcome this sporting spirit on the part of the opposition. I shall enjoy a spot of roughness. It will enable me to go all out and give of my best. Do you realize,' said young Tuppy, vermilion to the gills, 'that She will be looking on? And do you know how that will make me feel? It will make me feel like some knight of old jousting under the eyes of his lady. Do you suppose that Sir Lancelot or Sir Galahad, when there was a tourney scheduled for the following Thursday, went and pretended they had sprained their ankles just because the thing was likely to be a bit rough?'

'Don't forget that in the reign of King Henry VIII –'

'Never mind about the reign of King Henry VIII. All I care about is that it's Upper Bleaching's turn this year to play in colours, so I shall be able to wear my Old Austinian shirt. Light blue,

Bertie, with broad orange stripes. I shall look like something, I tell you.'

'But what?'

'Bertie,' said Tuppy, now becoming purely ga-ga, 'I may as well tell you that I'm in love at last. This is the real thing. I have found my mate. All my life I have dreamed of meeting some sweet, open-air girl with all the glory of the English countryside in her eyes, and I have found her. How different she is, Bertie, from these hot-house, artificial London girls! Would they stand in the mud on a winter afternoon, watching a football match? Would they know what to give an Alsatian for fits? Would they tramp ten miles a day across the fields and come back as fresh as paint? No!'

'Well, why should they?'

'Bertie, I'm staking everything on this game on Thursday. At the moment, I have an idea that she looks on me as something of a weakling, simply because I got a blister on my foot the other afternoon and had to take the bus back from Hockley. But when she sees me going through the rustic opposition like a devouring flame, will that make her think a bit? Will that make her open her eyes? What?'

'What?'

'I said "What"?'

'So did I.'

'I meant, Won't it?'

'Oh, rather.'

Here the dinner-gong sounded, not before I was ready for it.

Judicious enquiries during the next couple of days convinced me that the Servants' Hall at Bleaching Court, in advancing the suggestion that young Tuppy, born and bred in the gentler atmosphere of the Metropolis, would do well to keep out of local disputes and avoid the football-field on which these were to be settled, had not spoken idly. It had weighed its words and said the sensible thing. Feeling between the two villages undoubtedly ran high, as they say.

You know how it is in these remote rural districts. Life tends at times to get a bit slow. There's nothing much to do in the long winter evenings but listen to the radio and brood on what a tick your neighbour is. You find yourself remembering how Farmer Giles did you down over the sale of your pig, and Farmer Giles finds himself remembering that it was your son, Ernest, who bunged the half-brick at his horse on the second Sunday before Septuagesima. And so on and so forth. How this particular feud had started, I don't know, but the season of peace and goodwill found it in full blast. The only topic of conversation in Upper Bleaching was Thursday's game, and the citizenry seemed to be looking forward to it in a spirit that can only be described as ghoulish. And it was the same in Hockley-cum-Meston.

I paid a visit to Hockley-cum-Meston on the Wednesday, being rather anxious to take a look at the inhabitants and see how formidable they were. I was shocked to observe that practically every second male might have been the Village Blacksmith's big brother. The muscles of their brawny arms were obviously strong as iron bands, and the way the company at the Green Pig, where I looked in incognito for a spot of beer, talked about the forthcoming sporting contest was enough to chill the blood of anyone who had a pal who proposed to fling himself into the fray. It sounded rather like Attila and a few of his Huns sketching out their next campaign.

I went back to Jeeves with my mind made up.

'Jeeves,' I said, 'you, who had the job of drying and pressing those dress-clothes of mine, are aware that I have suffered much at young Tuppy Glossop's hands. By rights, I suppose, I ought to be welcoming the fact that the Wrath of Heaven is now hovering over him in this fearful manner. But the view I take of it is that Heaven looks like overdoing it. Heaven's idea of a fitting retribution is not mine. In my most unrestrained moments I never wanted the poor blighter assassinated. And the idea in Hockley-cum-Meston seems to be that a good opportunity has arisen of making it a bumper Christmas for the local undertaker. There was a fellow with red hair at the Green Pig this afternoon who might have been the undertaker's partner, the way he talked. We must act, and speedily, Jeeves. We must put a bit of a jerk in it and save young Tuppy in spite of himself.'

'What course would you advocate, sir?'

'I'll tell you. He refuses to do the sensible thing and slide out, because the girl will be watching the game and he imagines, poor lizard, that he is going to shine and impress her. So we must employ guile. You must go up to London today, Jeeves, and tomorrow morning you will send a telegram, signed "Angela," which will run as follows. Jot it down. Ready?'

'Yes, sir.'

'"So sorry –" . . .' I pondered. 'What would a girl say, Jeeves, who, having had a row with the bird she was practically engaged to because he told her she looked like a Pekingese in her new hat, wanted to extend the olive-branch?'

'"So sorry I was cross", sir, would, I fancy, be the expression.'

'Strong enough, do you think?'

'Possibly the addition of the word "darling" would give the necessary verisimilitude, sir.'

'Right. Resume the jotting. "So sorry I was cross, darling . . ." No, wait, Jeeves. Scratch that out. I see where we have gone off the rails. I see where we are missing a chance to make this the real tabasco. Sign the telegram not "Angela" but "Travers".'

'Very good, sir.'

'Or, rather, "Dahlia Travers". And this is the body of the communication. "Please return at once."'

'"Immediately" would be more economical, sir. Only one word. And it has a strong ring.'

'True. Jot on, then. "Please return immediately. Angela in a hell of a state."'

'I would suggest "Seriously ill", sir.'

'All right. "Seriously ill". "Angela seriously ill. Keeps calling for you and says you were quite right about hat."'

'If I might suggest, sir –?'

'Well, go ahead.'

'I fancy the following would meet the case. "Please return immediately. Angela seriously ill. High fever and delirium. Keeps calling your name piteously and saying something about a hat and that you were quite right. Please catch earliest possible train. Dahlia Travers."'

'That sounds all right.'

'Yes, sir.'

'You like that "piteously"? You don't think "incessantly"?'

'No, sir. "Piteously" is the *mot juste*.'

'All right. You know. Well, send it off in time to get here at two-thirty.'

'Yes, sir.'

'Two-thirty, Jeeves. You see the devilish cunning?'

'No, sir.'

'I will tell you. If the telegram arrived earlier, he would get it before the game. By two-thirty, however, he will have started for the ground. I shall hand it to him the moment there is a lull in the battle. By that time he will have begun to get some idea of what a football match between Upper Bleaching and Hockley-cum-Meston is like, and the thing ought to work like magic. I can't imagine anyone who has been sporting awhile with those thugs I saw yesterday not welcoming any excuse to call it a day. You follow me?'

'Yes, sir.'

'Very good, Jeeves.'

'Very good, sir.'

You can always rely on Jeeves. Two-thirty I had said, and two-thirty it was. The telegram arrived almost on the minute. I was going to my room to change into something warmer at the moment and I took it up with me. Then into the heavy tweeds and off in the car to the field of play. I got there just as the two teams were lining up, and half a minute later the whistle blew and the war was on.

What with one thing and another – having been at a school where they didn't play it and so forth – Rugby football is a game I can't claim absolutely to understand in all its niceties, if you know what I mean. I can follow the broad, general principles, of course. I mean to say, I know that the main scheme is to work the ball down the field somehow and deposit it over the line at the other end, and that, in order to squelch this programme, each side is allowed to put in a certain amount of assault and battery and do things to its fellow-man which, if done elsewhere, would result in fourteen days without the option, coupled with some strong remarks from the Bench. But there I stop. What you might call the science of the thing is to Bertram Wooster a sealed book. However, I am informed by experts that on this occasion there was not enough science for anyone to notice.

There had been a great deal of rain in the last few days, and the going appeared to be a bit sticky. In fact, I have seen swamps that were drier than this particular bit of ground. The red-haired bloke whom I had encountered in the pub paddled up and kicked off amidst cheers from the populace, and the ball went straight to where Tuppy was standing, a pretty colour-scheme in light blue and orange. Tuppy caught it neatly, and hoofed it back, and it was at this point that I understood that an Upper Bleaching versus Hockley-cum-Meston game had certain features not usually seen on the football-field.

For Tuppy, having done his bit, was just standing there, looking modest, when there was a thunder of large feet and the red-haired bird, galloping up, seized him by the neck, hurled him to earth, and fell on him. I had a glimpse of Tuppy's face, as it registered horror, dismay, and a general suggestion of stunned dissatisfaction with the scheme of things, and then he disappeared. By the time he had come to the surface, a sort of mob-warfare was going on at the other side of the field. Two assortments of sons of the soil had got their heads down and were shoving earnestly against each other, with the ball somewhere in the middle.

Tuppy wiped a fair portion of Hampshire out of his eye, peered round him in a dazed kind of way, saw the mass-meeting and ran towards it, arriving just in time for a couple of heavyweights to gather him in and give him the mud-treatment again. This placed him in an admirable position for a third heavyweight to kick him in the ribs with a boot like a violin-case. The red-haired man then fell on him. It was all good, brisk play, and looked fine from my side of the ropes.

I saw now where Tuppy had made his mistake. He was too dressy. On occasions such as this it is safest not to be conspicuous, and that blue and orange shirt rather caught the eye. A sober beige, blending with the colour of the ground, was what his best friends would have recommended. And, in addition to the fact that his costume attracted attention, I rather think that the men of Hockley-cum-Meston resented his being on the field at all. They felt that, as a non-local, he had butted in on a private fight and had no business there.

At any rate, it certainly appeared to me that they were giving him preferential treatment. After each of those shoving-bees to which I have alluded, when the edifice caved in and tons of humanity wallowed in a tangled mess in the juice, the last soul to be excavated always seemed to be Tuppy. And on the rare occasions when he actually managed to stand upright for a moment, somebody – generally the red-haired man – invariably sprang to the congenial task of spilling him again.

In fact, it was beginning to look as though that telegram would come too late to save a human life, when an interruption occurred. Play had worked round close to where I was standing, and there had been the customary collapse of all concerned, with Tuppy at the bottom of the basket, as usual; but this time when they got up and started to count the survivors, a sizeable cove in what had once been a white shirt remained on the ground. And a hearty cheer went up from a hundred patriotic throats as the news spread that Upper Bleaching had drawn first blood.

The victim was carried off by a couple of his old chums, and the rest of the players sat down and pulled their stocking up and thought of life for a bit. The moment had come, it seemed to me, to remove Tuppy from the *abattoir*, and I hopped over the ropes and toddled to where he sat scraping mud from his wishbone. His air was that of a man who has been passed through a wringer, and his eyes, what you could see of them, had a strange, smouldering gleam. He was so crusted with alluvial deposits that one realized how little a mere bath would ever be able to effect. To fit him to take his place once more in polite society, he would certainly have to be sent to the cleaner's. Indeed, it was a moot point whether it wouldn't be simpler just to throw him away.

'Tuppy, old man,' I said.

'Eh?' said Tuppy.

'A telegram for you.'

'Eh?'

'I've got a wire here that came after you left the house.'

'Eh?' said Tuppy.

I stirred him up a trifle with the ferrule of my stick, and he seemed to come to life.

'Be careful what you're doing, you silly ass,' he said, in part. 'I'm one solid bruise. What are you gibbering about?'

'A telegram has come for you. I think it may be important.'

He snorted in a bitter sort of way.

'Do you suppose I've time to read telegrams now?'

'But this one may be frightfully urgent,' I said. 'Here it is.'

But, if you understand me, it wasn't. How I had happened to do it, I don't know, but apparently, in changing the upholstery, I had left it in my other coat.

'Oh, my gosh,' I said. 'I've left it behind.'

'It doesn't matter.'

'But it does. It's probably something you ought to read at once. Immediately, if you know what I mean. If I were you, I'd just say a few words of farewell to the murder-squad and come back to the house right away.'

He raised his eyebrows. At least, I think he must have done, because the mud on his forehead stirred a little, as if something was going on underneath it.

'Do you imagine,' he said, 'that I would slink away under Her very eyes? Good God! Besides,' he went on, in a quiet, meditative voice, 'there is no power on earth that could get me off this field until I've thoroughly disembowelled that red-haired bounder. Have you noticed how he keeps tackling me when I haven't got the ball?'

'Isn't that right?'

'Of course it's not right. Never mind! A bitter retribution awaits that bird. I've had enough of it. From now on I assert my personality.'

'I'm a bit foggy as to the rules of this pastime.' I said. 'Are you allowed to bite him.'

'I'll try, and see what happens,' said Tuppy, struck with the idea and brightening a little.

At this point, the pall-bearers returned, and fighting became general again all along the Front.

There's nothing like a bit of rest and what you might call folding of the hands for freshening up the shop-soiled athlete. The dirty work, resumed after this brief breather, started off with an added vim which it did one good to see. And the life and soul of the party was young Tuppy.

You know, only meeting a fellow at lunch or at the races or loafing round country-houses and so forth, you don't get on to his hidden depths, if you know what I mean. Until this moment, if asked, I would have said Tuppy Glossop was, on the whole, essentially a pacific sort of bloke, with little or nothing of the tiger of the jungle in him. Yet there he was, running to and fro with fire streaming from his nostrils, a positive danger to traffic.

Yes, absolutely. Encouraged by the fact that the referee was either filled with the spirit of Live and Let Live or else had got his whistle choked up with mud, the result being that he appeared to regard the game with a sort of calm detachment, Tuppy was putting in some very impressive work. Even to me, knowing nothing of the finesse of the thing, it was plain that if Hockley-cum-Meston wanted the happy ending they must eliminate young Tuppy at the earliest possible moment. And I will say for them that they did their best, the red-haired man being particularly assiduous. But Tuppy was made of durable material. Every time the opposition talent ground him into the mire and sat on his head, he rose on stepping-stones of his dead self, if you follow me. And in the end it was the red-haired bloke who did the dust-biting.

I couldn't tell you exactly how it happened, for by this time the shades of night were drawing in a bit and there was a dollop of mist rising, but one moment the fellow was hareing along, apparently without a care in the world, and then suddenly Tuppy had appeared from nowhere and was sailing through the air at his neck. They connected with a crash and a slither, and a little later the red-haired bird was hopping off, supported by a brace of friends, something having gone wrong with his left ankle.

After that, there was nothing to it. Upper Bleaching, thoroughly bucked, became busier than ever. There was a lot of earnest work in a sort of inland sea down at the Hockley end of the field, and then a kind of tidal wave poured over the line, and when the bodies had been removed and the tumult and the shouting had died, there was young Tuppy lying on the ball. And that, with the exception of a few spots of mayhem in the last five minutes, concluded the proceedings.

I drove back to the court in rather what you might term a pensive frame of mind. Things having happened as they had happened, there seemed to me a goodish bit of hard thinking to be done. There was a servitor of sorts in the hall, when I arrived, and I asked him to send up a whisky-and-soda, strongish, to my room. The old brain, I felt, needed stimulating. And about ten minutes later there was a knock at the door, and in came Jeeves, bearing tray and materials.

'Hullo, Jeeves,' I said, surprised. 'Are you back?'

'Yes, sir.'

'When did you get here?'

'Some little while ago, sir. Was it an enjoyable game, sir?'

'In a sense, Jeeves,' I said, 'yes. Replete with human interest and all that, if you know what I mean. But I fear that, owing to a touch of carelessness on my part, the worst has happened. I left the telegram in my other coat, so young Tuppy remained in action throughout.'

'Was he injured, sir?'

'Worse than that, Jeeves. He was the star of the game. Toasts, I should imagine, are now being drunk to him at every pub in the village. So spectacularly did he play – in fact, so heartily did he joust – that I can't see the girl not being all over him. Unless I am greatly mistaken, the moment they meet, she will exclaim "My hero!" and fall into his bally arms.'

'Indeed, sir?'

I didn't like the man's manner. Too calm. Unimpressed. A little leaping about with fallen jaw was what I had expected my words to produce, and I was on the point of saying as much when the door opened again and Tuppy limped in.

He was wearing an ulster over his football things, and I wondered why he had come to pay a social call on me instead of proceeding straight to the bathroom. He eyed my glass in a wolfish sort of way.

'Whisky?' he said, in a hushed voice.

'And soda.'

'Bring me one, Jeeves,' said young Tuppy. 'A large one.'

'Very good, sir.'

Tuppy wandered to the window and looked out into the gathering darkness, and for the first time I perceived that he had got a grouch of some description. You can generally tell by a fellow's back. Humped. Bent. Bowed down with weight of woe, if you follow me.

'What's the matter?' I asked.

Tuppy emitted a mirthless.

'Oh, nothing much,' he said. 'My faith in woman is dead, that's all.'

'It is?'

'You jolly well bet it is. Women are a wash-out. I see no future for the sex, Bertie. Blisters, all of them.'

'Er – even the Dogsbody girl?'

'Her name,' said Tuppy, a little stiffly, 'is Dalgleish, if it happens to interest you. And, if you want to know something else, she's the worst of the lot.'

'My dear chap!'

Tuppy turned. Beneath the mud, I could see that his face was drawn and, to put it in a nutshell, wan.

'Do you know what happened, Bertie?'

'What?'

'She wasn't there.'

'Where?'

'At the match, you silly ass.'

'Not at the match?'

'No.'

'You mean, not among the throng of eager spectators?'

'Of course I mean not among the spectators. Did you think I expected her to be playing?'

'But I thought the whole scheme of the thing –'

'So did I. My gosh!' said Tuppy, laughing another of those hollow ones. 'I sweat myself to the bone for her sake. I allow a mob of homicidal maniacs to kick me in the ribs and stroll about on my face. And then, when I have braved a fate worse than death, so to speak, all to please her, I find that she didn't bother to come and watch the game. She got a 'phone-call from London from somebody who said he had located an Irish water-spaniel, and up she popped in her car, leaving me flat. I met her just now outside her house, and she told me. And all she could think of was that she was as sore as a sunburnt neck because she had had her trip for nothing. Apparently it wasn't an Irish water-spaniel at all. Just an ordinary English water-spaniel. And to think I fancied I loved a girl like that. A nice life-partner she would make! "When pain and anguish wring the brow, a ministering angel thou" – I don't think! Why, if a man married a girl like that and happened to get stricken by some dangerous illness, would she smooth his pillow and press cooling drinks on him? Not a chance? She'd be off somewhere trying to buy Siberian eel-hounds. I'm through with women.'

I saw that the moment had come to put in a word for the old firm.

'My cousin Angela's not a bad sort, Tuppy,' I said, in a grave elder-brotherly kind of way. 'Not altogether a bad egg, Angela, if you look at her squarely. I had always been hoping that she and you . . . and I know my Aunt Dahlia felt the same.'

Tuppy's bitter sneer cracked the top-soil.

'Angela!' he woofed. 'Don't talk to me about Angela. Angela's a rag and a bone and a hank of hair and an A1 scourge, if you want to know. She gave me the push. Yes, she did. Simply because I had the manly courage to speak out candidly on the subject of that ghastly lid she was chump enough to buy. It made her look like a Peke, and I told her it made her look like a Peke. And instead of admiring me for my fearless honesty she bunged me out on my ear. Faugh!'

'She did?' I said.

'She jolly well did,' said young Tuppy. 'At four-sixteen pm on Tuesday the seventeenth.'

'By the way, old man,' I said, 'I've found that telegram.'

'What telegram?'

'The one I told you about.'

'Oh, that one?'

'Yes, that's the one.'

'Well, let's have a look at the beastly thing.'

I handed it over, watching him narrowly. And suddenly, as he read, I saw him wobble. Stirred to the core. Obviously.

'Anything important?' I said.

'Bertie,' said young Tuppy, in a voice that quivered with strong emotion, 'my recent remarks *re* your cousin Angela. Wash them out. Cancel them. Look on them as not spoken. I tell you, Bertie, Angela's all right. An angel in human shape, and that's official. Bertie, I've got to get up to London. She's ill.'

'Ill?'

'High fever and delirium. This wire's from your aunt. She wants me to come up to London at once. Can I borrow your car?'

'Of course.'

'Thanks,' said Tuppy, and dashed out.

He had only been gone about a second when Jeeves came in with the restorative.

'Mr Glossop's gone, Jeeves.'

'Indeed, sir?'

'To London.'

'Yes, sir?'

'In my car. To see my cousin Angela. The sun is once more shining, Jeeves.'

'Extremely gratifying, sir.'

I gave him the eye.

'Was it you, Jeeves, who 'phoned to Miss What's-her-bally-name about the alleged water-spaniel?'

'Yes, sir.'

'I thought as much.'

'Yes, sir?'

'Yes, Jeeves, the moment Mr Glossop told me that a Mysterious Voice had 'phoned on the subject of Irish water-spaniels, I thought as much. I recognized your touch. I read your motives like an open book. You knew she would come buzzing up.'

'Yes, sir.'

'And you knew how Tuppy would react. If there's one thing that gives a jousting knight the pip, it is to have his audience walk out on him.'

'Yes, sir.'

'But, Jeeves.'

'Sir?'

'There's just one point. What will Mr Glossop say when he finds my cousin Angela full of beans and not delirious?'

'The point had not escaped me, sir. I took the liberty of ringing Mrs Travers up on the telephone and explaining the circumstances. All will be in readiness for Mr Glossop's arrival.'

'Jeeves,' I said, 'you think of everything.'

'Thank you, sir. In Mr Glossop's absence, would you care to drink this whisky-and-soda?'

I shook the head.

'No, Jeeves, there is only one man who must do that. It is you. If ever anyone earned a refreshing snort, you are he. Pour it out, Jeeves, and shove it down.'

'Thank you very much, sir.'

'Cheerio, Jeeves!'

'Cheerio, sir, if I may use the expression.'